FEAST OF CHAOS

✳ ✳ ✳

A Novel of Geadhain

CHRISTIAN A. BROWN

Copyright © 2016 by Christian A. Brown
Feast of Chaos is a work of fiction. Names, characters, places, and incidents are products of the author's imagination or are used fictitiously. Any resemblance to actual events or locales or persons, living or dead, is entirely coincidental. No part of this book may be reproduced or transmitted in any form by any means, electronic or mechanical, including photocopying or recording, or by any information storage and retrieval system, except as may be expressly permitted in writing from the author/publisher.
All rights reserved.

ISBN: 0994014422
ISBN 13: 9780994014429

For the children, poets, and protectors of Geadhain
(For the readers)

15
20
25
NORT
VALHOLOM
BONE
ARCHIPELLIGO
CARTHAC
EOD
EBON
VALE
SALT
FOREST
TAROCH
ARM
KORKHUL
SOUTHREACH
STRAITS OF
WRATH
BAINSBURY
MORKETH
MOUNTAINS
MEADOWVALE
FANGS OF
DAWN
WILLOWHOLME
LAKE
TESH
BRACKENMIRE
ZIOCH
MORKHUL
SORSETTA
GORGONATH
CHTH

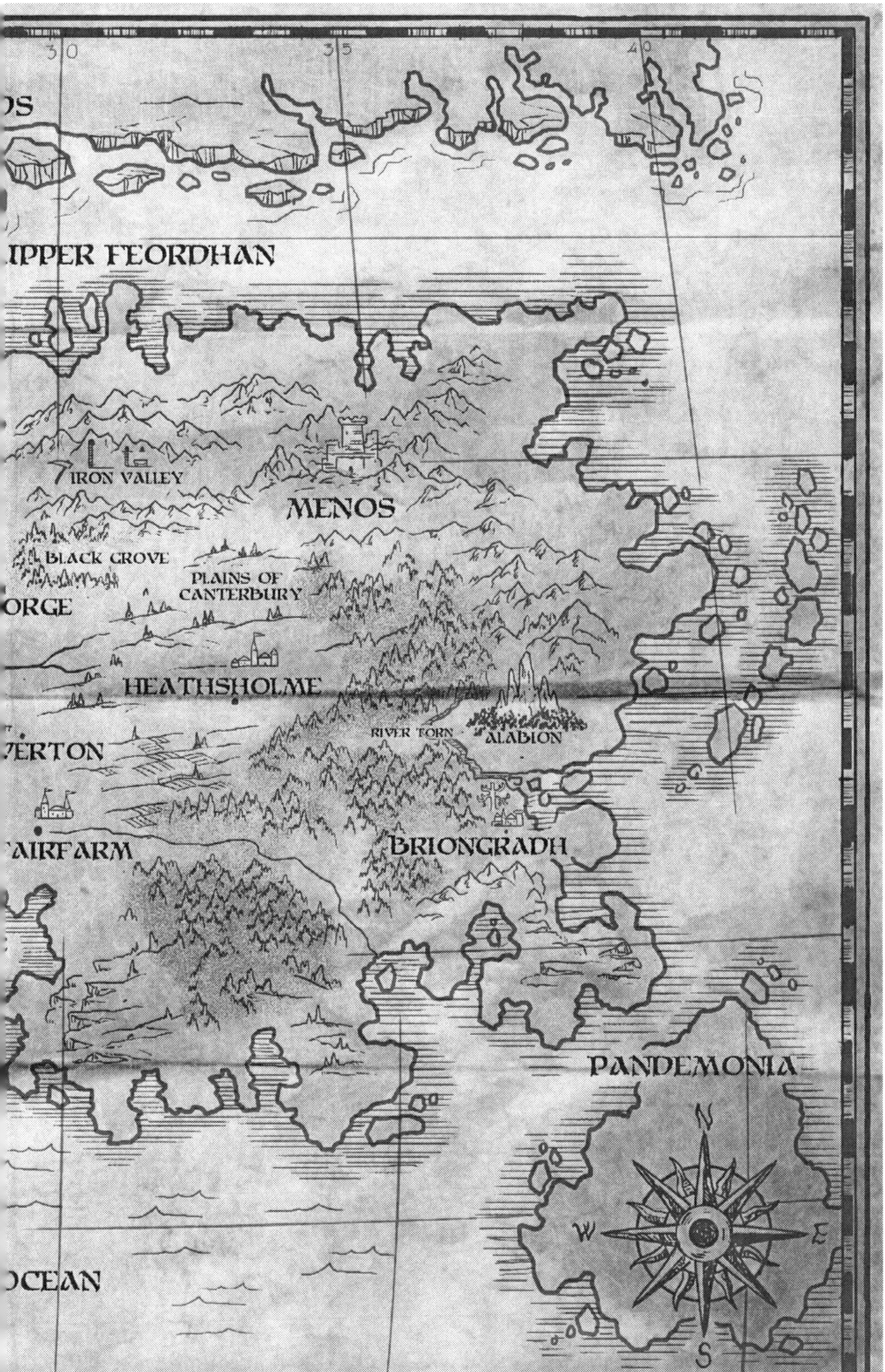
30
35
40
OS
UPPER FEORDHAN
IRON VALLEY
MENOS
BLACK GROVE
PLAINS OF
CANTERBURY
ORGE
HEATHSHOLME
RIVER TORN
ALABION
VERTON
BRIONGRADH
FAIRFARM
PANDEMONIA
N
W
E
S
OCEAN

CONTENTS

On Geadhain (Glossary)		ix
Foreword (A Recap)		xix
Prologue		xxxiii
I	The Cradle	1
II	Teeth	17
III	People of Glass	50
IV	Judgment	98
V	Red Riders	129
VI	After the Fall	176
VII	Taken	207
VIII	Memory's Burn	234
IX	Return of the Queen	265
Part II		293
X	Defying Death	295
XI	True Selves	331
XII	Sinner's Path	381
XIII	The Empress	404
XIV	City of False Grace	452
XV	The Hunt	479

XVI	The Descent	531
XVII	Queen's Justice	576
XVIII	Deepest Truths	629
XIX	A Trick of Fate	645
	Epilogue	657

ON GEADHAIN (GLOSSARY)

I: Paragons, Wonders, and Horrors

Brutus: The Sun King. Brutus is the second of the Immortal Kings and ruler of the Summerlands in southern Geadhain. Zioch, the City of Gold, shines like a gold star on the southern horizon and is the seat of his power. Brutus is the master of the wilderness and the hunt. His magik has dominion over the physical world and self. He is victim to the Black Queen's whispers and falls far from his nobility.

Lilehum (Lila): Magnus's bride. Magnus sought her when learning to live as a man independent of his ageless brother. Through the sharing of blood and ancient vows—the *Fuilimean*—she is drawn into the mystery of the immortal brothers and imbued with a sliver of their magik. She is a sorceress and possibly eternal in her years. She is wise, kind, and comely without compare. However, she is ruthless if her kingdom or bloodmate is threatened.

Magnus: The Immortal King of the North. Magnus is one of two guardians of the Waking World. The other is his brother, Brutus. The Everfair King—the colloquial name for Magnus—rules Eod, the City of Wonders. He is living magik itself; a sorcerer without compare; and the master of the forces of ice, thunder, Will, and intellect.

Morigan: A young woman living a rather unremarkable life as the handmaiden to an elderly sorcerer, Thackery Thule. A world of wonder and horror engulfs her after a chance, perhaps fated, meeting with the Wolf. She learns she is an axis of magik, mystery, and Fate to the proceedings of

Geadhain's Great War. In the darkest days that she and her companions must face, her heroism and oft-tested virtue will determine much of the world's salvation or ruin.

Thackery Hadrian Thule (Whitehawk): An old sorcerer living in Eod. Thackery lives an unassuming life as a man of modest stature. However, he is a man with many skeletons in his closet. He has no known children or family, and he cares for Morigan as if she were his daughter. Morigan's grace will touch him, too, and he is drawn into the web of Fate she weaves.

The Black Queen, Zionae \'Zē-ō-ˌnā\: A shapeless, bodiless, monstrous entity without empathy who seeks to undo the Immortal Kings and the world's order. Her actions—those who perceive these things sense she is a she—are horrific and inexplicable.

The Dreamstalker: A vile presence that haunts and travels the waters of Dream as Morigan does. She is the Herald of the Black Queen, Zionae's voice in the physical world.

The Lady of Luck, Charazance \'SHer-Ðh-zans\: The Dreamer of serendipity, gambles, and games. Alastair is her vessel.

The Sisters Three—Ealasyd \'Ēl-ə-sid\, **Elemech** \'El-ə-mek\, and **Eean** \'Ē-en\: From youngest to eldest in appearance, they are Ealasyd, Elemech, and Eean. The Sisters Three are a trio of ageless witches who live in the woods of Alabion. They are known to hold sway over the destinies of men. They can be capricious, philanthropic, or woefully cruel. One must be careful when bartering with the Sisters Three for their wisdom. There is always a price.

The Wanderer, Feyhazir \'Ph-āe-āh-ˈzi(ə)r\: The Dreamer of mystery, seduction and desire. He is Morigan's father.

The Wolf, Caenith \'Kā-nith\: A smith of Eod. His fearsome, raw exterior hides an animal and a dreadful wrath. Caenith is a conflicted creature—a beast, man, poet, lover, and killer. Caenith believes himself beyond salvation, and he passes the years making metal skins and claws for the slow-walkers of Geadhain while drowning himself in bitter remorse. He does not know it, but Morigan will pull him from his darkness and make him confront what is most black and wicked within him.

II: Eod's Finest

Adhamh (Adam): An exiled changeling of Briongrahd. Noble, loyal, and loving, his only hatred is for those like the White Wolf, who abuse and punish life. Humble Adam has a destiny beyond what he or others would ever expect.

Beauregard Fischer: A waifish, lyrical young man lost in the Summerlands with his father. In his past and soul lies a great mystery. His cheek is marked with the birthmark of the one true northern star.

Devlin Fischer: A seasoned hunter and Beauregard's father. He is as gruff and hairy as a bear.

Dorvain: Master of the North Watch and Leonitis's brother. He is a brutish, gruff warrior tempered by the winds of the Northlands. He is dependable and unflappable. He is an oak of a man who will not bend to the winds of change or war.

Erithitek \'Ār-ith-ə-.tek\: More commonly referred to as "Erik." He is the king's hammer. Erik was once an orphaned child of the Salt Forests and a member of the Kree tribe, but Magnus took him in. Erik now serves as his right hand.

Galivad: Master of the East Watch. The youngest of Eod's watchmasters, he is seen by many as unfit for the post because of his pretty face, foppish manner, and cavalier airs. He laughs and sings to avoid the pain of remembering what he has lost.

Jebidiah Rotbottom: A flamboyant spice merchant from Sorsetta. He sails the breadth of Geadhain in a garish, crimson vessel—the *Red Mary*. Currently, he uses different aliases, for reasons no doubt unscrupulous and suspect.

Leonitis: The Lion. He is thusly named for his roar, grandeur, and courage. He is the Ninth Legion master of Eod (King Magnus's personal legion). Once Geadhain's Great War commences, he will play many roles from soldier to spy to hero. Leonitis's thread of destiny is long and woven through many Fates.

Lowelia Larson (Lowe): The queen knows her as the Lady of Whispers. Lowelia seems a simple, high-standing palace servant, yet her doughy, pleasant demeanor conceals a shrewd mind and a vengeful secret.

Maggie Halm: Maggie is the granddaughter of Cordenzia, an infamous whoremistress who traded her power for freedom from the Iron City. Maggie runs an establishment called the Silk Purse in Taroch's Arm.

Rowena: She is Queen Lila's sword and Her Majesty's left hand. Rowena's tale was destined for a swift, bleak end until the queen intervened and saved Rowena's young life. Since that day, Rowena has revered Queen Lila as a mother and true savior.

Tabitha Fischer: The sole magistrate of Willowholme. She has assumed this role not by choice but through tragedy.

Talwyn Blackmore: The illegitimate son of Roland Blackmore (since deceased). Talwyn is a kind, brilliant scholar and inheritor of all the virtue that escaped his half brother, Augustus. Talwyn lives in Riverton. His thirst for knowledge often makes him cross boundaries of decorum.

III: Menos's Darkest Souls

Aadore Brennoch: An Iron-born survivor. A woman whose strange lineage comes from the far, far East. Once a handmaiden to the Lady El, she will leave that meager station behind and rise into a woman of prominence and legend alongside her brother.

Adelaide: Mouse's childhood friend from the charterhouse. The girl's fate is the cause of much torment for Mouse.

Alastair: A mysterious figure who acts seemingly in his own interests. He greatly influences certain meetings and events. To all appearances, he is the Watchers' agent and Mouse's mentor. He almost certainly, though, serves another power or master.

Beatrice of El: Moreth's pale and ghastly wife. After a glance, a person can tell this ethereal woman is not wholly of this world.

Curtis: A young, athletic man with a shameful, criminal past trying to make a better life for himself in Menos. He is taken with Aadore, though will prove himself more than a doting suitor.

Elineth: Son of Elissandra.

Elissandra: The Mistress of Mysteries. She is an Iron Sage and the proprietress of Menos's Houses of Mystery—places where a wary master can consult oracles and seek augurs regarding his or her inevitable doom. While she is wicked, she is also bright with love for her children, and she fosters a hidden dream and hope no other Iron Sage would ever be so bold as to consider.

Elsa Brennoch: Mother to Aadore and Sean.

Gloriatrix: The Iron Queen and ruler of Menos. Gloriatrix single-handedly clawed her way to the top of Menos's black Crucible after her husband, Gabriel, lost first his right to chair on the Council of the Wise and then his life. Gloriatrix has never remarried and blames her brother, Thackery Thule, for Gabriel's death. With her family in shambles, power is the only thing to which she clings. Gloriatrix has ambitions far beyond Menos. She would rule the stars themselves if she could.

Iarron (Ian): An abandoned child, unnaturally calm and still, who was discovered by the Brennoch siblings, on Menos's darkest day—he is a star of hope to them.

Kanatuk: A tribesman of the Northlands who had been stolen from his home and placed into a lifetime of abhorrent slavery, serving as a vassal to the Broker. Morigan rescues him in Menos.

Lord Augustus Blackmore: Lord of Blackforge. A deviant power-monger with grotesque appetites.

Moreth of El: Master of the House of El and the Blood Pits of Menos. He traffics in people, gladiators, and death.

Mouse: More of a gray soul than a black one, Mouse is a woman without a firm flag planted on the map of morality. She knows well life's cruelty and how best to avoid it through self-sufficiency and indifference. As a girl, she escaped a rather unfortunate fate, and she has since risen to become a Voice of the Watchers—a shadowbroker of Geadhain. Mouse's real trial begins when she is thrust into peril with Morigan—at that time a stranger—and Mouse is forced to rethink everything she knows.

Sangloris: Elissandra's husband.

Sean Brennoch: Brother to Aadore. Once a soldier of the Ironguard, now a one-legged veteran. Sean wants no pity, however, and is more capable and clever than most other soldiers.

Skar: An ugly, ogreish mercenary whose heart is kinder than his looks. Fate sees his path cross with the Brennochs, and to them he will become a sword not for hire but bound to protect them through respect and duty.

Sorren: Gloriatrix's youngest child. Sorren is a nekromancer of incredible power who possesses the restraint and moods of a petulant, spoiled child. He shares a pained past with his (mostly) deceased brother, Vortigern.

Tessariel: Daughter of Elissandra.

The Broker: All the black rivers of sin in Menos come to one confluence: the Broker. Little is known about this man beyond the terror tales whispered to misbehaving children. The Broker has metal teeth, mad eyes, and a cadre of twisted servants whom he calls sons. He inhabits and controls the Iron City's underbelly.

The Great Mother: Her Faithful are multitudinous. Her elements and the shades of her divinity—Green, White, Blue—are prefixes to her many names.

The Slave: An unnamed vassal purchased in the Flesh Markets of Menos. A dangerous creature, more than a man. Although property, he later became a free man and substitute father to the Lord El. Together, the men traveled into the wilds of Pandemonia on a most dangerous safari.

Vortigern: Gloriatrix's second son. This pitiable soul lives in a state between light and dark and without memory of the errors that brought him to this walking death.

IV: Lands and Landmarks

Alabion: The great woodland and the realm of the Sisters Three.

Bainsbury: A moderate-size township on the west bank of the Feordhan. Gavin Foss lords over it.

Blackforge: A city on the east bank of the Feordhan River. It was once famous for blacksmithing.

Brackenmire: The realm outside of Mor'Khul. It is a swampy but pleasant place.

Carthac: The City of Waves.

Ceceltoth: City of Stone.

Eatoth: City of Waterfalls.

Ebon Vale: The land around Taroch's Arm. It has fiefs, farmsteads, and large shale deposits.

Eod: The City of Wonders and kingdom of Magnus. Eod is a testament to the advances of technomagik and culture in Geadhain.

Fairfarm: The largest rural community in the East. With so many pastures, fields, and farms, this realm produces most of Central Geadhain's consumable resources.

Heathsholme: A small hamlet known for its fine ale.

Intomitath: City of Flames.

Iron Valley: One of the richest sources of feliron in Geadhain.

Kor'Khul: The great sand ocean surrounding Eod. These lands were once thought to be lush and verdant.

Lake Tesh: The blue jewel glittering under the willows of Willowholme.

Menos: The Iron City. It is hung always in a pall of gloom.

Mor'Khul: The green, rolling valleys of Brutus's realm. They are legendary for their beauty.

Pandemonia: The large island continent across the Cthonic Ocean and separated from most of Geadhain's other landmasses. Three Great Cities of immeasurable technomagikal power serve to bring order to this realm of chaos, a land where topography shifts and changes day by day from tundra to desert to lava field to wastes. Only these three Great Cities stand permanent in Pandemonia's constant flux.

Plains of Canterbury: Wide, sparse fields and gullies.

Riverton: A bustling, eclectic city of lighthearted criminals and troubadours. The city is found on the eastern shore of the Feordhan River, and it was built from the reconstituted wreckage of old hulls and whatever interesting bits floated down the great river.

Sorsetta: In the south and past the Sun King's lands. This is a city of contemplation and quiet enlightenment.

Southreach: A great ancient city built into a cleft in Kor'Khul.

Taroch's Arm: The resting place of a relic of the great warlord Taroch: his arm. The city is also a hub of great trade among all corners of Geadhain.

The Black Grove: The forest outside of Blackforge. It leads to the Plains of Canterbury.

Willowholme: A village located in Brackenmire and famed for its musicians and anglers.

Zioch: The City of Gold and kingdom of Brutus.

V: Miscellaneous Mysteries

Fuilimean: The Blood Promise. It is a trading of blood and vows and a spiritual binding between two willing participants. Magnus and Brutus did this first in the oldest ages. Depending on who partakes in the ritual, the results can be extraordinary.

Technomagik: A hybrid science that blends raw power—often currents of magik—with mechanical engineering.

The Faithful: Worshippers of the Green Mother. They exist in many cultures and forms, and the most sacred and spiritual of their kind, curators of the world's history known as Keepers, often lead them.

The Watchers: The largest network of shadowbrokers in Central Geadhain.

FOREWORD (A RECAP)

Four Feasts till Darkness is an expansive and complex work—even I lose track of things without my notes! It would be unreasonable, then, to expect perfect recall from my readers. To that end, I set one of my dear editors—Kyla—to scribbling down all the important bits of the story. Here you are: a refresher of the events of Geadhain's Great War leading up to *Feast of Chaos*.

—Christian

When first entering the world of Geadhain, we encounter a realm of magical smoke and metaphysical mirrors reflecting the darkest and lightest that its inhabitants have to offer. But as the pages of *Feast of Fates* turn, a deeper understanding of this mystical realm emerges, one that parallels the universalisms found in our own very real experiences in this world. It is a world unlike any other, where science and magic form a mysterious force known as technomagik. It is a land borne of a Green Mother earth, but ruled by the wills—both conscious and unconscious—of kings and queens that wreak havoc on their world. But there comes a time where even a mother must teach her children the hard way, even if it pains her. And so *Feast of Fates* sees the start of the Green Mother's tough love, depriving them of her protection for the anguish they have brought to her with their violence; it is the world's inhabitants alone who can save themselves.

Our story begins with the weavers of fate themselves, the Three Sisters—Eean, Elemech, and Ealasyd—who make their homes in the forests of Alabion. The Sisters represent life, death, and all its various contortions and permutations in the world. There, they both give birth to, and usher death upon, themselves and the world. With each renewal, they shape the twists and turns of our players' journeys, for better or worse. They represent destiny's infinite loop in a twisted sibling rivalry that will determine Geadhain's future. But even the Sisters of Fate cannot control the rumblings on destiny's horizon—the harbingers of destruction to come in the stormy and ethereal form of the Black Queen.

The scene shifts to the city of Eod—Geadhain's cosmopolitan metropolis. Nestled within Kor'Khul's oceans of sand, it is known as the City of Wonders for its host of technomagikal advancements and a skyline filled with flying carriages ferrying Eod's cultural and social elite. There we find Morigan, a young woman of character and strength who is traveling toward a destiny that was forged ages before her birth, and one that is intimately entwined in tapestries of the Three Sisters.

Morigan lives a simple life as a handmaiden until her world is thrown into tumult as she is drawn to the literal animal magnetism of Caenith, a wolf-man changeling whose initial gruff appearance belies his ancient origins and unimaginable power. The two are instantly bonded, each of them knowing that their attraction goes well beyond "love at first sight," and is more akin to having been written in Geadhain's starry skies. The two cannot deny what has been preordained, and the ripple effect of the Wolf and Fawn's union (as they come to know each other) as bloodmates begins to be felt throughout Geadhain. Their coming together stirs ancient powers of sight in Morigan, and inspires the beast in Caenith to reclaim its role in his life.

Morigan's nascent visions are a near-constant reminder that whenever there is joy, sorrow remains but a half step behind. She is witness to waves of destruction and death shadowing the realm, making their impending presence known not only to her but to all of Geadhain. In her mind's eye, she sees that just as we humans wage war against ourselves and the earth that has borne us all, so, too, does Geadhain face a battle against evil forged in blackness, smelted from the depths of all the worst the world has to offer. Chief among Morigan's visions is the emergence from the pitch of the Black Queen.

This foul, black entity exerts her power chiefly by wielding the bodies of others like puppets. Morigan is forced to watch as the Black Queen overtakes Magnus's body to mete out a brutal attack on his wife. She is also witness to her use of the Sun King, Brutus, to wage war against his own people, pitting him against his brother in kingship and immortality, Magnus, the Everfair King. The incorporeal figure of the Black Queen has set the wheels firmly in motion to bring drought and death to the Green Mother's world.

A witness to Morigan's symbiosis is Thackery Thule, a sorcerer who guided her in her youth and through the painful loss of her mother. Thackery forms another piece of the puzzling group that will either pitch Geadhain forward into light or see it crumble before them into darkness. For years, Thackery's past was concealed from Morigan, but unwittingly, she begins to reveal tragedies long buried. His is a history filled with loss at the hands of those closest to him, the details of which will play out over the tapestry of time. He quickly realizes that Morigan's powers extend beyond simple fortune-teller's tricks; she may hold the key to Geadhain's future. In an effort to safeguard this knowledge, Thackery takes them to see Queen Lila. There, in the royal palace's Hall of Memories, Morigan reveals that the threat that Brutus poses to the queen, the kingdom, and the entire realm is also manifest in Lila's spouse, Magnus.

But the sudden emergence of Morigan's long-repressed powers has not gone unnoticed by other powers that be, and fear that she might pose a threat to the hierarchical order of Menos quickly makes her a target. In those moments where Caenith and Morigan are pledging their blood to each other, others are plotting to capture the Fawn and subjugate her before the Iron Queen of Menos, Gloriatrix, a woman so driven by grief at the loss of her husband that she has ruled her kingdom with a fist worthy of her title. Never content to do her own dirty work, she instructs her son, Sorren, to become a party to the destruction of Eod and capture of Morigan. He sets off a number of explosions that destabilize the city not only physically but also politically and socially, and Lila is struck with the realization of Eod's vulnerability. For Thackery, Sorren's indifference to inflicting pain comes as no surprise. As his uncle, the sorcerer was not only a witness to his past violence but a victim as well. As the mysteries of Thackery's past continue to be untangled, we learn that not only is Gloriatrix his sister, but his nephew was responsible for the death of his wife.

Before the dust can settle, Morigan is spirited away to Menos, a city that breeds its own brand of filth borne out of fear. She is to be held captive there until she is subjugated to the whims of Gloriatrix. But even with her newfound powers still in their infancy, the Fawn is a worthy match for her captors. So, too, is her new companion, Mouse, a member of Geadhain's underworld network of spies. This diminutive woman has been shaped by the mean streets of Menos, the ones paved with slavery, exploitation, violations, and hate. Mouse had done her time in the city and sought out a new face from a fleshcrafter, only to discover that there truly is no honor among thieves, landing her in the same captivity as Morigan. Like the city of Menos itself, Mouse's moral compass is one that, accordingly, wavers with the magnetic pull of the tides.

The unlikely pairing of these two women is a reminder of how difficult it can be to cut through the obscurities of a world where appearances are never quite as they seem. Our impulse to simply dismiss the "bad guys" is constantly challenged by being privy to perceptions of individuals both within and without the relationships of all our players. Good and evil are never as simple as they appear. Each player is "othered" by those in opposition. Good is never just good. Evil is never simply evil. Perception is everything.

Neither does "dead" always mean "dead." There are brokers and fleshcrafters who deal in the undead and nearly dead, and these manner of men are holding the women in wait for Gloriatrix's interrogation. But even the zombielike slaves of these nekromantic death dealers have deep within them a spark of humanity waiting to be lighted once again. For no one is this more true than Vortigern, the dead man whose shackles of catatonia are broken when Morigan's psychic bees pierce into his mind. Buried deep below his death mask is a past and present inextricably linked to the group. He was no random victim of Sorren's psychopathy—they were brothers. Vortigern's present death was the consequence of having once loved Sorren's wife and fathered a child with her, Fionna, the mighty Mouse who is now a witness to his deliverance from un-death.

But these women are not stunned into inaction by their newly gained knowledge, for the world of Fates is not one in which women are the meek observers of the world's affairs, passively allowing events to simply happen to them. And so their escape comes not at the hands of Thackery and Caenith, who have ventured into Menos's dangerous underworld to rescue them, but through the women's own ingenuity and intuitive powers. In the process of their escape, they rescue yet another prisoner, Kanatuk—once a malevolent, mind-thralled servant to Menos's underworld kingpin, the Broker. Although before being enslaved and brought to Menos, Kanatuk was a peaceful wanderer of the frozen North. Through Morigan's grace and natural proclivity toward reweaving broken souls, he is rescued from his darkness and restored of his past.

Elsewhere, in their efforts to rescue Morigan, Caenith and Thackery also encounter a young changeling girl being exploited at the hands of the seemingly insane Augustus and free her of the bonds of child bridedom. A skin-walker without a skin, Macha is a sister of Alabion, and like her changeling brethren, she is possessed of visions of other worlds. Her dreams are ones that foreshadow the presence of an unknown, fanged warmother who has ushered an era of conflict and violence into their homeland. They form a troop of undeniable misfits that eventually makes its way out of Menos toward a destiny whose grandeur and importance is made increasingly clear through Morigan's visions and buzzing mind hive. She alone bears the full weight of those visions and the horrors that unfold within her mind's eye. Even the mental and spiritual link with her bloodmate do not fully spare her of that burden.

In an effort to secure what she believes is her rightful place in the halls of power, Gloriatrix has formed an alliance with Elissandra, a powerful sorceress and seer. She believes that the prophecies have foretold that when brother rises against brother, she will find her place in the resulting power vacuum. But even the Iron Queen is unaware that the powers that run deep in Morigan's veins also run in Elissandra's; we learn that they are both Daughters of the Moon, sisters in the providence of Alabion. And so

Gloriatrix's plan to wage war against the immortals may be undermined and her suspicions of Elissandra warranted.

Meanwhile, King Magnus and his hand, Erithitek, have been leading the troops of Eod's Silver Watch forward toward Zioch, the City of Gold and host to Brutus's throne. Magnus begins to appreciate the scope of his brother's burgeoning depravity, unleashing terror and chaos upon his own people. It also becomes clear that there is every chance that his journey is one from which he might not return. He thus elicits a hard-won promise from Erithitek to return to Eod and keep safe his Queen Lila.

But not unlike the two women who use their strength and cunning to escape Menos, the queen that Magnus left behind is no manner of shrinking violet. Shaken by Morigan's prophetic revelations, she is no longer certain that the man she loved is as virtuous as she once believed, and whether the choices she made were truly guided by love or something more sinister. She sets out on a dangerous journey upon Erithitek's return, steeled to protect her people against any offensive from Gloriatrix. Yet love of husband and love of kingdom drive her to commit acts of terror against those who would threaten either, reminding us that each one of us believes we are "the good guys."

As Magnus continues the Watch's advance, he knows that his brother is lying in wait, hunting him. Once the two are face-to-face, Magnus comes to understand that just as Brutus has transformed his kingdom into a wasteland, so, too, have the feelings of fraternity they once shared been transformed into intense hatred. Empowered by the Black Queen, Brutus overtakes his brother in a firestorm of destruction. Lest mortals and immortals alike forget: even with all the accumulated powers of the world, complete control over one's ecosystem is always an illusion. Magnus's vanquishment by his brother shakes the foundations of Geadhain, and the land spews forth a natural disaster, a storm of frost and fire that sweeps the world from end to end, triggered by the outcome of the battle between brothers.

It is a battle that produces no winners, since it takes place in a realm where even the very concept of death is malleable. And death, or that which resembles it, is the destabilizing force it always is, bringing with it both chaos and clarity. Thus the Black Queen's reign of terror begins with the fall of Magnus and the rise of her corrupted avatar, Brutus, from the ashes of that climactic battle.

When the smoke clears, a world lies in ruin. The line between coincidence and fate is wholly blurred. And the Three Sisters reveal that they are adding a new sibling to their fold—one by the name of Morigan.

In *Feast of Dreams*, we are greeted by the Three Sisters of fate who reveal that despite their best plans, the threads of fate have been broken, and by none other than our own Hunters of Fate: Morigan, Caenith, Mouse, Thackery, and Vortigern. We join the pack as they venture through the land of the Untamed, deeper into the protracted quagmire of a great war.

Morigan's mind has become a virtual hive of visions. The bees of her dream-walking are beating out a nearly incessant rhythm of prophecies that are becoming ever more burdensome. Her waking dreams show her that she is, indeed, of immortal origin, and that the woman she called her mother, Mifanwae, did not give birth to her but rather was a willing pawn in destiny's game. In many ways, Morigan has become a silent Cassiopeia, blessed with a second sight full of images she cannot, or dare not, share. With every passing day, she comes to realize that much of what she sees is unchangeable. She also peeks behind fate's curtain to reveal more about the woman in Caenith's past who once held his heart. Aghna, herself a wolf-changeling, had long ago ended her life when faced with a future of untold suffering. Morigan herself felt she had little to fear from a shadow of the past until she and her friends suddenly found themselves surrounded by an even greater legion—led by the long-departed Aghna.

Once again, it appears that death represents little more than a temporary transition for the lycanthropic being who now governs Briongrahd, the City of Fangs. She is no longer wrapped in the loving glow Caenith remembers from their last moments together but by a shroud of violence and hate. The changeling to whom Caenith had once devoted himself bears little resemblance to their glorious past, and he is forced to reconcile the woman he knew in life with the woman she became in death. Aghna has become the warmother of which Macha had warned, leading her species toward a battle against the Kings in which victory will represent the domination over other species in the realm. And much like Brutus allowed himself to be moved to slaughter his own kin, Aghna now appears possessed by a power that lives only to satisfy its carnal desires and lust for domination.

Unsurprisingly, there is little honor among those who are singularly focused on the advancement of their own—a kind of species-based nationalism—and Aghna betrays her former lover, killing Vortigern in the process. This is a death from which he will not return, and while the survivors escape, Mouse is scarred by the untimely loss of a father she had known only in his afterlife.

All the while, the undefinable, ethereal evil of the Black Queen continues to overshadow the land, reminding Geadhain's inhabitants at every turn that in the battle of man versus the forces of the universe, they are always the underdogs. Yet the machinations of the Black Queen and her cabal are not the only threats to peace in the realm. With Magnus either missing or dead after the battle with his corrupted brother, the Iron Queen, Gloriatrix, intends to launch an offensive against Eod, using all the forces of her technomagikal arsenal.

Gloriatrix's past has been so marred by loss that when her son, Sorren, suddenly disappears, she takes it as a signal that she is destined to live a life bereft of love, cementing her ire against anyone who would deny her the singular pleasure remaining to her: power. But Elissandra, who shares Morigan's gift of insight, knows that Sorren's disappearance was not of earthly origin. His essence has been given over to a power greater than anything Gloriatrix could imagine—that of Death itself. And while Gloriatrix is almost singularly focused on capturing Morigan and her fellow travelers, she is blinded to the dissent that is fomenting in the halls of Menos in her absence. The Iron Sages begin staging a revolt, targeting Elissandra and her one vulnerability: her children. The sorceress barely escapes with her life and fails to impress upon Gloriatrix the growing futility of waging war against Eod.

Queen Lila, Magnus's wife, has left the kingdom with her husband's hammer, Erithitek. She leaves in her stead her hands, Lowelia and Leonitis, who will serve the kingdom in her absence, both wrapped in a spell of illusion that tricks whoever looks upon them into seeing the appearances and voices of their departed queen and Magnus's hammer. Believing Magnus to have perished at Brutus's hands, Lila has taken it upon herself to acquire a tool of untold power: the arm of Taroch. Conjured out of the ashes of Magnus's despair, the ancient relic, like every tool of magik in the realm, possesses power that is easily abused and will extort a steep price from its user.

Approaching madness, Lila gives barely a thought to her once-beloved Summerlands or to those she left to safeguard its borders. She is blinded by her loss and pain, and Erik—her silent admirer and stalwart protector—is the only thing keeping her physical and spiritual being safe, as she wrestles with a faltering morality that is dizzied by grief. Both she and Erithitek—who is increasingly struggling to keep silent his intense feelings for the queen—are unaware that Magnus, in fact, exists in a kind of purgatory. There, Brutus has opened a window into his mind through which Magnus can view his rampages, in the hopes that he might seduce his captive brother into joining him as a vessel for the Black Queen. And so visions of Magnus that push Lila to the brink of sanity represent more than simple nightmares from which Erithetek must awaken her.

All the while, Rowena and Galivad, Queen Lila's Sword and the Master of Eod's East Watch, respectively, have been watching Moreth of El—a trafficker of all things dark and depraved in Menos. Also under their purview is his new bride, Beatrice, a woman not unfamiliar to Galivad. Beatrice, with her angel-like appearance and glowing aura, is more akin to a viper in her actions, her need for self-gratification finding purchase in the indulgent devouring of bodies and souls—one of whom was Galivad's mother. The couple are kindred spirits with Gloriatrix, both taking relish in exacting their own sick torments on those who have the terrible misfortune of crossing their path—and Lila's envoys are exactly such misfortunates.

Also caught in their web is one working for an invisible authority, guided by forces unknown in the corporeal world. Alastair, a man who had once granted Mouse her freedom from indentured service, appears to have a mission that extends well beyond that of underground trader of goods in Menos. His intrigue with Maggie, the owner of the Silk Purse tavern, leads him to pull her into his plots as well—the goals of which seem to shift along with his loyalties. While Alastair is another of Geadhain's citizens for whom dying simply represents a bump on the road toward his next death, there is little question that he takes no pleasure in seeing Maggie tortured at the hands of their captors.

As the pack's journey continues, Caenith comes to see that Aghna's treachery is but the first of many shocking truths he must absorb. Deep in a cave, the pup that grew into a great Wolf is reunited with his mother. There in the darkness, the great Mother Wolf divulges a secret about his father's identity that eclipses all the Wolf thought to be true about the world and his place in it. Brought face-to-face with the woman/beast who bore him, he learns that his father is none other than Brutus, the creature who would see the world's destruction as a vessel of the Black Queen.

But while the immortals are faced with challenges of an otherworldly nature, most inhabitants of Geadhain cannot shake their mortal coil. Amid Menos's murk, there are civilian casualties of a war they are simply trying to survive. A simple observer, Aadore does not see herself as a party to the jingoist frenzy into which Menos is being whipped. She seeks only to reunite with her brother, Sean, a man who has been ravaged by not only time but life's savagery. At the moment of their strained homecoming, the city is rocked by explosions, and rising up from the detritus, these new players reveal themselves as the sole survivors.

Another unwitting player in fate's grand theater, young Beauregard has a past that remains a mystery. But in the present, he and his father, Devlin, have been entrusted with knowledge that may secure the future of Geadhain's most precious and beautiful region: Sorsetta. They leave the Summerlands—a land now scarred by Brutus's fury—to act as messengers of the war that is bearing down on Sorsetta's peaceful land. But more than that, they bring with them a tool of magik that offers one of the few glimpses of hope for defense. As Brutus appears to them, he is cloaked in the shadow of Magnus's trapped spirit. Knowing that his son is strong enough to survive the hardships that await him, Devlin sacrifices himself so that Beauregard might wield their weapon: a wonderstone—a shard of condensed, ancient magik. Doing so releases Magnus from his purgatory, banishes Brutus, and propels Beauregard forward from peaceful poet to warrior of fate.

Meanwhile, as our travelers venture through the Pitch Dark groves of Alabion, they are met with three sisters of another kind. The three red witches whose taste for blood would see a meal made of each them can sense Morigan's ascendant power. They foretell that hers will not be a path paved by peaceful light but with crimson. They also sense within Mouse a growing resentment for a fate that would drive her further into darkness.

The immutable nature of that which is preordained becomes ever more apparent as the Hunters of Fate finally meet with the sisters whose shaping of destinies makes them both friend and foe to all they meet. There, Morigan's true calling as a Daughter of Fate is confirmed, born of Elemech and sister to Eean and Ealasyd. But the sisters also reveal that the darkness overtaking Geadhain is more terrible than the anthropomorphized version of the Black Queen could have led them to believe; she is The Great Dreamer, Zionae, whose roots run deeper than anything in their world. She is devouring Geadhain, and even immortals cannot halt her frenzy. Their only hope is to return to the cradle where life began to find a trace of Zionae's fall from grace that might reveal a weakness. Despite the incredible losses they have incurred during their campaign to find the Sisters, Morigan and Caenith know that their destiny is to take up this mantle.

Recognizing that he, too, bears a burden for Geadhain's fate, weary Thackery strikes a bargain for time. As an old man nearing the end of his days, Thackery declined across the miles, an effect made even more glaring in the company of immortals and beings who are seemingly beyond death. Each night as the travelers rested, he was enveloped by a vigil of companions wary that each breath might be the one that ushered in the end. But to add time to one life, it must be taken from another's. And as a now youthful Thackery emerges from negotiations with the sisters, the origins of his newfound years are unknown.

Mouse—seemingly unable to deny the dark roots that were nurtured during her life in Menos—also readily accepts a deal, albeit from the three red witches, that would see her avenge her father. She is so blinded by her grief that she fails to realize that even for the purest of hearts, it is all too easy to be led astray when the desire to exact revenge rears its head. There is always a price to pay for such caprices, whether in this realm or another, and early indications are that Mouse may pay dearly for acting as the messenger for a spirit of retribution.

Even knowing that much of what lies ahead is unchangeable, the Three Sisters pull at wefts and warps here and there, keeping the fabric of fate intact, but all the while subtly changing its pattern. They cannot help themselves from crafting deals designed to test the travelers' characters and push the limits of their virtues. Nor can they remain untangled from the affairs of beasts and men, even when their own existence may depend upon it. Even as sisters of fate, they make these bargains, largely unaware of the impacts they might have on the final tapestry for the future. But then again, these are not concerns for beings who are reborn as easily as a snake sloughs off its skin.

The only certainty that remains is that the Green Mother is angry, and what she wills, she wills...

FEAST OF CHAOS

—The Cradle—
What is this fire that bleeds and roars?
A babe of chaos.
Veins, cracked on a dusty plain;
O'er shield of ruptured ice,
Hideous garden bewitched in glittering grace.
A man does not know what to tell his wonder,
Of this sea of stars on earth.
Hollows—canyons, deep and dark as space—that echo with time,
And whispers
Foretell the fleetness of your life.
Here, there be the calling of ancient Kings
The Will of Starry Things,
Of beasts both real and beyond.
Know thy place, as ant and beggar
In the Kingdom of true rule—
False demagogues and would-be lords,
Know thy place.
The wise listen in silence,
Enraptured by the melodies of our damnation.
Oh, ancient voice
Oh, starry voice
Speak
I hear, I fall, I weep.
—Kericot, poet of Geadhain

PROLOGUE

"A red moon," noted Eean, peering up over Elemech's pale shoulder and away from the witchwater pool into which the sisters had been staring. The slowly undulating glass reflected a patchwork landscape of lush vales, rivers shimmering with queer, petrol-stained beauty, and hooked claws of rock. Pandemonia. Eean dismissed most of the vision, for there was too much strangeness within—all of it distracting. Besides, the moon within the image was her real obsession. Lidless and swollen, it glared at her like the eye of a Dreamer of Blood and Doom.

"A blood moon," said Elemech. Over a thousand years had passed since a moon like that last shone over Geadhain. Elemech recalled the celestial event's synchronicity with another ominous affair—namely, war. "Taroch's Moon," she said. "We saw that moon on the night the would-be king's armies went to war with the Immortal brothers."

Disturbed by the memory of the warlord's failed conquest, and by what omens his moon suggested, Elemech swished away the vision with her pale hand, then flicked the water off her fingers and tried to see where the drops landed in the dark. Not even her sight could find them. "Lost," she muttered, though it was unclear what had been lost—the water or her hope.

Eean sighed and took a seat next to her sister. Together, they gazed like sad children at the freckles of light dancing off the crystal corners of their home—often the same flicker entranced them. Ealasyd watched the pair from the nearby shadows; how alike they were in looks and manner—twins, to all appearances. Ealasyd frowned. When she lived with two dour sisters rather than just one, she especially hated the arrangement.

She stomped out of her hiding spot and, in a further display of disgruntlement, threw down the moist rag she held so that it made a wet splat on the stone. "Listen here: I may be nearly ageless, but I still have the hunger and needs of a youngling. Right now, I have two mothers who are no better than a couple of ravens watching a graveyard. Gloomy, awful creatures you two have become. I cannot eat worms, nightmares, and dust as you do. I need sunshine, joy, and food!"

"Why should we feel joy?" asked Elemech miserably. "All of our work is crumbling. The Daughter of Fate—"

"Your daughter," interrupted Ealasyd, pointing at her. "My sister."

Scowling, Elemech resumed. "Morigan follows her own agenda. Her soul is full of chaos. I have no idea how she will end this war; she may even be starting another. I cannot follow her or her companions either. Not even with my Arts. The interference from Pandemonia's rampant magik warps the currents of Fate. I cannot witness her success or failure in the East. We have never been more powerless. Indeed, our power wanes as that of our shadows grows. Hate is what now nourishes the Green Mother. Winter is here, my sisters. The Longest Winter. The Black Queen's star is not far from our world. There are omens, blood moons...And let us not forget Death, in her City of Bones, who has broken all the laws of her kind by possessing her vessel, her immortal vessel—a feint so well played that I wonder who is the greater threat, Death or the Black Queen. I do not know how much more the Green Mother can endure from all these terrors."

"She will break," proclaimed Eean.

"Aye," agreed Elemech.

"Horrible!" declared Ealasyd, storming away. "You two are horrible. I'll find myself something to eat. I'll feed our guest, too, since I'm now the only one with any sense!"

On the way back to the rock-cubby where she and her sisters slept, she picked up the rag she'd discarded. "Infuriating!" she fumed. "Useless!" she grumbled. In times past, whenever her sisters had shared this state of depressive reflection, Eean had at least managed to retain a shred of pride and sagacity. Perhaps the upheaval in the world had affected the balance of their ancient sisterhood as well, for now Ealasyd had two morose sisters instead of one. The pair would spend days mumbling wicked prognostications and discussing disasters occurring in each corner of Geadhain. Unless there were entrails to be read, neither sister ever left Ealasyd the ingredients needed to cook a wholesome meal. Lately, she'd been hunting rats to feed herself and their guest. As a child, Ealasyd had had no idea how to flavor her beggar's stew. Everything that came out of her cast-iron pot bore notes of shoe leather and stinky feet, and tasted about the same.

Ealasyd shuffled over to the faintly glowing hearth, a pit filled with warm egg-shaped stones, many dim with their witch-light. Soon she would need to stoke the stones' heat again, and Eean's magik would be required. *I can't be bothered to ask*, she thought, after glancing at the two mournful shadows by the pool. *I'll do everything myself!* she cursed—her charwoman's chant of late. Angry, she grabbed a cup full of simmering herb broth from a pot hung over the hearth. She burned herself retrieving the medicine but cared not, as she knew that the pain and wound would pass in a speck to Eean, as happened with all of her injuries, decay, and age. Then, feeling mean, she seared her knuckles a second time on the outside of the pot. Eean expressed no discomfort, from what Ealasyd could tell. *They don't even care!* she nearly screamed.

Finished with her small rebellion, Ealasyd took her rag and her medicine over to their guest's bedside. *Eean's guest*, she thought, since no one else had invited him. Although Ealasyd's memory was so spotty that she bordered on the senile, she recalled the doll of the man she'd once made. An effigy of a lord of torture and nightmares with a shadow—vast, cold, black—rising over his shoulders. She had called him Rotsoul, and was amazed that she remembered the moniker. She paused before bowing to the sweat-soaked pallet, before tending to the man who stank of sweetly unwashed and spoiled flesh. She took a sand to *feel* for danger—for a sensitivity to the true selves of all creatures was Ealasyd's gift. Nothing wafted from him but his smell and fevered warmth. She no longer felt the great, cold shadow of Death that had once haunted this man, but only a faded presence: a fire diminished to ash and smoke, which cloyed in scent and taint and would never be purged. Rotsoul was what she had called the simulacrum of him that she'd made. But he really was rotten now: a barely breathing corpse. It was a miracle that he'd survived, even with the Green Mother's blessing and Ealasyd's herbs. A dark miracle.

She somehow sensed him watching her. Rotsoul's eyes were closed, his body cocooned in blankets. His face was webbed in scars, and he shivered as if he were frail, though she was not fooled. Eean had brought this monster into their home and then shortly thereafter had abandoned the duty of his care so that she might sulk and ponder death. Since that time, Ealasyd had reluctantly nursed the monster. And as much as she detested the task, she found it impossible to turn away from any suffering beast. He surely suffered, even if he was deserving of the torment.

Ealasyd began her duties by cleaning the spit and crusted pus off his face with her rag. The body's expulsion of infection usually meant the pendulum swung the right way—he was healing. Once finished with his face, Ealasyd hovered and studied the monster further to see if she had woken him, but he remained still. She took a short breath, then brought the cup of sacred water and ancient herbs to the monster's lips. At least the curative carried a strong, sappy aroma that diffused some of his prune-sweet stink. Before becoming a gloomy old hag, Eean had told Ealasyd that Rotsoul had been on the very edge of darkness—a walking corpse. The stench gave credence to her sister's claim. Ealasyd looked away while she fed the monster, then squinted here and there to make sure that most of the curative had trickled into his mouth. Some of the medicine washed over his scraggly, unshaven chin. His facial hair was growing in strangely for a man—patchy. A few specks later, the curative in the cup ran dry and she shook what little remained over his face like raindrops. Peaceful. He looked so calm, but then suddenly his brow wrinkled with awareness. He grabbed Ealasyd's hand so violently and quickly that she dropped her cup.

"Where am I?" hissed Sorren.

Trying to temper her heartbeat and avoid showing fear—as one does when dealing with monsters—Ealasyd replied, "In the home of the Three Sisters of Alabion. Eean brought you here. You asked for her help, I am told."

Regret twisted Sorren's face into swollen putty, and Ealasyd repressed a yelp. "I...did," he finally said, and released her.

As soon as she was free, Ealasyd hurried to fetch a stool. She positioned herself out of reach, next to an iron rod used to poke the fire-stones. "Eean saved you," she said.

"I remember now."

Uncharacteristically stoic, Ealasyd watched him as he began to cry. Monster's tears—it was like watching a toad weep. She doubted that his grief came from anything genuinely kind; at best, he was weeping for something valuable that he'd lost. "She managed to save your flesh...in a sense," said Ealasyd. "She stopped the great decay, though she could not remove the piece of Death's great shadow that is within you. Doing so is beyond my sister's power. You let Death in, and now She can never be removed—even if the worst of her power and presence has gone. You are *tainted*. Or rather, I suppose, more tainted. Is that why you're weeping? Because of what you will become?"

"I'm not crying for myself—" Sorren began, but a fit of coughing overcame him before he could finish.

Ealasyd waited until he had relaxed into a wheezing submissiveness and then continued. "You can't be upset for someone else. It's not in your nature. I can see your insides, Rotsoul; they cannot hide from me. My oldest sister says that my heart is made of sunshine, and like the sun, I fear the darkness. I fear you, helpless though you appear." She tapped the poker on the ground, then drew a line like a river in the dust. "Hmm...Do you know the story of Frog and Viper?" She didn't wait for him to answer. "I'm bad with stories; I lose track of the details. But this one I remember as clearly as I do my lost sister's name, as clearly as I perceive your dark truth." Ealasyd leaned in. "Spring in Alabion is a terrible time. In that season, the Green Mother cleanses herself through forest fires, floods, and storms. One spring—I couldn't say when—Frog and Viper were racing from the disasters. On the edge of a floodbank, they met. Frog knew he had a decent chance of swimming for his life—from both Viper and the cleansing—and he leaped into the brimming River Torn. However, he was halted by a plea from Viper. *Please, carry me across! Carry me to safety and I vow never to harm you or your children again. A marvelous offer*, thought Frog. An eternity of never worrying about this predator again would be a gift to all the generations of his kind. Once the two were in agreement,

Viper slithered onto Frog's back, and they were nearly to the other side of the deadly waters when—"

Sorren began to groan, thrashing in pain and anger.

"Oh, you've heard this tale before," said Ealasyd, a little sly, a little menacing. "Or you're smart enough to guess how it ends. Viper bit and strangled Frog, and they both drowned in the flood. You see, you can't change the nature of a creature. I may not be as wise as my sisters, but I know how animals work. And you, Rotsoul, you're Viper. Worse than he is, actually. A predator, a defiler. A creature meant to kill and pleased only by killing. There's nothing wrong with that; it's what you are. I bet you thought of redemption, of penance, when you beseeched the Green Mother. *Siogtine* is our word for it; at least I think that's it. I'm very forgetful. Regardless, you thought you would find a path to absolution. I don't see that in you. I'm sorry. Your soul is simply too dark. For the life of me, I can't figure out why Eean and our Mother brought you back. Unless there is something for you to kill..."

Then it came to the sister of innocence and sunshine: the reason why the Green Mother had brought the monster back. Excited now, Ealasyd stood and searched for the missing cup. Rotsoul—her monster—would need his greatest strengths for what he was to hunt.

_# I

THE CRADLE

I

Back in Alabion, when Morigan and the Wolf had consummated their marriage, they had sworn they would steal whatever scant sands they could to worship at the temples of each other's bodies. A bounty of riches then presented itself during the voyage toward Pandemonia. Long days of flight and conversations quickly evolved into an opportunity for the bloodmates to spend as much time as they could together, mostly in their chambers. At breakfast, they'd make an appearance, and perhaps another around lunch. However, the barb—as released by Alastair—was that more turbulence occurred on the back end of the great skycarriage than anywhere else on the vessel.

Tonight, they'd come out of their foxhole and joined the company and ship's captain for a night of feasting, drinking, and song—the latter courtesy of Alastair. Deciding this was to be a merry occasion, the mysterious jack of all trades produced a potent elixir that managed to inebriate the Wolf after several draughts. It tasted like varnish. *A slow and staggering vintage of rare spirits from the East*, Alastair promised the grimacing Wolf. *Strong enough to drop a herd of cattle.* While the liquor didn't knock the Wolf over, it certainly flushed his cheeks and had him clapping and singing along with an uncommon levity. Once the revelry had ended, and after finishing off Alastair's gift, the heavy-footed Wolf carried his lover back to their cabin. For hourglasses thereafter—possibly until dawn—they made love in the slowest, wettest, most drunken, and delicious way. More of a brute when under the influence, he'd fallen asleep kissing and softly biting her breasts. Soon, Morigan drifted off to his half-snore, half-growl, and occasional suckling, thinking how much she loved this beautiful creature. One of Alastair's pretty songs from down the corridor—carried through the great metal halls of the skycarriage like music through a pipe—was her final shepherd to sleep.

Morigan steps out onto the cracked-dust desert plain and sniffs. Wider, farther do her perceptions reach than the grandest of wolves, her mate— he who sleeps in another place. Who am I? Where have my bees taken me today? she wonders. The land offers only the most mysterious of clues; whirling clouds, hewn steeps, dunes mossed over with spiny, straggling forests, and a rolling sea of sand that creeps toward a starkly red horizon. Rendered in the morning sun are the glittering threads of many rivers branching over the land—they look like pulsing veins of blood. How sweet and unusual is the air that flows through her nose and down her throat. Upon its current, she tastes the chlorophyll of leaves, the chalk of sand, the spice of mildew, and the refreshing salt of the rivers—inland water that bears the taste of an ocean. What place could be so strange as to hold all of these details and elements in harmony? The answer strikes her then: Pandemonia.

I am here. No, Brutus is here, she realizes, as her enormous galvanized host begins a thundering run across the landscape. It has to be Brutus in whom she resides, as if trapped with a storm in a bottle. For who else has lungs like bellows? Who else climbs gullies in a reach or two, bounding about like a spastic ape, but the King of the Sun himself? With an astonishing disregard for natural laws, the Sun King leaps from butte to butte, jumping so high and so far that he soars like a wind over the irregular valleys and dashes through waterfalls that pour from winding pinnacles of rock. Following his speedy journey is difficult, and Morigan refrains from flexing her Will to see her host's secrets or feel all that he feels, for she realizes she is not alone in his mind.

Zionae, the Black Queen, rides in Brutus, too.

Frozen, as still as a woman hiding in the closet while a murderer creeps through the house, Morigan holds in check her consciousness and her bees—a maddening effort to maintain. Zionae sibilates on every wind that whisks Brutus's ears. Zionae rushes through his veins like poison. Zionae perks his nipples and groin with infernal arousal: a need to hunt, kill, and breed. From her hidey-hole within the mad king, Morigan listens to the suggestions of the Dark Dreamer. More intimations and emotions than words are these whispers. Still, Morigan discerns enough of her enemy. Zionae's madness is a paste of crushed spiders, bent nails, broken glass, aborted children, and the tears and blood of those who have died screaming in horror, a madness so thick that it pours over Morigan, blocking her ability to scream. Better that she does not, lest Brutus's dark passenger hear, and thus know, of her presence.

Morigan buries herself deeper into the mad king's soul. She tries to creep elsewhere, to find a piece of his mind untainted by Zionae's lust. There is no corner of the Sun King's mind, though, in which wickedness does not fester. A black poison has washed through Brutus's soul. Even when Morigan flees to what should be sacred memories of Brutus and his brother, she finds no familial sanctity. Instead, she experiences her host pounding Magnus with his fists, tearing him with his teeth, and thrusting into his pale brother with his gargantuan sword of meat. Is this a memory or a dark delusion? She hopes the latter, as the acts Brutus is committing are depraved beyond measure. When she seeks out Brutus's memories of Mother-wolf, she finds that these, too, have been corrupted. Now the king fantasizes about devouring his mate, eating her innards, and stabbing his prick into her shuddering dead corpse. Perversion, lunacy, and repellent desires assault Morigan wherever she darts. The whole of Brutus's mind has become maggoty with death. He and his evil mother would rape the world. They would eat and feast on every meat in creation. Their hunger has no end. Mercy save us all, laments Morigan.

I must escape! I must wake!

But rather than soaring in a silver cloud to freedom, Morigan is caught in a darkness that clots and constricts around her. The light she seeks seems farther out of reach, a pinhole that vanishes in a blink. Now there is only the whispering darkness. Zionae has found her.

"Little Fly, I warned you against any return to my Dreaming," Zionae says—a screeching of rending metal. *"Come now, let me into your heart and feel the glory of a world without remorse. I feel it in you—a fear. Fear is the root of hunger. Indulge in it. I can show you the heights and depths of passion. Such glories do I see in your future. I shall offer you a spot at my Feast. Kill your pack. Make love with your Wolf on a bed of their corpses, and then kill him too as he empties inside of you."*

A red mist whirls around Morigan. It parts like a curtain to the Black Queen's cues, and Morigan appears in the grisly scene described by the Dreamer. There, upon a stage of blood, upon a mattress of tangled corpses, Morigan watches herself ride the rigid corpse of her bloodmate. From the pile of flesh beneath the abominable lovemaking, Mouse's waxen face glares up as Morigan uses her promise dagger to hack, with gusto and virtuosity, at what remains of her mate. If Morigan could vomit here, she would. The doppelgänger turns from her unsavory duties and smiles at Morigan.

"See what you can become, my child," says Zionae, through the doppelgänger's mouth. *"Such glory and beauty. Rise and find yourself anew."*

"No! Never!" screams Morigan.

Summoning her strength and her swarm of bees, and calling for her mate, Morigan shines. Burned by Morigan's light, hissing and gurgling, the darkness fades away to smoky tatters. Morigan bobs peacefully in the gray mist of nowhere, safe from Brutus and the Black Queen. But she is still not alone.

Who is that? she wonders, and drifts toward the figment in the fog. Is it a girl? Is it Macha? For the faded shape and distance feel familiar—evoking the moment she and the young changeling met in Dream. If not the young seal girl, it must be the gray, billowing spirit of some other young woman. For the figure is small, shrouded, and meek. Lost lamb, thinks Morigan, floating closer still. She reaches for her with hands of glass and smoke. Then, like a coat of pins, the bees sting her in reprobation; they warn her, too late, not to touch the spirit.

The girl turns to her. But Morigan does not see Macha's gentle countenance; indeed, what greets her eyes is far from a child. It is as if something bulbous has been stuffed into a child's body and draped in a robe of mist that fails to hide its deformity. The shape swells as Morigan beholds it, *growing from her fear. It stares at her from two soulless eye sockets swirling with winged insects—flies, though as loud and as large as bees. Beneath the crawling skin shine glimpses of a picked, possibly metal skull. A mask? What is this dream-walking monster? A Dreamer? Not a Dreamer, sting her bees. What then?* she wonders. *Cicada music hums from the verminously churning head, becoming sounds and words that Morigan can hear through her entire body.*

"You are not safe. You are never safe," says the creature.

Morigan shrieks.

II

"My Fawn! It is alright. Wherever you were, you are in no danger now."

Soft sheets, soft fur, and hard muscle rubbed against her flesh. The only sounds she heard were her cries, Caenith's voice, and the thrum of wind striking the ship's shell. No smells of blood and death. No buzzing nightmare person or whispers of Zionae. Morigan stopped her struggling and breathed against her bloodmate's body for a while. She inhaled his onion-and-pepper scent, soothed herself with the warmth of the prowling beast of fire in her chest, and relaxed in the cradle of his strength. When a few sands had passed, the Wolf pulled away a little, swept back some of Morigan's sweaty hair, and caressed her face. Caenith's eyes seemed grayer than normal—worried.

You called my father's name, more than once, he said in their secret language of souls. *I could not wake you until a sand ago. You were trying to scream, and yet no sound came out. Like the wailing women, the Banninshide, who shriek grief that only those of magik can hear. What did you see, my Fawn?*

Your father—and the Black Queen. In Pandemonia.

I see.

And another evil creature, too.

No matter, said the Wolf, and kissed her brow. *We shall hunt the meaning of these omens and dreams together. I regret that such a wonderful evening has been ruined by a visitation from my father and his wicked master.*

As she stared at his carved and gloriously handsome face, she had a flash of his eyes rolling back until their whites showed and of his neck decorated in a bleeding, raw smile—just as he'd appeared when she had murdered him in her dream.

Our flight of romance is over, my Wolf. She slipped out of his arms and off the bed, gathering her clothes. *We must discuss what I saw, and what it means, as a pack. We must prepare ourselves for Pandemonia.*

Leaning on one elbow, the Wolf watched his bloodmate clothe her lithe body. She did not glance at him, most surely trying to keep him from her sight. Tainting her sweet fragrance was an unusual, skunky note of sweat: the perspiration of fear. Mortal fear; murderous fear. It was a stink he knew well from his days as a gladiator in Menos. But what could she fear? He stayed on the bed for so long that Morigan finally looked his way. Then he caught it: a glimmer in her silver stare. With a sting of the perception inherited from their union, and a chill that pimpled his skin, he knew she worried for him.

III

While the majority of Eod's ships were constructed for military use, the *Skylark*, the vessel in which the company traveled, had been made to entertain dignitaries. Its generous hollow belly held all the comforts of a passenger vessel: private sleeping arrangements, running water, a kitchen. Even an expansive parlor had been installed, and it bordered on theatrical greatness with its echo, small stage, knotted-silk curtains, and rows of buttoned leather seats. A great deal of luxury and design had been dedicated to the great parlor, and quite often the company and their uninitiated members spent the day there. They drank, ate, and played games of Kings and Fates with Mouse's deck of cards (or *Crowns and Fates*, depending on which regional rules were in use).

Sometimes one of the company stared out of the portals at the streaming clouds and flickers of dark blue water far beneath. Often they contented themselves with Alastair's crooning. The shadowbroker did so love to sing; his voice was extraordinary, and no one asked him to stop. Thackery still hadn't received a plausible answer about how it was that Alastair so closely resembled a bard Thackery knew a hundred years past. "Are you a descendent of the man?" he might ask, at which point Alastair would, like a conjurer, produce an instrument—a flute from his cloak, a lute from under his seat—and deflect the inquiry with smiles and song. As the days dwindled, the sage began to doubt that Alastair would ever be forthcoming and stopped asking.

Despite the skycarriage's fleetness, the voyage to Pandemonia would be a long one. It would require crossing the whole of eastern Geadhain and then journeying over the Chthonic Ocean: the wet abyss that separated the fragmented lands of east, west, north, and south into isolated kingdoms. Following some snippy consultations with Moreth—who seemed to think everyone less intelligent than he—the companions learned it would take around three days of flight to reach the great island continent of Pandemonia. Beyond that, their journey to Pandemonia's first harbor of civilization, the city of Eatoth, would take many days to weeks of hard hiking inland. From Eatoth, they would reassess and plot their journey. For Eatoth, the City of Waterfalls, with its quicksilver towers and its encircling wall of ever-flowing water (*Balderdash*, thought Mouse), was said to be a repository of the world's most ancient and coveted wisdom—legends and facts older than anything in Central Geadhain. Surely, they would discover a course or thread to follow from there. Pandemonia…Eatoth…To many of the companions, it felt as if they were headed to the very end of Geadhain.

Aside from Moreth, no one had made this journey before, so each morning he prepared them with naught but the direst briefings on temperamental climates, bloodthirsty animals, and inconceivably chaotic landscapes. Magik wasn't to be wielded where they were headed, apparently, since the etheric currents surrounding Pandemonia amplified or warped its effects. And even the smallest scrape could summon a horde of ravenous animals—or so the Menosian claimed. Moreth's depictions of the land had received the company's greatest incredulity: deserts of ice, lakes of fire, fields that went from green to rotten in a day. Such strangenesses were a strain to believe among even the most imaginative members of the company; they sounded like wonders from the ages of Fire, Dust, Winter, and Wetness. After all, they'd survived Alabion—how much worse could Pandemonia be?

Given Moreth's propensity for gloating, Mouse was suspicious that he knew or was truthful about all that he claimed. This morning, she called his bluff as they sat around the parlor.

"How far to this city, Eatoth, from when we land?" she asked. "You've said days to weeks, which is quite a discrepancy."

"That depends on where we disembark," replied Moreth, not bothering to divert his attention from the whorls of steam rising from the mug of tea he held in both hands. "I assume you were eavesdropping on the captain and I during our cartography sessions, and you've attended my briefings. Despite all that, you seem to have missed the most important details."

Mouse scowled, but didn't deny the accusation. "Which are?"

"The problem with Pandemonia is that nothing stays the same," continued Moreth. All heads in the room now turned to him; he spoke with a slow and captivating lilt that the company had learned indicated a certain valuable, if arrogant, wisdom. "While this is true in life—with age, feelings, aspirations—it is even truer in Pandemonia. What was a shoreline yesterday could be a ravine today. Lakes dry up in weeks or months; some then fill with lava or, if the land feels frolicsome, flowers and herds of gentle beasts—though I would not expect to find many gentle beasts in Pandemonia. Such sweet-tempered creatures as do exist are quickly devoured by the more aggressive fauna of the realm. Kericot, who visited Pandemonia once, wrote of its nature in his poetic ramblings. If you dig through the man's florid nonsense, you'll find an occasional resonant gem:

Walled in water, gardened in flame, a wind that rails over earth untamed.

Fall upon the sword of reason, swallow your terrified shout.

Awe and weep for the fractured land, though never, ever, let the chaos out.

"You will see when we arrive. All that I've told you is true, and none of it half as tall a tale as you will behold. Still, I think Kericot's words describe best what to expect: total disorder. An assault on what you understand of nature. There is a reason why Pandemonia exists at the farthest reaches of our world, contained in a prison of the deepest water, in a region where the ethereal currents disable technomagik and the winds blow so fiercely that only the strongest ships or skycarriages can reach it. The chaos must be contained."

After a sip of tea, he added, "So, my dear rodent, to answer your question—I have an idea where to take us once we land. But only an idea.

Where to go next? Well…life is an adventure, and this will be one of your greatest. And perhaps your last."

Moreth laughed, feeding on the silence of the company.

If a man could be a fart, a fart Moreth would be, decided Mouse. She left the seats to look through the round windows, watching the peaceful flocks of cotton that floated beside the vessel.

A patient, silent presence stood beside her. Adam had been with her all morning, in fact, though she often overlooked him. Wherever she went, Adam followed, and his dedication was finally penetrating her callousness. Each morning, they now met to go on a long, speechless stroll across the metal decks of the *Skylark* before joining the others in the parlor. Mouse appreciated the company of a man who did not feel the need to talk; so many people felt the urge to ruin silence with blather. When she and Adam did speak, it was to exchange a comment regarding the technomagik that surrounded them: engines, decks, motors, and propulsion. The changeling thought all of it fascinating. His inquiries, though, often demanded answers beyond her schooling, and she added them to a mental list to be discussed later with Talwyn and Thackery. Most of the time, however, there were no questions. She and silent Adam simply walked down a humming tunnel, listened to the click-clack music of their shoes, and felt completely quiet and content.

Although they spent much time together, their intimacy had not grown past friendship. At some point, they had reached an unspoken acceptance that they were not going to be lovers. Perhaps Adam had decided that the time and situation would not permit a deeper companionship. Perhaps he wanted to know what other mates there might be in this great, grand world outside of Alabion. He also likely correctly interpreted Mouse's aloofness and flighty affection as signals of her lack of interest. In life, there existed a window in which circumstances could unfold, and that window of opportunity had closed. Mouse felt all this with only a soft sinking in her heart, even if at times she recognized how beautiful a man he was. She needed friends and family more than lovers. Yet, she was never without Adam, and his ability to calm her with his calm, to make her smile with his smile, was the mark of true friendship.

"How is the Wanderer today?" asked Adam after a while.

The Wanderer was how Adam and the others referred to the dormant entity in her flesh—Morigan's father Feyhazir, the Dreamer of Passion. Since they'd left Alabion, the Wanderer had not stirred. He slept like a hibernating creature in the depths of her mind. Unless she really paused and listened, usually in the darkness of her room at night, she couldn't hear him. A better use of these recent days of peace might have been to contemplate and test her covenant with Feyhazir, yet she found herself wasting hourglasses on cloud-watching and walks. For Kings' sake, a woman was entitled to a break every so often, and she had certainly earned hers.

"Quiet, mostly," she said. "He's there, deep down. Sleeping like a creature at the bottom of the sea. I'm not sure how to wake him; I'm not sure that I want to wake him. Last time I swear I lost a year off my life."

"Loss…In Briongrahd, while I worked story from stone, I would see pups grow into wolves, see them throw away innocence and kindness—they never cared or knew what they'd lost. I lost years upon years, waiting for something to chase. I felt my soul, if not my pelt, grow gray from age and sadness."

"What an odd—and gloomy—thing to say," replied Mouse. Turning, she slapped her companion's arm and he made a canine whine.

"Gray is, however, a fine color for a pelt," said Adam, touching her hair. On the voyage to Pandemonia, she'd emerged one morning with a gentleman's military cut, streaked along the sides with gray. The haircut gave her the air of a military commander. She'd said she barbered herself because she was *simply ready for a change.*

"A pelt?"

"None of us are above animals."

Mouse went to slap him again, but he caught her hand and made a small, challenging growl. Too easily she forgot that he was, truly, part animal. He held her wrist longer and more firmly than a friend should, and that flame they'd convinced themselves was smothered sparked up. Accentuated in the morning glow, his lean, tanned physique held a gleam of copper, and his eyes were as deep and brown as ancient amber. His charisma was poorly hidden by the light sash and kilt he wore. Down the valley of his sinewy, tattooed chest hung the dark stone talisman given to him by Elemech. He kept a trim and perfect beard, and Mouse saw the muscles of his jaw moving underneath, as if he were chewing or hungry. Feeling light and a little detached from reality, Mouse watched the man's gaze move over her slight hips, small breasts, and up to the sharp face people told her was pretty. All the while, the changeling's nostrils flared as he smelled her perfume of iron, roses, and sage.

They were interrupted by a strained and aggravated laugh—likely from someone responding to one of Moreth's witticisms, which were usually at someone else's expense and often led to arguments. The two returned to the half-circle of furniture set back from the more orderly rows of bolted seats around the stage. There, the company had gathered in typical fashion. Thackery and Talwyn sat beside one another and nursed porcelain cups of tea. Their lordly poses lent them an air of brotherly masters, kings upon thrones. Now that Thackery had cheated time, the sage and scholar looked similar; both had square high-browed faces and stares that glimmered with vast intellect. Still, Thackery's raven-dark hair and Talwyn's reddish-gold locks distinguished one from the other. Alastair sat next to the two, hidden in his cloak, tuning a lute. Legs crossed and oozing leisure, Moreth reclined in a seat many chairs away from the others and cradled a book in his hands. Physical separation from the group did not seem to diminish his need for a disagreement.

"What you've suggested is absurd," he said, not looking up from his book, nor repeating whatever absurdity Mouse and Adam had missed. "Street-level rumormongering. You are intelligent men; please stop embarrassing yourselves. How can either of you—you, especially, Thackery, Thule as you are—not see the connection between the disruption at Taroch's Arm and the doom of Menos?"

Not everything had been relaxation and measured preparation aboard the *Skylark*. Moreth, Alastair, and the crew had informed the lost wanderers of Geadhain's current events. Of all the ill tidings, the destruction of Menos had become the topic that circulated most often and provoked passionate discussions. Genocide on that scale seemed somehow even more dreadful when no one knew the identity of the perpetrator and all were unable to investigate the area thoroughly enough to venture an opinion. Ruins—everything lay in ruins, the companions were told. Foul entities were said to stalk the remains of the Iron City under a blanket of perpetual night made up of smoke and ash that would not disperse from the realm. Mouse wouldn't have believed such an old wives' tale herself if she and Adam had not seen the queer, distant globe of black smoke from out of one of the *Skylark's* windows one bright, beautiful day. They had run to fetch the Wolf and asked for his opinion, which had been grim. "I can see nothing but death," he had said.

"Taroch's Arm is missing, gentlemen and gentlewomen," declared Moreth.

A hush seized the company. Mouse took a seat before tempers erupted, and Adam knelt beside her chair—doglike and protective. Behind Thackery's blue gaze, thoughts furiously brewed. Mouse knew he would be the first to explode.

"Where did you hear this?" spat Thackery.

"What matters the source?" said Moreth with a shrug. "I cannot tell you where the eyes of Menos peer—what few of them are left—any more than you can speak for Eod's master or spies. What is important in what I have told you is that his arm was *stolen*."

"Stolen? By whom?" pressed Thackery.

"A woman and a large cutthroat," said Moreth. "If I were not needed to shepherd you six lost lambs, I would hunt the culprits myself. They are Geadhain's greatest game at the moment—perhaps the greatest murderers of any age. I am sure that a man as learned in magikal antiquities as yourself, Sage, could think of a few suspects. Put that Thule genius to work. Let me know what you come up with. Perhaps we can exchange notes."

Thackery puffed. Caution stilled his tongue, and he held himself in nervous hesitation. *Did he know something?* wondered Mouse. The fear in his eyes, the fading of his skin from red to pale, indicated he might.

"An arm?" she asked. "What's the harm in a dead man's arm?"

"I like an opportune rhyme, so I shall answer," replied Moreth, finally placing his book down and turning his waxy, expressionless face her way. He wriggled one of his gloved hands. "Not just an arm, Mouse, a talisman. Taroch was a sensualist and aesthete. He believed in the pleasures of touch. He was captivated by the beauty of the sculpture and sorcery he created with his hands. His arm, therefore, was arguably the most precious part of his body, his magik, his soul. Taroch was the lord of transmutation, a sorcerer who could whisper a wind into a hurricane, turn water into fire, or encourage a tremble in the earth into the mightiest quake. What do you suppose a madman and madwoman could do with a relic containing all of Taroch's power?"

"Nothing good," she said.

"Nothing good," repeated Moreth, and resumed his reading.

They sat in an unpleasant silence until Morigan and the Wolf arrived through a gilded arch. Mouse hadn't seen her friend very much beyond last evening's festivities. Just then, the *Skylark* seemed to pass into a cloud, or perhaps a hint of Morigan's mood manifested, for she flickered with darkness. While Morigan was as striking as ever—with her mane of fire and glittering gold, her buxom figure and sultry pout—she seemed tired after a night of tossing happily in the sheets. *Maybe not so happily*, thought Mouse, noticing the Wolf's stormy disposition. Unhappiness hung on his grand, craggy shoulders like pauldrons of stone, and fretting had turned his carved brows into a single ridge of worry that pooled his gaze with black. Both of Mouse's friends appeared slightly unkempt: Morigan's hair was twisted into the kind of pleasing spirals in which birds might make their nests, and the Wolf was looking wild and unshaven, even for him. Alastair had stitched for him a leather warrior's skirt (several attempts at pants had ended in burst seams and frustration), which complemented his sandals and gave him a gladiatorial presence. This morning his veins—the ones at his temples and the multitude on his arms—were full and throbbing. He marched toward the company exuding the menace of the Blood King he had once been. Even Moreth lost interest in his book and stared at the Wolf's approaching hulk.

"You two look miserable," commented Mouse.

Morigan, rattled by something, tried to settle into a seat beside Thackery, though she looked as if her seat's cushion was full of pins. The Wolf stood behind his bloodmate's chair with his arms crossed.

"An uncomfortable sleep," said Morigan after the long pause. "Bad dreams."

"Oh, fuk," said Mouse.

Thackery shushed her and laid a hand upon Morigan's forearm. Morigan did not glance at him. She didn't speak for a long, long spell, and then spoke only one word.

"Brutus."

That one word broke the spell of silence. "I saw him in Pandemonia," she resumed. "Either in the recent past or in our future. I felt the evil that drives him. I touched her, or she somehow touched me...the Black Queen." Gasps and shivers spread through the company. "I believe she holds great sway in Pandemonia. I believe we are headed into the territory of our enemy. And that is not all, my friends. I encountered...a spirit. Another walker in dreams. Dark and wicked, and willingly so. I cannot say what this creature was or whom it serves, but it is malign and grim and full of doom."

Done, Morigan hung her head. The Wolf brought a huge hand to her shoulder and squeezed. Having spent hourglasses in the Crucible conspiring with Gloriatrix and Elissandra, Moreth knew that seers often glimpsed a bit more prophecy with the right prodding, the right questions. This seer was still in the thrall of her nightmare, still attuned to the Fates. He felt as if he could reach out, wave his hand around her, and feel the invisible silver sparks leap from her eyes. There would be no better occasion to press this witch for truths.

"Would you say that we shall find what we seek?" he asked. "In Pandemonia?"

Using the fullness of her senses, the buzzing prophets that were her bees, the instincts of the fire wolf in her chest, and the primal rush of her heart as she considered his question, Morigan sought an answer. A specific, determined future could not be found, although the tingle of destiny ran through her. "Yes," she said.

Interesting, thought Moreth, and returned to his questioning.

"What is it? A weapon?"

"No."

"An answer?"

"Yes."

"Shall we meet our enemy?"

The tingle in Morigan became a jolt. "Our truth," she snapped.

Black blades of shadow suddenly crossed the room, and the skycarriage hit a surge of battering winds. The company was forced to ignore the implications of Morigan's doomsaying so that they could cling to bolted-down seats for safety. Imperturbable, Moreth raised a gloved finger and started to launch into another question for the seer, but the Wolf barked him into reconsidering. A few sands later, when the vessel had not calmed, but only intensified its rocking, Moreth quietly addressed the issue of the turbulence. Not many heard him over the rattle of wind on metal, or paid heed through the flickering darkness; they felt as though they were in a tin can being tossed in a hurricane.

"It's Pandemonia," he explained. "We've arrived."

IV

The company gathered in the supply bay of the *Skylark* as it sputtered over the sea. Its engines struggled to resist the magik-warping effects of Pandemonia; it could not hover here for long. The time for goodbyes was short. Morigan and Mouse, who usually joined in labor, instead allowed the men to pack their steel-girded and warlike oarboat. Sitting in the deep vessel, the ladies craned their necks to watch the black water sloshing over the ship's bay—a portion of the *Skylark*'s hull that had been separated and lowered into the sea as a giant gangplank. They wrinkled their noses at the burning stink of salt, brine, and soil that issued forth from the ocean. Caenith did most of the lifting; the other fellows mostly slipped about. Adam would never have a pair of sea legs, Mouse realized, trying not to laugh at his stumbles on the wet dock. Once the oarboat had been packed with supplies and all seven companions were aboard, Alastair untied the rope from its cleat and threw it to the Wolf to catch. The shadowbroker's contract had been fulfilled: he had brought them to Pandemonia's border. From this point on, they would be at the mercy of Moreth and Fate. As powerful currents pulled the company's vessel away, Alastair bid them fair parting.

"Good fortune and safe travels," he said, turning his gaze on Mouse. "Watch out for them, Fionna."

Strange and meaningful words, observed Mouse, as Alastair rarely misplaced his warnings. She waved back at the man, who was already a ghost in the ocean mist that covered the landscape. The vessel drifted until the Wolf hopped to the stern, grabbed the oars, and began beating the water with his strength. Their craft was deep, its bulkheads so tall only the Wolf got a proper view of the seascape. The rest of the company settled for peering out the unused oar slots.

For a time, they saw nothing through the fog. They swayed and huddled together for warmth like doomed slaves—with Moreth, perhaps, as their slave-master. He sat alone at the bow of the craft: primly upright, cane atop his lap. Even for this dangerous safari, he had donned his bowler hat. The man's poise appeared unshakeable. Mouse believed men like him to be the most dangerous breed, because they did not fear death or change. Morigan clung to Mouse, worried about either the Menosian's unnerving poise or some other terror. Mouse wished she could tell her friend that things would be all right, but she could not lie. The creeping fear of what they'd find here became a sickness in her throat. And she couldn't see a damn thing. She could hear only the hiss and splash of wind and sea, smell only the salty reek of an unfamiliar ocean. If her father, Vortigern, were here, she knew he would have inspired them all with his charm and composure. Vortigern, though, was dead. He could not be here to hold her hand or to gasp a potpourri-scented breath at the sudden lights in the distance, which flickered as the morning mist broke.

Perhaps the strings of this mystery were what pulled them like puppets to their feet and had them standing on the benches and leaning against the hull to peer. Spiny, glowing things swam alongside the vessel. The creatures flashed in and out of the dark waters like lures leading the companions on. The company stared, speechless, past the quiet shadow of the Master of El to an island shore that dazzled in places like diamonds, or ice. By the Kings, every tall tale of Moreth's suddenly rung true. Behind the shore rose a many-humped land of green, blue, and phosphorescent growth. Fuchsia trails, rolling purple clouds, and here and there, flashes of emerald lightning sparkled over the strange land like a colorful mirage. They could not grasp what they felt or saw; they were torn between extremes of awe, wonder, and dread. As they stared, they knew that what they witnessed—however queer—was but a taste of the bizarre, a prelude to the true feast of chaos they would dine on when they landed.

II

TEETH

I

A beach. That much, at least, the company recognized as they pondered their landing. Near where their boat bobbed, there ran a shoreline of ashen silt, pointed shale, and crystal rocks mixed together like burned and unfinished glass. Gray crabs congregated on stones, or poked their stalked eyes out of the sand like stealthy rogues, watching the strangers. Beyond the beach was a great craggy hill that would challenge each companion's strength. They shivered when guessing what awaited them atop that climb, beneath a skyline of dense, rumbling, violet clouds. On trembling legs, the company stood aside as the grunting Wolf splashed into the ocean and pulled the boat to shore. Moreth stood ahead, glaring and defiant.

Although he presented a front as brave as Moreth's, the Wolf suffered from confusion and doubt. Already, his senses seemed disordered. Warning smells—smoky, earthy, musky, honeyed, mossy—polluted the air with a near insufferable redolence. His hearing fared no better: he was unable to identify a single one of the innumerable animal clacks, tweets, and roars that sung down from the wall of rock. Suddenly, he realized that a hunter—no matter how great—without specific knowledge of his environment and all these alien smells and rainforest echoes, might be a blind and useless man. Morigan's star, shining steadily in his chest, calmed his nerves and anger a little in this realm of instability. Once the boat was ashore, he stood behind his bloodmate and mind-whispered his fears to her.

My hide crawls with danger. I do not know what to focus on, or where to bark. The chaos of this realm bewilders my senses.

I am no better at sorting through the madness myself, my Wolf. Fragments of memory and time are everywhere.

It seemed impossible that the day could become any stranger, but as she shuffled ahead over the silt beach, Morigan saw lines drawn in the sky—faint scintillating strings of glass, arranged in a definite convergence and pattern. She didn't know what they were, though her bees seemed to have an idea. Agitatedly, her bees pressed their stingers against their cage of flesh; they wanted to play those strings of fate or magik in the sky and hear their music. Morigan flailed and then found the Wolf's arm. Like his bloodmate, he'd walked on, nearly unaware of his own actions. He could not see the strings in the sky; instead, he fixated on what lay over the rise they needed to climb. Another mysterious instrument lay there, one with strings that twanged tunes of animal cries, nauseating stenches, and delirious sights.

The Menosian will guide us; that is why he has come, said Morigan.

Caenith growled and glared back at the man dusting the ashy sand off his overcoat. Moreth was totally unaffected by the strangeness around them, behaving as if he'd stepped off the deck of a pleasure cruiser to begin his vacation. In his shadow, the two scholars, Mouse, and Adam waited. The Wolf felt as if their positions were a subconscious acknowledgment of their new pack master. The Wolf did not know how *not* to lead. Was he to fall into step behind this wicked man? Could he actually listen to Moreth's orders and not rip out his throat? Morigan squeezed the Wolf's hand before he stormed up the hill.

I shall study this new hunting ground, and I shall master it, he declared.

I know, she replied.

"Follow me," said Moreth, with perfect timing. He slung his knapsack over his shoulder and strode past the pair, before moving up the rise in a puff of black dust. "And try and remember every warning about this land's danger you've been given. On the subject of which, is anyone cut or bleeding?"

The company checked themselves and their garments for tears; none were found.

"Good," Moreth said. During his briefings, he'd forewarned them that blood of any kind—from a wound, from a menstrual cycle even—would hold extraordinary allure for the creatures of this realm. The company presumed his caution arose from this.

"What about the boat?" asked Talwyn.

"No point in worrying about it," Moreth called back. "The shore—and boat—won't be here in a week or two."

"A week or two?" complained Talwyn.

Moreth hissed at the scholar. "We're not on a damned retreat, you fool. I'd have thought that you, with all your inquisitiveness, would've paid the best attention. Let me clarify: we have come to the very heart of chaos in our world, a land that never stays the same, save for a few points of order. All else is uncharted; unpredictability and death await us at every step. Whatever journey we have committed ourselves to shall take longer than a few days inland and back. I guarantee you that much. We shall be lucky if we see our homes again in a year."

"We don't have that long," said Morigan, thinking of Black Stars and doom.

"Then we had better quicken our steps," replied Moreth. Regaining the ghoulishly perfect carriage that he'd lost for a speck to spitting anger, Moreth threw back his shoulders and continued hiking. Climbing after the man as he moved with great athleticism up the rubbly path was laborious work for a few of them. When they'd all caught up with Moreth atop the rise, they quietly studied the land. *What am I seeing?* each asked their inner child. For their odyssey would take them through a realm of dreamscapes and wonder that only the youngest element within each could comprehend. Their vision scattered over the humps, spires, and valleys of Pandemonia, into the rainbow storms and queer will-o'-the-wisps on the horizon, not knowing where to focus in the phantasmagoria. Eventually, they restrained their wandering inspection and looked to their feet, where, separated by a line of black and a line of green, the ashen rise ended. The slope angled down into a field of tall grass, fat-budded flowers, and small swarms of insects that flickered like embers.

"Beautiful..." whispered Talwyn.

Farther on, the hillside meadow met a bank of rocks beyond which flowed a twisting rapid. Talwyn's gaze followed the rapid and its mysterious windings to break down the larger mystery into smaller chunks that his mind could digest. In the left of his vision, the water flowed into a creek, gentle and babbling. The creek then dried out, suddenly, as it entered a yellowish grassland with far-off steppes. Over that region of Pandemonia reigned the blackest of thunderheads, with lightning so bright it spotted Talwyn's sight as he stared. He wondered whether the tremor in the soles of his boots was caused by the thunder or his own quailing. He wondered what kind of rain would fall there, in that yellow desert. Perhaps a rain of fire, to have forged the enormous broken crystals that glimmered like the rib cages of giants ossified in crystal between the steppes. Dead crystal giants. Talwyn laughed, unable to disprove the lunacy of his imaginings. Faintly seen herds of animals raced across the shimmering, storming land.

Finally, he tore his attention away from the desert. To his right, the meadow broadened and surged wildly into thickets and trees wholly unfamiliar to him, despite that he had just come from Alabion and its strangling verdure. These shuddering trees—their branches like loose hoses draped and tangled in each other, the knots in their trunks spilling forth profusions of canary-yellow moss—seemed more suited to an expressionist's unfinished painting than to woodland. Birds circled above the rubber forest, warbling warnings against approach. The birds, too, seemed unfinished—ugly clay things that Talwyn could not fully distinguish, even when he squinted. These strange terrors were not hidden from the Wolf's sight, however, and he glanced at the sky-flecks and frowned.

Beyond the river lay the least objectionable terrain: more grass, scabs of stone, a smattering of dead-looking trees, a speckled trail of sunlight in which to walk. *Not entirely normal*, thought Talwyn, *though close enough*. He had a hunch they would head in that direction. Moreth proved him right.

"Deserts and dense woodlands we stay away from," said the Menosian. He stripped off his coat, revealing his male-blouse and buttoned vest; sterling matchlock pistol grips gleamed from the shoulder holsters under his sweaty pits. Very quickly, the weather had changed from ocean-cool humidity to sweltering heat. Moreth folded his coat and put it away, placed his pack back on, and then twisted the metal gargoyle head off his cane—a metal scrape and quick flash of light confirmed the presence of a hidden blade—before moving toward the river. The company followed him closely.

"Once more I shall tell you the rules," said Moreth. "They'll make more sense now that you're here and you've seen the lay of the land. First, we sleep only in the open. I know that sounds contrary to huntsman's wisdom, but here we do not sleep in hollows lest the earth seal them into tombs while we rest. Second, no fires, obviously, since we aim not to draw attention to ourselves. In Pandemonia, you'll find a million ways to die. Many of them are almost pleasant: death on a bed of poison flowers, or at the paws of a charming, furry animal with a musk or spray that melts your flesh like acid. Alabion is dangerous, as you all well know, although the realm of the Sisters Three plays by nature's rules. Nature can be cruel by mortal judgments, but we understand her and her laws. Do not attempt to understand Pandemonia—death will come more quickly if you try. You might not even know it's happening until the Pale Lady shows up to take your hand. So the third and most important rule is, do not touch, eat, or otherwise engage with anything unless I have confirmed it is safe."

Moreth spun around and poked his cane into Talwyn. The scholar had been bumbling along behind him, eyes wide, fingers trembling and ready to grab things to feed his scientific curiosity.

"I wasn't—I wouldn't just touch things!"

"You would; you will. I'll be shocked if you aren't dead in a day," replied Moreth. "Blood King, if you care for him, watch him, please."

The Wolf flicked Moreth's cane off his pack-mate. "I am the Blood King no more."

"Well, find out where he is, and get rid of the other fellow you're pretending to be. We need monsters in Pandemonia, not a lion who has gone and slept with the lambs."

After having offended the whole company, Moreth—unfazed—resumed his walk. Breezes and heat swayed his dandified attire; he somehow blended in with the fantastic vista ahead, seemingly as comfortable as the natives of this land. *What people could live in this kaleidoscopic delirium?* wondered Thackery, as he glanced from ember-bug, to rubber tree, to the terrifying desert over yonder. Noises, visual stimuli, and smells abounded. Thackery sensed that the Wolf struggled with this sensory deluge. When Thackery looked to the man, he saw his chest-fur matted, his hanging mouth huffing, and his eyes wild—the appearance of a frantic animal. They would have to help him find a way to filter out all the environmental static, or this place might drive him mad. All-seeing Morigan flashed a silver stare at her concerned friend as he pondered her Wolf. *It will be all right*, she seemed to whisper. And Thackery would have believed her—if he hadn't known her well enough to read the lie in her expression.

I shall look out for her again, too, until Caenith finds his bearings, he decided, and considered what in his arsenal he could use to uphold this promise. What of his magik? Aboard the *Skylark*, Moreth had suggested that magik wouldn't work properly in Pandemonia, that the etheric currents made sorcery too unstable. Surely, though, there was a way for him to invoke. First, he had to discover what was mechanically wrong with the process in this environment, before exploring how to fix it. So as not to embarrass himself through failure, Thackery waited until the others were ahead of him before summoning his Will. He conjured a memory of Theadora running in a green summery field not unlike this one (although without the freakish elements). It was a memory of love. She'd always loved stars, his Theadora. She'd called them wishing-spots. A little wishing-spot, then, he would make in her honor.

W*HOOSH*!

A pillar of white fire twisted in the air behind the company, and they scattered for cover. No warning, no tingle of danger from the Wolf, seer, or Menosian hunter had presaged the event. There was simply a violent, fiery assault. Mouse was wrenched away by Adam; the Wolf barreled into Morigan and Talwyn, taking them to the earth, and then leaped to his feet. Thackery! Where was the sorcerer? Neither he nor Adam had shielded the man. Angrily, he scanned the haze and screamed into the cindery clouds for his friend. Just as the Wolf was about to charge ahead into the black mist, Thackery appeared: soot smudged, coughing, and stumbling. The Wolf carried him to safety.

"You idiot!" exclaimed Moreth, appearing beside the huddling company. He brandished his cane like a mean schoolmaster ready to rap bones. "You used magik, didn't you?"

Thackery coughed. "P-perhaps."

"Per-fuking-haps! Obviously, you did." Spittle flew from Moreth's mouth. "I would not have thought that a sorcerer, a *sage*, would fling magik about—here of all places—without reason. I warned you."

Sooty, though indignant, Thackery scowled at the Menosian. "I had a reason. Furthermore, your warning was quite vague. A sage and scholar puts himself at the forefront of experimentation to determine causation and result."

"The *result* is that you nearly blew yourself up."

Caenith growled. He was done taking abuse from a Menosian master, ally or not. Besides, the Iron City had died: so, too, should its ideals and rulers. Once the others were on their feet, he told Moreth to get moving. Smartly, the Menosian made no rejoinder; he knew when not to provoke a violent animal.

When they were nearly to the river, Moreth resumed chatting. "Magik," he said. "Once more I find myself repeating lectures...Perhaps this time you'll listen. Putting things simply, you've gone from one polarity of magikal influence to the other: Alabion to here. In the Sisters' domain, magik is repressed, but in Pandemonia, there is no limit to the diffusion of magikal energy in the air. It surrounds us like a fine mist upon the sea. We breathe and drink in magik without our knowing. Scholars and wise men have said that the world is wrapped in threads of power—ethereal currents—and here, these threads converge in a knot. Whatever you conjure, Thackery, however small the release of magik, will be amplified one hundredfold. You will open a dam, and wash us all away."

"Threads, yes..." mumbled Morigan, and gazed again into a sky crossed with silver lines that the others could not see.

"I am sorry." Thackery glanced to the ground, ashamed. "I should have known better. I didn't believe most of what you'd said. I needed to see it for myself. We should have better prepared ourselves. We should have listened to you."

"Confession is the last act of the damned," agreed Moreth, mockingly. "You scholars and sages are such slaves to curiosity. Although, why prepare for the most dangerous mission in the history of man, when we could spend days waxing our pricks?" Moreth glanced to Caenith and Morigan. "Playing fetch with our dog?" Then, to Mouse and Adam. "Or wasting hourglasses on sophistry?" He finished his berating with a glance at the two scholars, who stood side by side. "When I wasn't being interrupted with nonsense, I devoted my hourglasses to *preparing*: strengthening my mind, recounting my inventory, remembering the bestiary of this realm, and testing the limits of my body's deprivation. For in the land of chaos, all faculties and strengths you have ever owned will be called upon and exhausted. You think you know death? Hunger? Fear? You think you know doom? Pandemonia will redefine the meaning of despair."

"Oh, stop," scoffed Mouse, tired of the man's self-flattery and insults. "I attended every one of your briefings, and I found them light on substance and heavy on scorn. I think you're withholding certain facts, because you know that without that reservation you'd have nothing to offer us. I'm still not certain that you do. We've faced worse than whatever picture you're trying to paint. I see loveliness amid the strange."

Life had enveloped them from the moment of their landing. Although the crabs, cinder-bugs, desert herds, and clay birds were the most notable fauna, countless other creatures also claimed the lands through which the company walked. At this very moment, a family of blue-furred rodents, long and sleek as marmots, flowing over one another in a stream of bodies, chattered nearby. They'd been following the company, slyly, though none slyer than the Wolf and the glances he'd kept to them out of the corner of an eye; he didn't consider them harmless, and they had regrouped and begun to follow the party again after scattering from Thackery's explosion. Persistent, possibly hungry, felt the Wolf. Realizing they'd been noticed, the creatures paused, rose onto their hind legs, and squealed. For a speck, Moreth and the company all stared at the creatures.

"There is nothing lovely here, remember that," Moreth said, and whipped a pistol from its holster.

Bang! Bang! Bang!

Each burst of blue fire sent a shell into the swarm. Apparently a flawless marksman, Moreth shattered three tiny skulls. The squealing of the pack became higher pitched—eardrum-piercing to the changelings—but the creatures did not flee. Instead, they opened mouths much larger than their tiny heads should allow, bared shining rows of serpent teeth, and began tearing their departed number into jellied shreds. Astonishingly speedy, they ate the dead in specks, and then returned to their squealing and watching of the company. They looked red and repellently adorable, like a band of cannibal squirrels. Mouse started counting them now; there seemed to be dozens. Dozens more could be watching from places unseen. To keep the creatures busy, Moreth emptied a few more bullets into the swarm; his shots caused an orgy of rending and devouring. He slid his pistol back into its holster. "Corpse-weasels," he said. "I don't know their official name, but that is what I call them. They're harmless until provoked or aroused by the scent of blood. They are like the monster peasantry of these lands—vermin no better than the rats that crawl through Menos's sewers. *Crawled* through, I suppose…"

Morigan shivered from the psychic ache of Moreth's regret; Caenith sniffed a rosy fragrance, too. Absurd to think an Iron Sage might feel any kind of remorse or empathy, yet the evidence of their senses could not be denied.

"They will eat you while you sleep," continued Moreth, walking on. "The slightest bit of fresh blood drives them berserk. If anyone starts bleeding profusely, or if one of our ladies, whose womanly cycles I've been tracking as best as I can"—Morigan and Mouse gasped, but Moreth paid them no heed—"happens to have a particularly heavy day, we may encounter a problem. Blood is law in the Old World, for its witches, rituals, and monsters."—*Suddenly Morigan spins through a curtain of silver, buzzing light and sees a gorgeous icy woman, white from head to toe, brushing her frost-spun, glittering hair before a mirror. Morigan trips, twirls with her bees again, and returns*—"I believe Pandemonia is the oldest of all the lands in our world, and here that law reigns the strongest."

By now, the companions knew that Moreth's reticence was a calculated manoeuvre, adopted to secure his position. They had themselves to blame, too, for any dismissal of his warnings. Many felt that Moreth was vile, arrogant, and only tenuously attached to the company's welfare. However, until the rest of the company had learned the rules and dangers of this land, he was all they could rely on for survival. The six followed the agile master to the bank of the river, where they undressed to check themselves for bleeding scrapes. On his calf, Adam discovered a red gouge, likely sustained during the rocky climb—it must have been the scent of his blood that the beasties had followed. "They should have attacked you," said Moreth coolly, and was otherwise uninterested in the miracle. Wading through the cold, salty water sealed Adam's wound and broke the trail between the company and the corpse-weasels. Once, Adam looked back to the meadow to see where the corpse-weasels were. Numerous black-eyed things watched him from behind a veil of green.

II

On the other side of the river, the land boasted rock and copses of emaciated trees in which no scurrying hordes could lurk. There, Adam's tension blew away like the brisk wind that stirred the new plain. The six were soon challenged by another elevation, a steady rise to the land, and they conquered it with spirit. Soon they stood on a new summit and took in a broad view of Pandemonia. The quilt of the land rolled wide, stitched with patches of the fantastic.

One region fumed with black smog, as if the whole of it had been razed. Another wavered with misty billows and sparkled with lush dells and lakes. A third was pale as if with snow and wreathed in golden clouds. Indeed, the sky and earth before them appeared stitched out of a riot of colors, textures, and elevations. Far off seemed the glass desert and rubber forest at the fringes of the vista now—wonders to be crushed beneath these new ones. Pandemonia's wind was as unsettled as its other elements. As they surveyed the vista, it raged and calmed, turned hot and then bitterly cold. Again, the profusion of flavors nearly overwhelmed the Wolf. He'd never encountered such a fecund and fetid musk in any city of man or realm of nature he'd wandered, but at least it smelled of life—of beast, water, sweat, and fur. No steel or grease soured his tongue, and no echoes of industry did he hear. *Or is that a distant din and shuffle of commerce and people?* he wondered, straining. The fickle wind seemed to raise a prickle of magik upon his hide.

"Eatoth," said the Wolf, frowning. "I recall your mentioning a city, son of El."

"Aye, Blood King," replied Moreth. "As I've said, in Pandemonia there are a few constants—eyes in the storm, so to speak. I'm only a road-scholar, so I'll leave the theorizing on these phenomena to those of you best at postulating magikal theory. There are pockets in Pandemonia where life exists unchanged—or, I should say, *places where certain elements rule in such excess that a kind of balance is upheld.* I speak of the fundamental energies of our world: earth, fire, wind, water. Great civilizations have been built on sites that possess particular elemental power; the tribes of Pandemonia have histories, cities, and hieroglyphs that make the Sisters seem young."

"*Claeobhan.* That's what the Sisters Three called this place. The Cradle..." mumbled the Wolf. Suddenly, the glut of sensory information compressed into a thought. "The cradle of life—all life."

"That may be true, Blood King," agreed Moreth. Each time he used Caenith's old title respectfully, without disdain, it bothered the Wolf less. "Eatoth is one of the four great cities of Pandemonia. It is known as the City of Waterfalls. The lands around Eatoth might change, but the city remains the same. On my last expedition, I marked its coordinates by the stars, which do not shift as the land beneath them does. Assuming the distance inland has not changed too drastically, I think we are a week's travel from Eatoth. I shall know better once night falls, and I can see our markers in a darker sky."

Moreth strode down into the valley. Theirs was a perilous trail, with slippery plates of mossy stone and entangling thorny growths that could tear a traveler's flesh. The skeleton trees grew here as well, often in tighter copses in which gaunt-fingered branches twined into one another. The pitiable scrubland went on for many spans. They hiked lower and lower, now unable to see what lay beyond this valley.

It's as if we're not really in the nightmare of Pandemonia at all, thought Mouse, comforted. Only the rumbles of thunder from clouds out of sight and occasional odd-smelling gusts of wind challenged this impression. After many sands of quiet, Mouse's churning Thule mind ruined her peace.

"Four cities," she said. "You've only ever mentioned Eatoth. What are the others?"

"Three cities, actually," replied Moreth. Once more the wind was hot, and he stopped and fanned himself with his hat. "Only three cities remain standing, one lies in ruins. There's Eatoth, the City of Waterfalls. It is home to poets, scholars, technomagik so astonishing the mind melts. There, men in blue robes contemplate the eternal mysteries in silence, and they are ruled by a queen of sorts: cold, equally silent as her consorts and sitting on her throne, I assume, in a tower of glass and silver. From what I gather, Eatoth is the capital of Pandemonia, and we shall likely be able to plot a course from there—one that might lead us to Intomitath, the City of Flames...What wondrous industry they have there: forges of pure magik and flame, arts perfected from generation to generation over the course of thousands of years. Or Ceceltoth, the City of Stone. My expedition never made it that far east. Think of the cities like points on a compass: West, North, and South. These points aren't quite at the edges of Pandemonia, though; they're still many spans inland, and are further separated from one another by a chasm, an uncrossable, forbidden terrain at the heart of this continent: the Scar."

"Dreadful name." Talwyn trembled. "Hopefully, we can avoid that place. What of the fourth city? The eastern point on this compass? You missed a city."

"City of Screams," said Morigan.

Stars glittered in her gaze. Rusty sounds—high, low, and as harmonized as a chorus—had breezed past her ear with the wind. Screams, she'd realized, though very hushed, as though from elsewhere. Morigan did not feel herself shivering, but was grateful when the Wolf enfolded her in a warm embrace. "What happened there?" she asked.

Reluctantly, Moreth replied, "Aesorath is its proper name—the city. What your eldritch senses deduced from the ether is a rough, though apt, translation for the sound the wind makes through the city's ruin. I don't know much beyond the more common lore. A woman, whose name is never spoken, betrayed her holy office with the Keepers—think of them as sages, sorcerers, esoteric spirit-men of a kind the West has never truly replicated. I think we have some similar ascetics in the West, in Gorgonath, though these Pandemonian folk are far more austere and militant. Nevertheless, this Keeper was consumed by madness and destroyed her city. Now the place is cursed, filled with ghosts and terrors that make grown men shake like little women."

"Madness?" asked Thackery.

"Again, I don't hunt history," confessed Moreth. "I hunt animals. Although I am a worldly fellow, what I learn of my environment is only for the betterment of my sport. The politics of nations do not particularly concern me. Not even in the case of my own fallen one."

The company could not press the master on this or any other issue, for he now resumed walking. New anxieties played havoc with their stomachs as they silently marched behind their guide. Each felt a measure of dread over Black Queens, mad kings, places called the Scar, and now a mad priestess and her doomed city. In their heads, Morigan and the Wolf consoled and counseled each other; after the Menosian's speech, she had a powerful sense of obscure but nonetheless aligned Fates.

Odd birds circled overhead, jarring her with their cries. *Screams...City of Screams*, she thought. In time, the sun vanished into a purple mist, and Morigan felt as if she walked in a nether-realm between Geadhain and Dream—a purgatory. Her wolfish senses could not hear the brouhaha that her mate endured, although her ears were attuned to the scuffing of the company's tread and the rasp of their breaths. To this somber music she walked for a time, while the Wolf's fire-beast tried to settle the unease in her breast with courageous roars and flares of heat and love. *I feel that we are headed somewhere dark, my Wolf*, she mind-whispered at last. *Perhaps darker than any place we have ever trodden.*

The Wolf stopped and kissed her forehead. He offered none of his prose or challenges to Fate, for he felt it, too. The subtle rattle of bones in the wind. Bone dice, inscribed with both their names, shaken in a cup before being cast on the Pale Lady's table. Until they left Pandemonia's soil, he would be ceaselessly vigilant. *Vortigern, my friend, I miss you*, he thought, suddenly and before the sentiment could be restrained. *I shall not lose another of our pack.*

Morigan squeezed his hand.

III

The clouds dispersed once the company had passed through the realm of withered life, and they strode out onto a sun-dappled highland. Here the ground rose before them in great green steps. Patches of spiny thistle and garishly pink, red, and orange flowers spilled about like a garden of twisting fire and blood. Most of the day was already gone by this point, and they took their time wading through the flame-like garden and climbing the giant steps. Misery was hard to hold on to in these climes, and the company smiled and talked among themselves. The changelings fared better in these highlands, where the nectars of so many plants dulled nearly every other smell.

Moreth, a stoic black specter in this colorful land, did not partake in conversation. He did speak up once, to confirm that these fields were not the kind that exuded lethal pollen; for him, that was almost sociable.

When the stars came out, he called for a halt. The company settled down in a lonely circle that had been cozily bedded in soft flowers. Vivid white moths—children of the moon above—entertained the travelers when they glanced up while eating their bland rations. Elsewhere on the highlands, singing things that trilled like loons gave the moths an enchanting tune to which to dance. The moths' wings made a strange thrumming to Adam, as if chanting was hidden behind the beat. After straining to hear a word or two, and drawing Mouse's perplexed stare from his exercise, he ceased trying to decipher the language to the song—and felt silly about believing there was one.

The company, particularly its largest member, restrained their appetites. In this ever-changing land, Eatoth could be days or even weeks away; their supplies would have to hold them until they reached their destination, as the fauna was unsafe for consumption. *Too unknown, too rich in life,* Talwyn mused as they'd hiked and chatted that day. *I propose that in an environment such as this, life proliferates and changes at a hyperactive rate, so each species, old or new, rapidly evolves its own defenses and properties to ensure survival in the face of absolute hostility.* In other words, almost all animals in Pandemonia were either poisonous or dangerous, even those, such as weasels, who occupied the seemingly harmless levels of nature's hierarchy. Moreth's vigilance certainly suggested this was the case. Even as the company rested in its pocket of tranquility, the master watched the white moths for signs of viciousness. He twitched at every call of the loon creatures.

"A few hourglasses of sleep," said Moreth. "We shall split the watches; I shall take the first."

"I shall watch my pack," declared the Wolf.

"Suit yourself," replied Moreth.

The Wolf settled into his familiar pose of a man mimicking a waiting dog—on his haunches, his hands on the ground, and back erect. Morigan and the others lay close to their protector, using their packs as pillows and cloaks as blankets to be shared. It wasn't long before snores were competing with the songs of the loon beasts. While the others slept, the Wolf and the Menosian maintained a standoff. They didn't speak or even look in each other's direction. Hourglasses passed, longer than Moreth had promised the company, but the Wolf could smell their vinegary fear and weariness, and felt no urge to wake them; his Fawn seemed especially far away, drowning deep in dreams. Without embarrassment, the Wolf had hiked up his kilt, in plain sight of Moreth, and began counting stars while he pissed; it was then that the master addressed him.

"What it must be like to be you," said Moreth. "All sinew and power—anger, masculinity, and lust. You are a storm of a creature. I know why my ancestors adored you, for you wear what you are without shame."

Snorting, the Wolf shook his prick and tucked it away. "Shame? Why would I ever feel shame unless I dishonored myself with my pack?"

"I suppose that makes sense," said the master, and walked toward the Wolf. Depending on Moreth's mood, he could be one of two men, noted the Wolf: a sophisticated master or a stealthy predator, like one of the cats that stalked Alabion.

"We are similar, you and I," professed Moreth. "I would not insult either of us, however, by calling us brothers. We are fellow predators, although we are different species of carnivore. I do not shed my skin and become something terrible, as you and the young changeling do, according to the not-so-quiet chatter of your friends. But we understand the scales of blood, you and I. We know how to kill and feel respect, not remorse."

Intrigued, and aware of nothing of deadly terror nearby, the Wolf crossed his arms and listened.

"As hunters, we observe." Moreth stopped and cannily looked him up and down. "We see patterns in the world and in our prey. We live in danger. When last I came to Pandemonia, I had a companion from the land of chaos. I bought him in the meat markets of Menos. He stood out like a lion in a field of lambs—as you do. Gloriously wild was this man, who we shall call the Slave...I never learned his tale, which I am sure was a legend in its own right, as his tongue had been removed before he and I met.

"Once, you won your freedom from my family's Pits, or claimed it, anyway." A low growl escaped the Wolf; Moreth dismissed the threat with a shake of his head. "I consider that matter as old and dead as the skeletons to whom it is owed. My father and forefathers were too despicable to be honored by any debt of blood. We shall have no quarrel over that. The Slave—he, too, won in the ring. He was one of only three victors. In what was the El Estate, we had a small wall on which we displayed the victors' portraits. The first was of Belladonna, the temptress of the pits. I am told men pray to her spirit, believing her to be a saint who can grant vengeance. Lesser known are those pictured in the other two portraits: the Slave and the dark shadow of a monster-man mounted on a pile of bodies; I think you know him well."

"Did he have a name?" asked Caenith. "The Slave?"

"No name," said Moreth, touching a finger to his chin in thought. "He did not file one with the Iron Crown after claiming his rights as a free citizen of Menos. We predators among men, though, do not need names. You do not name a lion, you simply know it is king. He was one such animal—a savage soul, a true hunter. I would have died in Pandemonia without him."

A brown man wrapped in earthy garments kneels in the weeds. When he is motionless, his lined skin makes him indistinguishable from a hunk of wood or a camouflaged lizard. He becomes one with nature—unseen. Only a flash of the stone talisman attached to the leather cord about his neck warns that he is neither bark nor lizard. But the Slave's prey never notices this glimmer, or anything about the hunter at all—not until its death has already been determined.

The Wolf caught a whiff of sand and blood, and tasted bitter wine in his mouth—the essence of whatever memory had distracted Moreth.

"You might not agree..." said Moreth, ending his silence. Moreth's fingers were under his shirt, touching something—a twine of leather, a necklace, the Wolf determined. "But fathers are mostly useless entities. We learn the most from those who act; my father, Modain of El, was not such a man. Now the Slave, *he* taught me skills most men never learn. After he won his freedom in the Blood Pits, he wanted to return here, to Pandemonia. I can't say what impetuousness or stupidity claimed me, but I also thought to challenge myself here. As a free man, the Slave had no obligation to teach me how to survive. If he had been wrathful, he could have let me play the fool from abroad, traipsing about in the jungle. But he chose to let me live; and it *was* a choice, I realize now. He brought me into his company as a lesser animal to a greater. He brought me into his pack."

Pack? wondered Caenith.

"You've used the term more often than you realize," said Moreth, smiling. "I know we see eye to eye on certain matters, wherever our allegiances have been placed in the past." Moreth slipped off his glove and laid a cold white hand on Caenith's warm granite chest. He felt the pulse and power trapped in the Wolf's great bronze cage of flesh. The Wolf, curious, did not repel Moreth's touch. Moreth's smile widened, revealing teeth unusually sharp for a man. "All that might," purred Moreth. "Like a fire made into a man. I would envy your power, I would seek to take it, if I did not understand that it was not my place to possess it. You are a king of men and beasts. But here," Moreth removed his hand, "you have lost control of your power. Pandemonia does that with all magiks, even those embedded in our instincts and our very natures."

"How did you know?" asked the Wolf, shocked.

"The Slave," replied Moreth, moving away from the Wolf and granting Caenith respite from his calculating eyes and cold hands. "Animalistic, he was—part of the reason why he did so well in the Blood Pits. The Slave tore men into the tiniest morsels, and the more the crowd roared, the greater grew his rage. He was like a dog in the midst of a feasting hall, howling and barking at every clanged plate. His symptoms and yours are the same: sweating, twitchiness, darting stares, jittering hands. You've displayed every one of these and more since we arrived in Pandemonia. That is a side effect of the gift of extreme sensitivity to one's environment;

a gift for which I can only train. However, the Slave was mortal, too, and I'd wager that the sights and sounds in *your* head surpass those afflicting even the most bestial of men. Your head must be full of bells, aches, and shitty smells."

"Yes," admitted the Wolf. Rather a friend to pain, the Wolf had thus far ignored the fist pounding behind his eyes, which had not let up since this morning.

"The Slave taught me how to embrace my animal through scribbled notes he always made. He told me of how he had learned to exercise serenity in chaos. He told me that Pandemonia was not loud; it was simply that I was not *listening*."

The Wolf scowled. "Listening? There is too much to listen to."

"Pick something," said Moreth. "One sound. A single wing flap. A howl. A spider's crawl. It doesn't matter what. One thing, and one thing only."

Scoffing at the idea that a mastery of Pandemonia's din could be achieved though a charlatan's meditative exercise, and despite having the pride of a beast that did not bow to suggestion, the Wolf nonetheless attempted what was asked of him. Finding a state of peace in which to begin reflection proved the Wolf's first obstacle. A sound, one not from Pandemonia, eventually beckoned his mind: Morigan's soft and unmistakable breathing, soft as cotton to his ear. Once he had discovered her music in the orchestra playing in his head, the pounding, surprisingly, subsided a touch. Next, and unintentionally, the Wolf began to smell her honey-and-onion sweat, and then the perfume that gathered at the back of her neck, rich as the dew of a rose petal. He must have been smiling.

"I see you've found a bit of peace," he heard Moreth say from somewhere nearby.

The Wolf nodded.

"Now hold onto that presence, use it as your anchor, and simply roam from smell to smell, noise to noise. Pick and choose from the market of many things, and remember that you are the one with the coin and desire. You decide what is worthy of your attention."

A market. Naturally, a Menosian would make analogies in coin. Still, the Wolf kept Morigan's sounds and bouquet circling in his skull, along with apparitions of their lusty tumbles—their sweats, the slap of their bodies, even the barbaric taste of her sweet blood, which he'd once or twice drawn in pleasure. Whenever Pandemonia's grotesque clamor cried for dominance in his senses, Morigan's elements grounded him. As a beast that ruled and did not wait, the concept of peace, of calm before action, was wholly new to the ancient Wolf. No wonder he could not steady himself in this realm, when he came to it screaming and snapping. For Pandemonia had teeth, too, and infinite mouths with which to bark back at him. After dwelling on Morigan's various wonders, the Wolf rolled his senses outward. He hunted and found Thackery's leather-scented wisdom, then the book-spice and new-baby smell of the innocent scholar. Then his senses moved on to Mouse and Adam, who shared some of each other's grease, rubbed off through a close friendship. Upon Moreth, he smelled blood and ether: strong, bitter aromas in keeping with his personality. No longer in doubt, the Wolf now flew his senses wide. In one heartbeat, he tasted the iron soil, shivered from the ruffling of the moths' wings that played in the night, and listened to the scaly shuffle of fat-bellied vipers as they slid along the earth. But far as he went in that instant, Morigan's faint scent clung to his memory like morning perfume. She was his anchor.

"Quick study," commented Moreth.

The Wolf woke from the casting of his mind. Moreth had settled on the ground near the others and was fluffing a pack as a pillow.

"You were a fine teacher," admitted the Wolf.

"Now that you're listening, and smelling, and all the rest, I shall get some sleep. Wake me in an hourglass. Dawn will come soon, and I need to see the stars before we set out. Although..." the Menosian smiled. "Perhaps you can lead us to Eatoth now."

Caenith watched the man remove his bowler and place it neatly beside his pack. Then Moreth shut his eyes, sighed, and breathed more and more slowly; he lay like a corpse: on his back, hands crossed on his chest. Freshly attuned to the world, and no longer distracted, the Wolf knew Moreth was not quite asleep. "Why offer your help?" asked the Wolf.

"The Slave is dead, and I was but his student," replied Moreth, his face frozen and only his lips moving. "I did not make it to Eatoth on my own, and I would not make it there again without aid. I need a true hunter behind whom I can stalk in the shadows. I know my own strength and that of others. I ally myself with the strongest. We are not friends, though we do need each other. Let us accept that, Blood King."

Thus the Wolf did. That night he watched over all six of his pack, even the stray coyote from Menos. Did he trust Moreth? No. Coyotes and wolves were natural enemies. He did, nonetheless, respect the wily creature.

IV

Who am I? wonders Morigan.

These youthful brown hands that she contemplates in her lap—clenching something dry and balled—and the curled wisps of dark hair fringing her vision, belong to someone else. Around her, dusty bookshelves gleam with a tarnished elegance—they are of gold or some other aureate mineral—and there are numerous pedestals stacked with scrolls. Morigan doesn't understand the reason behind the uncountable candles—a graveyard of candles—that clutter the tall, stuffy room. Many have been snuffed and snuffed again by the wind; their cooled wax has bled over tomes and tables like bulbous mold. A few candle flames flicker, casting shadow puppets in the dusty heights of the chamber.

How queer. Morigan feels as if she is two women at once. She has a daydream of the other body, the one that is held elsewhere, bouncing and warm in the arms of someone strong. Who is that woman? Who is this? In this deep and powerful Dream, she fights to remember herself as defiantly as she once screamed into the darkness of Death where Vortigern's soul floated—the forgetfulness here is nearly that profound. Defenders of their mistress, the bees buzz loudly their warning of walking in the Dreams of Pandemonia. In the land of Chaos, the barriers between worlds are as brittle as the paper scrolls that often crumbled in her hands while she tidied Thule's tower. Thule—yes, she remembers her sort-of-father, then her mind reclaims the man-wolf and the rest. How could she ever have forgotten Caenith, even for a speck?

Angry and wary, understanding that Pandemonia's pull is stronger than Alabion's, Morigan leaves the body of her host to observe the young woman who has summoned her here. Barely out of girlhood, she is pretty in an Arhadian way: tanned from sun, dark of hair. Her eyes are as deep and telling of pain as scars burned black. She smells of the spice of knowledge, as her Wolf would say—a fragrance that coils up the nose and would have made her host sneeze if the girl herself had not been inundated by the same must since her youth. Eighteen, realizes Morigan, in a sting of knowledge. The girl is eighteen summers old. At least that's how old she looks, but there is something eternal about her presence. Morigan receives a name, too, though not from her bees. Instead, she gleans this name from the note that her host unfurls and then crumples again and again in her hand.

Amunai.

The name is written at the top of the letter, its addressee. Morigan admires the beautiful writing: forests of long, tall letters, inconceivably intricate lines, surrounding pictographs similar to the scrawling in the Motherwolf's cavern—an ancient language, then. Morigan can read any language in this otherworld, and she scans flitting expressions of desire: my darling songbird...my dearest...another kiss, another whisper. A love letter, she realizes, of a kind any young girl would like to receive if the suitor was pleasing. Perhaps Amunai does not care for boys and their advances. Certainly, Morigan had no interest in young fools. Still, Amunai's agitation seems inconsistent with the frustrations of early love: she looks mortified and torn. Within, Morigan senses Amunai punishing herself for these flushes in her breast. Amunai flogs the images of a trickster's crooked smile from her mind faster than Morigan can see the rest of that face. Regardless of her apparent age, Amunai seems to possess incredible willpower, so ruthlessly does she repress her emotions.

She burns the note on one of the hundred candles surrounding the chair and dais upon which she presides and wriggles her fingers through the ashes, as if saying goodbye. Then Amunai closes her eyes and listens. She falls into a well of thought so deep and vacant that Morigan worries about following the girl.

Bzzt!

Morigan floats away from Amunai to seek out the noise. She drifts down the aisles of ancient lore, wishing she had fingers with which to peruse the enticing texts. These many books with inscribed metal covers, these scriptures that hum with secrets from within their leather tubes...Morigan feels as if all the information of the world resides here—or at least all the information one would wish to know. She realizes that this young sage—a Keeper, suggest the bees—holds the knowledge of this entire library inside her small self. After finding nothing of interest, no disturbance but for the wind ruffling through the oval windows that scares candle flames and papers, Morigan returns to the Keeper. The alcove is empty; the throne is bare. Papers drift in the air, suggesting the Keeper has just vanished in a gust of wind.

Bzzt!

A fly lands on Morigan's shoulder. Wait—how is it that she has a shoulder? she wonders. In Dream, she is most often a ghost, one that cannot touch or be touched by the past.

Bzzt!

A glimmering green friend joins the insect, and they crawl in a figure eight on her naked white skin. Morigan hears more buzzing behind her. Her bees spark the air like firecrackers, warning her too late of the danger. It takes much to scare Morigan, a woman who has delved into Death and confronted Dreamers. Although she musters her strongest steel and girts herself as she turns around, her bravery scarcely holds upon seeing the picked skull and fly-weeping eyes of the monster that greets her. Flies swarm all over the creature, like bees on a doomed honey-tender. More flies flurry toward Morigan, and she waves them off while stepping back from their master.

Morigan has managed not to scream; that would only let the vermin into her mouth. How is it that she has a mouth? Or a heartbeat that threatens to tear apart her chest? Among other aspects of the waking world, though, she can feel the Wolf. However distant, he still roars his anger at whatever frightens his mate. Caenith's heat makes her sweat, then glow with light. Morigan's silver aura blazes through the buzzing dark. In the wash of light, some of the hideousness of the monster is dispersed and exposed as a facade, as a veil of flies and evil. The creature wears a mask.

"This past is not for you to see," warns the cicada monster.

"I am the Daughter of Fate," declares Morigan, supremely radiant, and no longer afraid. "I see what I choose. Dream is my queendom, and I go where I please."

The Wolf's flame rages in her, and she shines even brighter. More chinks in the monster's horrid pretence reveal purplish clothing under the crawling mantle of flies, the glittering darkness of a gaze. Even the damp funeral-pyre stink is another layer of the monster's disguise, and hides scents that Morigan's part-wolf nose discerns as sweat. "Who are you?" demands Morigan.

"You will know."

"Tell me."

"Blindly, you swing the sword of the righteous," says the Dreamstalker, with what Morigan thinks is pity. "You do not see how cold Geadhain can be. You look only to her summer and never her winter. You will know this season, Daughter of Fate. You will see that love is the same as pain. You will know darkness in your heart and murder on your hands. You cannot be clean of sin forever."

The Dreamstalker moves forward, like a leech, shivering flies and dropping globs of maggots that squirm where they splat onto stone. Impossible, thinks Morigan, that this should-be-phantom can influence an echo, an illusion of time past. Is that an illusion too, she wonders—the way the Dreamstalker's glinting, skeletal teeth bend into a smile? What is truly real here? The sweat beading her body? The tremble in her legs? The reeking, rolling, buzzing, nightmare cloud? The Dreamstalker thunders now, shuddering in violence, as if about to explode.

"Back!" screams Morigan.

"I am not trying to hurt you, Daughter of Fate." The Dreamstalker shuffles nearer and extends a sloppy tendril of an arm. "You wish to see? You want to know what your devotion will cost you, its price in blood? Give me your hand and I shall give you the gift of knowledge. I shall show the seer her future."

Again, Morigan senses pathos, which she does not care to contemplate; she wants to flee. She does not understand Dream's new rules, or how they are being bent by the Dreamstalker; but she realizes that she, too, should be able to play this game. Desperately, Morigan calls to the bees that sting and dazzle her with warning bursts of pain. "Unmake my body," she Wills them. "End this nightmare; take me away before—"

"Begone, terror!"

Was that a shout? From whom? A sudden whirling rampage of light and wind smashes into the trembling Dreamstalker, who then erupts into a fountain of black flecks and filth. Morigan chokes on waves of crawling darkness. Her eyes squeezed shut, she blindly thrashes her hands from ears *to nose to mouth. The insects, though, cannot be purged, and their legs tickle and scratch as their innumerable bodies form a torrent into her mouth. At last, terror triggers Morigan's magik, birthing a silver pulse she does not see, but feels as an explosive heat, and that scatters the Dreamstalker's horde. In another instant, Morigan is cast into Dream's gray currents.*

Morigan wishes to wake, yet she cannot find the right path. Lost as a trout in a filthy stream, she swims from memory to memory: her mother's arms as a child, she and Thackery dirty from making her mother's grave, she and Caenith's first kiss in Eod. Cruelly, no matter the sanctity of these visions of her past, a buzz ever haunts her ears. So Morigan leaps again and again into the river of Dream, trying to flee the horrid Dreamstalker by immersing herself in these most sacred of memories. She tries not to feel fear, even though she is hunted.

No matter where Morigan goes, the cicada music follows her.

V

As promised, the Wolf stirred the Menosian while Pandemonia still lay in darkness. Moreth woke to a chipper and grinning Blood King, and for a speck considered the possibility that he was to be eaten. However, the Wolf had already taken care of his appetite during Moreth's nap—the master could smell blood somewhere on the man.

"What did you kill?" asked Moreth.

"Something furred and fast," replied the Wolf.

"It seems to have agreed with you," said Moreth with a yawn. For a man who'd slept a mere wink, Moreth seemed quite refreshed. After putting on his bowler, Moreth pointed at the stars with his cane. "Oria, Demeter, Prosperae...Under the last—the third and slightly red star—we shall find Eatoth."

The Wolf gazed at the red gem hanging in the heavens. It felt a thousand spans away.

"Have you been practicing what I taught you?" asked Moreth.

Indeed, the Wolf had practiced and honed the skill of funneling the maelstrom of Pandemonia into smaller channels. It was this new clarity that had allowed the Wolf to hear his supper snorting its way through the fields. That distilled concentration, still tied to Morigan's presence—focus on one thing before focusing on all—was also how he had known, from the clean ammonia musk of his kill, that its meat would not upset his stomach with poison. Once the Wolf had learned to use Morigan as his anchor, just as she so often held fast to his spirit while she wandered the nether-realms, he had discovered he could roam quite far on his new chain. Admittedly, he could not, and would never, hunt in Pandemonia with the same surety he could in the woods of Alabion. Nonetheless, he *could* hunt, which was all that mattered.

"Yes," he said. "Your lesson was valuable. I shall lead us, if you like."

Moreth shrugged, then woke the company with clapping and prods from his cane. Morigan would not wake, but the Wolf dismissed Moreth's concern. This was not the most unusual behavior for the seer; she was probably witnessing a grand Fate. Settling her in his embrace, the Wolf looked for the white sparkle of Oria, and then they set out into the highlands.

While the company walked, they drank and picked at what remained of their rations. During the night, the moths had prodigiously reproduced, and white, fluttering clouds filled the highlands. The moths tickled the travelers as they passed and left a shimmering dust upon them. According to the Wolf, this was a nontoxic powder. Their great leader appeared to have rediscovered his sense of authority, something for which all were grateful.

Talwyn murmured to Thackery about the marvel of the moths' procreation and proliferation, and cited earlier discussions on the fecundity of Pandemonia. Of course, neither scholar had thought of the other side of life, of how, to continue a cycle of rapid evolution, death must forerun each new lap. Pandemonia revealed this lesson to the travelers as the sun shined its greeting in a golden dawn. The light grew, and the flowers wilted, then wrinkled. The moths dropped in droves to the ground, and soon the company trod over a skin of dead life that had shriveled to blackness—an aromatic mulch. Soon, even that had decayed into dust that clouded around their feet. Noon arrived and the land was as dead as a desert. The elevations changed as well: the many steps in the land wore down into piles of stone, then sandy patches. When the land was stripped and whirling in dust, black clouds gathered, loomed, then finally released a rain gentler than anticipated, considering the fearsome rumblings that had preceded it. The misting, warm veil shrouded much of the land in fog. Eventually, that cleared and the company walked in a strange new realm.

Here, Pandemonia flourished at the peak of a season of life. A green and precipitously rising highland emerged from behind the rain's gray curtain. The company avoided the land's many vales—chasms that were rent like claw-marks across the land and that belched pungent winds of clay. Silver threads of rivers gleamed in the muddy dark of these crevasses, and angry life teemed and chattered within. Taking to the safer and higher flats of the land, the company wandered through rocky foothills crowned in woodlands. In these forests, songbirds chirped, wildflowers festered, and the trees shone silver, gold, and copper in the dim sunlight. *Metal plants?* wondered Talwyn. He investigated a few of the fallen leaves, which disappointed him with their pedestrian crinkling and left only pewter dust on his fingers, before Moreth reminded him, again, not to touch anything. Down from these hillocks and on the misty plains between tall hills, they mingled with herds of eyeless, hairy creatures—beasts as large and bulky as buffalo—that foraged the ground with prehensile snouts. Undoubtedly, the beasts used senses other than vision to scan their environment: the musk of the Wolf caused a lazy fear in their number, and they ambled out of the company's path.

In time, heaven donned the gray cloak of dusk, and Moreth suggested that they stop. He even broke one of his rules and proposed they make a fire, as a remedy for the dampness in their clothes. The company huddled near the heat of the flame and of the Wolf. They warmed their hands, picked at rations, and talked in whispers in a night that had fallen fast and dark.

"Will she ever wake up?" asked Moreth, suddenly, gazing at the seer.

The Wolf looked to his bloodmate. He brushed her hair with his hand, caressed her face and lips. She murmured and turned deeper into his body, yet did not wake—he could feel her wandering far from this world. He had felt her terror a number of times that day, and had sent her roars of strength to embolden her in whatever trials she endured. Sands passed as he observed his mate, as he read the pattern of her light, which was palpitating erratically in his chest. She was anxious and afraid; she was likely watching a dark Fate. As the Wolf did not reply to Moreth, and showed no intention of doing so, Thackery spoke up.

"Morigan goes away at times," he said. "As a witness. She will return when she has seen what she needs to see."

"Hmm," replied Moreth, and walked over to gaze at the seer. "Pandemonia has a strong connection to those with magik. We saw this with your fire starting, Sage. I believe we may be seeing it again. I think you should wake her."

The Wolf challenged the master with a glare. "I know my bloodmate. I feel her heartbeat, her passions, and terrors. I know how to care for her; you do not."

"Do not be blinded by your pride," snapped Moreth. "You know I can be trusted."

Could he? Since when? wondered Mouse, Thackery, Talwyn, and Adam. Flabbergasted and wary of intervening between a coyote and a wolf, the four watched in fascination. The Wolf pulled Morigan closer to his chest.

"Look at her," suggested Moreth. "Tell me if she seems like she's simply dreaming, witnessing, or whatever she does."

What if Moreth was right? Closer consideration suggested that Morigan's catatonia was deeper than normal. She still breathed, lightly, and he could feel her heartbeat, but it was fluttering out of pace with his. They should never be out of synch. Squeezing one of her hands and pressing their foreheads together, the Wolf whispered, *My Fawn, I need you to wake up. I need you to return to me.*

Nothing, not even a change in her lethargic pulse.

Morigan, wake up.

Still nothing.

Morigan!

Moreth stared, dark and pitying. The company rose and gathered around the Wolf, their faces distorted with shock. Surely, this could not be happening. Morigan must simply be lost in Dream, as she had been so many times before.

"Morigan!" roared the Wolf, no longer using a hidden whisper.

He shook her roughly. She did not respond, but lay like a rattled doll in his arms. The gazes of the company started to cloud with tears and fear, and their scents spoiled with the sour vinegar of terror. Having no other recourse, the Wolf surrendered to his beastliest urge. He did what animals do—what Macha had once done to him—when they are driven to the most hopeless extreme. He bit his bloodmate. Ripping down her garment so that it barely covered her breasts, he sank teeth that were now fangs into the meat of her pearl shoulder. At once, she bled. The Wolf screamed her name while sinking his teeth deeper.

Morigan heaved. A speck later, she shot up. Coughing racked her, and she leaned away from the Wolf and retched something into the grass. *That can't be right*, thought Mouse, for she saw some wriggling matter in the steaming puddle of sick. Then something buzzed in the vomit, and Mouse's stomach tipped. She quickly looked back at her friend. Morigan clung to the Wolf, collecting herself, shivering, unable or unwilling to speak. She was terrified, realized Mouse.

The Dreamstalker, Morigan whispered to the Wolf. *It chased me. It hunted me while I slept.*

Shame consumed the Wolf, for he had not known of her danger, and he wanted to tear this foe into wet red hunks. Growling away his tears, he licked and kissed the wound he'd given his mate. That would make the bite heal more quickly than usual, although the wound to his pride would not. *I did not know. I did not know. I did not know*, he chanted in her head. Though he had physically injured his mate, he might have harmed her more through his ignorance. Contracting with fantastic strength around her, he squeezed her until it hurt them both. Morigan tried to console him. Still, the beast ruled the Wolf in this moment, and he refused to hear reason.

Most of the company maintained a somber vigil around the bloodmates, hoping for, but not expecting, an immediate explanation. Moreth, though, had taken up the gruesome task of sorting through Morigan's sickness with the tip of his cane. After a while, his intrigued *hmms* became as grating as the Wolf's rocking and grunts of suffering.

"What is it?" asked Mouse quietly.

The Menosian gestured her to draw close. Holding a hand over her mouth, Mouse leaned in. Even though these bugs were now quite drowned and dead in the matted grass, their hideousness confirmed her delirious fear of insects. Moreth gathered the others away from the bloodmates to share the strange entomological finding. "Have you seen such a thing before?" he asked.

"Not really," answered Thackery vaguely. They'd been through incidents of phantasms and walking illusions with Morigan before; nothing seemed beyond reason at this point.

"And this seems normal to you?" whispered Moreth. They hardly responded beyond the barest of shrugs; their conspiracy to keep him in the dark was poorly veiled. Moreth's mask started to crack in rage. "I shall need to be let in on the secret handshake soon. I know we were once bitter enemies, but I deserve some scrap of truth. What is your objective—beyond discovering a mysterious relic of worship from an unnamed monarch of the past? A queen, was she? A Black Queen? We speak of royalty, yet your faces all pale as if we speak of nightmares. A nightmare queen, then, who shares some connection with Brutus, Magnus, wars, and a far-seeing woman who sleeps for a day, then wakes spewing maggots and flies. Surely, I cannot be expected to carry on trusting and supporting this lunatic cause while receiving little reason for any of my commitment." Moreth waited for one of the company to validate his fury, and again felt the sting of their silence. "Surely?"

Moreth spat on the ground and walked away. When no one else gave chase, Mouse cursed and ran to catch him. Moreth heard her swishing through the damp field, and he waited, leaning in a gentlemanly fashion against a tall rock standing alone on the plains. Mouse was sweaty and frustrated when she reached him.

"As a fellow Menosian," he said, while Mouse caught her breath, "you would know much about the art of keeping secrets. Gloriatrix, queen of our now doomed nation, is a master of dispensing information in exactly the right doses: never enough to cause panic or to overly illuminate a situation. When she told me that my services as a huntsman were needed in Pandemonia to locate a relic of indeterminable power, I assumed we needed it for use against Brutus, or whomever had leveled the Iron City. However, I see the fretful stares and whispers that pass so often among the five of you, and I wonder if we are not all marching to damnation. If I'm going to die, and in a manner worse than Pandemonia would grant me in even the best of times, I should be allowed to knowingly embrace that future. I don't like being kept in the dark. Tell me what is going on or I'll take the few far-speaking stones I carry—our only hope of communicating with the outside world and coordinating an escape off this cursed rock— and try my luck without any of you."

Calmly and eloquently, Moreth had given his ultimatum. Mouse respected the man for keeping so cool a front. She could not defend either herself or her companions against any of his accusations. Naturally, Gloriatrix had given him only the bare minimum of information, and unsurprisingly, the company he'd joined had chosen not to inform him of the more critical details: they hadn't trusted him, and felt any appearance of partnership would be false.

And yet, in these first few days of their travel, Moreth had already proven himself capable and trustworthy. Perhaps even more important was the commendation of trust he had mysteriously received from the Wolf, who could smell deceit. Mouse made her own decisions, too, and had her own mind. Mouse could think of few reasons why she should not tell the master something of the real forces they pursued. The benefits of having the whole company in possession of the whole truth about their quest now seemed to outweigh any possible doubts. Mouse claimed a part of the rock next to Moreth, sitting shoulder to shoulder with the man. While she counted the strange stars that the Dreamers had once placed in the sky, she pieced together a grand disclosure: one involving the Black Queen, the war of the Kings, and the bits of her and Morigan's journey a listener, and now fellow pilgrim, would need to comprehend the whole. It seemed right to begin with the moment she and the seer had first encountered each other, shackled together and as physically close as she and Moreth were now. "I had been taken. Held against my will by Sorren Blackbriar. While imprisoned, I met Morigan…"

Mouse was not a storyteller, although she'd picked up a variety of tricks from the Wolf's fireside orations. But her telling was more suited to the moment precisely because of its succinctness, its lack of embellishment. She outlined all the major occurrences related to the dark forces at play: Morigan's visions of the Kings, the revelations the company had received from the Sisters in Alabion. She made no mention of Caenith's father, her father, or any other of the companions' secrets—although she made a brief, strained admission that death had claimed one of their company in Alabion. Moreth did not ask who had been taken or why.

In all, her chronicling of events took little time. Finally, Moreth knew what they sought in Pandemonia was an object of Fate, a relic that Morigan could use to read the heart of creation's mother and destroyer: the Black Queen.

When Mouse had finished, he spoke: "We walk a thin road of hope. We face a primeval terror not even of our world, or at least not of the realms of the world that I understand—an enemy capable of corrupting the mind of an Immortal."

"We're quite fuked, you see," said Mouse.

They laughed.

"Why are you here? Other than because of an obligation to your liege?" asked Mouse as soon as the humor had died.

"Come now, Mouse," said Moreth. "Take away a man's wealth, raze his country, attack his pride, and then expect him not to strike back? I am no monster, unlike the creature we seek. I am a man, with values and possessions that I love. What of mine still remains I shall fight for, just as you and your allies do. Our pasts are different, yet we share a fate—an abysmal one, if we do not find means to avoid it. I am glad you have named our enemy. I now have an outlet for my hate and a creature to hunt." Moreth exhibited a bit of the Wolf's primal anger as he spoke. Mouse sensed him trembling through their small point of contact at the shoulder.

They left their rock and returned to a scene far nicer than the one they'd left earlier: the Wolf, his savage self-flagellation over, sat upright and proud with his arms about his now wholly aware and awake bloodmate. Their gray and silver stares greeted the two as they joined the others around the fire. Mouse felt as if Morigan had been waiting for her return.

"Twice now," said Morigan, "I have been haunted by a Dreamstalker, one who can move through the otherworld as I can. It claims to bring a message, although I feel nothing but disharmony and evil, and I do not wish to hear its words. The smallest whisper can become poison—" Morigan paused, assessing Moreth with a flicker of silver awareness, then deeming him worthy of candor "—as we have seen with Brutus. So I shall not listen to this Dreamstalker or hear her message."

"Her?" asked Moreth.

"Yes..." replied Morigan. "A *she*. I feel I spoke to a woman. A living creature, not a ghost."

"Then there is another enemy who conspires in the shadows," concluded Thackery.

Morigan nodded. "One bound, too, with the fates of kings and queens."

There was a sense that she would speak more. However, now that the bloodmates were again in harmony and united, the Wolf became her voice: "Thus far, our greatest challenges in this realm have been the faults and monsters in ourselves: our trust, our faltering or unusual strength, our insecurity over what we face. But I smell a calm upon Mouse as sweet as the breeze and grassy breath of summer. It is the scent of unburdening. I see that she has cast her vote of confidence for our new companion." The company looked to the Menosian, who preened a little from the attention. "This man has instructed us in magik, tracking, and survival during our journey. This man was our enemy not long ago, but it is the nature of wind to change, and we must be as the wind. We must not harbor divisions in our own company, not when we have terrors assaulting us in the privacy of dreams. Hereafter, we shall be a fellowship against the darkness. Perhaps not friends, but friends are not needed in war—only warriors and a code."

"What is the code?" whispered Moreth, captivated.

"We shall hunt and destroy this Black Queen and all who serve her. We shall trust one another, even if our beliefs would damn us to eternal enmity beyond this island."

Moreth went down on one knee, removed his hat, and said, "Aye. I swear allegiance to your code."

Moreth's posture of fealty had an instant effect on the rest of the company, each of whom went down on bended knee to the Wolf and Morigan seen waveringly through the flames. Strangely, the fire seemed brighter, the wind suddenly furious, the air sharply chilled.

"So it is spoken; so it shall be." The company could not tell which of the bloodmates had spoken, which only compounded the aura of mystery. What mattered, however, was the trust and promise that sat in their stomachs like warm porridge. The company felt curious rather than corrosively suspicious when they glanced at the waxy master of Menos, now sworn into their circle.

    Moreth, still rather creepy, smiled, at the faces turned to him, as if seeing the company for the first time. "So it shall be," he murmured.

III

PEOPLE OF GLASS

I

Carthac's winds were said to be the sweetest, saltiest, and most invigorating of any in Geadhain. *A true kiss of the sea*, said the men of boat and sail, these Jacks who often waxed romantic over the blue mistress. Kericot himself had once swooned over the beauty of Carthac, and had stayed in the city for a season to compose countless tunes, many still sung by the Jacks who toiled on boats in the thrashing sea. However, Kericot's original finesse was often lacking in the simpler, modern renditions of his works they sung: limericks and ditties that portrayed a mistress far crueler than the one found in the great poet's honeyed lyrics. For the Blue Mother possessed a streak of murder in her blood. She stormed often and without reason. She drowned men and made widows. Even when not wreaking havoc, the Blue Mother possessed a threatening temperament that could never be forgotten. The crashing, wailing Straits of Wrath that assaulted Carthac's western bank served as a constant reminder. Most fishermen chose to trawl the colder, safer waters to the north. Even there, though, and even if men were cautious, accidents and deaths were not uncommon.

For over a thousand years, the grand watchtowers of Carthac, battlements left over from a forgotten war against the world, had stood under the assault of the Blue Mother's catastrophic waves. The Lordkings, migrant Menosians, even more corrupt than their maleficent countrymen of the era, had built these towers when once Carthac's people bowed to their will. The Lordkings were all dead now—neither Lords nor Kings as they'd wished, and ruling only the earth cast over their burned remains. Gazing from afar upon Carthac, its bastion of salted stone, its sky-scraping pillars driven like pikes into a sheer plummet of rock, brought any observer to humbled awe. Many outsiders wondered how even so sturdy-seeming a wall could endure in the face of the wrathful elements, how it could protect a city of brick houses, which were as delicate as little gingerbread creations. Such speculations, though, were bandied about only by those who were not Carthacians.

Indeed, as far as the people of Carthac were concerned, there existed no livelier a place than the City of Waves. Anywhere less clamorous or dangerous, they thought, must be a sad place to live. To the Carthacians—men and women white with salt, pale of hair, blue of stare, and as tempestuous as their climate—a nearness to death defined life, making laughter bolder, music and wine sweeter, and lovemaking a bliss fit for kings. In Carthac, where drowning and doom were the order of the day, mere survival had a special reverence worthy of celebration. Come nightfall, the city became a carnival of lights and sounds that rivaled even the festivals of Willowholme—and its bravado hushed the pummeling of the sea.

II

A rhythm different from the beat of celebration echoed in the stuffy chamber of a barnacled, tired inn that eve. It was music of man and woman: their gasps, their grunts, the slapping together of their wet thighs and stomachs. Erik was a powerful lover, the fallen queen had discovered. After her assault, she had never thought she would touch a man again—or let one touch her. Still, this had been her choice. Like his father, the fallen hammer of the king was a storm of his own kind, one that drove deep lightning into Lila's loins. His whisky kisses roved over her flesh like the black, fulminous clouds he personified. When he wasn't clasping her wrists or twining their fingers together, his gritty hands coursed like stone over her caramel flesh. Often, during their extensive exercise, they slowed and changed positions. They stood and stumbled around; he would pump, while she stuck to his body like a spider. Later, they would each stand and take turns bowing like slaves while they ate—or swallowed—their master's sex.

There was no end to their deviancy, and neither the queen nor the hammer thought of any of their contortions as lovemaking. Their sex was torment given form; it was their punishment. Not unlike the veiled priests of the City of Waves, who flogged themselves to purge their minds of the sins they'd heard, Lila and Erik were sinner, confessor, and forgiver to each other. They were the queen of Eod and the hammer of the king no more. Their titles they had left in the ash under the Iron Valley. Now he was Erik, and she was Lila. They were the murderers of thousands, bound together by criminality and guilt, which, when shared, became an intoxicating and vile elixir, an impulse as grand as love.

Sometimes when they made not love, but loathing, a tear would threaten their numbness, a hitched breath of Lila's would tremble on the verge of becoming a sob. In these instances, Erik would hold her face as if she were a child about to be lectured, though never too hard, for he knew of the brutality of her rape. If it was his turn for weakness, rare as that was, Lila was less kind. She would claw her nails into whatever hunk of his hard back, buttock, or chest she could reach, usually drawing blood. Always, her violence acted as an aphrodisiac for this man drunk on self-punishment. Whenever she hurt him, he would increase the vicious tempo of his hips and the rude exploration of her body with his fingers. While she took little pleasure in it—except for the moments his hands tenderly caressed her raw nipples during the act—he occasionally drove his fat sausage of a prick into the place from which she shat. She remembered a similar violation from Magnus, but this was different, for she wanted it; she wanted to be punished. When they were alone in their squalid room, where rats scraped at the walls, the sheets reeked of month-old sweat, and the stink of a fishmarket wafted in through the shuttered, rattling windows from the streets below, there was no hedonistic perversion in which they did not wallow.

They had become monsters to themselves and to their world.

They had no other roles to play, no more kindness to pretend to feel, no other recourse. They had attempted suicide when they first arrived in

Carthac. Facing a red dawn, they'd held hands, intending to throw themselves from the ancient salt-wall—but neither had had the strength to take that ultimate leap. Were they cowards? Perhaps. But perhaps what honor they once possessed, the faint ghost of virtue that wept in their hearts, had kept them alive to see them punished for their crimes.

Tonight, after they'd finished their session of teasing and torment, Lila lay in the crook of Erik's armpit. Resting her tawny head upon his great scarred chest, she played—not romantically, only absently—with the curled hair around his dark nipples. Once more, without lust, she looked up and pondered his hard, square face, his unruly beard, his broken nose (which matched his slightly curved, cumbersome, and still erect prick), and the dark jewels of his eyes as he watched the creaking ceiling. One of Erik's hands cupped her breast, rubbing it with the same apathy that she expressed while caressing his stone-hard thigh with a silky leg. Satisfied by their refinement of the art of sex without love, Lila remembered the night the dam had finally broken, and all their anger, pain, and desire had transformed into a new kind of suffering.

Hourglasses before, angry that they could not end themselves, Erik had left her in their dingy quarters: chipped commode, stained sheets, buckled bed, and an air of mothballs, fish guts, and mouse turds. Far from fitting arrangements for a queen, but by then she was only a woman. She'd made peace with that devaluation many weeks past.

So she'd fluffed the sheets, washed herself in a rusted tub, then had put on a flimsy, cheap undergarment and slipped into bed. The outside world had sounded merry. She'd heard harpists and clapping and a murmur of conversation that tugged at her heart because it was mostly laughter. She hadn't been able to recall the last time she'd laughed; it seemed inconceivable that she had ever known how. She'd assumed Erik was among those celebrating, or drinking at least. She'd imagined him sitting in the shadows, dour as an old warrior at a ballet, and telling the women who might approach him, "Begone, wench."

He had been drinking a lot in those days. All down the long road through Fairfarm, particularly while traveling the sotted shores of Riverton and on the ferry ride across the Feordhan, her companion had developed his fondness for the taste she had introduced to him—liquor. Even in the Salt Forest, he had carried two waterskins and drunk from the one causing more urination and dehydration than his own wisdom had dictated. Aye, he had sulked and drunk away what no amount of poison—save fatal venom—could have smudged from the mind. She had preferred the simpler remedy of sleep, which, even if haunted with screams, explosions, and Magnus's pale face, had been a deep enough void that she'd recalled only hints of terror. Mostly dark and forgetful, sleep had been her only escape from what she had done. She'd closed her eyes and had been unconscious almost instantly.

Heavy footsteps had roused her from a nightmare of burned, broken, bone-jutting hands pulling her into a pit of rubble. She'd felt relieved to see Erik leaning over the bed, swaying from drink. However, she might have welcomed an assassin and his blade with the same sighing acceptance. "You're drunk," she'd said.

"I am."

They'd broken and pissed on the rules of civility by murdering a nation, and she hadn't felt herself in a position to judge him. She had wondered only whether or not she should give him the side of the bed nearest to the lavatory door. He had not become ill often; sickening him required as much alcohol as it would take to bring down a bull. But when the drink had sickened him, he'd heaved until blood ran from his mouth. She'd wanted not to play nurse and bucket-serf all evening. "Should we switch sides?" she'd asked.

Erik had performed a one-legged dance pulling off his boots. He'd struggled out of his shirt, then had stared at the crumpled pile of his belongings on the floor. A panting shadow, he'd neither turned to her nor answered. Ignoring her had already become habitual for Erik; for him to acknowledge even half of what she said was miraculous. She had figured that in order to cope with his grief, in order to avoid strangling her in rage, he had decided to block out the poison of her voice. Sometimes, she'd seen the flicker in his eyes of a passion she'd taken for bloodlust when he'd stared at her. It must have been murder he'd felt for he could not possibly have still loved her. Once, flecks of blue had dotted his irises, but his corruption had since turned them black.

As he'd seethed in silence, in the thin, dusky light of the room, she'd noticed the corded muscle of his back and the gnarled flesh upon his broad shoulders, wounds he'd sustained when he'd saved her from Menosian terrorists in the

Faire of Fates. She had not witnessed beauty in some time, had become almost unable to recall what it looked like, now that her march through life had become somber. But Erik's scars had beauty. The scratches left by shrapnel and sorcery had healed imperfectly, leaving bold white lines on his brown flesh—a writing almost as fine as the oldest scripts housed in the Court of Ideas. What would this book of flesh say if its scars were words? she'd wondered.

"You're staring at me," he'd said, turning around. *His eyes had glowed with a beautiful darkness.*

Maybe tonight he'll strangle me and end this sick charade of life, she'd thought. *A sacrifice like that would have been within his code of honor, and would have allowed him to live on and absorb the guilt of her murder into the already pulverizing weight he carried. Thoughts of beauty, suffering, and blood had shaken a bit of prose loose in her head—something once read in the Court of Ideas. She had found herself mumbling the words,* "Iron song, blood song, burning in my veins. Iron song, blood song, heathen woe my name. A gash of glory, and ye decry. Fear deep the love of death, have I…"

"What is that?"

"A poem. I didn't realize I'd spoken aloud."

"You did," *he'd said, climbing onto the mattress, unsettling everything with his mass before flopping on his back; he'd reeked of sweat and whiskey. Staring at the roof, he'd asked,* "What does it mean?"

"Ode in Blood *is a love song, believe it or not," she'd replied. "A tribute to the beauty and allure of battle."*

"Beauty is a lie," *he'd hissed, his manner that of an angry beast.*

She would have been a fool to stick her finger into his cage. Gradually, as though their old decorum had been part of a fantasy she'd once read, their demeanor between each other had hardened into the coldest ice. Erik had begun to say anything he wanted, to act with the brashness of a young man, and to behave with often dangerous violence. Never toward her, though her safety had come at the expense of a bloodied, toothless inebriate or a pack of groaning, crippled men that Erik had left somewhere. As darkly as his temper might have manifested, as beclouded as he might have become from drink, never, ever had he harmed her. She'd wondered if the shade of the honorable man he had once been had stopped him at the brink of rage. Daring to push him while he had been under the influence of darkness, in that moment she'd managed to coax forth the man he had hidden, by touching him on his shoulder.

Erik had snatched her dainty hand, rolled onto his side, and his anger had vanished. His rage had risen into a different kind of fire as he had beheld the golden queen wearing a shift made as thin as paper by her sweat, her curvaceous figure rendered in soft moonlight. She'd felt his eyes wandering over her hips, her bounteous breasts. She'd felt him dotting her long neck with phantom kisses. His desire to touch her candy-red lips and ruffle her golden curls had become as powerful as a vibration. "Beauty is a lie," he'd repeated.

She'd waited, trapped in pounding, drawn air, for something to happen; she hadn't been sure what. Slowly, he'd taken the hand he'd claimed and had pressed it to his hammering heart. He'd left her hand there, and she'd trailed it, lower, to the throbbing snake that had wanted to burst from his pants. "Will you lie to me?" he'd asked.

Noble even under a carnal spell, he had offered her a choice—to remove her hand, rather than adding another layer of damnation to their souls. If only refusing temptation had been so easy, she would have never listened to the whispers of Death and leveled the Iron City. She'd added one more sin to the pyre of torment and loathing as she'd freed all of Erik's meaty weight from his pants. She had never touched another man's hardness, save for the cold icicle of the Everfair King. Erik's meat had been incredibly hot, and different: the crown of it wider, the rod of it squatter, the balls heavy. Erik and Lila had shuddered from her exploration of his flesh, then had separated for a moment to shuffle out of their garments. The first thing he'd done, as they'd rolled together, was to press them close, so close: hot to hot—which she'd never felt with a man, as Magnus had been only cold. As if a woman on fire, her shame had peaked with the flames rushing along her skin. She had longed to touch him; she had wanted to press caramel to dark brown skin for more years than she'd known.

Staring into his gaze, she'd seen how deeply she had corrupted him, how powerfully and entirely her love had bewitched this man. Memories—flashes of wood rafters and twirling shafts of light, even distant scents of hay—had come over her as he'd stroked the side of her face. In tune with him, her fingers had played over the rippled tissue on his back. Had that been the instant he'd realized he loved her and would give up everything for her, including his honor and soul? What then had this moment meant for her? Redemption? Realization? She hadn't been able to resolve that question, for tenderly, he'd entered her mouth with his tongue and slipped his erection into her womanhood. A perfect fit in each place, like oiled chocolate into molten caramel. Sheer delicacy and bliss, she'd felt, and the revulsion and heat in her body had consumed her in a violent, shuddering fever.

That was their first night, and the most sensual of their dalliances. Since then, they'd used sex as a recreation for forgetfulness. In a slight turn for the better, Erik now drank less, though still regularly, and she slept with fewer terrors, though still fitfully. During the evening hourglasses, he took on hazardous jobs: the kind for which laborers weren't asked for proper papers, as they usually ended up injured or dead. While she never asked, she had an idea about what kind of work he did—protection and brutality for hire. Lately, with the horns of war wailing from west to east across Geadhain, men had much need of procured violence.

When Erik went off to break noses and bones, and on the days when Lila could drag herself from bed, she had taken to doing a bit of charity work at the Order of St. Celcita. The sisters at the old basilica found Lila quite useful, with her knowledge of nursing, herbology, and potion-craft. The latter was a passion of hers. Back in the secret groves of the palace gardens, there were plots of some of the rarest plants on Geadhain—herbs that would now die without her knowledge and care. Carthac's market, even its most exotic brokers, had a dearth of green mysteries. Still, the most basic plants one needed to aid with restlessness, pain, and tremors could be found. She used her herbology to tend to the dying and the ill.

She felt no squeamishness toward her charges. When she helped those who suffered to feel a shade less terrible, it was not under any illusion of piety—for she could never be redeemed. Instead, she wanted her eyes rubbed with the sand of suffering, so that she might never forget her crimes. Those who lingered near the veil of death evoked the strongest feelings of remorse in her. At times, she imagined them to be those she had doomed in Menos. She assumed Erik was similarly possessed by hatred and depression while wetting his fists with blood.

"I should be leaving shortly," said Erik, suddenly.

Another moment, and he was up making noise: stomping to the lavatory, splashing water, taking a piss, walking around the room on a treasure hunt for his garments. Sleepily, Lila listened from the bed. Eventually, Erik's shadow and tidier self hovered nearby, and she woke herself to see him standing over her, a bit sinister with his frown, dark clothing, and half-cloak. She repositioned her body in the sheets—into an alluring pose, from the way his mouth hung—and they played a game of stares before speaking.

"Will you stay in for the evening?" he asked.

"I think I shall see if I am needed at the Order."

"Be safe."

What he meant was, stay unseen, speak to no one. They were, after all, hiding in plain sight. Clever but risky. Fleeing to Carthac, using the same path Magnus had instructed his adopted son to take should the queen be threatened, might seem the riskiest road to travel for two genocidal fugitives avoiding justice. Excessively paranoid about the arrangements, Magnus had long ago ensured that any assistance available to them would come through anonymous partners—men who did not know from whom the coin came, men who would be loyal out of fear of that same anonymous, potentially wrathful sponsor. At roadside inns, Erik had whispered passwords to faceless strangers, who then gave him horses, supplies, and coin. In total, it had taken around a month to reach Carthac. First, they had trotted south through the long, empty green hills of Meadowvale, hardly encountering another soul; then, they'd made a push through the withering Salt Forests. They'd arrived in Carthac thanks to the generosity of no less than three unnamed shadowbrokers and perhaps a dozen merchants, who would know it would not be safe to remember the large warrior and his hooded companion.

Surely, Magnus didn't even suspect they were in Carthac. They certainly hadn't reached out to any of the king's most powerful allies in the city—the council of aldermen—for fear of his getting wind they were here. Even in Magnus's most devious moments, he would likely not suspect they would head to the City of Waves. It seemed probable, given the lack of wanted posters about the realms and bounty hunters hounding them, that Magnus hadn't mounted a pursuit. In a sense, knowing that was worse than being on the run, for it implied the king thought she and Erik were either irredeemable or inconsequential.

While Lila's mind wandered, Erik left, giving her neither a kiss nor a wave goodbye. After all, they were not lovers, only fellow sufferers. If he'd stayed, it would have been to roll with her in angry, savage forgetfulness. There would be more of that when he returned in the early dawn, drunk, and bearing the spiced and not unpleasant body odor gained from crushing skulls. Until then, she could ponder the notes of his smell, his fragrance of violence, which reminded her of an Arhadian clove she'd sniffed in her childhood a thousand years past. Before getting out of the sheets, she took a sniff of herself and smelled violence upon her flesh as well. They were in her nature now: blood and death. Her body, at last, had become as tainted as her soul.

III

At the base of the sea wall that protected Carthac from the Straits of Wrath, the Order of St. Celcita occupied a partially demolished basilica. It looked close to collapse, with its one ruined dome, two standing towers, and two fallen ones. The towers that remained erect looked as flimsy as bushels of straw. Lila wondered if it would be her destiny to die beneath their inevitably toppled mass. Against the grim sky and gray wall, the ivory basilica appeared as if it were made of clouds and faint light. *Holy.* It felt holy to her, every time she beheld it. Feathers of mist floated about the towers, and the sea beat upon Carthac's wall like an unyielding drum: it was a pretty and impressive scene. She stood and pondered.

Her trip to the hospice had been unremarkable. Once out of the noisy quarter where she and Erik lived, she had taken a slink down bricked streets, past cube-shaped dwellings with shuttered windows and chimneys piping smoke. She had passed an alley cat or two, and a few singing drunks, though hardly another soul more. Things had seemed rather quiet in the City of Waves. Wryly, she wondered if tales of a face-smashing thug who kept the peace for rich masters were making the rounds.

Chastising herself for thinking fondly of Erik—she was meant to suffer, not fawn—Lila focused on the basilica, which always required a small rousing of courage to approach. The peaked and ruined towers, which rose like talons toward the sky, and the shattered dome, fallen in like a broken egg, gave her a frightful shiver whenever she neared. If this was a place of divinity, then it stood to reason that here she would also find a gateway to the infernal—although she no longer feared the voice of a dead warlord or the whispers of Death. She had scraped from herself the mercy and love that her attackers had twisted to make her obedient. No more would she be controlled. She hardly knew what fear was anymore. What then spooked her? This was not terror, but...

Lila couldn't find the word, and the wind swept down over the wall, bringing with it a sudden hail of water. A peal of thunder also rang, and she hurried toward the basilica. Quickly dashing between tombstones and around rusted fences, Lila managed to reach the shadowed arch of the Order's sanctuary just as rain began dousing the land behind her. From her place of shelter, she watched the weather turn the grave markers slick and black, frowning as it blazed the sky with white rage. Storms reminded her of Magnus, and dwelling on the king summoned unwanted thoughts of Erik, too. She felt moodier today, less set in her resolute darkness than usual.

"Siobhan," said a woman.

Sister Abagail's voice was as cracked and ancient as a grandmother's. When Lila turned, though, she saw a thin, spectacled lass in a black frock. Religion seemed such an odd convention in an age of technomagik—these women, with their peaked hats, half veils, and gloved hands, struck Lila as especially anachronistic. Abagail and her sisters were relics of the past, which is perhaps why Lila had felt so drawn to them in the first place, being a relic herself. "Sister Abagail," said Lila.

The two women coyly watched each other, like cats deciding if the other were friend or foe. Lila sensed that the sister saw through some degree of her deception, which is why they often engaged in this contest. Then Abagail smiled. Friends, it appeared. Abagail gestured Lila forward into the ornate vestry where she stood.

"Come on in out of the rain, Siobhan. We have enough sickness to tend to in here already and don't want to have to make up another cot for you."

If only you knew, thought Lila, who hadn't sniffled from a cold in a thousand years.

While the two walked together at an easy pace through spacious dark halls, the fallen queen glanced at the surrounding remnants of a dynasty of yore: tapestries enchanted with witchstitch, torn, yet still garishly red and bright despite their age; pedestals displaying busts of burly men with chipped faces. Lila knew the tale behind these fallen generals, these men who had wanted to be kings—the Lordkings of Carthac. They had been descendants of some of the oldest houses of Menos, the founders of which had come and settled in Carthac when it was barely even a hamlet. The masters had been fleeing some enemy or retribution for their sins— no one knew the exact history anymore. The lords had lavished wealth on the sea-folk, turned a backwater hamlet into a byzantine metropolis. These ancient masters built the wall of the city—a dark reflection of Eod's achievement. This structure did not exist solely to protect the city from privateers—it also served to seal in the wealth that the populace trawled from the sea: fish, weeds, and ores from the furthest deeps (and, it had been said, even a wonderstone or two, although none was found after the masters fell).

And fall the Lordkings did, for the true nature of a Menosian could never be hidden and would ever be his undoing. After the Lordkings had entrenched themselves as the supreme benefactors and rulers of the City of Waves, they began to demand more and more of the people. Soon the city had swollen with ill-gotten gains and become an untouchable bastion on the tip of Central Geadhain. For a time, Carthac in its foul prosperity rivaled even Menos—until, that is, the sea-folk unseated the lords in a single bloody night. They burned the Lordkings' temples and dragged the masters and their families out into the streets to be gutted like fish and hanged. The prideful masters of Menos had forgotten that the sea-folk had wills stronger than those of average men. Carthacians were elemental folk, with an almost magikal connection to the Blue Mother and born with her temperaments. One could not truly know wrath until one had seen a storm on the ocean. Aside from the historians, no one in Carthac chose to remember these doomed lords of antiquity. Instead, they made gardens of their grand, toppled manors, and parks and hospices of the ruined temples where iniquity had once reigned.

"We have a strange patient," said Abagail. "A man from the East."

From the East? wondered Lila. They walked on, trading shadows for the occasional halo of firelight granted by a sconce. Overhead, rain drummed and dribbled through millennia-old cracks, filling the hallway with tiny lakes and ripening the mustiness of the building. Lila considered how unhealthy the mildew must be for those trying to recuperate. However, the argument could be made that most men came here only to die.

She and Abagail entered the great hall of the temple, once stunningly ostentatious. Their feet scuffed on tarnished plates of ivory and gold; from beneath the ancient grime flickered teasing glimpses of the gilded friezes upon the walls. Dull golden columns surrounded a wide court, which lay under the deteriorated dome of the temple. The area was sealed off with rope and tarps—tan sheets ruffled in the air like a ship's sails in a tempest. As they passed through it, making their way toward an arch and holding their garments against the wind and rain bleeding in from the night, Lila wondered how it was the whole place hadn't fallen down. Perhaps the nameless spirit that these sisters worshipped had truly blessed this temple.

In her great life, Lila had met idolaters and zealots before. These women were different. Neither Abagail nor the other sisters ever gave their patron spirit a name other than the Great Will, the Blue Mother. For religious folk, they were quite lazy about proselytizing. They did not recruit, and they observed little in the way of rituals from what Lila had seen. The sisters kept their beliefs to themselves and, perhaps because of this, the people of Carthac had allowed them to settle in ruins for which the city had no use. There, they carried on with their hedge-healer ways. They calmed the demented with herbal elixirs. They fed those in extremis with the blood of the red poppy that soothed all pains. They acted as wardens for the insane. Sometimes, they released the chronically suffering from the mortal coil—when such was the patient's wish. The Order of St. Celcita dealt with whatever runoff of sin and social refuse physicians, fleshbinders, and the Veiled Confessors of Carthac could not heal.

Lila felt at home with the sisters. She often wondered, though, what grief or suffering had driven St. Celcita to abstinence and asceticism. Furthermore, what wrongs had the current women of the order suffered or perpetrated in this age, that they embraced the same self-denying seclusion as Celcita? Perhaps all were secret sinners here.

In the hallway past the arch, the hunger of the wind died, and the women straightened their clothes. Before striding down the damp corridor, Abagail gave Lila a little smile. *Get ready; here we go.* As they continued, additional signs of faded grandeur met their eyes: brass door handles, white stone frames around doors for men as tall as Brutus, the shimmer of silver from spiderwebbed candelabras on the walls. Every door they passed was closed and barred heavily on the outside. Some of the portals thudded as deranged folk requiring sedation bashed themselves against the wood. Rarely was Lila assigned that duty. Lila's skills, Abagail declared, lay in preparing a man's soul for the long sleep.

"Black thistle?" asks Abagail.

Lila turns to see who is speaking to her in the marketplace. When she wraps herself up like a beggar, no one ever notices her, let alone pays her a word, although sometimes they throw coins in her direction. In the dusk, the woman and her loose dark clothing blur together with the shadows of passersby, the darkness cast by tents and their awnings, the smoke curling from outdoor tanneries and ovens. The woman's face is obscured by a veil, and Lila cannot make out her features. The stranger stands very close and speaks once more, her voice that of an ancient. "Do you know what it is used for?" *she asks.*

"Possibly." *Lila hands the sachet she'd been generously filling back to the scowling merchant, canceling the sale, and starts to walk away.*

"A dash in one's tea," *continues the woman, trailing behind Lila as she swims in and around the throng, trying to avoid conversation,* "and the aches of arthritis blow away like dandelion dust. More than a dash, however, induces calm and a sleep so deep that death is but a footstep away."

Angrily, Lila stops and turns, and they stand almost nose to veiled nose. Lila detects a smile under the black veil—a flash of eyewear, too. "I had no intention of killing myself," *spits Lila. She'd already tried that with Erik. She wanted the herb only to deepen her slumber, to deaden her to dreams.*

"I hadn't considered it," says Abagail.

"I merely sought a cure for my restlessness."

"Oh. Well, come with me, then. At the Order's sanctuary, we have herbs much better than this ditch-peddler's tripe at warding off fitful nights. Unless you fancy scoots and a headache."

Hooking her arm into Lila's elbow as if they are old friends, the odd woman guides her through the crowd. Men are getting drunk around them; merchants are closing shop and joining in. A herd of children and seemingly wild dogs races across the street, giggling and barking. In specks, the hints of sunlight leave, and the world feels dark, loud and spinning on an axis of giddy chaos. *What is going on? Where is this woman taking her?* Lila tries to pull away, but the stranger's grip is fierce.

"You have the look of the lost," says the stranger, without stopping. "I tend to the lost; I know what they need. If you want your herbs and the peace of a sleep without terrors, then you must work for them."

"Work? What?" Lila is aghast at the presumption that she has agreed to perform some kind of service. She hasn't engaged in manual labor since milking lizard-cows ten centuries ago.

"Just a bit of blood on the hands and a little sweat. I think you have a knack for it," replies her gleeful kidnapper.

The moment is so queer that Lila wonders if she's somehow already taken a lethal dose of black thistle and is right now lying dead on the floor of her squalid home. Embracing the nightmare, Lila stops asking questions and allows herself to be marched off through dark streets and into the darker reaches of Carthac.

"Always wandering off in your mind," said Abagail, tugging at Lila's arm as she had in the memory. The two had entered a large space separated from the rest of the room by drawn sheets that years of sweat and sickly breath had spotted yellow. This area of the hospice smelled worse than any other ward. In here, the most fevered, pustulant, and leprous sufferers lay waiting to die. Women dressed like Abagail, but also wearing heavy masks, rubber gloves, and splattered aprons, swept to and fro. The sisters carried bedpans, draining needles, and bowls that steamed with aromatic effusions of petal and herb. A nearby sister glared at Abagail for speaking.

Among their many mysterious oaths, Lila knew that for the Sisters of St. Celcita, their vow of silence was paramount. *We hear so much better when we ourselves do not speak*, she'd explained to Lila. Abagail herself was exempt from this vow, as the order needed an advocate among men. Lila felt that Abagail stretched that freedom further than she should with her frequent palaver, but she made no objection: such talk served her well, as it kept her abreast of happenings here and beyond. Around each other, the sisters communicated through a language of complicated hand gestures, stares, and the occasional written note.

"The Easterner," Abagail said as they continued to walk. "He came in a night or two ago, definitely after the last time you visited us. We found a wallet and papers on him, announcing him to be a man of certain means…" Her voice dropped low. "A man from Menos."

Lila stopped, and they huddled behind one of the curtains while a sleeping wretch wheezed nearby. "Menos?" she asked.

"Not just any man. A master."

"Who?"

Rather dramatically for a holy woman, Abagail waved her hands and said, "Sangloris Donanach, father of the House of Mysteries."

Someone shushed them. Abagail shushed back.

"Show me," said Lila.

Abagail nodded, and they moved through curtains and past the resting and nearly dead. They came to the bedside of a direly pale man, who was wrapped up to his neck in wool blankets and sopping wet with greasy sweat. His smell induced a small heave in Lila. He stank like the fish markets of Carthac in the morning, when yesterday's offal and blood were being washed into the sewers—tangy with death. The man's lips were chapped and flaked in white. His eyelids flickered like the candle by his bedside.

As a former companion to Death, Lila now possessed an acute sense of when a man's life would simply let go. This man was close to that release. Examining him, first with her eyes, then unknowingly with her fingers, she noted that Sangloris shared some of Magnus's attributes: the ivory skin, the uncommon hue and clarity of the eyes—silver in this case—the fineness of the nose and cheekbones. Abagail cleared her throat as Lila's fingertips drifted to the man's dry lips.

"How did he end up here?" asked Lila, and set her wandering hand to combing the man's white hair.

"We don't know. The Twelveswatch brought him in. None of the twelve aldermen will claim knowledge of a Menosian master hiding in plain sight. Even today, the City's hatred of the Iron masters burns as hot as a young man's passion. If you were here then, you will certainly remember that folks lit bonfires and danced in the streets when they heard of Menos's sad fall." The sister clucked. "So you can see why none of the aldermen will utter the faintest peep that could indict them. They'll likely remain silent until a moment comes when they can take credit for his glorious murder, whether they're entitled to it or not. I imagine the master of Menos was here doing business—as those iron folk always are. I would assume that events went sour, as he was gutted like a pig and then thrown to his doom in the Straits. A strong man, he must be. I admire that. To have held onto a slippery island—bleeding and wounded—while the world tried to drown him..."

"How terrible," said Lila, saddened.

"Not for much longer." Abagail touched the fallen queen's shoulder. "The rot has set in from his wound. No magik but that of the Everfair King and all the wonders of Eod could cure him in this state."

Lila shivered.

"You're trembling like a winter lamb, dear child," said Abagail. "I'll get you a blanket and fetch him some more poppy's blood. I doubt he'll wake up again. It's awful when he does—so much thrashing and agony. I shan't be more than a speck. You just talk to him, and let him know it's all right, and he can leave whenever he must."

Sister Abagail's departure conjured a gust that killed the weak flame by Lila's side. She could have sat in the darkness listening to Sangloris's sputtering gasps, but the sound of his ghastly rattle managed to unnerve her. Quickly, before Abagail returned, Lila flung a hand toward the gray smudge she assumed was the candle and readied herself to Will it to life. Trembling once again like Abagail's winter lamb, Lila found she couldn't bring herself to summon her magik. Would she summon flame or deepen the shadows?

Since the events at the Iron Mines, her magik had been polluted by its sinfulness; she now eschewed phantasms, preferring to disguise herself with cowls and scarves. On the road once, she had, though, tried healing a gash on Erik's shin, one he'd received while stumbling around partly drunk. The task involved only the most basic mending, demanding none of the complex anatomical knowledge of a fleshbinder. She'd frozen then, too. When she'd finally squeezed a bit of Will from herself, the light she shone—her magik and soul—had been so black and burning that Erik screamed. To this day, Erik wore the brand of her brief touch: a five-pronged marking on his leg. In time, she hoped the scar would blend in with his natural pigment.

It's only a flame, you child, she chastised herself.

Anger summoned her Will, and with a puff of black smoke and a scattering of sparks, the wick was lit. The act had not been marred by the appearance of dark forces, and that felt like cause for celebration. But then she looked over at the ghoulish man and any exhilaration that might have blossomed was stillborn. He was now sitting up in his cot, the sheets pulled down his torso to reveal a wound like a giant green bee sting on his stomach. His silver stare was locked on Lila, and he reached out and seized the hand she'd been using to conjure the flame. As soon as they touched, a buzzing cacophony and a dazzle of lights assaulted Lila's senses. She fell.

Onto a slick rock? She scrabbles to her knees, battling wind and salty shrieks, fighting the slippery ground for footing. A strong white hand hauls her up; for a speck, she believes it to be Magnus's. Then the illusion flakes away, her spinning vision settles to take in a dark night, and she recognizes the extraordinary pallor of her patient, Sangloris. However, he's not dying on a cot—instead, he's handsomely dressed in a sharply tailored silk shirt and pants. A fury of wind and spume roars upon the tiny mount of rock where she and Sangloris stand. Black crashing waves circle the island. Nonetheless, Sangloris's glossy boots have not a scuff of salt upon them, and the wind barely ruffles his free-flowing hair. He might almost be elsewhere. He is elsewhere, realizes Lila. He is with her in the basilica, as well as here in this Dream upon the Straits of Wrath. He stands with one foot in each world.

"What have you done to me, ghost?" she demands, and shakes off his hand, which feels convincingly real.

"I am not a ghost," he says, in a cultivated, gentlemanly voice. "Not yet. But this is where my journey into the Great Mystery began, where I found more clarity than a living mind can touch. The secret moon, the moon of spirits, shone over me one night as I lay here, bleeding and dying. While I have not my wife Elissandra's gifts for reading fate—none of the men of our line do—the moon, the magik of my blood, tapped into power from the deepest well: the well of time and eternity."

"I don't—" Lila nearly falls again, but the master instantly catches her in a whirl of white. They stare, face to face. "Whatever this is, send me back."

"I shall."

She waits and shivers in his arms, on this speck in the sea, while the half-ghost continues gazing upon her. A determining look, he gives, as if he judges her. She wonders how deeply the spirit can see into her heart, and suddenly she wants—needs—to be released.

"I know what you have done," he says.

Lila struggles against Sangloris.

"I am no wrathful spirit," he says, calmly. "I am not here to punish you. If you could see the horizons to which I shall soon sail, or hear the quietest voice that calls me to sunset, you would understand the futility of harming yourself with guilt over having ended a society of wicked men. I am one; I was one. I know what I have been. Death would have made her army, one way or another. Dreamers are toying with all these men and women as if they were playthings of glass; they are breaking everything they touch, cutting the flesh of our world with the bodies of the shattered. I am not here to punish you, Lilehum, most used of all Geadhain's glass creatures. However, there is something I need you to do for me—an act I cannot complete before taking my journey. Cease your resistance."

Lila has no choice; she feels paralyzed, as if a poison has been seeping into her through Sangloris's increasingly cold touch. In specks, her throat has numbed too much to shout anymore, and her fingers feel so deadened, they seem likelier to break off than to move.

He continues. "Open yourself: surrender to and embrace the fact that you are weak and imperfect. Let the tides of Fate wash and drown us both."

Only in her frozen skull can Lila scream when Sangloris, holding her tightly, leaps into the black water. Liquid ice fills her lungs, bringing hopeless terror with it. Every nerve is on fire. Her body spasms for breath. The ghostly master tightens his arms around her. "Surrender," he whispers, although it sounds more like a buzz to her water-clogged ears—ears that should not be able to hear. *Bees?* she wonders. Then the mystery loses importance, her body goes slack, and she and the master drift gracefully, their garments billowing, through sheer, cold blackness.

Death.

"Now you are ready to see," echoes Sangloris's voice.

She'd thought they were dead, so this, naturally, surprises her. The rude brilliance of light and a tremendous movement create a second dissonance. Suddenly, she is no longer underwater: she is hurled through panes of shattering whiteness, then stopped, then hurled and stopped, again and again. Each pause gives her a gasping moment in which to glimpse a scene.

S<small>MASH</small>!

A girl and a lad, both wrapped in furs and skins against the elements, stand on a hill of snow, gesturing toward the distance. Lila feels they could be brother and sister. Their tribal chatter sounds like the whine of a seal or the caw of a crow. She can't hear most of what they say—the wind beats her spirit ears for trying. Something about north, heading north, where there are glass forests more ice than plant, and mountains like jagged glacial molars chewing at a sky as thick and white as plaster. Oh, what terrible cold must stir there! Yet that is where the brother and sister must go. North. But who are those others with them? Two men and a woman, if their statures are any indication. She feels twinges of suspicion, as if she knows the shrouded trio. Then the vision propels Lila forward again, through darkness, then light, and the winter hill and the small shadows climbing its back are erased.

S<small>MASH</small>!

As another pane of reality shatters, she floats and twists like a wind over a deeply cracked and bleak plain of the coldest, blackest ice. Tormented eddies roar from grand white buttes, rushing under the irregular bridges of ice that arc the land and down into pits of sheer, gray doom. This is the heart of the North—the coldest place in all the world. Perhaps Magnus was born here. The brother crow and sister seal are gone; nothing could possibly live in the tearing, shearing howl that consumes this place. But something has called her there, from down in the blur of white, and she thinks she sees three black dots that could be the wandering trio from before. She's more intrigued by the noise though: sounds like brittle glass breaking, or grinding—a hundred tons of ice, crystal, and bones. It cannot be a voice, and still it summons her like a king's command. Down. A force pulls her through snow flocks and crevasses, pulls her down to the earth—

Smash!

A sparkling fantasia appears before her. Fractured looking-glasses, drifts of diamonds, and mist float around her. Tinkles, shattering groans, and percussive bursts of frozen stone exploding from pressure make an obstreperous song. Is she in some great crystal machine? What is this ether reek? A stink of minerals, salts, and purity—a mineral spring without the heat.

'Tis the smell of the beast, Sangloris's buzzing voice tells her. The beast? Then she spots a fragmented line of mirrors moving in the bedlam. A crackling slit shows a beautiful sphere of quartz with an accrual of sapphire-blue crystals at its center. The mirror line moves again, casting glitter and frost, and closes over the immense sphere. Suddenly, hysterical with panic, Lila grasps what it is she beholds: an eye. An impossible riddle: What has an eye as large as a moon? What more of this coiled thing lurks in the vaporous streams of ice and floating crystal? She knows it moves through the inconceivable reaches of this underground cavern like a water snake, but this serpent is immeasurably large. By Sangloris's oracular magik, she knows, too, the serpent's name, and speaks it: "Nifhalheim."

Speaking the elemental's name ends her journey. In a blink, she is bobbing once more, rigid and dead, in a black and watery grave.

"You must share what you have seen," says Sangloris's spirit. "Since you continue to choose the illusion of weakness, tell my wife, Elissandra Donanach, who has traded the Iron Wall for Eod's ivory one, what to do. No matter the inner circle, she provides her wisdom to this war. She is strong; she will guide the king. I cannot reach her, my fair daughter of the moon. My spirit cannot pierce the strange new shield of Eod so that I might say goodbye. Tell her that I love her. Give my children the kiss I cannot. You are to be our goodbye. Go forth, glass woman, and stir the world with change. You do not see how fierce your storm of fire can be, how cleansing. I warn you against straying from this path. An errant step and you will ruin more than Menos. You will ruin life, all life—here, and throughout the tree of stars..." Sangloris's warning echoes, and then begins to fade. "Fire against frost... Element to element...Mother to seer...Brother to brother...This is how it must be..."

Silence swallows Lila, silence that throbs with emptiness.

Lila took the longest breath of her life, an inverse scream; it was as if magik had suddenly revived a heart and lungs stilled by death. Sister Abagail was shaking her, shouting at her to release the body of the dead Master of Mysteries and pleading for Lila to explain why she was soaking wet and burning cold.

Lila couldn't answer, for nothing in life made sense at the moment. The memory seemed as staggering to consider as the monster of ice that slept in the North. An elemental; *the* elemental force of ice. She remembered the vision of its twisting, glittering lunacy. She remembered that Sangloris had charged her to find Elissandra—possibly tempting death at Magnus's hands. That didn't matter. For she needed to return to Eod, find Elissandra, and tell her how to stop the world from ending.

IV

Rather drunk, and further blurred by anger, Erik struggled to find Lila in the dim, unlit room. He had only the thin veins of a red dawn by which to see. However, after a moment, Lila's tawny, naked flesh gave off an artful shimmer. She sat upon their bed, her back turned to him. She seemed to be shuddering and rocking herself. Alarmingly, the room looked as if it had been torn apart: chairs had been tipped, their meager set of dishes shattered. Erik relaxed after he'd scanned the room and confirmed that no men had taken cover in its shadows. It was only Lila who had done this, then. After bolting the door, Erik rushed toward her.

"We have a problem," he said, and wondered if her distress meant that she already knew.

Circling the bed, he came and knelt before his partner in sin. She looked unhealthy; her olive-and-gold complexion had taken on a greenish hue, as if she were oxidizing copper. She shivered, refusing to look at him. A cold, damp towel lay discarded at her feet. Whimpers and watery eyes expressed her barely contained turmoil. "Lila?" he asked quietly.

They were not lovers; they were prisoners sharing the same sentence. Still, the broken hammer rose, sat on the bed, and put his warm, strong arm around the fallen queen. She must have bathed recently, and her honey-apple smell—and the whiskey in his veins—inclined Erik to a kindness out of keeping with the rough-and-tumble persona he'd adopted. Somewhere in the thick mists of his feelings, he heard musical notes, the melody of his early love for her. Songs of her incredible strength, but also of her frailty. A woman like a glass nightingale in a cage of the hardest steel; a woman who challenged the world with her beliefs, and at the same time became trapped by her hubris. Perhaps Lila had also found that woman again, if only for an instant, for she fell apart in his arms. She broke down, shuddering and weeping.

"You are not a weak woman," declared Erik, after she'd wet enough of his tunic with her tears. She stiffened up and pulled away a little, though she remained within the circle of his embrace. "Have you heard, then?"

"Heard?" She sniffled.

"I've been recognized. One of the aldermen. At the gambling house where I sometimes work, he saw me and called me by name. I denied it, of course. I would have thought a man his age would have brains like porridge, and yet...We should leave Carthac. I do not believe we shall be safe here anymore. Word will get back to Magnus, somehow. I haven't thought of where..." Erik paused, and images of a cool white tundra, swept with snow and bitter winds, charmed a smile out of him; it was a memory of their voyage near the Northlands. He spoke again, stirred by wistfulness. "Perhaps we could go to a place where men are too focused on warring with the elements to worry over war itself. We could go north. To a place where we would never be found, where you would no longer be a queen—and where I would no longer be a man who has lost his honor. We could be whomever we wanted. New people...not prisoners chained by our cultures and our pride, or sycophants bespelled by the charisma of an Immortal. I love my Kingfather, I always shall...But you and I both know that loving Magnus is not a choice. Why must we tie ourselves to his heart—a heart that beats strongest and truest for his brother? Why must we forgive him, forgive them? Why can we not love whom we choose? Possibly even—" He froze and stared at the woman of gold sitting beside him.

The question would not be answered; it hung there between them, its scope as deep as the wounded devotion they shared. Nothing could be clearer in that moment: he had followed her into doom, and she had wallowed with him in depravity. Their carnal suffering and sadism were another shade of love: a blacker one, forged in pain and blood.

Was it as the spirit of Sangloris had said? wondered Lila. Could guilt created by monstrous acts outside one's control—earthquakes, war, the damage done while she'd lost herself—be a distraction from following one's purpose in life? The purpose of life...What could that be? A mystery too grand to apprehend, and yet...

A revelation pulled at their souls, their flesh. She and Erik drew nearer. She saw Erik's scars—not merely the ones on his cheeks and on the sculpted, frowning lips that infrequently kissed her, but ones caused by wounds that bled deeper: his imperfections, his longings, the honor with which he fought. She wanted to apologize or confess an enormous secret. Then a weight of emotion that felt like a tangle of nettles, broken swords, and clotted darkness—the *poison* that they'd drunk together—forced itself from her body in a heave. "Erik, I..."

"Lila..." he said, and his hands were upon her. He touched her face, as he had that first forbidden time in the stables in Eod. "We can go tonight. We can catch a ship and sail north. We can forget Kings, our twisted vassalage, and wars. In time, the cold will make us numb to our memories of the Iron Valley and what we did. War and despair harm what is good in us. You told me that. You warned me and I followed you. I cannot blame you for where I have chosen to go, for where I shall always choose to go."

Torn between weeping and laughing, Lila trembled. Erik's entreaty, backed by the force of his black gaze, inspired a fierce yearning in her—to give in wholly to his suggestion, roam white nothingness, forget who they were, and choose who they would be. His appeal was as powerful as one of Magnus's spells—more powerful, even, as Erik's was a magik she had chosen to be bewitched by. However, fate demanded that she be strong, that she be the fire of change once more. At first, Sangloris's speech had ruined her with its pressure and expectation of what must be done. She'd fled the basilica, tried to scald the vision from her body in the hottest bath she could fill. Then she had agonized—catatonically, rocking like a madwoman on her bed—over the spirit's dire words. And here, now, as always, was Erik: when she most needed the strength and surety of a weapon, he shone as her sword. At last he had stripped off the wicked armor each had donned, baring himself, his feelings, and the desire to serve and protect her. He was a flame that would never die.

"Your patience is my greatest strength," she said, touching the hands that cupped her head. "We shall go north. To start again."

The huge, dark, often terrifying man wore a desperate, starved expression. In a sense, he had been deprived. Lila's golden touch, her amber stare that beheld him with awe, was a feast for his soul. "Do you mean it?" he asked.

"Yes."

Creeping closer, with the utmost hesitation, the two glass creatures grazed noses then brushed their cheeks together. Finally, each found the warm sanctuary of the other's mouth, kissing with a sigh. It was a kiss exchanged between the most intimate strangers: people who had known the darkness and ugliness of each other before tasting any of the other's light. Hands groped, bodies rubbed, and they tumbled onto the bed, blind with passion. A careful lust, a cautious lust, now that they knew it might mean something other than escape from the world. Erik kissed tender trails down her golden neck, but Lila stopped him, raising his panting face to hers.

"I must tell you something."

"Do you want me to stop?" The calloused wave of his hand paused its roll over her flesh.

"No," she replied.

"Do you doubt..."

Your passion, your truth, your commitment? Never. She'd broken this man so often that he could not tell whether fist or kiss would come from her next. No more punches, she decided, and kissed his cheek, then placed her arms around his broad back. Confused, though submitting to the pleasure, Erik rolled on the squeaking mattress and held her, too. After sands of that peace, Lila whispered, "I shall travel north with you. But we cannot go right away. There is someone in Eod who is waiting for a message—a message only I can deliver."

Erik grunted and pulled back, glowering. "Eod? Is it Magnus? What would you say to him?"

"Not Magnus." With her serpent's charm, sweet perfume, and red lips, she drew him into her spell once more. "The message is not for him," she half kissed and half said, "I could not reach him anyway. I do not know how the magik of the heart works, the magik that binds Magnus and I, but there is no longer a wall or chasm separating us. There is nothing. I have cast him out, or he has done so to me. I do not think he and I shall be together again without an invitation."

"Who then? Who is the message for?" asked Erik.

"While I've never met her, I know of her—it would be impossible not to, as she's been one of our enemies for years..." Lila gazed off, distracted by the strangeness of it.

Gently, Erik turned her head to meet his gaze. "Who?" he asked.

"Elissandra, one of the Iron Sages of Menos."

Erik gasped. "I would've thought them all dead. Who gave you this message?"

"The ghost of her husband."

A ghost? This mystery would have to wait, for Lila, his one and eternal queen, pressed her lips to his. In her kiss, he felt the purity he'd known was hidden behind her sorrow all these days. Behind her kiss, dazzling the darkness of his closed eyes, he felt the sacred light that had nearly made him bring steel upon his Kingfather. He had followed Lila's star on the darkest journey of his life; he would protect its beauty with his soul. At last, his queen was free to shine. And she had made her choice, which was to be with her knight. Ghosts, guilt, and secret messages evaporated in the fire that rose between their bodies. In moments, his clothes were off, their sweat and kisses lathered each other's skin, and slowly, sweetly, and for the very first time, they made love.

V

"Sangloris Donanach, a creature called Nifhalheim..." Erik muttered, struggling to pay attention to Lila's account of her ominous vision. The feel of their legs entwined, thighs caressing, was more interesting to the warrior than tales of ghosts and doomed promises. Thrice they'd made love, with such patience, that day had come and gone. He could taste her sweat and the salt taffy of her lower valley on his lips. How could a woman taste so sweet? Something in which she bathed? Even while they had been in exile, he recalled, his queen had stepped into water that steamed with exotic oils. The wonder of her elegance bounced around like a ball in his head. Never mind that: now he must listen and unsheathe the steel of his soul. It was time to be a weapon again—the queen's weapon. Lila watched the change happen—a military stiffness now commanded his body even as a certain part stayed rigid below—and knew she had most of his attention. "What would you have me do?" he asked.

"*We* must deliver the message to Elissandra." She walked two fingers up his chest while speaking. "We must tiptoe into Eod, as there is a protection of sorts around it. I have heard from local gossip of this Witchwall; it is a shield against magik. It must have been raised by an unknown ally, because Magnus was not present to defend his city from the sky monsters of Menos—Furies, as they are called. No matter; we shall find Elissandra and I shall tell her what I have seen. Then we shall head north."

"What of Lowe and Leonitis, stuck playing in our skins?"

"If Magnus had wished their phantasms dispelled, he could easily have broken my magik. We should assume he knows about the illusion; we should assume we are seen as criminals by most who once favored us, those who know of my act..." Sadly, Lila drifted off, her hand stopping atop the beat in Erik's chest.

"Our act. I helped you," he declared. "We destroyed Menos together. And think of the state Eod would be in now if you had not struck the Iron City first."

"Eod would lie in ruins."

"Yes."

They mulled over the sour truth.

"Promise me no more guilt, Lila," said Erik, and shuffled closer. "I do not have endless years, as you do. I have only now discovered, so late in life, *what* and *how* to feel."

Erik's adoration and confession humbled her, and she blushed. A knock and some garbled announcement saved her from any further conversation on mortality and commitment. The knocking rose to a violent banging.

This was definitely not a dainty maid come calling, and the lovers knew they were on borrowed time. Alert, Erik wrestled himself from the sheets, which clung to him, making him furious. Meanwhile, Lila scrabbled around for a scrap of clothing. Making sure he was decent was not a priority for Erik: he needed to get to the sword that he kept against the dresser. A thundering bound brought him to the bureau, and he crashed into it with his hip, hurling its mirror to a shattering death. Nonetheless, he managed to catch his weapon by its hilt before it fell, too. Suddenly, the door was kicked inwards, and Lila, frantically whipping her head about, saw men storm into the room. She could not say how many. Erik may have been drinking himself into oblivion for weeks, but at his core he remained a man of metal; steel sinews vibrated in every knotted brown cord in his body. As the queen glanced to her weapon and shouted his name, he protected her with a fearsome spectacle of strength. He drove his sword into the floorboards—releasing a humming twang—picked up the creaky piece of furniture he'd bumped, and then roared as he threw it toward the doorway.

The sight of a crazed, naked strongman hurling a dresser took everyone by surprise, particularly the men on the receiving end of the payload. A handful of thugs went down in a puff of dusty shrapnel and lay moaning on the floor. One dazed fool stayed on his feet, having sidestepped the dresser. Dazzlingly fast, Erik picked up his sword, moved through the chaotic room like a black monster of smoke, and bashed the man's face with the pommel of his blade. The warrior dropped. Erik strode toward the remaining crippled men, who crawled and stumbled through shattered wood. With kicks to their backs that made sickening snaps, Erik rendered two men unconscious. Once downed, the men did not move again. Erik caught the fourth and last failed assailant as he attempted to escape, grabbing the flowing tail of his cloak. Like a scarf dancer, Erik twirled the fabric around his hand, wrenched it tight with a grunt, and then unfurled it, throwing the man back into the room. The man lost his balance, fell, and dropped his sword. In a speck, Erik had his blade under the man's chin. "Who sent you?"

The gasping youth, red-haired and nearly beardless, could comprehend neither the storm of violence in which he'd landed nor the dark, powerful man threatening him—a man who smelled of both destruction and ripe, sexual sweat. Erik drove his sword's point a sliver closer to the lad's jugular, and the steel sparked a confession.

"Alderman Tretton! A b-bounty! He said there was a bounty on the hammer of the king! I'm s-sorry! I've never been sorrier! Please, I'm only following the orders of the Twelveswatch. I'm betrothed, I have a child—"

CRACK!

A pommel to the lad's head ended their discussion; but at least Erik hadn't killed or horrifically maimed him as he had the others. Shouts sounded in the tavern beneath them. Erik rushed around fetching boots, pants, his flask—but no, he felt no urge for drink, not now that he must defend his queen. Lila was dressed in a moment, fully hooded and prepared for flight. She helped him into his shirt.

"A bounty? I thought—" she began.

"That Magnus would leave us be? Forever? You forget that Magnus's judgment is as bitter as the Long Winter in which he was born. We have been judged, it seems, and found wicked."

Erik shrugged on his cloak and hood, then slid his sword into its sheath; they would draw less attention if his steel weren't flashing. Lila was not quite panicking, although she was clearly vibrating with worry; her mouth trembled, trying to give shape to unformed questions. Feeling impetuous and enflamed by the red, fluttering petals of her lips, Erik, the eternal sword, ruler and repressor of emotions, succumbed wholly to desire and kissed his queen. They were hot, dripping, hungry kisses; he grew hard against her leg. When they pulled apart, Lila felt breathless. She had forgotten her questions.

"We are fugitives now," he said. "If word of the bounty has spread, we are now the most wanted criminals in all Geadhain."

Lila was weak with shock and giddiness, but she smiled as they dashed out of the ruined apartment.

V

In their wake, the fugitives left a trail of unconscious and slumped men, bleeding noses, and broken limbs. When it had become evident that the fugitives would not be easily or quickly caught, the Twelveswatch intensified their efforts. Soon, the clanging naval bells atop the ancient watchtowers woke every man, woman, and child from their beds. Carthacians were unfamiliar with such disruptions, and they stepped timidly and sleepily out into the streets wearing their nightgowns and long johns. Rubbing their puffed eyes, they chattered about what in the king's name had woken them at such an unkind hourglass. A fire? Where, then, was the smoke? A burglary? If so, then Carthac's treasury must have been beset by privateers, given how many of the Twelveswatch had been called into action. They received no answers from the frequent patrols of cloaked, steel-baring men sweeping the roads and alleyways.

Foolishly, by rousing the rabble, the authorities had raised a clamor that allowed Erik and Lila to camouflage themselves during their brief scurries through populated areas. A phantasmal disguise from the queen would have allowed for a perfect escape, yet she still believed in caution when it came to using magik, unable as she was to foretell whether it would bring harm or aid. She needed time to test her Will, to see whether her connection with Erik—their *feelings*, she thought lightheadedly— would act as a counterweight to her instability. She felt as if she were a different woman from the one who had been haunted by a dark spirit for weeks. Occasionally, Erik glanced to her, or stopped to give her a rough, bearded kiss and some wanton caressing, and she knew that whatever reckless desire filled her filled his veins as well. Everything about their predicament was unsafe, undignified, and unseemly for a queen, yet still it seemed as if she was behaving like herself—not a woman-slave of the Arhad, not a gawking bride to an ancient king, but her real and buried self. And from what she could tell thus far, she liked this new Lila, even if her actions were unpredictable.

For hourglasses, they played cat and mouse with the Twelveswatch, while slowly creeping toward the Order's basilica. There, Lila felt they would find sanctuary among the women who distanced themselves from politics and wars. If they were given no welcome, she and Erik could always take refuge in the catacombs under the building. Leaving the city without magik and a devious plan would not be possible, and they would need time for her to construct them. One mercy was that the Twelveswatch appeared unable to deal with this level of emergency; they never patrolled in groups larger than four, and Erik alone counted as an army. While not prone to fawning, Lila found herself nonetheless marveling at the strength and viciousness of her lover. Astonishing that a man, one without magik or supernatural strength, could train and discipline his body until he had become a weapon.

She watched Erik dispatch one of the first patrols they encountered, a trio of the Twelveswatch, so fast that only sands later did she realize what he had done. After asking her to stay back, he had tiptoed through shadows, almost running, and then disabled two men with quick chops to the base of their skulls; they dropped like ragdolls onto the street. As the final member of this Twelveswatch patrol sauntered on, Erik kicked his knees out from behind, then smashed his face into a brick wall while he was still laughing at the joke he'd just told. Erik was a master of restrained brutality—he did not want to kill these men. If he were set on murder, or if he chose to use his sword...She shivered thinking about how red the streets would run.

Roughly twenty assaults later, her awareness had become smudged behind a grease of blood; she had grown desensitized to the cracking, meaty, pounding sounds and stifled whimpers. She knew whenever violence was imminent, for Erik would pause then skulk off. From somewhere up ahead would drift the notes of his violent music, and then he would return to her hiding place, usually wild looking and spattered in crimson. "Come!" he would hiss. Lila often kissed him. This new or *true* Lila was a warm and daring woman.

As they ran from their latest escapade, leaving behind a groaning heap of men and swords, she remembered a book. It was one of the millions in the Court of Ideas, an overwrought romance she'd once read in an afternoon. She had laughed at the contrivances and clichéd characterization: besotted women who fell over themselves, men who were uncompromisingly cold, but somehow harbored secret, hidden flames. She hadn't believed that people could reach such emotional heights, where the fires of passion transformed the metal of the soul into wondrous alloys. She had thought she might never feel anything again—and certainly not so soon— but perhaps she had wanted Erik for longer than she knew. Indeed, most of her ignorance and misconceptions about love and romance had come from marrying Magnus, a man of ice, always cultured and cool. Her time with Magnus had been a dream, and it possessed the consistency of vapors and illusions when she dwelled upon it.

With Erik, however, life was raw and terrifyingly tangible. The moments they stole, the warmth of his mouth, the exhilaration of their fear, the threat of his mortality…This last thought pricked her heart with a thorn. They would worry about his longevity later—if this delicate dream didn't shatter, if they managed to evade the Twelveswatch. *I think I might love you, Erik. Real love. The passion of a woman who knows herself, not the starry-eyed wonder of a girl beholden to a king.*

"A moment, my queen," said Erik, interrupting her reverie. "There are men up ahead. I need you to be both silent and patient."

As you have so dutifully been with me. The sentiment choked her, and she nodded, though she said nothing. Erik darted into the shadows, leaving her alone near the back steps of a noisy alehouse that stank of piss. She hunkered down behind a stack of kegs, and was not so dainty as to shriek as rats ran over her feet. Angry at her uselessness, she made the rats squeal with her kicks. With her magik, she should have been able to protect Erik as much as he was protecting her. She debated testing out a spark of her power—something small, a bit of flame, perhaps, like the one she'd managed back at the Order—when the clang of swords and a grunting scream from Erik jolted her. Damn his rules, and damn the man if anything happened to him.

Bolting from her cover, she raced down the narrow alleyway, as mad as a horse in a thunderstorm. She quickly came upon her protector. He was alive, thank the Sisters Three. The same could not be said of what lay near him in a twisted pile of shadows. Death had finally come to the Twelveswatch, she saw, appraising the jutting, gnarled hands and grotesquely crooked legs. A red, sparkling spray decorated the walls of the alley, and a ghastly iron stink farted up from the bodies.

Erik, strangely calm, leaned against the wall, his sword hanging limply from his hand. When she whispered his name, he dropped the blade, clutched his side, and stumbled toward her. As he stepped out into a flash of moonlight, he winced, and she saw he'd left gory handprints on the bricks. Lila ran to him.

"What happened? What did they do to you?"

"Two groups." Erik huffed. "Eight men. The second patrol spotted me creeping upon the first. One of them had a knife. I thought he was down, and then—"

Erik clenched his teeth in agony. Lila slung his heavy arm over her shoulders and helped him lean up against the wall, so that she might examine his wound. Eight men? She was amazed he still lived. Even more astonishing was Erik's composure in light of the fact that the dagger remained embedded in the lower left side of his stomach. Crimson circles seeped into his tunic. The blood looked so dark that despite Lila's limited medical knowledge, she was certain it came from an organ. The wound would be fatal.

"Erik!"

"If you pull it out, I'll bleed faster."

Lila hesitated, unsure, a thousand terrors suddenly in her heart.

"You have to pull it out," he said. "And you have to heal it."

"I'm not sure—"

Erik grabbed her hand and brought it to the rough bristle of his face, caressing himself with it. Her touch acted as a medicine on the knot of burning, numbing pain in his gut. "Then I die," he whispered.

"No. No!"

"Do it now, Lila. Remember the promise we made; remember your strength, my queen." After kissing the hand he held upon his face, he lowered it to the hilt of the weapon lodged inside him. "Remember that we still have to answer the question for each other. If we can love whom we choose—"

Unable to finish, he coughed, then spat out a wad of bloody mucus. Lila felt warm red syrup pulse against her fingers. In a speck, Erik's impressive discipline would crack, and either delirium or shock would seize him. *Do it. Answer the question; be the woman he sees in you,* she demanded. Suddenly, as she stared into the black shadow of death on her lover's face, the breath of their journey rolled out in a storm cloud of emotion that flickered with bright and dark memories. She saw a thousand dreams in one speck: the stables, their crossing of Geadhain, a hand steadying her on a sheer black cliff, the horrors of the Iron Mines, their beautiful sexual torments, and, finally, their salvation. That they had passed through the world's gauntlet unscathed was thanks to their need of each other and a force that had to be love. Lila knew the answer to Erik's question.

She spoke quickly. "You asked if we could love each other, Erik—but we already do. No other power could have brought us through such pain. I shall bring you through this pain, too. This will hurt, and terribly. Hold onto something, my knight."

The bells and shouting seemed to dim. They could have been adrift on the sea, they felt so alone.

"Are you ready?"

"Yes, my queen."

Erik gripped the stones behind him. He tensed, breathing quickly, as he readied himself for the pull and the rush of pain. Fate had decided that each would be granted an agony: as Lila swiftly extracted the metal, she sliced her other hand, the one not holding the dagger, and which was bracing the wound. *More blood and pain,* she thought: so had their story been written. With wet heat pumping against her hand, she fingered the squelching spot until she managed to touch skin, on which her magik could work. Attuned to his every shudder and flinch through her wounded, blood-soaked hand, she was bound to him in suffering and need.

The reknitting of Erik's flesh would be an agony for him. She pulled her tall knight down by his tunic and kissed him as her Will—golden and true, as Erik remembered it—wrapped them in tingling, tinkling light. When the twisting began in his belly and his muscle tissue writhed like a mass of disturbed earthworms, Lila's mouth swallowed the intensity of his shriek. Something was pulled from Lila, too, something then lost amid the shining transfer of pain that heralded the rebirth of this man's heart, body, and soul. She felt the mystery—an intangible, glowing essence—leave her flesh and enter Erik's body through the gash in her hand.

This magikal covenant of their bodies brought Lila screaming to tears as well. Erik drank in her suffering and wails, just as she had done his, and like souls on fire, they embraced in a rapture of agony, bliss, and love.

The sublime experience ended coldly. Suddenly, light, heat, and pain were gone. Again, they were themselves—less wounded, although still sore. Erik's hands came off the wall, and he bowed and kissed Lila's hand.

"My queen..." said Erik, glancing up and smiling in a broad, handsome show of teeth and beard she had seen but once or twice. "You saved me."

"It is what we do—save each other," she replied.

"Yes."

The knight stood, nodded his head in recognition of her service, then fetched his blade from the lake of the dead into which it had fallen. *I shall bear some of our burden. I trust myself now. I shall conjure a little phantasm for us both so that he might rest and not fight,* thought Lila, as he walked back toward her, his clothing torn and filthy with blood. Undisguised, he would be recognized the moment he was seen.

"What did you say?" asked Erik.

"Nothing. I said nothing at all."

"Then my ears play tricks," he said frowningly, wondering at the echoing sound of words he'd not quite heard her say, at her lips that had not seemed to move.

A flutter disturbed his chest, and he felt a bit heavy for speck, as if he were happily drunk. Then the heaviness passed, and he felt jubilant and agile as a circus performer as he began walking, his queen in tow. Give him a tightrope and he'd dance down its length. Queerer even than this sudden euphoria was the taste of brandy on his tongue. Brandy and perhaps...yes, the oils with which Lila anointed herself. "I feel off," he said.

Once they had reached the other side of the carnage, they paused. Lila looked him over. The bright light of the moon allowed for a careful inspection, but she wasn't sure what she should be searching for. Erik's dark, hard abdomen showed no tears; neither did the tanned hand she used to examine him, though she swore it had ached moments ago. All done, she glanced up and locked gazes with him. *Had a man's eyes ever been so black?* she wondered. A deep and timeless devotion shone in his onyx stare, which spoke of mountains that stood untroubled by the ages and black seas that swept in perpetual, ancient beats on the farthest beaches of shale and salt. Erik's gaze spoke of eternal things: love, honor, stone. Swept up in a rush of calm foreign to her recent fretting nature, Lila found herself daydreaming about undying forces. *I am a drum in the earth, the beat of the oldest heart. I am the wind, and I am the harp. I am music eternal. I am love. I am the mountain. Hear my promise; surrender to my arms. Dance, lover, dance, and never know fear...*

"A beautiful poem," said Erik. "Is it yours?"

"But—" The words had not been spoken, only thought.

"I shall be the drum, the beat, the wind, the harp, the mountain. You will never know fear, my queen, or loneliness, or the coldness of not being loved."

"Erik..." she murmured.

A little surprised, horrified, and delighted, Lila gasped and shook her head. Realizations clicked and shattered the locks barring her from what she knew. She had opened a door. Magnus had left the house of her soul, and she'd invited another to enter. On the bridge of death, she'd bled into Erik and he into her, while each prayed for a life with the other. Magik... the *Fuilimean*...Somehow, the wonder of an Immortal and of blood promises did not end with Magnus. The gift of the Brothers' eternal blood could be passed from king to woman to man, it seemed. Erik, a close observer of Immortals and their odd silences (during which much that could be heard by no other had passed between King and Queen) now knew whence the brandy and warmth—Lila's magik and soul—had come. When her poem had echoed in his head—the second time he'd heard her voice without her speaking—he'd understood completely and swelled with joy at this new miracle.

You see? It is really quite simple, my queen, said the warrior, his lips smiling, but not moving in speech. He pressed her to his chest so that they could feel each other's heartbeats, synched and resonating through their ribcages in a single throb. Lila could not say which beat belonged to her. *You welcomed me in. At last, you welcomed me in.* Indeed she had, and now the elemental calm, the silence of the gentle, empty escarpments of the North, and Erik's temperance and honor were all a part of her. With a whimpering laugh, she leaned in and kissed her knight.

"Halt! Drop your weapons! Raise your arms, and step forward, slowly!" cried a voice.

What a petty, irritating man, thought Erik. The knight ignored the command and the escalating voices of the other Twelveswatch until his queen bade him dismiss the interlopers: *Be kind, though,* she warned. *Do not harm the weak things.* For Lila was of his noble code now, and would not condone senseless killing. *Weak things,* considered Erik. Yes, men were weak things—but he was one of their kind no more. He had never studied magik, as he lacked both an aptitude for and an interest in it. However, the catalysts for magik did not always need to be taught. In Erik's chest and blood flowed the brandy and golden light of his queen, and he could succumb to its intoxication at any time, as easily as he had once surrendered to lesser liquors. Which is what he did now—surrender. He allowed her essence, her golden venom, to consume him. He shivered and moaned in the throes of lust. Much of the world shimmered away until all that remained was a thin metallic line of sight, reminiscent of the field of vision provided by the visors he had worn while jousting.

When Erik glanced at his enemies now, everything looked crisp and clear and was haloed in a golden sparkle. The shouts of the Twelveswatch turned to screams that sounded as if they were echoing through metal.

Lila watched as a miracle unfolded. First, he stood apart like a man embracing the sun. Then, pearl light like that of the rising dawn crept over his body from within, twining him in an ivy of magik. The magik incinerated his clothes and cocooned him in light. Finally, there came a flash, a pulse of earthbound thunder, and a rippling wind that blew her back, and he stood as a man remade. It was still Erik, yes, but an Erik transfigured and transformed by the bond of blood. He seemed sculpted of the oldest rock, like an unfurling, smoking, living meteor, as he stretched out new arms and took a flagstone-cracking step with his new legs. It was impossible to say whether he was man or golem, this giant donned in pauldrons of shale, wearing greaves of pronged black and gold crystal, and bearing gauntlets of molten metal and onyx.

After he had taken his first strides, the obsidian knight dropped his stalagmite-horned head and gave the kind of snort that foretold a bull's charge. The Twelveswatch screamed and bumbled backwards. The obsidian knight held his position, for he awaited the command of his queen. Although now buried beneath tons of rock and metal and illuminated by a glaring aura of light, he remained her warrior, her kind and considerate knight. At last, Erik's shape reflected what in his heart he'd always been for her: a weapon, a shield, a mountain that would not fall.

They are soft, so soft, next to your great self: remember that, Lila mind-whispered.

Her bloodmate charged.

VI

Considering she had just opened the vestibule door on this night of ominously tolling bells to a wild, dark-skinned, naked man wrapped only in a cloak many sizes too small and a woman who'd fled the Order soaking wet after possibly killing a man, Abagail seemed remarkably unconcerned. "Hmm, you," she said to Lila, adjusting her glasses, which had dropped during her assessment of the tall fellow. "I thought you would be back. Come inside, both of you."

Having grown used to surprises, Lila and Erik entered the sanctuary. While the sister hurried off to fetch an unspecified *something*, the new bloodmates shuffled their feet on the weathered tiles; Erik's felt cold on the stone, as he wore no boots. As the bloodmates waited for Abagail's return, they quietly reflected on their night.

During Erik's transformation into the obsidian knight, events had been veiled by a fog like that of inebriation—one possessing only the buoyancy of drunkenness, though, and none of the fumbling. After he'd rampaged through the streets, then a market, an ale garden, a coach house, and several other places he couldn't wholly remember, Lila's voice had brought him back into the shape he commonly wore. At that point, he had emerged from his stupor, seen first the golden dazzle of his queen and then the arch of an overpass trickling water, and finally become aware of the tickle of wind on his naked skin. They'd caused so much damage and confusion that the Twelveswatch would be too busy putting out fires and settling the crowds he'd terrified to find them. It seemed as if they'd managed to steal many hourglasses' worth of reprieve.

Reckless and laughing like two rogues after a heist, they'd made love in a filthy subterranean chamber. Neither of the bloodmates could render the passion and liberty they felt in words; instead, they rasped, gasped, and drank in wet kisses from each other's mouths. Steadily, the rhythm of their bodies faded to a dull, slippery thrum, as they went beyond their pounding flesh and wandered the vast spaces of each other's hearts. Lila hadn't found a corner of his vast sea out of reach to her, not a wind upon which she could not fly. Nor had he discovered a single rise on her sunny meadow over which he could not run. This grand intimacy had seemed extraordinary, even to a woman who had already shared another's heart.

My queen. My knight, they'd mind-whispered as they'd risen to a climax that spun their brains with stars and filled their noses with scents of sweat, honey, semen, brandy, and the charcoal ripeness of shale—Erik's scent, Lila'd realized, the fragrance of the bedrock of his heart. Their release had left them delirious and shaking, and they'd remained joined by the lock and key of their hips for many sands.

Eventually, the obstreperous bells had played on their raw nerves, reminding them of mortal terrors, even if mortals they no longer were. Thus, Lila had put on her clothes, dressed her bloodmate in her cloak— which covered enough of his modesty but none of his greatness—and the two had resumed their escapade. They'd taken the shadiest paths in the city. Fearless with her magik, Lila had woven deeper shadows upon them, so that darkness veiled them in sheer black; not even the alley cats had paid them any heed. The two had run for the Order's basilica holding hands, aglow with irreverent, youthful love.

Having left off remembering, they were kissing when Abagail returned—kissing as if eating a thick delicacy from the other's mouth. Seeing their lust, the sister stumbled. "Excuse me," she said.

The bloodmates turned, sleepily.

"Queen Lilehum, and Erithitek, hammer of the king," said Abagail, whipping an immediate propriety into the pair. Erik pulled his queen close. "I must have your attention."

"You have it," declared Erik.

"How did you know?" whispered Lila, somehow not wholly shocked.

"I knew before the bounty went out," she replied, and came forward to deliver a bundle of boots and men's clothing to Erik, who took the offering and began to dress. Covering her eyes, the sister continued. "We of the Order, and those of the body from which we've splintered, are historians, listeners, and keepers of the truth. Folk see us and think we are sexless women, with nothing better to do than knit and tend to the disadvantaged who weep for our ministrations; they think we couldn't find husbands to put rings on our fingers and babies in our bellies. It's insulting.

"We choose to be here, Lilehum. We forgo children, drink, pleasure—" cannily she peeked, then pursed her lips at Erik as he stuffed himself into his new pants—"even conversation, so that we can hear what our world needs and set our hands to nurturing the vast garden of life. I do not claim to know everything; there are mysteries not even the Blue Mother herself can fathom. I can, however, spot a queen, a woman who shines as bright as dawn over Carthac's waves.

"Likewise, I can recognize the weary honor of a man who has bathed in and anointed himself with ritual and virtue. And we have pictures of you, Lilehum, artistic renderings drawn by hand before the age of phantographs; they were left among some of our older documents from the second era of the city. I'd tell you that you haven't aged a day, but you know that." Abagail again peered through her fingers, determined Erik was clothed, and then removed her hand. "You've held up quite well for a mortal, too, Erik. A phantograph of a far younger you in company with the king still hangs in the offices of the aldermen, memorializing the time the king ended a bloody civil quarrel here. I believe that was after you and he first met in the Salt Forests. It's remarkable that you've managed to maintain your great vitality; warriors tend to be so quickly hobbled by arthritis and gout. If I had to say...if I stop and listen, I think I can hear that you've changed the rules of your nature, hammer of the king."

"I am the knight of my queen, and you listen well," said Erik.

"I do," agreed Abagail. "A knight; very well. I've dressed you as a thief, though, or at least that was the vocation of the last fellow who wore your clothes. Sister Seraphine stitched up the knife marks in that tunic, and it's good as new. I suggest you play a thief for now; it's much safer to be a petty criminal than a wanted felon."

Quickly sliding her hands into the sleeves of her habit, Abagail strode ahead. Before following the sister into the cavernous antechamber, Erik draped the queen's cloak upon her again and fastened it around her cast-gold neck. His handsomeness made her blush—it was if she saw him with new eyes. Black was Erik's color. It drew on the ebon of his gaze, now wholly and undeniably obsidian, and emphasized the sheen of his shaved head and brown skin. In truth, his darted silk shirt, black pants, and tall boots made him look more like a brigand king than a robber.

You have more charm than you know, she said.

You are beauty itself, my queen.

In they leaned, for a kiss—

"Hurry-ho, you two!" called Abagail. "I would never judge, as it's not my place to say what the heart should feel, but you are each still bound to Magnus by certain oaths. You should sever those oaths before swearing them anew."

Abagail's prudent counsel raised burning doubts in the queen. How long could they play lovers on the run before this fantasy collided painfully with the hard wall of reality? Lila felt they must face Magnus. That would be the honorable thing to do, although it could mean their end, if the King's fury were stoked: one storm for Menos, a second for the betrayal of his marriage of a thousand years. But what of Magnus's betrayal of her? What of the attack she had suffered? How would he answer for his deception, which had led to her marrying not one brother, but both? She would welcome a confrontation with her former bloodmate.

We shall face my father, your husband, our king, said Erik. *I can see no other way for us to live with ourselves. I am with you now; we are not alone. We are shamed and punished, proud and weak together.*

Erik's strength, his calm and gray sea, settled her anxiety. Most certainly, she, Erik, and Magnus were fated for a devastating confrontation. Whatever danger awaited them, though, Erik did not fear it, and so neither did she.

They had not yet reached the familiar section of the basilica with its tarps and columns, and Lila was beginning to wonder where they were headed; just then, Abagail took a torch from the wall and turned down a mysterious hall. The passage was thickly pasted in dust and lined with shattered doors that Lila could imagine having been smashed by angry kicks and small battering rams, before the screaming men inside were dragged out. A trail of small footprints led forward through the decay, but the flickering glow of Abagail's torch revealed no other indications of life. This path was used then, but not often. The wide hallway, the placement of the doors, and the stacked beds that could be spied in rooms utterly curtained in spiderwebs, left Erik thinking this had once been a barracks.

"Men loyal to the Lordkings of Carthac slept here," said Abagail, suggesting she might again have been listening with more than her ears. "Great warriors, all of them. Valiant to the end, each bred with the slave-mind of a

Menosian vassal. They died with their masters, and none has ever touched the bones that lie beyond. I suppose this is a mausoleum."

Erik's senses were much sharper and more sensitive now, as if they had been enhanced by magik. Although it was dark, he could, without straining, spy bits of whiteness amid the threads of dust and spider silk in the burial chambers of the fallen Lordkings' servants. Bones. When he clamped his jaw and flexed the muscles behind his ears—had those always been there?—he could hear the clatter of mice claws and the scuttle of things smaller even than rodents.

It felt as if his body had grown stronger as well. Musing on this strangeness, and taken aback by none of it, he thought of the legends of Brutus, including those that told of the man's mutagenic flesh: limbs that could transform into golden blades, armor that sprang from beneath the skin. That blood was within him now, too. They were all cousins now, he supposed: he, the mad king, Magnus, and Lila. All part of the same strange family tree.

Are you well? You feel distracted, whispered Lila.

*Not distracted. I am...*Mice scurried to his right, at least six of them. In the air, he could taste the sulfur of ash mixed in with the motes of dust and understood there had been a fire here, many ages ago. From farther on, a whiff of briny algae wormed into his nose, and he sensed a dampness, so light it was only a shiver upon his skin. "Water. There's water up ahead," said Erik.

"There's water most everywhere in Carthac," Abagail muttered.

"Indeed there is," replied Erik, surprising her. He stopped walking and crossed his arms, frowning. "I have no urge to bite the hand that feeds; however, I must ask where you are taking us."

Sister Abagail turned, and while Lila saw a frail, spectacled woman holding a torch, Erik could pick out lines around her eyes and mouth that suggested the deepest ruminations. Abagail was a woman burdened by knowledge, responsibility, and the weight of each. He knew he could trust her—the easy pitter-patter of her heart suggested as much. It was not the pulse of a liar or someone ready to deceive. Erik lowered his arms, his expression softening.

Abagail sighed. "We shall arrive faster without the banter. I'm sure it won't take long for even the dullest fork in the kitchen to poke the morsel that tells of your trips here. Lilehum—"

"Why do you call me that?" asked Lila. "No one calls me by that name anymore." Erik could feel his bloodmate's annoyance; her golden light burned his esophagus like strong bitters.

"It is your name," replied Abagail crossly.

"My old name."

"Your *name*," stressed Abagail. "A woman can change her nature, her looks, her status, her future. A name once given, though, can never be rescinded. We wear its mark on our *souls*. Lilehum is who you have always been. I would urge you to rediscover her again, because she was as bold, brave, and daring as any heroine of whom I have read."

A silence fell, and Erik broke it. "A beautiful and strong name, yes. Now, where, Sister, have you brought us, and how much farther will you be taking us?"

"Beneath this building lies a port," replied Abagail. "An ancient route of escape planned by the Lordkings, although those doomed souls never used it. Some of the wicked masters died in this wing of Bastille Dermoch— that's the old name for this building. The masters and guardsmen who died here endured a kinder torment than those who were caught in the city. Lordkings were crucified and burned in the great square where Carthac's quaint market stands today; where you and I first met, Lilehum. Funny how history makes playgrounds of cemeteries, how life is grown from death, and we never see...Sorry, I ramble and am often easily distracted. I also wander *physically*, not just to the market, but anywhere a cat's curiosity would lead her, and many times to places where no animal would tread. I found the secret port. It's quite a wonder if you've never seen Menosian architecture of ages past, still marvelously intact because of the feliron used in its construction. You can almost feel the magik humming beneath us. Hurry along, and you won't have to wait to see of what I speak."

Again, they swept into the darkness, Abagail banishing the gloom with her light-bearing brand. The passages changed: widening, growing taller and framed in ornate gold-inlaid arches. They saw banners, muffled poles that could be spears, and other humps made brown and shapeless by an accumulation of velvet dust. Distracted by the game of deciphering the weaponry, it took a while for Erik to realize that their guide had not quite answered his question. "Why the port?" he asked.

"So you might sail to freedom, face the Blue Mother's trials thereafter, and complete your pilgrimage."

"Pilgrimage?" he exclaimed.

Abagail did not turn, though she slowed her pace. "My sisters and I listen, as I have said. Some sisters listen better than I do, as my proclivity for gabbing drowns out most of the Blue Mother's words. We know you have been charged with something, Lilehum. A pilgrimage, a holy quest—if you credit the oldest legends of our realm. As Keepers, it is not our place to serve the secret, only to observe and protect the seed of it, so it might grow into the promise the Blue Mother sees. After you left in a hurry, I could almost hear a whisper from the dead Menosian: *Queen of Eod, Queen of Sand*. Whatever he said had such power, such meaning, that even after you'd fled and I tended to his body, I could not stop myself from shaking. The chills he gave me were like splashes of cold water. Now, Sister Seraphine is stone deaf and can't hear it if you clap your hands next to her ears. It's possible her disability aids her, though, for she, too, heard the Menosian's secret. Seraphine knows of the seed of hope you carry, Lilehum. A message from a dying man that should never have been delivered has found a messenger in you. I think you also know that you and the hammer must return to Eod to face the pains that have been wrought by all."

Lila knew she could perhaps have arranged for a surreptitious courier to deliver the cryptic prophecies of a dead witch to his wife. She knew she must attempt the journey herself, though, and not simply because Sangloris had charged her with this task. As Abagail had said, the pain she, Erik, and Magnus shared needed to be cleansed. She straightened her shoulders. The importance of her mission only strengthened her resolve. *Our mission*, noted Erik, who had been creeping alongside and inside of his queen, his onyx now threaded into her heart.

"My sisters are waiting for us at the port," said Abagail.

Lila and her knight would no longer keep the sisters in suspense and strode ahead quickly. Dust and time rose and fell to the thud of racing feet. Abagail's torchlight whipped across the relics of the old regime. Glimmers from tarnished helms shone like sunlight into Erik's newly sensitive eyes. As they hurried, even their racing pulses became audible to him. *I wonder whether this sensitivity will grow more bearable—or become increasingly intolerable.* Lila squeezed his hand in reassurance.

Abruptly, they passed out of the dry gloom and into a dank chamber. Here, moisture had blended the omnipresent filth into a limy paste, and Erik spotted infestations of pale white worms and spiders dropping on silk cords around them. Condensation dripped from a high, grated ceiling, and the place echoed like a prison tower when Abagail said, "Down there." With a sweep of her torch, she gestured toward a square opening in the floor, which revealed a flight of steps descending down into the earth. Abagail led them across stretches of mossy decay that moistened their boots and then down into the dark. It wasn't unrelievedly black, Erik found, as he had both Abagail's torch and his feral eyesight to guide him. Regardless, he kept hold of his queen's hand: the stairs were slippery and in some places more powder than stone. They descended lower and lower, moving carefully toward a fleck of light in the darkness beneath them. Soon, the distant will-o'-the-wisp expanded into the pulsing light of many flickering torches. Salty winds quenched the must, and the air became cleaner and fresher, the breath of open spaces. The stairway ended, and the travelers shuffled out onto a landing before a great square arch. Certain parts of the arch gleamed as black as the stone of Erik's soul—not onyx, though, but feliron, which not even aeons and salt water could corrode. Beyond the arch, they saw displayed one of the wonders of Old Menos.

It was an awesome sight, even for a woman a thousand years old. Lila slowed as they walked out onto the pier, arm in arm, like a lord and lady of the Old World. Marveling at its stability, Lila tapped her heels on the "T" slab of feliron-buttressed granite that spread for hundreds of strides into a cavern—a swollen womb of darkness with a fanged roof. Truly, the dock was steady as a mountain. It did not sway even as the roughest of waves dashed themselves to foaming pieces a hundred paces below. Only a faint spray from the waves' misty deaths reached the queen and her knight. *Eternal, it is, and always will be, till Carthac itself falls into the sea*, the queen mused.

You have an aptitude for pentameter, or whatever the scribes call it, said Erik, and the queen smiled. *Perhaps you should try your hand at it one day. I feel that we shall have plenty of time in which to explore your talents, ones you have not dared to use or even dream of in your long life. Look, my queen. What would your poetry make of that?*

A hulking shape loomed out of the mist at the end of the pier. It was largely obscured by darkness; the embattled torches locked in iron clasps along the pier cast only a dim and wavering light. However, Lila thought, as with nightmares, many details were not necessary for the conjuring of fear. But inspiration came to her quickly and apt words spilled forth. *Eater of waves, eater of light. Oh nightmare ship of blackest scorn. Do cleave and brashly beat with thy might, through wildest sea and deepest storm.* That would do, she felt. Her verse seemed florid enough to do justice to the lordvessel; struck by its grim stature and incredible size, this was the name she gave to this ship. *What a grisly majesty it has*, she reflected, walking closer to the metal titan. Its bow faced them, barnacled with bulls' horns, thorns, and spikes. The horrific encrustation was concentrated most heavily on the front of the vessel and along the trim of its lofty deck. *What foolhardy master would ever saunter above and risk impaling himself on the railing?* she wondered. The lordvessel possessed no mast and surely operated under power of some technomagikal engine.

In the lordvessel's shadow stood six women in black, awaiting their arrival. Wind screamed in from a cavern mouth elsewhere in the blackness, though it died as they entered the lordvessel's numb, cold presence. The ship hummed, Erik noticed, creating a tingle that prickled the hair on his arms. The static of sorcery.

"Sisters Seraphine, Georgina, Teravella, Lucinda, Gabby, and Frossetta," said Abagail, "these are the pilgrims." Abagail turned, and she and her sisters bowed their heads to Erik and Lila. "If you allow us, we shall give you our blessing, and set the wind of the Blue Mother herself at your backs."

"We shall need every blessing on this journey," replied Lila. "Thank you."

She and Erik were not sure what to expect, and at first the blessing seemed nothing more than a long silence. As they listened, though, they could almost make out the echo of faraway calls. They closed their eyes, and it was as if they'd been transported elsewhere for a moment, to a place where gulls cawed in their ears, winds stirred their clothes, crisp salt filled

CHRISTIAN A. BROWN

their noses, and glee infused their hearts—the kind of glee sparked by the thrill of adventure, the sight of a blot of uncharted land on the horizon, a vision of the dance of clouds in an endless blue sky. After experiencing these powerful sensations and daydreams, they stepped once again into their own flesh. The blessing completed, Lila and Erik stared at the sisters in wonder. The sisters maintained a watchful quiet for a time, perhaps wanting to dwell a while longer in the dream they'd conjured, but then they finally stood aside. Abagail walked on, and Lila and Erik knew to follow her.

"The ship is propelled by magik," said Abagail. "The engine should work, although we have no means to test it. You, Lilehum, will have to be the ship's navigator and possibly also its engineer. I believe you already know, or at least will quickly learn, whatever is required to command the ship. What she wills, she wills."

Lila recalled something Thackery had once told her: all technomagikal engines were powered by sorcery, their metal merely a chamber for the fuel of magik, so to speak. She had plenty of magik, and, therefore, plenty of fuel.

Abagail continued. "We've packed some food for you, which we've left just on the other side of the landing plank." Barely visible along the hull was a tongue of darkness, a ramp leading up into the ship. "My sisters wouldn't board the vessel. They didn't like the sounds it makes. We haven't been able to give you much, but you won't need more than a week's worth of supplies, assuming your journey goes well."

The three stood at the gangway. Closer now, they saw it was another of ancient Menos's queer structures: metal had been stretched like spittle or the excretions of an insect, then hardened into a thin bridge.

"We found it that way; the door has been open for years." Abagail tipped her head toward the portal into the ship. "I have no idea how to raise the gangway, and no knowledge of what could be waiting for you deeper inside. Nothing very terrible, I should hope. Good luck on your journey, pilgrims. May the Blue Mother guide you with her wind, and keep your souls warm with her sun. I know you will brave the Straits of Wrath and emerge unscathed from the trial."

"What?" exclaimed Lila.

"Come again?" said Erik.

Abagail waved and continued talking as she walked away, her figure and light fading into a ghostly silhouette. "Where else did you think you could go? Up through the northern Feordhan? Out through the gates of Carthac? Privateers, mounted hunters, and skycarriages will be watching every northwestern channel, road, and sky on the continent. You're worth a queen's ransom, and the bounty on your heads will be paid from the Iron Queen's purse. Lilehum is to be captured alive; in the case of the hammer, the rules are not so demanding.

"You two, then, must go where no one will follow, where even skycarriages buckle from the wind—through the deadly Straits of Wrath. After that, you can head down into the summery beaches of Meadowvale, then up through the desert. You can lead there, Lilehum, in the land of your people. I know you'll make it, both of you. I have faith."

Abagail vanished then; even Erik's keen eyes could no longer find her. Troubling, deeply troubling, was this news of the Iron Queen's ransom and what it suggested about Eod's political situation. Deeply troubling, too, was the knowledge that those who hunted them would not hesitate to kill Erik. The burning brandy of the queen's anxiety stuck in Erik's throat, and Lila clutched his arm with sharp talons, scowling. Most of the northeastern continent, then, was closed or being closely watched. As Abagail had said, if they were to reach Eod with the greatest possible haste, they would have to cross the desert of Kor'Khul, the lands of her people. Once more, she must become an Arhadian. Of all the perils and threats confronting her, she dreaded most what awaited her in Kor'Khul.

A homecoming.

IV

JUDGMENT

I

"We must make up our minds. We are nearly out of time," said Leonitis. The soldier's voice cracked, wavering between that of the husky fellow he was and the even gruffer voice of the hammer he was supposed to be.

For the queen's magik was fading; the effects of her spell were unraveling. The deterioration had begun earlier that morning: while shaving, Leonitis had sleepily spotted himself—his real self—in the glass of his hand mirror. Over the hourglasses that followed, the phantasm had disintegrated so dramatically that he could no longer show himself in public. He'd hurried to the king's chamber as soon as it was dark. He sat on the edge of Magnus's bed next to a crestfallen Beauregard, who had no comfort to give. Lowelia Larson was huddled in Lila's old chair, which had been pulled close to the two men. She herself had spent the day hiding and covered in layers, like an Arhadian bride. Fatigued and shrunken, she stared at her hands, waiting for them to flicker again from soft brown-sugar skin to the pale things with which she'd been born. *What a fine trio of frowning wretches we make*, Leonitis thought. Magnus, who stood apart from them at the fireplace, bore twice their darkness and gloom on his ivory face.

"Why is this happening?" Lowe asked sadly. Had something happened to Lila? She didn't have the courage to ask that particular question of Magnus; his silence felt dangerous. Rather, she asked: "Can you fix it?"

Magnus began pacing by the fire, stopping occasionally to take draughts from a decanter of wine on the mantel, but he didn't offer his troubled guests anything for their nerves. Certainly, he could restore their magikal disguises: as a master of the arcane, he was probably more knowledgeable about magikal theory than was any other creature in existence. Because of this, he knew the failure of Lila's illusions could have been caused by only one of two things: either the sorceress had died or she had ended her own enchantment. If she still lived, she could have broken the enchantment either intentionally—or, as magik was born out of and ruled by emotion, unintentionally—through the severing of ties, the breaking of the bonds of love and fealty. The former was less likely: the circlets worn by the matron and legion master still retained some of their power, and objects were generally stripped of all enchantment when their enchanter died. The more probable and damning explanation was that Lila herself had terminated this magik. Magnus stared into the flames, his mind drifting down a distant river. Through the open window, a night wind crept into his chamber and chilled his skin. After a moment, he took another swig of wine, hissed, and then spoke. "Do you know the tale of Esmerelda? Witch of the black highlands?"

No one drew attention to the fact that Lowe's question had gone unanswered—this was their king, and he was clearly preoccupied. Instead, they attempted to respond to the king's apparent non sequitur.

"I may faintly recall a song or two…" Beauregard mused, "about an ancient witch of the highlands whose moods could weave, or break, great enchantments."

"Esmerelda…" said the king. "It's a tale taught to initiates in Eod's Royal Academy of Magik; I'm surprised that you know of it, Beauregard. Clever lad. All magik is born of the heart, and as the heart changes, so, too, does sorcery, often on its own accord. Like most tales, though, Esmerelda's legend is based on a very real, if faded, history."

Magnus quickly drank more wine, and the temperature in the room abruptly plummeted to a prickling chill. Knees knocking, each of the three listeners rubbed their hands together to stay warm. Magnus resumed. "Back in the early days of Central Geadhain, before the introduction of our philanthropic system of law, when Menos starved and idolatrous, warring chieftains ruled, there lived a woman: Esmerelda of Clan Swannish. She made her home in the green hills of Swannish, over the River Feordhan and just outside the edge of Alabion. A true white witch, she practiced ancient medicine and magik for her clan. Esmerelda served her people and her warchief faithfully, until Caer Swannish was overrun by their rivals, Clan Derrdoch. At the time, I knew nothing of this war and I was too far away to stop it, in any case. Let that be said."

Magnus drank more; the decanter was nearly empty. "In the battles that followed, the Swannish lost their lands. Their warchief was killed—beheaded and piked. Esmerelda, though renowned for her talents, even by her enemies, was raped, beaten, locked in felirons, and left in a dungeon. But because the age was so primitive, its perils so grave, and medicines so scarce, the conquering warchief of the Derrdoch eventually let Esmerelda out, under tight guard, to work her craft. Alas, her time in the dark and her savage treatment had changed her. She'd been twisted and her magik was no longer white, but rather the coldest black. She loathed what man had done to her and to the land. She became fury itself. The speck Esmerelda's felirons were removed, she cast a spell, a summoning of hate and rage. An illness flowed from her and spread through the land, a black storm that rolled over the hills, withered life, bred violent animals, and sickened any man not of Swannish blood—of which precious little remained. What had once been one of the most fertile realms in Geadhain became a doomed waste circled by crows and winds of ash.

"It is said the land stayed that way for a hundred years. One day, a child, then a young man, who was born of a Swannish woman and a warrior of the humbled but surviving Derrdoch—each line much diminished—traveled into the witch's highlands in search of a way to end the curse. Possessing as he did some Swannish blood, Esmerelda's hatred could not poison him. Also a child of Derrdoch, he was a brutal fighter who could face the worst of the land's terrors: the hideous beasts and flights of pecking crows; the dreadful sandstorms of cinders; the swamps of fetid, leech-filled water. At last, the lad came to the crumbled ancient bastion of the Swannish. There, he confronted Esmerelda, who was still very much alive, having sustained herself all those years with her radiant hate."

Magnus finished what remained of his drink. His audience was a captive one, in thrall to both the cold and to his fervor. "The lad could not win with might, for, aged as she was, Esmerelda could still easily have smitten him with a word." Magnus snickered. "The brave boy would not be cowed by the hideous hag's promise of thunder and threats, though. He strode toward her ruined throne. During his journey to Esmerelda's lands, the boy had collected certain trophies: the head of a once-beautiful elk, decayed into a fanged, mutated skull crowned with horns; a handful of the ash that had once been loam and fern; and a vial of the sour poison that had replaced the sweet waters of the Swannish lands. At Esmerelda's gnarled feet, he bowed, dropped his blade, and spread out these items."

Magnus's strong voice suddenly became that of a young man: "Great *Cailleach*, do you see what your anger has wrought in the land? Look once more upon the reason for your hatred. You have destroyed all that your arts were meant to preserve. Before you, I stand: a child half Derrdoch, half Swannish. Half my blood is that of your people, whom you drove from their land. Great *Cailleach*, the war is over. Both clans have been defeated, and your cold lesson has taught us how to live as strong hunters, yet without violence between us. Allow us to show you that we have changed, that we have earned the right to live on this land with you again. Look into my heart and see I am a man made not of my forefathers' sins, but of the promise of tomorrow."

Magnus snorted and said nothing more; the fire seemed to hold all of his attention. The listeners shivered and waited for their storyteller to finish. Soon Lowelia found she could no longer stand the silence. "Did she k-kill him?" she asked, knowing that most faery stories ended in blood.

"Kill him?" Magnus whispered. "No. The lad's appeal touched Esmerelda's dark heart. His entreaty and honesty shattered her magik. Once she had shed her grudge like a butterfly emerging from a cocoon, both she and the Swannish highlands changed before the lad's very eyes.

Years and wickedness fell off the witch and the land like the sheddings of a snake. Esmerelda stood before him looking as she had hundreds of years past, once again a comely maiden. In that instant, she and the young warrior fell in love—true love. They soon wed. The remaining clans celebrated the end of the long curse with a festival we honor still, though its origins are now a mystery to many who celebrate it. Even today, the animals, rivers, and hills of the ancient highlands are among the most bountiful in Geadhain. The lands you would call Fairfarm were once the highlands of the Swannish."

As Magnus turned, the fire at his back leaped and streaked with green magik, and the three listeners saw that a misty emerald light had claimed the sockets of his eyes. Beauregard gasped. Leonitis and Lowe were so alarmed they barely noticed a sudden pressure on their wrists. When they glanced down at the metal circlets given to them by the queen, they found that the jewelry had shattered into diamonds of ice that now lay scattered on their laps. Magnus had annulled the magik and they were again themselves. Although the legion master and mater were relieved that the long lie had now officially come to an end, they both watched their king warily, not yet able to read his intentions.

Magnus noted that pretending to be queen appeared to have been good for Lowelia's health: she looked as if she'd lost quite a bit of weight, although she'd gained a few years, since he'd last seen the real her. The pretty, silver-and-black haired woman, round only in her cheeks now, dusted the frost from her lap; she'd be back to dusting as a matter of course in the days ahead. Truly, he'd been sick of looking at the face of his treasonous wife whenever he beheld the matron in her disguise. Behind Lowe pouted Leonitis, once more a grand hunk of frowning, snowy rock. He had the pallor of the North, and frazzled, untended braids ran down his scalp. Leonitis's pale face was a sight far more welcome to the king than the dark countenance of his adopted son. *Can I still call Erik that?* wondered Magnus.

How stupid and blind he had been not to see the symptoms of Erik's infatuation. His devotion to her had arisen not from duty, but from an infantile attraction; Erik was a naive, simple, love-struck fool. But what of Lila's feelings? Was she the puppet master of Erik's heart? Or was it possible that in shutting her out, he had driven her to Erik? Needing to be alone, sick with disgust, Magnus dismissed his council. "Go back to your chambers," he commanded. "In the morning, we shall tell Gloriatrix of this whole sordid mess."

"My king, is that wise?" protested the legion master, rising to his feet.

"Wise?" snapped the king. A blast of wind buffeted the room, turning the curtains into flapping ghosts, throwing sparks from the fire, and whirling papers into tornados. "I am your king. Do not question the wisdom of my judgments. Menos is our ally, and we shall need its aid if we are to match Brutus's power. Handing over to Menos the war criminals they seek would be the sincerest offering of friendship we could make. Hatred, not love, is what creates strong bonds between enemies. Lila no longer wishes to deceive herself or her people. That is why her magik is evaporating, much as Esmerelda's once did: her heart has changed. She no longer loves me or what we've built." Anger ripped apart Magnus's beauty. "I shall honor her wish and grant her a life without lies, without a crown, without me. Lila and Erik must answer for what they have done—to me, to Gloriatrix, to the world."

Leonitis nodded. After helping the trembling matron rise from her seat, the two left the king's chamber. Beauregard hovered near his master like a ghost, but didn't speak. Magnus turned back to the fire. No matter how hard he concentrated, how tightly he shut his eyes, he was unable to stop picturing Erik and Lila writhing together. Was it a fantasy? Or was the reality even worse? Once, in a moment of weakness—or clarity—he had dived into himself and reached out for his queen. He had toppled the grand wall, the twisted thornbush of black ice, he'd erected in his soul to keep Lila at bay. He had then called for his wife of one thousand years. Called and called until his spirit waned from the effort. Alas, the cold plains of his soul had remained empty; only the wind had shouted back. No other voices could be heard; no longer could he sense the warmth of Lila's spring. What else could he have expected? He had told her she was damned. What else could she, a prideful creature, have done? She would endure; she would live to fight again. He'd shut her out, he'd cast her out, and she'd left. Like his cursed brother, with whom this great splintering of love and trust had begun, Magnus could weep only for himself. No one remained to care for him now.

II

"Almost ready, my liege."

Beauregard buzzed around Magnus's head like a gnat, industrious, and largely unheeded in the sunny, breezy chambers of the king. Morning had come early, or so it felt after a long night of talks. The king, still drowning in conflicted vengeance from the evening's discussions, appeared to be in a waking sleep from which he would or could not stir. Thus, Beauregard played valet today.

He had become used to a certain flexibility in his role as the spellsong of the king, and adopted different jobs from day to day. Without the queen or hammer around, the king appeared to have lost much of his patience for life's menial grind, and had grown increasingly irritable with the servants. And so Beauregard, used to mending and fending for himself, took up the roles of both household and military companion. He brought Magnus his food, and often stayed to ensure it did not go uneaten. He stitched trousers, took dictation, and composed letters. More and more frequently, he had to help the king bathe.

This morning was no different. Beauregard puffed as he went about his duties: lacing Magnus's shirt, folding up his sleeves, adjusting the lopsided tilt of his silver crown. Throughout the process, Magnus's hewn ivory face maintained a sad pout, and the king's emerald gaze seemed to narrow in and focus on some dark thought Beauregard could not see—probably last night's explosive revelations. Magnus brooded, and his bleak mood conjured a chill in the room.

Beauregard, shaking, completed his work in silence. He understood the agony assaulting his king. "My king, I'm sorry, but it's time to go," he said.

Perhaps not everyone is lost to me, thought the king, as he beheld the patient but charismatic friend and savior who'd stood beside him during his daydreaming. One day, after the war, this comely young man would win the first lass he wooed; it would take only a gleam of his handsome teeth, a toss of his full, dark hair, or the first notes of a song to make his chosen swoon.

"Magnus?" prodded Beauregard.

I shall see that you find happiness, even if I am doomed never to feel it again, decided Magnus, smiling at his spellsong. His smile was so dazzling and kingly that Beauregard barely noticed its underlying sadness.

III

On their way to the Chamber of Echoes, the king and the spellsong met with Rasputhane. The spymaster's face was grayer even than his clothing. News of last night's events had reached him, and he had only terrible things to whisper in the king's ear about what had been done. *Are you sure? It's not too late to postpone the meeting and devise another plan. What will Gloriatrix do in reprisal?* he asked. Magnus's answers were terse: Yes. No. We shall see.

In silence, the three men made the rest of the trip through serene, green archways lit with indoor stars, over crystal-inlaid mosaics on the floor, and past glorious frescos of battles and winged warriors—but the palace's oppressive beauty had no effect on them today. Occasionally, faint choral music could be heard, and soldiers and white-robed fellows bowed to the king and company. After a winding march through the palace, they arrived at the Chamber of Echoes and walked up the grand stairs into the subterranean garden, which struck them for once as annoyingly bright, with its rainbow-casting boulders, stones, and flowers of glass.

A sanctuary from the light and the frothing noise of the falls called to the men from under the shade of the distant white yew; there lay the stone table raised during Queen Lowe's reign. Five recognizable figures had taken seats around the ancient stone. Lowelia was dressed in her standard charwoman's attire of apron and white linen shift. She held her own next to Leonitis against the three glaring Menosians on the opposite curve of the table: the Iron lord and frowning gargoyle, Gustavius; the ghastly specter, Elissandra; and the queen of iron, who sat between her two ghoulish totem poles.

As soon as the king and his men entered the muted awning of the great yew's branches, Gloriatrix barked at Magnus; she'd managed to affect the air of courtesy and respect due an immortal for at most about a day. Magnus considered the astonishing audacity of this woman. The king couldn't recall ever having encountered a person who had lost everything in one moment—city, people, land—yet still kept all of her pride.

"You're late, again," said the Iron Queen. "And you've sent a chambermaid and a man in your hammer's armor to insult me with their bovine stares and seats at a table of rule. I expect an explanation—of this and a number of other things." Gloriatrix waved her hand at the many empty stone chairs. "Where is the rest of your council? Why have you asked only Elissandra and I to come? Why are we alone?"

Beauregard's keen senses caught the Iron lord's hand reaching toward a pistol or blade beneath the table, and he gave the man a warning shake of his head. Although the Menosian seemed to understand, his hand remained where it was. The spellsong chose to match the silent threat. While the king seated himself next to Leonitis and Rasputhane settled in beside Lowelia, Beauregard stayed on his feet, gripping the hilt of his foil.

Magnus rested his pale hands on the table and leaned toward the Iron Queen. "I am not so barbaric as to invite you to my hall, feed you, clothe you, and care for your troops, only to murder you in cold blood without reason."

"Speaking of provisions," replied Gloriatrix, apparently no longer concerned she might be at risk, "have you thought further on my plan to reclaim Menos?"

Rasputhane spoke with a hint of irritation. "Only yesterday did we receive word of the first of Menos's survivors from our joint encampments on the front lines of the disaster. It was difficult to make out from the far-speaking transmission what kind of shape they were in. As you know, when our skycarriages and magikal instruments enter the region, they encounter a peculiar interference, one more disruptive than the usual etheric noise. We do know, though, that a handful of survivors have come through the dark fog of your realm. My king will correct any misguided assumptions of mine, though: we shall not blindly move our forces into a disaster we do not understand. Whatever energy or force destroyed the Iron City could still remain in the region."

Gloriatrix puffed and curled her lip. "Then arrange for an *exploratory* mission at once. Furthermore, I would like the survivors brought to the

Furies. We are well equipped and more than capable of treating our own citizens."

You mean interrogating our citizens, thought the king. "They will be treated by our finest fleshbinders before being released into your care. We shall all hear their accounts, together, before formulating any strategy to confront the darkness that has claimed Menos." Magnus savored a long breath, and those who knew what was coming also enjoyed their moment of peace. When he was ready, he said: "You asked why we have sequestered ourselves away this morning, with only the most important advisors and champions of our realms present—"

"And a chambermaid, and some warrior—" added Gloriatrix.

"*The* most important advisors and champions," boomed Magnus, angrily, sending out a flash of cold that pimpled the scalps around the table. "*I* shall establish their importance. *I* shall explain to you how these men and women have been manipulated by a traitor of our kingdom, a serpent in our garden." Magnus needed to stop, rein in his rage, and grit his teeth before continuing. "My bloodmate, Lila, is this snake. Aided by the betrayer of his title and honor, Erithitek, the hammer of the king. I say these next words in the spirit of peace and transparency between our nations. I say what I must with my darkest, deepest sympathies and regrets: they were the ones who brought the Iron City to ruin."

Gloriatrix was speechless.

"I had a dream last night..." muttered Elissandra, air whistling through the gap in her teeth that she refused to fill. Ethereally, as if made of wind chimes, the leaves of the yews rustled above her and lured her attention. Glancing up, she cast herself into the vision: "I see a wall of twisting shadows. A woman, golden, though worn with mud and travel like an old coin, brandishes a scepter. No, an arm—one heinously pulsing with veins of green, radiant blood. A man clings to her, desperate and weak. What strength has bound him to this madness is finally spent. He could be much stronger; one day, he will be. But now, he is weak, and then hit by the tarnished woman. She strides forward and nearly throws herself into the abyss with her talisman of horror. By the Makers! The light! The fire! The howling! Such horrible cries screech from the pit. So great a roar echoes, it is as if Mother Geadhain has been gutted. Flames grow like vines of light from the crevasse. This is the first tolling of Menos's doom. Here, the end begins."

Elissandra smiled at the beauty of her dark vision and continued. "Sweetly, the woman—now free of the whispering horde that has possessed her—clings amid the chaos to the man she has condemned. The man and woman whisper soul secrets to one another. They shine, too, with a light, a warmth I've seen but once or twice. It is the fire of the truest love." Magnus's heart shattered; if the others hadn't been so bespelled, they would have seen the king slump and swallow a whimper. "Oh, what glorious fanfare: the chorus of the abyss, the rain of rubble, and the spumes of sparks herald the arrival of doom. Death herself has come to see. She wears a skin that I know. So ruined...so ruined. At her feet, the soul-bound lovers cower and clutch at each other. Death speaks to them in her voice of hurricanes and earthquakes. And then a red and radiant doom is born in the hollow under the Iron Valley. And so tolls the bell. So rings the end of Menos."

An argument began at once. Explanations and protestations were made, although none were heeded. Gustavius stood, drew his pistol and pointed it across the table at the king's men. His targets rose, waving swords and fists, shouting obscenities at the Menosians. Honoring their elements—ice and iron—the Everfair King and Iron Queen sat calmly amid the storms of their men and exchanged murderous gazes.

"I have seen the Pale Lady, you nattering twits! I have seen Death herself!" roared Elissandra. Her sudden ejaculation produced an immediate hush. Shocked faces gaped at her. With her missing tooth, the stub of a wrist that she'd decorated in silk bandages, and the patch of baldness that she concealed with a scarf, Elissandra commanded the onlookers with an eerie soothsayer's charm. "Were you not listening? She walks among us now." She pointed her bound stump at Magnus. "I have seen her poison the ear of your queen." Next, the stump of doom pointed to Gloria. "I have seen her reap your sons. She wore one child's skin, and now she wears the flesh of the other." Finally, Elissandra touched the stump to her face to catch a sudden trickling tear. "I felt her take my Sangloris, and I know there was something he wished to say to me, something I now shall never hear."

She closed her eyes for a moment, vibrating with emotion, and twitched as a shriek tried to wriggle out; her willpower triumphed. When she opened her eyes, they twinkled with tears and silver currents from rivers deep and distant. "Taken, and yet I could not see him as he went... The rules are breaking. Order is falling apart. I know not what to tell my poor lamblings, though they must hear of their father's journey into the Great Mystery."

Elissandra stood up and drifted off on a breeze only she could feel. She did not return to the table. She left behind a vacuum spinning with questions and fear.

"What did she mean?" asked Magnus, very quietly. "Death?"

Remembering back to when he and Lila had touched minds, before their fatal silence, he recalled something in the frenzied mania of her thoughts. Amid her blinding hatred of Menos and her twisted righteousness and grief, had there been a whisper? Or a whisperer? A black tongue licking at her ear? Telling her...*what*? What did the whisperer say?

"Death walks among us? Poisoning and reaping?" muttered Lowelia; she shivered.

"One never knows what Elissandra means," said the Iron Queen. "Not even the lady herself. I shall ask her later, once the Fates have lost some of their hold upon her wits. In light of what you have told me, Magnus, I expect justice for my people. What justice do you offer?"

"Justice?" said Magnus, slumped in bewilderment. He wondered if anything that he had done was fair. "I shall offer my queen the same justice I would my brother. A trial for her crimes, and punishment after."

Gloriatrix slapped the table. "Ha! I deny this *justice*. What of the hammer? Will he, too, receive the shelter of your mercy? I want blood, King Magnus. Give me blood, or I shall take it for my people."

"More blood? Is that what you want? Will your people never change?" spat Magnus.

"We are iron, we are blood; we do not change. Meet my demands, or I shall take my Furies and fly to the Bone Archipelago or some place even farther beyond the map edges we know. I shall leave this apocalypse, this messy family affair between a pair of Immortal fools; you and your bleeding-heart soldiers will have to sort it out. I shall start a new Iron regime among the dimmest savages, who will worship me as an Immortal after I descend from the heavens. You may visit this neo-Menos and I shall show you how rule is properly cultivated. That is what will happen if I do not see justice. Do not question whether I am bold enough to do all this and more. You know that I am. *Blood*, Magnus, or this meeting is over and will be our last." Gloriatrix stood up when he did not answer her. In a speck, she would leave and never return.

"Wait!" he cried.

The Iron Queen turned, raised an eyebrow, and waited for Magnus to buckle under her pressure. She displayed the most horrific smile—the wrinkled delight of a risen cadaver eating its first flesh—as the king spoke.

"I shall give you blood," he said. "In my court, Lila and my brother will answer for their crimes; that decision I shall not revoke." For a moment, Magnus battled a half-century of emotions and guilt over the sentence for his foster son. Someone needed to suffer for the fall of Menos; a name must be given. "However, as for Erithitek...as for my hammer's fate...I leave his life in your hands, Iron Queen."

"His life? His execution," replied Gloriatrix, walking away. "Your terms are sufficient."

While the others left, some bidding muted goodbyes, Beauregard stayed with his liege. Winter seeped from his master. A skin of frost grew over the slowly breathing king and the toes of Beauregard's boots. Still, the spellsong did not move. He held, trembling, to his spot. At one point, thinking he saw a glimmer on Magnus's cheek, a clear gem that could be a frozen tear, he reached out to the Immortal. The gesture dispelled Magnus's winter, and broke the king's shoulders with a sob.

IV

"A fuking fortnight!" hissed Gloriatrix, sneering passersby out of her path as she swept down the palace halls. "For a fortnight or longer, we've been bargaining with a charwoman and a soldier. The arrogance and chicanery!"

"Chicanery indeed," agreed Gustavius.

After a sand of angry striding, Gloriatrix pulled her consort into the first vestry they came across. It was a placid hollow, like an outdoor temple moved indoors, with a circumference of pillars decorated in ivy, fragrant blue roses, and the light buds that were ubiquitous in the palace. A pair of scholars contemplated scrolls on an alabaster bench set before a bubbling fountain of white stone wrought into a coiling, razor-backed serpent. Gloriatrix and her gargoyle companion cast their shadows over the couple. "Leave," she commanded.

The fellows seemed poised to object, but when they gazed up into the cold countenance of the Iron Queen, they lost their nerve, gathered their papers, and fled. Gloriatrix took the bench, while Gustavius settled on the lip of the fountain. He removed his gloves, splashed a hand through the water, and studied the monstrous fountain-snake, appreciative of its beauty and surprised to see something appealing in this kingdom of toddlers and coddlers. Gustavius sighed and took a moment to reflect on the cruel styles of Menosian design—works such as the black armor he wore, the likes of which might never be seen again.

Gloriatrix would punish those who had defiled Menos, he knew. Although she seemed appeased by Magnus's decree, Gustavius could decipher the nuances of her silence. He'd noticed, for example, the narrowing of her eyes when Magnus had mentioned showing leniency toward his queen. The Iron Queen's present calm, he decided, likely resulted from the fact that she was even now mentally attempting to find a way around the king's stipulations. Gloriatrix would not let the shaming of her nation—and by extension, of herself—stand.

Balthazar, thought Gustavius, *if you could see how large your little spider has grown.* Unfortunately, Balthazar Thule, Gloriatrix's father, had fed the maggots of centuries ago and was currently no more than a bit of bone, dust, and brown meal in the coffin where he lay—or had once laid. His peaceful rest had almost certainly been shattered when the earthquake and dread sorcery had destroyed the cemetery housing his remains. *What would Balthazar, one of Menos's greatest masters, have done in retaliation?* Gustavius asked himself. He would have demanded blood, just as Gloriatrix had; she was truly her father's daughter. The Iron Queen understood that some crimes, some freedoms even, came only at the cost of death. Gustavius wandered into a long, ancient memory.

In the gardens tending to the metal flowers, Gustav takes care not to break the blossoms from the stems; he and the other gardener slaves are given the nine-tails for such clumsiness. Gustav is not clumsy, though: he is quick and attentive. Only once has he been threshed, and that was because he had not yet understood the rules. He knows the rules now, and more, for he is clever. While the other slaves of the North bemoan their predicament, he ignores the language of his people and listens to the language of his captors. He spends the afternoons absorbing the chatter of his Iron masters: a woman, her children, and a powerful warchief, he gathers. As he clips hedges and climbs trees, he comes as close as he can to the family. Although he is tall and broad backed, he does not stand out like a pale giant. Instead, he blends in with the slender branches he prunes. His presence goes unheeded, except when the clip-clip of his tools is heard, and he always turns his head downward whenever someone turns to look. The warchief and his offspring do not notice him at all.

They are a curious family. A mother, fair and always wearing a whimper on her lips. A father, dark, preened and always shining in his tight, regal clothes. The children are far more interesting than their parents. Well, one of them is: a little girl with a strange, beady stare and the soulless awareness of a hawk; her eyes are purple, and he wonders if she is a witch. Her brother certainly is, though he has blue eyes and is too lighthearted to be interesting. It is the girl Gustav studies most in the garden. Sitting in her black dress, gazing around observantly, she is often as quiet as he is. She listens like a hunter. She possesses a majestic and dangerous presence for so small a creature.

As Gustav does his job exceptionally, better by far than any of his fellow slaves, the warchief treats him well. The other Northern slaves hate him. Men of snow and frozen rocks as they are, they are inept at the tending of green things. His fellow Northmen receive far more beatings, and far less food, than he. One night, several men had attacked him while his rested on his threadbare mattress, his eyes closed. What fools they were: often he closes his eyes to listen, not to sleep. Gustav had broken the jaws and arms of several attackers before the Iron men came and beat them apart. In the morning, the Iron warchief had summoned the garden slaves to the courtyard. He had strutted before them and said: "In a society of the strong, those who work are rewarded. Those who falter become steps for the strong."

Only Gustav had understood his words, as he had spent so long listening. The rest of the Northmen had been terrified. Nonetheless, they had known *something bad was going to happen even before the warchief pulled a fire-stick off his belt, and then, with three smoky bursts of loud magik, shot dead the men who had instigated the attack last night. Fair, Gustav had thought. A fair man, this warchief. When an ox no longer pulls its load and begins to kick, it is put down for meat; a man should be no different. Gustav had nodded his gratitude and respect, and the warchief had nodded back. In another sand, and after dragging the corpses away, Gustav had been back to working in the gardens.*

And so it has been, for a season of summer to the wet rain that passes for winter in the South. Snow does not penetrate the purple shield of poison above Gustav's new home. During this spell of time, Gustav has listened much. He now knows the slang and colloquialisms of his new masters. He has learned that the warchief's name is Balthazar, his mate's name is Isabelle, and the two children, Thackery and Gloriatrix. Gloria, her parents call her for short, though she signals her dislike for the abbreviation with frowns.

One sweating summer day, while high amid the iron oaks with their thorny leaves and trunks as hard and sharp as fractured onyx, Gustav hears voices he should not. Men. The warchief's men, yes, but they are speaking of treachery. They whisper of guns, murder, and treason: the whole family is to be killed. The dishonorable warriors lurk behind a barricade of bushes below Gustav. There are two assassins, and Gustav hears them rustling their fire-sticks through the foliage. Balthazar and his family are nearby enjoying an afternoon of sport: father and son toss a ball, mother and uninterested daughter work on needlepoint. The family do not realize death draws near—except, perhaps, Gloria, who gazes to the tree where Gustav's white shadow hides and possibly even beyond, to the black hedges where the murderers hide. Perhaps she sees her assassins.

"*Frightful little bitch. I'll get her right between the eyes, then the mother. You take Balthazar and his son,*" *whispers one of the assassins.*

Gustav had been destined to be neither great nor villainous. In Menos, however, he has learned skills and discovered a pride he never thought he could possess. Although he is no friend to the family, he does not enjoy thoughts of where he might end up next, should his indentureship end. Very quickly, he considers his options. Then, like a white bird of prey, he drops from the branches. His swinging descent carries him over the hedges, and he lands with only a soft thump behind two crouching men, catching them totally unawares.

Lean, fast, and strong from years of hard labor, Gustav leaps on the spiny back of one man. The man's armor cuts Gustav as he grapples, though it hurts no more than would breaking the shell of an arctic crab. He has held onto his pruning shears, too, which when closed are as sharp as a shucking knife. Like an arctic crab, the armored man is soft in places, such as beneath his chin, and it is there that Gustav begins his shucking. Blood warms his knuckles, a gurgle plays in his ears...Gustav realizes he has missed the music of the hunt. Red mists and spurts over his flesh, painting him in tribal markings.

He rises from the corpse, and his appearance is so horrific and surprising that the other traitor freezes in shock. The assassin's hand starts to move, to free his rifle from the bushes. Gustav's hand is quicker. He watches the second assassin's gaze and helmet fill with blood. For a few specks, Gustav twists the shears around in the man's skull and squats on the twitching body until it stops its dance. One of the assassins had shrieked while dying; the fatal cry will no doubt summon the master or his men.

Gustav does not flee. Instead, he remains hunched over the two bodies, one hand still clasping the instrument of murder, until the master and little Gloria come running down a green lane toward him. Gustav bows his head to Balthazar, who approaches him with a flame-tipped pistol. "Master Balthazar," he says. "These men spoke of hunting your family. I am happy with my place here in your gardens. I do not wish my servitude to end." Gustav's Ghaedic is perfect, albeit thick with Northern inflections.

"You speak!" exclaims Balthazar.

"Of course he does," says young Gloria.

Balthazar and his daughter walk around the lake of blood that soils the garden path. Gloria picks up a stick from the gardens and prods one of the dead. Gustav waits, unwilling to move until he instructed to do so.

"You're quite talented with a sharp implement," notes Balthazar. "I could give you a real blade to swing, something more civilized than garden shears."

Is this an offer? Gustav wonders and stays still.

"Clean up the bodies and go see my men at the gatehouse," says Balthazar, as he slips his pistol into the folds of his velvet coat. Taking the hand of his daughter—who gives Gustav a smile and waves her bloody twig—he adds, "Welcome to the Ironguard," then turns and walks away.

"Welcome to the Ironguard..." mumbled Gustavius. He hadn't thought of that memory in maybe a hundred years, but it had lost none of its clarity.

"Pardon me?" asked the Iron Queen.

"Balthazar. I was remembering him, and you, when you were young. When *we* were young, I suppose."

The mention of her father calmed her demeanor. She sighed, then gave a pinched smile. "I sometimes forget how long you have served our family," she said.

When Thackery had left his station, the Thules had been stripped of their seat on the Council of the Wise. When Gabriel had died shortly thereafter, they had lost his seat, and with it their remaining power. Through all that turmoil, however, Gustavius's loyalty had remained unshaken. Gustavius—an appropriate disambiguation from Gustav to denounce his northern ties—had been absorbed into the ranks, had killed any rumors that arose about Gloriatrix, and sometimes their propagators as well. He had warned the opponents of the Thule line that the family was far from forgotten. They did not know, as he did, of the iron in Gloriatrix's soul. She had faced death, dishonor, and absolute ruin with the attitude that some problems were only more complicated than others. When she said that Menos would rise again, Gustavius believed her. For she had risen, over and over. No matter the depth to which Fate cast her, she clawed her way higher. A throne was where Gloriatrix deserved to be, and he would help her achieve that greatness.

"'The kings and queens of our world,'" Gustavius said, "'Those who claim the right to rule, through whisper and guile and blood of Thule.' Isn't that the rhyme you and your father made?"

"It is. I'm surprised you remember that."

"I remember everything. I remember how you gave me my title after I'd spent decades prisoner to the whims of weak fools. You gave me a true chance to serve again. I am honored that *you* remembered *me*."

"I would never forget the slave who saved my life."

They snorted, done with sentimentalities.

"I know what I must do," said the Iron Queen. "Thank you for this talk; it has inspired me. The men that tried to kill my family and me so long ago...Do you recall how father flushed out the rest of the traitors?"

"A murder pool?"

An old Menosian tradition among mercenaries: offer a bounty so large, a target so tantalizing, that no money-thirsting monster could resist it. At the close of such a pool, the number of dead mercenaries often exceeded that of their assigned quarry. After the attempt on his family's life, Balthazar had offered half of his estate to whomever could root out all those allied with the council. It became the largest purse ever, a prize so gross that it had become part of Menosian legend. *A murder pool of riches.* Gabriel, a mercenary prince of the time, had won the pool, and years later, Balthazar's daughter. Gustavius felt that Gloriatrix was brash for even suggesting such a thing, but was nonetheless curious to know what she would offer.

"The first step in defeating your enemies is to put them on the defensive," said the Iron Queen. She rose, straightened her skirt, and walked over to the pillars, where she picked glowing buds off the vines and watched their lights die. "Fear makes people sloppy, and a messy criminal is easily caught. But it is not enough simply to steer your enemies, to wither them from starvation and exhaustion: they must be humiliated. I want the world to know what the Everfair Queen and the king's man have done. I want the entire world hunting them. A murder pool would do just that—one with a prize so grand it would draw an army of mercenaries, villains, and thugs..."

She made Gustavius wait for her genius, caused him to stand upright and tight as a steel solider. Children were such awful disappointments, realized Gloria. It would be better to groom an heir through a process of careful selection instead: a trial of ascension, with a murder pool as its first gauntlet. She'd quite outdone herself. At last, and after killing another dozen flowers, she whispered her thoughts to her companion: "I won't live forever, Gustavius. I want to live for a hundred years more, so that I can ensure a world free of any Immortals, a world prey only to the kinder vices of men.

Still, I would be foolish to bank upon the notion of living another century. Who, then, will lead our broken nation when I am gone? Who will build it, brick by iron brick, from the ashes? Sorren is gone and may never return to me. Even if he did…he might prove not to be the child, or man, I recall. Our council had been destroyed in all but name. We have no city to rule or return to. All of Menos, all of the history of our people resides within us, the Furies, and Fort Havok. There is nothing more of Menos in the world." She paused, panting with passion. "Menos will rise again. You and I know this shall come to pass. Menos needs a steward, a person of iron will and ambition: A soldier, a shadowbroker, man or woman, who does not shy away from blood. A student of politics, economy, and war. I don't know who amongst the current scraps of our army I would deem to possess such varied skills, or be worthy of such a mantle—they're all such terrified little things—aside from you. I know, though, that you prefer to serve and not rule."

"True, my queen," replied Gustavius.

"Menos needs a soldier, thief, and spy. Menos needs a mercenary. If we are to hunt the queen and the hammer, I want more from the pursuit than vengeance: I want insurance for our future. I want someone who will carry on the legacy that I, my father, and the great leaders of Menos began. I want an *heir*." Gloriatrix strode to her Iron lord, who bowed reverently. "Capturing the hammer and a wild sorceress powerful enough to level a nation should be enough of a trial of ascension. Do you not agree?" she asked.

"Indeed."

"More tests will follow, though I expect only the most ruthless and brilliant person will be able to apprehend the Everfair Queen and claim the prize. I foresee a grave champion, a Menosian in spirit, if not in blood pedigree. We must spread the word far and wide. Magnus did not tell me to be silent. Whoever brings me the queen, alive, and the king's man, in whatever state, will win the Iron crown and all it represents—in tomorrow's tense, not while I still have a head upon which the crown can rest."

Smiling wickedly, she wandered back to the bench, pondering the dark traits of her future heir.

"What if the chosen heir somehow fails us? By not learning, and heeding, the Iron way?" asked Gustavius.

Gloriatrix had already considered this outcome. "It's not as if we would be bound to our promise," she replied. "If the heir proves unworthy, we may slit his or her throat and be done with it. I'm sure you have lost none of your skills with garden tools. If necessary, we can always find a less elaborate and entertaining way to fill the throne of Menos."

V

After the miseries of Blackforge, imprisonment, and months away from home, Galivad could think of no greater pleasure than a walk on the east rampart of Eod's great wall. He waved to men he recognized, and burned his fair skin under the unforgiving sun. Perfecting the moment, his mother, Belle, was present—or rather, a shade of his mother wearing Beatrice's skin strolled beside him. She held his arm, and got more than a few queer looks from the soldiers they passed. Galivad and Beatrice weren't friends, enemies, or even mother and son; he wasn't sure what to call their relationship. He didn't care.

At each day's end, as evening draped a silver shroud over the land, and after Galivad had finished his duties, he and Beatrice somehow found each other. No matter where they were in the palace, they were drawn together by the invisible threads of family. Although they acknowledged that in truth they were strangers, and that she was a monster, they nevertheless recognized they were bound to each other. Galivad would sing for the Lady El to feed her and cure her of her tremors and hideous urges. She hadn't murdered or eaten anyone since he'd known her, which he assumed represented progress. And Beatrice, once satiated, would sing along with her kind-of-son in a voice that was only slightly different from the original Belle's—colder, sharper, and meaner to a tuned ear. Sometimes, they played a game of Kings and Fates. Beatrice was unbeatable, and certainly not letting him win as his original mother would have.

Sometimes, Galivad was overcome by a revulsion that urged him toward matricide. That bloodlust, though, like Beatrice's monstrosity, always passed. The one sad consequence of Beatrice's companionship was that it appeared to have driven Rowena away. Staring down from the ramparts at the black behemoths parked in the desert, the hive of campfires and tents, and the streams of little black men during their daily amble along the wall, Galivad and Beatrice were unexpectedly greeted by Rowena.

"Galivad, there you are!"

The broad woman, looking a bit like a burly athlete in her undershirt and pants, hurried toward the pair through the haze of dying sun. She accidentally elbowed a soldier in her haste and then patted him on the back, throwing him off balance even more. She did not stay to help the fellow right himself. Rowena seemed to be burning with news when she met Galivad and his companion, though her lips kept her secrets tightly bound. Nervous, she gazed from Galivad to Beatrice. "Can we have a moment? Alone?" she asked.

Beatrice gazed at Galivad tenderly and touched his fair skin with one of her bloodless, gray-fingernailed hands—the claws of a corpse. Rowena loathed the woman.

"Is that necessary?" replied Galivad. "Beatrice is an ally."

The Lady El gave him a smile that should have frozen his blood; it certainly froze Rowena's. "Fine. As you wish," spat Rowena. "Wherever you have been all day?"

"Working, training my men, in my quarters with Beatrice, then here. My movements are not secret," said Galivad.

In my quarters with Beatrice stuck on a gear in Rowena's head. Disgusting, whatever it meant. It felt like old times—she and Galivad together again, bickering and pecking at each other. They'd been playing shy around each other since their return to Eod, although Rowena admitted that the distance between them was mostly of her own creation for her friend, almost her lover, was never without his pale new mistress. Could this be a sliver of jealousy stinging her heart? She didn't know, and wouldn't be able to examine her feelings until the two of them were alone—which, considering how he and Beatrice stuck to each other, would be never. Rowena wondered what spell the Menosian witch had cast upon Galivad.

"There was a private meeting of the council this morning," said Rowena, finally.

"I know; I was not in attendance," said Galivad. "Only the king, the Iron Queen, and a few others were present."

"The results of that meeting have since come to light. I'm assuming you haven't heard?"

"Heard what?" asked Galivad.

Beatrice slipped an arm around his waist, and the casual embrace was enough to distract him from today's politics.

Malevolent temptress! "The queen and Erik," said Rowena. "They have been named as the ones who destroyed the Iron City."

"What?" exclaimed Galivad.

Rowena could almost have sworn that a shadow had found them in the final flash of day before night. A hideous rage wrenched at the Lady El's throat, pulling down her chin and revealing a mouth filled with what looked to Rowena like ivory nails. Not teeth, they couldn't be; snakes had teeth like that. Surely, it was some trick of the dazzling sunfall, for when darkness fell specks later, the impression passed. Beatrice glowered, still lovely in countenance, although unsettling in her hunched carriage. She had no fangs. The lurking rattlesnake of Lady El's anger could be heard trembling her voice. "The Everfair Queen…" said Beatrice slowly. "But why?"

"I don't know," admitted Rowena. It was unbearable, hearing servants mumble curses about the queen. Even worse, people were already spreading rumors that the tie that bound Erik and the queen involved more than fealty. The sight of Galivad's face, pasty with shock and revulsion, pitched her through the glass window of what she held most dear. All had shattered; all was lost. Galivad's sickness became her own. Before this moment, she hadn't allowed these feelings to consume her. Propped on her elbows and staring sadly into the desert, Rowena hung in the gap between two white crenellations like an ancient dog ready to die. She did not understand her mistress's intent. Furthermore, she felt like a fool for having been tricked by the mater's impersonation of the queen.

"How do we know this is true?" asked Galivad.

Sighing, Rowena said: "The king. Magnus has accused her of the crime."

"Shite…" replied Galivad.

"Shite, indeed," said Rowena.

"What of the Iron Queen?" wondered Galivad. "What will she do? I mean, there must be a trial. That is our way in the West. They must be allowed to face these allegations, to explain or deny them, and then face judgment."

"Trial?" Rowena snorted. "Whatever trial they are given will be a mockery. There is still so much you have to learn."

She stared off into the desert—the scarab shells of the black Menosian army gleamed amid the three earthbound mountains of darkness that were the Furies—until sandy wind blew into her eyes, forcing her to tears. *I doubt my queen will get any kindness from this court, not when Gloriatrix has put so much at stake, not when all the vile, mercenary killers in Geadhain will be stabbing each other for a chance to become her protégé. I hope you survive, Lila. I hope they never find you. All of them deserve to die.*

Holding in a sneer, Rowena turned to look at Galivad and Beatrice, who leaned on each other in a loose embrace. "Gloriatrix has offered the Iron Crown and the remains of her nation, still sizable and fearsome, to whoever captures Queen Lila. Erik, well...he's to be brought in however is easiest."

There was a long silence.

"Gloriatrix has called forth a warband of criminals, then. Central Geadhain will be overrun," muttered Beatrice, stating the obvious.

The Lady El seemed genuinely appalled, and Rowena didn't hate her so terribly in that moment. The three wore their gloom like heavy cloaks upon their shoulders, cloaks with invisible hoods that shadowed each line in their faces.

That was how Alastair and Maggie found them when they came strolling down the stone path, materializing, it seemed, out of nowhere. Maggie pulled on Alastair's arm, trying to force him onward and past them. Alastair did not yet understand why Charazance had urged him, in the midst of his return-from-the-frontlines romp with Maggie, to retract his prick and go for a walk on the city's eastern wall. His sexual frustration now abated, Alastair found himself enjoying the fresh desert air and Maggie's conversation, which had remained as lively as her charm. He'd missed their chats and squabbles. He hoped Charazance hadn't demanded that he come up here to talk to any of these sad-faced hound dogs.

"Let's not bother them, Maggie," whispered Alastair. "I don't care for depressed folk, and they look like they're ready for a funeral, perhaps their own."

Rowena glanced at Alastair and snorted. "Hmph. You."

"You've returned," said Galivad, remembering where the man had been. Pandemonia. Beatrice also turned toward the cloaked rogue and his sultry, middle-aged companion, asking, "How are they, the heroes?"

"Is that what we're calling them?" scoffed Alastair. He and his lady paused beside the trio. "They are simply men and women doing what they must. They're no better than soldiers, really, but feel free to dress their duty up with the trimmings of honor if it makes their sacrifice seem more meaningful."

Galivad rolled his eyes and weakly waved his hand. "I asked for news of them, not for one of your interminable speeches on the nature of heroism. They are doing what *you* are not: seeking an end to this war."

"You have no idea what I've done, or what I would sacrifice to see all of this end," declared Alastair, his chest rising.

Rowena had seen this kind of man-to-man conflict before: two men puffing up and volleying insults like rotten tomatoes at each other. When this pair of fops were involved, though, it seemed more like ladies slapping each other with their evening gloves. She shouted over their bickering: "Alastair, I could use a breath of good news. Tell us about our allies in the East." Rowena separated the men, who had been huffing into each other's faces, their passionate anger mirrored in each other's expressions. "Did they arrive safely? Did they find what they were seeking?"

"Yes and no," replied Alastair, relaxing. "I doubt they've reached the City of Waterfalls yet, and they will not be safe until they do." He was met by blank stares and a glare from Beatrice. "It's one of Pandemonia's Great Cities, and it's where the *heroes* are headed. They should be able to contact us using a far-speaking stone once they are within a pocket of stable energy. I hope to hear from them before the week is out."

The company breathed a sigh of relief.

"I suppose you've heard," said Rowena.

"About the queen and hammer?" replied Alastair. "Yes…Shame, though."

"Shame?" asked Rowena.

"Shame that she didn't kill them all."

Rowena's opinion of the shadowbroker climbed a few notches, while Beatrice's fell, though neither she, nor anyone else, objected to Alastair's statement. Alastair felt the urge to leave. The Arhadian barely tolerated him; the fop always had something to say. And Moreth's wife, with whom he'd spent little time, gazed at him with an unreadable affection. Alastair, master of emotional inflections, couldn't decipher what lay behind the intensity of Beatrice's expression. Within a short time, she'd made him so uncomfortable that he absolutely needed to take his leave. "Well, we were only out for a stroll," he said. "Good night, then."

An echo of children's laughter in the air surprised everyone. Moments later, little feet ran past Alastair, and an errant limb got caught on his cloak. A young, pale creature with pink lips, slicked gray hair, silver eyes, and dressed in gentlemen's attire of vest, blouse, slacks, and cravat tugged free the cufflink responsible for the issue. "Quite sorry, mister," said the boy.

"Lamblings!" cried Elissandra. Sweeping in like a white breeze, she took her children's hands. "Eli! Tessa! Do leave those folks be."

"Hello, Lady Elissandra." Alastair gave her a short bow. "I was about to leave. Good evening."

"Not yet," said Elissandra.

"Do you see it too, Mother?" asked her daughter, equally pale and odd, and clothed in lacy finery. Frowning and craning her neck like a pecking bird, she studied the strangers. "What do you make of that color, Mother? An owl gray? A graveyard mist? They all have this soul-light; those three do, at least." She pointed in turn to Alastair, Galivad, and Beatrice. "Death? Fate? Doom?"

Elissandra, swaying hypnotically, said: "I see it, too, child. Death… fate…doom. I'd say a little of each, Tessa. But there's something else. A thread of light? See how it weaves between them? See how they all are bound?"

"I do," she said, nodding solemnly.

Elissandra squinted. "We're missing a shade."

"Yes. A grand, golden shade. I think I saw him earlier."

The two Daughters of the Moon contemplated the group. They frowned as one face. They touched their temples like women checking their appearance in a mirror. Their synchronicity felt as chilling as their prophecy, and the objects of their stares could not move. "Death and life," said the seers. "Doom and strife. A glass of light to wash down the blood."

"I see only people," complained Eli, and pointed to a few, starting with Alastair. "Sneaky, and hiding something." Rowena. "A bit like a man." Galivad. "A bit like a woman." Maggie, he simply called, "Lost." Finally, he pulled back his hand as it pointed to Beatrice. "Oh, and she's not a person."

"Very good, Eli," said Elissandra, breaking the spell.

Tessa shrugged and kicked at the flagstones. "Not terrible."

"It's quite drafty up here, such a strong wind," noted Elissandra, lisping a bit because of her missing tooth. "I don't know why we even came. Terrible evening for a walk." She drew her grandmotherly periwinkle shawl tighter and pulled on her children's hands again. The three pale seers left. Their passing left a nervous rumble in the stomachs of all who remained. Each time they saw her, her strangeness seemed to have grown by degrees. What had the witchfolk seen? Why had they come? How had any of them, these eight souls of differencing alliances and moralities, come to this crossroad of Fates tonight?

"What a strange evening," said Galivad. "Quite chilly, as she said."

"Quite," they all concurred.

"Best to call it a night," said Maggie.

Looping her arm into Alastair's, Maggie started to walk once more down the rampart. She sought the curve of a darkened arch that led away from the cold night. Trapped by intuition, drawn and drowning in the icy sea of Beatrice's presence, Alastair betrayed his lover and gawked at the beauteous ghoul while being led away. Lurching in his heart, weak in his knees, and gasping from the warm exultation of desire, he gazed upon Beatrice, who was, and was not, two women. One was white, one dark; one had a mane of spider silk and the other a sweep of hair like nightfall. That other woman—the dark-haired shade hovering within Beatrice that he could almost see as if she were real—he loved *that* woman. He loved her with the kind of fire of which epic ballads were made, with the unquenchable flames that burn only between bloodmates.

"Forgetting is often more forgiving," whispered Beatrice.

Bewildered, horrified, and completely stripped of comprehension—who, how, why?—Alastair turned his head away before he began to weep.

V

Late that night, while snuggling her children into their blankets, Elissandra spoke to them about the *Moon of Spirits*, which floated above them this eve. "Once every hundred years or so, our moon moves through a passage of ancient stars. The moon turns away from Geadhain, and is lost in her shadow. In this great, dark night, when we should be blind, we of the true sight see most clearly. All that is concealed loses its disguise. All the secrets and horrors of men flow through us. It is then, my lamblings, that the eyes in our souls open, ripped free of their lids, and we look to the sky like the old lords of Alabion. We howl and go mad, but mad with prophecy, not bloodlust. We are no less the Children of the Moon than are the changelings. Which is why you must sleep now: you are as tired as I am after sniffing fates and barking at fortunes. So sleep, my lamblings, sleep."

After tending to her now gently snoring children, Elissandra settled into a weak imitation of comfort under her coarse wool sheets. She repeated to herself her own advice: sleep…sleep. Behind pinched eyes, she thought of Sangloris and his effeminate citrus-and-vanilla perfume, the sensation of his satin hands, his sharply staccato voice. Perfect. She had conjured a perfect illusion, a tease of what she would never know again, as these were memories and not a visiting spirit. If she sent her seekers out into Dream, even under the moon of spirits, they would fly and fly and find nothing save the objects and persons touched by her husband in this life. They would never find Sangloris himself. Could Elissandra travel beyond the grayness of the Dreaming, if she were to break into the stars with her mind, she might discover the sparkling fragments or sound wave that his soul had become. She'd felt it when he passed; she'd gasped, breathless and choking on tears. There had been a screaming in her ears that might have been either a warning or a curse, but she'd never know, for the Witchwall had corrupted Sangloris's call into a static roar. He was dead. That much her love and the Fates could tell her; it would have to be enough.

Farewell, my love, she mouthed. This was not the goodbye she wanted, though it was the goodbye she must have. Tomorrow, she decided, she would tell the children. Tomorrow. She was crying softly when sleep and Fate seized her.

Dream is a rough, dark river tonight. Rudely, like a twig tossed in a rapid, she is thrashed in the currents; her silver seekers do all they can to keep her sound from shattering. A million memories dash against her, and her consciousness splinters into visions. She sees faces, some familiar, many covered in blood. Too many sights and sounds engulf her. Among them, she hears the cries of her children, a sound of glory or a wail of doom. Suddenly, billows of smoke surround her—a fire?—and she stands in a street, while horrible, shambling things slump forward over white topples of rock. The riotous streets are almost familiar, though they are unrecognizable in their state of ruin. A thick fetor, the crack and whiff of a week-old casket, blasts Elissandra's senses, knocking her out and then casting her into another sweeping tide of Dream.

"A kingdom on fire; brand this onto your mind," command her seekers, who speak to her in a loud choir of voices. "Now, witness the Dreamstalker."

After a more relaxing, peaceful flow down Dream's river, she's spit out on a shore—a time, a place, a reality. Elissandra's spirit wakes in a library gilded with wealth and fat with knowledge. She sees Morigan nearby, naked and shining with light. The Daughter of Fate converses with a creature buzzing in flies. Man? Woman? Possibly a child, or something pretending to be one. No, this is the Dreamstalker, Elissandra realizes. She hears the grisly threats it whispers. Morigan seems uncertain, when she should be blazing this monster with her silver wrath. For she must not listen to a word from this Queen of Lies. The creature has mastered the art of tweaking truths into profanities, of destroying empires and Kings with the smallest suggestions. A wind under the door, a whisper in the ear. Yes. She speaks as the Black Queen speaks. She serves the Dreamer who would eat the world. Morigan! You fool! Get away from her! *thinks Elissandra. Alas, Morigan's pride makes her deaf to her danger. Each buzz, each wingbeat of the million flies, vibrates an insidious suggestion to murder, fuk, and gorge. The music is hypnotic, and Morigan has been beguiled.*

Elissandra's seekers have almost gathered the name of this enemy, plucking out letters from the ether. A...nnn...Anne? Mann? Who cares about a name? *thinks Elissandra. If this is a reality, a Dream within a Dream, she must help Morigan, who will not raise arms to defend herself.*

"Begone, terror!" shouts Elissandra.

Elissandra flings her Will forward. She alights with the silver radiance of her seekers and strikes the monster as a cloud of light, which explodes the cloud of vermin. Elissandra does not see if her assault has been successful. The Daughter must fend for herself now; the shining dew of Elissandra's being is scattered back into the waters of Dream. A moment later, the current spits her out again over a ripple of turquoise ocean. Inconceivable colors of land pass under her ghost in a pastel and brilliant smear. At last, she slows and descends into a valley of what appear to be colossal black skeletons, or mountains of osseous black stone. It smells of death, of the charnel house: singed. A most horrible and ancient disaster has occurred here, and its gravity and scope have cursed and wrought this land into the wreckage she sees. Roving billows of ash twist below, and winds howl like the agony of the land given voice. I am burned, *says the Land.* I have been ruined. I shall never be whole again.

Where am I now? asks Elissandra. What must I see?

A star twinkles down in the dark storms roiling over the land.

Ah-ha, she thinks, and prepares for her descent into the mystery—her final stop, she hopes, as this trip into Dream will leave her empty of energy come morning. But instead, she hovers, unmoving. Time...stretches...on...

Nothing is happening; there are no further revelations.

Well, this is new, she thinks.

As there is nothing else to witness but the land, she studies that: the black crannies and smoldering hillocks, the aeries flocked with winged lizards that caw as if they are crows. Of all the wondrous horrors she has seen in this end-of-days era, this scenery is the most magnificent. She turns and turns, absorbing all that she can see, and smell, of the charcoal valley.

Her seekers sting her insistently. "Remember," *they urge.* "Never forget the creature you faced tonight; you will face her again. Remember that glimmer—the star in the dark—and remember, too, the city in ruins. Know, mistress, that when you see the northernmost star shine bright in Eod, it will be shining also in the heart of Pandemonia. When the world is aflame, the star shines and the Dreamstalker strikes. That will be your call to arms. Be the sword to swing back. Know thy time."

The proclamation echoes; she can feel it trembling in the valley.

My time? wonders Elissandra.

"You must be here, and there," say her seekers. "Both places, and one body. You must be the bird of sun and moon, mother and sword to the Daughter of Fate. You must soar and strike."

While Elissandra floats over the desolation, she arranges the incoherent clues: dying men, the shrieks of her children (not in pain, she decides, as that is a possibility she cannot accept), abominations sacking a city aglow in destruction, a monster in a mask of pests, a bright star in Eod, and a glimmer in a land of desolation. In the Dreaming, in her state of all-knowingness, patterns interweave into a picture of her destiny.

Two wars; two places. I must be the bird of sun and moon, mother of my children, and sword for Morigan. It can be done, though it will cost me everything. It is my duty, yes, and will perhaps prove to be a blessing. Men have long pondered on and sought to know their Fates, and this would bring the ultimate knowing.

She is unafraid. Until this type of vision has been met and faced, a witness to Fate cannot claim bravery. And while she has not seen her precise ending, she knows that this valley, this moment, will be where the road of her life will run out of track. She decides to hold off on telling the children about their father. Before hearing of the war in Eod, the miracle of splitting herself between two places at once, her clashing with this Dreamstalker, dear Tessa and Eli deserve to be showered in joy and peace.

"Oh, my children..." she sighs.

Her seekers do not rush her back to waking, instead allowing her to drift and grieve in the wasteland. Better that she bleeds out her sorrows with invisible tears now; the grief will douse the brand of her soul so that she may wake as newly wrought steel tomorrow. She will need all of her strength to face her destiny.

Her death.

V

RED RIDERS

I

The trip through the desert was a suffocating crawl, a heave through winds that burned the throat like sandpaper, a hike through sand that scorched through leather soles. This realm of Pandemonia felt hotter than any other, as if it were a nightmare purgatory and not a real place. Often, Morigan thought of the Dry Season once endured by Magnus and Brutus, and wondered if this heat could be worse. She kept this, all her thoughts in fact, to herself. She left conversation to the hissing sandstorms. Even she and her Wolf maintained a tense silence with each other, their bodies and minds focused simply on ploughing onward.

Night came, and with it the bitterest cold, cold that would have frozen the land if a drop of water had existed. The company huddled around the Wolf, and leeched heat from his inner fire. At some point, a few of them drifted into a delirious sleep. Sonorous horns soon awoke them, the cries of beasts whose movement was signaled by bursts of sand across the yellow plain. As they looked to the collapsing dunes, they saw amid the whirling a herd of lanky, monstrous creatures that looked like hundred-pace-tall storks covered in scales. Many times that day they saw one of these gigantic herds. Once, the great storks grew angry for reasons unfathomable, and the Wolf whipped his weary pack faster, farther away. Last night, and for many nights, in fact, he had not slept. While he did not appear to need rest as a normal person would, sleeplessness gave him an ill temper, and he growled, cursed, and scowled. After a day of following their leader's brutal pace, the company's only prize was exhaustion. Sleep came fast and hard for the others, but not for the Wolf, who stood watch with the moon.

Dawn and bloodcurdling shrieks from soaring horrors served as the morning's alarm. On through dunes, alongside perilous, dusty chasms, and beside waves of white stone rolling down into a sea of dust, the company trod. Come whatever danger, the Wolf kept them together and moving, herding them like a mean sheepdog. Moreth, too, did his part. He was the first to stir, and now and again he offered to take the Wolf's guard so that the man could eat, pee, or hunt. In the desert, days ran and melted like frost in the spring, turning into a trickling mire of delusions. Moments came when much of the land blurred; the eyes of the company puckered, their tongues felt like plaster lumps, and they could feel each drop of sweat crawl over them like maggots. Was this life? Was this death, or some kind of interminable undeath? Finally, when the sun and its daze vanished, they were able to savor a speck of modest, cool wind, before the crushing cold of evening arrived. At least then they knew their question had been answered: they lived and would sleep to endure another day. How much longer, though? How much farther till the end?

When Morigan closed her eyes, she slept the deepest sleep of her life.

Morigan's fatigue has affected her soul, and she cares not where she drifts in Dream. Down, up...anywhere Dream chooses to take her. Time passes, and then she awakes to sticky, wet heat. She is not trudging through sand, but moved by desire. Unusual, alluring, and not what she expects: a red, velvety vision of sin, of her and the Wolf rolling on clouds of gray warmth, on—the tides of Dream, over meaningless scenery, in a fantasy crafted from real moments of their time together. Beneath her, gloriously spreading his arms, exposing the bulging majesty of his beauty to her, he lies. When they are together and at the peak of intimacy, she can feel every thought and urge in him, as though she were a man, a wolf, and not herself, and he were woman, a temptress, a fire on his breasts. Absolutely lost between bodies, she leans, or he rises to kiss her—

Bzzzt!

She manages to catch the fly on her tongue and spit it out. When she looks again, the Wolf's once-handsome form crawls with black, glittering shapes, which hum as they masticate on the bone. She does not question how much of him has already been consumed, for there are pits in the churning, ebon blob of his skull. Even confronted by this horror, her devotion overrides the madness, and she wipes what she can away from his remains. She cries and begs and kisses the maggots and flies to get to a patch of skin or bone, but her mouth fills only with the mulch of dead bugs. When she is defeated, when she is sobbing and can fall no further into the moral abyss, the Dreamstalker's voice drones in the air, a spine-seizing sound wave of evil.

"Will you see now? Do you see the cost of your quest? Answers await, but you must be wary of the price of virtue. Death by the Black Queen is a release from the cruelty of fate. Love does not win; love never wins. It dies. Look."

At this command, the horde scuttles, buzzes, and then whirls past Morigan's face, returning to its source—the Dreamstalker, who stands behind her. Mist marks an empty grave where her Wolf's body should be. Nothing of her bloodmate remains. In this nightmare, Morigan cannot feel his purring fire-beast; she cannot even recall the wood, fur, and sweat of his scent. She remembers so little of he who claimed her heart.

"Sorrow makes a better mate," suggests the Dreamstalker. "Come, wed yourself to the dark with me."

A hand is laid upon Morigan; voices shriek inside her head. Suddenly, Morigan remembers her mate, his touch, his love, and the fire that roars in her chest. In a flash of light, she holds metal in her hand—her promise dagger. Whether it is real or conjured by Dream, she cares not; it will serve her purpose. "Out of my heart, you witch!" shrieks Morigan. She spins, slices—

And woke hissing and swinging a dagger at her mate. At once, the Wolf caught her wrist and subdued her, though it took more than a moment for the beating of their hearts to synch, and for the horror to fade from their faces. Luckily, they hadn't woken the others, who slept in a pile nearby. Morigan dropped the dagger and fell, but the Wolf swept to the ground with her, circling his arms about her shaking body. As their rush of adrenaline subsided, and her sobs ebbed, he asked: *My Fawn?*

*I could've…I could've…*Morigan was at a loss for what she might have done to her mate.

The Wolf dismissed her worry. *My hide is like iron. Now, what did you see?*

A nightmare.

What have you seen?

Seen? Too much.

With that, she finally unlocked the door in her soul that her pride—a bit of his pride, as well—had kept sealed. He shuddered as her memories came over him, as he saw all her terrors: the masked and buzzing face of the Dreamstalker, and not one, but two of his deaths. When the red images had vanished, the Wolf gave a sigh of dread. *She wants you to end me?*

Love never wins, she warned me.

It does, my Fawn. He kissed her head. *In those visions, I smell pain on her, deep as the rot set into green flesh. She loathes because she once loved. I do not fear her, though I do not think she is a cat without claws, either.*

I want her out of my head!

I know. I know. He kissed her crown again. *And we shall find a way to cast her out. Until then, tell no one of this incident. I would not want our pack doubting you.*

Don't you? Doubt me?

The Wolf glowered at her. *Never. Now sleep, if you are able.*

I cannot.

I am here. I am always here. You are the true compass of our voyage, and will lead us through the darkest seas. I shall need you to save your strength for that. For now, you must sleep. He gave her another kiss, and as if it possessed some faerytale magik, all of Morigan's weariness and nerves swelled in a wave of fear that then receded in a tide, pulling her to sleep. He carried her back to the nest of the others, and settled himself in amid their bodies. When his bloodmate felt distant enough in his heart, he left her and the others sleeping and sniffed the night. Baring his fangs and rumbling in his throat, he harked for the rattle of cicadas. Into the night, he cast a silent, blood-sworn promise to the Dreamstalker: *Come, broken soul, wounded child. Come and be eaten.*

II

"Beautiful," observed Moreth.

The unthinkable march through the endless desert had soiled the Menosian's waxy perfection; he looked as if he had melted. His hair was soaked to his temples. His vest had been wrung out and placed in his pack. His blouse clung to him with patches of yellow perspiration. At least the heat had infused a pleasant pinkness into Moreth's cheeks, making him look almost like a normal man.

The lush vale below them seemed to be a prayer answered. Beneath the sandy ledge from where the Wolf gazed down watchfully—hand on a knee, leaning in to smell the view—the desert suddenly dried up and festered with emerald life in the way common to Pandemonia. Long, curly weeds, as sinewy as seaweed, rose from step to step of an inverse basin, stratified like a great mine. On these stairs, each of which would take hourglasses to climb, the growth evolved from the fields of seaweed into bush and strange scrub, and then finally into tall tangles of green with white spires. "Trees," announced the Wolf, responding to the sap-scented tease of these odd ivory twists. "Unicorn trees," exclaimed Talwyn. Warm hands of wind caressed the cheeks of the tired travelers. Winged shapes fluttered and glided over the basin, more and more of them appearing as the land ascended, and a chattering chorus from both sky and wood called the wanderers to enter. Mouse spotted some teal bushes with yellowish spots. "Looks like fruit down there." She set off walking. "And, King's mercy, I think that's a creek. Hopefully, it's nothing strange. I'm going to find out."

Grumbling an uncertain warning, all noise, no words, the Wolf followed her, the others in his wake. Once they had descended a little, they were swallowed by wet fronds that tickled their faces. Down in the basin, they stopped at the stream that Mouse had noticed. There, the Wolf had a sniff and drink of the creek, then nodded his approval and waved to his companions to partake. They refilled their waterskins, splashed their faces, and cleaned off a little of their stink. After plunging again into the veldt, the Wolf led them over and through lands rich with moss and thick undergrowth, his presence deterring whatever hissing things waved faraway trails through the grasses. The Wolf spotted one, and didn't care for it: a skulking cat-lizard as large and dark as a panther, patched with both fur and scale, and surely as dangerous as each of its parent species. Aside from the calls of those hunters, or the cries of the animals they killed, only toads and strident crickets could be heard.

The land was densely vegetated, and they were long in coming to the first major elevation: a step of risen soil, dangling roots. After slinging Morigan into his arms, the Wolf leaped like an ape up the cliff. At the top, he waited, sometimes scrabbling halfway down the crumbling dirt wall to carry a slipping pack-mate up. The stubborn members of the company, Mouse and Moreth, accepted none of his assistance. Once everyone was up, they took a moment to rearrange their packs and cloaks, and to gaze around this new woodier terrain.

Far and wide the woodland stretched. Underbrush loosely framed pools of mirrored water around which clustered purring, quilled creatures that glanced at the company, then away. Unicorn trees punctured the blue-green turf, a grass higher than wheat and tall enough that the Wolf could hide in it without hunkering. Moisture gleamed upon every leafy surface, and the land buzzed with noise. The land's sheen and sounds enticed the imagination with thoughts of rainforests. The Wolf didn't care for the thickness of the air or the tang of split and spoilt fruits that suggested the presence of some insidious rot. Still, the animals seemed harmless, and nothing leaped to kill them as they continued onward.

In some places, the greenery was near impassable, and they formed a chain and held hands while swimming through a bluish haze, numbed by the swish of fronds. In one wider, freer opening, they rested on a cracked and toppled unicorn tree and scared a few of the spiny critters away from a pond, where they then refreshed themselves.

For this they could be grateful: the water was always pure and, although the Wolf assured them it was free from enchantment, it grew seemingly sweeter with every taste. After their repose, they marched through grass and ferns, wrestling with each step to pull their feet from the increasingly marshy ground. Insects harassed them, the large, buzzy kind with stingers and a thirst for blood. A refreshing evening breeze soon blew through the grasses, though, and they managed one more taxing climb onto the next plateau. The Wolf assisted all of them this time, as the company had grown very tired.

They made camp for the evening on an island of sorts. It was moated by a fork in a shallow stream, and upon it stood a small unicorn tree surrounded by easily trampled bush. As they gathered around the tree, the Wolf declared the night safe for a fire. He'd sensed danger only on the lowest range of this realm where the cat-lizards had roamed. Up here, no predators seemed to hunt. That there could be two separate ecologies so near to one another yet completely independent of one another perplexed him. Pandemonia made no attempt to conform to the natural order. He rather missed the voracious cat lizards, for those beasts, at least, he understood.

Why the frown, my Wolf?

Throughout the day, his bloodmate had said little. Morigan's sudden mind-whisper made him choke on the quill beast meat in his mouth. *I seem to have surprised you*, she continued, then smiled and rubbed his great back. Her mere touch made his heart race, and he realized he had been lonely for her company all day. She'd been so quiet, speaking less and less since her terrible dream.

I do not like this land, he replied. *It does not know what it is, or should be. I feel as if it divides and confuses us.*

Not entirely. Bonds have been made, as well as broken. She nodded at Moreth, Thackery, and Talwyn, so engaged in arguing that they were neglecting to touch their dinners, which lay on a picnic blanket of cloaks. Mouse and Adam, like a pair of city-wise dogs, were leaning in as if to hear the discussion, all the while using the argument as cover for stealing bits of uneaten food out from under the men's noses. When the pair of thieves noticed the bloodmates staring, they offered no apology and continued their pilfering.

In times of war, the greatest enemy is the one who commands the most death, said the Wolf. *While that is my father and the Dark Dreamer now, it could easily be Menos again. For now, the son of El fights with us. Tomorrow, I may have to rip out his throat.* The Wolf threw down the raw shank he'd no interest in, leaned back, and tumbled with Morigan until their noses touched. Her scent intoxicated him, and he tingled in pleasure: love, not desire—though for a beast, the feelings were near the same. Voices on the other side of the fire quieted. People surely watched, yet he cared not for impropriety. *But I do not wish to speak of traitors, Iron rulers, or Black Queens. I wish to speak to my bloodmate, the other half of my soul, who was as silent as a brooding owl today. Why do you keep to yourself? Are you worried still over that masked coward? If she comes for you again, I shall hunt her in your dreams.* Harmlessly, he snapped his teeth, summoning a smile from Morigan.

An idea struck the Wolf and he smiled—sharp, dangerous, and full of wicked charm. *I shall sleep,* he said. *How else can I protect you from this creature that stalks you in dreams, but by entering your dreams myself? We are close, close enough that I feel my fingers as part of your hand at times. Close enough that I feel you inside my loins when we are together. If we share feelings and sensations, we can share everything else that is unseen. Tonight, my Fawn, you will sleep soundly, as shall I. If she comes for you, I shall be there, too, a call away or perhaps already in your presence. We shall end her.*

It was the simplest of remedies, one that required only that they surrender certain prideful habits: her need to conquer everything herself, and his obsession with vigilance. Their companions were not children or cubs; they could care for themselves tonight. Mumbling orders to their companions, snuggling tight, and placing bearded cheek to velvet one, the two rocked themselves into a swooning darkness.

The Dreamstalker did not come for Morigan that night. It was possible she watched and waited, hovering in the clouds of Dream and cursing the bloodmates' union, for love was anathema to her soul. She remained a whisper in a graveyard, though, a faraway terror. She could not harm what was united. She would have to break them apart.

III

The following morning, the Wolf yawned for the first time in recent memory, and spent a sand playing with the flow of his bloodmate's hair in the radiance of a fresh dawn. He ran his fingers through her tresses as if unfurling red silk. He pulled her closer, sniffed at her ear, then her nape. She turned sleepily to him, a puppet to his desire.

"No, thank you," said Mouse, who saw something large and quite frightening creep up under the Wolf's kilt. "If I wanted to see a woman swallow a snake, I would have visited one of those peepshows in Menos." The bloodmates ignored these jibes.

How did you sleep? he asked.

Perfectly.

They kissed quickly. A tiring day lay ahead: steep, sheer walls of mud daunted them from afar. The unicorn forest, veiled in a light fog, felt muffled with humidity. Moreth appeared with a smoking pistol and a pair of dead quill beasts, and they sat down to a quiet breakfast. They ate everything, down to the bone, to build up their strength for the day. Adam, strangely, was the only one not to finish his meal. Morigan and the Wolf buried the bones, said a small prayer—some habits never died, no matter how far from home they were—then set out into the swaying morass. Surprisingly, the sun seared away the fog, but the day never became too hot. A general air of levity accompanied the morning breeze. The other allies could sense that the bloodmates, the heart of their company, had mended a tear in themselves, though no one said a word.

As usual, the Wolf took the lead, clearing a broad path for his pack. Mouse, Moreth, and Talwyn—who'd been given a thin rapier back on the *Skylark*—hacked at whatever foliage was left still blocking their way. Trailing Mouse was Adam, her guard dog. Watching them from behind, Morigan could not decide whether or not Mouse and Adam were meant to be lovers. Certainly, the bees had no opinion on the matter. An indifferent *bzzz?* came if she asked her sixth sense about the destiny of the two. What most held her attention, though, and gave Morigan the greatest enjoyment that morning was neither the memory of her sleep without terrors nor the confidence of her Wolf. Instead, she took a personal, selfish pleasure in the companionship of Thackery, who walked quietly next to her.

When she thought he wasn't looking, she examined him. The mystery of his renewed youth was a fascination to which she hadn't paid enough attention. King's mercy, he looked so *dashing*. Thackery's face held the perfect etchings of time: a scratch of gray at the temples, a slight spiderweb about his eyes, and deep lines set where he laughed, currently hidden by many days' worth of unkempt black beard. Messy beard aside, the chest-proud posture of his lean body bespoke an ancient, dynastic royalty: Thule royalty, dark royalty. In his gaze of blue-white lightning shone the weight, worry, and gravitas of a ruler. *Perhaps he will rule again, one day,* thought Morigan, and the bees made a sharp sting in her heart. She didn't have time to press her bees for a fate because Thackery caught her staring. "My dear?"

"You look so noble," admitted Morigan. "I see you, and I have known you all my life, and yet I feel as if I am seeing you anew."

"We have all been through a spell of *growth*," he replied. "Mine is simply more evident than yours." Thackery nodded toward the Wolf, who hiked ahead. "Even your bloodmate has changed. Your love has given him a strength, and a softness, that he would never have found without you."

Morigan blushed. She interlocked elbows with the man, and they strolled in a gay and forgotten way along the path.

"I feel as if an age has passed since you and I were together," said Thackery.

"Too long."

"Far too long." As he paused to study the woman on his arm—she was truly a *woman* now—he became misty-eyed.

"What?" asked Morigan.

"I see you, and yet I feel as if I am seeing you anew."

She laughed. "That's my line."

"You really are a most remarkable woman," he continued. "I am so grateful for this journey, hardships and all. I am grateful you made an old man young again, and I do not mean my body, as the Sisters must be credited for that. I mean my heart, and my soul."

"Thackery..."

"I mean it, Morigan. You have a gift for renewing what you touch. I feel that I can love once more." The words made him cringe as the ghosts of his Theadora and Bethany stirred in his memory. "Not romantically. I do not feel I shall ever again find that commitment."

"I wouldn't be so sure," said Morigan.

Thackery was afraid to inquire about the silver flicker in her eyes, so he brushed off the statement and considered a better use for her prescience. "I think of Macha often. The fourth of my many daughters." They smiled. "I hope that she and Kanatuk fare well in the North. I have thought many times of asking you of their fate. Can you...I mean...Do you *feel* they are happy and whole?"

Morigan paused, thinking of their friends in the North. She Willed her servants of Fate to seek out the nectar of her Kanatuk and the young daughter of Dymphana. Magik snatched and then hurled Morigan's consciousness so quickly she could not understand anything of the brilliant landscape—all knots of silver and flashes of light—through which she careened for an instant. Across the ocean, on a wind up the Feordhan, and into the wintry deeps of the North flew an aspect of the seer. There, her spirit drifted like a snowflake amid white dunes, trees laced with ice, and woolly creatures bleating against a vociferous wind. She noticed two flecks of black on the ivory swath of a distant rise, and her heart danced with joy. One fleck, smaller than the other, she knew was a young girl wrapped in furs. Macha. The other taller dot—bravely strutting, at last free in his frozen home—kept one hand on the young girl to guide her. The two had become the brother and sister they'd never had.

Through her sudden tears, Morigan said, "Yes, I see them. They are happy."

An ugly smear of black twisted with a flash of white tore into the pleasant vision. She saw a handsome Northman's face: blond, amber eyed and dripping in blood. She saw Magnus, the Queen and a very dark man—his skin black as obsidian—screaming. She cried out as she heard in her head a terrible shattering roar like ten thousand glass plates breaking. She collapsed, feverish, but with Thackery present, she was never in any danger of hitting the earth. He caught her, then knelt and held her until her swoon passed. *Whoosh*! The Wolf appeared, snuffling, angry. From Thackery, he stole the task of tending to his mate. The bloodmates conversed in private while the others stopped and waited.

What did you see?

I don't know. It all happened so fast. Very unusual. There was a beast, I think...a roar in the north. I have never heard a thing so loud.

What were you doing?

Thinking of Macha and Kanatuk. Thackery wondered how they were. She touched his face and met his stare, silver sparked between them, and the vision passed into his head. He shook off the experience, its loudness, and made no answer. He had none: better to leave these mysteries for another time.

He brought Morigan to her feet, left her with Thackery, and then returned to the head of the pack. Morigan explained to her friend what she'd seen, and had nothing more to say. From her frown, Thackery assumed she now worried about their friends in the North and portents of loud, angry monsters. Whether that assumption was true or not, Thackery couldn't leave the strange business unsorted; it wasn't in his nature to leave threads unpulled. While he and Morigan walked along, again linking arms, he thought of Macha and Kanatuk. Were their distant fates still part of the pattern being woven by Morigan? Would he see Macha again? Were they in danger once more? What was that roaring thing? Why were the king, Lila, and those other two strange men involved—and in what? Perhaps he should instead have been pondering the question of his own destiny, for suddenly the Wolf hissed at them to stop. He ushered them quickly into the concealing depths of the grass before dashing away.

My Wolf, what—

Hunters.

The underbrush swallowed him, and his mind went silent, too. Thereafter, Morigan could feel only the throbbing of his pulse. Her Wolf was hunting, in a mind state similar to the one that governed her when she wandered the gray netherverse. Squatting together, the six companions listened for any disharmony in the morning's music of ruffling stalks, wind songs, and heat haze. Nothing out of the ordinary for Pandemonia's queer wildlife could be heard. Morigan didn't feel that it was any such creatures that had alarmed her bloodmate. "Adam, do you sense anything?" she whispered, at her wits' end.

The changeling shook his head. "I do not smell any predators, although my senses are not what they should be in this land."

"I can help you with that later, skin-walker," whispered Moreth. His cold, narrowed gaze then slid to Morigan. "You're a seer. Why are we hiding, waiting, and guessing, when you could simply *tell* us of our danger?"

"I..."

Morigan's mouth hung open: she had no good answer for the man. In the heat of the moment, she had forgotten that only a few sands ago she'd thrown her mind across spans of Geadhain to find, unerringly, the souls of her friends in the North. Once, Elissandra had claimed that Morigan did not know the full extent of her powers. *"A fat-fingered and fumbling child,"* Elissandra had called her. The white witch had had cause to denounce her, for Morigan tended to call upon her magik only when it was needed, not seeing it as useful in everyday life. Perhaps she feared becoming too reliant upon her magik. In truth, she hadn't contemplated the matter deeply, though she supposed her stubbornness, humble upbringing, and determination to be in control of her life had contributed to her reluctance. Besides, more often than not the Fates made use of her, and not the other way around. But if she wanted to master her gifts, it was time to stop being afraid. *No better moment than now*, she decided.

"Well?" pressed Moreth, having waited all this time for a reply.

Somewhat angrily, Morigan answered, "Yes. Yes, I can."

Morigan shut her eyes and released the swarm of her magik. She left her flesh entirely this time; her body collapsed and was quickly caught and cradled by Thackery. *I am the master. I am the Queen of the Unseen*, she told herself and her swarm. *Show me who or what threatens our pack*. Into the air her spirit spun like a maple key.

Pandemonia's atmosphere was radiant. The sky glowed with a thousand silver rivers of coursing light—etheric currents, each one of them a vein of raw magik, and not so different from the riches buried in the earth. Here, though, nothing was entombed: power flowed freely through the skies and rained down with the water into the soil. Little wonder that Thackery's earlier attempt to conjure a light had spun beyond his control. He might as well have lit a match in an oil-soaked apartment. *All this power...*, she thought. She wondered where the silver rivers converged, at what glorious sea of energy, of possibility, they arrived.

She sensed that this place was similar to the Hall of Memories. It was a nexus of time, space, and magik. She even felt a comparable, though far more terrible, pull and began to float upward and away from the vaporous outlines of her companions and the mumbles of their underwater conversation.

No. You are in control. You will not be led. You have only one thing to discover here, and the mystery of where the thousand rivers of light converge is not it.

She sought the fire of her bloodmate, and in the realm between worlds she saw his strong flame burning on the upward slope of a transparent valley. She blew herself toward him, and in a speck hovered over his broad crimson outline.

Morigan, he said, surprised. He touched his heart, where he could feel her, then looked behind him, sensing her but seeing only fields of blue fronds and unicorn spires. Somehow, she stood near him, although his eyes told him different. The Wolf reached out, lightly, and his hand passed through a breeze that tickled his flesh like the softness of her lips.

I am here, my Wolf.

The Wolf snorted in shock. He quickly composed himself. *How? I have known shamans and witches who can cast their souls, but even they cannot interact with the living. I felt you. I know that I did. Your warmth... Your kiss?*

Although she had no mouth in her current state, a flock of warm, unseen butterflies fluttered over the Wolf as she thought of kissing him. The Wolf grinned. *How?* he asked again.

It is as Moreth said, I believe, and as Talwyn speculated. Pandemonia is a source of magik, life, and fate—a fertile bosom of possibility. I feel that anything I do here will be multiplied untold times. Think, my Wolf, of how your senses found these creatures even over the enormous roar of this place.

These creatures, thought the Wolf, and became sullen once more.

In no time at all, he'd found their hunters. A wind sour with ash and the musk of an incredibly sweaty, rancid animal had drawn him to them like a shout. Six riders, huddled in dusty red cloaks and mounted on patient, horned steeds formed a lined guard over the top of the valley, on the final hill the company would have to climb to get out of this patch of Pandemonia. At first, the Wolf had considered dashing up and disabling the riders. It would not have taken long to do, and at most, one of them might have had time to scream. However, the unsettling odor that blew from the six, and the motionlessness that they exhibited even as he began to fidget amid the ferns, held him back. The Wolf could nearly place the smell—the reek of oily scorched meat left to fester atop dead coals—but it reminded him of something from a dream, not a memory.

Do you not recognize them? asked Morigan's ghost.

No.

To Morigan, who floated in the membrane between realities, everything appeared dazzlingly clear, sharp, and bright. She could not only see the shapes of things—trees, beasties, and her handsome, hulking Wolf—she could spy the secrets that lay beneath the flesh. She glimpsed the fire of her bloodmate's spirit: a gold-tipped, wild light contained within the glass lantern of his chest. Indeed, the Wolf's soul was as beautiful as she had always known it would be.

With her heightened perception, she could easily look to the six riders upon the hill and peer past their glass shells into the matter that constituted their hearts. Each of the six beings was empty, mostly, save for a pointed and black spot. It was a star, or anti-star, the very opposite of life. Each mark was as intricate as an ebon snowflake, as complex as the greater celestial body from which it had come—too complex for even Morigan's incredible mind to apprehend, for these marks were shadows of the Mother of Creation: Zionae.

You do not see it, my Wolf, though you sense it and smell it. These are not men, not anymore. They are hollow, and they have been marked.

Marked?

By the Black Queen.

Now that the Wolf knew Zionae's smell firsthand, he would never forget it. A growl burbled from his hate-curled mouth, and he prepared to leap from concealment and ravage the slaves of the Black Queen with already bared claws and teeth. Morigan's sensual, tickling wind blew against his face, giving him pause.

Hold, my Wolf, she warned.

If her spirit had not manifested here, if he had discerned the nature of the men upon the hill by himself, as he probably would have in time, he wouldn't have been able to leash his beast. He wanted to ravage the horsemen, for they were the agents and foul children of his father; they were the embodiments of corruption, monsters bred to consume. He'd seen Morigan's vision of how Blackeyes were conceived. These creatures were almost siblings to him. This thought so unsettled the Wolf that his iron stomach heaved. Still thinking of brothers, sisters, and wicked families, he suddenly detected the stink of man musk upon the riders. From that whiff, he knew that a huge, reeking animal must have been near them. Brutus. That was his father's smell—the musk of war, sex, and doom.

I yearn to shower myself in their death. I yearn to howl over their corpses until Brutus comes to challenge me.

Hold, she commanded.

For as angry as he felt, he must hold himself back. Morigan looked once more at the black stars in the distant glass men. They were not six separate men, but six roots of a great dark tree. Attacking these roots would alert a larger force to the presence of the company. Now that her bloodmate had evoked the name of his father, she noticed signs of Brutus's taint on the bodies of the corrupted vessels—powdery markings, as if the six riders had been molested by great gold-dusted hands. Quite possibly, that's exactly what had happened. At least the soulless riders could not describe to Morigan the terror that had come before their deaths. She found that viewing them abstractly, as little glass and ebon soldiers, brought her some small comfort, too. She'd been spared the sight of their scars and mottled flesh.

They are of many bodies, but only one mind, she said. *Each is an eye and hand of the Black Queen. We must know why they are here before we reveal ourselves. Somehow, they have already come this close*—Morigan thought of the Dreamstalker, another pawn or servant of the Black Queen, and realized she must have been tracked, either by that villain or any number of creatures or forces they'd yet to comprehend in this strange land. *Please, my Wolf, I know you want your clash with your father, and I am sure you will have it. But we are not prepared. For now, you must be calm.*

The Wolf stayed low to the earth, swallowing his growls and making himself as still as the soil. *Good, my Wolf, good,* whispered the breeze of his soul mate as it caressed his back. Morigan knew she would not be able to placate him forever, that this was a temporary respite. Glaring at the glass monsters atop the spectral hill, Morigan wished these evils away. *You have brought us enough pain, Zionae,* she thought. *Leave us be. We shall have our reckoning with each another soon enough.*

As though they had heard her, the horsemen reined in their mounts, turned around, and rode off into the crimson dazzle of the sun.

They have left...said the Wolf, as he rose up and sniffed the air for scents of the riders.

Why did they leave?

I don't know.

The Wolf smelled the enigmatic, cloying incense of a mystery. *Did you Will them away? Or has something else made them give up the chase?*

Morigan had no explanations for him; she felt she'd worked no magik, and there could well be other threats out there to attract the riders' attention. Paranoid, the Wolf decided to hurry back to the others. Down the hill he strode, embraced by the gentle living wind of his bloodmate. Despite the worries he carried with him, he found himself grinning at the newest wonder of their love.

IV

After the Wolf had returned to the company, and Morigan had, with a gasp, announced her spirit's reintegration with her flesh, the bloodmates explained their narrowly avoided encounter with the Red Riders.

"Your vision was true, then?" asked Mouse, referring to Morigan's dream on the eve of their landing in Pandemonia. She was shaking. "Brutus and his forces are here?"

The seer nodded.

"Yes, my father is here," growled the Wolf. In a fury, the Wolf stomped off, tearing a path through the grasses. The companions hurried after him. A hard pull on Mouse's arm held her back.

"Father?" hissed Moreth. "His *father* is the mad king?"

"Small detail!" Mouse freed herself and tried to put Moreth at ease with her smile, lovely when she used it. "You and I didn't have the time to go over *everything* the other evening. Certain bits may have been withheld out of a sense of discretion, a discretion I see I need no longer maintain."

"No more secrets," warned Moreth.

Half hidden in the fronds nearby, Adam crouched, watching their exchange. Noticing this, Mouse decided to move before the changeling felt she was being threatened. As she and Moreth continued along the path cleared by their company, Adam circled her in silence. Mouse ignored Moreth's presence. She didn't entirely know why, but she felt guilty about not having trusted Moreth. "I suppose you have questions," she said, at last.

"I doubt we have time for all my questions," he snapped. "Will there be any other surprises? Is there anything else I should know? You know, the kind of details one might feel compelled to withhold for discretionary reasons. Not knowing things tends to be the quickest route to death. I am not a man content to exist in isolation from reality, no matter how cold and unpleasant that reality may be. I know for a fact you are missing one, or more, from your number. I hear the whispers about those who have come and gone from your company. The steward of the Blackbriar estate, who went rogue; and he was a reborn, which is strange, since that kind never stray. I have heard that one of the Broker's men defected, as well. Were they, too, left to flounder? Would those men be with us today if the wisest among you had not kept your secrets in such tight reserve?"

A hitch formed in Mouse's chest at the mention of her father. She hadn't stopped thinking of Vortigern—she felt she never would—but she wasn't as tormented by his ghost these days. Every night before going to bed, she would recall his cold hands and yellow smile, and feel a twinge that was more of happiness than sorrow now.

Moreth read her wince, saw her suddenly watery eyes, and realized he might have spoken too harshly. "I don't know when to stop myself, at times," he said. "My father used to call me *Lingua Serpens*...Snake Tongue. Indeed, my mouth often runs away with my mind. A gentleman should know better."

From somewhere, he produced a pristine monogrammed kerchief and passed it to Mouse so that she might dry the few tears she couldn't recall having produced. She made quick work of her grief and returned Moreth's cloth to him.

"Fathers..." she muttered, then let the whole truth leak out. "I lost mine, shortly after I'd found him. He was one of those damned by the secrets they kept. Vortigern Thule...that was my father's name, and he was the reborn you mentioned. He was Sorren's brother—the man who kidnapped me, if you recall...Both men are Thackery's nephews, Gloriatrix's sons. It's all such a glorious mess."

An astounding confession. Here was the lost heiress to the Blackbriar fortune, the granddaughter of the Iron Queen, a child rumored to have died of a fever. Here was a royal offspring who'd surely been shuffled into hiding amid the politics and paperwork of Gloriatrix's Charter for Freedom. Little wonder, thought Moreth, that the Iron Queen had ordered him to support this seemingly charitable cause. Such a lapse from mercilessness made sense now that he knew a child of her own blood was involved.

Tucking away his kerchief, which had been left dangling in the wind for a moment, Moreth walked onward, tipping his head toward Mouse to follow. "Fathers..." he said. "It sounds as if you loved yours. I would say that it is better to have loved deeply and briefly than never to have loved at all. When I think of my father's death, it is only to regret it did not happen sooner, for he was such a wanton wastrel of a man."

"I...Thank you, that's kind of you to say. What you said about my father, I mean, not yours."

The pair, and the changeling stalking them, had fallen behind the others and now hastened to catch up, while still keeping to themselves. Adam left the pair and joined Talwyn in beating down whatever brush the Wolf hadn't crushed with his stomping. Mouse discovered that the Menosian's company was oddly relaxing. Moreth spoke with a shrewd elegance, unadorned and unsentimental. His was the acerbic candor of her people, and he possessed a conversational savvy that she had missed. Perhaps Moreth felt homesick, too, or more at ease with a fellow countryman, for he began to open up. Or perhaps speaking of fathers had loosened the bolt on the door, keeping in many forgotten memories from his childhood. Frank and often bitterly funny, Moreth wove for Mouse a tale of an age of grotesque decadence: The Age of Discovery.

Stunning breakthroughs in technomagik had occurred in quick succession. Within one decade, organ transplants, skin swapping, and even spinal and nerve tissue replacements were being performed without causing crippling, adverse effects. Any piece of a man could be traded with any other, down to his prick and the market for sizable slave genitalia suddenly boomed. The advancements in fleshcrafting made it possible for a man to live three or more times his natural years. For the first time in history, man stood within reach of the Immortals. Beyond these medical wonders, Menos had profited from the height of its Iron Valley excavations (it would be many years before the great quake would shake humility into the ancient masters). Never had the Iron City been so bursting with wealth or so in demand by those eager to trade for Menosian secrets. Into this era, Moreth Eustache El had been born.

Which makes you about two hundred years old, give or take, thought Mouse. The fleshcrafting wonders conceived during that age had served Moreth well.

"You wouldn't believe the parties," he said, laughing wickedly. "Fountains of liquid ether, flavored with whatever was then the voguish narcotic. Grab a glass and hallucinate to your heart's content. Chase a golden faery out a window, race with your long-dead lover down a flight of stairs and probably break your neck...You know how our people are, we like our death. It wasn't a proper party unless at least one person died by misadventure. Perhaps food, and not mayhem, was your pleasure instead. In that case, you could wander to any hall in one of my father's soirees and take your pick of pickled oesterich eggs, Alabion tufted wildcat, or black-tailed pheasant—species nearing extinction at the time, and surely living only in the history books now. But that was the allure. Without the rarity, the taste was not worth having. This applied to appetites of passion, too, and as he was a merchant in blood, my father often rang a gong to clear the great hall, then made ten or twenty of his warriors gut and decapitate each other on our beautiful Basadora marble floors. Last man standing, and all that. Our house staff would spend days cleaning the hall afterwards. Blood soaks right into untreated stone, you see, and innards can fly as high as chandeliers. Where Father truly outdid himself with perversion, though, was with his showstopping orgies. Come the peak of the evening's intoxication, naked slaves would be brought forth, oftentimes to the same gory battlefield as father's gladiators. The poor souls would stand there, pumped like breeding livestock full of aphrodisiacs, the men's rods raging, the women fondling their breasts. Then the slaves would be forced to fuk—well, not really *forced*, considering their states. The slaves would engage in rabid pleasure before an audience of esteemed perverts that usually fuked and fondled themselves as well. Most of the slaves were so inebriated and foreign that they did not realize there would be a cruel endgame to their exhibitionism. The slaves didn't understand that Menosians are aroused primarily by violence; if the savages did figure that out, they never stopped fuking anyway, not even as molten feliron was poured upon them from on high, and chanting earthspeakers cast and set their bodies into horrific erotic reliefs. The slaves screamed in pleasure and then finally in terror as they died. I still remember their noises and the murmurs of the spellcasters—like a priest's chanting, which I now hate—echoing up through the halls of the El estate. For a time, until I inherited the House of El, Father kept a wing filled with his pornographic iron trophies."

Mouse almost pitied the master, although he seemed dismissive of pity, as if it would be beneath him. Far more astonishing than the violent debauchery Moreth had witnessed as a child was the apparent disgust he felt at this cycle of entitlement and sin.

"To the disappointment of many, I did not continue my father's ways," he said. "Those heinous traditions died with him," said Moreth. "My Blood Pits had men of valor, men fighting to break the system that had enslaved them. We all deserve a chance to be something better than what Fate demands we should be."

"I agree," said Mouse.

They walked in silence for a few specks, then Moreth spoke softly. "Nearly every night since the fall of Menos, I have thought of what comes next for what's left of the Iron City, and for our people. I think about our soul, mostly, as all else has been lost—our wealth, our technomagik, our culture. All those things must be rebuilt, but our soul—made of our faith and our endurance—is our only virtue, and we must not lose it. I'd like to believe that when Menos rises again, we shall do more than find new ways to destroy our morality. I'd like to think that we shall..."

Mouse finished his thought. "Not be so fuking terrible?"

Moreth cackled.

V

For the remainder of the day, the company hiked with caution, worried that the Red Riders might return. As evening covered the land in a cool crimson glow, they camped at the base of a muddy cliff. Reaching the top would involve great exertion: to inspire his pack, the Wolf hunted and killed several quill beasts and then started a cooking fire. While they sat and ate their dinner, a few of the company found themselves rubbing their shoulders and huddling closer to the Wolf or the flames. At last, the first white flake fluttered down and landed, then melted, upon Mouse's cheek. Neither she nor the others found the arrival of snow surprising. "I guess we should bundle up," she said.

The idea of wandering amid a snowy wonderland appealed to Mouse; they had never had much snow in Menos, only gray slush at the best of times. Eager to meet the snow, she left what remained of her meal, threw on the heavy garments she'd packed away, and began her ascent. The company soon followed her. As the Wolf had anticipated, this climb was harder than the ones that had come before; the sloped wall rose taller and grabbable roots were scarce. Often the companions had to kick and dig for footholds and handholds in the cold, dense soil. Winter awaited them above, and the company finished the climb with fingers numb and pale. Afterward, they stood breathless, collecting themselves before going on. There seemed to be only one path this time, and not the cornucopia of choices, colors, and terrains with which Pandemonia usually presented its travelers.

Ahead of them, grass surrendered to great black tiles of stone that tilted like fallen dominos. Frost consumed the land, and the path looked glassy and precarious. In the distance, the black tiles turned gray, then white, and were soon buried in snow. As for the storm that had caused this massive snowfall, it seemed dormant in the strange evening sky; the clouds were a shade between purple and blue and flickered as if with fireflies. The storm would be dangerous when again unleashed. However, they all sensed this was the way to go—this was the way to Eatoth.

A nasty-tempered wind rudely assaulted the company, and they pulled their hoods and cloaks tight. In the bluster, Mouse didn't notice Adam undressing until his clothing was thrown in a pile at her feet; Thackery did him the courtesy of collecting it. A moment later, after a little screaming and growling, a lean brown wolf panted by her side.

"I think Adam has the right idea," said the Wolf. "I, too, would serve us better in my other skin. The night is dark, and I sense something wicked ahead."

Something wicked? They watched the miracle and spectacle of the Wolf as he undressed and then started bristling with muscle, hair, fangs, and claws. Even the unflappable Moreth felt an unfamiliar reverence, shaking uncontrollably when a rending howl tore from the Wolf at the climax of his transformation. Morigan calmly retrieved the discarded clothing of her lover while the huge ebon monster looked around with his paralyzing gray stare. The bits of crystal braided into his hair by the faeries in Alabion glittered about his head in a mane of diamonds. He was beautiful and terrible. The Wolf barked, then turned and padded over the uneven land.

"That means we follow," said Mouse. "Let's go."

"Oh, yes…Yes," mumbled Moreth, who'd forgotten how to walk for a moment. "He's bigger than a horse…Bigger than an ox…than two oxen, even."

"You should have seen his mother," quipped Talwyn.

A hard push lay ahead. The storm conspired to fight them, and an hourglass into their trek the clouds flashed and released flurries and wind. Against the whirling paleness of the land, the Wolf's black hide was easy to spot, even when obscurity claimed all else. At times, Adam strayed ahead with the Wolf, or ran in circles around the rest of the pack like a dutiful sheepdog to ensure no one would be lost. Making a chain, the two-legged company held tight to one another with blue hands, took careful steps in unison, and focused on the black dot of their pack-master. They were united and strong: no one tripped or allowed despair to sink into their bones along with the chill. Eventually, the daze of traveling up and down over irregular snowdrifts ended, and a brown wolf was nudging them down a gully formed by two of the giant stone dominos, which had fallen against each other, creating a formation like a lean-to. Here the snowfall was lighter, and the company had a moment's grace from the elements. They huddled together and warmed their hands. Moreth, the only one clever enough to have brought gloves, chose not to gloat.

Of the changelings, only Adam was present, thumping his tail. The Wolf had not joined the company inside their stone tent.

"Where is Caenith?" Moreth asked.

"He's…caught wind of something," Morigan replied, her attention divided between Moreth and her bloodmate, wherever he had gone. "Blood."

As the company had seen neither hide nor hair of another living creature in this snowy wasteland, Morigan's news came as a shock. Tense, and slowly warmed by their excited heartbeats, the six waited for the Wolf to return. Moreth thought he saw a dark flicker, and then the Wolf's blackness materialized out of a sheer white curtain; the storm was growing only more furious. The Wolf spat an ice-coated length of something out onto the ground, and it rolled in the fluff. Then the Wolf began to lap at a mound of snow. He swallowed none of it—it was as if he were cleaning his mouth of a taste. The Wolf did not seem inclined to revert to a man, so Morigan acted as his voice. "He says there are bodies up ahead. Corpses that have been mostly buried by the weather. He had to dig to find the remains. He took this from the dead."

Scowling, the seer kicked the object her bloodmate had discarded, sending it rolling toward the company. She didn't want to touch it. Some of the snow tumbled off, and the companions saw a frozen L of an arm, snapped and pink at its cleanly broken-off shoulder. The limb looked as if it had once belonged to one who had practiced scarification and burning, for the skin was patterned, mottled, and mostly black, though possibly this was due to the temperature. Even from afar, they could smell its snuffed, wet odor, which curdled next to the Wolf's strong, comforting musk.

Talwyn stated the obvious. "That's an arm."

"Yes, but to whom did it once belong?" asked Thackery.

"A Red Rider," replied Morigan. "Can't you tell? The stain on the skin and those scars were caused by the corruption bleeding from within. I shan't tell you what that stain looks like, what it *feels* like, to my senses."

"All right..." said Thackery, rubbing the seer's shoulders as she trembled. "Are these our would-be hunters? The ones from whom we escaped earlier?"

The bees stung Morigan with a truth. "Yes. All six of them...No...More than six..." Kneeling and ignoring her revulsion, she grabbed the scorched, dead thing. A vision entered her mind.

A dozen riders wander the waste of snow and ice—six red slashes moving toward six dots of red through the endless white. The Red Riders have not abandoned their pursuit, no: they have left to gather more of their swarm. Six have met with six who will meet with six, and so the cycle goes. Mother

Elemech had once compared Zionae's army to Oroborax, the snake that eats itself. Far as he is from his fallen seat of power in the West, the Sun King has built a new horde.

In a ripple of repulsive images, dreams within dreams, Morigan sees Brutus stealing the bodies of Pandemonia's nomads; he initiates them into his army through rituals of fire, agony, and sex. She witnesses chained men drinking a concoction that from its putrid stench she concludes must contain both the essence of Zionae's madness and a squirt of Brutus's seed. Morigan realizes that the mad king must have arrived in Pandemonia long ago to spread his taint and raise his reserve army of Red Riders—a legion hidden and waiting.

"Look, mistress," say her bees, and she returns to this Dream. "Don't blink or you'll miss them: the ghost men."

The ghost men? Of course: the figures to which she's been psychically alerted would never be spotted in the wild. No normal sight would discern the creeping, shrouded hunters in their cloaks of white, cloaks that Morigan knows will adapt to the pattern and hue of any surroundings. The hunters are movements in the snow; they are not men. Despite Morigan's omniscience, and regardless of the many truths she possesses in the Dreaming, she finds herself unable to focus on the ghost men. She cannot strip away their disguises and find their truths. They are slippery, their souls unreadable, as if their cloaks or some other magik ward them from her second sight. She cannot tell if they are friend or foe—at least not until one of the ghost men sweeps like a leaping spider up and out of a white cranny and wraps a Red Rider so tightly in a weighted net that he becomes a spun cocoon. Metal flickers, and the Red Rider's entangled horse has its knees cut. Suddenly, the Red Rider is being gored in a dozen places, and warm, winey spirals decorate the soil. And then the ghost men are everywhere, erupting in plumes of snow, slashing, hacking, and decimating the servants and mounts of Zionae's army.

As Morigan drifts, staring down at the battle, the elegance of the slaughter—so effortless, neat, and quick—impresses her. As soon as all necessary death has been dealt, the ghost men vanish. Morigan loses track of the killers in an instant; their presences and souls are gone.

Gone.

Releasing the dead limb, Morigan explained what she had seen: ten men, maybe less, maybe more, slaughtering two groups of Red Riders before disappearing like ghosts into the storm.

"It was all so...efficient," said Morigan. "I've never seen such killing."

"I have," said Moreth. "From the natives of Pandemonia, the people who decline to congregate in the safety of her Great Cities. I speak of the tribes who wander and live off this land without a great changeling to hunt for them. They are the sturdiest folk in all of Geadhain, I would say—sturdier, even, than the people of the Iron City, for they encounter death with each passing moment. I do not know much about the many tribes of this land, though I would think that if they are hunting the mad king's army, we should consider them allies. The enemy of our enemy..."

Morigan's bees stung a warning. "We need to be cautious. I don't know if that is quite true."

"Do you think they are still here, these hunters?" asked Talwyn.

Morigan reached with her extraordinary senses out into the deepest white. The Wolf, too, leaned and sniffed the bitterness of the storm for the pungencies of men. Neither of their attempts to divine nearby hunters proved successful. Morigan shook her head. "I don't know." Morigan glanced at her bloodmate, and they had a silent conversation while locking gray and silver stares.

"Caenith suggests that we rest here for a time," said Morigan, turning back to the others. "It is a dark night, and the storm goes on and on. This may be the safest haven we shall find. If hunters remain out there, we shall be able to better spot them when visibility returns, perhaps with the morning light." She paused, receiving another look and instruction from the Wolf. "Caenith would like you to keep watch tonight, Moreth. I assume you are up to the task?"

"I am at your service," replied the Menosian.

Already he'd perched himself on an icy hump opposite the others, looking quite comfortable in his fur-lined overcoat and bowler. As no fire could be started in these conditions, the company sought warmth from their pack-master, who lay down and generously allowed the company to snuggle into his furry nooks and muscular pillows. Tonight, the Wolf would have to sleep: he could protect Morigan from the Dreamstalker only if he, too, dreamed. The reluctant Wolf closed his eyes, folded his ears against his skull to muffle the screaming wind, and attuned himself to the breath and beat of his bloodmate.

Moreth will keep us safe, mind-whispered Morigan to her Wolf. *I trust him, and so do you. Back in the desert, the first time you really watched over me while I slept—my breathing, my heart, my soul—I felt you near, watching me like a shadow through the glass of my dreams. Last night, when you joined me in dreaming, I saw you as an intimation, a phantom in the corner of an eye, in many places that I wandered; we were barely a breadth apart. I believe the Dreamstalker sensed your shadow, too, on each occasion, which is why she stayed away. This time, my Wolf, I want to be with you. Together. Let us dream the same dream. I feel all these doorways opening within me, revealing as many wonders as there are silver roads in the sky over Pandemonia. I feel my power swelling like a tide. I believe I can do almost anything now, my Wolf—including taking you into my Dream. Come, we have a Dreamstalker to hunt.*

The Wolf didn't quite understand this desire of his Fawn, though he felt the pull of her need. Tumbling—he was tumbling through darkness, surrounded by a halo of silver that flickered and buzzed.

From his nearby perch, Moreth watched the enormous beast slump, snort, and begin to snore.

VI

Of all the tales of magik and mystery the Wolf knew, there were only a few in which two lovers wandered the same dream. For he and Morigan, though, there was no barrier to such a communion. They needed no magik, only a joint desire to stay together in what lay beyond. Together, the two of them awoke within Dream.

Their subconscious minds had conjured a wood, one not unlike the rich and tangled one where they'd first made love. The faintly shimmering trees and the smoky trails of their bodies told them they were not on Geadhain. Morigan looked radiant in her slightly silver skin. He kissed and ravished her starry body: he wanted to make love. In the Dreaming, Morigan saw the fire of his soul flooding his glass fingers, for he was transparent and shining, too.

"Wait..." she panted. "Remember why we are here, my Wolf. Remember whom we are to hunt."

A hunt, yes. That got the Wolf's blood boiling as much as had his lust. From within, flames burst and consumed him. Morigan stepped aside as he shuddered, stretched, and groaned into the second shape of his soul. A wolf of searing light stood before Morigan. Mounting him, clutching his curling mane of wispy flame, Morigan reined him into a run. Like a wild shooting star, they tore out of the woods and into the gray ether. Morigan felt confident that her power had blossomed, for with the speed of her mount, and with the expansion of her mind, it seemed there was nothing in creation she couldn't find, no secret too precious or hidden.

"We want the Dreamstalker," she declared to her bees.

The Wolf roared in agreement, spraying fire and sparks. Nothing could escape the two of them, united in this hunt of hunts. If they chose, they could soar to the center of the universe, move through dreams and realities as did the Dreamers themselves. In a single leap, the fire wolf bounded through an orchestral chamber glittering with stars and echoing with sonorous hymns. Such queer and mystic beauty. Whose Dream was this? For they knew it was not their own.

Morigan and her living chariot of fire continued their phantasmal gallop through more recognizable fantasies: a rusted playground in Menos, where a young, petulant, dark-haired Mouse played catch with a girl who looked as if she had eyes made of seawater and skin and hair made of sunshine: young Mouse and Adelaide. This must have been one of Mouse's favorite memories, dreamed of often, for it had the clarity of a phantograph.

A gallop through a sudden silver rip in the fabric of this dream took Morigan and her fiery mount into a new scene: Talwyn sitting in a glowingly white room, upon a cube. For a moment, all was silent, but then listening with her sixth senses, Morigan heard it: a low thrum. With that, she began to see the faint filaments and flickering mathematical patterns whirling in the air: these ephemeral, inconstruable formula. Even asleep, the man's mind continued to churn. Talwyn's intellect was a universe unto itself, and Morigan's amazement might have held her there, perhaps forever, watching the extraordinary cosmos of thought surrounding the genius. However, the Wolf was an animal who had no interest in higher disciplines, and he dashed off through the whiteness until Dream's grayness enveloped them.

Leaping through another suddenly opening seam, the bloodmate's perspective shifted, and they filled the head of a man. The man's gaze was turned toward his navel, where a pale woman forged entirely of ice, teeth, and rage licked a trail of blood on his chest. Morigan could see only the hands of their host: bony, elegant fingers she believed belonged to Moreth.

Freeing themselves from Moreth's head, the bloodmates traveled to countless other dreams. They were ghosts alongside Thackery, who hummed as he sailed a one-man vessel on a crystal-blue sea. They saw Adam's secret vision of himself as a gloriously wealthy man of leisure strolling down the streets of a fantastically gleaming city, a dainty-dressed Mouse on his arm (some dreams weren't dead yet, it seemed). Wistfully, Morigan visited pasts as well as futures, appearing in Mifanwae's kitchen, which smelled of buttery, breaded delights, before soaring into dreams of knighthood, sainthood, motherhood, and deviancy.

They were hunting fates madly, frenzied from all the scents suddenly there to chase. Morigan concentrated on getting the beast in her heart and beneath her thighs under control. She repeated the name she knew was right, and conjured the crawling face of her foe.

"Show me the Dreamstalker."

The Wolf's next leap landed them in a smoking desert, with blowing sand as blinding as the snow they'd seen that day. Confidently, the fire wolf stomped over the dunes; he was invulnerable to these angry elements, which should have sheared off flesh by the handful. Indeed, the Wolf possessed no fear of what lay beyond the sandstorm, festering at its heart. As they prowled forward, the bloodmates listened to the song of this desert, a magnificent keening. Then the sandy curtains ahead were wrenched apart, and a yellow moon shed a ghoulish light on the scene. Somewhere amid the crumbled buildings and the leaning, sky-scraping towers—bent over like shattered masts, howling like flutes of horror through their many perforations—their prey would be found. They had discovered the Dreamstalker's lair: Aesorath, the City of Screams.

"Come forth!" demanded Morigan. "You have been hunted and found. Do not cower, servant of Zionae."

Everywhere and nowhere, the wolf of fire and light could smell a sickly stink of sweat, rotten fruit, and scorched roses. The Dreamstalker was here, watching. The fire wolf challenged her with a terrible roar. At last, a shape stepped forward in a flourish of gritty winds. It was a small woman, wrapped in a crawling black cloak, a living mantle; her face was hidden behind a silver skull-casing. Much like the bloodmates, the Dreamstalker was incandescent, but her light was gray. Morigan sensed she was not of the Dreaming or the waking world, but from somewhere in between. The Wolf snarled, wanting to attack and find out just how much of this despicable creature was composed of meat that he could tear apart. Morigan restrained him for the moment. The Dreamstalker, sensitive to her own peril, stopped far away from the glowing seer and her fiery mount.

The cicada music buzzed. "Well done, Daughter of Fate. I did not think you could travel so true, so far in this land warped by magik. Welcome to our kingdom."

At this, Morigan's mind's eye swelled with images of dry dungeons, walls splattered in blood, and chained folk of all ages and sexes being force-fed a vile pink concoction that would transform them into Zionae's slaves. Morigan watched as black-eyed, burned souls worked naked in a shredding desert storm under a sizzling desert sun. It was a deplorable existence; they had been scarred and burned as much by the elements as by dark magik. Morigan shut her mind's eye. She wanted to see no more of this *kingdom*. Morigan urged the fire wolf forward, and he proceeded across the desert, plodding and snapping his teeth.

"Your kingdom is wanton and black as your heart," said Morigan. "You offer us no compelling reason to spare your life."

"As much as you fight, as hard as you struggle," buzzed the Dreamstalker, "you will never win against the Will of my master. She fights for love lost. She fights for a grief that eclipses any and all mortal suffering—including yours."

"Zionae is without love. She has lost her mind."

"No. She is the sane one, the fairest of her kind. She is the one most like those of us with blood, hearts, feelings, and flesh. You will see, Daughter of Fate. You will see the dark games these Dreamers play. The Pale Lady, the Gray Man, Charazance—they care only for the game. Wait until you see their visions of the future. You think you have found your enemy, when you have actually found your salvation. Zionae offers unity. She offers an escape from the pain."

Strange references had been made to the Dreamers, but Morigan dismissed them as more of this creature's deceptions. "Zionae offers slavery and sin. We reject every ounce of her vision."

The Dreamstalker laughed tinnily. "You refuse to see the truth."

"You have shown me nothing but nightmares in which I harm those I love."

"That is what your future holds. You cannot be warrior-mother to the world and not come to know loss. Send out your Will and discover the truth for yourself. Love dies, leaving only pain. Better to revel in that red, glorious truth than to deny it. Better to end your loved ones with your own merciful blade than to leave their deaths to chance. Death, in Zionae's kingdom, is only a bit of pain before true immortality. Zionae will show you the way to eternity."

She's raving mad, thought Morigan. *And we must put her down, as we would any sick animal.*

The Wolf, feeling none of his bloodmate's compassion and overwhelmed by a murderous urge, cleared the twenty yards separating them from the Dreamstalker in a single leap. As his flaming jaws clenched shut, he tasted insect mulch, fabric, and a little blood, which was sweet and tainted with agony and misery. But an instant later, the Dreamstalker vanished in a puff of sand and flies. The bloodmates heard her call from somewhere in the desert; she sounded rattled. "I shall not be ended by you! I am the Herald of the Black Queen, her very voice! Do not think you will find me again so easily!"

Herald? thought the bloodmates. Here, then, was Zionae's very lieutenant: killing her would be a glorious achievement. She should not have revealed her importance; her execution was now inescapable. The Wolf sniffed, savoring the blood in his mouth. As if it were a delicate wine, he rolled it on his palate, trying to identify the traces and source of its flavor.

"I have come before you to accept your surrender," boasted the Herald, "and to end this war. You will not be offered such mercy again!"

"We shall not barter with you," warned Morigan. "You sound scared, and you should be." Because of her intimacy with her bloodmate, Morigan could taste the Herald's fear and blood upon her tongue as well, and she wanted another drink. She looked over at the cloudy sandscape to their left. That was where their prey hid. Feeling her impulse, the Wolf leaped. A dark form faded into view, and he snapped his teeth down into solid, warm matter before it dissipated and buzzed away. From somewhere, the Herald screamed.

"Stay quiet or our hunt shall not be as challenging," taunted Morigan.

Wisely, the Herald said nothing more. The Herald would have fled from this dream, if she could. However, Morigan, peaking in her power, flushed with the sexual anger and rage of her bloodmate, possessed more control of the unseen than she'd ever believed possible. By her Will alone, she denied all exit from this dream, and turned it into a trap. Now Morigan made the threats as she and her fire wolf casually stalked the sands and tracked their bleeding victim.

"You thought you could corrupt me," said Morigan. "You believed you could horrify me, weaken me, bring me down to your pathetic level of depravity. I am stronger than I once was. I am far stronger than you were when Zionae broke you. I am stronger than the mad king. I am stronger than Zionae. My bloodmate and I are stronger than anything this world has ever seen. Your master once warned me that I must never again enter her Dream. I have met her since; I survived her threat. *I* bring the threats and thunder now. I look forward to meeting her again. I shall show the Mother of Creation how angry and destructive a child I can be."

Power shone from the entwined forms of the maiden and her wolf. The winds stilled, the earthbound clouds of dust fell and settled, and all that moved in the desert was revealed—including the Herald, who cowered and stumbled in the sand, holding her arm, bleeding gobs of flies and tarry blood.

"Look at you." Morigan and the Wolf shared a bestial, elemental laugh that sounded like a thunderclap. "Nothing but a weak, pitiful thing. Where is your master now? Where are your grim warnings? Time to end this. I shall let my beloved devour you now. I hope that in his stomach you will at last find peace."

The Wolf roared.

In a last and desperate attempt, the Herald shielded herself, crying out, "Fool! While you judge me and declare my Fate, those you love, those you say you will not lose, are being taken from you! I may be ended, but my truth shall be my vindication!"

Truth? Those that Morigan loved being taken? Even the Wolf paused in his crouch, not quite ready to leap and eat the wretch.

"What lie is this?" demanded Morigan.

"No lie," said the Herald slyly, realizing she may have bought herself a reprieve. "While you've dreamt and hunted, much has happened in the otherworld, deceptions and danger not brought by the hand of my master. I warned you of the Dreamers. I told you that Zionae, brutish and single-minded as she seems, remains the most honest of her kind. Now, you will see and learn that cold lesson for yourselves. Even a speck spent on my murder could cost you a lifetime's regret. Your friends, your pack as you call them, are not safe."

The company was in danger. Morigan took a speck, a precious speck, to listen to her bees. She and the Wolf had traveled far, so far, from their bodies and the mortal world that it now felt more like a dream than this. What she saw of that otherworld was no dream, though, but a confusing nightmare with flashes of silver light and screams: ghost men were swarming two of her friends. For once, the Dreamstalker, this Queen of Lies, had spoken a truth. The Herald's death could wait. Morigan spurred on her fire wolf, and the two galloped off and vanished into a ripple in the sky.

With Morigan gone, the magik that bound the Herald to this vision suddenly ended. She shrieked in rage and then disappeared in a twister of bugs and sand.

VII

The Herald awoke, torn back to awareness by a jolt of pain and fear. Rarely did she experience either, and she lay entangled in her sheets in a cold sweat. The heaving of her breath and the hammering of her heart dazed her. She could not recall the last time she had felt her mortality. Or tasted the bitter liquor of fear in her throat. Or smelled her own fear-rank armpits. Interesting; irritating. That damnable Daughter of Fate and her mongrel lover.

Cursing and groaning from the deep, raw tooth marks and claw marks in her forearm and shin, she rolled from her bed and onto the dusty floor, landing hard and groaning again. After a moment, she stood and stumbled across her wide room, which was lavishly decorated with crimson veils, tiles trimmed in glossed red ceramic, clay statues of men and women engaged in penetration and murder, and sometimes both. During her progress across her chamber, she added much of her own blood to the ruby patterns on the floor. The animal-son of Brutus had grievously harmed her.

At the other end of her chamber hung an oval mirror framed in an orgy of small gargoyles. Since she looked at herself many times each day, she knew what she should see. The maroon punctures, seeping red trails, welts, and one glistening fissure that winked with a hint of bone exerted a pull of fascination she could not resist.

She called to the power that lay within her: the divinity of the Black Queen. Zionae's glory filled the chamber with a dark aura, and veins of black spread over her. Although the Dark Dreamer was the Mother of Creation, her magik was primal and unkind, and the Herald cried out as it twisted her guts and flesh, ripping her matter. Then, in the inferno of pain, the Herald was reborn. The shadow enveloping her pulsed, then faded, and she rose from the floor to which she'd fallen.

In the mirror, she examined the tanned, unbroken skin on her arm and leg. She swept back her tumbling ebon hair and cast admiring stares at herself through catlike eyes while tilting her small chin from side to side. Finally, she did a slow spin to check her voluptuous backside and then her small, brown-nippled breasts. A hundred years and then some, and she looked the same as when Zionae had first spoken to her.

Morigan and her misguided fellows fought the wrong enemy. They knew not the benevolence, honesty, and purity of Zionae's rule. The Dark Dreamer offered many, many gifts, and every one of them came free if a person had the Will, the *right*, to live. The uninformed daughter did not understand that the Dreamer crushed only the Wills and souls of the weak, the ones of no worth. Men and women of the greatest mettle, however, those who could withstand the screaming presence and shattering grief of the Mother of Creation, those who were as fierce and wronged as Zionae herself...those champions were forged into paragons.

Paragons like myself, thought the Herald.

From an age ago, she remembered the voice of the Keeper Superior, chastising her for having taken the briefest of glances into a pool of still water, telling her how immoral it was simply to like oneself. *Child! You vainglorious whore. A Keeper's role is to watch, never to intercede. We are the ear, but not the voice—the wisdom, but not the hand, of justice. Do not cultivate an appreciation for your flesh, for what men would consider beauty. Looking outside too often will damage your ability to look within, much as I shall now damage you with this cane. Pray for your sins.*

"You would have me be nothing." The Herald scowled. "Now, I shall become everything."

Once this bout of mad passion subsided, the Herald realized she argued with the ghost of a woman ages departed from this life. She went to dress herself. Brutus would need to be informed of last night's intrusion, if he hadn't already sensed the disturbance himself. She and Brutus shared many experiences, as each had been touched and chosen by Zionae; however, they rarely spoke in each other's heads for his mind was a whirlwind. She preferred to report to him in person.

She came to a grand cherry-lacquered cabinet carved in hideous motifs—screaming women, horned men with pronged genitalia—and threw it open with a gesture and a burst of Will. Hanging on a peg within were many fashionable garments: ball gowns, frocks of emerald lace, flowing satin shifts. The Herald dallied while deciding what to wear, ultimately selecting a hooded gown so sinfully maroon that it seemed black. It almost resembled one of the bland habits commonly worn by a Keeper, but it had been darted on the bodice, laced like a corset, modified to have princess sleeves and flow at the waist—it was far showier, fit for an appearance at court. She'd embroidered the hood and trim with feliron thread: an enchantment to deflect blades and magik. A shame she couldn't wear such protections in Dream, where her only defenses were illusions and horrifying disguises. Morigan appeared to have figured out her game, the clever girl.

Illusions still served their purpose in this world, however. Hastily, she picked out a pair of amethyst-studded sandals from one of the many rows of ornate, stilted, and strange footwear in her armoire, then strode back to the mirror. She fluttered her fingers over her face in a motion that suddenly puffed her visage with a black cloud like a lady's powder. When the shadow dust had wafted away, her face appeared bronzed, her eye-sockets arced in purple, her cheekbones highlighted, her lips painted in a glossy, winey hue. "Mirror, mirror..." she said, thinking of the ancient faerytale of the West.

This time, though, it was the villain who would enjoy a happy ending: this time, the Daughter of Fate would die.

VIII

The Herald walked along the windy ramparts, her garments flapping in the sand and storm. From over the broken crenellations to her side, from all the way down in the dilapidated jails beneath the city, came a chorus of screams from the newly captured tribesmen—music to her ears. *What grand suffering*, she thought: metamorphosis could not be rewarding without pain; her own transformation had been no less agonizing.

Such an abundance of voices meant good tidings for the army they built here. As more men and women were hollowed out, more Blackeyes were born and sent to harvest bodies. Given the hardiness of Pandemonia's natives, she and Brutus had seen even greater success here than in Central Geadhain: some of those who survived the often fatal transformation retained a shred of individuality, were capable of freethinking, as she and the king were. Thus she and the king had not only fodder now, but also generals and heroes for their cause. Brutus's blood and seed, the essences of an Immortal, possessed mutagenic wonders and properties that she continued to discover to this day—wonders that had allowed Brutus, not a sorcerer by definition or study, to raise enormous golems of flesh and seared ruin to assault Gorgonath. Brutus had reanimated dead matter through a rudimentary rite of bloodmagik, simply opening his veins over a charnel pit of corpses, and then sculpting the sloppy, malleable decomposition into gargantuan worms.

That, at least, was the tale told by the Sun King, and she had no reason to question it. After the blood rite had been performed, he had commanded the monstrosities to move, to rise, and they *had. Amazing*, she thought; his magik seemed more art than discipline. The blood of the Immortals could change the building blocks of life itself; it could transform man into another species. Such an opportunity must not be wasted. The Herald imagined what miracles of meta-engineering could be achieved with the winter secrets embedded in Magnus, and regretted that she had not been present for his brief capture.

The Herald passed a few of the new breed: men shrouded in scarlet cloaks, their eyes aglow with fire, all visible body parts branded in incandescent runes. A diminutive Redeye opened a creaking, half-shattered door for her as she exited the outdoor path. The gesture was not an extension of the mindless automation of most of Zionae's vessels, but a conscious act of courtesy. She sensed the vestiges of the proverbial cocoon still clinging to this pupa, and did not bother him for anything more. In a few days, the Redeye would be able to speak, if necessary, and to engage in the planning for war.

The Herald considered herself a modern, and quite liked that the terms for her soldiers had been imported from the fearful flocks of the West: Blackeyes and Redeyes. Simple and clear in their distinctions. She gave the new Redeye a smile, and he responded with a stiff and ghastly grin before she passed into one of Aesorath's great towers. The whole of the ancient city was made such that, bridge to tower to bridge, it stretched across the land like its own horizon. Reaching back through her ancient mind, she recalled how the city had shone before its fall. She would make it shine again, if with a redder, more ominous light. She remembered the first time she'd witnessed Aesorath's majesty, through the glass of an airborne vessel—another wonder among wonders she and her sister had seen after being taken by the Keepers.

When the Keeper Superior herself, the Holiest of Holies, comes for her, "relieving" her from her simple life of hunting and surviving, she resents her. She feels as if her fate has been ordained for her, that she has been robbed of choice. In the sleepless nights that follow, she misses the songs and joy of her tribe. She misses the simple act of speaking, which she is told she will need to start learning how not to do. For she has inherited the great calm, they say: the ability to hear the world's most ancient and buried secrets—or something like that. She doesn't care. She has never felt special. She has never wanted for any wonders beyond her mother, father, and sister. At least her sister has been taken, too, so they are fellow sufferers. Not to speak or to sing—that is a sentence of eternal misery.

But as she is shaken awake on the skycarriage, she feels her first pang of excitement. Out in the desert rises a shimmering gold line; great spires and glorious twists come off of it like rays from a sun. Can this be a real place? What is she seeing? More of the City of Winds comes into view, more of its auric towers with pointed crystal roofs and lines of windows wrapped like ribbons of glass around great cylinders. The whole horizon shines, and dawn has only just begun. As she watches, dawn creeps behind the shimmering city, and her eyes are dazzled with rainbows and spots. She cannot glance away. She doesn't want even to blink. She holds her sister, also awake now, and their joy grows to hysteria as the wind rises and flows through Aesorath's carefully, artistically crafted channels, archways, and smokeless piped chimneys. The whole city sings for the sisters: high and low flutes, whistles and wordless gasps that are nearly voices. She and her sister are scolded by the Keeper Superior for laughing, then separated from each other.

An unpleasant voice echoes in their heads once the wards have finished giving them a cursory beating: "Do not corrupt yourself with mirth. Do not surrender to even the smallest vice. You are to be ones on high; you must be above mankind. This is only a pilgrimage to the four Great Cities; you will find no enjoyment or permanence here. You may never see the greatness of Aesorath again; you may not survive your training in Intomitath. Remember every whistle, stone, and grain of sand; your memories will be all you have on your journey to the afterlife."

I shall see the city once more, decides the young woman. *I shall make it mine.*

According to what she could remember from before the blackness had clouded her memory, she had fulfilled that vow and ruled Pandemonia's most glorious city. Some of Aesorath's grandeur had survived the fall of the city. Between the larger pillars supporting the dizzyingly tall tower through which she walked shimmered vertical strings as fine as those on a glass fiddle. There had been a time when musicians, talented Faithful, had sat on the age-softened, deteriorated benches near the wall of music and played warming melodies that had made the whole of Aesorath hum. It would become one great hymn, one grand meditation, sometimes lasting for hourglasses, in which the city could share. The space was empty now, filled only by the tapping of her feet and the faint chattering of sand vermin. The vacancy would have disturbed a woman of lesser character, but she found the silence comforting, as if it were a promise waiting to be fulfilled. As she passed through the song tower and out onto another brittle walkway and crumbled parapet, a screaming wind tore at her and banished her wistfulness.

Sandstorms clouded her view of the desert, but she could hear the tapping of fine tools and the dragging of stones as Blackeyes labored in the dark courtyards below. Brick by brick, they were clumsily rebuilding the fallen city. A hum of machinery purred under her feet: in the subterranean depths, her workmen were restoring Aesorath's ultimate achievement, the ancient Gate of Wind. She remembered its ornamented beauty: it had been like a wreath of glowing serpents and mist. She'd ordered that the Gate be restored with newer, darker touches: carved, lamprey-like figures and winged horrors. The last time she had been down to see how far her workmen had progressed, she'd sat upon a gargoyle statue waiting to be worked into the great ovoid frame of the Gate, and lost an hourglass or more to gawking. With this technomagik, and sufficient energy, Brutus would be able to transport himself anywhere in Geadhain. Once the Gate was complete, no realm on Geadhain would be safe from his army.

Although the workforce was made up of brainless automatons, progress had been made in rebuilding the city and its ancient technomagik. The Blackeyes couldn't be blamed for their awkwardness: the weakest of Zionae's children were but remotely operated puppets. It was a miracle that the Blackeyes could handle warfare and complex tasks at all; that they could do so was a credit to her master's Will. The Herald expected that the pace of work would increase in the coming weeks as more and more people were converted and more Redeyes emerged from the chaff. In the months since Brutus's return to Pandemonia, they had raised nearly three thousand men: an alchemically bred army birthed from the perfect elixir of Brutus's blood, seed, and magik (the recipe was another of her masterstrokes of genius)—no raping required, though try telling the king that. The tribes of Pandemonia had forsaken her many lifetimes ago, or so it felt to the Herald; they had left her with nothing, *as* nothing. The Keepers forbade the use of her name: it could not be spoken or recorded in their sanctuaries. *She-who-will-not-be-named.* She had been purposefully forgotten by her people, erased from history. Soon, though, the wretches would remember, would speak her name in horror. *I am no sad story. I am triumph. I am glory.*

The Herald's haven lay a fair walk from the nest of Zionae's son, and while she was Lady of the Winds, a supreme master of the element itself, and could have transported herself to Brutus in an instant, she wasn't above a good stroll. It was good practice to clear her head of wandering thoughts before engaging with the king, who required her absolute attention. So she entered and exited another empty, music-less song tower, then moved from the higher tiers of the city down an ancient stairway built into the battlements. After reaching the ground, she traveled along the outskirts of Aesorath. The winds and howling lessened at this elevation as she bade them to be quieter; the yellow moon's shadow revealed here and there the faint shades of Blackeyes and of the sand pits and shifting dunes that had once been verdant landmarks. Neither tree nor green could survive without the arkstone's magik. When she'd smashed Aesorath's arkstone, she hadn't realized the destruction would be so complete. In a handful of hourglasses, this city, which had stood untouched for thousands of years, had crumbled like a wet sandcastle overwhelmed by a tidal wave. Without the magik of the arkstone, Aesorath's graceful glass towers and courts had no protection from the furious elements long kept at bay. Hiding in the catacombs beneath Aesorath as the city tumbled in upon itself, she'd had no view of the destruction. She felt it was better left to the imagination anyway, as she wandered through dust and sneered at the bones of her enemies ground into small granules under her feet. *I did this,* she thought, relishing the destruction. One woman—only a girl, then—had erased an entire civilization. And she had done more than that, even: she had heeded the voice of the Dark Dreamer and recruited Brutus to the cause.

After a long battle with the elements, the Herald returned indoors by way of an arch that appeared in the sandy haze. A deep, warm hallway tunneled through strides of stone and led her into a long hall lit with braziers and laid with a torn runner that gleamed with hints of gold thread. Other signs of opulence lay all about: dust-filled goblets, a huge, cracked globe of Geadhain drowning in a small dune, and metallic bookcases with grimy crystal shelves. Some of the real treasure of this realm had once been displayed upon these shelves, lore now scattered and lost along with a million ancient candles in heaps of sand. Directly across from the Herald as she entered stood a tarnished copper-and-feliron portcullis that could have withstood a blast or two from Magnus himself. The vault was opened now, its treasures no longer sealed or safe. She'd read much of that forbidden knowledge, here, or in many of Aesorath's cloisters of contemplation; cavalierly absorbing the wisdom of these tomes and scrolls while dribbling crumbs or wine over the holiest of papyrus. The Faithful were denied most worldly pleasures, and she was now free of their rules and shame. As the Herald thought back to her lessons with the Keeper Superior, back to when this vault of sacred wisdom had glittered and shone with vainglorious wealth, she felt the same contempt now as she had then for the Keepers' convenient bending of morality.

For a moment, she stood ruminating while she fluffed, shook, and stomped the grit from her clothing. The Herald always hesitated before entering this hall, not because she was afraid of walking into the warm darkness ahead, but because of a memory she could not clearly recall. Mother Zionae had taken that memory from her, mercifully removing it from her mind. The Herald could remember much of her life and mistreatment. She could remember as far back as the blurry days when Zionae had first whispered to her. She could remember entering into a pact with the Dark Dreamer...she had spoken the words, the vow, to let Zionae in, to free herself from an inconsolable, immeasurable pain...That agony, though, was now a cipher to the Herald. Any trace of the incident had been excised from the soft matter in her skull. Surely, that memory must have been one of horror itself, an event so wretched, so miserable, that the Dark Dreamer herself had been stirred from slumber and moved to mercy.

Whatever it was that had happened, she never wanted to remember it. So she stood there, shaking, fighting tears, clutching and caressing her belly for an unexplainable reason, as traces of this unfathomable terror crawled over her flesh.

"Herald!"

Brutus's roaring summons came from the deep darkness of the hall; he must have heard or sniffed her presence. Blending in like a chameleon with the bloody shadows, a Redeye in his black-and-red garments lurked nearby; she hadn't noticed him before. The gaunt, burned-smelling fellow strode forward to take her arm and lead her into the inner sanctum. The Herald left her dark past in the dust where she'd been standing, and strode with confidence to meet the Sun King. The future was meant for those of strength, not sorrow.

Suckling noises could be heard, and the sweaty, bestial reek of the Sun King intensified in the air as she approached. The bloodbath around her was mostly concealed by the dark. Brutus had been either angry or lustful, perhaps both, and the carpet that lay before him was thick with footprints, scattered tomes, and the red, sandy porridge of offal and death. Those who had avoided the full consequences of Brutus's appetite cringed in the shadows, mewling and bleeding. A few rattled their chains and mumbled prayers; the Herald hoped they would stop, as pleading tended only to enrage the Sun King, and if they kept it up, they would not live to receive the Dark Dreamer's gift of rebirth. Getting close now, she stepped around a headless, steaming carcass torn in twain from shoulder to hip, and held her nose against the stink of shite and piss.

The Redeye left her to meet the king on her own. She walked ahead, stirred by the carnage, pondering. The Dark Dreamer's gift brought out the deepest, most untamed desires of one's heart. Zionae mined from the soul pleasures and urges, both pure and depraved, men had not even realized they possessed. Zionae bequeathed to her chosen their truest desire. The Herald thought Brutus's must have been to live free of mortal grief and regret, to become a beast unchained. And the Sun King had certainly that wildness.

As for the Herald herself, she'd wanted to forget her darkest pain and to have power over those who had wronged her. She also wanted to live in luxury and elegance, which is where she and Brutus differed. Still, there was room for all desires under the Dark Dreamer's reign. Brutus would have his kingdom of animal pleasures and endless hunts—elsewhere, back in Central Geadhain, she presumed. The Herald, for her part, would realize her designs for the resurrection of Aesorath, making it a queendom of cold rule and refinement.

Now that Brutus had returned to Pandemonia, they were forced somewhat to impose their desires upon each other. Neither the acolyte nor the son had struggled with the arrangement so far. Holding on to the knowledge of their mutual esteem and the temporary nature of the arrangement made it easier for the Herald to squelch her way through the soupy slop of blood that surrounded the Sun King's throne. She approached the king as close as she was able, her footwear and toes becoming slicked with blood. Then she bowed to the giant shape before her.

Flames danced in the many braziers placed around and behind what had once been the throne and dais of a Keeper, their light revealing the great shadow that sat on the blocky, hewn throne—a shadow that seemed itself to be made of crude rock. Brutus could always be smelled if not seen: his buttery, lusty funk might have come from a herd of animals. His fiery warmth made the Herald break into a sweat whenever she was near him.

On the wall behind the king was carved a mural that depicted the earliest tribes of Pandemonia scattering from a flaming cataclysm hurled from above: the Day of Skyfall. A scene that had once impressed the Herald with its grandeur, it now seemed childish next to the dark presence of his highness. After bowing, she rose. Brutus came forward to greet her.

A nude, hairy leg, twisted with muscle, thick as a tree, emerged first from the shadows. After a moment, the remainder of the gargantuan king was exposed by the warm light of the chamber. Brutus was always a shock to one's sight, with his chest as broad and veined as two marble slabs, skin sheened in bronze, hands each of which could crush a ribcage. Upon his chest grew a pelt of the blackest fur, like the proud tufting of a lion, while on his handsome head were curls like those of a king of beast's mane. What handsomeness the king still possessed was dwarfed by the elemental rage contained behind his tense, snarling facade; his eyes were like spheres of trapped lightning, ready to storm; his jaw could snap bone as easily as bread. A blood-stained sash and kilt made of copper scale covered little of his great glittering flesh. In spite of his grisly traits and odors, the Herald still found the Sun King impressive and alluring: for he was man, sex, power, and death—everything carnal in the world contained in one being.

Once, the Herald had whispered the bitterest truths into his ear. Like a mother bird regurgitating food to her young, she'd nourished him with the secrets of Zionae that had once been fed to her. She and Brutus, therefore, shared an intimacy that transcended respect. He knew this, and now ceased his bellowing and adopted a more temperate demeanor. He stopped, towering over the tiny woman, and spoke. "Herald, I smell worry upon you."

"You smell anger, too."

"I do. Why?"

"I was attacked in the Dreaming, nearly killed in an ambush."

Brutus unleashed a torrent of abuse, examining her with his great hands, his sniffs, and his thunderous stares. She held still for a time, then finally waved him off.

"I have mended what wounds were caused. Your son's teeth are sharp."

"My...son..."

He spoke dreamily, as if he did not fully understand the concept of offspring and parenting. As she did every time his child was mentioned, she suspected that part of the memory Brutus sought had been eaten, for his sake, by the Dark Dreamer. There was also a chance that Brutus had evolved so far into his bestial nature that he no longer understood attachments of heredity. It was as if he had become the lion that mated and left his cubs to the care of his pride. She felt she should remind him a little of this attachment, as it related to what she would suggest next. "Yes, your son," she said. "A child of great power, great promise. A creature of two natures: man and beast. A creature much like yourself."

"No creature shares my throne. I sit alone," declared Brutus, with a growl.

"I do not mean to imply that he is greater than you, only that he is great."

"Strong?"

"The strongest I have seen, other than you."

"Savage?"

"His bloodlust is art in motion."

"Hmph."

Undecided, Brutus paced around in a circle. Hunger often clouded the king's mind, and clarity would come only with satiety. He called for a Redeye to bring one of the praying natives to him. A man was dragged into the light. Brutus snapped the scream from the scrawny man's neck, twisted off his pulpy head, and squeezed the essence from him as if he were a sausage. The Herald looked away and busied herself with a study of the mural. She tuned out the king's gurgles and slurps. She didn't have to wait terribly long until a freshly crimson king stormed over to her, again ready to talk. She took note of how he clenched and unclenched his hands, still yearning to squeeze something, and prepared her most delicate words.

"Why can I not remember him?" demanded the king. "This son of whom you speak? I should remember a child born of my greatness."

"I cannot say. Mother Zionae has also taken memories from me, to make me strong."

"Why do you mention him now?"

With a finger, she beckoned the king nearer. He obeyed her and knelt. She crept around his grand shoulder, brushed back his oiled mane, and whispered poison in his ear. "I have mentioned him before, my king, only you forget. We forget what *we* have asked Zionae to help us forget. You would not want memories of him anyhow, shameful and bound like a dog as he is to the Daughter of Fate."

The king stood up, snarling. Time and again, Mother and the Herald had warned him of this woman, Morigan, a creature as willful and spiteful as his brother. The Daughter of Fate had dedicated herself to unraveling each and every thread of Mother's great tapestry. This woman had nurtured alliances and thwarted the greatest of Zionae's feints—often unwittingly, as if her very existence affected destiny. Now, Morigan had claimed his son. Whatever a son was, Morigan's taking of it felt like another slight to his pride.

"I feel your anger," said the Herald, trembling, aroused by the rage of the Immortal. Sinuous as a snake, she slithered around the huffing giant. She coaxed his madness with sensual touches to his lower back, stomach, and the inside of his thigh. "As you know, the Daughter of Fate is here in Pandemonia. She has exposed herself. Never have our paths aligned so perfectly; we now have an opportunity to strike. Zionae wanted me to offer the Daughter of Fate salvation, and I have done my best to carry out this duty. However, Morigan is too stubborn, a woman without ears. She will not hear me. Like your brother, she allows fear to deafen her to greatness. I do not know whether either of them can be saved. We are left, then, with only one choice, should Zionae permit us to make it..."

Pausing, the Herald listened with the whole of her heart for an answer. In the windless, stale chamber, the flames of the braziers suddenly flickered, the shadows churned and thickened, cringing men still sane cried out as a warm sickness passed through them, and the Dark Dreamer whispered to her Herald. The whisper was strong tonight, a hammer in the Herald's head that stunned her with lights and sounds.

Into the deepest dark, a velvet stream of stars and space, she spins. Where have you taken me? she wonders. What do you want me to see? The Herald stops spinning and hovers. A wide plane of darkness, like the mirror into which she often stares, floats before her. A terrible crackle fills her head, like thunder and lightning and broken glass shaken in a bag beside her ears—the voice of her master. As she watches, the shadows painting the mirror of darkness are ripped apart, like gift paper torn by claws, revealing scenes beneath. She must look quickly if she would see them: the Dark Dreamer is not a prophet, and these possible futures will not be clear.

A woman of ivory and fire—Morigan—walks toward a shining dot on the land. The image is rent asunder, and the Herald hears what could be the howl of a wolf before the sounds of thunder and broken glass deafen her once more. From under the torn image emerges a view from within the city Morigan approaches: someone looks upward, awed by the silver towers that reach into the storm clouds. This is Eatoth. The Herald knows the city from the memories Zionae has allowed her to keep. What must I see in Eatoth, master? What? she wonders, as the mirror-pane trembles and readies to break. The glass into which she gazes shatters. Fragments fly toward the Herald, and she is thrown from Dream. One spinning triangle of black glass thrusts into her eye. In the dazzling pain of blindness, the Herald somehow sees a blue glimmer, a light so pure it can only be the shine of one of the greatest of wonderstones: an arkstone.

Brutus watched the Herald. Tonight, Zionae did not speak to him; in fact, Mother had communicated with him little of late. Nonetheless, he felt Mother's presence surrounding them in the chamber. A less animal mind would have questioned the Dark Dreamer's confiding in the Herald so much. Instead, impatient and twitching, the king waited for the Herald to awake.

Soon the Herald snapped into alertness, returning from where she'd been; her nose had been bleeding, and she dabbed at it while talking. "Yes. It has been ordained. She has spoken. I know what must be done. I have watched Zionae's grand designs unfold in a vision. We have a great many tasks ahead of us, my king. First, we must find another arkstone to counter any future threat from your brother. The army we are building here will not be enough; we may need to summon the sleeping Father of Fire again. Of paramount importance is that we stop the Daughter of Fate from reaching the Scar. Our riders lost her in the West, but I know where she intends to go: Eatoth. There, we shall end the Daughter of Fate and reclaim your son. We shall anoint him with the blood of his bloodmate and forever swear him to our cause. Think of that glory, my king, of storming the City of Waterfalls and making its waters run red."

Brutus was disappointed there would be no immediate action or violence. To soothe the frowning and grumbling beast, the Herald gave the king a sly smile and another caress on the fur trail on his abdomen. "You should be happy, my king. Your son is coming home."

Brutus felt neither happy nor sad. In a few sands, after the Herald's hand had descended lower, he forgot everything about this son.

VI

AFTER THE FALL

I

The world as Aadore and Sean had known it was gone. Menos, the eternal city of iron, had fallen. They lived in the aftermath of that apocalypse. The city was filled now with shattered and smoke-shrouded mounds, the muffled red auras of buildings still writhing in fire, and the groaning, sloppy tumble of those iron-boned structures that had withstood the earth's heaving, splitting, and swallowing. What would this place look like once the smoke faded? It would be yet another nightmare. But they couldn't think of that now: they had to think of life.

With the ruins of Queen's Station at their backs, and only smoke and doom ahead, Sean needed to decide where to go. He picked a direction and strode forward. Sean's leadership was unwavering even when they were out in the wrecked city and wandering amid billows of ashy smog. A soldier, Sean performed at his best during crises. The loud drowning grumble of the city's slow decay surrounded them, making it feel as if they walked through a thunderhead; the noise was calming and dreadful all at once. In the smoking horror of their city, amid the smoldering pyres, the charred statues that could be men, the burst pipes spraying filthy water and shite, they could not tell night from day. They knew not whether they were sane or insane. It was easier to feel hollow, they decided, though there was really no other option. Only the hollow could have avoided leaping at the sound of that first mortal cry and rushing toward its source. Neither they nor the babe they'd rescued earlier from the collapse of Queen's Station had cried out in response. Instead, they'd waited, Aadore rocking the baby. The adults almost smiled at their canniness when the screaming intensified beyond a summons, suddenly carrying notes of raw terror. After that, an abrupt silence had fallen. Whoever had screamed was dead. Brother, sister, and somehow even infant knew what to expect now, and they moved more cautiously through the fog of death, ignoring all further screams. They steered away from any contact, lest they met whatever hunted unseen.

Brother and sister stuck to the shells of buildings and carefully tiptoed through the warm soot that remained in the carcasses of ruined houses. They waded through sewage-filled alleys. They walked along great rubble-banked splits in the city that had eaten homes and streets. Throughout their explorations, the infant remained still, content to suck a finger when one was offered. Occasionally, the child coughed because of the bitter, barely breathable air. At some point, brother and sister had wordlessly decided that this child was, and forever would be, a part of their family. They reaffirmed this through glances whenever they peered at each other's filth-stained faces in the mist. During their prowl, they spoke mostly through such gazes and expressions. They nodded at holes in which to scurry, narrowed their eyes and shook their heads to indicate a need for caution when shapes shuffled nearby in the murk. These shapes did not suggest living men, and neither sibling wished to probe the heart of that mystery; they sensed it would be revealed soon enough.

Whenever the fog of death cleared for a speck, Aadore would look for signs—not actual signposts, although a few of those still stood, but for indications of where they were headed. At one point, they raced across a broad stretch of warm road that ran with blackish-red oils. The oils were slippery, and she almost fell. Yet Sean, even with his wooden leg and hobble, caught his sister. Aadore reserved her thanks, for there were shapes moving in the streets, and silence was the language of survival. As they hurried for the cover of an alleyway, she saw a ruined storefront with a broken sign: the filthy loaves and trampled tarts littering the ground told her it had once been a bakery. RAMUS, read the half of the sign she could see as she and her brother cowered behind a heap of roofing and wood. She guessed the shop was likely Ramusen's, one of her favorite patisseries. If that were the case, they were on the right path and making toward home. A combination of Sean's keen senses and instincts and her wit might just lead them there, she realized. Suddenly, she felt grateful that the Lady El had sent her on so many shopping expeditions throughout the city. Because of them, she carried a map in her mind, though she'd need to be on alert for clues in this chaos. There would be no carriages to expedite the journey this time; reaching her neighborhood might take a day or even longer—

Dead, she thought, her throat dry as bone, all her plotting at a halt. *They're dead.*

Shadows shambled past their hideaway. Like iron children, she and her brother remained motionless, managing somehow not to gag as they were assailed by the bouquet of raw flesh that followed in the wake of the horde. They tried to master their revulsion when they glimpsed bowlegged humanoids with burst ribcages spilling swollen entrails, eyeballs swinging on corded stalks from their sockets, bones jutting through torn green skin—or heard snarls from chewed-up faces. As she clung to her brother and shielded the babe, Aadore could feel only her own trembling. She wondered what, in his time away, Sean had seen that could keep him calm when confronted with the walking dead. Regardless, now brother and sister knew what hunted in the fog.

Before they set out once more, Aadore tore off part of her skirt to fashion a beggar's satchel, which she stuffed with bread, befouled tarts, and anything else that looked even slightly edible. Sean shushed her and then motioned with his cane toward the alley; he'd heard something else. They ran. On and on the day-night went, as they slunk like city coyotes toward Aadore's home, hopeful that, if nothing else, a payload of canned foodstuffs and various emergency supplies awaited them there. Aadore refused to consider that her reinforced locks might have been broken or her home sacked. She needed a glimmer of hope in this black night. Night indeed came, bringing a miasma darker and deeper. Soon, she and

Sean moved as if through a sandstorm, every step uncertain, hands acting where eyes could not. The wandering packs of damned wailed in celebration of the dark. This was their hourglass—the time of the dead. The living would have to find shelter, brother and sister realized.

After stumbling through a haunted square, splashing through lakes of filth, and picking their way quickly around toppled carriages, past stands reduced to incomprehensible trash, and over bodies too eaten to be turned into unliving vessels, the siblings entered the shadows of an enclosed arcade. Aadore was confident she recognized the square through which they ran; she believed it had been the site of a market where she had once bought fresh produce—a place not very far from District Twenty-Two. If her memory served her well, they would find laneways branching off the wall she could barely see to her right, exits that led to properties of moderate wealth. In order to get past these private gates without being electrocuted, a person would need to possess the feliron key of a city servant—or of a highly placed handmaiden to an Iron Sage's wife, one who was often sent on shopping errands for her mistress. Aadore praised the perks of her indentureship and checked her tatters for her keys. Their jangle both alarmed and excited her.

She was towing Sean along now as he seemed to be faltering. He looked terrible, white enough to stand out in the dark, and she felt him shivering. They reached a quaint iron gate set in a tall brick wall. Quickly, she unlocked the barrier with a square key and a spark of magik. Once they passed through it, she closed the gate, which squealed a rusty summons to the monsters in the mist. *Did they hear?* she wondered. She wasn't sure how these monsters even hunted; they were missing eyes, ears, the organs necessary for perception. Perhaps some other supernatural power gave them awareness. At least the fog of death and the bunkers of refuse had granted the three inconspicuousness thus far.

"Aadore!" hissed Sean.

As they'd said little to nothing for hourglasses upon hourglasses, his croaking voice startled her. Bloody Kings! She'd been standing still and dumb as a mule. Aadore remembered to move, and fast. She hurried into the clouded courtyard and squinted, hoping to squeeze shapes from the murk. A cobbled road made for foot traffic wound off into the gray nimbus ahead. The neighborhood throbbed with silence, and the air felt stale and thick in Aadore's lungs. Her cheeks were icy cold, and the infant she held shifted and snuggled into her warm breasts. At least the stink of the dead, which had begun to creep through Menos, seemed lighter here; Aadore hoped this community had somehow survived what had happened elsewhere in Menos. Then she and Sean noticed glittering trails of broken glass and dark smears upon the road. They followed one sparkling trail through a gap in a wrought-iron fence with bars ripped apart like straw, and over a trampled flowerbed before coming to the whistling window frame of a grand dark house.

Sean examined the damaged casement. Scraps of flesh and blood hung off teeth of glass—its inhabitants must have been dragged either from or into the manor. There might be no one left here to fear what the day would bring—Death had already paid a visit. While likely futile, Sean listened for any signs that a breathing creature remained inside the manor.

After years of being drugged, strapped to a table, prodded with needles, submerged in ice-baths, and subjected to a psychopath's litany of further torments, Sean's senses were extraordinarily developed. When he'd gone blind from pain the first time, he'd passed out. When he'd gone blind from pain a hundred times, though, his body had adapted, and his mind had liberated itself from his flesh. He'd learned to seek distraction in the many noises, scents, and curiosities of the laboratory. Soon, he'd been able to see past the spots that blinded him and stare into the masked faces of the fleshcrafters and physicians leaning over him, including the smug, piggish face of that monster, Dr. Hex. "Is he conscious?" the master torturer would ask as Sean's fishy eyes flicked open, and he stared into the doctor's unmasked face—conscious indeed, though neither Hex nor his comrades really believed he could be. During his horror, Sean had learned how to see, hear, and smell incredibly well, transcending the normal sensory limits of man. He was no longer a man, though, not really. He did not feel pain as men did. It was likely that he could not feel pleasure, either. These days, he used the organ between his legs only to piss.

As Sean could hear only a small huffing that might be a draft, he threw his cane over the windowsill, and then lifted himself up and over the frame in a movement surprisingly graceful for a scrawny one-legged man. Aadore noticed a bit of his sinister nature then, and reflected he was like a mink in a man's skin: lean, clever, and vicious. Sean reached down, took the infant from Aadore, and then managed to offer her his cane to use for the climb. Aadore clambered through the bay window without harming herself. She thanked her brother with a nod and reclaimed the infant. She wanted to say so much more to him, wanted to express her need and love for him, commend him for his bravery. Were the world calm, and had she the time and materials, she would have written him a poem—one of her silly, stupid attempts at rhyming, like the ones she used to compose for him when they were young...

Just then, cries from unliving throats ripped apart the silence. The dead were nearby; she and her brother had to hide.

Inside the manor, the air held less weight and smoke, and the siblings could better see where they were going. The window through which they'd crawled had once been the centerpiece of a grand living room filled with chairs piled high with velvet cushions, walls adorned with silver damask patterns, and polished teak tables cluttered with cards, board games, and ashtrays. Leisure and laughter had been welcome in this room. Sean could smell the sweet smoke of old witchroot over the stink of the fog of death.

Sean counted two exits from the room. Through the one on the right, he could see a stone slab and glimmers of kitchenware. He ignored it; they would raid the kitchen later if they had the opportunity. Instead, he motioned to his sister and turned left, entering a regal hallway flanked by a stairway going up. He considered going to the end of the hall, but a small oval table gave him pause: once used to display portraits, it had been tipped onto its side, blocking his path. Around it were scattered crimson phantographs, images drowning in a pool of blood. Pausing and listening in his disconnected way, he thought he could hear things—clawed, hungry things—shambling toward them. Sean couldn't say how close the noises were, but he could not afford to take any chances. The dead he'd seen roved in packs like wolves. He and Aadore would need to find a rabbit hole in which to hide until those animals passed.

Sean shoved Aadore up the stairs and quickly followed her. Although he tried to move stealthily, Sean soon found himself dragging his limb. The stump of his leg felt swollen and raw against his prosthesis. Every step was like a knife driven up his femur and into his groin. The pain was endurable; he wished only that his stupid wheezing body would just shut up and obey him. Sean nearly fell at the landing and cursed his flesh. Aadore hauled him up by an elbow, and they stumbled down a barren hallway.

Signs of a great struggle were visible through open doorways, and many of the doors themselves had been splintered by some terrible force. The beautiful damask wallpaper had been splashed with sprays of red. A quick peek into each room they passed revealed no survivors. They saw a collage of horror: messy bedsheets, discarded slippers, shattered lanterns, a teddy bear gummed in blood, a hand clinging to the foot of a bed—as if someone had been dragged from beneath it—and an amputated leg, which lay on the hallway carpet. That last sight made Sean's stump twitch with phantom pains. What the siblings couldn't find anywhere was a viable hiding place.

Suddenly, they heard a warbling from the street below. It was the unmistakable call of the unliving. There must be a horde right outside the manor.

*C*REEEEAK*!*

Dust sprinkled from the ceiling at the end of the hallway. The siblings froze, hearts slamming against their chests. Heavy footsteps and several thuds shook the roof, followed by a painful quiet. Aadore clenched every muscle and screamed inside her head. Sean pointed down the hallway toward a door that stood at the hall's end. The pair stepped around the severed leg and approached the door. Sean motioned for his sister to halt, pressed an ear to the cold wood, and listened. Once more, he heard a drafty sound...an intake and outtake of air...Not a draft at all, he realized, but labored breathing from a real and living person. Sean wasn't certain whether to be excited or terrified. "I think there's someone alive in there," he whispered.

He settled for caution as he tested the handle of the door, which turned. When he tried to open the door, though, he was met with immediate resistance. A great weight stacked against the door prevented him from entering. Still, he was a child of Menos and a man of war, and he would not give up without breaking himself first—which was exactly what

Aadore sensed and worried he would do, as he put aside his cane, drove a bony shoulder against the door, then huffed, strained, and showed the wood just who was the most stubborn.

Aadore was amazed at how much strength he possessed for such a slight man. In a moment, she felt like clapping as the door buckled and relented, and cumbersome furniture fell away with a thudding crash. Sean was able to open the door no more than a pace or two: it seemed that whatever jumble lay in the room beyond would not permit more than that.

Aadore, thinking of getting the child to safety, pushed past her brother, and announced herself to whoever might be inside the room. Then she waved her hand through the space before she tested its safety with her body. While she encountered some nails and wood, it was nothing that could seriously injure her. What Aadore didn't realize was that her declaration and little exercise in arm-waving had saved her from a brutal death by the giant blood-soaked man who waited in the shadows of the chamber beyond. Shivering with bloodlust, he hunkered by the remains of a bed frame that he'd hacked up earlier for parts. When the man heard an actual *living* voice, and saw the flailing arm, one that did not resemble that of a rotted being, he relaxed his guard, repressing the impulse to throw the hatchet he held. He then watched as a woman carrying something wrapped in rags shimmied through the opening.

Aadore glared about the room, alert for danger. The lavish chamber had probably belonged to the keeper of this estate. It had tall ceilings, extinguished chandeliers, and thick plaster mouldings, though all its richness showed signs of destruction. Every piece of furniture aside from the wooden skeleton of the bed had been piled together, forming a heap of bedposts, boards, cabinets, and broken chairs that had then been pushed up against the door. The curtains had been torn down, their rods and fabric bundled into the mess. In place of curtains, the bed's mattress rested against the windows of the chamber, and very little light illuminated the room. *Muggy*, thought Aadore, for this place was warm with sweat. She could not place the smell—a fresh, farmy odor—that congested the chamber. Nor did Aadore spot the man who watched her. The man blinked and gaped as he scanned her features. Could it be?

Sean slipped into the room. At once, his sharp eyes spotted the lurker—a man squatted in the farthest shadows, heavy and strong. Sean placed himself in front of Aadore and held his cane as if it were a sword. "You're not dead, and neither are we," he said. "We mean you no harm. Step forth and declare yourself."

The shadow moved, expanding to great dimensions, nearly scraping the ceiling with its head. Sean worried he'd awoken a giant or ogre, and mythic blood might indeed run through the body of the man who now moved into the meager light of the black room. Shirtless, hairy, tattooed in markings of blood, and wearing only ill-fitting gentlemen's pants and boots, he certainly looked like a monster. On the man's rock-shaped cranium ran scars in zipper patterns. His twisted lips and oft-broken nose told a tale of endless brawling. He smelled as if he were wrestler and butcher in one. The cleaver the man carried—a full-sized ax, in fact—looked small in his hand and spoke of no kind intent.

"Skar?" said Aadore.

"I'll be fuked...Aadore," replied the mercenary. He looked Sean up and down. "And you, lad, must be her brother. I can see the Ironguard in you. Nothing save for a soldier's will would have kept you alive out there."

"You know each other?" asked Sean.

Aadore nodded. "Yes—in a fashion. Why...how is it that you are here?"

Skar put down his ax and moved past the siblings. "Never mind that for now. We need to get the door blocked again, then stay quiet for a while until the dead leave. I can hear them out there. They're close."

"Yes," agreed Sean.

Wasting no time, the soldier and the ogre pushed the largest piece of the barricade, a solid oak drawer, back into place. A true Menosian woman, Aadore was both mother and worker: she rocked the incredibly serene babe while gathering the smaller bits of furniture with her free arm. Between the three of them, they rebuilt the jigsaw jumble quickly and with tactical precision. Aadore had no idea if the structure would hold, but Skar tested the blockade with a shake and then grunted his endorsement.

A window shattered in the rooms below. Like a herd in the wild, the three held for a moment, waiting. They soon heard the slithering, flopping, and groaning of dead horrors dragging themselves through glass, over carpets, and up the stairs. Skar picked up his ax and gestured to the rear of the chamber before heading there himself. At the back and right of the chamber were two doorways. The first led to a lavatory that glinted with hints of chrome. The second opened into a large square closet. Skar vanished into the closet. A moment later, the siblings discovered it contained a ladder that rose to a hatch in the ceiling. Blindly and awkwardly, they followed Skar up—one of them one-legged, the other using a clawed arm so as not to drop the baby. Aadore had to fight to keep herself from slipping on whatever wetness was on the rungs. It was a relief when Skar's long arms suddenly appeared and hoisted her up. Skar helped Sean into the attic as well, then pulled the ladder up without so much as scraping it and closed the trapdoor.

In the attic, a hint of light stole through drawn curtains powdered in dust. Cobwebs and memories hidden in boxes filled the wide space, along with draped portraits, chests Aadore imagined filled with valuable heirlooms and keepsakes, and ladies' racks and dresses. In this space, sounds were muffled. Even with their especially keen hearing, Skar and Sean couldn't make out what was happening in the house below. They had escaped death for the moment. The horde would have to break down a barricade and then somehow climb into the attic in order to harm them. Aadore didn't think the creatures were that clever, not from what she and her brother had seen. *We're safe*, she thought, and her body sighed from head to toe. Aadore kissed the infant on his sweaty scalp. What a good boy; what an unusual boy to have been quiet through all this terror.

While the men stationed themselves around the hatch, Aadore looked for a spot to feed and tend to the child. She decided upon a square pirate's chest covered in a sheet, which she removed, fluffed, and shredded to fashion a new diaper. Although the Lord and Lady El had never had children for her to care for, as an older sister, she had much experience changing a baby's bottom. The baby grumpily pawed at her as she changed him. There was hardly any shite, though the rags were so filthy and the place so dark, it was difficult to tell. Aadore unslung the beggar's pack tied under her armpit; the knot had left an aching mark. For the little man, she made an inadequate paste out of a crushed jam-filled pastry and some water from a silver thermos, which she'd filled at one of the few broken water pipes that hadn't been spewing filth. She had no utensils, and had to feed the baby using her fingers. He suckled more than he ate, but got at least some food inside him. She gave him a few dribbles of water, too. *He really should have milk*, she worried. Aadore finished off what remained of her concoction, which tasted like a mashed strawberry tart and actually wasn't half bad. She packed up, burped the child, and then prepared to head over and offer the shadows near the hatch a loaf of bread. Footprints suddenly noticed in the dust distracted her: glistening footprints, impressions from large wet feet, like Skar's. Wondering where the footprints might lead, Aadore followed them around a labyrinth of tall draped mannequins till she arrived in a different area.

Blood. Blood everywhere. She tried not to step in any of it, and turned the baby's face toward her breast although he would not understand, even if he could see it. The mad artist from the hallways downstairs could have learned a thing or two from this macabre master, who had used buckets of gore, strands of viscera, and a flayed confetti of skin to decorate his canvas: the floor, sheets, and concealed furniture of this small space. A small person had been butchered here, possibly a child from the size of the carcass, and quite recently, she gathered, from the reek of the freshly opened body cavity that lay before her. It smelled of earth, shite, raw meat, and cooking oil. She'd smelled it even when they were a floor below, though she hadn't been able to identify it then. The scene was brutal: head and limbs had all been separated from one another; why, she did not know. It looked as if the murderer had wanted to purge this person from existence, entirely.

Aadore took the carnage in stride; there had already been so many atrocities. Only the smell was really making her ill—the same smell that lingered on Skar, whom she was sure had committed this violence. On her way back to the others, Aadore used the shadows to hide her search for a weapon with which to defend herself. She was lucky, luckier than the mutilated victim she'd found, and discovered an old Menosian military blade that had been leaning up against a pile of bland landscapes. The guard of the weapon, an entwinement of silver snakes around an iron hilt, was what caught Aadore's attention. Cooing to the baby, she paused and slid the blade from its sheath inch by inch. She needed to hurry, though, in case her absence was noticed, in case Sean was in danger. Once unsheathed, the weapon gave her a gleam by which to see and the courage to move faster in the dark. She retraced Skar's steps and crept past the chest she'd seen earlier. Two shapes appeared ahead: her brother and Skar engaged in a whispered conversation. Aadore slipped between them and tapped the ogre's side with the flat of her blade. Aadore's arm, shoulder, and back ached from holding the infant, her body felt ready to shatter, and she'd been chased by the dead after watching her city fall to chaos and evil. Still, she looked as fierce as a sword-maiden to the two surprised men.

"I found a dead body," she said. "Sean and I heard a thumping and scuffling not long ago. I know it was you. Do you have an explanation for what you've done?"

Sean reached out and tilted his sister's blade away. "I know. Skar and I have been chatting. He had to do it. He had no choice."

Aadore stepped back from the men, keeping her sword at the ready. "You haven't seen what he did, Sean. But go on, you brute. Go ahead and explain why you dismembered that..." She couldn't remember the sex of the victim: all she recalled was red, torn meat, and that the body had seemed small. She decided upon "child."

Aadore was entirely unprepared for what happened next: the ogre shook his head, drew up his knees, put his face into his hands, and trembled either because he was crying or because he was trying not to weep. Skar began to mumble. "You're right...I killed her. A little girl. I'm horrible. A monster. I was paid to protect them—the family. But it was impossible. When the streets began to fill, we fled back to the manor. Kings be damned, the children wouldn't stop screaming because of the things in the streets...eating coachmen, horses, dogs. I got her away from the windows... the youngest. I pulled her out of the fuking claws of those things when they broke down the door! We watched the master and his lady die—her father and mother. They couldn't be saved. Couldn't be saved. From the dead men. Dead men walking and eating. I think her brother died, too. I saw him hiding under his bed; he refused to come to the attic with me. I should have saved him. We made it, she and I. Clarissa is her name. *Was* her name. The little lass even helped move a pillow or two in front of the door. It kept them out. They're not smart. I don't think they can climb anything more challenging than stairs. I knew to take her to the attic. That's what her father wanted me to do with the children. Take 'em to the attic. The children. The child. Only one. Couldn't save the boy. Only one. Only one..."

"What happened up here?" whispered Aadore.

Skar stopped rocking and looked at Aadore; his face twisted with sheer ugliness as he attempted to hold in his tears. "The poison. This darkness that has cursed our city...it gets in them. I don't know how. A bite, I think. Maybe just a scratch. Clarissa was clawed, and deeply—when they grabbed her at the window. I think that's how the poison gets in. You'll find no cure on hand. No magik that can fix...There's nothing I could do—" At first, he'd made the little girl as comfortable as she could be, though she'd continued to suffer blood loss and delirium—the wound wouldn't stop bleeding, no matter how much pressure he applied. She'd babbled about eating worms, tasting ash, and seeing a thin lady in a dark cloak. She had been quiet for a while after her rambling, then grown grayer and grayer in pallor, and finally stopped breathing. Dead. She'd passed on; Skar wept. Then suddenly, she'd begun thrashing about, tearing at the floorboards, while foam erupted from her mouth. After another speck, she had flopped onto her stomach, her limbs snapped and twisted at the joints, her body hunched as if she were a spider, and then she had scuttled toward him. In Clarissa's eyes, once brown and kind, he had seen nothing that lived. So he had swung his axe again and again, without thinking twice. "She turned."

Poison? Turned? "Iron Queen's mercy," said Aadore.

The baby chose this of all moments to finally cry. Aadore put down her blade and lowered herself to the floor so she could quiet him. Perhaps it was her weariness, perhaps her nerves had finally been rubbed raw, but she couldn't calm him. Although his cries were not loud, they might still be heard or sensed by the creatures crawling through the house. Aadore began to panic. *Stop crying! Stop!* willed the handmaiden. She was no sorceress, though, and her thoughts had no effect. Frustrated, she passed the child to Sean, but his bounces and burbles seemed only to enrage the tiny terror.

"Give him here," said Skar. He did not wait for Sean to hand him the boy, instead snatching him from his grasp. At the touch of Skar's murderous hands, rusty with gore, the infant stilled. Skar held the boy up, and they stared, face to face, ogre to infant, and reached a silent agreement. The two sealed their peace with a smile; Skar's grin was almost as gummy and toothless as the child's. The ogre then patted and rocked the babe, who made no more fuss. "No more noise out of you until the monsters are gone," whispered Skar.

Everyone knew to stay still after that. They weren't sure how long they waited. Darkness stretched a cold blanket over them, tempting them with sleep. Sean's head bobbed, and occasionally he snoozed for a speck, maybe even a few sands. Aadore removed her beggar's satchel, found her brother's skinny shoulder, and slumped against him. Awful dreams haunted her that night. In them, she wandered the streets, calling for her brother in a voice alien to her. While stumbling about, she saw her reflection in a partially broken window: a rotted, swamp-haired thing that looked wet and bedraggled as if from an accident.

Aadore awoke, gasping.

"It's all right. They're gone," said Sean.

Grayness had chased away the attic's deepest shadows, and something resembling morning was happening outside. Aadore took stock of herself. She felt rested, though she was full of aches and pains, and her stomach cramped from hunger. Her brother looked especially haggard in the light. Sitting cross-legged, he massaged the flesh by his knee where his bone met wood, wincing every time he kneaded it. Skar lay on his side, curled up like the babe in his arms—knees in, hands together. Big baby and small baby. If Skar had been sucking his thumb, Aadore might have laughed.

"Let him sleep a while longer. He's had as horrible a time as we have," whispered Sean.

Aadore looked around for her pack. "Have you eaten?"

"Yes. A bit."

"What about him? He looks as if he should eat a lot."

"He ate a few bites—didn't appear terribly hungry. We fed the child as well. Water-soaked bread. I don't know how good that is for the boy, but food is food." Sean reached over and took his sister's hand. "We're all together in this now. The four of us."

"I know. I was thinking only about supplies. What we have won't last more than a few days."

"I'd like to think we'll be out of the city in a few days."

Aadore squeezed Sean's hand. "Is that the plan?"

"I believe so."

Skar snorted, groaned, and sat up; he and the baby shared a yawn. "Well, if that's the case, we should get moving. I can't seem to sleep much anyhow. I'd like to make the most of this light...if you can call it that."

"Gloom," said Aadore.

The three smiled, enjoying a moment of silence together in which vows were made but left unsaid. Menosians had heart when it mattered, when they were at their lowest. *We are all in this together*, they thought.

"We should search the house for anything of use," suggested Aadore.

With that, they moved. Sean found his cane and rose. Aadore collected her satchel and the ornamented sword. Skar set the baby down, opened the hatch, and lowered the ladder. When it came time to descend, Aadore dashed off, remembering that the scabbard had a belt that she should collect. By the time she returned to the hole, strapped and suited up like a proper sword-maiden, the men and child had already gone below. Back in the master's chamber, the three found their barrier still undisturbed. Skar had spoken with wisdom about how easily the creatures could be deterred. Perhaps others as clever and lucky as themselves had also weathered the apocalypse. *How far does the ruin reach?* wondered Aadore, while picking detritus from the barricade. *What if Menos had not been the only victim of this calamity, and all of Geadhain—*

"Aadore, come on," said Sean. He motioned his distantly gazing sister through the gap they'd created.

Aadore blamed her moment of distraction on her exhaustion and starvation, not on the horrors she'd seen; she felt she could deal with worse. A few specks and a small squeezing of herself later, she joined the others. Aadore wondered how Skar managed to navigate the hallway so easily, burdened, as he was, with an ax and a baby. The ingenious fellow had fashioned an old-style sling, a small hammock, in which the infant now rested; she should have thought of that contraption herself, she realized. Burbling and clinging to the man's chest, the babe looked quite content with his mercenary nanny. Aadore put her industriousness to use and started foraging through the trash of the manor while the men followed along at a slower pace.

There wasn't much of worth upstairs, just curios and personal belongings of the dead that she poked through with her blade. She and her sword discovered a letter opener, a little girl's tea set—saucer, cup, and spoon—and a bag of toffee-sweets. She added all of the items to her satchel. In the oak-and-steel kitchen downstairs, Aadore found canned goods, powdered supplements—including milk for the baby—smoked meat, and preserves stashed in a larder. As she could only encumber herself so much, she suggested the men fashion another pack or two out of the curtains in the drawing room. After their happy raid had been concluded, Sean suddenly paused and tilted his head toward the shattered kitchen windows through which the haze leaked in; he'd heard a noise from outside. Up went everyone's make-do packs: the dead were near. They raced through the house, crushing glass and mementos with their careless feet as they moved from kitchen to sitting room to hall to great hall. Finally, they stepped over a shattered, clawed-down door and emerged into the city.

Outside, they were immediately swallowed by the fog of death. But they were not afraid. They knew they could survive; they had so far. With Sean's senses, Skar's might, and Aadore's cunning, they made quite a pack—one great wild hunter that silently stalked the deserted neighborhood of the damned.

II

Although they were brave, they were also cautious. During the night, the terrors of yesterday had bred, and now the streets were infested. The three crept under the billowing cover of fog to avoid the larger roaming hordes. They hid behind ruined walls, hunkered down in hollowed-out sewer pipes, and turned chameleon by pressing their black filthy bodies against the ruins of charcoal buildings. At one point, they waded and then swam for a small stretch across a submerged section of Menos that looked like a scrapyard after a tsunami. All the while, they willfully ignored the bobbing turds, limbs, and trash floating around them. Skar paddled with one hand, holding aloft both his pack and the infant, who giggled in delight. Aadore carried her brother's pack in the same manner, while Sean focused on keeping the pollution out of his mouth. The unremitting reek of garbage and manure, the slimy skin they had to slough from themselves after reaching a junky shore, demanded that they rest. They camped beside a piece of scorched metal that might have come from a crowe, and shared food and sips of cleanish water. Sean sensed no dead nearby, and they felt safe enough to whisper.

"You're good with him." Aadore nodded to the baby, who was back in Skar's sling.

The mercenary stopped chewing, debating whether or not to speak, then said, "I had a family once. I know how to care for children."

Neither sibling inquired further. It was the way of the world to know loss and death; no one escaped that lesson. After the three had finished eating, Aadore used the stolen tea set to make a paste for the infant out of powdered milk and water. It felt proper, this way, lent a bit of dignity to an utterly undignified situation. Aadore let Skar spoon-feed the lad for the man continued to impress her with his paternal care and kindness. *How strange that this child is even here*, she thought. His mother and father were likely dead. She refused to believe the child's uninterested caregiver, killed in the collapse of Queen's Station, had been any relation. Why had they saved him? And why did they all care for him? She didn't need to look far for an answer: in this darkest of nights, he was a star. He was life. He was a keepsake of their civilization. He was the Menos that would rise anew. Aadore would protect him, because he was hope. She believed the others felt the same.

"I never did hear how you and Aadore came to know one another," said Sean. "Or how you ended up at that manor."

Skar wiped the infant's chin, and pinched and tickled the wee lad while answering. "I did some work for the lady Aadore. What was it... two, three nights ago?" Aadore shrugged. "I thought about catching a coach and heading back to the spot I rent uptown. I don't have much of an attachment to any one place; I tend to move around and lay my head wherever it gets tired. So I didn't wander far from D Twenty-Two. I found lodging in Beggar's Court—a neighborhood just up the way from yours, milady. Good digs, good food, good whor—" Skar smiled. "Anyway. I slept there and then asked around for work in the morning. I'm guilded and bonded, so I hire easily. Masters aren't scared that I'll sell them out to the men they've hired me to protect them from. Professional standards, you might say. This job, though…It was supposed to involve shuttling people quickly from one place to another…people on the move, running from some shite they'd put their boot in." His face turned grave. "I wasn't told much, and you learn not to listen when you're for hire—listening leads to knowing things that others want, which is never good. But the master…He was in real trouble, trouble that reached all the way up to the Crucible and the Iron Crown. I could be wrong, but I might have heard the word *rebellion*."

Rebellion. A calamity, a rebellion, a city of unliving monsters. They spent a moment pondering: were all these things connected?

"My employer never made it to Queen's Station," mumbled Skar. "The quake struck before the ladies were able to pack their bags. Then came the ash, and the dead…"

"He wouldn't have gotten anywhere from there, in any case," said Aadore. "Queen's Station is now"—Aadore cringed at thoughts of that place, its shrieking metal, smoke, fire, and heat—"much as you'd expect."

"Well, that's enough of a rest," said Sean. "If you're done feeding little…little…"

"Bugger," exclaimed Skar. "What's his name?" Brother and sister each gave embarrassed shrugs. "Not much of a surprise. I figured he doesn't belong to either of you. Seems as if he's just another casualty in the game of Fates. We really need something to call him, though. This farce of a world is cruel enough even if you do have a name, a few letters with which to declare yourself."

"I'm terribly uncreative," said Sean.

"I don't have much of an artful way with words," admitted Skar. "I tend to hit poets when they speak."

By default then, the duty of naming their small charge fell to Aadore. The men looked at her with great expectancy, each waiting for her mouth to open and speak something wise. Aadore worked her way through the problem aloud. "I hate Fate. It means we are destined to live and die, our existences counted and woven like threads by three old hags at a great loom. What a shite faerytale. I refuse to believe it, for here in the ruins, the four of us found each other. Some might say it's *fate* that we've found one another, though I believe it is determination. We have defied death, and I feel we can continue our revolt against her, and against Fate. We can win the game of Fates, as you called it, Skar. This child has the same spark of insurrection. He will not be defeated. He barely cries; any other child his age would scream to high heaven until we denied our morals, thought only of ourselves, and left him in a heap of ashes somewhere. But he is true and Iron-born. If I could remember the word, the old word, the true word for that metal, I would call him just that...Iar...Iarrin..." While pondering the riddle, Aadore walked over to the child, bowed, and kissed his forehead as the revelation came to her. "I remember now, Iarron. But I think that Ian will do."

"Ian," repeated the men.

They beheld Aadore with a queer, canny respect. She had an air of greatness about her. She gripped the guard of her sword with assurance. Each man's head was filled with thoughts of courts, knights, queens, and noble inheritances. The men blinked and the moment was gone. Aadore was no longer a queen, but once again a dirty woman, who now began striding into the fog-muffled ruins ahead. Sean followed in her wake. But he would not forget what he had seen. They might have lost their capital and their countrymen, but if nothing else survived, within Aadore resided the soul of their nation.

III

The dog had been dead for some time. Its carcass lay in the street, buzzing with flies. Its yellow ribs stuck up from a matted brown husk. All of the good stuff—the organ meats, fats, and entrails—had long ago been eaten. The three survivors and their child waited in a hideaway of rubble and beams for the fog of death, which had the temperament of mist over a lake, to thin and reveal what lay farther down the street, beyond the carcass. This was not the first dead animal the three had seen, not by a long chalk. Most of the alleys and roads featured similar hollowed-out taxidermies. Reborn horses, freed from their nekromantic commands and left aimlessly wandering the streets, had not escaped the hunt: the lonely, inedible hooves of these beasts were visible here and there, along with what remained of their bodies. Whatever force poisoned the air and haunted the city appeared interested in turning only men into the unliving.

Across the way, just past the dog, Aadore could see a familiar building, or at least familiar parts of what had once been a building. It now leaned sideways out of the heap of concrete into which it had settled when it fell. The structure's familiar boxiness, its iron shingles and black windowsills, reminded her of home. At last, and just before the dreaded fall of night, they'd arrived in District Twenty-Two and her apartment was only a heart-pounding dash away through the street ahead. However, they needed to be calm. They needed to be as gray and silent as the fog. For District Twenty-Two crawled with the unliving.

On the way here, their progress had been slowed by chattering hordes of the damned. Sean's awareness had helped prevent any encounters; on two occasions, the creatures had been busy eating a screaming wretch, or wretches. At the moment, Sean looked tired. They had not stopped since leaving the swamp of filth, and Aadore knew his senses must be overtaxed. Whenever he walked now, he needed to lean on both Aadore and his cane. He could no longer run—another reason they moved so slowly. It had taken them hourglasses to slink a mere ten city blocks. *One to go*, thought Aadore. They were almost there.

Hoisting Sean up, she moved out from the protective shadows and into the street. Her brother wheezed in her ear, and the clacking of his cane on stone sounded like a cowbell summoning the monsters in the fog. Aadore tipped her head, silently telling Skar to hurry onward to the concrete shelf she spotted in the distance. It looked as if it had once been a wall, but it had tumbled onto an aqueduct that itself had been vomited up from beneath the cracked street. With each tremble of his body, Aadore could sense the bursts of pain her brother endured; it took all the energy he possessed simply not to fall. As she assisted him, his skinny hands sank like an eagle's claws into her flesh. "We're almost there," she lied; in fact, they'd barely passed the dog.

Sean looked down, counting steps, focused only on putting one foot in front of the other. The game worked for a while, until his wooden toe hit the edge of an upturned cobble and he stumbled, flinging his cane and nearly taking his sister to the ground. Aadore saved them both from the worst, her grip and footing strong enough to keep them from tumbling. Up ahead, Skar—almost sheer and intangible now, a ghost in the fog—came to a stop. Aadore motioned him onward with a hand. She and her brother had to rest a speck. Sean panted against her neck, and she rubbed his back. In her arms, his body felt like skin stretched over a skeleton. She dreaded the conversation they must one day have about his years away in the military. "I had a whole evening of fine things planned for you, Sean," she whispered. "A phantograph show, your favorite foods. I even found an elusive fragrance...a silly gift, the smell of the Feordhan. Do you remember that? From when Father, Mother, you, and I took a vacation with the Els?"

Sean did. Memories of ripe salt, spume, and earth were among the few that had not been damaged during his tortures. When his mind had drifted from his body and off into the past, driven away by pain, he had sometimes splashed in the frigid rush of the Feordhan with a younger, smaller Aadore. As the hungry night drank what light there was and the shadows deepened by the speck, Sean thought of what that memory meant, and of what this experience meant, too: devotion, family, love. All too abruptly, the memory of salt and innocence was dispelled by the stink of rotten, wormy meat. Although Aadore hadn't yet seen them, Sean noticed the shadows lurching to her side. Because Sean loved his sister, no matter how distant in years and experiences they were, it was easy for him to whisper, "Leave me, and run."

Suddenly, Aadore saw the hunched shapes. *Shite, fuk, and damn,* she thought in a flurry of curses. Three unliving creatures materialized out of the grayness to her right. She didn't scream at the horror of their scabby bodies, their blood-soaked clothes, the waggling entrails in the emptied gourds of their bellies, their hanging jaws, concave heads, or wobbling eyes. She knew she could run. Sean, though, would be able to manage a few steps at best. She debated dragging him, but the creatures were only paces away now, too close for her to cover much ground. Fighting seemed the best option, and she gripped her blade. What Aadore never considered, not even as her brother pushed at her and the rotting creatures staggered forward to eat them, was leaving Sean to die alone in the streets like the dog they'd seen. They were brother and sister of iron. If they were to die today, they would do so proudly and bathed in the spoiled blood of their enemies. Aadore hadn't fought a person before in all her life, and yet her heart galloped in excitement. She prepared to unleash her steel—

Ding! Ding! Ding! Ding!

Objects that rang with the hollow acoustics of metal bounced and spun in a symphony somewhere on the street. Brother and sister couldn't tell from where the noise came. The unliving, with their disintegrated noses, ear-nubs, and gelatinous eyeballs, somehow sensed the shrill sound. They seemed confused for an instant, torn between pursuing their original prey and hunting this new ringing. The ringing—its crystal echo, its vibration— won out. Before Aadore had drawn her blade more than a finger from its sheath, the creatures had dashed off like mad wolves after a bleeding hare. Aadore and her brother didn't move until they were sure the unliving had ventured far enough away. They then hurried to retrieve Sean's walking stick and made an athletic lurch toward the sanctuary where they hoped Skar and Ian now safely hid. Aadore was still wondering what it was that had saved them when they reached the stone shelf and ducked into its shaded embrace. The sound? The pitch? The echoing? One or all of them had led to their survival.

Skar lurked in the dark against a boulder of wreckage. The great man pulled the brother and sister down into his squat. "They appeared right after we'd settled in," he whispered, "dropping off the top of this tunnel. I feared they were going to come at us and got my ax ready. Ian and I froze. What a good lad he is; his silence is unnatural, but good. I watched the dead things from here, watched them turn back the way we'd come. They were wriggling their disgusting faces, holding out their hands like old maids lost in the dark. They can't see shite, I'd wager. Can't smell either. I figure they sense only sounds, the kinds of sounds you don't need ears to hear."

"Go on," whispered Sean, fascinated.

"I'm an army man, as you know. But I spent some time in the navy, too, and had a few tours sailing above and under the great blue wonder. Had to stay on a submersible for a week—feels as if you're a tinned fish. Anyway, while I was down there, I heard the noises the great lords of that domain make. We used to shoo them away with our own noises and horns when they got too close to the submersibles. Some of the sounds were exceedingly strange—not noise so much as force—and came in quick succession. I don't have anything in the way of fancy technomagik to draw on here, but I figured if I made enough noise, created enough vibrations, I might scramble the hearing, if you can call it that, of these dead folks. I threw away all of our drinking cans, and some spoons and other trash. Hope you don't mind."

"Mind?" said Sean. "You saved our lives."

Aadore contemplated the behavior of their enemies. Was it possible that the monsters would have shambled right past her and Sean if they'd kept perfectly still and silent, or if she'd thrown her clattering sword as a distraction? She couldn't think of a scenario in which she would want to test that hypothesis. Nonetheless, her thoughts lingered on their seeming luck thus far. She wondered if the cold, determined silence that the three of them had employed every sand—their bravery and refusal to shriek and flail like ordinary victims of doom—had been as much responsible for their survival as Skar's bombardment of cans. Regardless, the man had acted quickly, made every effort to save them.

"Thank you," she said.

"Think nothing of it, milady," he replied.

"I'm a lady's maid, not a lady," corrected Aadore. "I suggest we keep moving, and keep quiet."

Confident that the creatures couldn't see her, Aadore took out her glinting blade and pointed it down what looked like a concrete underpass of sorts, which wasn't very long and seemed to emerge into a gray, smoky space. The sword served as a poor torch, though she wielded it as if it were one. She strode ahead, no longer afraid of the things in the dark.

IV

Night reigned in the misty city, and Aadore could see only the shadow of her building. The rectangular edifice tilted to one side, though it appeared sounder than the complexes to the left and right of it, which had been pulverized and swallowed by the earth. Curtis and Master Jenkins had been in those buildings, Aadore realized, and an angry sorrow pinched her heart. Once they'd entered her building, they tried to move quietly, but they were not alone for long. Windows shattered, bodies rose from blood-soaked mattresses, corpses crawled out from under boards. In sands, a swarm had appeared out of nowhere. Although the creatures could not see, they could sense life nearby. The three survivors stumbled up a rickety hallway, which was groaning from its cracked plaster walls, and felt as if they were running through a funhouse. The last push required a delicate shimmy along a toothy ledge of wood, created when the staircase had collapsed into a heap several floors below.

It was a good omen, Aadore decided. She and her companions had been able to prevent themselves from falling: the clumsy dead things below would almost certainly not be so fortunate. From beneath came the commotion of the dead blindly hunting for food, dragging their wet feet, stumbling into walls and each other in their race to find something warm and red to consume—and not only to consume, she remembered, flashing back to the shrieking, bleeding, amputated men they'd passed during their travels. Dozens of men not quite dead, being hauled by the unliving deep into the fog. Perhaps they would not all die, or turn. Perhaps some had Wills that were too strong. Grim and quiet as graveyard mice, Aadore and her new family had watched those abductions from the shadows. Even now, armed, with the cans and scrap metals they knew could distract the monsters, they doubted they would have chosen different. Those diversions—forks, wire, metal twists, nuts, and bolts all capped in glass jars—must be held in reserve for themselves, for use in moments such as this one. Once they had moved free of the ledge, Skar reached into the second sling-bag under his arm, produced two jars filled with rattling trash, and then threw them down into the dark.

Smash! Crash! Spin! Rattle! Spin!

The noise was extraordinary and continued resonating for a few specks until all the scattered bits had settled. Under the broken landing, voiceless hunters squeezed cawing sounds from their carcasses, and rushed toward the noise. Skar peered over the edge and watched a flock of lumpy shadows converge and claw at each other, before creeping back to the others. "That should keep them busy and off our trail," he whispered.

"Let us hope they're all down below," replied Sean.

Taking Sean's caution under advisement, they skulked through the halls of Aadore's building. This place, once so familiar to Aadore, now made her skin crawl. Apartments had been abandoned, their doors flung wide open. Their upturned tables, unpacked suitcases, and knocked-over furniture told tales of hasty flight. Some of the disorder could be blamed on the earthquake, although it seemed most of Aadore's building had survived the shocks and aftershocks. Dust fell upon them as they walked, and the walls groaned and creaked, continuing to lament the need to hold themselves together. Aadore wondered if the building was sound. The frenzy downstairs dulled, the dark muffled their senses, and the three felt quite alone up here. They encountered no life or unlife on their way to Aadore's apartment.

Her door was closed, unlike the others. Aadore stepped toward her home, but was suddenly restrained by Sean's bony grip. Tired, pale, and clinging to consciousness as he was, he had immediately heard the noise coming from behind the wood—the small bellows of lungs. Someone was sleeping, or trying to be still. Using military hand-signals, Sean held up two stiff fingers, then swiped them from Skar toward the door. Heeding the command, Skar handed the child to Aadore and pulled his ax from his belt. Aadore passed Skar her house key, then stepped back to grant him control of the situation. Skar put the key in the lock, turning it so slowly that the click might simply have been a natural creak. Skar tested the handle, placed his shoulder to the door, and pushed it open a few fingers. As the door swung open fully, Skar flew into Aadore's apartment. Outside, the two heard a yelp, then a small scuffle that ended with a thud. Aadore and Sean knew who had won the contest even before Skar emerged, lugging a moaning, slumped man out of the apartment.

"Seemed to be squatting in there," said the ogre. "You know this fellow?" Skar pulled the man up by his collar.

Aadore at once identified the brown-haired, dizzy man. "Curtis," she hissed. "I thought you were dead."

"I've managed to avoid that fate thus far." Curtis groaned. "Although this gent here almost ruined my luck."

"He's fine," she said. "He's a friend."

"A friend?" Skar wasn't convinced. "Friends don't break into their friends' houses. How did you get in there, anyway?"

"I know how to pick a lock; it's hardly a science." Curtis fought to wrestle the hand from the back of his clothing—about as successfully as a kitten trying to free its collar from a low-hanging branch. "Tell him to release me!"

Aadore nodded to Skar. "You may let him go."

Skar had one more question for the man first. "You have any bites? Any scratches that won't heal? Any touch of a fever?"

"What? No. I was perfectly healthy until you clobbered me on the head."

"I guess you're all right then," said Skar.

After releasing Curtis, the ogre tried to make peace by straightening the fellow up a bit and sharing his crooked smile. Curtis wasn't interested, and hurried to Aadore. He clasped her hand. "It's so grand to see you," he gushed.

"A bit of a miracle," replied Aadore.

"I couldn't think of anywhere else to go. I don't know if you've seen what happened to my building."

"I did."

"Who are your companions?"

"My brother, Sean. The gent that bashed your head is a friend of ours. His name is Skar."

"He has a mean punch. I'm glad your brother is alive. I didn't want to ask the question." Curtis tapped the head of the little fellow peering up at him; the baby grabbed his finger and grinned. "And this?"

"His name is Ian."

"Another miracle."

"Yes, he is."

Curtis finished shaking Aadore's hand, which he had meant to do instead of engaging in this prolonged caress.

"Enough jabbering, you two, we need to get inside and stay quiet," commanded Skar, and shoved Curtis ahead.

They moved into Aadore's simple apartment: open cans littered the kitchenette, and the reek of piss came from the open-concept lavatory—though none could blame Curtis, as there was no water for flushing. There was also an odor of wet, mossy sewage that Aadore could not place. She did not ask what her pink negligee was doing balled up next to the pillow and rumpled bed sheets. She didn't recall leaving it there. Perhaps Curtis was lonely; and she'd always known he was a bit of a pervert.

Curtis had thrown extra sheets over the windows, and the makeshift curtains were parted, letting in soft slats of gray light. Aadore noticed that Sean's foldaway bed and her privacy screen had been shoved into a corner near the lavatory to make room for a bit of construction or destruction in the wall. Dewy pipes tied in dripping tourniquets gleamed in the hole there. Several glass bottles littered her table. Inside them shimmered clear liquid—not the milk or brewed summer teas for which they were generally used. Nearly every bottle she owned appeared to have been taken from her cupboards and arranged on the table.

"Oh, that," said Curtis, watching her stare from the wall to the bottles. "I'm handy with a wrench and a hammer, as you know. Well, you probably don't know that, as we don't know each other terribly well. But I am handy. Locksmith, builder, repairman: I've done it all. I've been called on by my neighbors to fix their awful plumbing more than once. All the pipes in our buildings run to and from the same reservoir and sewage. However, to save crowns on the bills, the water doesn't flow constantly, but sits in the pipes on each floor until there's a large enough demand or accrual of shite. A weighted valve is then triggered, and everything starts to move. That's why some days, the tap runs nearly dry and last night's dinner floats in the bowl for longer than it should. I tapped into a few of the water mains on this floor and drew out as much as I could. Seemed a smart thing to do, as there's no technomagik to purify things now."

"Very smart," agreed Aadore.

"Clean water?" gasped Sean.

He hobbled to the table and helped himself to the contents of one of the glass bottles. Sean moaned in pleasure as he drank. Skar joined him, signaling his delight in the indulgence even more sloppily and noisily. Water had never tasted so sweet, so nourishing to these men. Aadore wasn't as interested in clean water as the men were, though she grabbed a bottle on her way to the bed. There, she removed her weapon, her shoes, her pack—anything that felt encumbering. Free now, she sighed. Aadore took a few sips of water, spilling more than she drank, and then gave Ian a few draughts, too. Once they had sated themselves, Aadore lay nose to nose with Ian and stared into his warm gray eyes. His gaze was the color of uncertainty, the color of change, she thought, before losing herself to sleep.

V

At the table behind Curtis, Aadore's brother and the large man snored in their chairs; they'd fallen asleep at the table. From a stool by the bed, Curtis watched Aadore and the child as they slept. She was lovely, perhaps the loveliest creature he'd seen in his life. With an innocent vulgarity, he studied her, stirring with lust as she shifted her long, muscular legs suggestive of pieces of alabaster broken from an androgynous statue. Occasionally, he wondered how her frowning hard mouth—her beauteous scowl, as he'd once called it—would taste and feel against his lips. Now and then, he felt jealous of the babe that nuzzled so close to Aadore's plump breasts. He thought of kissing the pale arc of her neck, which was exposed as she rolled her head and spilled her dark hair to and fro.

These were the inconveniences of being a man—a youngish one, at that—and of never being able to turn off one's raging sexuality. But though his thoughts were tinged with passionate red, the focus of his study of Aadore was how much respect was owed to her. She had survived this disaster. She commanded worship from him even while she slept, even while patterned in oil and filth and dressed in rags resembling a ballerina's burned and tattered tutu. Curtis hoped that Aadore hadn't thought he'd done anything untoward with her negligee, which she'd modestly tucked under her pillow once at the bed. He'd kept it close to him only while he slept, much as the babe now slumbered near the warmth of her breast. In the darkest of days, a man needed an anchor; he needed a reason to survive. Curtis frowned, remembering the day before last, or however many days ago it'd been when Menos had fallen: the moment Aadore had become his reason.

Curtis stands on the shaky metal floor of a turbulent skycarriage. This crowe has been built for luxury and has the posh, gleaming interior of an expensive passenger train: brass bars, buttoned seats, and small windows leading to a cloudy outside. Curtis must stand, for the seats, while not all fully occupied, are reserved for masters. He would be a fool to ask for an empty spot on these comfortable-looking benches. He would be beaten simply for asking, and he wants to keep his face handsome for his and Aadore's date. She's inspired something in him: a bravery, a desire. He doesn't care if she's older than he, and spends no time worrying about the complications a pairing such as theirs would probably create.

You should be proud of yourself, he thinks. *Cleaned yourself up. Living in a proper neighborhood, with a proper job, maybe even a proper lady.* Curtis feels so proud of himself at that moment that the bloody flashes of a brawl and a man lying face-down in the mud—still, deadly still—don't make him cringe today. *Nothing you could have done*, he tells himself. *You were only defending yourself from that madman. He was drunk and ranting. He would have killed you.* All true, surely, though now he is a murderer, forced to live in a realm of murderers and madmen. There's some justice and penance in that, he decides.

Men of great importance fill the skycarriage. Although he rather hates men like this—they are willing villains, he thinks, not hapless ones like him—he enjoys taking their money. His masters, though, appear pale and afraid today. Perhaps they find themselves questioning their continued importance: no one, including these men, who are Horgot's accomplices, has heard from Curtis's employer, Iron Sage Horgot. Curtis wishes he were at home, and could see Aadore glancing at him from her window. He'd rather exist in that fantasy than be here with men congealing in sweat and expensive perfume. They smell like tropical fruit that has spoiled.

Boom! Boom! Boom!

Three gongs and the world ends. Fire and dust scream outside the craft. Men scramble from their seats and rush over to the windows on each side of the cabin, babbling questions: what, how, why? Curtis pushes for a view as well, unable to comprehend the roiling smoke and glowing rents that appear beneath him in the city and sanctuary he has known for years.

Bang!

A humming blast hits the skycarriage. The crowe must have been struck, for a hurricane of wind now gusts around him. A sizzling hole has been punched in the side of the ship. Too stunned even to flail, Curtis finds himself spilled out of the frenzy and suddenly swirling through space. The last he sees of the crowe is alight with flames and veering through the sky.

"I must have come from there," he thinks, still stunned. Delirious, he falls. He descends toward a landscape of brimstone explosions and toppling metal towers; with each whistling inch of his plummet, he realizes he is about to die. The impact comes abruptly, shattering him with stars, but he has landed on something softer than concrete. Curtis rolls and rolls, falling unconscious after an instant.

Darkness. Muffled commotions.

He surfaces and finds himself in darkness. How sensible it has been of him to do daily exercises including push-ups, leaping squats, and chin-ups off his doorframe. His athleticism has saved him from his fall onto a wooden roof softened by rot, and then down into an alleyway piled with crates, which have both been broken by and broken his fall. Curtis stares up at a swinging eaves trough and contemplates the mathematics of his incredible drop. He praises the Fates for his luck in being alive. However, he has praised the Fates too soon: the sky is black, and as the buzzing leaves his head, sounds of destruction—screaming, wailing, crashing, crumbling—come to him. Taking a deep, aching breath, Curtis lumbers to his feet. Every part of his body complains, especially his back and his ribs, of which a few are probably broken. He stumbles down the alleyway...

Into madness. Men on fire, running. Geysers of smoke and stone. Ground that will not stop shaking. Slumped things moving in the haze. What is real? What giant has smashed the home across the street into rubble? What has happened to Menos? Too many questions. Curtis calms himself, wills his pains way, and asks only one question: Where is Aadore? The question rises from the deepest part of him. Sometimes a man who has nothing needs something to hold on to, no matter how irrational the attachment. Aadore can be his guiding star. There is nothing else in his life that could drive him to live. His family has disowned him; he doesn't have a favorite whore in town, nor even a pet that would miss him. Aadore might care. He marches into the fog of death to find her.

And I did, he thought now, and sighed.

"Curtis the Worthless," his father had always called him. May, his mother as well as Riverton's cheapest, nastiest whore, was never any kinder. His parents had each told him he would amount to nothing. They'd stressed he was as worthless to the world as they were. They'd laughed when he had confessed to the fight, the accident that had turned him into a murderer. Then the wretches had told him not to waste his tears and to set his feet to running before they went after him themselves for the bounty. They were horrible people, and had made him a horrible person through the curse of their blood. However, he had decided he could do better. He would do better.

Aadore caught a sudden shiver and Curtis flew to her, slid a blanket over her and the child, and then returned to his stool.

VII

TAKEN

I

Mouse dreams of a long white room with walls of fluttering, transparent sheets; they tickle her skin as she floats by them. Warm, diffuse light streams in from somewhere. Mouse feels partially blind, as if she's walking beneath the sun of a gorgeous summer day. A dark and dapper man sitting in the room's single white chair beckons Mouse forward. If she were not in a dream, she would be able to move faster. She would race to meet the gentleman in the chair. Alas, she moves as slowly as a lazy wind, and her insides clench with excitement and fear: she is to see her father again. She can tell who the dapper man must be, even though he sits with his back to her. A back ramrod straight, shoulders squared and proud, and a tumble of softly twisting hair: these can only belong to her elegant father. Mouse will indulge any illusion that allows her to see him. She's aware that she's dreaming, and that this billowing hallway does not exist where her body lies. Who cares? she thinks. She reaches the man in the chair and moves to grab him. He surprises her by turning around in a juddering ripple that suddenly flips chair and occupant to face her.

Mouse recoils from the stitched-up countenance. Black thread sews up the face's eyes, nose holes, and mouth; the needlework is messy and imprecise.

Vortigern had already appeared doll-like; the stitches make him seem even more surreal. Not until he thrashes in his seat, somehow bound without rope, and starts moaning and screaming through his vile restraints, does Mouse leap with the awareness that he isn't a simple nightmare. She had not experienced a vision this clear and biting since her time in Alabion, when she'd encountered Adelaide once more.

"Father? Father? What's wrong?"

In a howl of force, Vortigern is pulled down the hallway and spun as if he were a kite in a hurricane through a passage now black and violent with wind; the summer day is gone, eaten by a terrible crackling storm. A fragment of her father's plea pierces the blustery noise of the tunnel. Vortigern's words jar his daughter, who at last understands his muffled plea: "Help me!"

Help me. Mouse cannot battle the winds with her body of air and dreamy matter. She cannot Will herself toward the whirling epicenter of gray light in the storming chamber. But to the heart of this terrible tempest is exactly where she must go, for that is where her father is. Lightning shatters the hallway into fragments of glass and smoke, and Mouse wakes—

Inside another storm. Has she traded nightmare for nightmare? Her flesh remains leaden and beyond her control. Groggily blinking, Mouse catches glimpses of herself walking through whirling snow. Her head tilts down, and she notices the shuffling of her feet and the occasional flash of a hand. People are calling to her. They sound quite far away. Who is that? Must be Moreth, whose acerbity competes with the blizzard's stridency. What's happening? Is she awake? Dreaming? At some state in between?

"Sleep, my vessel. It is not your time. I have called upon our covenant of flesh," says her master, Feyhazir.

I don't want to bloody well sleep! Now Mouse realizes she has returned to the waking world, at least partially. But she seems to have left the safety of her pack, and she is wandering the realm of ice and frost, the unsafe tundra where the Red Riders and the ghost men who hunt them roam. **"Sleep."** Feyhazir's command comes again, and Mouse feels her eyelids sliding shut like stone sarcophagi, feels her mind spinning into a river. Her last sliver of consciousness, her final dreadful blink, captures a host of pale shapes, men of white shadow and snow, who rise out of the winter hills around her.

"Kratístoch, Chamyóskyngós!" (Hold, Doomchasers!) *Feyhazir shouts through her stolen mouth, using a language unfamiliar to her, but one she somehow understands. The power of the Dreamer's command shoves Mouse into the hungriest torrents of Dream, and she sleeps.*

II

Vigilant Moreth stared out into the blizzard. A hand on his pistol, he stood ready to shoot anything that wasn't a brown tail-wagging shape coming out of the whiteness. A sand ago, Adam had run off, barking as if he'd heard a noise. The rest of the pack still slept, even the Wolf, who growled and flexed his claws as if he chased something in a dream. Moreth wouldn't wake the Wolf, wouldn't embarrass himself just yet by asking the great hunter for assistance. Moreth assumed that if a truly terrible danger neared, the Wolf would be roused from any depth of slumber. This was his night, his watch, and nothing would escape the net of his senses—

Mouse breezed past him, striding out into the blizzard. Fuk!

She moved quickly and faded into a white shadow. In another step, she'd vanish. Hissing, Moreth raced after her. Mouse's sleeping partner, Talwyn, had stirred when she rose, and the scholar joined the chase. Neither bloodmates nor sage woke and followed them, each being lost in the deepest of dreams, and Moreth and Talwyn were too harried to care. Talwyn threw a shout back to their shelter to alert those they were leaving behind, though he was now a few paces out into the storm, and he wasn't sure they'd heard it. Regardless, the scholar caught hold of Moreth and joined the man in the futile calling of Mouse's name into the white abyss.

By then, Moreth knew he should rush back to the stone hovel and wake everyone. However, a soft gray light sparked ahead, accompanied by a tingle of music. The queerest music: a song of sorcery. It prickled their skins: he forgot summoning the others, as queer visions of starscapes, spins through weightless space, and a glowing moon washed over his and Talwyn's sight. They stumbled a bit, blinded by snow and swatting at the hallucinations.

When they saw once more, they were standing in a pale, roaring sea of nowhere, with no encampment in sight. They would never find their way back in this blizzard. The silver light—a figure—shone farther on, and a tingling enchantment remained in their bodies. They pursued the glimmer, stumbling, laughing. For a time they wandered, never catching up to the silver woman, to the mirage they felt compelled to follow. *What of Mouse?* wondered Moreth, abstractedly. The silver woman did not remind either man of anyone they knew; they wanted only to catch her and hear more of her skin-tickling song.

The pair entered a pocket of peace where the storm stilled: white dunes and gentle whorls surrounded them. The softly silver woman stood and spoke in a voice that sounded a little like Mouse's, but even more like a choir heard through the delirium of wine. Again they stumbled and laughed their way toward her, wanting to touch her, to drink more of her sweet music. The wariest part of Moreth, the canniness that couldn't be quashed, saw white and blue shapes rise from the dunes. Then netting entwined him and his drunken partner, and they tumbled down in a puff of white.

Using a language neither man had heard before, but which both somehow understood, the voice told them to sleep. As if each man had suddenly passed the point of happy intoxication, the music blared, their heads swooned, their stomachs twisted, and they took a nauseating trip somewhere dark, deep, and cold as space.

III

Wind and harsh light woke Moreth. Shapes moved. With spots still clouding his sight, he sat up, reached around on the floor for the comforting hardness of his cane-and-sword, realized it had been hopelessly lost, then for the iron of his pistols, which hadn't been removed—although his overcoat had been. He leaped to his feet, snarled, and aimed his weapons at the shape holding open the folds of a tent and ushering in winter's breath. The big bluish shape threw a parcel down at Moreth's feet, and snarled back. "*Kratísoch ta óplac sae!*" (Hold your weapons!)

Moreth's trained finger didn't twitch, even as he surveyed the horns, size, and stunning aspects of the blue giant. He glanced at the bundle of clothing—heavy, furred, stitched with lining—that had been tossed on the floor. By the time he looked up again, the giant was gone. If he was a prisoner, he was certainly a well-treated one. As was Talwyn, who, having been woken by the fuss, now yawned and sat up in his comfortable fleecy bedroll.

"What? Ooh, my head. Were we drinking? Wait..."

Fate had played a cruel joke on Moreth by trapping him with this bumbling fool. However, any ally was better than none. Moreth walked around their tent cautiously, examining the makings of the structure: bone frames, a patchwork of skins. Objects of ritualistic design lay around the shelter: brass and bone dishes, wooden figurines, even a swinging hexagonal object crossed in a cat's cradle of twine and hung with feathers. Moreth looked these over carefully, then listened to the voices that could be heard through the leathery walls; he could hear chattering in what sounded like the strange language they'd heard before their minds went dark. He couldn't translate full sentences, understanding only snatches here and there, but it seemed as if they were in an encampment of Pandemonian natives. Talwyn, now more awake and slightly scared, had blathered on while Moreth perused their confines. Moreth finally chose to answer him. "As you can see, we've been taken somewhere. I don't know whether the others are with us, but I don't think so. Adam ran off, in case you don't remember."

What did he remember? wondered Talwyn, scratching his head, where memories floated in a haze of phantom shapes that escaped his shrewd recall. "Well, we're alive," said Talwyn, "and cared for, even. That must be a good sign."

"Not always. Some predators enjoy playing with and fattening their prey before eating."

Talwyn shivered and pulled tight the warm cloak he'd picked from the scattered bundle on the floor. Within the furs, he'd also discovered a bit of jerky and a hard round gray thing that might be bread, but looked like a stone. After Moreth's glum caution, he put the food he'd been about to eat aside, and instead dedicated himself to wandering their tent and seeing what he could learn. While picking up engraved bone bowls, sniffing piney incense fizzling in copper burners, handling the totems of mutated creatures too terrible to be real, but probably representative of Pandemonia's wildlife, Talwyn mumbled to himself about indigenous cultures and Ghaedic-style Cyrillic.

Suddenly, both men sensed the approach of the silver being who'd lured them into this cage. Each turned his head toward the split in the tent through which the day peeked. The light became more luminous now as the being entered; they became drunk once more on phantasmagorical visions of moons and stars, and were beguiled by the music of heavenly choirs. In that moment, they would have obeyed any demand from this creature, believed anything it said. The figure before them was Mouse, yet more than Mouse: wrapped in silver radiance, it poured black mist and gazed upon the men with star-laden pools into which they fell.

"I am the one to whom Fionna has pledged her body and soul," said Feyhazir. *"Be assured my daughter and your companion, Morigan, knows of our quest. You will, too, in time. I have given her a quest of her own: she must save the souls of Eatoth. She will fulfill this duty, for she is a miracle. She will save your tiny souls as well, if we can stop our enemy. For now, I ask that you go forth and meet with your new tribe. I have called you here to serve as Fionna's guardians—you have been chosen for your talents to protect my vessel. She will be returned to you as soon as I have accomplished what I must."*

With that, the divine being wearing Mouse's body left, likely to discuss matters with mortals more important than the ones who now lay gasping, groveling, and moaning on the floor. Moreth regained his sense and sanity first, and was appalled by his response. He wrenched a sniveling Talwyn to his feet. "Get up, fool. I believe we've just been given free rein to investigate our captors."

"Investigate, yes," agreed Talwyn. "Do you really believe we've been taken, though? Are we truly captives? I'm not sure what to think; I've never been so confused."

"Our actions have been determined by the will of that creature. Our company has been divided. What would you call this behavior other than hostile?"

"Mysterious?"

"I don't care for mysteries; they generally involve lies."

"Let's figure out who's doing the lying, then."

For a brief speck, Moreth admired the scholar. Then the two stepped out into the winter day to trail their friend and unravel this mystery.

IV

Days later, Mouse heaved and woke, covered in sweat. She gasped and threw the smothering blankets off. Hands restrained her. Mouse couldn't see faces in the dark, warm wherever-she-was. Aggressive as always, she swatted and struggled until her foggy vision conjured two shapes, two men that were holding her down on either side: Talwyn and Moreth. They appeared clean and washed, almost like gentlemen. Unlike gentlemen, however, they'd been shouting, trying to calm their thrashing friend. The sleep from which she'd woken, though, had been so deep that her hearing only now returned.

She relaxed when she recognized her companions, and the men now relaxed as well. Mouse sat up in bed. She tried to speak, ended up yawning several times, and then ungraciously burped because of her angry, empty stomach; she'd never been so hungry. After her belch, she found her voice. "Pardon. Now where the fuk am I? What happened?"

Talwyn touched her shoulder. "We are safe. Let me get you some water; you're probably quite thirsty."

As soon as he mentioned thirst, Mouse noticed the dryness and pain in her mouth and throat; it felt as if she'd been drinking mouthfuls of sand and wind from that damn desert they'd passed through to reach here. Wait, where was *here*? She remembered tatters of a nightmare: a white chamber, her father's ghost. Then she'd stumbled through a snowy tundra…

Mouse, frightened at the void that came after that event, looked here and there for familiar elements, but nothing was familiar. Around her gleamed lavish fur rugs and metal chalices that sat atop the angular shadows of furniture. Copper burners effusing fragrant, sweet, and exotic scents hung from the bones of the dome-shaped tent. She lay upon a raised bed of hides and blankets, which she pawed with a dreamy pleasure, for they'd found civilization, or at least something that passed for it. A suggestion of day leaked through the heavy skins of the incredibly hot, small dome, and winter's wrath shuddered the walls. Dimmer noises, too, came from outdoors: clangs, laughter, and chatter in a language she didn't recognize. Looking over to where Talwyn had gone, Mouse noticed two other pallets placed lower on the ground next to hers.

Talwyn hurried to a small table, and she heard him pouring water. Mouse continued to rub her sheets and her throat, to wake into this body of hers that creaked as if she'd been dead and resurrected. She knew what that felt like, as a matter of fact—and her resurrection in Alabion had been positively exhilarating in comparison to this. After Talwyn had returned with the water he'd promised—it was in a decorative chalice that piqued her curiosity with its ancient engravings—Mouse drank all she could, until she felt refreshed and alert.

"What is the last thing you remember?" asked Moreth, taking her cup.

"I had a dream about my father. Then...I was walking through the snow. That part felt quite real to me. I remember—" Mouse paused. How much had she told Moreth about the being that slept within her flesh? After a moment's hesitation, she recalled that she'd promised this man, their ally, that she would no longer withhold any truths from him. Sighing, she continued. "The divinity who sleeps in my flesh, Feyhazir—I remember hearing his voice. Then a horde of ghost men appeared. Feyhazir wanted me to sleep. I did, and here we are."

"That was the last moment you recall?" asked Moreth; he didn't seem disturbed by the news of Mouse's possession, though his waxy countenance was hard to read. "Nothing else?"

"No. Why? What *should* I remember?"

Talwyn, sitting on the edge of the bed beside Moreth, reached over to claim Mouse's hand. Looking sorrowful, he rubbed it as he said, "A whole lot, my dear. We've been without you—the real you—for three days now."

Mouse snatched her hand away from Talwyn and swaddled herself in the blankets, shaking. A woman who'd known rape, violent rape, and the accompanying sense of utter powerlessness and rage, Mouse found her total absence of memory, the black space in her head where three days had come and gone, to be just as traumatic. Possibly, it was worse. What sick men had done to her in the past could be explained—though not forgiven—through lust, misogyny, and a culture that elevated coin over decency. She would not *allow* those faceless bastards to haunt her. But what the Gray Man had done to her, stealing days from her life...Mouse couldn't understand that. Were they not partners? Vessel and Dreamer? Avatar and divine? Moreover, she'd willingly invited the Dreamer into her body. Now there might be no evicting what could prove to be a most unwanted guest. Right then, Mouse wanted her family and their comfort; she wanted the rest of her pack. "Where are Morigan and Caenith, my great-uncle and Adam? Surely, they cannot have forsaken us."

Both Moreth and Talwyn raised their eyebrows while exchanging a glance.

"You've communed with them—with Morigan," Moreth said, before deciding to forgo empathy for a bitter slap of truth. "Correction: the Dreamer that resides within you has communed with her, or so the other-you has informed us. We've been separated by your—the Dreamer's—orders. We are to meet our company in Eatoth, in time. First, we must collect something at the behest of your master: a relic for use in the battle against the Black Queen."

A quest? Kings save her, she remembered none of this. "Wait. How did we even get here? How were we separated?"

"There was a storm. You ran away, quick as a hare from a rifle shot; we barely even saw you go. Talwyn and I chased you, and then before we could either contemplate our foolishness in charging out into a winter storm or summon the others, we succumbed to the queerest music…bells and faery songs. It intoxicated me like a cloud of witchroot. Both of us fell down like drunks, and then awoke here—as clueless and scared as you are now."

She shuddered. "Feyhazir. Yes, those are his tricks and trade. Still, why have we been separated? Why fracture our company?"

"War," said Moreth, grim as a mortician's ghost. "The Doomchasers have been tracking Brutus's movements since his arrival in Pandemonia, and the movements of his allies for longer than that."

"Doomchasers?"

Talwyn explained. "Allow me to help. That's a rough translation, but still a more proper name for what we've been calling 'ghost men.' You see, I've been working on understanding the nomenclature of this subsect of the natives of Pandemonia—the many tribes of which are broadly and collectively referred to as Amakri—who've taken us in."

"You're not helping." Mouse threw up a hand to stem his words and turned back to Moreth. "You said something about Brutus's allies?"

"An army," he replied, "if our blue friends are to be believed. One made up of soldiers reaped from the harvest of Pandemonia's peoples. In Eastern Pandemonia, the tribes have been most heavily hit. They've been nearly exterminated now, the survivors driven to the other end of the isle. We've put our foot into the middle of another warzone, you see. No realm on Geadhain is safe from this conflict between the Kings, and now Eatoth, the City of Waterfalls, is imperiled. The Doomchasers claim it will fall, claim they have seen armies of thousands of Brutus's damned amassing in the East. However, they won't warn the city. They would rather honor a stubborn and ancient class-based feud than save the people of Eatoth."

"Doomchasers," mumbled Mouse. "Doomed cities. I feel as if I've woken up in another world."

"You have," snapped Moreth. "And there's still much you need to understand; there's so much we don't yet know ourselves."

"Better to show her," suggested Talwyn.

Over the howling of the wind, Mouse heard a boisterous laugh from outside, one that sounded as if it had been born from a creature with a horn for lungs. Had it really come from a man? He must stand as tall as Caenith. What strange new terrors awaited her? Rather than agonize over her bitter and bewildering separation from her pack, Mouse asked the men where the chamber pot was (thankfully, these people used such things), and then went to release three days' worth of piss.

While squatting, she menacingly reprimanded the entity that had stolen her skin. *Wear me like a puppet again, and I'll find a way to get your hand out of me for good, pact or no pact. I thought we were to be allies in this war, champions for your daughter and for your love of all the green reaches of Geadhain. Or was that a superbly told lie, the greasy lines of a seducer who knows how to coax forth a woman's desire?*

The Dreamer was silent.

V

The monstrous laugh she'd heard had come from one of the many people walking through the noisy snow-blasted day. But they were not people; they were monsters. Accomplished at hiding her fright, Mouse restrained her shriek when the first grand, lean, blue-skinned giant greeted her—hand on chest, knee to the fluffy ground—as she and her companions exited the tent.

"*Megáli Paraphach*," said the blue man.

"Great Wanderer," whispered Talwyn into her ear. A combination of Moreth's rudimentary lexicon and his own voracious mind meant he'd already learned more than a few bits of this tongue.

Mouse shrank deeper into her hooded, furred cloak, which had apparently been a gift from the Doomchasers—not that she could remember. She couldn't remove her gaze from the Doomchaser guard. He was huge, though a bit lanky like an underfed Northman, and his skin was the strangest, prettiest blue. While she stood there, his color seemed to fade into and out of different shades. If only his pigmentation had been the strangest thing about him! But his powder-white cloak and garments, the cluster of short black horns and keratinized growths about his bald forehead and brow, and his nictitating serpentine eyes were equally queer. Man? Snake? Giant? After his bow, he stood and resolved the last question: he towered over Mouse by at least two paces. He wasn't as tall as Caenith, although he exuded a similar sense of the primal. Mouse gave the Doomchaser a stiff nod and turned away.

"That was a Doomchaser?" she whispered behind her hand.

"An Amakri, technically," replied Talwyn. "Doomchasers are a rather unique tribe, even within their collective. Let's walk."

Mouse quickly forgot the other questions she had been on the verge of asking, her mind wiped clean by the sheer impressiveness of the land. Claws dipped in ice reached out of the hilled shadow that lay beyond a village of tents, conjuring a sense of lurking peril. Although the vista was bleak, Mouse felt that this winter realm was calmer than the one in which she'd fallen asleep. Less wondrous than the backdrop were the many tents sewn from variegated hides—yellow, rough, furred, and scaly, representing all the herds of Pandemonia—that scattered the snowy land closer by. Men and women such as the one she'd just met strode through the gentle storm as if its chill meant nothing. Some of the Amakri bared blue-nippled chests inked in ornate circular designs. Others eschewed the conventional tattered white garments, having stripped right down to loincloths and sandals. Little children ran untended in packs about the camp, brandishing sticks and throwing stones at one another as part of seemingly cruel games. They hissed and barked while they played. Elsewhere, fire pits puffed savory smoke from animals and pots hung over the flames. To form these many outdoor hearths, the land had been stomped down to its frosted, gemlike green bedrock, creating a foundation as strange and scintillating as the people who tended the fires, ate, laughed, fought in circles, and tinkered with weapons and nets. The Amakri were beautiful, in a way—bald and hairless as lizards, every one, though that was their sole similarity. Tribesmen stopped whatever they were doing to bow and mutter *Megáli Paraphach* as she passed, and she stared into every strange face.

Over by one of the fires, an Amakri noticed the lost and daydreaming Mouse, and stood to mutter a greeting. The Doomchaser possessed two grand sleek horns like those of gazelle and a star of black ridges on her forehead and nose. The woman leaned on a long weapon, a cross between a spear and a quarterstaff. They were fighters, these folk, and the woman's stare was steely. Finally, one of Mouse's companions urged her to break the stare and move.

As they wandered between fires and tents, they saw more evidence of this people's martial ethos. Indeed, everything about them appeared to be tuned toward war. Those who worked by the fires either cooked food or made and mended hunting nets of thick, braided rope—gut, according to Talwyn—which would be used for trapping and killing. Nowhere did Mouse see idle hands. Even those Mouse thought might be Doomchaser artists—men and women who painted the skin of their fellows with markings of valor while singing throaty, grating chants—were actually preparing the tribesmen for combat. At almost every fire, animals were being gutted and hacked apart upon the white-and-green butcher stone of the earth. Mouse watched as one of the butchers carried freshly peeled skins into a large tent, which was smoking from a hole at its apex as if it had a chimney atop it. The butcher bowed to her as he walked past and mumbled the now-standard greeting. She made a mental note to ask Talwyn later about her apparent holiness, if an explanation failed to present itself.

Right now, she was too busy staring. The general savageness and lack of civilized recreations here reminded her of the people of Briongrahd. While these folk didn't appear to change forms, they were no less tribal or attuned to their inner beasts. This truth was made brutally clear in the fighting circles: there, bald youths and maidens clashed fists, staves, and swords wrought of a chiseled, dark stone that clanged like steel when struck. The combatants roared each other on, and the matches didn't end until blood had been spilled, often through no small injury. Then another competitor would be thrown into the miniature ring of blood.

At least their blood was red. Mouse wasn't sure why that comforted her, but it did. Perhaps it made her feel less like an outsider in this already outlandish realm. When she and her companions passed the fighting circles, the warriors didn't pause to honor her, or the entity they believed her to be—they were too engaged in snarling and spattering the snow and each other with their spit, sweat, and blood. They were extraordinary to watch, fighting with both an animal's speed and wildness, and a man's cunning and strategic awareness. They appeared not to be bound by rules, no chivalry. A man could win his match by throwing his weapon at his opponent, clawing the other man's eyes, or kicking up snow. *Perhaps the Amakri are changelings who have simply forgotten their other skin,* she mused.

Talwyn, evidently taking to his new role as amateur anthropologist, commented, "All so incredible, is it not? Their social conventions are similar to those of our tribes in the West, although their racial traits differ greatly because of the climate and chaos of Pandemonia. However, their songs and focus on battle remind me of the war-hungry, though deeply spiritual, indigenous peoples who once settled in the Swannish Highlands south of Menos. Over the centuries, they were pushed to cultural extinction. Some fled to Alabion, but most were assimilated into the existing populace. Here, I see a preservation of the past."

"Indigenous people?" scoffed Mouse. "Men of Iron and men of Eod have always lived in Central Geadhain."

"Spoken like a thoroughgoing colonialist." Talwyn laughed. "Men of Iron and men of Eod were not the *first* residents of Central Geadhain. All of our stock stems from the ancient tribes, whom we've conveniently dismissed from our history."

"What do these natives want from us?" she asked.

"*Amakri*, not *natives*," scolded Talwyn. "And you will know in a moment. It took us a while to figure it out, but we did all the necessary legwork during your nap. These Amakri have a leader. We were told to bring you to him as soon as you awoke, as soon as you were *you* again. Think of him as a shaman. Charming, entrancing fellow. Something like a Keeper, I suppose, which is what the Sorsettans call the holiest of the Faithful. We talked about that a bit before; I don't know how much of it you recall. Still, applying what I understand of Sorsettan beliefs, which must surely have their roots in Pandemonia, I gather that the fact that this Keeper is a man is but one of the many differences between the wild tribes and the city ones. Strictly speaking, of course, those who live in the cities shouldn't be referred to as "tribes," which brings us back to that cultural divide Moreth mentioned. Also, Pythius speaks, which is another anomaly, as Keepers take vows of silence. I'm certain that he practices magik and medicine, too—"

"Pythius?"

"Right, that's the gentleman we are to meet." Once Talwyn became excited about a topic, it was almost impossible to put a stop to his lecturing. "Although I suppose you met with him many times while you weren't you. Where was I? I don't remember, there's so much to discuss! Take the assignment of duties according to sex, for example. The Amakri, Doomchaser or otherwise, do not distinguish between men's work and women's work, as so many other cultures do. Look around, and you'll see that men and women share the same burdens, laboring, battling, and char-womaning—*charpersoning*, I suppose—equally. The only exception is when it comes to more spiritual positions, such as Pythius's. Anything involving magik is strictly in the purview of men, though these people don't think of their shamans as sorcerers. Still, women can lead warbands as much as command the evening hearth. Other than that small wrinkle, I'd say this is, therefore, neither a matriarchal nor a patriarchal society. Fascinating! Wouldn't you agree? Oh, we're nearly there—that's his tent up ahead."

After meandering through the camp, they had finally reached its busy center. Here, warrior circles and hearths were plentiful. In kneeling, muttering droves, tribesmen now prostrated themselves in front of Mouse. She found the reverence they had for her—for Feyhazir, rather—unnerving. Mouse wondered what the Dreamer's association with this tribe could be to have inspired the kind of fealty generally reserved for a king.

"In there," said Talwyn, who'd taken the lead.

The scholar strode toward a tent no larger or smaller than the others, and curiously devoid of activity. Talwyn slipped between the flaps. Mouse hurried after him and past a few kneeling Amakri, whose worshipful attitude she found increasingly bothersome. She entered the tent. Within, a sweltering robe of air wrapped itself around her, and she immediately undid her cloak. The dwelling was far more cluttered than the one in which she'd awoken. Aside from a scattering of fur rugs, the floor was mostly bare; twine and bone talismans hung from the white supports of the dome. The fetishes clattered like mad wind chimes as Mouse and the others came inside. Incense burners, clay and metal pots, urns, and arcane phylacteries carrying misty, whirling substances behind their glass lay jumbled around the outside ring of the tent. The tent smelled of must, pepper, body odor, and unrefined dirt. She turned up her nose at none of them, though, for the fragrance was one of knowledge, magik, and toil. Mouse found the smell welcoming compared to the cold, mildew stink of sorcerer's towers and ateliers in the West.

The Keeper of this sacred space bade them welcome. Although he'd been sitting in the center of the floor when they arrived, no one had noticed him until he greeted them. *"Kalasi, Feyhazir."* (Hail, Feyhazir.)

How could he not have been seen, if not for mystic forces? For when he stood, he would be a tall man, even for an Amakri. Mouse knew that when he was enraged, his long veiny limbs would swell with violent strength. At the moment, however, his cobalt countenance wore a peaceful smile. Still, in his greenish eyes flickered the tempestuousness of a sea storm. This spark was one of magik, for gazing upon him and his iridescent, scaled face, Mouse felt the thrall of enchantment, as if she were being lured in by the twisting dance of a snake. Indeed, he seemed to waver as he sat there, dizzying the watchers with his shimmering allure, his coat of scales, and the mystic inks drawn in circles upon circles on his mostly nude flesh. His face was beautiful, at least for a man: a hard V of a jaw, slashes for cheekbones, a small scowling mouth, and heavy eyebrows that looked made for brooding. From his hairless skull protruded two grand ebony horns like those of a ram, though these spiraled upward to sharp points. This man was dangerous, Mouse felt.

Suddenly, the shadows seemed heavier, and the noises outside—winds, chatter, fighting—fell to a thrum. The shaman swept a large, elegant hand through the space between them. "*Vlépoóti sae ékei apomeína. Eímas sígour óti échet erotis. Parakaló, kathís.*" (I see that he has left you. I am sure you all have questions. Please, sit.)

As Talwyn wrestled with the string of words, Moreth beat him to a translation. "I believe he is asking us to sit. I don't know about the rest."

The three came forward and formed a semicircle around the shaman. Teasing fragrances of cinnamon, dried apples, and an oil sharper and sweeter than lavender wafted from small black pots that lay around the shaman. The fumes of which caused warmth to rush from their groins to their chests. Patiently, the shaman watched and waited for the three to settle, to feel comfort in their bodily beats and to become distanced from the commotion happening elsewhere. He waited until they had inhaled enough of the *ísycho vótan*, the quiet herb that burned in the black pots. When he sensed they were calm and in a state to listen, to hear with more than their ears, he Willed the shadows to be a little darker and the smoke to be thicker and to curl about him. He then shone in the haze like a glittering being of light.

"Greetings, vessel of Feyhazir," said the shaman. "I am Pythius, and I shall answer the questions you no doubt have. We have only so much time to speak with our souls as we now do, because the quiet herb can be dangerous to those not used to it."

Mouse understood him, somehow. "The quiet herb?" she asked.

Pythius bowed his head. "A gift from Feyhazir many, many ages ago. When the Amakri first lived on these lands, after the Great Fall and the ruin of the Cradle, times were grave. The land would not tolerate us. Feyhazir, however, walked amongst us, bringing with him many wonders of knowledge. He showed our elders how to cross any barrier of language so that we might make peace and not strife. Feyhazir showed our elders how to mend wounds with medicine, how to unearth the rarest of flowers, roots, and plants—things that grow less than once each season, in each changing climate of Pandemonia. Our land may seem chaotic, but it has its own rhythm and seasons, an order that cannot be seen by those unfamiliar with chaos. Feyhazir taught our cast-out Keepers to do more than listen for secrets—he showed them that their gift was a doorway to possibilities and to other Arts. He showed them how to use the secrets of their souls, how to make miracles with their Wills. The Amakri, and many other tribes of Pandemonia, owe the Dreamer for the preservation of our people."

The last time Moreth and Talwyn had entered this space, the conversation had been much less informative. Mostly, Moreth and the scholar had strained to translate a jumbled tale about Feyhazir and some relic of the Dreamer that was hidden somewhere in Pandemonia. Thanks to Moreth's skulking about the camp, they knew that the Dreamer had often taken private counsel with the shaman, though they hadn't been privy to the fruits of those discussions. Moreth had made almost a hobby of tracking the Dreamer, while Talwyn had blundered about the camp like a nosy traveler, murdering the natives' language while attempting to know more of their aims, history, and relationship to Geadhain and this war. Here and now was their first opportunity to know more—about everything, really. Talwyn leaped into the conversation. "Feyhazir taught your people magik?" he asked.

"Yes," replied Pythius.

The serpents of smoke and scent twining around Talwyn had sedated him enough that he refrained from jumping to his feet. "He has walked here before? As a man, or using a vessel?"

"All of the great Wills in the sky once made Geadhain their garden of joy and sin. Feyhazir walked here, many times, through many bodies cursed to be vessels."

"Cursed?" said Mouse, with a spike of fear that the herb and sorcery couldn't calm.

"Breathe deeply, Mouse, and call upon your lion's heart. Your master is not the same as his kin. There are those who would rule through ruin, such as Zionae, and there are those who value the preciousness of every soul. Feyhazir does not seek to harm you or me. He seeks, rather, to free us, to answer our every desire. Look to the legacy of the Doomchasers, and see what our ancient pacts with Feyhazir have granted us: immunity to the taint and influence of those who would seek to control their creations. We live by our natures and desires; we are free."

Taint and influence? Does he mean the corruption Zionae is spreading? wondered Talwyn. *Can the horrifying transmogrifications of living men to*

Blackeyes be stopped, stalled, or reversed? Have these tribesmen been inoculated against Zionae's corrupting power?

The group listened raptly as Pythius continued. "In our blessed silence, I hear your clever thoughts well, West Sun." He looked at Talwyn as he spoke, though the title he used was obscure. "All of what you think is true. We cannot be claimed either by her darkness or by the deceits of any Dreamers. Long ago, when we wandered, when Feyhazir walked among our elders once again, after we'd been cast out of the Great Cities for refusing to honor their laws and accept meekly and quietly the secret wars the Dreamers wage, he granted us this gift—a gift so strong that even after thousands of years, our bodies still carry the essence of his wish. His wish was for us to be free and fierce, to become the hand that fights the untouchable. Our bodies cannot be claimed; our Wills cannot be swayed. So it is that we chase the darkness. We hunt the doom. We are Doomchasers."

A tribal pounding suddenly rose and thundered, as if a single-instrument orchestra were bashing drums outside this cozy cocoon of magik. Perhaps it came from their hearts, or perhaps it was generated by the passion of the shaman's words. He spoke low and emphatically, his eyes glinting, his form grander than a mountain's. From everywhere at once, it seemed, the three heard the drumbeats of ancient war, the screams of men spearing their enemies. In the furls of smoke, they could almost glimpse the ghosts of these warriors.

"Look at our bodies, and see men who are weapons," said Pythius.

Sudden fury twisted his handsome beauty, revealing the sharp teeth he had been hiding and causing his sinews to ripple.

"Look to our souls and to the light and truth from which we were born."

They now looked past his great glowing figure, toward a point of light hanging like a Northern star—if this were illusion it was more real than life itself. Frenzied by an irrational need, they grabbed for the star, which seemed within reach. In a moment, each held it: a chalice, possibly of bone, carved with inexplicable runes and an orgy of grotesque designs. Had they not been so bespelled, they would have recoiled. The cold earthen feel of the cup chilled their hands, as though it had just been pulled from a tomb.

"Look to your hands, and see what we seek, what Feyhazir has returned to reclaim from the lands where it was lost when last he walked Pandemonia."

A chalice? they wondered.

"The Covenant!" declared Pythius, who'd turned into a shivering colossus of light.

The three cowered, dropped their phantom chalices, and raised their hands to ward off the brilliance. Following a burst of savage wind, the drumming stopped, and only the sound of their heartbeats and breathing could be heard. Some of the darkness and smoke had cleared, and they faded back into their bodies, still in a deeply confused state. They saw Pythius waving away the plumes from the potted incense. Nothing had really changed. He wasn't any more of a giant than seemed normal for him, and there was no chalice to be seen. They even sat exactly as they had before the strange cacophony of visions. Pythius welcomed them once more with a smile. "I hope that answers some of your questions," he said. "I am afraid that our time with the quiet herb must now end, lest you develop something worse than a headache."

Ow, thought Mouse, as pain shot through her head on cue.

"I think I understand," said Talwyn, but the others couldn't say the same. "I have further questions, though."

Pythius tilted his head and stared at the scholar, like a reptile deciding on a cricket to eat. "Very well, West Sun. Stay and we shall speak. You will not have the advantage of the quiet herb to assist you; however, I feel you will do well enough with your wits and perseverance."

"Wonderful," said Talwyn, rubbing his temples, where an ache had now settled. "Where to begin…"

Heads pounding, needing fresh air, Mouse and Moreth left the scholar and the mysterious shaman to themselves. She had more questions, though any more mysteries and her head might split from pain or the burden of those secrets. Talwyn would be a better sleuth than she. Glancing back as she went, Mouse was struck by the voracious gleam that appeared in the shaman's eyes as Talwyn started to pour out his hundred questions—a look of hunger, one she'd seen in many men before. *Should I be worried?* she wondered.

"He will be fine," said Moreth, catching her lingering, troubled look. "If Talwyn was to be eaten for his inquisitiveness, it would've happened days ago."

Somewhat assured, she and Moreth wandered off to find a quiet place of their own, where they could have a chat and clear the rest of this quiet herb from their skulls.

VI

Pythius proved himself to be outstanding company. The Amakri possessed as good a mind as any Talwyn had ever known. Not that he'd encountered many intellectuals outside of formal, academic, or technomagikal settings; he wasn't convivial, and had been virtually friendless before meeting his new pack. The two of them sweated, gestured, and cursed, often laughing at one another as they tried to tackle ancient history and the world's greatest secrets without the benefit of a shared tongue—an exchange so exciting that Talwyn's pain quickly diminished to an easily dismissible irritant.

Strangely enough, they made do. Pythius proved as patient as he was aggressive. Like a man of two temperaments, two spirits, he took his time sounding out words and phrases, but often grew enraged during other passionate discussions, usually regarding the Dreamers or the other people of Pandemonia—the Lakpoli—who inhabited the Great Cities and who'd spurned the wandering tribes in an age long past. Like an angry snake, Pythius hissed the word, *Lakpoli*, whenever it came up. He showed a similar anger when discussing the concept of honor, which arose often, especially when the city-dwellers were mentioned. For pride, honor, and the very fact of being alive were all the same to an Amakri. If you could not live honorably, you should not live. Pythius did not believe that the Lakpoli had ever known honor. Talwyn never felt brave enough to ask what it was that had caused this rift between the civilizations; he would just have to suss out the answer in a subtler fashion.

A bit of verbal stumbling occurred at this point in the conversation, as the men explored concepts of excommunication and social exile. The Doomchasers never killed one other, not even for reasons of justice or dishonor. They did, though, mete out what was perhaps a colder punishment, banishing a wrongdoer forever from his tribe and branding him with a mark that would declare him untouchable to any and all Amakri he might encounter. Pythius showed Talwyn the brand—a metal rune like an inverted cross with a circle of metal in its middle—which he pulled from somewhere among his arcane clutter. With a snarling smile, the shaman demonstrated how it would be used. First, he stood the scholar up, then he spun him around, wrenched up his shirt, and placed the freezing metal stamp on his flesh, saying, "*Símac delhiós.*" (Coward's mark.)

If Talwyn had not felt a conflicted, unexpected enjoyment at this aggressive handling from an attractive man, he would have objected sooner. Instead, he waited until the lesson had ended before anxiously tucking in his shirt. Pythius put the rod and its flesh-burning stamp away and made apologetic gestures. When Pythius realized he hadn't offended his companion, he came nearer and helped Talwyn tuck in his clothes. The intimacy and freeness that these people exhibited around each other and the spice of the shaman—sweat, sweet-grass, and tree oils—gave Talwyn a second bout of nerves.

"*Akoúoch to fóva sas, lypámani. Misótous adýnamoch.*" (I hear your fear, and I am sorry. I hate the honorless.)

Talwyn gathered the "sorry" part, and guessed some of the rest. "I'm fine, really," he said, and hazarded a phrase. "E-eímai gennaíoch." (I am brave.)

Pythius howled at that, whether because of the sentiment or because Talwyn had pronounced the words incorrectly, Talwyn couldn't tell. Pythius walked to the entrance, pulled apart the flaps, and shouted to his men, leaving Talwyn to worry over his gaucheness. In a moment, the Amakri indicated he should sit once more. Talwyn sensed the kinder side of Pythius's soul as the shaman knelt with him knee to knee and gave him the smile he now often wore when the scholar had said a silly thing.

Lightly, they picked up the strands of their conversation, with Pythius making inquiries about Talwyn's "tribe." "A *pack*," corrected Talwyn, causing the shaman's smile to deepen. When chatting about his pack, Talwyn was almost certain he referred to Morigan as a milkmaid and the Wolf as a dog, but he didn't know how to correct these mistakes without making more. In the end, he supposed the picture he painted of the company for Pythius was rather odd. In his turn, and in the spirit of swapping tales—and slaps, for the Amakri slapped him so frequently that Talwyn's arm ached, and the scholar slapped him back once or twice—Pythius explained to the scholar the wonders of his tribe.

Some of what Pythius told him supported observations Talwyn had made during his investigation of the encampment, although it felt good to have his perceptiveness validated. The Amakri, Pythius explained, were not single-minded warriors, but also storytellers: each and every one of them, not only the elders and learned people elected to lead. True, Pythius knew the most tales, the longest threads of history, but they were handed down from shaman to shaman: his knowledge wasn't hoarded. Unshared secrets and tales were thought of as poison; they needed to be circulated in order to cleanse the bearers' souls. This belief stood in stark contrast to the philosophy of the silent Lakpoli, their Keepers, and their soldiers, who lived protected in their bastions of elemental power; those dishonorable men never shared their stories, but hoarded them for power. As such, they were considered poisonous, every man, woman, and child among them. A toxic culture. For there was only one law in Pandemonia, one truth, declared Pythius: *"Típotae deen eínnai aiǵnioch."* (Nothing is eternal.) Whereas the Lakpoli thought of themselves as above the order of time, nature, and the elements—they ruled, and did not respect these forces.

Once more, the conversation became heated as Pythius described the differences between the cultures of the Lakpoli and the tribes who wandered. Here, then, was at least a partial explanation for the hostility between these peoples. Talwyn listened as Pythius shook his fist and hissed, asking few questions. The colonial attitudes of the Lakpoli weren't all that different from those shown in the West toward the now vanished indigenous folk. Here, though, the original inhabitants had managed to protect their culture, avoiding assimilation by the apparently civilized societies walled up in Pandemonia's Great Cities. The Great Cities...Where stood crystal towers, silver eggs that flew through the sky, bridges of fire, rivers of molten rock...The wonders of these places sounded greater than anything in Eod, and Talwyn fantasized about, as much as he dissected, what was said.

However, the Amakri wanted none of these cursed wonders, were interested in nothing that would weaken or sever their connections to their land, community, honesty, and honor.

There were numerous tribes, but none quite like the Doomchasers; however, the Amakri did not war with each other. Their cursed countrymen in the Great Cities were foes enough. The Amakri were one people, of many colors and tastes, who were united no matter how far across Pandemonia they spread. Once every few seasons, Pythius explained, the Amakri met and held council and celebrated together, reaffirming their vows over campfires, trading wares and knowledge gathered in whatever corner of Pandemonia they'd come from, and singing and dancing long into the night.

"*Énaólokai* (The Becoming)," said Pythius.

Food came; Pythius must have called for it earlier. The meal was another serving of the green-leaf, meat-chunk, and gristle porridge that Talwyn had come to enjoy. Whether actual oats were involved in the recipe, Talwyn couldn't tell, though it stayed in the stomach like porridge and a warm glass of milk. One meal a day was often enough for him.

They were quiet while they ate, and afterward sipped the invigorating minty tea that had accompanied the food. The shaman and the scholar hadn't run out of things to say, and Talwyn had learned more about Pythius and his tribe in the last few hours than he had in days of careful observation. However, as day dragged into night, Talwyn continued to withhold his more important questions. Dreamers walking Geadhain? What was this chalice? How had it changed these particular Amakri? Had it turned them into blue-skinned giants with horns?

Talwyn fussed over voicing these questions, wondering if he were wasting the man's time. A leader couldn't fritter away his hourglasses chatting with some stranger. The Amakri didn't waste time; they moved. Already the entire encampment had packed up and relocated once in the days they'd been with it. Occasionally, warriors had come and gone during his and the shaman's talk, briefly claiming Pythius's attention. Outside, he could hear dragging and clanging as tents were disassembled and wares were packed. Soon they would be moving again, probably to find Feyhazir's relic.

A few more sands, he promised himself, before asking a question unrelated to wars, Dreamers, or affairs political or mystical. After a few verbal fumbles, he managed to inquire why it was that Pythius called him "West Sun." It seemed such a strange moniker to bestow upon anyone. Startled,

Talwyn held still as Pythius reached over and wonderingly caressed his coppery hair. *"To chrṓm tou anatéllontos ilíous. I sofiach tou dytikoú anémo."* (The color of the rising sun. The wisdom of the west wind.)

Embarrassed, Talwyn laughed a little too loudly and then took another sip of tea.

VII

Four solid planks of emerald rock stabbed up out of the glacial terrain. Mouse thought the markers seemed like good places to sit two tired arses after a long walk, so here was where she and Moreth came to rest. Far now from the warmth of the encampment, they huddled close to each other, thinking about chalices, the Black Queen, and Mouse's increasingly unwelcome possession. Neither spoke nor had spoken in the hourglasses of their stroll. Each loved a companion who never felt pressured to talk. Even now, they looked to the twisting winter lace that lay atop the far-off shadow-clawed mountains. For many sands, this diversion entertained them. Winter's song, a slow howl that rose and fell, was quite sedating.

Finally, Mouse said, "I keep reaching for memories of the past few days, for anything at all that I've missed, and my hands come up empty."

"I cannot imagine the feeling," whispered Moreth. He nudged her with a shoulder. "I need to possess a feeling of control at all times, even if it's false. I sense that you are the same way."

"I am."

"Again, the last thing you remember is falling asleep?"

"Yes...Feyhazir." Mouse grunted, while fondling, beneath her shirt, the cold iron talisman that represented her covenant. "Dreamer of amnesiacs and dementia sufferers."

"I don't like it. I wasn't able to even come near you to see what he was up to...when he was in there." Moreth tapped Mouse's temple. "I became groggy and disoriented whenever I tried. I think he's hiding something, this master of yours." He recalled Mouse's shining and terrible form, and the thunderous authority with which Feyhazir had spoken. "What bothered me most was how he spoke of you as if you were a thing, a vehicle to be driven."

"I'm not a thing!" spat Mouse. "Fuk!"

Mouse leaped off the rock and wrestled with the amulet around her neck. For such a thin chain, its strength was incredible. Despite making a desperate, thrashing display, she could not snap it. Instead, she slipped it over her head and threw the damned relic into the snow, where it lay gleaming, refusing to be buried. Moreth waited for Mouse to calm down a little, then hopped down to join her. Together they stared at the relic.

It was because of the angle of her head as she looked down at the amulet that Moreth noticed it from his eye's edge: a stark streak of white along the back of Mouse's skull that matched the streaks on the side of her head. "Probably not the best time to mention this, but a bit more white suits you."

Moreth watched Mouse run her hands through her snow-and-slate hair. Although the change was dramatic, Moreth felt that Mouse had retained her prettiness; her thin mouth, her childlike nose, her great brown eyes were all sized to perfection. The stripes in her hair drew attention to her simple, often overlooked, comeliness. It made a man look. There was not a wrinkle or spot to suggest she'd aged, but that might not be a blessing: age and decay could be happening deeper, in her soul.

She glared at the amulet, trying to melt it with her hatred. "I'm changing. In small ways, I'm changing into something I was not before."

"Into what?"

Mouse couldn't answer him.

Moreth wanted to press. Sometimes, though, silence was a better remedy for upset, he decided. Within a moment, Mouse had defeated her anger.

"I guess I've been a professional messenger for most of my adult life." She sighed. "At least being the toady of a divine being gives me more status than a Watchers' pet. Don't even remember where I lost my old Watcher's trinket…Somewhere along the wild road we've walked. But that cursed amulet of Feyhazir's carries more authority, more meaning, than any the Watchers' jewelry. I am a survivor: I have cheated death, and that is my trophy. I'll cheat this Dreamer, too, if he gets out of line again."

Mouse bent down and reclaimed the amulet. She brushed off the snow, then slipped it back on.

"I shall help you with that, should it become necessary," said Moreth. "We're together for a reason, though I don't know what that reason might be. We were chosen by your master for our skills, or wits, or because Talwyn and I might somehow serve you. And serve you we shall. We can play games, too. I'm a scoundrel at cards. I count them all. I never lose. Beatrice hates to play me."

Thoughts of his icy wife and their hot, red pleasures built a fire in Moreth's chest that shielded him somewhat from the growing wrath of the winter night. Could it be night already? He mused over the play of violet waves that rolled through the clouds. Their walking and talking had taken up most of the day, and there would be no rest for them now: Moreth knew the tribe was soon to move. He and Talwyn had already been through this ritual before since the Amakri never settled in one spot for long. On his and Mouse's way here, he'd seen tents being dismantled, rods bundled, furniture broken down, tarps rolled and tied with leather. Those parcels would be carried by the tribe and its temporary members; Moreth's shoulders still groaned from the weight he had borne on previous days. Before they set out, he wanted to make sure his companion—almost a friend now, he would say—was mentally ready for whatever journey the Dreamer had in mind. "Are you...Has our conversation been fruitful?"

"I think we're both in the dark a bit," said Mouse. "I don't trust the Dreamer or the Amakri, though that could just be my nature. But I trust my pack, and I sense there is something honorable about you, despite your darkness. We shall trust one other, then—you, Talwyn, and I—until we reunite with our company. We should both keep an eye out for Talwyn, actually; I worry that his curiosity will make him vulnerable."

"I'm astonished he's not dead yet. Astonished." Moreth's unflinching sincerity surprised a laugh out of Mouse. "You can trust the Amakri, though," he continued, his head echoing with thoughts of his own relic of past ties, the necklace of the Slave, which rested against his breastbone. "I'm still quite unused to this idea of lords and ladies of creation running amok on Geadhain. I shan't claim to know what motivates your master or his kind. But I have known the Amakri before, and they value honor and sincerity above any vice. They cannot be corrupted, at least not willingly. I would like to see whether Talwyn has anything to say on the matter."

"Aye, we should—"

"Hullo!" cried the scholar.

Shuffling onto the scene came a red-cheeked, puffing Talwyn. Wisely, the Amakri had made use of his generally unexploited natural muscle, the genetic boon of the hearty Blackmore line, and burdened the man with more packs than a mule. Perhaps he'd taken on too much weight, for Moreth noticed sweat beading along his brow, and his frame seemed bent. The fur cloak surely wasn't helping to ease his strain. Still, Talwyn possessed a spirit of eagerness and he greeted them with a smile.

"We were just talking about you," said Moreth.

"I'm flattered!" Talwyn's grin grew wider.

"You shouldn't be," said Moreth. "I was sharing my amazement at your continued survival. I had you marked for dead. Good thing I didn't bet any crowns." Moreth looked past the man to the scraped green surface left in the wake of the milling tribe. It didn't appear as if they were waiting to leave; they seemed already to have made their exodus. A snake of Amakri, each person bearing twice as much gear as Talwyn, wound away from the campsite toward the fuzzed purple glow of the sun, which was now falling behind the distant range. "It seems it is time for us to go. Do give us some of those packs, lest you break your dainty self in half."

"I can…I'm not dainty!" declared the scholar with a stomp of his foot.

"There, there, my dear." Mouse reached up and relieved him of one of his burdens. "You are a most delicate thing. All that meat is just for show and play, I figure. Your mind is what you flex most to impress the gents." Mouse paused. "It is *gents*, right? I get that sense from you. I've caught you staring at Caenith; you're not exactly subtle. Have I embarrassed you? I don't mean to offend."

Talwyn's redness spoke for him as they hurried after the Amakri caravan.

"Of course it's gents," scoffed Moreth. "Good Kings, we used to catch ones like him waiting to give a five-fingered tug in the lavatory at the Iron College."

"I don't do that!" shouted Talwyn.

As the three travelers caught up with the Amakri, the sun died suddenly, casting the land into blackness. It was an omen that they missed.

VIII

MEMORY'S BURN

I

Morigan tasted the iron-and-wine tang of the Herald's blood in her mouth as she awoke, frenzied. She and the Wolf leaped up and then glared at the winter storm into which they sensed their friends had disappeared. Disappeared...or taken, just as the wicked woman in their dreams had warned. The Wolf growled, dashed off in a black streak and disappeared into the whiteness. Morigan strode outside their rock shelter. Wind and flurries attacked the seer, but she sneered her defiance of the weather. Only her pack-mates mattered. Mouse, Talwyn, Adam, and Moreth were all missing; soft melted spots marked the places they had rested. *Where are you?* she demanded, and threw her swarm of Fate-seeking bees into the storm. Silver light irradiated her.

Thackery, who'd slept like an old man even though he was no longer one, was woken by the Wolf's departing growl. The sage's deep, drowning dream—filled with a queer music of bells and tintinnabulations—faded from his body, some mysterious spell dispersing. *Danger*, he realized, throwing off his fogginess. Something had happened. He looked around for familiar faces, and noticed more than a few missing. He'd neither heard nor sensed his great-niece and the others leave. Stumbling a bit, still unusually heavy with sleep, he rushed to Morigan's side. Upon reaching her, Morigan's light faded and she returned from her otherworld hunt. Thackery noticed, then, a dribble of red running from her mouth and wondered if she had been hurt.

"What's happened?" he asked.

For a time, the seer didn't answer. Instead, she scowled at the twisting ivory sheet that had fallen over the land. She wiped her mouth, having felt her lipstick of blood. She wanted more of it—on her, in her throat. Surely the Dreamstalker was responsible for taking or luring away her friends. Who else could be? An echo of the Dreamstalker came to her: *I warned you of the Dreamers. I told you that Zionae, brutish and single-minded as she seems, remains the most honest of her kind. Now, you will see and learn that cold lesson for yourselves.*

"Morigan? What is going on? Where is everyone?"

"They have been—" Morigan fought with the word and with her failure. "Taken."

"Taken? By whom? Why?."

She hadn't a clue. Morigan's prescience had thus far proved marvelously useless when it came to locating her missing companions. She could sense they were alive somewhere, alive and afraid—though not filled with the dread of mortal danger. Otherwise, her impressions of them were so indistinct that her companions might as well have been old memories or people she called to across a foggy, windy lake. Distance lay between her and her missing pack-mates, and one not simply of spans. It was the result of an artificial separation: a force shielded them from her sight. Some magik as great as her own had interfered. She felt nothing save for fury. At least Thackery remained with her, by whatever miracle.

The Wolf suddenly returned from out of the white void. His great shadow seemed hunched and downcast. He shook the snow and icicles off his coat and padded over to his bloodmate. Before they touched, she felt all of what he knew: disappointment, trails that could not be tracked. They came together; he pressed his cold, wet nose to her hand, and they whimpered in unison. Their melancholy and mournful admission of defeat irked Thackery. They'd met and conquered tougher challenges than an abduction or three. Adam, whose brown and shivering figure Thackery now noticed behind the Wolf, seemed of a similar mind, and began to bark.

"Stop it right now," demanded Thackery. "No one is dead, I assume?"

"My senses tell me that they're alive," replied Morigan.

"Well, that's one blessing. Can you tell me nothing else? With your senses?"

"I have pushed my Will as hard and as far as it will go." Morigan pouted, lost in self-pity. Once again, she was a seer without sight.

"Push again! Push harder!" Thackery snapped. "Only yesterday, you reached across the world to find our wandering friends. I've seen you cross into the gray nowhere of death and bring my nephew's spirit back, and you did the same with a changeling girl near as gone as he. You continue to doubt yourself, but I have seen you evoke miracle after miracle. Finding the ones to whom you have sworn your heart and allegiance should be a parlor trick next to raising two people from the dead. No more sad faces and defeat. Shine, my silver daughter, and find our companions."

As Morigan pondered, she grew braver, shedding humility and fear. She was chaos, the maker and unmaker of all things. She was not fumbling to light a match in the dark. She knew intimately the souls of her friends—Mouse's especially. They had touched minds and Fates. They called themselves sisters. Finding Mouse should be as difficult as finding her own nose. *No more incompetence*, she told her bees sternly. *Find my friends. Tear apart Dream itself if you must, but do not return to me without traces of their spirits.* Sizzling light, so bright and hot on his skin that Thackery reeled and threw himself into the cold, pierced Morigan's flesh and flooded the stone lean-to. The radiance blossomed and then fired a gusty, twisting lance of silver into the heavens, taking with it Morigan's mind and soul. Morigan's body fell upon the furry back of her bloodmate. After scrambling his way out of a snowbank, Thackery rushed over and helped the Wolf with the burden of Morigan's empty body. Thackery laid her flat and rested her head upon his lap while brown and black wolves curled up next to him, waiting.

Into the sky, past the pulled cotton of the clouds, beyond the scorching barrier that surrounded Geadhain, Morigan flew. In her fervor, she seemed to have overshot her mark. The echoing resonance of space titillated her with cacophonous songs, and the stars twinkled and tantalized her with secrets. She didn't want to travel there, not yet, though she suspected she could. She Willed her silver comet to slow. She paused, taking in the beauty of the green-and-blue globe of Geadhain, more vivid and transcendent in its glory than the phantasm once conjured by the Sisters Three, and almost lost herself to that mystery, too. While she whisked around the ephemeral skin of the globe, she looked for her sister.

A star down below teased Morigan with a glimmer of grayish silver. She dropped her Will upon the spot, descending like a screaming comet, seeing red, then white, then blue, then flecks of pepper on pale earth. One of the black dots held the gleam she desired, and there her comet crashed. She'd entered a mind—a vast network of threads, lights, and strong winds. As she spun, weightless and out of control, memories rushed in and out of her like radiant ghosts. Each gust warmed her with love, chilled her with hate, or stole her vision and replaced it with images of dark streets, yellow-toothed men, and, once, a creaking, sad merry-go-round and the inharmonious accompaniment of a young girl's laugh. That laugh had been Adelaide's, she realized. Morigan was inside her friend.

"Daughter," said the Dreamer.

The golden void slowed and became threaded with gray. Suddenly, Morigan bobbed in a fulminous mist. The heart of this thundercloud floated some distance from her—possibly near, possibly far: everything felt distorted and deceptive here. At times, the heart resembled a man with streaming arms and legs. The more she looked, though, the more unsure she was that the shape was a man and not a snake, or an enormous eye, or a hunched lump of a creature that would be horrible to behold without the mist.

"Father," she said. "You are awake, and yet your vessel, my friend, has been abducted."

"Your Will would wake the deepest sleeper," he replied. Lines snaked and curled in the nimbus as though the Dreamer smiled. **"The vessel has not been abducted. Your—"** the Dreamer appeared to consider the word **"—friends have been set upon a different path."**

"A different path? On whose authority?"

"Mine."

The gray storm rumbled, its flashes threatening. Morigan had felt cowed by this side of her father before: his grandeur, his authority. Still, she was a storm unto herself; she blazed silver light and rumbled back. "Return your vessel and the others to me. Now. My companions are not to be taken and then used as pawns in your game of Queens and Castles." Morigan hated that game, cringed every time she saw one of those checkered boards and their wooden playing pieces on a table, as she had never been any good at the lying and trickery necessary to win. She sensed her father would have no such difficulty. Deeper, a dissonance in her consciousness she avoided considering, was the whisper of the Herald warning her of the games Dreamers played.

After an ominous silence, the Dreamer spoke. *"Eatoth is poised to fall to the forces of Brutus. If this should come to pass, his army will overrun Pandemonia, and you might never make it to the Cradle to uncover what you seek. I have told you—and you have felt—how much I strive to distinguish myself from my brethren. I would embrace and kiss every corner of this world, if I had the flesh and senses necessary to achieve that glory. Alas, I am without shape and flesh. I look through a window at a garden I can rarely touch. When life is lost, I weep, and stars die. Much life will be lost, and many stars will disappear, should you choose the path that serves your need for kinship.*

"My vessel travels with those faithful to me in Pandemonia—some of my oldest children in this world. They will keep her safe. Together, the vessel, the clever one, the cruel one, and my children seek an artifact that I left here when last I had form and fingers to embrace Geadhain's beauty. That artifact must be reclaimed for it alone can end this war. Eatoth, too, must be saved. Two choices. Two roads. Two potential destinies. You will not have to carry the burdens and expectation of Fate alone, my daughter. I, too, shall make decisions that shape this war. I have planned for this war since Geadhain was a crude poem, a few lines of primitive rock and crashing sea. Trust in my wisdom. If we are to win against the Black Queen, we must be unified in our hearts, but divide to conquer. We must become many hands so that we can strike many parts of our foe at once. Do you understand?"

Calmer now, like a child coming out of a tantrum, Morigan reflected on what her father had said. Visions drifted into her mind's eye: reddish landscapes shimmering in flames, thick with the stink of charcoal and murder and the clamminess of fear and heat. Something was destined to burn, and she presumed it was a city, as her father foretold. Morigan wrestled with what the Dreamer had told her of her duty. "I cannot simply abandon my companions," she said uncertainly.

"They have not been abandoned. I watch over my vessel. I shall watch over the others as well—they, too, will be needed."

"Why didn't you tell me of this plan, give me this warning, earlier?"

"Would that have made you more decisive, or less? How many sands would have been wasted? You see time in such slow, miniscule increments, Daughter. For my kind, tomorrow has already come and gone. The Black Queen rules, the tree of stars has been devoured, and we are all doomed. Time is an open road to me: I go in either direction as I choose. Still, that road grows shorter. The ends of it fall under a veil of black. I fight every echo of that hungry future with a ferocity that you cannot comprehend. Trust that I shall take care of your friends. Do what you know is right: protect Eatoth."

Finished now with their discussion, the Dreamer blew his daughter from the Dreaming, out of Mouse's head, and back into her own body with a roar like one hundred thunderclaps. Morigan thrashed about, striking Thackery on the chin. After a moment, the shivers and shock of her violent travel passed, and she settled on the ground and was able to speak to her companions, two of whom had reverted to their two-legged shapes and dressed while she'd been away. Three frowning men hunkered around her.

"My father," she said, also frowning; vestiges of their conversation unnerved her as she reflected on its hints of hidden meaning. "The Dreamer has...sent Mouse, Moreth, and Talwyn on a quest."

"A quest?" asked Adam. "Then Fionna is safe?"

"Yes. He has sworn to protect her, and the rest."

"I'm fairly sure your father knocked me out like a sleeping draught," Thackery involuntarily yawned; he felt as if he could lay down again. "Seems like a rather one-sided alliance."

Adam, also concerned, gazed out into the white buzz, remembering. "I heard a noise—slithering and rattling. I chased it. I smelled her scent in the storm, and chased it, too. Then it vanished. She vanished, and I circled the cold white land barking for her return. It seems cruel. And wrong. I care not for this father of yours."

I suppose he didn't need your talents, or Thackery's, thought Morigan, loathing how her father had commoditized and manipulated the members of her pack. Morigan's anger leaked into the silently raging Wolf, though neither bloodmate showed it except in their cold stares.

"Where did the Dreamer send them?" asked Adam.

Feyhazir had mentioned something about traveling with his faithful. Morigan didn't believe he meant anything resembling the Faithful of Gorgonath. Could he mean the ghost men? They had encountered few others in Pandemonia. Ghost men. The bees stung her with this truth. "The hunters, the ones in white capes who kill Zionae's brood. Mouse and the others travel with them—I'm certain of it."

The Wolf wrinkled his nose. "I care not for the stink of this. It would explain, though, why neither Adam nor I could find a trail: those ghost men leave none. I detect something in their nature that is either magik or designed to deflect magik."

"We must trust in what my father told me," replied Morigan. "We have no other choice." She wanted to stand and take action; Caenith sensed her need and helped her to her feet.

Mouse, she explained, had been called to action by the needs of her master, and Eatoth was apparently about to become another of Brutus's battlefields, a scorched ruin. There was also mention of an artifact, one they'd never heard of, that could supposedly change the course of this war. The Dreamer's story was riddled with holes like a coat from a moth-infested closet. If nothing else, they were beginning to see how self-serving and autonomous the Dreamers were. Even Morigan's rose-tinted glasses had broken. Of her conversation with her father, what she remembered most was his obscurity—and the amorphous monster that had lurked in his gray storm. What beast was that? What side of his nature?

Adam was having none of these careful deliberations and paced in sad restlessness. Leaving him to his temper, the others started picking through the belongings of their missing friends for foodstuffs and valuables. Moreth's cane couldn't be found, though Morigan was mostly concerned with Mouse's favorite deck of cards, which also appeared to be missing and were hopefully in their owner's possession.

Adam watched them, growing darker and meaner until his venomous thoughts erupted. "Stop foraging through their lives," he demanded. "What now? Do we not pursue our pack? We are to trust this great snake? For that was the scent on the wind; his very nature smells of scales and mystery. Snake betrays. Snake loves only himself. What am I to do without her?"

"I have seen the fires and smelled the death, Adam," replied Morigan. "I know that much of what he told me is not a lie. I don't know how much else to trust."

The Wolf snorted and spat. "Dreamers. They have made a mess of their creation, and now they return to raze more of the forest." In a low voice, he added darkly, "I shall see us triumph in this war if it costs me everything." The Wolf glanced at his bloodmate. "When this war ends, I shall see the Dreamers removed from this world. It may take much magik or sacrifice to banish them, but Geadhain should be left to the care of its children, not its fair-weather, neglectful creators." As he spoke, he was undressing again, and becoming more deeply irritated over having to jump in and out of clothing and skins. "No more walking, no more measured and careful steps in this land. We shall need you to run, Adam, if we hope to arrive at Eatoth before it burns. I am broad enough. I shall carry my Fawn and Thackery." The naked giant, already rippling with metamorphic twists under his flesh, kissed his bloodmate, then patted Thackery's shoulder. "Cling tight. Make knots of my fur for your hands to hold, for I shall run as fast and free as when I was lord in my realm."

Caenith stepped back to complete his transformation. He buckled as the worst of the ecstasy and pain stabbed him. Morigan collected his garments, and those discarded by Adam, and placed them in her pack. It pained her to leave the empty, rifled-through knapsacks of her friends in the cold hollow, but they were an unnecessary burden. She stared out into the winter world, thinking of those who weren't with them—including Vortigern, who was always just under the topsoil of her consciousness. *I promised him I would protect Fionna. I'm warning you, Father: I shall hold myself to that oath at the cost of whatever family you and I may be.*

The Wolf nudged her hand with his wet nose, and she knew they must leave. She also knew that the Wolf and their companions, present and missing, were all the family she would ever need. Woe betide any—Dreamer or not—who came between them.

II

Once the wolf-carriage had been prepared, Morigan and Thackery mounted Caenith's great, shaggy back. The two of them took up at most a shoulder blade and a strip of his ribs down to his flank. He smelled of comforting, peppery sweat. The Wolf's stone drum of a heartbeat and his tremendous heat also brought reassurance. With a whoosh, they were off, and the strength of their handholds was immediately put to the test. For such a massive beast, the Wolf moved lightly, though, barely shaking the ground and his travelers. If they'd proceeded at a slower pace, Thackery might have fallen asleep, the Dreamer's enchantment persisting in him still. Instead, he fought the vestiges of that unwanted magik and turned his neck to see his fellow passenger's bouncing head. They smiled to each other at the implausibility of this journey.

Beyond his pink-cheeked companion's head, Thackery could see tides of snow and wind. Looking anywhere for too long prompted dizziness. Thackery did what he remembered doing while crossing Kor'Khul: he closed his eyes. He occasionally clenched and unclenched one and then the other of his hands to prevent cramps from settling in. Every so many sands, he turned his head from left to right. Finally, he started regularly moving his pelvis to keep the blood flowing. No longer afflicted by the deterioration of age, he found some thrill in once more riding the wolf-carriage. Youth made everything in life easier, he supposed.

After a stretch of travel through whistling cold space that chilled only the side of his face not buried in the Wolf's fur, Thackery peeked at the skies. They looked clear, and were tinted with the light-blue shade of dawn. He counted stars for a bit and then stopped when that began to make him sleepy in what at last felt to be a natural urge. His mind and body drifted along with the beat of the Wolf's exertions. Many heartbeats and heavy pants later, Thackery felt warmth on his exposed cheek and looked up to see sun threading through gnarled, leafless branches that resembled withered hands. It was a sort of forest, filled with glistening trees. Splashes came from beneath the Wolf as he moved through stagnant water that stank like rotten vegetables. Thackery appreciated not having to wade through that brackishness himself.

But he had rejoiced too soon, for a short time later the Wolf stopped and lowered his haunches. Morigan dismounted from her bloodmate and landed with a splash. Thackery took the cue as well, and shivered as his boots left warm beds of fur for cold water. They had discovered a forest of drowning, broken trees and tumults of driftwood hung with spidery moss. Flies buzzed through the dead swamp, and slick shadowy birds—or other winged creatures—cawed and swooped from wasted tree to wasted tree. *A dying woodland,* he thought, *in the final stages of putrefaction.* Its decay would provide rich nutrients for Pandemonia's next bizarre iteration.

"He suggests that we rest here," said Morigan. "Caenith can smell a city up ahead. Eatoth." She paused, and she and the Wolf traded silver and gray stares. "He claims it smells like spring and winter's frost all in one."

"Interesting." Thackery gazed around the swamp. Adam had found a nearby tree against which to lift his leg, and Thackery waded over to join him. Thoughts of his youth and fitness surprised him while he urinated, enjoying the weight of his prick and the flush of warm sun upon his face. Even the buzz and churn of the swamp made a pleasing kind of song. All things, from his virile body to nature's resplendence, appeared restored from their faded beauty. As an old man, he'd often reflected upon beauty: Morigan's, Theadora's, Eod's. But he'd done so without any great appreciation. When a man grayed, it wasn't simply his sight that went, but also his passion for what could be seen, heard, and smelled. However, Geadhain had given him a great gift. He was Geadhain's knight, had been anointed as such by Sister Eean herself. And yet, what good was he, really? If he could figure out how to light a damn fire here without blowing up a field, he'd be far more useful.

Around him the crow-like things left their roosts, screeching. Their grating cries, though, sounded to him as golden as songbirds' songs. Down near the warm stream of his piss wove a curious snake: a living ribbon of red and green. The reptile was small enough not to alarm. Thackery watched its synchronized elegance, as though the world were new to him. A little sorrowful, he contemplated all that he'd shunned since Bethany and Theadora had died. Perhaps Morigan was right, and he would love again, too. For he now thought of his autumn nymph Bethany—of her smiles, her songs, and her smell—without his breath hitching and his heart racing in nervous grief. Indeed, his blood had recently begun flowing from his heart to somewhere else entirely. Lately, he'd been waking up with a sword in his pants; the experience was unsettling to him as the discovery of his first creamy-wet bedsheets or the sight of the strange black hair that had one day started growing on his loins. Thackery quickly tucked his manhood away and returned to the others, who appeared amused—even the wolves, with their doggy smiles and flicking tongues.

"They say if it's in your hands for more than a sand, you're playing with it," teased Morigan.

Thackery turned red, and the wolves made him hotter with their huffing laugh-like barks. "I wasn't...I was only thinking! Lost in thought."

Morigan playfully nudged him, and then started searching Caenith's fur for the loops she'd braided there. "I am glad that you seem to have once more found a zeal for life. For how many years did you just sit about like a sad old owl? Too many, I say. Now I can feel your magik; your Will and passion blaze from you like heat from a fresh forge. You are new and vibrant...I always saw that flame in you, Thackery, even when you did not." The seer found her grips. "Mount up, my friend. Eatoth awaits."

Thackery continued to dally. He had no prick in hand this time, he was simply pacing in the filth. Words twitched like flies in the web of his mind: zeal, passion, magik, blazing Will. He thought of the small apocalypse he had caused when he had last attempted magik in Pandemonia. Had he been too eager? Too casual with it? Although he could not say why, he felt that failed event held significance that, if properly understood, could lead to a breakthrough. Failures always preceded successes. What was he reaching for?

"Thackery?" called Morigan, sprawled like a spider on Caenith's back.

"Coming!"

He hoisted himself up, and they resumed their journey. He hoped he would soon grasp the logic behind that nagging thought. Soon the decomposing wood lay behind the speeding Wolf, and without the loom of branches, sunlight spilled over Thackery. When he turned his head and chanced a look, he found the sky quite crisp and clear, a pastel swath decorated with a golden-white dot of sun. Dank water had dried to dust, and clouds billowed around them. Sand stung Thackery's eyes whenever he opened them, so he mostly refrained from doing so.

Once, though, he felt a gliding shadow pass over them and braved another peek. Above, enveloping the sky with its vastness, was a lumbering chain of avian flesh; he could think of no other description for what he saw. It was as big as a train, lumpy and hideous. Parts of the beast shimmered as if mirrored, and silvery appendages like the wings of a dragonfly festooned its body. These gigantic window-wings refracted light, casting beautiful rainbows that made the gargantuan thing not entirely terrible to behold. As the Wolf ran beneath the monster, a crumbling rain of gritty matter fell from the creature's undercarriage. The monster then startled them all with a long cry, deep and rattling. Thackery quivered with fear and glee.

Even after they were away, free of the shadow, Thackery strained to look back incredulously at the ship of dragonflies, mirrors, and flesh that moved across the sun in an eclipsing line. It must be a wyrm, he thought, though he could place neither the species nor the elemental properties of the creature. Thackery watched it for as long as he could, until it was a mere squiggle, a serpent's slit across the eye of the sun. Then he was forced to clasp the Wolf more tightly, for the beast had picked up speed over this flat, dry terrain.

Thackery's exuberance was tested by the day's wearing travel. Hanging on to a moving thing was hard work, after all. The Wolf didn't stop for hourglasses. Each sand began to echo as it dropped. Thackery heard Morigan grunting from pain, and when he looked at her, he saw that her face shone with sweat and strain; by then, the sun had fallen, but the night remained warm. Thackery nearly asked for a halt, but the Wolf knew his bloodmate's needs better even than the sorcerer did. The wolf-carriage padded to a stop. Thackery dismounted first, then helped Morigan, who appeared quite pallid and trembled in his arms.

"How did you endure it?" she asked, once again standing on her feet. "When you and Caenith came for me, all the way across Central Geadhain in what—a week?"

"Less," Thackery boasted, grinning. "I did it for you. I would take that journey again, with all its perils and thrills."

Morigan laid her head upon his shoulder, and they watched sand whirl out from dunes and then spiral across the dark, bleak plain before them. Winds wound down into the blackest cracks and soared up over the buttes—puckered with holes like coral—atop which lanky beasts called. Thackery wouldn't call those creatures wolves, because they trilled as birds did. He preferred not knowing their species. Likewise, the black, scuttling pools here and there inspired only horror in him, especially when he realized these stains on the sand were great clacking swarms of insects.

"We should avoid those carrion creatures," boomed Caenith from behind him; he must have returned to his man-skin during Thackery's gawking. Without bothering to dress himself, the nude giant strode barefoot across the rough desert toward the base of the nearest butte. It was a ways off, and Caenith soon turned and picked up Morigan. In his arms, she struggled against sleep. Thackery, bemused, watched the Wolf's head nod as well, although Caenith regularly shook it to ward off this sympathetic fatigue. That man was never fatigued. A run and swim around the circumference of Geadhain wouldn't tire him. *How close they have grown. They are almost one being now*, thought the sage.

Under a dusted plate held up by stones, they made their camp. The space wasn't quite a cave, but it could accommodate all four of them. Familiar with the Wolf's behavior in times of pursuit, Thackery knew they wouldn't rest for long—he'd better make the most of it. The Wolf left them and shortly returned with a curious lizard as large as a doe and covered in brown feathers. They skinned and ate the creature raw. Gulps from their increasingly flat waterskins helped to wash down the bitter, gamey meat. Adam gnawed on what bloody bones were left, appearing content to remain as an animal. *Without Mouse around, perhaps he sees no reason to be a man*, Thackery thought.

After dinner, the Wolf exercised some civility and put on what for him constituted clothes. Usually, there would be a fire, tales, and laughter, but tonight there was only the threnody of wind through the wastes. Morigan commented on the dreariness. "A cold night. A dark night. I miss our companions." Adam dropped the bone on which he chewed to whimper, then laid his head down. "I wish we had a fire," she added.

"There is no wood in this dry land with which to make one, my Fawn." The Wolf kissed her head, which lay against his chest; he lingered to smell her hair and sweat. He tightened himself around her like a greedy crab. "I shall keep you warm."

"A fire would be nice…" mumbled Thackery. Then the thoughts from earlier—magik, Will, age, Pandemonia's etheric currents, and his having nearly blown himself up—coalesced into inspiration. "That's it!"

Morigan glanced over. "What's what?"

"I think I can do it," said the sage. "I believe I may have figured out how to use my magik here."

Adam whined his concern.

The Wolf wasn't convinced, either. "I recall a lot of fire and smoke when last you attempted to use your sorcery." Still, the spruce-hint of genius emanated from the sage, so perhaps Thackery was onto something; the Wolf's nose never lied. "I can tell that you're determined, all full of sprites and ideas. What did you have in mind?"

"A demonstration," said Thackery, clapping.

"Are you sure this won't be like the last one?" Morigan warily asked.

Flashing a bit of pride, Thackery stood and crossed his arms. "I'm a sage and a Thule—no mystery is beyond me. I was reckless last time, though I've learned my lesson. Mine is a theory only proved through the act. You've carried us so far, Caenith, so many times. Please, allow me to bear my shoulder of the burden on this journey. I am one of the greatest sorcerers in this world, and it's high time I acted like one."

The Wolf raised a hand as if he'd offended his friend. "Go ahead then, element breaker. Outside, preferably with a bit of space between us, though don't wander so far that we cannot keep an eye on you."

Thackery ran from their shelter and into the desert, stopping when the Wolf called for him to do so. Thackery pondered how to begin, his palms sweating, his heart pounding. Youth involved strange chemistry: it made one all excitable, gave one hands that shook and erections that spontaneously formed in the night. Thackery could only imagine what it would have been like had Eean given him still more years. He might once again have become the man who'd broken the ruling class of Menos and run away with a pleasure maiden to live on the outskirts of Alabion. That man had been a rebel, a lover, and a passionate father. There was a certain irony in the fact that he might have fared better in Pandemonia if he were still a doddering sorcerer, a man whose feelings were dull and bitter, rather than the gallant fellow he had once again become.

Instead of allowing his passions—his fire, his light, his Will—to burst forth, he dwelled on tranquil scenes. He envisioned babbling brooks. He thought of a sleepy-eyed read through a long, slightly boring novel. He even recalled how he had labored to cut back the growth that had snarled the site where he and Bethany had built their home. But he resisted further thoughts of Bethany, as they might conjure a magik too pure and strong, causing Pandemonia's wild currents to ignite like a river of oil. Thackery needed to blend creativity with dutiful devotion. He needed the calm and concentration of a master smith hammering at his anvil. As Thackery contemplated all these productive, slow, utilitarian exercises, he let his magik hiss out of him in measured, small steps that would eventually allow him to make the climb.

After watching the sorcerer stand still for many sands while making tranquil faces, the Wolf finally smelled the sulfur of his magik. He heard a hiss, and then from the man shone a weak, pale light like that of a lamp under lace. Thackery moved his hands. The Wolf clenched and held his Fawn, for this was the moment when something might explode. Yet the light dimmed away, bringing with it no disaster. During the invocation, Thackery's hands had come together, and they now held an object of trapped brightness. Beaming as he returned to the rock shelter, Thackery revealed what he clasped. In his palms lay a twisting complexity of points and whorls and radiance—a subdued light, like that of a tired star. He bowed and offered it to Morigan. "A light for you, as you requested, my daughter."

Morigan took the tingling star and kissed the hands that offered it. She and her Wolf curled up together and slept. They dreamed of racing through meteor showers. They dreamed of howling together at halos of green suns that dawned over the hemispheres of strange planets. They dreamed of freedom and love and all that they would hunt, once their quest was over.

III

Morigan and the Wolf awoke before dawn was even an orange thought in the sky. Morning seemed as heavy and slow in rising as were they. Even the Wolf found himself more tired than usual, and he suspected his union with the Fawn was the cause. By dreaming together, they were crossing the borders—the last border—that separated them. They were never apart now. For a man so accustomed to his ways, his wants, and his needs, the Wolf was quite complacent about this usurping of what he defined as self.

We are changing into something new each day, my Fawn, he mind-whispered. Then he kissed, pawed at, and rolled with her while they were still drugged by sleep. Adam wagged his tale at the randiness. Finally, Thackery made a few ah-hems before anything too untoward occurred, and Caenith roared his way into his bestial shape. Once packed, and while braiding grips in the Wolf's fur, Thackery made a playful jibe about having Caenith fitted for a proper mount and bridle, to which the lord of Fang and Claw responded only with a ferocious growl.

They left while the sky was still painted black, and raced until the gold strokes of noon came. By then, they had cleared the sands and reached greener pastures. Here, the travelers dismounted and hiked up knolls that were dressed in gowns of moss and bonneted with flowers. Morigan, already sore from another day of clinging, reminisced about the ease with which she'd ridden her mate in Dream; they might have to seriously consider Thackery's harness suggestion if this sort of travel continued. The steep hillsides were more treacherous than they appeared, and the land's delicate green skin often ripped off, causing Morigan and Thackery to stumble. They were never harmed, though, for the Wolf and Adam stayed in their four-legged forms and nudged their less able companions along like a pair of sheepdogs.

When the sun reached its zenith, the land stewed in a haze and nattered with life. Choruses of crickets made the loudest song, though they were often silenced by the springing, hissing lizards that leaped from rock to rock and ate the noisy carolers. Sometime into the afternoon, Morigan kicked over a rock and surprised a bed of wild cockroaches, little monsters with purple antennae. The insects were pretty until they shrieked like terrified persons and scattered. Morigan shrieked as well. Because of the density and humidity of the air, it felt as if the four climbed a mountain. They gradually headed upward; this land of many hills sloped only one way. Farther off, the land appeared to crest, then drop, into a shady emerald pit. Quite a lot of noise and scent welled up out of that valley: howls, musk, mushroom-fragrant earth. Most of it troubled the Wolf. Moreth had warned them against traversing any forests, especially the dense and primal ones, but Eatoth lay on the other side of this valley. They had no choice.

They reached the lip of the valley and stared down into a milky green sea of unclassifiable conifers and flat-leafed giants. Little could be seen of what lay below the forest's roof, even by the Wolf. It all felt too dense, thick, and entangling to the hunter. On the other side of the towering morass, the trees suddenly disappeared, defeated by a scrubland, whose yellow nothingness ruled until it reached a dot on the horizon. A shining dot; a bead of glass. They could all see it, wolf-blooded or not.

"Eatoth," said Thackery.

A breeze that only Morigan could feel whipped in from the east and slapped her in the face. Smarting, she closed her eyes—

And opens them to beauty, to a glimmering city of crystal, mist, and water. So much majesty cannot be taken in quickly. Beholding Eatoth is like staring into a glass ornament on a sunny day. She is dazzled and blinded. Then clouds descend, bringing a hungry darkness that rumbles. The slender glass buildings weave and wax from yellow, to gold, then to a furious red. She knows that the towers will fall, that a cacophonous shattering will soon begin.

"We have to hurry," said Morigan, and began hiking down into the trees. "Brutus is nearly there. They're all going to die."

The four descended into the chattering emerald dark.

IV

Feeling both dread and wonder, they slowly explored the new land. Here, trees grew as wide apart as a giant's legs, the rainforest dew collected in deep black pools that swam with spiny-backed shapes, and nets of corded moss fell from the overgrown canopy. They could not see the treetops. Sunlight trickled through as a jaundiced glow. The yellow dusk conjured long shadows, and while there was space to walk in the great paths between the trees, the dimness created haunting illusions. The four could see deep into the woods, but never far enough. Every path looked the same. Creatures haunted the heights of the trees. Even the changelings received only vague impressions of the beasts that swung from vine to vine above: lean, glistening, covered in protrusions. Once, these tree-dwellers threw down the steaming fresh carcass of a wild beast and screeched.

Morigan and Thackery held hands and walked together, the great Wolf at their fore and the smaller wolf at their back. Their pride and fearlessness must have shone brighter than the lights Thackery conjured for himself and his adoptive daughter, for the tree-dwellers' shadows eventually ceased passing overhead. *Or perhaps we've simply moved into the lair of a more frightful beast*, thought Thackery with a gulp. He noticed something white tangled in the hanging lattice of the forest—surely it was a bone. For Thackery, it evoked nauseating memories of a spider-filled tomb in Alabion.

Further inspection revealed it was poking out of a dried corpse—one of the tree-dwellers, the Wolf determined. The body appeared humanoid, though it had spines on its shoulders, and its limbs were as long as an ape's. Otherwise, the corpse resembled a man left to become jerky in the sizzling sun of Kor'Keth. What features it might once have possessed had shriveled upon its skull, but its teeth remained, their sharpness accented by the corpse's grin. Looking carefully up and around, they found several more tree-dweller corpses. The Wolf sensed there was an order, a biological meaning and precision to this pattern; it reminded him of a spider's web. He didn't believe that spiders were the cause of it, though, as the bodies appeared to have been dried through a natural process of decay, not drained of juices.

TCH-TCH-TCH-TCH-TCH-TCH.

Soft and sinister came the tapping, clacking sounds. Brows knotted with worry, the four looked at each other. Some horrible beast or danger lay ahead, a presence dark enough to scare off the pests in the treetops. Thackery snuffed out the small star he held, then wandered over to a hedge and snapped off a long gnarled piece of wood that would serve as a staff—the kind an ancient sorcerer in a tale would wield. More chittering swirled through the dark, and the tension grew suffocating.

Trying his best to ignore the noise, Thackery focused on his magik. After he had carefully dusted the moss and dirt off his stave, he coaxed his sorcery into the wood. He thought of an oceanfront, calm and bleached by the sun. He could almost feel a soft breeze upon his cheeks. The songs of the phantom gulls made him smile; he much preferred them to the escalating chatter in the real world. Instead of releasing his magik all at once, he Willed a fragment of the radiance and purity of that scene into the wood with each pass of his hand. After several sands, a golden-white light fluttered to life inside the staff. Thackery then stirred from his trance and found the Wolf, once again a man, staring at him.

"A sound idea," said the Wolf. He recalled what Thackery had been able to do with a stick of magik and thunder back in the Iron Mines. "We may well be needing your power soon. I could race us through these woods, but I would rather not leave any of us exposed and unprotected." He sniffed and then sneezed as he inhaled the staggering spice of loam mixed with an astringent musk. He could hear the shifting and clatter of chitin. However, he still saw nothing in the trees or in the green webbing between them that might cause such disturbances. *My eyes cannot find what I know to be out there. What is it, my Fawn? What do you see?*

For Morigan held onto her star with a carelessness that would soon cause it to drop. She stared up and out into the woods. She peered and peered, feeling something but not able to see it clearly. She had a sense that horrific things surrounded them: scuttling, clinging shapes, with parts bent and wriggling—tentacles or unnaturally flexible limbs. The shapes hung somewhere in the arboreal ceiling; they tricked her eyes and could only be spotted in the corners of her vision. Each time she whipped her head around to follow a movement, the creatures seemed to vanish. "Things," she whispered, and the company drew close. "Large and prowling above. Not spiders, for they're too limber. Not men, either, for they're too odd. I cannot see them, my Wolf. They deny both your senses and mine."

"Invisible?" hissed Thackery.

"Intangible," replied Morigan. "I would say they exist somewhere between this world and Dream."

"These bodies are certainly real enough," said Thackery, aiming his bright staff toward the tree webs and revealing wall upon wall of webs dangling with dried corpses. They would have to either turn back or pass through them. The Wolf was done with stalling and made the necessary decision. Onward, he strode. The others followed.

They pressed forward until they could no longer skirt around trees or find creative paths under the webbing. The Wolf confronted the barrier they could not avoid and then tested it, finding it stronger and more elastic than he'd anticipated. Mustering his strength, he ripped through it, and desiccated body parts rained down upon him. For a moment, he wrestled in corpses and tacky threads. Nonetheless, a hole had been made, and the four moved through it. Although the invisible lurkers clicked their displeasure, the things latched onto trees did not assault them. Perhaps Thackery's golden staff, which pulsed brighter from his fear, kept them at bay; or perhaps it was the huffing, sweating, grumbling Wolf, whom no beast had yet tangled with and lived, or the woman whose eyes gleamed silver and whose figure blurred as though it, too, could remove itself from sight. Adam remained close to his pack, growling.

They journeyed for a time, making holes, becoming slick with sweat, moving deeper and deeper into a giant cradle of mossy strings. The tangle showed no signs of lessening, and the stir and nattering of the lurkers above didn't abate. Indeed, the land seemed to be doing its best to confine the travelers, to suffocate them with the dewy soupiness of the air, to make their bodies fail from all the squirming and exertion needed to move but a few paces. However, they would not be beaten. They'd braved the Pitch Dark, and this trek through strange woodland was a summer stroll by comparison.

In time, their efforts were rewarded. Lesser creatures faced extinction farther into the city of webs. They neither heard nor saw any of Pandemonia's unique avian life, and the scattering of tree-dweller remains above them dwindled until it vanished entirely. A chilling calm befell the woods. Flowers, verdure, and moss became scarce upon trees and shrubs. Every now and then, a dashing, furry thing popped out and then disappeared in a brown streak. The four wandered through colonnades of trees without many leaves or needles—plants, spotty and stripped, like animals with mange. Moonlight dripped into the woods, though it was hindered by the ornate tapestries of emerald vomit strung about. The webbing now hung higher up, meaning they could at least cease their hunching and begin to walk upright.

Shining his light about, Thackery studied the fatty pods hanging in the boughs. Some of the pods moved and he shivered: any wind that might have stirred them had long since died to a hiss. These larger bulks resembled the crafts of silkworms or weaver ants. They were made of a knitted substance formed of verdure mixed with a secretion of some kind; perhaps a mucus borne of the chlorophyll extracted from the plants of this land. Even without his scholar friend present, Thackery was able to develop some hypotheses about this ecosystem. He realized that he missed Talwyn as he said, "I cannot conclude with certainty that these creatures are carnivorous or harmful. It is possible they are benign. There are no dead animals to be seen, and we have not been attacked thus far. Perhaps the dead tree-dwellers we encountered earlier had done something to upset the balance that these creatures maintain. Nothing involving territorial encroachment, though—we've been tramping about in the territory of these creatures and met with no retaliation. Perhaps the entities in these woods consider us too great or obscure a threat with which to engage. For the moment, I believe we are safe."

"I have the same sense," said Morigan, her head buzzing with accord. "We are, for the moment, safe." Still, she gripped her promise dagger, which she'd unsheathed some time ago.

Thackery continued. "We should watch our steps and try not to do anything rash. But I think we can make it through these woods unscathed."

"Hmm..." grumbled the Wolf.

Woof! The bark came from Adam, who'd run ahead while the three chatted. Down a moonlit road, they found the brown wolf. Here, the space was brighter, a piece of the green mesh having recently fallen from overhead. The Wolf growled and warned his changeling companion away from the quivering green-and-black mass. It glistened in the moonlight like a giant placenta, a sac of jelly as large as a small pool. It juddered and bled. An unfathomable birth was occurring. The Wolf pulled them all back from the mound just as it deflated with a flatulent *whoosh* and poured a silky stream of mucus and swimming worms out into the soil.

Aghast and amazed, the four stared at the abortions that flopped in the slime. They reminded Thackery of smelt, but fish did not have legs like centipedes—or were those little prehensile tendrils? Fish didn't waver between being seen and unseen in rolling flashes of silver, either. However, the monsters did give off a sharp fishy smell that also suggested semen, blood, a woman's fluids. Despite the terrible sight and smell, and no matter the comparisons that came to mind, the writhing pile still made the changelings' mouths water.

The company watched the last of the life spill out. They stayed until the flickering children had stopped their awful squealing. At their feet, there now lay only a great lumpy puddle. Within moments, even the membrane that had once protected the creatures began to break down into slop. The Wolf grunted. "The woods end not far from here," he said. "I believe Thackery is right. We shall be safe. Let us hurry to Eatoth."

The companions set out, but after taking only a few steps, they realized Adam was no longer with them. Turning, they saw the changeling sniffing and pawing at the green pool. As he'd worn his furry skin for many days, the beast now almost completely controlled his mind. Adam's wolfish appetites and desires had blocked the instincts of a man. He had the hunger of an animal, and the great soup of fishy matter was enticing to him. Although he could see only the broth and not the morsels themselves, that didn't keep Adam from searching through it with his paws and snout, and then lapping at the slime, which was apparently harmless: changelings had a nose for poison. Adam ignored the Wolf's summons, for he'd now found what he sought: a lump in the slime, an invisible slug. He ate it, then found another and ate it as well.

TCH-TCH-TCH-TCH-TCH-TCH.

An alarm bell rang in Thackery's mind, and he formulated a deduction of which Talwyn would be proud: animals were free to scavenge here, as long as they didn't eat the tentacled slugs. Perhaps the tree-dwellers had made the mistake of feeding on them. Alive or dead, these creatures were off limits, and Adam was now consuming, defiling, the dead.

"Oh no, no, no," blathered Thackery. "No, no, no! I think they're peaceful unless threatened—interested only in eating plants, breeding, and whatever else such odd creatures might do." Thackery shook his stick of light at Adam, who continued to gorge himself on slugs and slop. "Tell him to stop, Caenith. Make Adam stop!"

The Wolf roared. Adam leaped back from the pool, crawled to join his companions, then pressed his belly to the dirt and whined his subjugation to the lord of Fang and Claw. The Wolf's action, though, came too late and was not fearsome enough to quell the chattering in the trees. The great brood had been defiled; their precious young dead had been consumed. In one grand chattering storm, like a flurry of bats woken from a dark sleep, the creatures roared back to the Wolf, to the eaters of their young. In the cloudy green eaves of the wood, shadows madly slithered and arranged themselves.

The creatures' fury reduced their camouflaging abilities, and finally Morigan could see them—an impossible army of them. Slithering masses had been silent and placid this whole time while hanging over their heads. They were similar to crayfish, but grotesquely large and possessed of a sinewy fatness that reminded her of caterpillars or snakes. In their adult forms, the cray-squid bristled with tentacles. These appendages must have been what she and the others had heard clacking together, for they were armored and hardened to points. At once, the bees filled Morigan's spinning head with flashes of starving tree-dwellers, driven to desperation by hunger, raiding tree-bound wombs, only to find themselves entwined and gored by swarms of wriggling cephalopods. The damned things could leap, she realized. As she turned in circles with her companions, she caught only intermittent glimpses of the cray-squid. With each blink, though, the preposterously large size of the army was more fully revealed. Soon they would drop, leap, wheedle their way down on threads. "We cannot fight them all," she realized. "There are too many; it's an infestation."

"Can you run us out of here?" asked Thackery, and grabbed the Wolf's arm. "We need to escape."

"I can run," he replied. "But the forest is alive. I can smell the rage of the things we have disturbed. I cannot guarantee our safety. I cannot guarantee that nothing will drop down upon us. I sense the weight of them as if it were a net. We shall have to tear a hole through it."

"We have no option but to defend ourselves," declared Morigan. She shivered as the men looked at her. She was ready to dart in and out of Dream, and the glimmer of steel in her hand was as ruthless as her expression. The blood of the Wolf pumped as fiercely as fire and liquor in her veins. "Protect each other, and do not worry about me. Here is our final gauntlet before Brutus—" Morigan stopped speaking as the bees shrieked in her head, ordering her to look up, and then she vanished into a crackling silver wrinkle. Materializing in a silver flash a stride away, she screamed, "They are upon us!"

A shivering weight of air landed where Morigan had just been. It clacked and thrashed. While neither sorcerer nor changeling could see what was there, Thackery brought his blazing staff down upon the spot, and the Wolf crushed it with a heel. Their actions produced a small explosion of fire, warm plasma, and steaming pieces of shell. More invisible weights of air began to descend like phantom bombs. Clouds of dust—screeching, clacking dust—scuttled toward the panicking company.

Thackery spun, drove his staff into the soil, and Willed the creatures away, making no effort to restrain his magik. He was hoping to trigger a surge from Pandemonia's channels of ether, and he received one. A shimmering light erupted from the spot and threw whirlwinds of soil around the site. The Wolf staggered. Adam yelped and rolled like a teddy bear in a hurricane. Sensing Adam's peril, Morigan shivered her body into Dream, again, and caught the tumbling changeling by his scruff. She clung to a tree and held the frantic wolf, a feat made possible by her bloodmate's sympathetic strength. The wind howled. Trees rocked and groaned, raining splattering cargo onto the bare floor of the forest. A dusty Thackery scrambled out of the small scorched pit his sorcery had dug. He coughed out some dirt and shouted, "Everyone all right?"

They were, for the moment, although the forest creaked and croaked like an ancient shipyard in a storm as the nests dislodged by Thackery's telekinetic blast continued to drop. Morigan released Adam and ran with him to the others. By then, her bloodmate was helping the sorcerer dust himself off. They looked around at the windblown carnage: branches snapped, green placentas everywhere, gooey spurts bleeding from piles of shattered cray-squids, whose purple blood was visible, though their shells were not. Evaluating the carnage, she sensed they had killed dozens, maybe hundreds of them. Whatever the number, it hadn't significantly dented the remaining horde, which was even angrier now and rapidly drawing closer. She kissed her bloodmate, and seemed wilder even than he when she pulled away. The Wolf's heart did a dance as she asked him a question, a version of one he'd once posed to her in Eod. "Will you run with me?" she asked.

"Yes," he replied.

The Wolf and his Fawn ran ahead, a blur of speed and a flickering woman. Thackery and Adam ran to catch them.

V

Free of the woods and slathered in sweat and gore, the bloodmates made straight for the first glint of water that the Wolf spotted on the dry, grassy plain. Their companions were close behind; Morigan and the Wolf had gone ahead only to clear a path, keeping them always within range of their senses. All would be safe for their companions' passage. Knowing this, the bloodmates raced in a wind of passion toward the pool. They desired to occupy it for some time alone before the others reached them.

Almost casually, Thackery and Adam walked through the final stretch of the forest, encountering little in the way of further threats. A few lingering cray-squid (the term had stuck in Thackery's mind; he must share it with Talwyn) had survived on the path after its trampling by the Wolf and Morigan. With his glowing, smiting staff, Thackery put the beasts down as they lashed out weakly, their rage now feeble. He did so from kindness, knowing they would only have died more slowly otherwise. Most of the creatures had been split and damaged so badly that their own blood acted as a paint, enabling the sage to see the glistening corpses.

While administering death, he examined them: their hard shells, their many twisting limbs. It was unfortunate that he and his companions had been forced to disrupt one of the more peaceful habitats he'd encountered in Pandemonia. However, it had been either them or the cray-squid. If the creatures had been smarter, they would have clashed neither with the woman who unwove and rewove Fates, nor with the son of both a mad Immortal and an Ancient. Here and there, Thackery had seen the bloodmates' copper and silver shadows dancing a waltz of death while clearing the road ahead. It humbled him how much Morigan had transformed since their time together in Eod. She was no longer the doting, clever girl he'd known then. Now, she was a force of nature, a great warrior.

Morigan and the Wolf didn't abandon them until the plains came into sight. At that point, she and the Wolf vanished, moving so fast that Thackery and Adam couldn't keep up. The bloodmates wouldn't have fled if they hadn't determined the land was safe, so Thackery relaxed. He counted strange stars and enjoyed the refreshing kisses of the wind on his face. In the distance lay a small blue lens of water. It shimmered in the night's glow, and rocks stood around it like soldiers. Thackery believed this was where his companions must have gone. A crestfallen Adam, his head and tail down, seemed to be leading him there, too.

"Cheer up, boy," said Thackery. "You were only hungry. Could have gone much worse."

Adam whined; apparently, he did not agree. After a great many steps across the pleasantly windy expanse, Adam stopped, and his whines turned to grunts; within moments, Thackery was joined by the two-legged form of his friend. Thackery paused to pass the man his clothing, sandals, and the ebon speaking stone from Elemech that had been stowed in his pack. Once Adam was dressed, they continued on. Thackery sensed the weight of the young man's contrition, though he did not broach the topic. In time, Adam gave voice to his regrets. "I have been foolish," he said. "I have been an animal too long, and it's made me selfish and hasty."

"Sounds like a general affliction of the young," said Thackery with a smile. "Lately, I've been afflicted in much the same way myself. I understand your frustration and why you've chosen to hide in a wolf's skin. I know the feelings that you have for my great-niece."

Adam shrugged, surprisingly indifferent. "I know seasons: summer and winter, spring, and fall. She does not feel the summer for me; I doubt she ever will. I have come to accept that, element-breaker. I shall therefore dedicate myself to honoring the season she has chosen: autumn. I will foster an autumnal bliss, full of companionship, friendship, fellowship. Fionna has never had those things. I haven't, either. I lost all that was dear to me when I was young, as she did. I can be her brother-wolf without bringing any great pain to my heart. Sometimes the love we seek is not the one we need. I do miss her, though. And the chatty man, too. Even the Menosian was starting to grow on me."

"Like fungus," said Thackery, and the fellows laughed. Thackery's mirth faded, and he placed his hand upon the changeling's back. "I misjudged you, my friend. You have great and stoic wisdom for one your age. I believe you will be exactly the brother and friend my great-niece needs in these times. Ahead are our leaders. We should hurry: I know not how much time we—or Eatoth—have left."

After picking up their pace, the two soon came to the watering hole. An oval of silver with a shore of swaying flowers and feathery bushes resembling fanned, exotic plumage welcomed the men with an embrace of steam and mineral freshness that blew off the water's skin. They finally spotted the bloodmates hidden in the deep shadows thrown by the great rock-soldiers standing guard around the water. Thackery and Adam jogged toward them, but soon realized that their haste was unwarranted. The lovers made no secret of what they had been doing during their sands apart from the others. Morigan rested against Caenith, who had his back against one of the stones. Lust and passion filled the air like a musky fog, thicker than the breath of the pool, and the pair appeared relaxed and wet. Most of their clothing lay scattered around them. Morigan's hair tumbled in shining ruby ringlets that the Wolf combed his fingers through and smelled. Her naked body was wrapped in her cloak, but one alabaster shoulder was exposed, and the Wolf kissed it hungrily. He, too, was naked, but he was tastefully covered by his lover's body.

"Eatoth?" asked Thackery. Their carnality no longer discomfited him.

"We were only waiting for you to arrive," replied Morigan, running her hand up and down the hairy ripple of one of the Wolf's tented legs. She started to stand, but the circle of warm iron love that was her bloodmate constricted and held her.

"You must rest, my Fawn," said the Wolf. "If only for a few sands. Shut your eyes and let your body heal." Although his blood and their lovemaking had energized her, she did not have his powerful constitution. He could sense, even if she could not, that she was leaden with exhaustion from their journey and battle. As she considered his suggestion, the aches in her arms and the weight of her eyelids became apparent.

"How odd," she remarked. "I didn't feel tired at all until you mentioned it."

We blur and flow into one being, one body with two halves, whispered the Wolf, pressing his hardness against her. For a moment, she felt a pressure, a throbbing rod rising from her own pelvis. *Yet we are still ourselves, despite this marvelous gift. The closer we grow, the easier it becomes for me to know your every desire and weakness. I see the chinks in your armor that need repair, just as you more clearly see my faults.*

"What about the city?" asked Thackery curtly. The bloodmates were gazing blankly at each other, clearly chatting, albeit inaudibly.

The seer's eyes flashed with silver, and she pondered, hunting fates, weighing probabilities. "The smoke is not yet on the horizon," she said dreamily. "Thanks to our haste, I think we have managed to outrun Eatoth's doom. For the moment, at least. We can rest." Morigan sighed as the visions left her, and she nuzzled into her bloodmate.

"Adam, why don't you see what you can hunt for supper?" asked Thackery. "I shall start a fire. You two—"

But they'd already fallen asleep, tangled, calm, and beautiful like lovers cast in bronze and pearl by a master artisan. Had he ever seen anything so harmonious as the shades and contrasts of their beauty? He had not, and probably never would again. Thackery watched them, proud to be their caregiver. Eventually, he made a fire and waited for Adam to return. He occupied himself by naming strange stars, relishing this rare instant of peace.

VI

Adam was distracted tonight, and the hunt was going poorly. He couldn't place a finger or claw upon the reason why, but since reverting to his two-legged self, he'd felt different. Distracted. As if being his two-legged self once more after having been a wolf for so long had reminded him of all the pleasures one could savor only as a man. He was supposed to be hunting—already a difficult enough task in Pandemonia when one was attentive—but instead he wandered the heathlands.

Sometimes he fell to all fours and sniffed or rolled on the earth. Sometimes he brushed the long, silky grasses against his cheeks. Often, he thought of all the beautiful and magikal things his mother had wished he could know beyond Briongrahd. Pride at his accomplishments and at the journey he'd taken filled him. *I am about to see one of the greatest two-leg civilizations of our world, Mother. I can be every dream you ever dreamed. I carry your spirit, your season of change, with me wherever I go in this world. One day, when the storm of Kings has passed and the forests of Alabion are safe, I shall return for your bones, now drowning beneath the Weeping Falls. I shall return for them and bring them on my next adventure.*

A haunting species of ebon moth with golden patterns on its wings proved the changeling's next distraction from the hunt. He chased a living cloud of them for a time, all the way to one of the strangled, solitary, jarringly ugly trees that grew on this plain. The damned moths moved as fast as hummingbirds, and he couldn't catch even one. Vexed, he called out, "Please, I only want to see your wings of sunshine and night. They are so beautiful. If only you would stop and let me look."

The cloud of fluttering, sparkling things paused, hovering. Adam walked into the shade of the tree, feeling a little cautious, but still mostly giddy from the thrill of having hands instead of paws. He used his hands to reach up into the moth-cloud, and then used his voice of man to praise the beautiful creatures as they tickled his fingers and palms like faeries of cotton and static.

"Thank you, my friends. You are beautiful." Adam smiled and spun like a silly child in a rainstorm, letting the insects fly around him. "Go on then," he said finally. "You've entertained me enough, and your lives are short."

Absorbed in his frivolity, it did not strike him as strange that the cloud obeyed, although it probably should have. *I must hunt*, he suddenly remembered, and raced off to tend to that demand. Thackery would surely be hungry by now.

However, he soon found another diversion when a herd of loping mammals appeared on the plain. Adam darted to a rocky throne of the land, climbed it, and watched the herd. Although the creatures were merely shadows with long legs and huge strides, he felt they would be as soft and gentle as the night moths he'd recently met. Adam considered hunting them, but then thought better of it. There were dozens of them, and they moved as a pack—they were a family, and families should never be broken apart. It wasn't like the aborted cray-squids, which he also now regretted eating; even if he wasn't sure whence that regret came—the repercussions of his act, or the act itself. He heard a lone chortling creature, perhaps blood relative to a hog or quill-beast, snuffling on the grassy knoll below him. It sounded old and tired. Ready to die.

Adam's sentimentality surrendered to his instincts, and the wolf reigned for a spell. A red haze fell over his sight; when it had dispersed, he found himself in a shady dip in the land, on his knees, pinning a bleeding porcine beast down with his still half-clawed hands. It squealed in terror, not quite dead despite the brutal tears on its belly and throat. Its watering, rolling black eyes found him.

"Preeease..." the creature wheezed. "No die. No kill."

Adam shook his head. He was hearing things.

"No die. No kill."

Or perhaps he'd gone mad. The wolf in his spirit seized control once more, making the decision the man would not. Adam's claws ended the creature with quick, deep slashes.

As his bestial self subsided, the smell of blood and sweet perfume of his kill sickened him. Adam turned into the grass and heaved. Afterward, he staggered up, unable to look at the steaming corpse. *Preeease...Preeease—* the words seemed to echo. Adam slapped his face and chest to dispel the insanity. It worked for the moment, and he cautiously prowled around the carcass.

Adam assumed his sentimentality had tricked him. There were downsides to being a two-legs and to pretending he wasn't an animal. It was known that repressing the beast within could have consequences, though he'd never heard of anything as bizarre as hearing one's kill plead. Quite puzzled, Adam arrived back at the campsite with a vacant expression on his face. Thackery noticed the young man's detachment. Concerned, he stopped poking the flames with his glowing staff, stood up, and went over to his friend. The changeling was greased in clammy sweat. "You look a bit haunted," said Thackery. He peered into the night. "Something out there?"

I think I spoke with butterflies, and then a boar begged me not to slay it, Adam replied in his head. To Thackery, he gave a less-complicated response. "Pandemonia," he replied. "Strange."

"I'll say," replied Thackery.

Thackery watched the young man drag his kill to the fire and was surprised when he left it there, making no move to eat. Instead, he walked over to the pool and washed the blood from his hands. *Scoured* the blood, rather. Thackery was familiar with the sneers and pinched eyes brought on by self-disgust: Adam appeared to have mastered the expression.

IX

RETURN OF THE QUEEN

I

Following a single path forward down the great gullet of the lordvessel seemed the only way to go—Lila and Erik needed to find an engine room, or whatever passed for one, on the ancient Menosian warship Abagail had given them. It was hard for them not to fall to distraction and wonder at the simplicity of the design: the dark, hollow cavern, arced and strutted in feliron ribs. Along the ribs gleamed dead metal gaslights, which Lila lit with her magik every so often so that she could see in the dark.

Erik had no such difficulty with the shadows, but it pleased him to see how golden her magik was once more. Many cross-handled portals led from the interior. Erik opened a few, and they peeked into dustless metal quarters with bunks built into the walls—slots for bodies similar to those found in a mausoleum. The lordvessel seemed to defy every rule of shipbuilding he knew. It had been constructed to impose itself, not to conform. It was a wonder, as well, that ancient Menos had birthed such technomagik. Erik wondered, though, whether ancient shipwrights and technomancers had been wholly responsible for the lordvessel's advances. With his new senses, he could smell something under the tons and tons of feliron and salt—a reek older than feliron, a hint of something bloody and sour. Erik couldn't place the faded scent; his instincts told him only that it might be otherworldly. Erik mentioned this to his queen.

"A smell, you say?" she replied. "Older than Menos? That is indeed very strange."

"Aye. It could be that this ingenuity was not entirely the result of Iron minds. I cannot explain it, my queen; I am filled with sights, sounds, and smells that I have yet to understand. Some of these are more like impressions: it is as if I can see, hear, and taste secrets. I know many things about nature that a man should never know."

"The *Fuilimean* changes us, Erik, in ways we can't even imagine." Lila felt stronger, more secure, with his obsidian bedrock of support inside of her, but she retained her sense of self. *I don't need a man who will change me drastically—only one who makes me a better version of myself.*

"I believe that I do," whispered Erik, having heard her thoughts. Erik slipped his hand around her waist and spun her around for a kiss—not taking, but waiting until she pressed her lips to his.

You do. Lila smiled and kissed him.

The lordvessel was long, and they took their time exploring it. More than once, they stopped to entertain their lust. Although they shivered with arousal, Erik did not once slip his dark sword inside her. They'd discovered they didn't always need to engage in the physical act of sex in order to experience euphoria. As they exchanged spit and touches once more, Lila found herself swimming in the cold, gray ocean of her lover's spirit. She'd never been this intimate with Magnus; with him, there'd always been a wall in his heart beyond which she could not penetrate, beyond which Brutus lurked. Erik, for his part, found himself floating in fantasies—of running through swards aglow with sunlight, of chasing a wind spiced with Lila's apple and brandy scent. Intoxicated by each other's passion, they faded from the world and stumbled about the ship. Eventually, they came up against an unyielding table, sprawled on top of it, and laughed.

"My knight, we need to remember our duty," she said, caressing his pouting face. "Our great duty. We have a secret of all secrets to deliver to Elissandra. The lives in Eod depend on our level heads."

"I am sorry, my queen. I have wanted to taste this all of my life. I have now been given more of a feast than any man could eat." Erik kissed her, and the shadow of him surged within her, driving as hard as the meat against her leg. *I shall try to have my fill. I shall eat and eat your beauty… When there is time.*

Erik assisted his queen from the table. They had blundered into a dining area; the hall had veered abruptly, and they were now in the heights of the hull. Across the room stood many tables and benches that seemed made of some stretched mucous-like metal that resembled black putty or wax. The furniture's eerie style extinguished some of Lila's passion. Again, she thought of Erik's suspicion that a culture older than Menos had inspired these designs. Hand in hand, they walked across the deserted hall, imagining the place once again filled with fierce, black-armored men gobbling gruel.

In Erik, the vision created a sense of confinement and suffering. Strange as it seemed, he felt as if he could smell misery—stale, foul sweat, and the salt of tears. On the other side of the feasting hall was another throat of metal, ready to swallow them. Through that passage, toward the tip of the hull, was where Lila felt compelled to go. They passed more portals, Erik sniffing as the ozone-and-matchstick scent of magik intensified. Lila lit fewer lights now. It seemed as if they had been walking through the engulfing darkness for an hourglass, though surely it hadn't been that long; likely the feeling was the result of claustrophobia induced by the steadily lowering roof.

Finally, they came to an archway, an end to the road. They hurried inside, and Lila lifted her arms and threw her Will at the clotted shadows. A shimmering dust of golden stars flew like powder from her hands, dusting the walls, ceiling, and floor of the chamber. The pulsating yellow light unveiled the ancient deck of command that had been built into the bow of the ship.

Little could be seen in the chamber except for a sudden pyramid of steps that led to a dais upon which stood a single, thorny chair. On one side, the platform curled up into a skinned arm of black metal—all sinewy cables—the hand of which clutched an eye of crystal. With a glittering wink, the orb refracted the light Lila had summoned. Whatever sorcery the orb had originally been imbued with had not faded through the years, and it called to her.

Touch me. Command me, it said in an intimate whisper almost like that of a bloodmate. As he was bound to his queen, Erik sensed this gravity, this force that drew her. A hand always upon her, Erik followed his queen up the steps. Once they'd reached the small circular summit, Lila stood between the throne and the sphere and gazed deeply into the latter. Erik cared for neither relic. Sickly sweet sin wafted from the cruel and twisted iron throne, while the orb crackled with invisible power. As Erik stared at the orb, he was reminded of a glass skull as mist eddied within, forming nose and eye sockets, and little shadows for teeth.

Lila resisted touching the surface of the crystal, though it pulled at her hand like a magnet would metal. She wandered over to the throne and drew a finger over its barbed-wire twists, wondering how a person could sit on such a contraption; he would have to be wrapped in similarly evil skin, she supposed. She would stand to pilot the vessel, and Erik would be her moorings. She turned to face the orb. Feeling her intention, Erik moved into position behind his queen. Erik braced his legs and held her waist.

"Someone sitting there," she said, nodding at the throne, "would command the orb with his or her mind. It desires to be used, that orb, as if it were a living man. It wants me to touch it. I wonder how such a thing was ever made."

From somewhere in the room, perhaps the orb, Erik thought he heard a noise other than the gentle groaning of the lordvessel. A heartbeat, perhaps—one that was not theirs. "Living, yes," he said. "Although it must have a cursed kind of life, the life of a reborn."

Lila sighed. "Are you ready, my knight?"

He was, and she felt his eagerness. She leaned against the hard rock of her bloodmate, forgetting the body he so tightly held, and extended her Will to the unliving, cursed presence in the orb. Throughout the chamber, the radiance she had cast flickered, and Lila slumped. When she touched the presence within the sphere, it pulled her spirit from her flesh and threw her up through the ceiling to the jagged deck of the lordvessel. There, she hovered as a white-fringed cloud of vision. In this form, she could see anything she wanted, things that would not have been visible to her eyes, or even to Erik's. She could somehow see in many places at once, as if she were a gemstone and her beveled edges were windows showing everything above, beneath, and behind. Although she was having difficulty reconciling these various panes of sight, *the Mind*, the presence of the sphere, welcomed her.

Greetings, Navigator, said the Mind.

She was too stunned to reply; too many wonders were emerging at once. The voice echoed in her head like that of a second bloodmate and immediately filled it with technical information. The Mind whispered, *There are seven female organisms of bipedal standing gathered at the prow of the ship*; it must mean women. It then mentioned that a portal was ajar, and offered to close it if she had no objection. She made no response, because she continued to reel. In one of her many panes of perception, she had a vision of the black outer hull of the ship: its feliron was running wet, softening, and sealing itself over like melting wax. Wind power density, wave speed, temperature, and forecasting data whirled in her mind in a confusing burble, but the Mind soon quieted the storm and began dispensing the information to the slower neurons of its host one drip at a time.

Erik hadn't been terribly concerned thus far, because he could feel his bloodmate's calm and awe, but suddenly her body rose up in his arms. Her consciousness, though, was still elsewhere, chatting with the strange, busy thing: perhaps there was no cause for alarm. The ship then lurched without warning, giving him no time to further contemplate this uninvited stranger. What power the ancient lordvessel had—a strength the Straits of Wrath would rue. Like a black sword, the lordvessel tore ahead. Erik trembled from the might of the technomagikal engine that rumbled through the metal. He trembled, too, with excitement and rage as he thought of where they were headed: to Eod. Magnus would pay for what he'd done to Lila, and now Erik had the power to punish him.

II

After the ship had lurched away from the dock, actually shaking the stone and nearly tipping Sister Abagail into the water, it sped out of the underground port. Time and rising sea level had shrunk the once-great cave leading out of the harborage, but the lordvessel would brook no opposition: it simply burrowed a new tunnel through the rock. The citizens of the city above, still recovering from the bloodmate's rampage, were set to screaming again by this second terror. The Mind told Lila, though, that none of the Sisters of Celcita had been harmed, and that the resulting tremors would neither seriously damage property nor bring about any loss of life.

From there, the lordvessel struck open sea and turned on a skate's edge toward the black rock towers and storming skies of the Straits; how swiftly it could maneuver its bulk! From her metaphysical all-seeing crow's nest, Lila watched the black towers draw nearer and form jutting fingers, spears, and islands of the darkest rock. Any wooden or normal metal boat would have shattered like a toy there. In a speck, the lordvessel was upon the dangerous rubble and testing its hull against it. Erik noticed a few bumps, but nothing else: the ancient rocks that had claimed so many lives were ground to pebbles and swallowed by ravenous whirlpools of water. Nothing could stop the lordvessel, it seemed.

Neither the glowering thunderheads nor the screaming sheets of rain obscured Lila's vision in the nest. Indeed, the eyes of the lordvessel—now her eyes—pierced the maelstrom and revealed every sunken island razor-backed in stalactites, every black mast and ship's skeleton floating in the path of the lordvessel. The Mind steered the lordvessel away from the worst of these obstructions, and the ship's feliron bulkhead simply ploughed through the others.

As they sailed, the Mind continued to play second captain to Lila. It would relay a new piece of information to the queen every so many specks. The delivery of the statistics was timed to perfection: the Mind never overloaded her with thoughts, as if it had somehow measured the pace at which her cortex could accept information. It must also have read in her their destination, for they were headed south and east. Even as Lila contemplated the possibility of an error in charting, the Mind whispered that they would be arriving on Baldringer's Point, at the southwest shore of Meadowvale, in approximately six hourglasses.

The more sands Lila spent in the crow's nest with the diligent, diagnostic presence, the more convinced she became of its benevolence. Not all products of Menos were bred from evil; perhaps this creation was merely another slave to the Iron Will. It certainly aimed to please her, in much the same way that a hunting dog would—with unwavering obedience. She regretted that the Mind, having just had its first contact with a master and a mission in centuries, would once again be lonely when they parted. Sitting there, waiting to be touched for another thousand years... She was being absurd, and she stopped herself. She resumed studying the glowing veins in the terrible thunderclouds, and scanning the shearing horizon for a land that was green instead of black and blue. What could make a land so tortured?

The cataclysm, said the Mind, which listened.

Pardon? Lila didn't feel intruded upon, only surprised.

North, south, east, and west were all connected, Navigator. In a time before your body's cessation of age.

She wondered how it knew so much about her makeup, including her immortality, but she was more intrigued by the cataclysm of which it spoke. *Please explain. What cataclysm? I don't remember hearing anything of this history.*

The Mind went quiet as it unearthed old data, and Lila was left with the howling rain. A few specks later, it returned to her. *P.E. Zero. Landmass fractured by impact of meteorological phenomenon. Many primitive cultures and species on the geostratic surface eradicated. Twenty thousand years after impact, the four great ages end.*

P.E. Zero? Four great ages? A meteorological catastrophe that split the lands of Geadhain? Neither Magnus nor her studies of history had taught her anything of the sort. The Mind detected her confusion and, quick to serve her, fished for additional data. Efficiently and in a matter of specks, it processed and collated its information into a single explanation. *Primogenal Era, abbreviated to consonant "P" and vowel "E." Counted backward from an unspecified date—the origin of the world—to arrive at point zero, when the impact and the birth of the second era occurred. Chronological classifications thereafter may be confusing for you, Navigator, as I see that you adhere to the calendar of the West and count your sands by the A.E— After Eod—system. P.E. Year Zero occurred long before such measurements had been implemented by your preferred culture. Iron Sages theorize that an enflamed mass at least as large as a mountaintop struck the southeastern hemisphere of the world. The impact resulted in massive tectonic shifts, an* underwater bleed of magma that formed rivers, seas, and oceans, as well as a swelling of clouds of ash that blocked out the sun. Iron Sages refer to this as the Age of Fire. Very little sentient life survived the P.E. Year Zero impact, and at first, evolutionary and cultural progress was impossible in such a hostile environment. It has, though, been suggested that the Immortals lived through this period, albeit as tribal wanderers, and I see from the images stored in your memory banks about your former mate's trials through these Great Ages that this is true. Thank you for this information of your time in the Hall of Memories; I have added it to my repository. After P.E. Year Zero, uncountable geological, agricultural, and zoological transformations occurred as Geadhain found its balance—periods of excessive cold, saturation, and dryness. I have measured these periods from the millennia after the Age of Fire: each took several thousands of years.

Amazing, thought Lila, unable to pick a single aspect of the genius of this entity that didn't impress her.

I am glad that you think so. I am happy to have served.

Was it? Could it be? To what was she speaking?

I am a biological imprint of minds bound in a durable encasement of technomagikal crystal. The metascience is complicated, however, and the procedure could not be replicated in this age. I was made by the Lordkings of Menos, the men who fled to Carthac to rebuild their empire. They took with them, from Menos's treasury, a crystal of an old empire—though no one from that time before had been able to use its magik. My makers, though, were able to use that magik. They awoke the stone. I am the result of their ritual.

But why? For what purpose were you made?

The Mind contemplated her existential question, leaving her to be assaulted by the obstreperous music of the Straits. Lila believed she could see a glimmer of gold off in the dark. Then the Mind spoke. *I am sorry, Navigator. I do not have information on that subject. Much of my facility and use I am determining only now, since you are the first to have woken me. The souls of which I am made—*

Souls?

A neurological imprint cannot be created without impressions derived from a biological matrix. To make a brain, one requires brains. To make life, one requires the spark of life—or of many lives, in my case.

Of course no Menosian invention could have been ethically produced, Lila reflected angrily. How many people had died to create this fascinating entity?

May I continue? I hear your thoughts, and sense fluctuations in your telemetric currents that indicate a state of sadness. Do not feel sad. My biological components were all quite young, their neural networks hardly formed. I believe my creators showed what you would call mercy. My components' youth was necessary to facilitate the gestation and development of my pathways.

It was talking about children, a sacrifice of innocent lives. Somewhere, Lila's stomach heaved. *Why?* she asked once more.

I regret that I still do not possess the information you have requested. I was never touched by my makers; they never awakened me with their Wills as you have. I know little about the reason for my being. But I possess many memory banks of data on the western seas and on many of the archipelagos of that region. It is possible that my makers wished to pilot me there.

Lila could think of nothing to say.

Is that all, Navigator?

Yes.

I am happy to have served. Please enjoy the comforts of your journey.

Even as the golden spot she'd seen grew into a pool of sunlight in the clouds, and the black hands of the Straits finally surrendered the lordvessel to compassionate waters, Lila was unable to find peace. She was thinking of children—those she'd murdered in Menos, as well as the many she'd saved and adopted during her reign as Queen of Eod. Finally, she thought of this one child of many souls that had waited in a dark tomb in the earth for a thousand years for the simple pleasure of a touch.

III

"I won't leave him," declared Lila.

"How do you know it is male?" replied Erik.

"I simply do," Lila replied. "I have adopted and raised enough urchins through the centuries to know how children work. I can tell the sex of a child even if he or she is covered in the grime and ash of an atrocity." A thought pricked Lila's heart: two filthy infants, young Dorvain and

Leonitis, saved from the pyre that was to end them. She stared off into the distance, remembering.

Erik huffed. After the lordvessel had made a grating landing upon the southern shores of Meadowvale and Lila had returned from the crow's nest, they had begun disagreeing over what should be done with the Mind. It swirled with misty twists and pulsed with occasional dim light, as if listening to the two hiss back and forth. Erik felt the relic should remain as they'd found it: in the dark and forgotten. Erik had even considered shattering the Menosian object, but Lila's pleas had stayed his hand. Caught in this deadlock, they'd wavered for many sands.

"We cannot leave him, Erithitek," said Lila. "What if another were to find him? Someone wicked? You do not realize the brilliance, the uniqueness, of this artifact. I can think of no other comparison but Eod's Hall of Memories. Even that intelligence displays none of the extraordinary sentience I have seen in the Mind."

"The Mind?"

"That is what I am calling him, until we can think of a better name."

"You want to name it?"

"Possibly. Every creature deserves a name, my knight."

She slunk over to him, her serpentine grace and stare enchanting him, and then ran her hands over his shoulders. Erik knew he was being manipulated. He smelled her pheromones blossoming like flowers, teasing him with sweet pleasure. Connected as they were, he could sense her need to beguile him. There was a different aspect to her allure today, a magnetism that was more than carnal. Under the queen's candy, spice, and brandy aromas, Erik smelled a puff of sulfur, of magik. Whatever spell this was, though, he was able to resist it. Drawing determinedly upon his willpower, he pulled the two of them apart and held her by her wrists.

"There's no need to coerce me with your charms," he said. "I shall do as you desire. You need only ask. If you wish to bring the artifact with us, the only question that remains is how to remove it from its clasp." He paused, and his gray sea and rumbling storm inside of Lila turned turbulent for a speck. "I warn you, my queen, that if your attachment to this relic becomes anything like your fixation on Taroch's hideous curse, I shall smash it into splinters neither man nor magik could put back together."

Erik's ferociousness, his awareness of the games she usually so adeptly played with men, flushed the queen with shame. "I am sorry. I did not... Magnus never caught...never chastised me for wielding my influence—"

"I shall never be like him." Erik scowled, but then his face quickly cleared. He smiled as he said, "Your charm is certainly like a sword to the heart...and loins."

Doomed, soul-bound fools in love, they felt emotions run and melt like ice every time passion flickered between them. The knight and queen came together, and their caresses and tongues expressed forgiveness for any criticism and ill behavior. In a sand, they sank down upon the cold metal stairs. Unable to escape their clothing quickly enough, they pulled their pants down just far enough for his prick to enter her. The heat of their connection whirled them away: to seas and storms, to golden fields and candy-scented breezes. They each came in specks, Erik thumbing her secret switch of pleasure while he pulled in and out of her inch by inch. But their release soothed none of their lust, especially not Erik's. She was a marvel to him. Even her mouth felt extraordinary: harder, somehow, as he probed it deeply with his tongue.

This was their final carefree moment: soon, they would face the world and the legions of enemies their actions had created. Recklessly, they fuked and kissed and tumbled up and down the iron stairs. By the end of their dance, they were naked, soaked, and shivering like a couple in a rainstorm. They held one another, whispering sweet promises in their heads.

Throughout their lovemaking, the Mind had sat pulsing on its perch, busily analyzing their curious auras and physical exercises.

IV

Erik was able to extract the Mind from its clawed base by using his brute strength to peel back and then snap off the pedestal's black fingers. As soon as the bloodmates were in possession of the artifact, they left without lingering for romance. Lila fashioned a sling from her torn cloak and swaddled the artifact in it, carrying it as if it were a baby. She sensed that this intimacy bothered Erik, but he held his tongue. The Mind could apparently create access and entry points anywhere on the ship. Thus, they were only mildly astonished when they stopped in the hall at a spot the Mind recommended to Lila—who could hear its voice whenever she touched it—and watched the metal wall vertiginously spin, then flow into a gangway that led down to a noisy shore.

The lordvessel had driven itself right up onto a beach of crumbled granite. Gulls, busy cracking open clamshells, squawked angrily as Lila and Erik left the lordvessel through the newly ejected tongue of black metal. They walked down a rubble bridge. Lila spotted swarms of sinfully red crabs fighting the draw of heavy dashing tides. When they had descended lower, standing now amid seaweed-strewn pools, Lila, still touching the Mind, asked it to seal the hull. The lordvessel could not be entered again without the Mind's command. The bloodmates splashed a path to less water-pitted shores and left a trail of footprints on a beach that glistened in defiance of the sun's might.

That light and its heat, Lila feared, were simply a prelude to all that Kor'Khul would bring. *Do not think about tomorrow. Do not think about yesterday. Only the here and now matters.* In response to that thought, Erik's hand found her back. Onward they strode, silent and united, each supported by the other's strength.

Soon the beach was behind them, and they climbed a gradually rising green hump that met with other mounds and stretched into a rolling horizon. Once they had descended the first hill, Meadowvale's charm blew over them in honeysuckle breezes. They walked through grass and wildflowers, and tried not to bother the hidden finches, the wild horses that grazed atop exposed granite skulls in the land, the many rabbits Erik saw poking white-furred heads up and down in the grass like moles. These creatures noticed the dark warrior, too, or smelled his obsidian grit and sweat, and they gave him and the queen a wide berth.

Welcome to the new natural order, said the queen after noticing the animals' behavior. *You've become a lord in this realm.*

The afternoon passed in a gentle lulling flow. Before long, the sun readied for its sleep in the west. Night's red hand reached for the travelers, and they bunked down for the evening in a valley between two great hills, one partially stripped of green like some of the others in Meadowvale. Erik made a mercifully swift kill, bringing back a pair of hares that were then strung up over a fire lit by Lila's Will. Firebugs came out to play for the audience of two, and the bloodmates watched their dances, Lila wrapped in Erik's arms.

Lila felt as if her heart should be grieving: she had once watched a similar performance from these dancers with Magnus back in Willowholme. However, that moment was now centuries past. When she hunted for emotion in those remembrances, she returned only with anger for Magnus, anger stoked by his rape of her, his pretense of being a man, his deceptions about his brother and their connection. *Finally, I know how it feels to be with one man, one soul. I do not feel myself splintered and lost anymore.* Indeed, Erik's hale arms and the smell of his stone-powered sweat upon his tunic crushed these other reflections, and they were the last impressions Lila knew, or desired, before dreaming.

Her knight heard her thoughts, yet commented not. He'd loved her since the day she'd touched him in Eod. She still fought with terrors from her past, but to him, their tale was unfolding as it should.

Erik waited until he felt her presence far away and dreaming, then kissed his sleeping queen upon her forehead, her cheek, and her hand, which he lifted to his lips. "Goodnight, my queen," he whispered. He himself, though, did not sleep. Now a lord of strength and stone, he no longer felt the need for it. Instead, the unnatural knight watched the firebugs whirl in helixes, correctly intuiting their next patterns. He listened to the heartbeats of the animals around him—they could echo like thunder, but he was quickly growing accustomed to absorbing a thousand scents and sounds every speck. Occasionally, he shifted to comfort his queen or to adjust the burden of the crystal eye she refused to release. Catching sight of her gold cameo in the moonlight, he fantasized about a world in which there were no Immortal kings to damage everyone and everything with their puerile thirst for identity. *Damn Brutus and Magnus*, he thought.

V

The next day they continued their travel through land that was sunny, peaceful, and full of nature's songs and creatures. Around noon, however, they came to a point in the hills that was split by a road. Warily, they took the path; it would make for a faster journey, though they would have to remain alert for other travelers. Lila offered to mask them in sorcery, but

Erik rejected the idea. Erik felt he would be able to sense any approaching beings. Something about her knight appeared harder today, Lila found, and his insides were a quiet, brewing storm. He didn't seem partial to conversation. While padding down the dirt-trodden trail, Lila's hand wandered to the sphere trundled up and bouncing against her chest. The Mind spoke to her the instant she touched it.

Good afternoon, Navigator.

Good afternoon, she replied. *I am surprised you are still attuned to the passage of time. I thought you were blind unless awakened.*

I am always awake. Always seeing. However, I have no one with whom to share my sights when there is no connection between your skin and mine—I need the kinetic spark of your telemetry interacting with mine. Otherwise, we cannot speak.

Intriguing, alarming, and slightly sad, thought the queen: this entity inundated by experiences it could discuss with no one. *How much can you see? How far?*

Far. Ten thousand and ninety-six paces ahead, for example, I detect friable soil and a growing stratification of silt. A desert. If the barometric pressures do not change, I predict a storm will form in the desert, bringing winds of one hundred spans per hour. At your current pace, though, you and your mate should safely miss it.

My mate? You use the most curious terms.

The one with whom you swap blood and other excretions. The patterns when the two of you copulate are elaborate. I would say they resemble snowflakes, though I am only referencing data related to winter precipitation; I have never seen snow. There are astra that form in clusters—singing clusters—within the chambers of your forms. I do not understand the concept of beauty, but I find the complexity of your union a subject worthy of further scrutiny. The Erik is not like the Magnus. I have seen the Magnus's pattern, too, in your memories. It is very complex; it contains so many astra and molecules I cannot analyze its makeup. A universe to your galaxy. I believe it is beyond my analysis.

Yes, Magnus is a mystery. A sneer darkened the queen's face.

Palpitations and increased circulation indicate a state of hypertension or rage. You are angry when you think of your other mate. Is that because of what he did to you?

Lila gasped and took her hand off the Mind. Through her exposure to it, it had mined her soul and extracted her darkest pains. Erik turned, showing concern and tepid rage. Lila sensed a sympathetic fury behind his glower, a fury directed at Magnus and the event that had fractured all of Central Geadhain. One incident of incredible violence from her husband—possessed or not—was all it had taken to send every old reign crumbling into the sea. She'd neither confronted this pain nor dealt with it. Instead, she'd hidden, gone mad, and ruined a kingdom. She had become the horror that she'd suffered. *I have raped and reaped the world: of its children, its culture, its history.*

Lila stopped in the road, frozen by remorse. Her feet no longer obeyed her. Her heart would not heed her and stop its hammering. Surely, she would have wept, screamed, or fallen into the dirt if the man of obsidian had not forced her to speak.

My queen, you mustn't condemn yourself.

I have been fighting the wrong enemy.

Menos had to be stopped. We had no choice.

I do not mean Menos, my knight. Am I no better than the man who soiled me?

Magnus?

Yes.

Together, they rumbled. She'd become a cloud in his storm. Lila leaned into him. At last, she whispered the thorny secrets she'd borne since Magnus had left her for Zioch. *I want to know why he chose me a thousand years ago. I want him to apologize for what he did. I want the world to know of the crime that drove me mad. I know that he blames himself for succumbing to the primal temptations and influences of his brother. But how sincere is his guilt when he declares you and I criminals, and the world remains ignorant of his sin?*

Erik allowed the beast of his jealousy, the black side of his thoughts, to bleed out into his queen. *As a matter of pride,* he said, *as a matter of justice, as part of the code I have always upheld, he should not be allowed to keep this sinful secret. I loved him, I worshipped him, and he betrayed every virtue that he extolled. Would a better king have been able to resist his brother? Was Magnus ever as strong as I believed? Or merely weak, a puppet* to Brutus's—or his own—sick desires? *I want to fight him. I want to beat the answers from him with my fists of stone until he is as bloodied as you were when he left you. I would have killed him that night or died trying. I want to humiliate him as he did you. I don't want him dead—*

Not dead, she agreed.

But he should suffer, and be more humbled than he has ever been. With their minds and souls working in tandem, they weren't sure who spoke, who fanned whose fires of wrath. A dark plan was being spun in their heads. A vision of revenge against the King. *We must call him out of his ivory palace. We must bring him into the streets where all of Eod will see him bow, will see him stripped of the virtue he uses as a shield. You want to be a man, Magnus? Then be judged as one. Be treated as one. Be scorned and praised as one. An age of truth. Let the people decide who is guilty of what. Let the people be our court*—they smiled, then kissed, flooding each other with a delirious, shivering malice—*and his*.

Their purpose was now twofold: they would deliver the message to Elissandra from her dead husband, Sangloris, and they would cleanse themselves of their past with Magnus. Why sneak into Eod like cowards when they should come to the gates screaming for justice for the people of Menos, for her rape, for Magnus's lies?

Drunk on their black kiss, Erik didn't sense the two men coming down the road in their cart; Erik was again distracted by the rigidity of his lover's mouth and throat, as if she were becoming a woman of rock, as well. The strangers walked to within tens of paces of the pair, then stopped to stare at them. It was an arousing sight for two men: a comely lass tipped backwards, hood fallen—hair radiant as a falling cascade of sunshine—and held by a broad-backed, swarthy warrior. Young and aimless fellows, the wandering peddlers were in no hurry to make it to Meadowvale's shores to scavenge for crab shells and pearls. They cared not if their mothers complained about their laziness, and this sight was worth a pause. At first, the louts guffawed and elbowed each other. Then they quieted down so they might watch without disturbing the show.

Unwittingly, Lila had held on to the Mind while Erik dipped her; one finger grazed the sphere's cold crystal skin. *Navigator, two bipedal humanoids are displaying signs of increased temperatures, agitation, and sexual arousal. I believe they wish to see you and the Erik mate. I did not mean to disturb you, but I thought you should know.*

The bloodmates rose. The queen moved past Erik and strode toward the aroused voyeurs. One of the men gasped, then nearly choked on his tongue when he realized who this extraordinary golden woman with the amber eyes was—and by extension, who the dark and terrible man looming behind her must be. Lila gazed upon the unwelcome guests with pure detestation. She whirled through visions of all the men in her life who had spat upon, chastised, or otherwise scorned her. She remembered the sour-butter stink and sticky heat of spinrex milk on her fingers, and the warrior who had slapped her black and blue for not squeezing teats quickly enough. She remembered her former chieftain and how he'd laughed at her, then beaten her, when she'd asked to become a warrior. An Arhad woman was never meant to hold a weapon, only a prick. She recalled the many gray and ancient fools who'd silently mocked her, with their stares and carefully worded reprimands, when she had first begun to chair at the Chamber of Echoes. Wise men, they were supposed to be—but none of them were. All of those withered bastards were dead now. She remembered the state in which she'd found Rowena in the desert: dry and cracked, blisters from head to toe. Men had done that to her because of her sex. Finally, Lila dwelled in a waking nightmare where a man—towering, fat with muscle, and reeking of beast—and a pale, pretty prince of ice took turns raping her. It hadn't happened like that, though close enough. The fantasy was not so far from the truth.

As she neared the men in the road, her scent—her poison of spice, rage, and sweetness—became a field of blooming oleander. Erik could almost see the pollen of her power, a glittering particulate in the air, and he cringed from the reek of sulfur and the crackle of great magik. Was she set to destroy these men? He wanted no such wrath or blood upon her. Either his wish or her temperance helped them avoid this end. She did, though, walk toward the quaking men, who bowed and buried their foreheads into the dirt with such force that rocks and filth made their faces bleed. Her voice sweet and lethal as a tea of sugar and nightshade, she said, "No man shall look upon me but one: my beloved. My rock. My black mountain and gray sea. He has earned my love, as I have earned his. You have earned nothing, not even a glance at our greatness. Cower, and know that the queen of Eod has spared your wicked, weak lives. Cower, cry, and wriggle on the earth like the worms that you are."

The men mewled, their hips exploded with spastic jiggling, their hands came to their sides, and they snaked on the earth in senseless circles, as commanded. The queen motioned to her knight, and by the time he reached her, the strange scent and toxic cloud seemed to have disappeared. Lila didn't address what she had done, what kind of magik she had used on these men—for it was magik of a kind unfamiliar to Erik that had broken their wills and turned them into puppets. When he glanced back over his shoulder, he could see them still worming and weeping in the dirt.

VI

An ancient breath of sand and death doth hiss across in haste. Vultures cry and all men die within Kor'Khul's great waste. Another of the queen's lyrical ramblings flitted into Erik's mind as they climbed the peaks and valleys of sand. The drifts flowed in endless white waves toward a shimmer of gold. It became difficult to know how far they had traveled, how much farther they would have to go before the shimmer became Eod. The heat made them dizzy and conjured strange twists on the horizon that never turned out to be anything more than mirages.

When Erik and the queen had last ridden by caravan through the region, the going had been pleasant as they relaxed in the shade of a coach. Traversing Kor'Khul by foot was a fool's exercise. Already the waterskins they'd brought with them from St. Celcita had begun to shrink. Erik counted the drops they drank and took less than a mouthful of water for himself. Thankfully, Erik was more or less impervious to the pains of deprivation. He drank and ate only because he felt that he should. He supposed that was an aspect of now being a stone man: stones didn't eat or drink; they endured. Likewise, the winter cold that came with night was a nuisance to him. Lila slept in the warm rock of his embrace while he stayed awake, haunted by hissing sand ghosts and a bold, glaring moon. In the morning, his queen woke and smiled at the sandy face of her bloodmate. Erik didn't tell her that he hadn't slept in three days. They each kept certain silences.

Since the incident on the road, Lila had been reserved, but occasionally a thought wafted to Erik. She realized now, as did Erik, that she'd invoked a hitherto unknown sorcery upon those men in the road: a magik similar to that of legendary enchantresses. The queen, though, was no such enchantress. So from where had she summoned such power? She had little to say on the matter—to her knight, at least. Erik sensed her speaking to the crystal babe she cradled, and could not repress a certain amount of jealousy and concern.

Lila and the Mind made peace soon after the incident. Although it had been invasive about Magnus, and when it had warned them of the leering men, she could not deny it had been helpful. Also, she would need its insight to understand how and why her magik had suddenly developed new branches after hundreds of years. By her understanding, magik, once developed, never changed. It matured, perhaps—an earthspeaker, for example, might learn to move and manipulate larger and larger rock into ever more extraordinary shapes. She had always been an emotional sorcerer, one whose power manifested as light, fire, and smoke—physical elements of passion. Her sorcery produced a wrath gentler than the ice and thunder of Magnus.

That morning, at her request, the Mind explored many theories that could account for her metamorphosis. When it reported back around noon, though, it was able to offer nothing conclusive or comforting. *I apologize, Navigator. I do not have the information you have requested. I cannot deduce what metascience could animate a transmorphic matrix such as yours. I shall search my memory banks for evidence of similar transmorphic matrices. If I am successful, we may know more about the cause of your transformation. I hope that pleases you.*

It does, thank you, she replied. *And you may call me Lila; it's less formal, and I prefer it.*

I hope it pleases you, Navigator Lila.

She produced a harsh laugh from her cracked throat.

The next day, the Mind was quiet all morning as they pressed forward across the sizzling desert. As soon as she touched it while adjusting her burden, though, it jarred her with speech, blurting out a summary of the theories and information it had been processing since their conversation yesterday: *Navigator Lila. I have discovered information related to your condition. Basiloriverflax. River basilisks. These cetaceous lizards found in the deltas feeding off the lower River Feordhan have been known to molt not once, but two or more times each season. Biological markers and strengths often persist in subsequent generations; however, each generation is just as mutable as the preceding one. Basiloriverflax are among the only creatures that radically and rapidly alter their biological matrixes according to stimulating environmental factors. If the spring thaw of the Northlands is considerable, and the temperature of the Feordhan dips too low, they develop insulated carapaces. Likewise, if the waters become overly warm, they shed their extra layers and produce pliable, thin skins, even growing additional appendages to help them speedily navigate waters filled with saltwater predators migrating up from the Scarasace Sea. In one recorded season, when mudslides and runoff from the war with Taroch polluted the Feordhan, Basiloriverflaxes developed quadrupedal appendages—flippers with webbed toes—and climbed out of the water and onto dry land. During that season, until they returned to the water to breed, they moved farther inland and preyed on the river fowl and mammalian life found in the Feordhan's glades and swamps.*

Lila knew of these rare creatures of which the Mind spoke. Still, the comparison remained unclear. *What does this have to do with me?*

Your biological matrix has changed.

Changed?

Since your union of blood and sweat, the exchange of bodily humors with the Erik. Your matrix—and the Erik's—has become brighter and more complex. Yours is now as complex as the Magnus's, and it grows more elaborate with each sand. Your condition, your metamorphosis, has accelerated.

Metamorphosis? Into what?

Nigrum plectum. The black quill, continued the Mind, leaping to the next fact it had uncovered. *A peaceful herbivore of the Ebon Vale that has a highly toxic natural defense mechanism. Its spines—which have small, flesh-tearing anchors—can be detached and then flung by way of a sub-epidermal contraction of the intramuscular system. A lesser-known fact is that this is not its primary defense against the most dangerous predators. The spines deter the smaller nuisances of the forest: foxes, wolves, ravenboars. When confronted by* the bears that would crack their slow and spiny forms open like sea urchins, though, they release a musk, a cloud of psychotropic toxin. Animals under the influence of this poison have been known to ram themselves into trees until their skulls shatter, to drown themselves in rivers, or to engage in other self-destructive behaviors. The poison alters perception and usurps the host's natural survival instincts by issuing its own commands to the parietal cortex—

Pardon?

The section of a creature's cortex that controls action and, theoretically, free will. The toxin specifies its own protocols to the parietal cortex and in so doing disrupts its natural function. That is why the animals go mad. Lila felt as if her feet were sinking into quicksand. Her stomach flipped and flopped as the Mind ambled toward a conclusion she did not want to face. I have identified bio-sympathies between the attributes of these two species of animal, Navigator Lila—between the river basilisk's propensity for transmutation and the black quill's toxins. You exhibit the adaptability of the basiloriverflax, though you exist in a sphere of complexity all your own. As for the parallels between you and the Nigrum plectrum, I was able to analyze your spray—

My spray?

A diffusion of phosphorus-laced chemicals that can be released from the engorged salivary packets now found in your throat.

Lila gasped and clutched at her neck with a hand. She shrieked when she discovered the small fat caterpillars burrowing alongside her trachea. Whipping around, Erik ran to her side and demanded that she speak. But she remained silent, fearing that if she opened her mouth, she would spew poison, even though she wished her bloodmate no harm. Both the sick, suffocating heat and her fear drained her strength, and she fell into Erik. Nonetheless, one of her hands remained upon the crystal sphere, and she soon discovered the enthusiastic Mind was not yet finished with its analysis. *May I resume? When it comes to the order and bioactivity of species, however, your behavioral patterns are inconsistent with those of the black quill. The bipedal humanoids on the road ten point five spans back in distance were not threats to you, but you nevertheless released your distinctive spray. Because of the location of your glands, and your aggressive behavior, I would invert the order of predator and prey and name you as the former.*

I'm a predator?

My data suggests so.

"Lila! What's the matter?" When no answer came to him in his mind, Erik ripped her hand off the relic. Lila blinked, and her eyes found her bloodmate. She remained afraid to open her mouth, and definitely noticed a thickness in her throat now when she swallowed. *My poison sacs*, she thought.

"What poison sacs? What are you talking about?" Erik demanded.

Fumbling for footholds in the strangeness, Lila reached out and caressed the hard, bearded face of the man who'd changed her. She felt only love, the purest, deepest love, even if their marriage in magik and blood had brought out the reptile in her sprit. At least Erik wasn't her natural enemy; she realized that because he was part of her, he was therefore immune to her poison. However, the same couldn't be said of the species Erik had left behind, those who wronged, chased, raped, and enslaved the weak: men.

As she kissed him—not deeply, merely pressing her lips to his—he understood in flashes what it was she was uncovering within herself. Erik shivered in sympathy with her chills of self-disgust. Then he pulled away and forced her to open her mouth and look up at the sun. In the far shadows of her throat, past the vacancy that had once been her tonsils, the flesh appeared ridged, like rings chipped in stone. He remembered, then, how odd and hard her mouth had felt when he'd kissed her back on the lordvessel, and then again on the road. Shocked, he then noticed she had two small teeth like those of a cat tucked away behind her canines. Lila stopped his examination, turning her head away from him.

"I have become some kind of monster," whispered Lila, looking down.

"I am a man of rock." Erik took her hand. "You—Lilehum, Lila, my queen—are the beautiful and exotic serpent who charmed me decades past. We have finally become our truest selves, and we should be grateful."

Should she? She needed to think about what he'd said. If she was a monster, then she was a monster who knew love, fear, and all that it meant to be mortal—unlike her cold, former husband. She strode away from her bloodmate, pondering, watching the desert, thinking of all she'd been before now: slave-bride, queen, outlaw...Erik drifted to her, when he felt the turmoil in her heart subsiding. A warm black hand, as hot as the passion from the sun above, stroked her neck; she turned and Erik wiped away the tears she'd not felt herself weep.

"I am myself, finally," realized Lila.

They stood in the sands, caressing. Stone man and serpent. In a moment, the serpent began to hiss her darkest thoughts. "If I can do that to two men...what might I do to ten? Or twenty? Or a hundred?"

Ancient and ingrained traditions of brotherhood and subtle misogyny were not so easy to dispel, even in the progressive city-state of Eod. The majority of the Silver watch was male—even the term "watchman" was gender specific. Rowena was one brave challenger to this order, and the queen could come up with the names of perhaps another hundred women who possessed her determination. Menos, for its part, was no better. Gloriatrix was to be admired for her daring, at least.

"My queen?" he gasped.

For suddenly, her skin had taken on a sheen, a dusting of iridescent pink, amber, and green that resembled scales. Her fearsomeness enticed Erik, as did the puff of cinnamon and prickle of magik she misted into the air—her toxin. Then the monster within Lila retreated into its basket, and she was again all softness and beauty. She slipped a hand into her sling and chatted with the crystal child there, before speaking again. "Come, my knight. The Mind senses a grand encampment several spans to the north. *Arhad.*" She practically spat the word. "I would like to return to my people and offer them the chance I once had." She held her breath, and her stare glittered. "The chance for freedom."

She felt enflamed with purpose. Reborn. She spoke for the *khek*, the lizard-milkers, the first to seventh wives, the sewn-up, mutilated women who dragged themselves low to the ground and lived every moment in shame—a shame they had never deserved. Lila knew who it was should suffer.

VII

A stillness had fallen over the Arhad encampment, which lay scattered over the sands like a spilled pack of dull brown and beige cards. The warriors had spent their seed and filled their bellies with food, and now slept fat and fit as children. The children themselves slumbered, too. Boys and girls lay in their separate tents, both groups watched over by humming old crones—wives no longer needed or desired for coital duties. Some of the old wives' husbands were dead and once they began to fail in their wits and wakefulness, they would be cast out and left to wander the desert until they met their former mates in the afterlife. The old wives told themselves this would be an honor, yet their hearts were full of dread. They were the first to sense the presence. A wind of fragrant spice and dangerous sweetness blew through the encampment. It ruffled the tents, slithered through any tear in the fabric walls, and entwined the late-night guardians in a coil of scent.

Kali, the youngest of the disgraced, was slopping around in the wet shite of the nearby spinrex pen. She arranged the buckets and rags for the workwomen tomorrow; she could rest only when the task had been completed. Kali dropped her bucket and gasped as the invisible snake of scent wove around her. She was assaulted by images. She thought of fresh air, green life, a woman's smile, and the happy cry of a newborn. At once, the dull, eternal ache of the scars in her groin faded.

As soon as she had recovered her senses, she bolted past the roped-in square, forgetting to tie up the complicated mesh that kept the beasts inside. The less reckless voice in her head said she would be dead on the morrow when it was discovered the beasts had escaped. However, Kali cared not, for the scent, the perfume, drove her and warmed her with a sensuous heat. She'd never experienced lust or bliss, so she could not accurately explain her body's flush—but she wanted more. She wanted the source of this heat. Something must be baking, or cooking, she felt, although nothing the culinarians created from leathery meat and spinrex curds possessed such piquancy. The Arhadians' sweetest dessert was a bitter sap collected from the cacti found in the hidden oases. Smoke billowed up ahead, veiling the moon and creating an omen of doom. She didn't care. She had no sense. She wanted only to chase and capture the aroma. Tents flew past her. A glow was visible near the chieftain's tent, and it called to her. It had drawn others as well, for a large crowd had formed and now stood murmuring.

It was all so strange and amazing to Kali. Women, girls, and young boys had gathered here by the hundreds; surely, all of the tribe was present. Where were the warriors? Where was the chieftain? Suddenly, the memory of his sneering, painted face stirred her from her spell. The chieftain had been the one to cut and sew her womanhood when she refused to marry his eldest son. *If you will not be with the greatest, you will be with no man*, he'd decreed, and the shadows of her assaulters had pinned her as he went to fetch his knife and needle. She would never forget his face or his voice, which was how it was she recognized his scream. Kali pushed through the ring of watchers; doing so took most of her strength, as they seemed immovable and bespelled. The cinnamon sweetness tried to seduce her mind away from her body again, but she waved her hand in front of her face and puffed to cast out the slightly burned, acrid smell. *Magik*, she realized with a jolt of wonder.

As she shoved herself toward the chieftain's tent, her wonderment exploded into awe, floating as high as the flames of the moon-tickling golden pyre into which shivering, naked men were now throwing themselves. The men screamed for a speck as the flames kissed them and the spell cast on their minds waned, slightly—yet each one of them remained in the flames to wail and die. What was this? She reeled. Her mind was tugged back and forth between reason and delirium, madness and glee. She could see no tents, only the massive fire. All of the warriors' lodgings had been leveled, their scraps and bone struts brought to build the pyre. She saw one entranced warrior—a horrible man, who often slapped her for sport—lugging a sack of his favorite trophies and leathers toward the flames of judgment. He took out his glories and, one by one, threw them into the outdoor furnace. Finally, he stepped in himself, and the screaming began. The chieftain was nowhere to be seen. He must already have lunged to his death; Kali was disappointed that she'd missed his end. Still, dozens of atrophied shadows twisted in the fire, a fire so high and bright it could not possibly be a natural phenomenon. A sorcerer's fire.

No, a *sorceress's*. For there she stood: a woman as bright as the flames. She glittered and beguiled; she looked crafted of raw amber and beauty. She could not be real. And yet, the evidence of her magik was real as could be.

The sorceress turned to Kali. She gazed at the wounded, tormented workwoman with a warmth and a pity that said she understood every punch, every slap, every glob of spit to her face. As though in a dream,

Kali wandered and stood before her. Behind the golden sorceress stood a shadow of man whose devotion to the sorceress was as clear to see as his stone-carved rugged self. A rock, Kali thought. He was a living black rock. In a sling, he held something that resembled a cracked and glimmering stone Kali had once seen. Kali glanced back and forth between the sorceress and the man of rock.

"Are you real?" she asked, and reached out to touch the glittering woman; her skin felt ridged, scaled. When the sorceress smiled, Kali noticed the yellow slits of her gaze, the darting forked tongue, and the large white fangs next to her canines. Kali pulled back her hand as if she'd touched a snake.

"I am," the sorceress answered, her Arhadic exotically accented but perfectly spoken.

"What have you done to my people?"

The sorceress touched Kali's cheek as if reassuring a confused child. "My dear desert flower. I have freed them. I have broken the chains of man. I shall break them all if I can. I shall take you to a new future—a future where warriors do not punish to please. A future where girls are given loftier duties. A future where boys and girls will decide which roles and freedoms they wish to pursue." She hissed in pleasure. Kali tried to step back, but the woman held her with the intensity of her stare. "You resisted most of my spell. You are strong. You are already unbroken. What is your name?"

"Kali."

"Kali." The golden woman's stare flashed, and Kali was free of all magik—she spun and gawked, now fully herself again. "I am Lilehum. Look around you. Look and see the glory we shall build together."

Kali looked. Was this glory or horror? She saw women of all ages studying the flames into which their fathers and husbands had dived. They wore squinting expressions of flint and vengeance. She saw young men, not yet warriors, witnessing the cost of arrogance. A few were weeping—behavior unheard of for a boy. Other stronger lads had surrendered their spears and hearts to the sorceress. These were the men of tomorrow, these sons who watched the sins of their fathers burn while holding onto their mothers. Kali spotted young girls gazing bravely into the flames or up at the moon, now thinking of things beyond their small world. Although all were under the influence of the sorceress's spice and magik, their feelings were based in truth.

Lilehum—that's what the sorceress had called herself. The name from fireside memory now echoed in Kali's head, from a tale told to warn young girls of the dangers of corruption. *Lilehum* came the mnemonic beat again. A pale Arhadian princess who had been stolen by the sinful King of Eod... Kali turned back to the sorceress and laughed and cried with the wickedest joy.

PART II

X

DEFYING DEATH

I

The men were whispering when Aadore woke. It was their conversation that had stirred her from a deep sleep. Opening her eyes to the gray milk of dawn, she looked at the three gents gathered in chairs around the table. Little Ian slept on, though he reached for her warmth, and Aadore was careful not to disturb him. Gently, she pried his tiny hands off herself and left him in the hollow where her body had lain. On her tiptoes, she crept over to the others.

"An escape?" she asked; she was certain that was what she'd heard.

"I think we can get at least as far as the market and the Iron Wall," declared Curtis.

"The whole city is in ruins; it took us days to reach my apartment," she said.

"Not the whole city," replied Curtis. "Certain roads beneath us remain traversable; that's how I came this far."

His explanation made little sense to Aadore. "The Undercomb?" she said. "It might have weathered the Storm of Frostfire, as that took place above ground. But this chaos came from below. I imagine the Undercomb would have suffered the worst devastation. How would we even enter it, assuming it hasn't collapsed?"

Sean looked excited as he spoke up—he had a bit of color today, she noticed. "Father worked for a time as a city custodian, remember? Back before his time with the Els. He used to tell us all about the Undercomb, though it seems you were too bored to pay him any mind."

"I was."

"Well, you should have listened, Sister. If you had, you would know that between the Undercomb and the streets of the Iron City is an area that contains access points, tunnels, and passages for city servants. Rumor has it that the Broker's men used them, too. In one of his stories, Father mentioned he could feel the walls hum when he placed his hand against them. The whole sublevel is reinforced with feliron, just like the Iron Wall. You can't break magik that old and securely woven into the ground, not wholly. Not even with an earthquake spitting fire from below."

Now Aadore began to share his enthusiasm. "You're saying it's possible that this sublevel survived? That we could use it for transit?"

"Aye," said Curtis. "That's what I'm saying. Furthermore, what your brother heard about its use is true. The Broker's men—whatever has become of them—used the same passages as Menos's prized civil and political servants. Such passages are restricted at every entry, sealed by unpleasant wards to deter lock picking...Or the ravenous dead."

Aadore thought of the key she possessed, which to her knowledge would not be suitable for this task, even though its purpose was similar. However, she guessed from the smiling faces around the table that the men knew something she did not. "Political servants...Second Courier to the Third Chair...Curtis, you bastard, *you* have a key?"

"I do," replied Curtis.

Aadore stood straight as an iron rod, and commanded the men as if they were her vassals. "Let's not waste the light, then. We're leaving the Iron City."

II

All good plans encountered a few hitches, Aadore knew, and their escape from Menos was no exception. Curtis had taken the sublevel across the city, popping in and out of it like a rabbit in a warzone running between holes. What Curtis hadn't mentioned was that the city sublevel could be accessed only through tunnels or arcades that were already underground. The sublevel could not be accessed directly from the street, and many of the paths leading to the Undercomb had collapsed or been flooded with filth. As the city continued to collapse, these tunnels and the access points within them would become ever more unreachable.

Even finding such places was a terrible chore. In the three days since Menos's doom, more buildings had sunk into the ashy mire, streets had crumbled into the rents left by the earthquake—leaving chasms that could not be crossed—and pipes spraying putrid juices had turned what was left of the city into a bog. Although many of the fires appeared finally to have settled, the abundance of wet smoke had only swelled. With every dash they made, the cold, sour air of Menos slithered deeper into their throats. Doom ruled the city with a billowing hand, spreading the kind of fog that made ships wreck themselves upon rocks. Indeed, Aadore was reminded of sunken ships many times as she slogged through water and peered at the cement and metal wreckage that poked up in the mist like broken vessels and masts. It was day, although it didn't seem so as the land was steeped in grayness. Their eyes of little use, the survivors relied on their ears to hear the chattering hordes and their noses to smell the farty rotting dead. Curtis had been lucky to make it as far as he had, Aadore realized.

But the four met with far more frustration and dead ends than Curtis had on his earlier journey. Hourglasses of patient skulking through the gray gloom led them to two different roads to the Undercomb, but each was blocked with rubble, water, and hordes of the unliving. Legions of the dead were out today. Many must have been born just last night. What worried the travelers was that a select few seemed faster, more agile today.

If the dead had been bumbling kittens yesterday, some had since learned how to balance on their rotten legs and use their bony claws. A particularly dangerous, seemingly sentient unliving usually led each pack now—a creature that could turn its neck quickly and walk nearly with the grace of a man, and that would hiss when Aadore and her companions made noises in the fog. *How fast and aware would the dead be tomorrow?* wondered the survivors. *Or the day after next? What would their odds be against this horde?* The dead were the real citizens of Menos now for the living had gone extinct. All that day, they heard neither another living scream nor a scuffle in the afterlife of their civilization.

Little Ian, beatifically calm and soothing himself by gumming a ring of rubber pulled from a jar cap, became their talisman. Whenever their wills threatened to tremble, they looked to the suckling, sleeping child carried under Skar's great arm, and drew from him a draught of peace. Another small miracle Skar noticed, was that when smelled up close, the child somehow retained the powdery perfume of an infant. It made the ever-growing, spoiled reek of Menos less nauseating. Secretly, Ian's scent reminded Skar of his own infant children. In silence, he battled the memories of the screams of the wife and infants he had not been able to save from the home that had become his family's crematorium.

You'll not suffer a fate like theirs, he promised Ian.

Curtis quickly moved them around a burned railing and down a wide concrete staircase. As they descended, the darkness consumed them, and they fumbled for a moment. Curtis assured them this was the way, and so, hands linked, ears alert, they negotiated their way to the bottom in safety. There, they found themselves in a hollow space that pattered and dripped with haunting songs. They moved ahead, finding a reason for the strange tune when their feet splashed into water. There had been a flood here. They waded on, cold ripples shivering their knees, and waited for their senses to make something out of the swirling nothingness of their environment.

Folds of darkness warped into straight, bold lines: square pillars, running in rows to nowhere. Gleaming, curved shadows outlined entrances to tunnels that branched out from the tall, square chamber. Humped, unmoving heaps were strewn about the chamber; they could have been anything. Then Aadore noticed the soggy newspapers and bobbing trash—a glittering pinwheel toy floated up against her legs—and she guessed this had once been a marketplace. They heard water coursing in from elsewhere, a slow and constant stream like a brook. They would have to hurry: that brook would soon turn this shopping arcade into a lake.

"Which way?" asked Sean.

Curtis considered their choices, and tried to squint clues from the dark. Finally, he threw up his hands. "I don't know. We're in a commercial square. Beverly's Court, I believe. There should be an exit somewhere along one of the walls, but I don't know where. We shall have to feel the walls."

"A light would be helpful," whispered Aadore.

The men moved into the dark, leaving her wish unanswered. Aadore waded after their shapes and caught up with Curtis after a moment. Without asking, he took her hand. She felt neither shocked nor displeased by the feel of his warm, strong fingers interlaced with hers.

"You're cold," he said.

"You're not," she replied.

In the dark, they could not see each other blush. Aadore envisioned her companion as she had last seen him in Menos's funereal ambiance. He was quite pale, almost as white as a Northman, and he possessed the broad-painted features of those folk. His untamed beard had shone with the same soft animal texture as his thick head of hair; his hirsuteness, his wide-shouldered body built for exertion, or another aspect of him—his deep brown eyes, perhaps, or his seeming loyalty—evoked in Aadore the impression of a loyal hunting dog. At some point in their race for survival, Curtis had lost his jacket. But, apocalypse notwithstanding, Curtis had kept up his gentlemanly aspirations along with his suspenders. She even caught a hint of his sandalwood cologne; he must have doused himself in it before racing off to keep the date they'd yet to have.

Even if it weren't true, the thought made Aadore smile. She was certain if she were to lean in and sniff her companion, not the sandalwood fragrance but a thousand olfactory offences would cause her nose to crinkle. Nonetheless, she was grateful for the phantoms playing tricks with her, grateful for Curtis's touch. *What would we be to each other if the world hadn't ended?* she wondered. Would this old maid and creaking valet have led blissfully mundane lives together? She squeezed his hand. He squeezed hers in return. They continued searching the dark together, and their grip did not falter.

Their slow search became lulling in its monotony: splish, splash, fumble, and then pray that the glimmer up ahead is not a threading of water against brick but instead the shine of metal. For a time, their hopes were continually dashed, but eventually they saw a lighter shade of gloom up ahead. As they splashed nearer, shadows twisted and revealed an obstruction: tiles, wires, and stones had fallen down, along with an iron rafter. The rafter slanted up out of the rubble like a lazily planted flag; they would have to walk under it. The tear in the ceiling let in a sickly light, and finally they could glimpse one another's waxen, weary faces: five ghastly shades of white, with Curtis the palest. As they crept under the obstacle, the slight illumination revealed many shadows standing motionless at the fringe of the gloom beyond the heap. The four stopped, abruptly aware of their splashing. They were seasoned survivors now, and knew what these shadows were even before the figures shuffled about and emitted chilling gurgles. As the companions retreated behind the beam-and-rubble embankment, Sean caught a glimmer from a rectangle in the distance, a shape he was certain was a door.

The four held a whispered council on how to proceed.

"I saw a door," said Sean.

"What did it look like? Be specific," asked Curtis.

"Tall. Metal. I'll have to take another peek."

Sean hobbled through the mire, picked an inconspicuous spot, and peered ahead. He stared and stared, squeezing his eyes, ears, and mind until a headache formed—but the pain helped to sharpen his perception. He counted eight wandering dead. Beyond, on the far wall stood a door. It was metal, with small sparkling bits that might be bolts surrounding its frame. He could discern no handle. Returning to the others, he told them what he'd seen.

"If there's no handle, it's an access point," said Curtis. "Doors swing open by way of magik once the key's inside."

A near-silent debate raged among the four, while they contemplated various possibilities. What if that wasn't, in fact, a door? Where else would they find another? Not back the way they'd come, surely. Climbing out into the streets again where night would soon be upon them would be suicide. However, they'd crossed through the swamp of death; they were four survivors where no other life lived. If they needed to defeat a handful of dead soldiers to take that one next step to freedom, then that was just what they would do.

Aadore gripped her sword, Sean his cane, Skar his axe, and Curtis the hammer that had hung on his belt, the same hammer he had used to dismantle Aadore's apartment. Curtis was ready to start another project with his hammer's claw now, to deconstruct bone and pulverize rotten flesh. The four nodded and struck a silent agreement by holding up their weapons. Skar passed out rattling jars—the newest batch they'd made in Aadore's apartment. Each of the fellows armed a weaponless hand with a noise-making bomb. Without further discussion, they moved.

They dashed round the heap, no longer caring about their splashing footfalls—

CRRAAAAWK!

A funhouse face lurched out of the dark, missing a nose, lips, the cap of its skull—it was all teeth. An eyeball swung out from a socket as it shrieked. It was one of the unliving, one of the smarter of its breed, and it had heard them and then crept up to them. The monster shrieked again, then flailed about and threw its naked, gangly body toward them.

CRACK!

Aadore astonished the men by hurling her noise-rattling bomb. She had unerring aim, and the glass jar shattered against the creature's face, spraying it with shrapnel. Disoriented, the unliving stumbled and swiped like a fool at the silver and glass gnats that had attacked it. Aadore's action awakened her fellows, and the four quickly descended as a phalanx upon the flailing horror. The men bashed, hacked, and sliced the monster as it crumpled into the water. Twitching bits of the dead floated here and there when the men's frenzy had diminished.

But bloodlust quickly filled them once more, for the noise of the battle had reached the other wailing atrocities ahead. They raced toward the unliving, as howling and mad as those damned souls themselves. The unliving met their charge and came forth into the brightness in a rage, splashing and hissing. As had the monster the fellowship had just returned to death, these horrors moved with evolved gaits, loping and sweeping their limbs. Perhaps it was here, in the wet wombs of the city, that they grew stronger, cocooning themselves in rot, wetness, and death. Somehow, the fellowship of Iron souls was not afraid. Anger shivered its power down their arms, which they swung with untold strength—a strength inspired both by fear and by the thrill of meting out bloody justice.

Aadore and Curtis reached the horde first. He hurled his noise bomb, and it struck the soft shoulder of one of the horrors. Unfortunately, its flesh was too soft to allow for a proper impact, and a hunk of it dropped into the water with the intact projectile. Skar's throw was more successful; his glass jar shattered against the chest of the horror Curtis's had left unfazed, and a glittering explosion added to the tumult of this small war. The creatures faltered, some spinning in the water. The fellowship realized that not all of the unliving could see, and others were disoriented by the bombs. Sean hurled another jar of trash, sending the pack into fits of shrieking. By now, the noises had woken Ian: he giggled, though no one paid him any heed. The distance at last bridged, the seven horrors and five survivors clashed.

Aadore and Curtis remained side by side, while Sean and Skar stood back to back—with the brute keeping his hand on little Ian the whole while. The two former soldiers knew how to fight in close quarters. Sean wielded his cane as if it were the righteous sword of a king. Nothing touched him; no assault could break through his spinning, black defense. The creatures that did not receive a cracking riposte from Sean met with gory ends through the swift, true strikes of Skar, who chopped as if he were a forester possessed. Together, the soldiers whirled in a tornado that brought decapitation, evisceration, and amputation. A man with an appetite for gladiatorial sport—Lord Moreth of El, for example—would have found their brotherhood and the blood they shed sublime.

Aadore and Curtis performed their own dance of crimson. Fetid fingers that reached for Aadore were given a flashing reprimand from her sword. Aadore swung without her brother's finesse, her sword strikes more hackings than pointed attacks. But the difference was of little consequence, as they faced not trained swordsmen but rabid, slobbering beasts. Aadore's fury and strength were more important. She wielded her sword like a club—sometimes its edge connected, and at other times, she stunned an unliving with the flat of its blade. Like a mad gardener, she brought her weapon down on every lumpen face and limb she saw, tenderizing them to pulp.

Curtis proved a more adept killer. After all, he'd killed a living man before—not with intent, but with an innate ferocity that had turned a push into a lethal fall over a railing. He shoved the reeking carcasses with the same brutality into which he'd tapped before. Whatever Aadore didn't haphazardly dice, he finished off with tackles and brutal swings of his hammer, careful always to get away before he could be scratched.

Once, his hammer hooked into the jaw of a leering skull, and the creature's head was torn out by its roots and flung into the murk. The horror abandoned its assault and tapped the sappy pit where its neck had been. It bumbled about, almost comically, until a spittle-foaming Aadore stepped in and thwacked it in the chest. The dead thing dropped, splashed, and did not get up. Already, another horror had filled its place, this one reaching out to grapple with Aadore. Curtis leaped and shoved Aadore to the side. He caught one of the horror's soggy wrists and smashed back its other clawing hand with his hammer. Curtis snarled, kicked the horror in its stomach, and concentrated his full, terrible strength on the limb that he held. Off popped an arm, which the man then used, along with his hammer, to beat the creature back and down until it met a true death.

He then heard Aadore struggling, and turned to see a horror wrestling with her sword—trying to pull it, by its blade, from her hands. Aadore saved herself by abruptly letting go her grasp: the creature, a victim of its own force, then impaled itself on her weapon. Such a wound would not kill what was already dead, however, and Curtis hurried to turn its skull into a meaty pulp, for he'd realized that removing the head neutralized the other monsters. While Curtis completed his handiwork, Aadore placed one foot on the writhing horror and pulled her sword from its guts. Silence. They noticed that the fighting had ended, at least for the moment.

Aadore turned and saw Skar and Sean, panting, wet with sweat and rancid blood, standing in a hacked tumble of limbs and bent corpses. She felt no surprise, only a little rush of triumph—but then the underground plaza suddenly came alive with the inquisitive screeching of other hungry dead. A horde was nearing. The survivors hurried toward the door.

Curtis fumbled for the key. After a click and a spark of magik, the iron portal opened in an oiled sweep, and they shoved themselves into cold, dank safety, pushing shut the door. Within a moment, they heard the scrape of claws on metal—but the door could not be opened without a key. They wandered through the pitch black, guided only by their huffing. The tunnel stank like wet metal. At last the noise of their pursuers faded, and they found themselves alone with the chattering of rats. *Rats*, thought Aadore, rejoicing at the sound of a living thing, even if that living thing was vermin. She needed to stop for a speck, not to indulge her sense of relief, but because her leg had developed a stitch. As she leaned against a freezing metal wall, her shoulder protested and screamed with pain. She blurted out a small cry.

"Are you well? You're not hurt, are you?" asked the ghost of Curtis in the dark.

Perfect soldiers, Sean and Skar had already appraised themselves for injury while shuffling along the passage: blindly groping themselves and checking for pain. Both men reported on their fitness. Aadore had yet to speak.

For a wound throbbed in Aadore's shoulder. Consumed by the glory of battle, she hadn't noticed it until now. She tried to avoid confronting the unthinkable, to prevent herself from wondering whether the injury had come from teeth or claws. However, her head teased her with a heinous, hazy picture of that last horror pulling at her before she used her sword to push him away. Pulling and clawing.

Sean whispered in the dark. "Aadore?"

"Just a stitch," she lied.

III

Once, a long time ago, Aadore had visited the Royal Opera House. Shortly after Sean had been sent away, kindly Beatrice had sensed her handmaiden's sadness and decided to delight her with a satin frock and a ticket for one to *Un Balle Sanguia*: the Blood Ball. Aadore had never felt so fancy, so much like a lady, as on that evening. While ascending the palatial steps into the theater, and throughout the night, gentlemen tipped their hats to her and opened doors. They had no idea, these men, that she was the one who spent her life opening doors and ingratiating herself. Aadore remembered how her hands had trembled with joy as she'd held the yellowed programme, which in calligraphic script described the opera she was about to see. The opera had been unforgettable.

The Blood Ball was an opera in three parts, and both began and ended at grand dances. The opening act was set during Menos's Age of Discovery, and its action took place on the sprawling estate of Master Gestault, an Iron lord and hero of that era. Gestault was playing host to his friend and wartime companion Ferdinand, an uncommonly kind feliron mogul, and his new bride, the Lady Ingray, whom Ferdinand had met while traveling through distant continents in one of Menos's new crowes. The Lady Ingray was exotic and beautiful, and the diva who played her had been radiant. Gestault, like the audience, found himself seduced by her charms. From there, the plot promised to develop into a fairly standard examination of a love triangle—but a twist came when the Lady Ingray rejected the handsome Gestault's advances.

Well, this is new, Aadore had thought. A Menosian master rarely failed to capture his prize. After his spurning by the lady, prideful Gestault resorted to the services of a witch in the hopes of bespelling her. Before giving him her potion, the witch warned Gestault that love couldn't be forced, only offered, and that her concoctions at times induced not passion, but madness. However, Gestault cared not, and he snatched the elixir from the witch. At the first opportunity, the Masked Ball of the third act, Gestault dosed Ingray's wine with the love potion. Within moments, the elixir took effect, and the pair stole away to a suite within the mansion, where they removed their masks and clothes and engaged in lustful sex. Wild with passion, Ingray sang to Gestault that he would be hers and hers alone forever. Post-coitus, Ingray left the spent, drunk, and sleeping Iron lord to seal her promise.

As the opera approached its finale, Ingray's madness was revealed. Under the influence of the spell, she started a long, strident song about the trials of her love with Gestault, about how many sought to keep them apart. Mad Ingray then locked and barred the mansion's doors, collected Gestault's rifle and cutlass, and commenced "honoring" her beloved. Still gloriously wailing, she cornered her husband in a pantry, shot him into mincemeat, and then gouged the eyes out of his skull. But he was not the only one she felt stood in the way of her love: a similar fate awaited all the others in the manse. The guests fell to her sword blows and bullets, each dying a screaming and bombastic death. No one escaped Ingray; she proved herself unstoppable. For the Lady had been possessed by Gestault's selfish, prideful desire. She loved Gestault as he loved himself: she became his perfect bride, a living mirror of his narcissism. Even when the surviving folk rallied in the great room, broke apart furniture, and assaulted her, she did not succumb to her wounds. Instead, they fell to her bullets and blows. Soon, nothing could be heard in the mansion but Ingray's song and the loud snoring of Gestault. As *Un Balle Sanguia* ended, Ingray ascended the crimson staircase, which was draped with fallen bodies, wearing her wedding dress of blood.

It was this moment that played over and over again in Aadore's mind: Ingray walking up a staircase of death and ruin. Aadore felt as if she and her fellows had just done the same. She fixated on the image as she huddled in the darkness of their new hideaway: the Royal Opera House. She rocked Ian, listening to the creaking beams that somehow held up the ancient building in defiance of Menos's apocalypse. When she looked over at the dim and empty stage, spotlighted by the moonbeams penetrating the chamber's fractured roof, she could almost see and hear the ghostly Ingray singing her heart out. *Un Balle Sanguia's* makeup, scenery, and effects had been remarkable, reflecting what Aadore now knew of true violence. Ingray's victims had looked just like the unliving horror after Aadore had hacked it to pieces with the blade that rested in the empty seat beside her. Unconsciously, she adjusted the pack hiding the throbbing wound in her shoulder. *How long before the poison sets in?* she wondered. *How long before my brother hacks me to bits?*

"Aadore?"

Someone tugged at her, and the nightmare disintegrated. From the shadows beside Aadore glowed Curtis's white countenance. Curtis rubbed her back with his hand. "You look as if you're dreaming, but I can see that you're awake."

"I wish I were dreaming. I wish that this nightmare would end already."

Curtis could think of nothing to say. Out in the night, in the clouded ruins of Menos, shambling creatures called to the moon and to each other. The hordes had become an army. Although he and the other survivors had been able to make it as far as an access point leading to the Royal Opera House—a hatch that opened up right behind the stage—they were not yet free of the city. And the sublevels were now closed to them: water had found its way even into those feliron-reinforced tunnels. If they were to pass the Iron Wall, they would have to navigate the fog of death. Curtis pulled Aadore and the child into a one-armed embrace as he, too, succumbed to melancholy.

After a speck, Aadore poked him. "Where did you go? I watched you fall asleep with your eyes open."

"Did I?"

"What were you thinking about?"

"How much farther we must go. What were you thinking about before?"

"An opera." She laughed.

Whenever Aadore smiled, which wasn't often, her happiness spread like a fever. The little lad in her lap burbled and gave a gummy grin, and Curtis smiled, too. Curtis's prolonged staring made Aadore feel shy. Pretending to pay him no heed, Aadore tended to the baby: checked his nappy, spoon-fed him a few scoops of the powdered milk-and-water concoction. But Ian's food was nearly gone, as were most of their supplies. Aadore's caregiving painted a motherly, fierce image that only intensified Curtis's attention. *Lovely*, he thought. He wished that her thin pianist's fingers would touch him with the same kindness as they did the infant. He wondered what her hard-set mouth would taste like, how it might part and gasp in pleasure. As a gentleman, Curtis knew he should stop eyeing her. However, his baser impulses demanded he appreciate every moon-hued, voluptuous curve of this Iron maiden: her long and shapely legs, her strong shoulders, the full breasts hidden behind her tattered gown. Curtis refused to believe it was a lack of sex—he was rather choosy—or the absence of other women that made Aadore so appealing. These conditions simply allowed Aadore's inner light to shine. A gray light, surely, as she was a woman of the Iron City.

307

Aadore scraped the last of the baby's meal from the battered saucer, then placed the feeding paraphernalia back in her beggar's pouch. Strange, thought Curtis, that she refused to put down the pack—doing so would make the task far easier, would save her from the awkward game of arm-bending and wincing that she played. Afterward, Aadore burped little Ian, and he settled into a nap. Once the infant appeared to be fully asleep, Curtis and Aadore leaned upon each other, their heads and shoulder touching. They watched the ghosts of Menos perform on the grand stage in twirls of dust and ash.

"We smell like absolute rubbish," said Aadore.

Curtis couldn't disagree. "We're lucky to be alive. We're lucky to have found one another."

"Lucky...yes."

Aadore's mind drifted, lulled by Curtis's warm body at her side. Sleepily, she considered luck—and the fact that hers was about to run out. Relaxed and comfortable, Aadore nearly confessed her cursed future. *Not now. I'm still myself and not a monster.* Now, her brother and Skar were out in the city, which was thriving with so many dead—and more being born by the speck—that the men had risked scouting in the night for a way through the Iron Wall. To distract herself, she glanced at the blemished beauty of the grand opera house. She used her vivid memory to recall the polished balustrades, the gold-leaf balconies, and the red-velvet seats—features all now smothered in darkness and soot. What an effort it would take to make Menos majestic once more. Gloriatrix hadn't been present in the Iron City for the calamity, and Aadore believed that her queen still lived; she must still live. Had Gloriatrix been successful in her quest to conquer Eod? Did the world know what had happened? She worried that the lack of any rescue and restoration efforts was a sign that the whole world lay in ruins. Aadore banished the thought and prayed that had not come to pass: she had to believe there was something green and living beyond the fog of death, and that she and the others would see it again. Aadore whirled in this maelstrom of thoughts, hopes, and fears, all the while rubbing her shoulder. The claw marks burned.

Curtis sensed her restless shuffling and knew that her actions were odd. When they'd gathered at Aadore's apartment, he had learned of Skar's most recent employer and the complications surrounding the death of the master's daughter. *Aadore is fine*, he repeated, but he believed himself a little less each time. Consumed by their brooding, neither noticed the gray shadows of Sean and Skar moving through the orchestra and up the stairs to the balcony where their companions rested.

Sean startled them. "Enough with your long faces. We think we've found a way through the Iron Wall."

Curtis sat up. "Through?"

"Right through," said Skar, and grinned. "There's a tear in the untearable, a rip right down the wall. It's a small one, but your brother here has eyes that a hawk would envy. He thinks it runs all the way through. I'm hopeful enough to believe that."

I want to see fresh air and a blue sky before I must close my eyes forever, thought Aadore. "We've had enough of a rest. We don't need to spend the remainder of the evening in shelter. I'd like to leave. Now."

Aadore stood and passed Ian back to Skar who slipped the lad, still asleep, into his arm hammock. She gestured to her fellows to mobilize themselves, but Sean and Skar stayed where they were, frowning.

"Sister," said Sean. "We must take a moment. The night is hungry and thick with terrors. The damned are everywhere. Skar and I were nearly spotted at every turn. You know that the dead have eyes now, ones they can use. And there is something—"

"All the more reason not to wait. We don't need more eyes and more dead," snapped Aadore.

She seemed unreasonably angry and volatile. Sean came forward, hoping she would respond to his caution, listen to certain bleak details of what he and Skar had found. Sean took hold of her shaking hands. Oh, how dreadfully cold her flesh felt. Darkly, and with a flash of the empathy that only the closest siblings possess, one never dulled by time and years, Sean sensed a whisper of Aadore's terror. She hadn't been afraid this whole journey: not of the shrieking and rotting unliving, not of the asphyxiating clouds of death through which they'd come. Yet, at this moment, she trembled with mortal fear. Something was terribly wrong in her, something that felt like the dark secrets of laboratories and experiments he kept in his own head. While he couldn't guess what vexed her, he would honor her desire. "Very well, Sister," he said, and kissed her clammy hands.

"Hold on!" barked Skar, balling up his fists and puffing himself up with importance. "Just a damn sand! We would never make it, not at night. You know what's out there, in the marketplace. You need to tell them—"

"We shall live," declared Sean. "And they will see soon enough what final trial we face."

Sean's fieriness quieted Skar to a grumbling obedience. The four walked down and through the decayed opera house, making their way around burned detritus, kicking up trails of ashes, until they came to an antechamber. Together, they worked to hoist open the bent and buckled doors of the theater. As soon as they went outside, Sean knew that they'd have to be quick. At least his stump wasn't complaining today; he might be able to manage a hobbled-run. Stealth would be an ineffective tactic against an army of the dead. And where there was an army, there was also a commander.

He and Skar had been the only ones to see it: the mount of bones, cinders, and shadows. Atop the jutting throne had sat something resembling a man, though the companions couldn't determine anything more specific than that. When it had moved, they had run back to their hole. Now, they would have to run again: past the shambles of the market, past the gnawing hordes, past that mount of ashy dark, and past whatever sat and reveled in the kingdom's rot and doom. Sean prayed to the Kings, Sisters, Iron Queens, Saints—whatever or whoever might hear him—that what sat upon the new throne of Menos would not notice them.

IV

Although the metal creaked and screamed as they tore open the doors of the opera house, the clamor didn't summon as many unliving as they'd feared; only a couple of curious, noseless horrors came sniffing about the entrance. Skar rushed ahead, bouncing baby and all, and prevented their imminent wailing with two messy head-severing blows. The remaining companions crept out onto the rubble-strewn stairs and into the cold kiss of the fog of death. Sean and Skar had spoken truth: the night echoed with terrors. They ran.

As they'd already exhausted their supply of noise-bombs, the four tried to stay quiet. Tonight, the moon's bright light pierced through a layer of the gloom, and in the foul glow, the crumbled shells, fallen columns, and teetering piles looked like nightmare versions of the houses, lampposts, and carriages they'd once been. They not only had less cover, but also more cause to fear the moving shadows, the *legions* of moving shadows about which Sean had warned them.

How many of the dead have been reborn? wondered Aadore. It was impossible to count the lumpy, shuffling things they skirted in the fog of death. Moments later, Aadore saw what she thought was a heap of trash that filled the scraped-out ruin of a building. Then the mound moved, splitting into caterpillars and milling shapes, and she realized it was a gigantic orgy of the dead—which had been sleeping or insensate until they sensed the life of her and her fellows. The sleepy dead started spilling out from the fissures in the walls and through the building's shattered windows. The company raced away before the hissing things could catch them.

They made a number of narrow escapes, most made possible by Sean's acute reflexes and senses. Despite his leg, Aadore had seen him fall only a few times, when they'd pushed themselves to the limits of exhaustion. Indeed, Sean's soldier's grit gave him the strength of a man far haler—that and the darkness that rode within his soul, for fear and hatred were the most potent of fuels. It was incredible to Aadore how quickly her brother could move: a spring and a pivot off his cane with naught even a grimace to show any exertion. Still, even her rage-powered brother couldn't protect them from an army.

The night reeked with the earthy putrescence of a split, fly-buzzing carcass, the kind of smell that conjured vomit in the back of Aadore's throat. And the stench was intensifying. The fact that she was able to deafen herself to the droning of so many flies and the squelching and flatulent shifting of tons of rotten, maggoty flesh was a testament to her willpower. At any rate, the appalling music served to muffle the sounds of her company's footsteps, huffing, and heartbeats. A blessing? A curse? Who knew in this madness? Glancing at Ian—the eternally quiet child—Aadore noticed that Skar had swaddled him almost to the point of suffocation. Aadore assumed that Skar knew what he was doing, and there was no time to check, for they needed to run, run, run.

The company raced past shelled-out houses, waterlogged paths, and sloppy shapes. They took any shelter they could find—behind ruined walls and shields of sheet metal, and in dips and crannies in the road—but hid only for specks. Then they were on their feet again, outrunning the packs of wild dead things like a herd of fleet deer darting through a wolves' den. They never spoke, for doing so would have brought death upon them. They began to breathe in the shallowest rasps and ran until their oxygen-deprived muscles screamed and burned. But the four soon reached the marketplace of which Sean and Skar had spoken.

Tipped stalls, shattered glass and cookware, scattered weapons, and barricades of trash and wood fluttering with soiled silk flags emerged from the fog of death like a grand battlefield. Indeed, a battle had been fought here: signs of struggle remained in the form of long smears of both dried and freshly glistening gore, and severed hands clutching daggers. At least the people of Menos had taken a stand, however doomed, against the darkness. The devastation went on for some distance, illuminated by the ghastly moon. Aadore suddenly remembered a bold-lined image of a wolf atop a cairn, possibly from one of the books in the Lady El's library, but she couldn't say for certain. Even as Curtis pulled her ahead, she gazed up at the moon, captivated.

At first, the Black Markets seemed deserted. However, the hunched backs of Skar and Sean and the lightness and slowness of their tread told Aadore that her companions were aware of a potential threat. They crept through the misty battlefield, which was curiously empty of walking corpses. Every hair on and nerve in their bodies thrummed with danger. They brandished their weapons, prepared to attack the first rotten face that appeared. Soon the faint squares of houses faded away, and they skulked around the edges of black cracks in the flagstones and wove around mounds of filth. When a civilization fell, all of its baubles and riches were reduced to a slag of putrefied, buzzing matter. *How meaningless is man's desire to rule and conquer*, she realized. *Like a fortress in the sand, which the tide will claim in time.* Aadore couldn't distinguish rags from riches, or bones from meat. An alarming baby doll stared at her from atop one of the many piles of ruin on this beach of despair, pointing at her with its only remaining hand. She could almost hear it whisper, "Look what the wrongs of men and Kings have wrought."

Sean stopped in what felt like nowhere, and urgently motioned everyone to hunker down. They were forced to stow away their armaments and from that point on, walked low to the ground like crabs. Sean, who could not easily hold such a pose, handed his cane to Curtis, then crawled on the earth. Agony racked him when he touched the swampy hard stones; what he'd experienced these past few days could easily have killed someone with his disability. Aadore wanted to tell her brother that she loved him, but he shrugged off the pain and scrabbled away too quickly. She vowed to tell him how she felt before the ache in her shoulder developed into a worse affliction. Curtis, Skar, and Ian, too, should know her heart as well. A woman shouldn't go to her end without a slate free of unspoken truths.

As their slow worm inched onward, Sean repeatedly stared at something off to one side. *What are you seeing, Brother?* wondered Aadore. *What do you see that has the power to frighten even a man who's endured the dark torments you have?* They crawled between two trash dunes, and Aadore froze as the moon shone so brightly that the tattered veil over the land was burned away.

Deep in the gray plumes of this valley of evil lay a heart: a mountain. A hundred strides away, maybe? Aadore felt as if a force pulled her forward, as if she were being compelled to kneel before this monument. It looked as if it had been constructed out of the slag and ruin around them, perhaps even out of countless bodies of Menos's dead. Whatever its building blocks, it was magnificent in size—as tall as the Iron Wall. Radiant and ethereal, the moon cast its glory upon the gruesome tit. There was almost a feminine harmony to this symbolism: moons, the breast-like shape of the mound, the nipple at its apex...What was that? A structure? A figure? Surrounding the mountain of death were the children of this apocalypse—tens of thousands of dead. Aadore no longer wondered why the dead seemed to have vanished: they were all here. They had all come home and were...worshiping. Indeed, the rows of rotting, standing things swayed and tilted like the gentlest waves on the ocean. They were united in their movements and focus. They were not restless now, but still and reverent. Aadore couldn't believe what she was witnessing and smelling, the gagging rot as the dead rejoiced in their odious faith. In another speck, Aadore would either have vomited or passed out, so she was grateful when Curtis nudged her along to the next mound, behind which Skar and her brother were crouching. Pallid and sweating from any number of aches and fears, the four dared to rest a moment.

"Now you have seen," whispered Sean.

None of the four could grasp the absurd logic behind a dark mountain, an army of faithful dead, and a series of calamities that had unmade the known world. The crack in the Iron Wall, their planned escape from Menos, and their fellowship were the sole reasons for their hearts to beat, for their hands and feet to start moving though the muck. Aadore resisted the temptation to look back at the tit of darkness a second time. Instead, she exhausted her mind by fantasizing about what they would soon see: a crack, and beyond that greenness and starlight. She knew the fantasy would never come to fruition, at least not for her, but she held onto it desperately nonetheless. Knees slapping mud, hands squishing putrid garbage that puffed wet spores into her face as it crumbled, Aadore thought only of her dream as she crawled. They were all moving the same way as Sean now, and all likely daydreaming about realities less horrid than their current one. Little Ian didn't make a peep.

Finally, Aadore felt a fresh untainted wind and looked up from her scuttling. Through the fog, she noticed a black scribble that didn't waver or dissolve like a mirage as they drew nearer. The blackness widened, becoming a lightning bolt carved through iron, through a barrier that even now dominated the landscape and commanded awe: the Iron Wall. They'd made it. The dead must have been worshipping still, for the fellowship saw none. Perhaps no one else had made it this far. They would be the first to escape, they decided, and they stood and ran.

The Iron Wall and its great tear loomed in front of the gasping survivors. At the base of the titanic split, they noticed a quarry of waste and cindered iron, which they'd have to climb. However, no obstacle seemed impassable now. Their little star, Ian, was finally awake and gurgled as he bounced against Skar. Escape was within their grasp. They stopped at the base of the opening to assess its safety, and then stared up at its misty heights and deep into the canyon through which they would head.

"We've made it," exclaimed Aadore.

"Almost," said Sean.

Though they felt the urge to cry or scream, they climbed instead. People of Iron, to the end.

Screech!

What felt like the coldest wind in Geadhain suddenly blew up their spines. It circled around them, stinging their eyes with the ashes it bore, pushing them back. Terrified and battered, they held onto each other as the hurricane of black grit solidified into a blob of shadow on the rocks before them. The shadow stretched, and darkness fluttered from it like ravens. It faded into the shape of a man, one striding down the broken ruin of the Iron Wall toward them. Sean saw him most clearly: black eyes, strong, tall, and regally handsome, like a master. He was clothed in a rippling, tattered garment that wafted and dissipated like the shadow-born gusts that had transported him here. *Is he some kind of sorcerer?* they all wondered. Then the being's icy presence withered their genitals and skins like naked children thrown into the winter. His gaze arrested them with its pulsing dark power. They reeled with impressions of whistling emptiness and crumbling dynasties; tickling breaths of bone dust blew across their faces. This was no sorcerer, they knew now: this was a force beyond their ken.

"Worthless maggots," it said. **"I have offered you the chance to reign in my kingdom. You have seen what awaits you, what you will become, and you flee from my gift? Did you think you could pass without my knowing? There is not a star in the sky whose fall I have not ordained."**

Its words were thunder and knives that stabbed the skulls of the lesser creatures it approached. Curtis fell. Skar curled up and wrapped himself around Ian, trying to protect the suddenly wailing child. Inexplicably, though, the creature's words registered with Aadore and Sean only as a tinny, distracting hum. It was merely an annoyance, not an aural assault. Iron born and Iron proud, hearts in their mouths and hands shaking, brother and sister drew cane and sword and faced the uncanny horror.

"Fall!" commanded Death from within her vessel. **"Fall before me!"**

The storm of ashes and slicing talons of wind kicked up once more, and the land was consumed by a frenzy of twirling trash and smaller, dashing stones. Those of the fellowship who had fallen screamed as the

Dreamer's Will drove further into their heads; blood trickled from their eyes, ears, and mouths. Sean refused to obey the command, and when the monster slunk toward him like a snail, he charged the horror and stunned it by cracking his cane across its head.

The fury stopped; debris scattered. Death was flabbergasted, her host's skull ringing. The insolent maggot swung again, and this time Death caught its tiny stick and crumbled it to ash with her touch. Death snarled and snatched this grub, this pest that had somehow managed to strike a giant of the cosmos, and she filled it with her black Will. Aadore screamed and raced into the crackling bosom of ebon fire that had suddenly consumed both Sean and the entity. She was already tainted and dead; she had nothing to lose. If she couldn't save Sean, then she would willingly burn in this pyre with him. A shrieking Aadore entered the warm, but not searing, haze of twisting ether. Immediately, she saw two fuzzy shapes, one throttling the other, and she stabbed the aggressor.

"G*raaaaah!*"

An unforgettable cry sounded: the ear-shattering frustration of Death denied. The flames fizzled away, and the world slowed to a pace that allowed Aadore to become aware of her trembling naked body—her clothing had burned to molecular ash—and of the nude, thin figure of her brother. He clung to her, the wood below his knee having also been incinerated. However, they were alive and their flesh had somehow been left untouched by this unholiest of powers.

Brave and united, they stood, scowling at the destroyer of their city. Death moved back from the maggots that had rebuked her. Her vessel had been run through with a blade; she pulled it out of her abdomen and reduced it to flakes of rust with a touch. Death spat at the maggots and at their disregard for her order.

"Cursed blood! You should not exist on this side of Geadhain! You should not exist at all! I shall eradicate your line forever! I shall—"

Curtis and Skar continued to scream with each word; they could not endure much more of this ranting. Even Ian's wail had grown wet and choking. Aadore, somehow knowing she could not be harmed, challenged the unearthly horror. She left Sean to balance himself for a speck, dipped and picked up a rock, the only weapon available. Then, she and her brother took a step and a hop forward.

Death fled in a spiral of ash and a blast of foul wind.

Aadore and her brother limped over to their fallen comrades. She lowered Sean down onto a trash heap, and, a steadfast survivor, he set to work rummaging through the refuse upon which he sat. Eventually, he found an Iron City banner that could be worked into coverings for himself and his sister. Meanwhile, Aadore helped the cringing, weeping, bloodied men to their feet. As if she were a sainted mother, Ian stopped crying as soon as Aadore retrieved him from Skar's weary arms. Curtis and the larger fellow took a moment to breathe and wipe the blood from their faces. Soon, Sean hopped over and handed Aadore some soiled shreds that she could tie about her chest and waist. He had fashioned a wrap for himself, too, but both would have to make do with bare feet. They did not discuss the unearthly encounter, wanting only to make good their escape. Helping one another—mostly Sean, who was without a leg—they climbed up the feliron rubble and out of the city of death.

V

After what felt like hourglasses of scrambling and stumbling, the company found itself in an ashen meadow: there were no traces of anything green in this new land of smoke and darkness. They wandered, none could say for how long. Perhaps they'd died back in Menos and this was Purgatory. But then, off in the distance, there flickered something white—a flag? Aadore and her companions knew it could not be, but ran toward it anyway. They were further convinced that their eyes deceived them when, drawing closer, the shape resolved itself into the white and black banners of Eod and Menos, flying together.

There were structures below and behind these ensigns—tents and ramshackle lean-tos. The four blinked and shook their heads in disbelief as they saw figures moving toward them: men, nearly a dozen of them. And they walked upright, not shambling or lurching. These were not unliving, then, but fellow survivors. Some were elegant white-and-silver warriors and carried bows that crackled with electrical magik. Delirious with relief and exhaustion, Aadore almost mistook them for divine saviors.

Beside these shining warriors strode the familiar spiny Ironguards of the Menosian military. Instead of aiming their weapons at each other, these soldiers of rival nations were pointing them at her and her friends.

The men were not actively hostile, but they were certainly not welcoming. It seemed that before the comrades would be allowed to enter this armed encampment, they would have to be examined. An Iron marshal appeared wearing a black apron, black gloves, and a mask that looked as if it had been designed for underwater breathing. The company feared a harsh sentence: had they managed to escape the dead only to be judged and convicted by the living? While the Ironguards and Silver watchmen stood nearby with weapons raised, the marshal lifted the companions' arms, prodded their flesh with his cold, rubber-mitted hands, and generally treated them like potentially diseased specimens. They knew what he was looking for: scrapes, bites, signs of black-threaded infection. He sounded disappointed when he didn't find anything that would justify either a quarantine command or a sentence of death. "Hmm...you all seem fantastically intact." The Iron marshal did, however, poke the brown lines of the wound, now sealed by an ugly scab, on Aadore's shoulder. "How did you come by this?" he asked.

"A scrape," replied Aadore without flinching. "From rubble."

She could not tell whether his face expressed disbelief behind the foggy windowpane of his mask. But apparently her explanation had been convincing enough, for the soldiers lowered their arms, and the Iron marshal waved the company ahead.

"You were scratched," whispered Sean, as soon as they were a safe distance behind the soldiers who marched them through the camp. Although she'd made no mention of the injury, they'd all spied it after the fire had left her naked—but their breathless escape had left no time for questions. Sean realized that in her desperate push to reach civilization, she'd been trying to outrun the shadow of death. "How long ago?"

"Does it matter?" she muttered. "It's healed. Let us not speak of it here."

"You could have endangered us," hissed Sean. Quickly his anger lost its battle with reason. As a prisoner, many times, he'd contemplated and accepted death, but on his own terms. Perhaps Aadore had only wished the same freedom of choice in an untenable situation. *We shall speak of this elsewhere*, he decided.

One of the soldiers who escorted them proved more talkative than the others, and they began questioning him eagerly, curious about how it was that so many had survived. It turned out that some people, including a number of Ironguards, had been caught along the Iron Road when calamity befell Menos, and managed to flee. They had then spent some time wandering through the fog of death, which had spilled well past the Iron Wall, extending for spans and spans across the Fields of Canterbury and beyond. For a time, the land had heaved, spouting walls of fire and dribbling molten spit. But eventually, they, like the company, had caught sight of the white flicker of a flag and arrived at a makeshift camp established by advance guards from Eod. There, they were informed that an alliance had been forged between Eod and Menos. The Iron Queen had consented to overlook past wrongs in exchange for an offer of military might: together, Eod and Menos would confront the mad king. Silver watchmen and Ironguards were to be allies now, it seemed. The laws and conventions that had governed this land for centuries had fallen along with Menos.

Still trying to absorb the magnitude of these developments, they absent-mindedly bade farewell to their escort, which left them outside an empty tent. Inside, they collapsed with weary gasps onto four damp cots, content merely to sit for a sand without speaking.

"So..." Curtis sat up on one elbow, and gazed at Aadore in wonder, although there was a spark in his eyes that might have been something deeper. "How are you not dead? I thought it only took a scratch, and yours looked deep. Why have you not risen? Is there still a chance that you might..." A look of pain crossed his weary face; he couldn't finish the question. "How could you not tell us and just allow yourself to suffer like that?"

Curtis's eyes watered, as did Sean's and Skar's. Aadore had been selfish in her silence. She'd nearly left these men without saying goodbye. "I'm so sorry." Aadore hurried to each man's bedside, kissing him and apologizing. Ian, too, received a word and a caress. The men were all crying when she'd finished, but laughed at their soppiness a moment later.

"You're in the clear then?" Curtis grinned. "I'd hate to bash in such a pretty skull."

Aadore wandered over, intending to lightly slap the cheeky man. Instead, she held out her hand, and Curtis knew to kiss it. "We have unfinished business, you and I," she said, and her half-smile summoned from the young man the deepest blush.

"Unfinished business," muttered Sean.

Aadore didn't attach any importance to her brother's mumbling. Not until she, Curtis, Skar, and the baby had filled the tent with raucous mirth and her brother remained apart, watching them, frowning, and rubbing his stump did she notice his gaze—so distant and dark that the light feared it. Now witnessing his grim mood, Aadore went to her brother. "What are you thinking about, Sean?"

"Unfinished business. Secrets. I'm angry that you kept yours from me."

Aadore waited, for she saw it then: the hungry shadow in his heart, his own secret. It veiled his thin, handsome face; it shadowed his gaze. Seizing the moment, she said, "We could all be in the grave tomorrow, Sean. If there is something you would say or do, tell me now or you might lose the chance, through fate or pride, to make peace."

Sean snarled. "I don't want peace. I want him dead. Murdered by my own fuking hands."

Everyone froze and hung on the moment, waiting for Sean to continue. Sean's face twisted like a frenzied animal's. After some of the violence left him, Aadore whispered, "Who?"

Sean took her hand. "I'll tell you everything. That way, if I am to fail in this life, you will know of my enemy beforehand and thus be able to avenge me. Swear that you will." His grip became crushing. "Swear to me!"

"I do. I swear. Please, Sean, tell me, tell us, who we must end."

"A doctor. A madman." Sean paused, panting. The door in his head creaked open, revealing the darkness, and he spoke, low and with a sneer. "I should start at the beginning. I'd been stationed in Conway..."

Conway. A small hamlet, one not marked on many maps, in the far northern reaches of Ebon Vale. He'd been as green as spring grass, one of the few gay Ironguards who greeted locals with a smile rather than with the shove of a shoulder or cold words; his parents had raised him to be better than that. It was his first assignment since graduating from the Iron College, and it would prove to be his last. A lode of truefire had been discovered, he explained, and once the earthspeakers had completed their excavation, it had lain there, throbbing, a vein of pure elemental fire. The last thing he recalled of his time in Conway was standing upon the heights of the dig site like a man at the rim of a volcano, his face warm and tingling with crimson magik. Then some fool tripped or kicked a stone, igniting the truefire, which detonated with an incredible blast. Conway, already obscure, was obliterated. Sean had been the only survivor. He'd been dragged from the ruinous inferno, or most of him had: his leg had had to be amputated so that he could be pulled from the rubble. "We'll take you somewhere safe," a phantom solider had promised amid muttered exclamations of amazement that anyone had survived. That man had lied.

"I didn't wake up in a hospice," spat Sean.

He'd groggily stirred in a sterile steel room, strapped to a table. In a drugged stupor, it had taken him a few sands to realize he had tubes running out of his body, and that the distorted faces looming over him weren't denizens of the afterlife. But they acted as though they were arbiters of eternal damnation, for they cut him, carried out technostatic treatments, inserted cold objects into his rectum, throat, and ears. The potent narcotics subduing him ultimately proved unequal to the task, and he screamed himself unconscious.

Between treatments, they'd fed him—force-feeding him when he was too weak to eat. One kind, hefty soldier with the countenance of a sheepdog, whom Sean thought of as a "Horace" as he had no idea of his real name, would move his leg and arms and massage away the tremors caused by the experiments and the botched technomagik that wreaked havoc on his nervous system. Sean angered the doctors, especially that pig-in-an-apron Dr. Hex, the chief madman and torturer in the sick laboratory in which Sean had been sequestered. Hex had to develop ever more creative tortures to test Sean's uncanny resistance to magik.

"I never broke," said Sean, his expression wild. "I learned how not to crumble from the pain. I became the strongest soldier in all Geadhain. A good soldier saves his strength and chooses his battles. I saved my strength. I learned how to restore it by increments, in the short sands I was given when Horace left me, after the treatments, alone and in my quiet prison, assuming I'd rest. But I didn't rest. I practiced my balance. I stumbled about my cell like a drunk trying to do ballet until I had enough strength in my leg to hop. I strained my scrawny arms against the shivering metal of my cell until I could push my nose away from the wall. Most of the time, my arms weren't as strong as my will, and I ended up with a bloody nose. I didn't care. I had to be strong. I would have to be strong if I were going to kill him."

"Hex?" whispered Aadore.

"Yes." The tension Sean held inside him suddenly collapsed. He'd jittered on the edge of his bed throughout his tale, and now his head fell between peaked shoulders; he looked all bones and weakness. "And then one day, I was free. Madness. There's no reason in the world, I see that now. Horace simply let me out. I believe he was weeping. I don't remember what he said. He'd brought me clothes, though, and I had to remember how to put them on. Like an animal that had been caged, castrated, declawed, and then suddenly set loose, I wandered through the empty, flickering bunker. Horace was with me, of course. I do wish I knew what happened to him, where he went afterward. There had been some kind of terrible violence: blood was everywhere. I searched and searched, hoping to find the doctor among the heaped bodies in lab coats, but I only ended up covered in gore. We walked up steps toward a gleam of light…I remember how the sun blinded me as I emerged onto a roaring shore belonging to no place I'd ever seen: frost and ice everywhere. I was so used to the cold by then that it barely tickled. There was a crowe on the beach, guarded by soldiers of the Iron City, and Horace took me to it. I assumed they were shuttling me somewhere else, somewhere more terrible even than this place, and I began to resist, to draw upon the terrible fury I'd been forced to repress.

"Then Horace, who kindly endured my punches and thrashing and asked the Ironguards not to fire—all while trying to keep me upright, no less—repeated a question until I had heard it: 'Where can we take you?'" Sean paused, and the black vomit summoned by these dreaded memories receded back down his throat, returning to the dark place that was home to all his terrors. "And I said *Home*."

The word shattered him.

"You're here, brother. I'm here." Aadore held him. She asked nothing more. Surrounding the siblings in their tense embrace was their family of survivors. Aadore crawled into Sean's cot, laid him down, and snuggled into him as she'd done when they were children, when he'd just been scared of the dark, and not faced it, eaten it, and become it. Perhaps he remembered that innocence, too, for after trembling and wetting his cheeks with tears for a while, he slept—as he always did after his big sister came to comfort him.

VI

They emerged only to acquire new clothing and a pair of crutches; there was no woodworker around able to make Sean a new prosthetic. The four adults and little Ian mostly kept to themselves, holing up in the drafty tent they'd claimed and scaring off new would-be inhabitants with curses and scowls. Winter had come, bringing with it a cold deeper than any this region had ever known. An astonished Skar told them that as there were no longer any mountains to act as bastions against the wind, the Northland's fury was now free to travel wherever it wanted. While they huddled indoors, Skar occasionally ventured forth in search of information and food. Sometimes they peeked through the tent's flaps and imagined they could see Heathsholme's humpbacked white fields in the distance, though nothing could really be glimpsed beyond the fog of death. There was nothing to see, nothing to do. But why bother going anywhere now that they were finally comfortable? Geadhain, her warring kings, whatever entity was responsible for the destruction of Menos—none of these problems were going to be solved, at least not immediately. They had survived a nightmare. They would rest, recoup, and heal their bodies if not their souls, which might never be free of scars.

One day, Curtis snuck out, and from somewhere in the camp he borrowed or stole a pack of cards. They spent the second morning playing Crowns and Fates. Aadore and Sean seemed to win every match. Brother and sister both had devious minds and knew exactly what decisions needed to be made in moments of crisis, whom to sacrifice, whom to send to safety. Whenever the two were paired together against Curtis and Skar, their triumph was assured. Watching the siblings play each other, therefore, was far more entertaining for the fellows who'd lost their proverbial shirts, shoes, and underwear after a couple of rounds.

"A draw..." said Aadore.

"Hmm..." grumbled Sean. Aadore was as unhappy as Sean with the outcome of their game. Wrinkling their faces, they stared at the cards, as if trying to force a result, to divine a strategy that hadn't yet been played—or that had been played incorrectly by the other and so would lead to defeat. Sadly, the Everfair King and his glossy counterpart, the Wildman, were the only two cards still in play on the floor of their hovel. The rest of the deck had been discarded in the graveyard pile. Neither card could trump the other. The game had ended.

Curtis applauded from his bedroll. He'd been lying on his side and watching the match with tired eyes, concentrating mostly on Aadore's charming frowns and pouts. "Well done. I've never seen a draw before."

"Keep it down," hissed Skar.

Little Ian slumbered in the arms of the snarling ogre. Most of Ian's hourglasses were spent in this position and activity. Ian was surely as fatigued as the rest of his new family and did little but sleep. When they'd wandered around earlier, gathering supplies, the soldiers at the encampment had asked them who the child belonged to and whether they could be of any help. Skar told them to *fuk off* in a tone that no one wanted to challenge. Later, Skar and his company had briefly discussed who among them would shoulder responsibility for the parentless child: Skar announced he was prepared to be Ian's primary caregiver, and the others made no objection. Damn whatever complications might arise from four rather mercenary folks rearing an infant. They'd make it work.

"My apologies," said Curtis.

He yawned, stretched, and left the grumpy nanny to sit down cross-legged with the others in the dirt. As the siblings remained focused on their impasse and would not speak to him, Curtis plucked up the Everfair King and began to examine it. Regardless of the age or manufacturer of the deck, Magnus's depiction was always one of glory and beauty. In this instance, the king was pictured standing atop a white rock amid a crashing sea. Green lightning wreathed him, running from earth to sky—not the natural direction of such currents. It was as if Magnus had birthed the elements himself.

"Do you really think he looks like that?" whispered Curtis. "So...beautiful, for a man. So regal. So powerful."

Wind hissed through the tattered walls of their shelter, and they shared a good shiver that finally distracted the siblings from their game.

"We shall find out," said Aadore. She collected the cards and placed them back in their tin. When she glanced up, she discovered the men staring, waiting for her to elaborate. "Where else do you think the soldiers will take us, but to the one great city still standing in Central Geadhain? Even sequestered, we've all heard the whispers among the survivors that we'll be shipping out soon. And where else can we go but to Eod, given what we've seen and what we know? We must take our words to the Iron Queen and to Magnus, her...ally. He should hear our tale, too. Of that I am certain."

Their tale...Flashbacks to unholy flames, an arctic wind, shadow crows, ashes, and horrid maggoty faces made their new haven seem bleak. The unthinkable had resurfaced, stretching the shadows into tentacles, clogging their noses with phantom putrescence.

"What *did* we see?" asked Curtis; they'd done their best to ignore their looming memory for days.

Aadore and Sean contemplated the mystery; he rubbed the purple bruises on his neck, and she scratched the bumpy scab on her shoulder. These wounds were inextricably and unfathomably linked to what they had faced in Menos. *I am a man who can feel neither blessing nor harm from any magik of this world*, thought Sean. *I am a woman untainted by the poison that killed my countrymen*, she thought. *I am a woman who walked into an inferno and emerged untouched and naked as a babe*. Each thought of the being that had obliterated Menos, and of what it had said of their lineage. *Menos's destroyer had been a man, though not exactly a man, who was made of shadows and ravens and brought ruin through the thunder and lightning of his voice. And yet he had somehow also been female; the birth and horror of Menos had both been marked by a sinister femininity. He spoke of our cursed blood. What does that mean? We are simply children of the Brennochs, a family from the East. But where, exactly, in the East? Who are we, and how is it that we still live, given all that we have confronted?*

Brother and sister stared at each other, speaking many truths with their eyes.

"A nekromancer?" Aadore suggested at last. "I say that, and yet I think he must have been something worse, for his power was greater than that of the most wicked sorcerers from both our history and faerytales. I've heard of no other who possesses the power to ruin a city, other than perhaps the Everfair King and Brutus. Perhaps Magnus will have insights into this creature, this Unmaker. That is why we must find Magnus and our great Iron Queen. If they can find new purpose after centuries of war, then we, too, can take on new duties—to our countrymen, to each other, to Ian. We shall have no future until the atrocities that walk our city have been stamped into dust. That is my purpose. I would sacrifice whatever grace has saved me, if that would bring us peace."

"Be careful, Sister," said Sean, once again feeling the ghostly scrape of scalpels against his skin. "You do not know how far men will go in pursuit of science. They become mad, drunk with discovery, believing their genius rivals that of the Immortal Kings. Do not be so quick to offer us up on their table."

Aadore took her brother's hand. "Us, of course. You are right. I shall not."

"It will be our secret," declared Curtis.

"I've held my tongue for some dog-born masters," said Skar. "I'll gladly keep your secrets, milady."

"You need to stop calling me that; it's embarrassing."

"I shall do no such thing," replied Skar, grinning.

After that, the four no longer tried to deny the unthinkable. They talked about their fears, and began discussing the main challenge now confronting them: somehow, this undignified company of mercenaries, soldiers, and services people—none dressed much better than a beggar—would have to arrange a meeting with the most esteemed leaders of their world. If an audience were not immediately granted, they would just have to arrange one themselves.

VII

Neither of the two remaining sisters noticed Ealasyd and the tall shadow leave. Elemech and Eean, pale twin ladies in kirtles of mourning black, sat together at the edge of the glowing witch-water pool. They dipped their feet in it and wept as they watched the world's sorrows.

Scenes rippled across the skin of the pool, shimmering for only a moment before being replaced by another. They saw a maiden riding a wolf of flame and light: Morigan and her beloved, transformed and glorious. Then a sultry woman, hissing poison into the ear of a roaring, bloody giant: the fallen Keeper and the mad king. And most interestingly, a vision of a naked woman and a maimed, scrawny man walking out of a blooming rose of black fire. The sisters did not recognize these two; for some reason, they were unable to read these mortals' secrets and could only study their faces in the watery glass. It was odd, although not the oddest thing they'd seen in these end days. They would like to have known more about these two—their tale, they felt, must be both grand and sad—but the Fates then overwhelmed the sisters with terrors. They endured explosions, shrieking men on fire, promises made from dying lips, and the thunderous commands of the Dreamers. So many Dreamers. The sisters whirled down and through the many currents of destiny, all of which wended their way toward the great confluence of this age: the War of Wars.

The sisters cringed as a silver searing light burst from the pool. They lost their earthly sight and tumbled end over end in a void that buffeted their ears with sandpapery winds and assaulted their senses with mouthfuls of scorched dirt, sweat, metal, and shite. Their bodies crumpled, burned, and fluttered off into ash. Fire and wrath had come to Geadhain. Then came a shattering, as if a glass kingdom were being hammered down to its foundations, and a blast of violent winter air. Of course, they realized. Fire to Ice. Brother to Brother. When the sisters were cast out of the vision, they clung to each another and panted for some time.

"Did you see that, Sister?"

"I did. An end."

Their mimicking of each other was impeccable, and even they lost track of who spoke as Eean and who spoke as Elemech. But Ealasyd, returning now to her sisters, had no difficulty telling them apart. Because of what she had to witness, Elemech's face always held more shadow, more darkness around the eyes. Eean's gaze, though, maintained its gleam of wisdom. Slowly becoming herself once more, Eean became aware of Ealasyd's approach and of certain elements in the room around her: an empty pallet, a missing patient, a space on a shelf of curious wares where three very small and powerful stones in a leather purse had once sat.

"What have you done?" asked Eean.

Ealasyd puffed and crossed her arms. "What have *I* done? You choose this of all times to ask me? I've sent our little bird out of the nest! His wing's all better now. He's ready to fly. Furthermore, I didn't like his being here. He's not nice, you know. His soul is rotten. He stinks our home right up, and there's something terrible whispering in his head. He's as mad as they come."

Eean resisted the urge to stare once more into the glowing witchwater, which had again enthralled Elemech. The Fates were too powerful these days; the future screamed with calamities and omens, demanding to be heard. Of all the times for Eean to be trapped in the likeness of her deeply brooding sister, this was the least opportune. Eean rose, walked away from the pool, and then sat on a bench at the stone table with her back facing the prophetic waters. She needed to create distance between herself and them before she could give Ealasyd her full attention. Ealasyd joined her and sat on her lap. Speaking kindly and earnestly now, Eean continued. "I apologize, my little hummingbird. You know what she is like, and what I am like when we are she."

"I do, and it's terrible! I haven't had a good stew in weeks! Maybe longer, I don't count sands all that well."

Eean caressed her sister's shining locks, which felt as warm and tickling as sunshine against her hand. "You're right to accuse us of neglect. I shall hunt tonight and make you a fatty feast. Perhaps boar or bear."

"Delicious!" beamed Ealasyd.

"First, however, you must tell me what you have done with both the son of the Iron Queen and my three wonderstones."

Ealasyd squeezed her eyes shut and puckered her mouth, trying to remember. Memories didn't stay in her head for long; they flew in and out like flocks of chattering birds. Ealasyd had already forgotten that she and Eean had been bickering a moment ago, but she did manage to remember their guest and the fact that she had sent the unpleasant man away. Why? Why had she done this? "I..." she mumbled. "Something about threes...

Everything comes in threes, even us. I wanted him gone—yes, that's it. I've been trying to find a use for him: after all, he should have one. A creature that lacks a purpose does not deserve the breath of life. He should have died, blown off and away, like a fall leaf on the wind..."

Eean snapped. "Focus," she commanded.

"Right. Rotsoul, or whatever his name is—can't remember—told me what he wanted, what he needed to find most in the world: his mother, his brother, and the monster that wronged him. I thought to give him those old stones we have as a parting gift. I can't say why. At times, dear sister, I hear this beautiful whisper, like a butterfly made of music that flutters in my ear, and I chase it...I'm not sure what happens when I do, though I often wake up in strange places. What were we talking about? Monsters, I think. Imagine that, monsters hunting monsters! Seems like a good fit to me..."

While her sister rambled, Eean thought back to Sorren's indignant gasp against the darkness, where he'd beseeched her and the Green Mother for a chance at redemption. *I want to ask my brother to forgive me. I want to see my mother smile and feel something more than the cold burn of iron in her breast. I want justice and honor and glory, not for myself, but for those whose souls can still be saved. In the sand of my doom, I see every folly, every deplorable act and greedy sin with which I have fed the beast of my damnation. I cannot be saved. I do not ask to be saved. I ask to save those who possess hearts and souls, who possess the buried light and hope that I shall never find in myself. I thought to curse my brother with living death, and yet it is I who rot and crawl with worms inside. Please, great witch, granter of miracles and curses, curse me with another breath of miserable life so that I may be a miracle for my family.*

Much like Morigan's mate, Eean could smell the stink of a lie. But Rotsoul's words and his withered, ruined self smelled of nothing but honesty. Indeed, she sensed that this moment had contained Sorren's truest confession, expressed his most sincere self. And so the Green Mother had honored the fallen creature by granting him the chance he sought. Redemption...not for himself, but for those whose souls were lost in the dark. Could he do it? What would he do now that he was loose and in possession of three of the oldest wonderstones ever picked out of the vegetation, mossy crannies, and aeons of Alabion? The questions sparkled with the promise of both doom and greatness, humming with a resonance of Fate that lured Eean over to the glowing water-mirror, which revealed at least some of all truths. Poor Ealasyd would have no bear or boar for supper tonight.

Elemech welcomed Eean to her side, and they stared and fell as deep as the witch-water would take them.

XI

TRUE SELVES

I

News of the hunt for the fallen queen of Eod had reached the ears of the populace: such a scandal could not be contained, and murmurs ran like rats through this city plagued with fear. Opinions on the matter were divided. Most people were already finding the stress of the war with Brutus to be intolerable and could not envision waging a civil war, too. It was easier, then, to paint Lila the same villainous color as Brutus. *She's probably in league with him*, they whispered. *At least the Iron Queen came to us when the hourglass was darkest for Eod and extended the olive branch.*

There were also a few more seditious voices, those most loyal to the crown, who attempted to rationalize the queen's act of genocide. What she'd done was horrific; no one contested that. However, war itself was wicked, and in wartime, good women—even queens—were sometimes called upon to do terrible things. Any fool could walk to the Gate of Eod, look east, and see the three iron colossi sleeping in the desert and glowing with strange fires and lights: technomagikal monstrosities that had been created to destroy Eod. These loyalists suspected that once the war with Brutus had ended, a new one with Menos would begin. And Magnus would be at a disadvantage, too, as he had invited the enemy into his sanctum.

Those who held such unpopular opinions learned to whisper them only in trusted circles. For the eyes and ears of Menos walked the streets, and one never knew what a black-suited master or wandering group of Ironguards would repeat to their Iron Queen. Other more unsavory characters had passed through the ivory gates of Eod and taken up residence in the city in recent days. Rough men, angry men; women dressed in padded leather and crisscrossed in belts glinting with throwing knives. Yet there was no circus in town, and these women and men weren't performers. From far and wide, cutthroats and assassins had come to Eod, lured by thoughts of winning the Iron Queen's murder pool and becoming heir apparent to Menos.

The prospect of hunting a queen and acquiring the Iron Crown had drawn even the reclusive, legendary assassins from the sandy islands northwest of Central Geadhain: the Isles of Terotak, a chain of islands that cartographers drew like a string of black pearls. Indeed, the women of that land were as rich and mysterious as that rare adornment. Strutting through the white streets in loose black robes and capes of ebon silk, they seemed more specter than mortal. Only the beautiful coal-rimmed eyes of these women could be seen: the rest of their features were hidden by veiled hoods. One wouldn't have wanted to peer beneath the wrappings in any case, for these women were *Marith,* an old Ghaedic word meaning "Death-eaters." Their veils concealed their teeth, filed to points and capped in bronze. Their hoods hid the whirling, thorny tattoos on their bald, scarified scalps. And though the Marith passed by in clouds of petals and spice, the saccharine odor was not a pleasant one: it was reminiscent of a mortuary, the kind of pulverizing fragrance necessary for masking the stench of rotting flesh. For beneath their concealments, their silks and spices, these women stank of the death they ate and of the blood in which they washed their sunless skins. Like the other mercenaries, the Marith had come to Eod to hunt the queen; they had, however, no interest in the Iron Crown. They sought only to determine whether Lila should be consumed or sainted for the death that she'd brought to the world.

The moment of decision could soon be upon them, for the queen and her fugitive lover—how the scandalmongers reveled in the heady mixture of sex and sin!—had been spotted by two men on the roads winding through

Meadowvale. Both men had initially suffered from delirium, and one of them continued to crawl on the ground of his sanatorium cell, believing himself to be an earthworm. The other fellow, however, had recovered a few shreds of intellect and provided what information he could to his caregivers. Something—greedy pockets, likely—had led to the breaking of a hospice worker's vows of confidentiality, and his news had soon reached mercenary ears. Brigands had then descended upon the site of the encounter. There, they ferreted out a trail that led to the rocky beach alongside the Straits of Wrath, where they discovered a docked and ancient Menosian vessel powered by a kind of technomagik that none present could understand or operate. Only a great sorcerer or sorceress could have piloted it, they concluded—a queen of the City of Wonders, perhaps. After these discoveries, the puzzle pieces were easy to assemble. If the queen and her consort had come through the Straits of Wrath—a clever way to elude detection—then charted a path up through Meadowvale and away from Brutus's tainted realm, they could have only one destination: Kor'Khul. Perhaps the queen believed she'd be able to outwit an army of mercenaries in the land of sun and sand where she'd once lived as a mortal.

Naturally, the troupe of ruffians who'd first unearthed this series of clues was unable to keep its findings from the shadowbrokers for long; within days, the game changed from a hunt across all of Geadhain to a hunt focused on Kor'Khul. Southreach, the outskirts of the Salt Forests, and Taroch's Arm were also being closely watched: there would be no returning to Carthac for this queen. She and her lover were now fenced in on all sides by brutes and murderers.

As madmen, killers, and ritualistic cannibals flooded the port of the once safe and sacred Eod, loyalists unbeguiled by Gloriatrix's crocodile charms met with greater frequency, finding ways to communicate secretly in this world gone insane. They wore a random array of ornaments, such as white hairbands or woven-cloth bracelets, that they threaded with gold, for white and gold were Queen Lila's colors. Sometimes, even a mismatched pair of earrings—one pearl, the other gold—would be the only clue to one's alliance. They hailed one another using coded greetings and farewells that spoke of golden days, amber skies, and hope. *A fine amber dawn*, perhaps, or, *May your sleep be golden and full of hope.*

Late at night, the loyalists would meet in the basements of homes and taverns. Mostly, they simply talked and prayed for better days. However, from discussion, a dash of oppression, and a flicker of rage a rebellion can grow. And those loyal to Lila certainly felt angry when they thought of their silent king in his glittering palace. Even now, Magnus was entertaining the Iron monsters who would like nothing better than to see them all in chains. The loyalists' anger had not yet swelled into open dissent; they had no armaments and no real organization, although many were members of the Silver Watch dissatisfied with the toxic Iron men polluting their palace and city. And still Magnus spoke not; he remained hidden away in his fortress, mired in sorrows and in political fencing with the Iron Queen. He was neglecting the garden of his city—which had now been planted with the seeds of revolution.

II

Magnus stared down upon his city and felt lost. The maze of sun-dazzled silver rings and white circles bewildered him as if it were an optical illusion, and he couldn't seem to settle his gaze on any one place. He couldn't remember why it had been so important for him to build something so grand. Mercy for the uncivilized? Philanthropy? In hindsight, it all felt like a vainglorious, empty experiment. Eod's grandeur now seemed nothing but a testament to his pointless ambition. The city had blinded him to life's most valuable resources: love and family.

"Magnus," said Beauregard, from behind him.

His voice sounded as if it came from far away; much in Magnus's life seemed marked by a sense of distance these days. Magnus turned to the handsome, frowning lad. "Ah, I see that I have been in one of my states," replied Magnus. "Your expression rebukes me for my withdrawal, my isolation. If I could, I would freeze myself in eternal winter and numb the pain of thousands of years of memories. I could then forget who I am, who I was, who I foolishly wanted to be...And when I awoke, the world would be different. I would be different. All would be new..."

These rhapsodies about disappearing, about ending this eternal life and beginning one anew, sent the king into a smiling, morbid state. Since Lila's betrayal, Magnus's heartache and his removal from the world had worsened. At times like this, he would sit or stand while sands ran to hourglasses, chasing memories and regrets on the horizon of his dreams.

Eventually, Beauregard marched up the steps to the balcony, seized his king, and led him back to the shady recesses of his quarters. Magnus still needed to be dressed: he wore only a throw over his lower half, which was certainly not appropriate attire for a king. Wistful and melancholic, the king continued to ramble as his naked body was exposed, his arms were tugged and forced into sleeves, and he was made to step like an indignant toddler into pants, then boots.

"Rowena told me everything, you know," he said, "about those entities from which Brutus and I were born…Beings of starry matter, hands like smoke…When last in the Hall of Memories, she saw them, with the seer, the sage, and my queen—my former queen. Those four know more of me than I know of myself. I have lived through millennia. I am as old as the mountains that surround us, and still, I am a stranger to myself. What I wanted was to be a man. A man in all the ways that mattered…You would think that being above men, being greater than they are, would fill me with a sense of disdain for the faults and weaknesses of those who must age and die. Yet all it has done is make me yearn for them even more, Beauregard—because they are what define life. I stand here, *undefined* by the countless days through which I have marched. I stand here far more of a child than you with your twenty-some summers."

Beauregard wanted to slap his king, but instead roughly fluffed Magnus's collar. "Twenty-*three* summers," replied the spellsong. "You missed my name day last week on account of your gloom-mongering. Whether what you have, Magnus—these endless years—is a gift or a curse depends only on how you choose to view the matter. You have the opportunity to unmake any mistakes you've made. You can live through a war of one hundred years and see the peace that the soldiers of that era will never know. You can watch over the children's children of your closest friends. Normal men are not given such graces. Mistakes aside, you've done more good for Geadhain than any of the lords, sorcerer kings, and tyrants who've walked this world. Furthermore, you promised in no uncertain terms to be the father I have lost. If you want to live like a mortal, then act like one. Learn to conquer your failures and to wear your bruises like badges of pride. Mortal men, good men, see failure as a chance to do better. Be a role model; show me someone worthy of my pledge to protect him. I once knew that man. My father died to save him. Who are you now? The grieving, sad, haunted creature before me is an insult to your greatness. He's not a man I wish to serve."

A winter wind blew through the chamber, thrashing the curtains and speckling Beauregard with frost and his next breath was white. The cold eased as Magnus took the young man's shivering hand from his collar and said, "I am sorry."

He was sorry for this spell of sorrow that had enchanted him for weeks. Sorry for forcing this boy to do everything but wipe his arse. Sorrier still for having missed the lad's name day, and for not following through on his promise of stewardship. Magnus was supposed to be the father, the teacher, the leader to this boy, but he'd allowed their roles to become reversed. Magnus's gaze became pure and unclouded, and in its well of emerald green, Beauregard saw storms, wisdom, and power: the true attributes of his king.

"G-good, you're back," said Beauregard, his teeth chattering. "I've missed weeks of swordplay and magikal theory exercises—all the lessons of knighthood I was to learn from you."

A gray blush mantled the king's face. "War comes, and I have left my knight unprepared. I shall try to make amends for my neglect once our meeting in the Hall of Memories has ended."

"Glory!" cried Beauregard, keeper of appointments and maker of excuses for his master. "You have remembered where you are scheduled to be today! I shall take that as the first true sign of my king's return."

"I have returned," promised Magnus. "I have wallowed in regret for far too long. I worry my kingdom will have rusted in my absence. I am haunted by vague visions of murderers wandering our streets—"

"Death-eaters," said Beauregard. "It's all true, my liege."

Magnus sneered. "Have we fallen to that depth of vulgarity? The Marith? Cannibals and worshippers of darkness now terrorize my people? Come, my spellsong, we have much work to do every sand of this day, and a tireless night of sparring and teaching to look forward to."

Sounds exhausting, thought Beauregard, and grinned as they left the king's chamber.

III

Her hair coiffed high and her body attired in a tight suit and buttoned overcoat, Gloriatrix appeared ready for a cabaret performance. She even carried a sleek black cane. Beauregard doubted she could sing, at least not anything prettier than the shrill, ear-bleeding songs of a harpy. The king and the spellsong met the Iron Queen in the limestone cavern deep within the Court of Ideas, past all of the nose-to-book scholars and dusty walls lined with tomes. She stood just outside a stone arch that produced auric light and tintinnabulations. Wonders lay inside, felt the spellsong, and the music tinkling from the arch stirred his nerves and his hair and sparked awe in his soul. Only Gustavius, Gloriatrix's tall iron-clad ghoul, attended the queen today. The strange white witch had not reappeared since her doomsaying many meetings past, though he believed he'd occasionally glimpsed her flitting around the palace out of the corner of his eye, like a ghost that didn't want to be seen.

"Hmm, not late. How unusual," said Gloriatrix. Apparently, she considered this greeting enough. She poked her cane against the metal stomach of one of the two Silver watchmen who guarded the Hall and suggested that he move.

"Hold, Gloriatrix. A word before we proceed," commanded Magnus.

In a voice of thunder, no less. Disconcerted, the Iron Queen glanced at the offensively handsome man, dressed so simply in workmen's wear, which emphasized every curve of his perfection. Magnus met her glare of iron with one of lightning; his air of command made her lip curl. It would seem the king had at last remembered that he was a king and not a moping child. This was an unfortunate development, as he would now be able to pay closer attention to what was happening around him.

"What is it, Magnus?" she asked. "I thought there was something you wanted me to see in this strange place up ahead. Let's get on with it."

"Rules. There are rules we must go over before we proceed."

"Of course there are," she scoffed.

Magnus stormed over to her. "We are entering a sacred store of learning and history. There is no other place like this anywhere else in Geadhain, and although our nations are now at peace thanks to our mutual enemy, there are secrets therein that could destroy lives and nations. They must not be tampered with or abused. If I discover that your agents have come to this place without my consent, I shall end our alliance, and you will face my darkest wrath."

Static pricked at Gloriatrix's face and eyebrows. Lights in the star trellis above flickered erratically, and the air's sudden sulfurousness made her sneeze. When she'd recovered herself, the electrical irregularities and odd smell had vanished. Gustavius handed her a black tissue, and she dabbed at her nose.

Secrets that could damn nations, you say? "I shall welcome your wrath, should I break your rules," replied the Iron Queen.

While this was by no means an ideal answer, Magnus accepted it. Silently, he led the two Menosians into the tunnel of light. As a woman of the Iron City, which never saw sunlight, Gloriatrix loathed the excessive brightness of this realm and preferred to spend her time under as many layers of stone as she could find. She wished she'd worn a hat to protect herself from the glare; both she and Gustavius had to shield their eyes while following the outline of the Everfair King. Finally, their hands fell, and they allowed themselves to be dazzled by the wonder into which they'd walked.

A chamber—domed, echoing, grand, and constructed of crystal tubes and technomagikal struts—gleamed through the glitter-dappled golden fog breathed from the mouth of the giant divinity above. She could immediately feel some kind of presence: there was a rhythm to its puffing tubes, a pulse in the glassy floor that encased the starry void at her feet and a full-bodied hum that gave her the kind of tremors she had not known since she'd last tumbled in bed with her now-deceased husband. It all had to be illusion, unless Magnus had somehow trapped the universe below. Yet, the Iron Queen was certain that the Hall of Memories was somehow alive. Gustavius escorted the still gawking queen over to where Magnus sat on a glass bench worthy of royalty. There, she rested and whipped her astonishment back into poise.

"Quite splendid. But what's the point?" she asked.

Magnus looked up at the storm softly rolling overhead. "I have thought deep and long on this war: on how it began and how I was defeated in Zioch. My brother has attained power he should not possess. He has mastered magik that bends the elements, fuses together flesh and metal and souls. He is not a sorcerer as I am. Therefore, this magik must stem from another source. I believe I know from where he has claimed this power. I almost remember a cry…"

It is the moment of his capture and doom at Zioch. Fiery cyclones whirl around him, the earth splits, flames and lava burble forth from below. Through the cascading, roaring decimation walks the shivering shadow of his giant brother. What is the maddened chant that Brutus shouts? An incantation? A summoning? What is this word that brings an earthquake with every syllable? Ig-ni-fax!

"When he and I battled, I heard a word," said Magnus, his mind returning once more to the hall. "A name. The name of a creature, a force. I believe Brutus has harnessed its power, and we must discover how he has done this. I am hopeful that in one of the many learned minds that have shared their knowledge with the Hall of Memories, we shall find the answer to this mystery. In our past, we may find the key to our future, or so I hope."

The Iron Queen watched as Magnus's alabaster complexion became even paler. What could an Immortal possibly fear? She needed to know. "What kind of creature?" she asked. "What is this force?"

"An elemental. A wyrm," he replied.

Gloriatrix had heard of the great wyrms that burrowed in the far-off reaches of Geadhain, although she'd never seen one. They were so foreign to her culture as to be almost mythic, and as they could not be easily chased or exploited, they were of no use to Menos. She knew that earthspeakers and sages traced the causes of natural phenomena such as tidal waves and seismic disturbances to the movements of wyrms in the earth: when larger wyrms rose too high in the strata, they displaced the magma and waters of the world. A few of the smallest wyrms had reportedly been seen swimming in the shallows of Kor'Khul's sandy ocean. These creatures were considered a vital part of Geadhain's ecology; functioning much like antibodies, wyrms defended the Green Mother from infection. The accidents brought about by the movements of wyrms could often be traced back to some manmade catalyst, some disruption in the environment that demanded a response. The legendary city of Veritax, which was an abomination against Nature as the tales said, had been destroyed by the wrath of these elementals.

"You're thinking about Veritax, are you not?" asked the king, staring at her.

"Perhaps," replied the Iron Queen. "Although that is just cautionary balderdash that was no doubt invented by dramatic historians."

The king touched her leg as if reassuring an innocent child, and for a brief, deplorable instant, Gloriatrix felt as if she were twelve again and full of curiosity and life. "When I was building my kingdom," he began, "when it was barely a plot of sand and populated only by whatever tribes had wandered into my company, Veritax was at the zenith of its achievements. Its people had mastered magik and technologies that appear new to us even today, but they had less care and compassion than the most notorious of Iron masters—no offence."

"None taken," replied Gloriatrix, hoping, in fact, that he had indeed been referring to her.

Taking a moment, she recalled old history books in her father's library that told of the City—the Empire—of Truth. Ritual blood sacrifices. Coats of mortal skin worn as the latest fashion. And the image, drawn in black ink, of an atelier hundreds of stories tall and made entirely of bones. She was almost certain she was not imagining the picture, that she'd actually seen it. The empire sounded glorious, if horrific. "As I said," she said. "Cautionary tales. Fluff."

Magnus brushed off her disbelief and stood, before captivating the three once again with his words. "The empire lay in far Western Geadhain, past the Isles of Terotak. Yet, if its despicable rulers had desired anything beyond hoarding of otherworldly power—arcane atrocities that man should never seek to master—they could have conquered all of Geadhain in a single sand. But they did not. Instead, they built their sky-scraping towers of bone. They sacrificed tens of thousands of men, fueling themselves with the exquisite power produced only at the moment of death, until the streets, stones, and rain turned red. They tainted the land through their pursuit of greatness, their desire to pass through doorways beyond time and space. I know not all of what they found, but I am glad they did not discover my brother and me as we wandered with the tribes an ocean away. I do know that they twisted the art of windspeaking into stormcalling, perverted firecalling into an incinerating summons so terrible it could rip through the matter of our world and open portals behind which waited ancient forces. The beings that whispered there gave the sorcerers of Veritax more secrets, more power. Their greed makes a Menosian's venality seem about as corrupt as a child's desire for his rattler."

Either the intrigue or the splendor of the king's tale made Gloriatrix tingle. She leaned forward. She needed to hear more. "How do you know all of this?"

"I did not gather this knowledge through direct experience," replied the king.

He walked, spreading his arms open to the Hall of Memories, which swirled and pulsed in a dance of mist and lights as if directed by a great conductor. "I have, though, seen glimpses of one man's life—a shattered, decrepit man, preserved only through some foul sorcery. Centuries after the fall of Veritax, when that city was myth and Eod stood as the world's pinnacle, he came to me. He confessed himself to be a *Mortalitisi* of the empire, a sorcerer supreme. His pacts and kingdom having been destroyed long before, he was doomed to meet a much delayed death, and he confessed to me—and to this great mind and machine in which we stand—all the horrors and glories of his kingdom. The Mortalitisi wanted his knowledge to be preserved; I wanted to seal it away so that no others would ever be tempted by it. I would like to have kept his story locked away forever. But now, we must peer inside that box of horrors."

"Incredible," muttered Gloriatrix.

"I was able to see only fragments of the transmission when it occurred," whispered the king, bowing down close to the three as if sharing a secret. "In my long life, I have seen crimes, tragedies, wars too numerous to count...but this Mortalitisi's memories are unequaled in their filth and darkness. Madness, doom, howling storms with tentacles and eyes. It is a history into which I have chosen not to delve."

"Then why must we do so now?" asked Beauregard, shivering.

"My knight," said the king, rising and cupping the boy's cheek with a hand, "Veritax fell because it lost control of its source of power: the elementals. The great beasts whose blood and magik the Mortalitisi had tapped into broke free of the chains of their masters."

Gloriatrix snapped her fingers as the deduction came to her. "I see: you're proposing that in this past we shall find a means to eliminate your brother's control over his elemental pet, which represents his greatest advantage in this war."

"Indeed." Suddenly, Magnus crackled with green static and his luminous stare flashed to the Iron Queen. "Do not think that I shall allow you to exploit the twisted wisdom of these madmen. You are here only because you have an eye for darkness, as you are mostly wicked yourself. It is possible that you will see the smaller strokes that I may overlook in these maestros' works. We shall witness the past together. We shall discover how it was the Mortalitisi enslaved the elementals, and, I hope, how they managed to break free. We can employ the same tactic on my brother's pet, thus robbing him of his power. We shall make this journey together into the past, as allies. Are you prepared?"

"Yes," hissed the Iron Queen.

The other men stayed silent.

Opening his arms wide and calling upon his Will, Magnus woke the great presence of the chamber. *Ancient mind, wondrous mind, bring forth the chained and wicked box. Show me the memories we have sealed. At last, I must look into the heart of the Mortalitisi. We must see the final days of Geadhain's darkest empire. We must learn how this seemingly unstoppable power met its end.*

As the Hall of Memories searched for the entombed box—buried deeper even than the record of the king's own birth, down so deep that even the Daughter of Fate could not have retrieved it without a map—the chamber grew still, its pipe sounds subsiding into hisses. The Hall of Memories searched its own infinite pathways, traveling through deaths, births, wars, and acts of heart-breaking compassion. Finally, the Great Will found the black tumor nestled in layers upon layers of its oldest, most decayed tissue. These were memories from the demented, senile, and wicked—and among them was the cancer they sought. Although the Great Will was not capable of feeling mortal emotions, it paused, considering and calculating the risks of opening this pocket of disease, this pulsing knot of evil. After determining various probabilities, it sliced open the tumor with a scalpel of Will, and the bile and blackness leaked out, screeching.

Thousands of holed tubes whistled steam, and mist whirled in the chamber's heights. Booming golden thunderheads descended from above, raining electric warmth that prickled like dew on the onlookers' flesh. This was Magnus's beloved instrument; it was beholden to its master and did not simply present images of the past. Magnus preferred to *live* in the past, not merely to look at it. Lower and lower the storm came. Its magik mist burned Gloriatrix's eyes like Menosian rain. Its swells swallowed her in a golden typhoon. Scared, she reached for Gustavius's cold iron mitt. He gripped his queen's hand tightly as they were buffeted by the worst of the winds and electricity. She leaped up into his arms as the winds blew away their seat; she clung to him as the gusts blew away the Hall of Memories itself and sent the howling golden storm and the passengers whirling off into space.

IV

Through a haze of glittering threads, the Iron Queen saw another storm, this one of nightmares. *This cannot be real*, she told herself.

For one thing, they seemed to be levitating. In between neon flashes, she tried to study the sky whose etheric undercarriage they nearly touched with their heads. It was as black and red with corruption as a cauldron of tar and gore. Bulbous swarms and ripples moved in the clouds, and the night ululated like a living tormented beast of incredible proportions choking on lightning. *Could those be creatures in the clouds?* she wondered. *Snakes of thunder and doom?*

Spinning in awe, Gloriatrix then discovered a new horror below: an ocean. Everything about it was wrong: it was a moaning, gelatinous maelstrom, an assault of tidal waves further distorted by rubbery, flailing tentacles. What she saw made no sense. A jellied ocean filled with octopi? She had no time to absorb all of these insanities, for just then, an appendage of one of the leviathans swept down in groaning, whooshing doom upon the floating ghosts of her company. Gloriatrix screamed and the sores that covered the thing shrieked back at her, sending out a putrid waft of salty rot like the stench of a barge packed with dead fish. However, they were travelers to this time, not part of its reality, and the leviathan's tentacle passed through them in a breeze before smashing down into the gibbering orgy of chaos below.

"Save your screams," warned the king, whose form wavered in front of her. "We have not yet seen Veritax. Nothing here can harm us, as horrific as it may appear. Look deep, and remember every terror." The phantom king pointed ahead. "That lighthouse of darkness...We head there."

A lighthouse of darkness, thought Gloriatrix. How was she to spot a shadow in this blackest of nights? But sure enough, far away, a thin rectangle rose from the horizon, pulsing blackness as a lantern would light. Suddenly, their quartet was moving alongside the howling winds. They crossed tens of spans in moments, and then abruptly stopped. They hovered above what might be a city. The realm's shadows could be spied only through a crimson gauze—a mist of rain that carried telltale traces of the sharp scent of offal and rust. Blood. It was a rain of blood, as the legends told.

Through the downpour leered grand towers that thrust all the way up into the cumulonimbi clot above. Their vast proportions humbled even the Crucible. Although constructed of white brick, the towers were sheathed in throbbing black ether, which ran upward in currents. Gloriatrix knew that the pale bricks beneath hadn't been made of the smooth iron her countrymen used: these jagged, irregular blocks were formed of femurs, skulls, spines, and hipbones that had been crushed into mortal mortar and cement. How many men and beasts had it taken to build one tower, let alone this fogged, clustered cityscape of white and black fingers? Gloriatrix could find no words. She was shocked, awed, appalled, and the ethereal body she inhabited played a song of fear in her heart as they descended into the terror, drawn by the truth Magnus sought.

The haze thinned, revealing dwarfed off-white huts clustering around the bases of the Mortalitisi towers. Veritax wasn't as quiet as it first appeared. She began to hear crackling sounds like whips of lightning, but they were too jumbled to clearly distinguish. A speck later, she realized they were screams—the shrieks produced by Mortalitisi construction.

Somewhere on the red land below must be the factories that stripped skin and technomagikally molded bone.

As she and the other ghosts drifted lower, closer to the bases of the bone towers, she caught sight of winding arrangements that spun outward from the massive towers like the layers of a fossilized shell. Despite their horror, they felt a sense of awe that men had built an empire so grand and monstrous. The Iron Queen knew that a civilization such as this could not have been built in mere decades. Even with their magik, the Mortalitisi and their bone-grinding artisans must have needed centuries to produce this empire that predated all other known cultures.

Gloriatrix's head whirred with questions and suppositions. *From where had the Mortalitisi knowledge come?* Gloriatrix wondered. At the time this remarkable culture had flourished, the kings had been wandering with and amongst the savages of Central Geadhain…How had these diabolical geniuses established supremacy during an age when most of the world had still barely mastered the secrets of fire? The king had been right to bring her into this past. There was a mystery here. She tasted the sweet blood of it in her ghostly mouth along with the rain.

Gurooooh!

Something gargantuan and wailing blew through them, flapping slow, leathery wings, and sending their ghosts into a spiral. They spun and spun. Sheets of lightning startled them, and once more they were twirled by the flying, fleshy steam engine. It had tubes of meat, mouths, tentacles, and rubbery membranes stretched between bony autopods. Gloriatrix knew not what else to call it but *Mallum Eruca*—caterpillar of evil. As her spin slowed to a steady descent, she saw a swarm of the creatures weaving through the red skies above.

Although now numb to fear, she was nevertheless unnerved by the sound of the keening of thousands of dying slaves, a noise that was growing louder and louder. All the tribes on this side of Geadhain must have been rounded up, bound in chains, and then lined up in front of presses and conveyor belts in the mortal-mortar factories. Gloriatrix wondered if the tribes were forced to breed so that they might continuously feed the Mortalitisi empire with the flesh and sacrifice it needed for its power. What was it that Magnus had said? About the essence, the extract, of death that the Mortalitisi coveted? That was it—he'd stressed that it was unusually potent. So potent a resource, she figured, could well be capable of raising a million tall towers, of binding elementals. What they needed to learn, however, was how it was that all this had been lost.

Bone buildings now came into focus. Some were conical, others squat and square. Gloriatrix saw structures like giant eggs with cracks in them that glowed with red light. As her spirit-wind floated over these hatcheries of horror, the gristliest of cries confirmed these were indeed the factories she'd imagined. Gloriatrix peeked inside one as they floated past, but couldn't discern much beyond gleams of red light and hints of movement. Crystal? Metal? She couldn't tell.

She could, however, now better see the mortar of which the Mortalitisi empire was made: a papier-mâché of white paste and jutting bits in which traces of remains could be glimpsed. An intact skull grinned at her as her wind caressed the curved shell of the hatchery. Then the wind swept them up once more and sent them speeding along the great egg's curve so fast that its details blurred, before depositing them into a street.

Immediately, a shadow strode directly into them on all fours. Gloriatrix was able to stifle a scream, but the king's foppish knight gave a cry as the monstrosity lumbered through and past them. If she and her fellows had possessed bodies, it would surely have crushed them. As the dust kicked up by its passage subsided, she studied one of its stomping feet: three toed, about the size of a tree stump. She couldn't crane her spirit-neck around to follow the creature with her gaze, and had time to note only its swaying armored body that was fused with plates of hard bone, and the lashing shadows that flailed upon its back as it moved farther away. It bleated like a sea king, and other colossi answered in the red mist. But it was not the queerest of the terrors in the street.

Wandering in packs, one of which followed the trail of the colossus, were things that looked like men. However, as the things shambled closer, she could see that their skin was loose and quivering, that patches of it had been roughly stitched together. Fumes of black sorcery leaked out through their eyes and the seams of their sewn-up bodies, forming a lingering black exhaust around each pack. While this made it difficult for Gloriatrix to clearly make out anything below their waists, from what she could tell, these un-men had no genitals. Those who were un-women had deflated, raisiny flops for breasts. The things' mouths were sewed closed; their eyes, too, she realized. Sight and speech were apparently unnecessary for creatures stripped of their individuality and sexuality. These must be worker drones, balloons inflated with dark Will, servants of a make far more efficient than Menos's reborn. *How clever*, she thought. *Not an ounce of flesh wasted. A person's skin itself turned into a slave. I suppose in a cannibalistic, all-consuming society, measures must be taken to fully exploit one's resources.* Not as interested in the horror as she, Magnus Willed them along.

Agog with sick wonder, they floated down the streets paved in slabs of bone-crete. Gloria was struck by the lack of evidence of technomagikal machinery. Could all this have been made through the labor of the puppet-men and the four-legged gargantuan beasts whose wriggling, humped backs she saw moving in the fog? Through sheer omnipotent Will and the extract generated by generations of blood sacrifice? There were no sky-carriages, no obvious waterways or sewers—although the reek of excrement poured from the small, cubed houses, which had no apparent access points or doorways and only slits to admit air and light. Occasionally, dirty fingers poked through these openings, and whimpering lips were pressed against them. Sometimes a whole arm pushed through, desperately reaching for freedom, only to be snapped off by a silently drifting pack of skin-golems. At times, she thought she could hear snatches of bittersweet songs, prayers muttered in foreign languages. Could culture have embedded itself even here, amid such madness?

Once more, Gloriatrix examined what she'd learned, thinking only as a Thule and Menosian could. Hatcheries, echoing with murder. Cubicles, to hold the meat. Workers and oxen of the most horrid sort roaming through organized areas. She hadn't yet deduced the purpose of the conical silos, which were surely also cogs in this great machine, but the purpose of all this grisly agriculture was clear: mortal harvesting.

"One...great...farm," she whispered, sharing her thoughts with the others.

Gloriatrix's logic was convincing, but so hideous it was difficult for them to accept it at first. The king was perhaps most easily swayed, as he'd already had a sense of the truth of this evil empire. He'd seen enough truth, though, and he now Willed the Hall of Memories to show him its downfall. Up they were swept, then fired back up into the sky. In a blur, they traveled spans across land and sky and approached one of the bone towers. Like divine arrows, they punctured the edifice's sheath of writhing black flame and soared through its thick wall of crushed death, before finding themselves in a lighter, clearer space aglow with crimson light.

It was an orchestral space, as grand as the opera house in Menos, and equally as refined. Apparently, Mortalitisi social life was largely conducted inside the bone towers. The four visitors saw figures moving throughout the hall. It was difficult to tell whether they were men or women; they lacked hair or defining features, and all wore similar body-hugging, corseted black-leather garments tightly cinched with belts. Gloriatrix doubted that this leather had come from animals. The beings all wore crowns of which the Iron Queen was jealous: thorny whorls that entwined their heads in cages. Whether this was for fashion, or to protect their greatest treasure—their minds—Gloriatrix cared not to wager.

Across the dim chamber, which resembled an open amphitheater, the Mortalitisi busied themselves with their rituals and arts, if their atrocities could be so named. The ghosts of the present drifted toward them. The shadows spared the four the sight of every horror, but even so, they saw too much. Scholarly folk sat around ornate tables ringed with skulls and supported by legs of bundled bone. They focused on red shards, seemingly broken from the iceberg of frozen blood that hovered above each table at the center of their axis of minds. Occasionally, the Mortalitisi would turn to one another—all at the same time—and nod, or in some other way indicate agreement. They were speaking, Magnus knew, in much the same way he and his brother did. Somehow, the Mortalitisi had mastered the art of mind-whispering.

All present seemed to be communicating in this way, and aside from the shrieking of the savages being spread on bone tables and flayed as one would a deer, there was no sound to be heard. Once he and his fellow spirits had floated past the ring of surgeons and crystal enchanters, the agonized cries of the dissected were replaced by harsh and sinister music.

The four then entered a new layer of the amphitheater, one dedicated to art—of a kind.

Here, the four were bombarded by sensory offenses, each one graver than the last, until their souls were forced into hiding, and they gratefully retreated into numbness. Men lay splayed on bone racks, gasping as their skins were peeled back to reveal the glistening feast of organs within. Lounging, mind-speaking Mortalitisi chatted with one another while nibbling on the delicacies offered by these living creatures, or filling bone cups with blood from their wounds. At one disgusting dinner party, a pair of Mortalitisi argued over which one would get the sweetmeats; eventually, the greedier, stronger sorcerer knocked the other down with an invisible fist and then tore off his prize through the force of his mind. The Mortalitisi seemed unwilling to bother themselves with manual labor, and skin-golems could be seen billowing around and attending to the needs of their masters.

Although this was merely a dream of the past, Gloriatrix could smell the earthy fart of death to which these Mortalitisi had become immune. Even she knew them to be horrible beings.

Next, she and her companions came across the Mortalitisi musicians responsible for the cringing harmony. Now that the travelers knew how and what these people ate, they found these entertainers less shocking. The musicians played in small trios amid the grim feast, and their instruments were, like their meals, made of man. Seated in tall, bone chairs, Mortalitisi cellists swept their bows across hardened vocal chords, from which flaps of skin had been pulled and stitched aside. These throats belonged to men still living, held just shy of death by sorcery, and their wails added to the dry screech of the tune. Limbs had been snapped backward and frozen into tables; the hollow carcasses of men were banged on like drums, producing whimpers, for they were also still alive. The simplest and least repugnant instruments were the bone flutes that were being played here and there.

These atrocities were too much, too overwhelming for the travelers, and even though they knew this empire had later fallen, they couldn't rid themselves of a sense of horrified, almost paralyzing fascination. Magnus no longer Willed them along; instead, they were drawn by the hand of the Hall of Memories toward the penultimate moments of this society, of these monsters who had no idea their doom was imminent.

Suddenly, a mind-whisper reached each member of the Mortalitisi collective, and many carcass drums were struck at once out in the dark amphitheater. The guests at this half-living feast, the crystal enchanters, the vile musicians, and all the other wicked beings left their pursuits to hurriedly descend the stairways leading to the stage of this theater of horror. As the four wandering spirits also neared this destination, the Mortalitisi took seats on bone benches, joined hands with one another, and glared down into the red dark with what might have been pleasure, or reverence, on their alien faces. Science, culture, worship, unity...there was an order to this madness, though only Gloriatrix and Magnus perceived it.

A scene had been set in the reddest, deepest depths of the arena floor, in a space surrounded by totem-poles of twisted bodies. Despite all this butchery and doom, Gloriatrix didn't feel that the Mortalitisi worshipped death: they worshiped their own majesty and magnificence.

Upon the stage stood an emaciated grandmaster waiting for his flock to become attentive and still. Wearing no constricting gear, he was nearly nude but for an undergarment and a mantle hanging over his sharp shoulders. Clearly, the man needed no head cage to shield his intellect or fancy trappings to declare his eminency. Like Magnus, the grandmaster shone with kingship, but in his case, an unholy one. He was commanding, embodying a force as strong as that of the Hall of Memories, a force that pulled his audience, even the travelers, toward his presence. Magnus and his company wanted to see this evil king, too; they wanted to meet him.

Then Magnus realized he already had.

The wide brow, hollow cheeks, and pallor of the Mortalitisi leader made for a bold, attractive face like a stone carving. Still, the man's charisma was most evident in his sunken eyes; they might have been brown, but they flashed black as he produced and restrained flickers of power. Restrained was the right word, for more than any other Magnus had ever encountered, this man held within him the force of a storm. Hundreds of years after the fall of Veritax, he'd come to Magnus, far less proud than he appeared now. He'd come and asked Magnus to create a record of his people's vanity. Then, as now, Magnus had felt his power: a magik that no man should possess, and an evil, too, which was why Magnus had sealed the Mortalitisi wisdom away. But the confessor of Veritax's corruption—Arimoch, he'd called himself—had been no mere servant to his empire, as he'd claimed. He had, Magnus realized, been its king.

Beside Arimoch, pinioned to a bone altar by an unseen power, was a woman. Even so near the grandmaster and his captivating charisma, she commanded attention. Magnus had never seen her before, but when he gazed upon her, his heart did something queer and unpredictable and leaped into his throat. She was bald—her freshly cropped hair lay scattered about her—and so dark of skin that her movements looked like those of an ebon statuette held to the light. Much more than that he could not tell. She might have been beautiful or hideous. He suspected the former, although he hadn't yet looked at her body, not all of it. Again, as with Arimoch, something about her eyes held him.

She then seemed to look through the vapors to where his ghost drifted. She couldn't see him. Such a thing was impossible—as impossible and inexplicable as the feelings of curiosity, wonder, and hope that now swelled within him. Even in this darkest of moments, she shone with glory. With her innocence and passion, she might have been soul sister to Beauregard. Magnus thought of a bird of prey soaring over black mountains, of a stream's burble and a lion's roar—beauty and nature, purity and pride.

The woman thrashed against her magikal restraints, and the air hummed with the reckoning force of her Will. She was a sorceress, then—a powerful one. However much she struggled, though, she couldn't Will herself free of the weight of Arimoch's mind. Indeed, Arimoch's sorcery was as powerful as Magnus's, and enabled him to change the weather with his mood. Arimoch did not want the young woman to rise, and as a result, the air respected his wish and weighed her down like a coat of lead. Arimoch's Will created reality.

Who are you? the king asked each of the phantoms before him.

Neither answered, though the woman shouted ferociously, *"Tai tek hei!"* (I shall not become!)

In her barking inflections, Magnus recognized echoes of many of the ancient languages he'd mastered, tongues that sounded much like the cries of animals or birds. She was from an old tribe, then, one from the lands of the West, which he and his brother had never chosen to explore. Although he stood in a dream and could influence nothing here, Magnus reached out and placed a smoky hand over that of the struggling woman. A person's bravery could not be determined until she faced death, and this woman was looking into her darkest fate with fury.

But Arimoch intended to break her strength. He placed his hand on the woman's forehead, and she immediately became rigid and still. The four travelers noticed the crystal then: it had been floating unnoticed in the background between the totem-poles-of-flesh, its presence overshadowed by more captivating events. It struck them as strange even here, even in this realm of appalling strangeness—an irregular red jewel the size of a man's chest, it was strung up on a thorny metal rack that hung between two pillars.

Arimoch walked over to the crystal, his pace measured and ritualistic. As he approached, he opened his arms wide, and the crystal's bloody-black heart beat with a lover's welcome. Small winds and hisses came forth from nowhere, then greater gusts, hammering dins, and languorous, grating noises. Sounds like those of a metal giant awakening from his nap of one thousand years and bursting forth from the earth surrounded the four phantoms. Something was coming. Something was being called forth from a horrible pit. Both the infernal red glow above and the radiance from the crystal intensified into a dull and smearing light.

The four could not fully make sense of what they saw. Events wavered in the undulating tear, the pointed star that had formed in the vertical space containing Arimoch and the crystal. All four phantoms sensed great winds that could tear flesh from bone, infernal temperatures, cold sweats, and gut-roiling terror. Yet each was also confronted by a different impression not received by the others.

In the shivering light, Gloriatrix watched as a gigantic tumorous fetus emerged and unfolded. Now large enough to fill her entire frame of sight, it was so grand that she tried frantically to absorb every massive, dripping detail. Bleating came from the many heads that crowded its surface—unformed skulls set with spidery patterns of unblinking black eyes. The horror babe hovered, wet and gobbed in black matter, and began unfurling a cephalopodic network of umbilical cords, rubbery fins, veiny feelers, and tubes. Fantastic in its repulsiveness, it made her simultaneously shriek and laugh; she reached for her eyes, intending to pull them out and stop the madness.

Beauregard saw a woman: naked, jet black, and with hair that was a whirlwind of the whitest light. She was the most beautiful creature he'd ever beheld. Then she spoke, and from her mouth came the clanging din that was tearing up the chamber. He reached up to his head, hoping to rip off his ears to stop the noise.

Gustavius dropped to his knees and cowered before a mouth: a moon-sized hole ringed with cracked yellow teeth out of which poured a vomit of skittering, shapeless shadows—roaches of darkness. The wave rolled over him. It scuttled over, nibbled at, burned, and dissolved his flesh. Crazed, he clawed at himself, trying to strip himself of his new crawling skin.

The mighty Immortal was the last to fall victim to this power. He attempted to maintain a facade of royal power; the ant with the hardest carapace might escape crushing. While he did not succumb to complete madness like the others, he doubled over and retched as he was hit by the stink of tons and tons of ancient oil—fossilized, raw—flowing out of the deepest crack he could fathom. How deep? What was it that crouched there? Frantic, he thought of wells that swirled in stars. He dreamed, while waking, of slithering, wet, force coiling him, pulling him down into the endless dark. With the brunt of his Will, he fought against that pull, which, somehow, regardless of this not being real, threatened to drink his memories, his identity, his power.

In a speck, though, they remembered who and where they were. Although not even a sand had passed, they might as well have endured a decade of torment, considering how debilitated they felt. What had they just witnessed? What was the atrocity that had touched them? This experience inside an ancient memory had somehow felt more real than it should have. Magnus, who'd experienced the Black Queen's venom and knew the fever of corruption firsthand, understood that whatever they'd borne witness to was even wickeder than she. The four were unable then to speak of what they'd experienced, for there was suddenly more to see.

The crimson brightness ebbed, the tears in reality closed, and Arimoch now walked back to the altar where the woman lay. He held in his hands a grayish cup, filled with a substance darker than ink, darker than the lightless reaches of space. As the four watched, mesmerized, the horror king and his treacle of evil neared the woman for whom it was intended. Arimoch was going to feed this unholy substance to his victim—for what purpose, they could not yet say. But Gloriatrix had drawn threads between the hair-clippings on the stone, the bald monsters in the audience, the Will of this woman, and the behavior of the Mortalitisi. Perhaps they didn't intend to end her, but to remake her in their image, as one of their ghastly flock. Gloriatrix, a woman who had scorned pity save for the occasion on which she had secretly saved her granddaughter—the single act of kindness of her life—wished she could help this woman.

Alas, there would be no salvation for the saint upon the altar. She was to drink the milk of darkness. She was to become Mortalitisi. Arimoch held the chalice aloft and looked up and around to the leering creatures on the benches. They communed in the unspeaking way, smiling and showing their teeth, all sharpened for the eating of meat. Once it was time, Arimoch lowered the chalice, and the woman on the bone slab sat up, obeying his Will. She extended her hands and took the chalice. The four phantoms noticed a fire of rage in her eyes; as if she were gathering her strength for some final desperate attempt. Though it would never come, and Arimoch nodded, bringing the chalice to her lips. Tears ran down her face as she drank.

Arimoch closed his eyes and communed with the Mortalitisi watchers and surely, too, with the darkness that had taken her.

But she hadn't swallowed, realized Gloriatrix, who rarely missed a feint. Although the woman had taken in the draught, she held it in her throat as if she were a vulture. She wept, but her tears were called forth not by sorrow, but by the agonizing effort of clenching the devouring, evil treacle in her esophagus. Then, in the speck that lay between being consumed and remaining herself, in the flickering moment when Arimoch's arrogant self-absorption had bent his armor to expose a perfect chink—a time when his magik, his Will, was at peace and her telekinetic restraints were weak—the woman struck.

Magik was emotion. Magik was life. The sainted one screamed. A burbling black puke sprayed from her mouth—a vomit that tried to pull itself with sticky tendrils back into her throat. With her scream came her spell, and her Will was made manifest: a spear of white, sizzling sunshine burst forth from her head as she turned it skyward, and she sloshed herself in sick. She could have aimed her magik at Arimoch's head, as he was right in front of her. However, the travelers didn't question her judgment. They watched as the star-spraying javelin of lightning tossed by the Will of a true hero soared high from the altar and came down upon its mark: the heart of crystal.

The heart of this empire, the four phantoms realized. Arimoch spun around in time to watch the impact, shielding himself with a lens of dark magik against the nova of purest white, the waves of fire and smoke that now irradiated the chamber. The four ghosts watched as the nameless hero grinned in defiance and then vanished in a howl of flame. They felt the world beneath them erode into ash. Amidst the shattering detonations, they heard the mortal agonies of the Mortalitisi. Bellows, thunderclaps, and groans rumbled the quickly vanishing floor with the thud of a million tidal waves: the roars of the elementals, at last unchained. An army of rabid wyrms was now loose in their master's kingdom. The vengeance of the Green Mother had been unleashed.

There could be no hope for the Mortalitisi. Everything they'd cultivated had been destroyed in one instant by one woman, whose name they'd never know. Magnus thought of her bitter grin as the tides of fire and ruin turned golden and kind, and returned him and the other spirits to Hall of Memories.

V

It took some time for the four to be restored to themselves, to once more recognize their own forms and minds. Wounds were found on three of them: claw marks around Gloriatrix's eyes, throbbing soreness and blood coming from Beauregard's ears, and torn fingernails from when Gustavius had thrown his gauntlets away to scratch at his armor. Of all the travelers to the past, the king alone appeared unharmed, though inside he was tormented by what he'd experienced. The memory was too vivid, too engaging to the senses.

He glanced at the others as they examined themselves, and could arrive at no explanation for the harms they'd suffered, as he was unaware of the apparitions each had encountered. He would have to seal off the Hall of Memories until a team of technomagikal minds could attest to its safety. In a sand, the other three had assembled their wits and bodies on the bench—sharing it equally, all needing to sit. The king remained standing, brooding and glum.

"Who was he?" whispered Beauregard.

"That was the man who came to me," replied Magnus. "Arimoch. The man whose memories I sealed inside the hall. I see now that he was far more than he claimed."

"Without a doubt," said Gloriatrix.

"Who was she?" asked Beauregard.

"I know not," replied the king.

"She was a hero," continued the lad. "Perhaps the greatest of any age. Her sacrifice saved us from a future with those..." Monsters? Dictators? Menosians? Defilers? Nothing he could think of felt evil enough to describe what he'd witnessed.

Though Gloriatrix agreed with the lad's sentiment, she would never admit it. Instead, she stood and straightened out her suit and hair, which had somehow become quite windblown in the unusual illusion. "Whoever she was is unimportant," she said. "You brought me on this psychedelic nightmare to make use of my masterful deductions. We were to discover how these Mortalitisi chained their elementals; the rest of the experience is best forgotten. And I believe I have your answer, Magnus."

"You do?" asked the king. He'd been so consumed by thoughts and impressions—that saint, her eyes, her Will—he'd not yet considered the fruits of their quest.

Gloriatrix had now finished smoothing her hair. "Rather obvious, isn't it? The crystals. The large one, I imagine. While I have never seen technomagik or sorcery of that kind, that is what I must conclude: the crystal was what the woman shattered with her spell, and its destruction was what set the elementals free and allowed them to wreak revenge. Perhaps Brutus has some such crystal."

"From where or how could my brother have acquired such ancient power?" replied Magnus. "With its loss, Arimoch must have been stripped of whatever resources and relics he had or he would have raised his empire again."

Surprisingly, in a room of quiet, pondering, royal luminaries, it was Beauregard who presented his liege with a revelation. He shot to his feet. "Amara...My friend from down south, the Keeper of Sorsetta. We chatted, she and I, before the war came to Gorgonath. She spoke quite openly to me about matters generally kept private by her order. The stone with which I freed you, my king—there are others, larger ones to which she alluded before silencing herself on the matter. I have seen what a wonderstone small enough to fit in my hand can do. Something larger could well possess the power necessary to chain an elemental."

Magnus and his spellsong had discussed the power responsible for his liberation back in Gorgonath. Magnus had heard legends of the *Ioncrach*, these "wonderstones" that worked miracles, but he had seen none in his lifetime save for the one Beauregard had showed him after the battle: a smoky gray fragment drained of any magik it had once possessed. Sorcerers rarely used talismans, as all of their magik came from within. Such relics and foci were associated only with magikal grade schools, carnival illusionists, and faery stories about witches and vengeful sprites. They would be of no interest to a true sorcerer at the height of his powers. Unless that man were one such as Brutus, who could use magik, but not as well as his brother...

More and more, the king felt as if he were a child still figuring out his feet and words. How had he lived for so long and yet learned so little of the world? Wonderstones. Dreamers. Civilizations that had risen and fallen before his own long history had even begun. Entities that evoked madness in the strongest minds. The list of unknown things fattened every day. Each morning, he saw more clearly that he'd been mistaking contentment for achievement.

Beauregard shot him a glare of steel, and the king was reminded that he must not fall into another spell of gloom. Snapping back to alertness, he commanded, "Beauregard. Travel to Sorsetta, and see what else can be squeezed from the tight lips of this friend of yours. I met Amara briefly, but found her as unreadable as a shadowbroker. She seemed uneasy in my presence. I doubt she would be willing to speak as openly to me as to you, who saved her people."

Beauregard rose and bowed. While disappointed he would again miss training with the king, he felt excited by the prospect of seeing Amara once more. "Yes, my king."

"Do stop in Bainsbury, too," added the king. "To provide a service long overdue."

Bainsbury was where Tabitha Fischer, Beauregard's mother, lived, and she was indeed owed a visit from her son. Guilt twisted his guts as he realized he'd been postponing telling her about the death of her husband, his father. He'd been lying to her in letters lately, saying that Devlin was *at peace* here in Eod—not a complete fabrication since that statement was never untrue of the dead. Beauregard frowned.

"Gustavius will accompany your man," said the Iron Queen, surprising everyone. Call her suspicious—and she certainly was—but she didn't want the king's man running clandestine errands and listening to secrets alone and unsupervised by an eye and ear of her own. None of her Iron children was more reliable than Gustavius.

The Iron lord stood, bowed, and accepted his assignment without a wrinkle of consternation. "As you wish, my queen."

Beauregard scowled, less at ease with this arrangement. When he looked to his king, Magnus gave a nod.

"You won't solve the mystery standing around," said the Iron Queen, almost playfully nudging the two aides into a trot with her cane. "Run along. The masters of the realms have matters to which they must attend."

As the men left the glittering chamber, Magnus turned to the violet eyes watching him. "Matters? What matters?"

"Didn't I tell you? I suppose the morning's events stole all the attention. The survivors of Menos will return to their Iron bosom today. A ship full of them is scheduled to dock in an hourglass or two. I would think that the heads of both nations should be in attendance. And I believe you did want us to hear their tales together."

Wearing a seemingly patient expression, Gloriatrix folded her hands atop the ball of her cane. What in all the unholy horrors of the world was she scheming at behind that pleasant smile? The king was reminded of

Thackery's stare and the webs that were woven behind it. The Iron Queen possessed her brother's intellect, if nothing else. As they walked toward the arch leading out of the Hall of Memories, Gloriatrix cast a sly, covetous look over her shoulder at the great, mystical chamber that hummed with music and puffed golden mist—and thought of what she could do with all that knowledge.

VI

"We have a guest tonight."

The broad, unshaven man rose to his feet. Kings, how wearying these days had been as the locusts of the Iron City and the mercenary rats from all corners of the globe had scuttled in, filling their city with plague. But a cure had come tonight, a medicine of hope for the fledgling resistance. Brock looked at the draped shadows just outside the cone of light that shone down the cellar stairs. From there, a cloaked woman came forth. As she drew closer to the circle of twelve tired men and women with their accoutrements and jewelry of gold and white, she removed her hood. Her face was round-cheeked, flushed, and pretty in an understated way. Brock stayed on his feet, and the others rose as well.

If any of these men had known Mater Lowelia before the war, they would not have recognized her now. Her demeanor was cold and stern; her glare flashed steel and fire. Gone was the doughy, sweet caregiver. In her place, rising from the grave of that ghost, was a woman who'd embraced the castration of her sinful husband as an act of justice. A woman who'd killed spies. A woman who'd led a kingdom through the first of its darkest wars, when no other royals had been around to shoulder the duty. Lowe could no longer remember that other woman—that happy woman. She was dead and buried.

However, she'd lacked purpose since being exposed and cast out from her position as queen. She'd soon discovered, though, that her official status as a pariah involved a much softer fall from grace than she had expected. She'd become invisible again to the king. Normal men and women continued to look up to her, though. In dark hallways, or while elbow to elbow in the kitchen chopping vegetables, they whispered seditious thoughts to her about the unholy alliance of Magnus and Gloriatrix.

They secretly praised the mater for her reign as queen, however fraudulent it had been. For a time, she dismissed their heresies and held on to her anger toward Lila, feeling used because of her unwitting complicity in the queen's act of genocide. Then, as the days drifted on, and Magnus acceded further to the demands of Menos, even going as far as to declare his own queen a traitor when her crimes were still very much in question, Lowe started to take these whisperers seriously. When one of the loyalists had told her of a meeting of like minds and souls, Lowe had known that she must attend.

Brock bowed. "Mater Lowelia, you honor us by being here."

"There is nowhere else to be," she replied. "The city is buried under piles of shite and sin."

Those assembled took their seats as she spoke.

"Now," said Brock, glancing with pride at their guest. "Let us discuss how to reclaim our city."

Disappointingly, if predictably, the formality and excitement of the clandestine meeting soon degenerated into protests of rage and aimless threats against the Iron menace. Lowelia remembered these kinds of spiraling arguments that led to the center of nowhere from her days dealing with sages and watchmasters, all of whom had had very conflicting ideas on how to execute a war. What were these people doing? What did they hope to accomplish? Talking in a basement wasn't a productive use of her or anyone else's time. After a few sands that felt to her like hourglasses, Lowelia stood and slapped her fist into her palm. "I hear a lot of talking, but we are not building a road to *doing*." Her audience cringed, but no one replied. "Our city is now filled with villains, criminals, cannibals, and thieves. Our queen, the one whose role I was blessed to play, the one who saved us from certain enslavement, would never have allowed such a travesty to come about."

"What *can* we do but talk?" a frustrated, heavy-set man asked and threw his hands up in defeat.

Lowelia punished him with a scowl, and he looked down at the floor. She considered long and hard what to tell these people. She assessed their fitness, spirits, and pride, and found each of them sufficient, except for the man who'd so readily accepted his uselessness. He would have to go before she said anything more. She tipped her head to burly Brock, who worked nights upstairs as tavern enforcer and was familiar with the body language of his superiors; he hefted the struggling man up and out of the room. After a moment, Brock returned and sat down, huffing. Lowelia allowed a beat or two of threatening silence to pass, a trick she'd learned in council.

"Does anyone else share his attitude?" Murmurs and headshakes indicated *no*. "Cowards are not welcome at my table, so I shall assume none of you will ever voice reservations again. We are at war, my countrymen. In the South. In our very homes. War can be seen on every horizon. What can we do? The answer is simple: We can prepare. We can arm ourselves in the shadows. We can await the return of the true guardian of Eod, she who smote the Iron City with the fury of nature herself." Lowelia paused, panting in passion, and her eager audience leaned in as if it sensed what was coming. "Our queen is coming home."

"We've heard the rumors," said one poised older woman with dark skin and cropped hair like a soldier. Wearing a pale gown and gloves, she looked quite fancy for a revolutionary, though who was Lowe to judge? "What have you heard, matron?"

"You ask the right question. Ms...?" Lowelia waved her hand, fishing for a name.

"Miss Abernathy. No mister worth mentioning. Dorothy will do."

"Dorothy," repeated Lowelia, and the two women smiled, perhaps recognizing a familiar determination or darkness in the mater.

"And the answer to my question?" asked Dorothy.

"I've heard the voice of the queen, and she tells me she is even now making for Eod," Lowe hissed. "She is not alone, but brings with her an army."

The grouped gasped and exclaimed as one. "An army?"

"Yes," replied Lowelia. "Queen Lila intends to march into Eod and demand, through a show of military force, if necessary, an audience with Magnus. However, she cannot breach the gates of the city on her own, not without causing terrible casualties on all sides. In fact, she swears that nary a man, woman, child, or even housecat will be harmed so long as she needn't break down the gates. Whatever rumors you may have heard—and

I once struggled with such doubts myself—she is not an enemy of life. If she and Magnus are to meet peacefully, someone will need to let her and her forces into the city."

Awe, shock, and fear spread like a pox through her listeners; their complexions grew pale, and some bit their nails and twitched with electric thoughts. Dorothy and Brock remained the most composed.

Tapping her chin thoughtfully, the graceful Dorothy asked, "From where did the queen get her army? She couldn't have hired mercenaries, as they'd be more interested in the Iron Queen's bounty."

"From the Arhad, I've been told," replied Lowe.

"Impossible," spat Dorothy, losing her composure. Lowe traced the woman's anger—for Miss Abernathy was brown of complexion, like the desert wanderers—to some detail of her ancestral or personal history. Dorothy continued, "The Arhadian warriors would never bow to the will of a woman, not even a queen."

"Miss Abernathy—"

"Dorothy."

"Dorothy," continued Lowe. "When I was placed on the throne of Eod, the queen left in my care a handful of far-speaking stones for use in case of emergency. I never heard from her during that time, or for some time after. I kept them in my nightstand, however, out of a fool's hope that she would one day reach out to me to say..." Lowe stalled on a thought of what she'd wanted to hear from Lila: *I am sorry. I am grateful. I am proud of you. I forgive us both.* It was all a fantasy. Lowe resumed speaking. "To say that she'd survived the unmaking of Menos and that she was well. Then, finally, the Sisters Three themselves sent me a sign not even a blind woman could miss. Last night, only an hourglass after I'd learned of this meeting and settled into bed, one of the stones spoke. Its message burned so hot that it singed the wood of the drawer in which it was kept—the smoke was what woke me. I could hear only so much; if you're familiar with far-speaking magik, you'll know that unless you catch the speaker right at the moment of communication, the message will already have been recorded, and you won't be able to say anything in return. So I listened, with my ears and all my heart, and this is what the stone said..."

Coughing herself awake from a deep sleep, Lowe realizes there's a fire and throws herself out of bed. She quickly notices, though, that it's a small fire; only her squat two-drawered dresser appears to be under threat. Smoke puffs from the cracks: her papers, knitting implements, and even the picture she was never able to tear up and throw away of Euphenia's child have almost certainly already been reduced to ash. The stones! The far-speaking stones are in there, too! she realizes. Lowe braves a grab at the hot metal handle, fans away a rush of sooty breath, and then bats down flames with an empty pillowcase in order to see what remains to be salvaged. There, lying in a nest of scorch marks and ashes like the egg of a mystical bird of fire, glows a far-speaking stone. It pulses while the other stones cluster around like stillborn eggs with nothing to say. Whoever is speaking through this stone is doing so with so much power and conviction that its message will not be unheard. Risking a second and more severe burn to her already red fingers, Lowe reaches into the drawer, hisses as she touches the sizzling crystal quail egg, and then raises it to her ear. Contact opens the channel, and the queen's voice floods her head. She nearly collapses from the twist of joy and shock.

"I come to face the judgment of both my husband and my Fates. I come from the desert bringing an army of a thousand Arhadian women and men strong—and it will have grown larger still when you and I at last meet again. We are ready to face the defilers of our world. If you do not crack the gates for us, we shall pound on them until they are opened. Justice cannot hide, and neither shall I."

"A thousand Arhadian women and men strong..." puzzled Dorothy. Along with her companions, she pondered the dangerous unknowns implicit in the queen's proclamation—or threat.

"That's what she said." Lowe nodded, then stopped rubbing the blisters on her fingers. "I would never mistake her words. I have learned that our queen is a lady of action. If she says that she marches to Eod with an army of Arhadians—as absurd as that sounds—then roll out a grand carpet and ready your minds for a parade of the absurd. We have already crossed the Feordhan, in that regard. Riffraff and Iron rats are everywhere. She will not stand for it: this city is as much her creation as Magnus's. And there are things that you do not know about our king...imperfections in his seeming flawlessness..."

Before the king had left Eod to march against his brother, Lowe had heard horrid screaming and grunting coming from the royal wing. She and Erik had shooed all eavesdropping servants away, and then she herself had been shooed away by Erik. The next day, she had been secretly summoned by a mysterious fleshbinder to a cold recess of the palace, a wing no one went these days, where no one would look for a woman beaten and shamed. Sickened by the memory, Lowe remembered her first sight of the battered queen. *Oh, my fair queen! What has he done to you? What has that monster done?* For the woman before her had been nigh unrecognizable. In a room dank with sweaty fear and nauseating ointments, Lila had lain stiffly on a bed, breathing quietly, her face so shattered that she looked like a swollen victim of plague. Lowe had fallen, then crawled, to the bedside and wept for sands, while the queen—despite her condition—reached out a bandaged hand and stroked her hair. It was this memory that had allowed her to forgive Lila for manipulating her, to forgive her for everything.

"Magnus has also committed sins," said Lowe after a long pause. "Sins of the darkest kind, for which he must answer. When the queen returns, she will do so as a ruler who does not bow to men, the Iron Queen, or the backward ideals of a society that treat women like cattle." Dorothy's face formed the perfect mask of rage. Lowelia looked at her for a moment, then at each of the other men and women in the room. "In telling you this secret, I have made you all complicit in it. You have signed yourselves to Lila's service. I know the feeling of being trapped by the machinations of espionage. I also know the feats that even the smallest hands can accomplish. Look at what I, handmaiden to the queen and a mater, have managed to accomplish. Think of what wills like mine—working wills, honest wills—could achieve working in concert with one another."

Lowelia fell silent, allowing her sermon to sink into the spirits of her listeners. She could tell they were listening in the manner of those confronted by fundamental and important questions of freedom, worth, and life. They looked at their hands, the floor, the ceiling. They looked beyond the physical to mysteries, histories, and fears. They looked inside themselves for glimmers of steel that would echo the flash held in the gaze and soul of the woman who stood up and awaited their answer. When at last they found that voice within themselves, the calling to be greater and not lesser, they looked to Lowe, rose, and then pledged their loyalty to the values of Eod—the ones now forgotten by its king. Dorothy and Brock were the first to rise and salute Lowe with the fist of the Silver Watch. They were also the first to offer input on how to proceed.

"We'll need weapons and information," said Brock.

"I have a connection I can call upon for those," replied Lowelia.

"We'll need disguises," said Brock.

Dorothy snorted. "You won't find a better seamstress in Eod. Tell me what you need, and I'll have it to you by tomorrow."

"What we need, yes…" said Lowe, and gestured at them to sit. This assemblage, small though it was, boasted tailors, carpenters, bruisers, bakers, earthspeakers, and couriers. And this was not the only band of loyalists conspiring behind closed doors. They would need to find the others, to amalgamate many fragmented groups into one large body. Imagine, she reflected, how many skills and tools such a collective of artisans, working sorcerers, civil servants, and likely even a few soldiers would possess. There must be at least a hundred such rebels. A small number, yes, but enough to start an uprising.

VII

Again, and as with every sand since a chance encounter in the hallway that morning, Beatrice's pale ghost followed Alastair through Eod's starry halls. Had she been *waiting* for him? As a shadowbroker, and a man who'd lived and cheated death for many hundreds of years, Alastair believed he'd mastered the art of stealth, but he could not seem to shake the woman. He took the mustiest paths and darkest hallways he could find. He dashed through crowds, and once tried to lose her by plunging into the raucous lunchtime crowd at the White Hearth. But every time he turned around, he saw the same white head still bobbing behind him.

In the Court of Ideas, he'd played a game of masks and stolen the overcoat of a scholar who'd been paying too much attention to his books to notice the offense. Then he'd joined a huddle of sages and bullshitted his way convincingly through a conversation on the fluctuation of northern etheric currents. Alas, Beatrice's white countenance emerged from behind a bookcase, and he threw off his disguise and elbowed his way through the knot of learned men.

The maze of bookcases should have provided ample opportunities for evasion, but however much he tried, he could not free himself of his pursuer. Every time he looked over his shoulder, there she was.

Bloody Kings! What sort of hunter was she? Most Menosian ladies were devious, but vapid; they were like pretty snakes—venomous, powerful, to some degree cunning, but with the tiniest of brains. Yet this wife of an Iron Sage was determined and clever; she was of a breed much closer to that of Gloriatrix. She would simply not give up. Feeling the heat, running out of options in a palace that seemed to be growing increasingly smaller, Alastair darted into one of the many indoor arboretums. Shining with green life, it boasted cloisters twined with crystal flowers, splashing brooks, and many other distractions that might throw a pursuer off the scent. Tucking himself in amongst a row of tall, lanky hedges, he closed his eyes; smelling the rich soil, he wished he could sink into the stone, that the earth would swallow him entirely. Make him disappear. He was not practicing magik, only trying to remain so still and silent that he would go undetected even by the sharpest senses.

Rustle. Rustle.

"Hello."

Fuk. Creaking open his eyes, he saw that with one lean, pale hand, Beatrice had parted the bushes that screened him. She stared at him curiously. "Are you going to come out? It seems a bit tight in there for two."

Alastair settled himself in more firmly, gripping branches. "What do you want?"

"To talk, you fool. Now come out of there."

He dawdled, but Beatrice—having none of it—with the same fiendishly strong, icy hand that had pushed aside a row of greenery, yanked him out of the hedges. She used a little too much force, and Alastair tripped and rolled on the grass. Beatrice swept over to the downed fellow. "I do apologize. Sometimes, I do not know my own strength," she said.

Alastair crawled away from her kindness. Up close, he could sense more than strength beneath the white skin of this woman. Her sickly sweet smell—apricots and overly dried sweet things—and her glimmering, edged beauty were obfuscations that hid a darkness within her flesh. As he so often lied himself, Alastair knew how to spot deceit, and part of the lady

El, the part that looked like a woman, was false. Alastair glanced around for other people, and noticed the garden was empty.

"We are alone," she said and strode forward.

"You're not normal! I shall—I'll tell someone!" he shouted, hoping a threat would scare her off.

"Oh shut up, you spineless shite of a man," she hissed. He tried to leap to his feet, but she moved in a smoky ruffle of shadows and spinning silks, and somehow restrained his arm with fingers that had become icy daggers. "I was trying to be polite, but there's no reason for that now, I suppose. Running away! Ha! That was always your way, though, wasn't it, Alastair? Is that your real name? It's certainly not the one I recall. Another lie, of which you've told plenty."

Beatrice dragged him to a stone bench, around which flocked birds that had flown in through some hole in this deceptively sunlit place. The creatures actually turned their small heads and cheeped in fear at Beatrice before fluttering off. Alastair wished he, too, had wings, and was suddenly dizzyingly afraid. What was happening? He contemplated rolling the dice with Charazance for a translocation, but Beatrice, although violent and powerful, didn't seem to want him dead. Instead, like an angry mother scolding her boy, Beatrice forced him to sit and kept her hand upon his forearm—bruising the flesh, clamping off all blood to his forearm and hand. What was she? Alastair dared not ask. A speck later, she surprised him by releasing her grip.

"I shall let you go, but know that you cannot run from me," she warned. "Indeed, running only makes the fire rise in my veins. If you antagonize me, force me to hunt, you will bring out the side of my nature that knows no restraint. I caution you against ever meeting my shadow." She turned upon him a shivering glare. "A second warning for you, man who has lived for hundreds of years, man who"—she waved her hand, her claw, through the air around him as if grasping the unseen—"is not entirely mortal. Do not try your lies, tricks, or whatever magik to which you have bound yourself on me. I shall tolerate none of it."

Alastair nodded and risked her wrath by shuffling to the other end of the bench. Carefully and with a hunter's focus, she watched the man reposition himself. "Why so shy? Don't you recognize me?"

He most definitely did not. "What do you mean? I know who you are. I know of you and your husband." With fury, he added, "I've listened to enough whispers in my day to know of the sick appetites you two possess."

"Sick appetites?" Beatrice smiled; her teeth seemed larger and sharper than they had been just a moment ago.

Alastair swallowed. "Whips, harnesses, instruments that look as if they're made for pleasure, yet are intended for no pleasure I—or any sane man—would crave. You and he are filth."

Beatrice laughed. "Oh. I thought you meant the people I *ate*."

Without a doubt, her teeth had narrowed to needled points: her smile had an ovoid quality, and her mouth was now more a hole than a pressing of two lips. Suddenly, her hair twisted from white to black and blew around her head in a wavering mess, reminding Alastair of the fanning of a dangerous lizard's crest. A gust of blackness, twin and tattered scarves that expanded into much greater shapes—sweeping things—flew from Beatrice's back. A wind assaulted him from nowhere, carrying with it Beatrice's stench, the sweet decay of fruits. Terror choked his breath. Gasping, he fell off the bench and crawled for his life. Shouting to the sleeping master within him, he pleaded for Charazance to intervene. Although static—a tickling, a laugh—prickled in his chest, he received no reply but a vague sense of mockery. Doomed. He was about to be eaten by a monster in the gardens of Eod.

Beatrice called from behind him, her voice distorted, likely by all the teeth now clustering in her mouth. "I asked you not to incense me! I asked you not to wake my shadow! Idiot! Graaah! Now I must eat. I must taste passion; I must chew meat." A skin-scraping wail escaped the tortured blood eater as she tried to fight back the goring agony in her stomach, the hunger that she was compelled to satisfy. As her slavering shadow fell upon his back and her claws reached forward to rend his spine and spill out his gushing redness, she called upon the last of her mortality and offered the wastrel a last chance at life. "A song! Sing for me! Sing for your miserable life!"

Song? A song to save his life? A claw tore through his cloak and tunic like a knife through paper. Alastair cried out, but he was a performer—and a desperate one, at that—and he forced the scream into a note. He sang.

Madness, terror, pain and all, he sang whatever tune popped into his head. "A Moonless Night" spilled from his mouth. Alastair slithered out from under the cold shadow and managed to stand while continuing the verses, hopeful now that he would not be murdered. The five lines of pain on his back, throbbing with a numb ache, gave him a forceful timbre and imbued the song with the passion, real passion, the monster had requested. After "A Moonless Night" had ended, though, Alastair discovered he hadn't the courage to turn around.

"One more," she said, sounding normal again, and farther away. "How about 'All the Fair Ladies and Gents?'"

The request wrenched at Alastair's heart. For a moment, he simply stood there, stunned. It was a song he never performed. To sing it would mean calling upon all the deepest pains in his life, and so he had always laughed, connived, and gambled his way out of every request to do so.

Who is the beauty by the fire? The woman who strums and wavers notes that somehow have all the black-hearted, grizzly murderers in this grungy tavern enthralled? Her fingers move over the guitar, creating a dark breeze that echoes her hair. She does not so much pluck the strings as caress them. In her patchwork skirt and peasant's blouse, she makes him think of wanderers, of the Romanisti—the old bards, soothsayers, and thieves of Geadhain, who once moved in caravans and lit the night with tambourine music and gin-soaked howls. These had been his people, long ago. They do not exist anymore...and yet this tanned, night-haired, and sultry bard, she who enchants with her voice, she who sparkles and smiles with her eyes, could be one of them. She stirs him with her gaze, and her thick hair of curled black ribbons, her hourglass curves, and the earthen lows and giddy highs of her voice possess a Romanisti essence he remembers. She summons her music from her soul. Her song, her ancient song, brings him back to the campfires, the chatter over Kings and Fates. He thinks of the first time he felt a young lady's hand upon his body, tasted the burn of liquor in his throat, told a lie, picked a pocket—all the ancient, secret, and beautiful moments of his life.

When the music ends, the whole tavern is silent. Men are too bewildered to clap. In time, though, they remember their manliness and clap and make comments about what else the swarthy temptress might be able to do with her mouth. He wants only one of two things from that mouth: another song or a name. Still enchanted, he finds himself standing before the woman, who is tuning her guitar and not paying him much heed.

"What is your name?" he asks.

She looks directly at him. He'll be damned if the woman doesn't have a Dreamer of Chance inside her, too, because she smiles as confidently as if she does.

"Belle," she says.

"I told you to sing. I shall help, as you seem to have lost your voice," said Beatrice.

As she approached Alastair, she opened herself to the memories, to the spirit of the woman she'd long since eaten and who now lived alongside the monster in her flesh. Every now and then, Beatrice found it impossible to distinguish between Belle's memories and her own. There were instances when she'd mistaken Moreth for a stranger, even as she had his prick inside her body. There were times when she'd woken from her dark dreamless sleeps wondering where her sons were—only to cruelly recall that her womb was anathema to life. As she sang in the rich tones of her spiritual passenger, she felt as if she were, in fact, the woman who'd kissed Alastair's shocked pink mouth that night in the inn.

Belle and Alastair had spent almost a whole season together in Menos, a golden summer in a city of gloom. By day, they had shopped markets and collected food and drink with which to replenish themselves after their exhaustive tumbles in bed. She remembered his skilled fingers, his kisses, even the way his armpits smelled after they'd heated the room and their bodies too much. By night, they had continued their lovemaking on stage. They had slid their voices over each other: kissed notes, thrust chords. Their duets had lulled the Iron souls of Menos into states of slowly applauding wonder. Then she'd woken one day, reached for Lucien—that's what he'd called himself then—and grasped nothing save for emptiness and heartache. The rogue had vanished without giving her a note, a kiss, or an explanation. Belle had never learned why. Although she'd desperately prowled the streets of Menos, she could not find him, and she was eventually forced to return to Heathsholme. She'd never been given a chance to tell the wily bastard that he'd left her with more than a broken heart—he'd also left a seed of life in her womb. Belle's memories continued to flash within Beatrice, even after the music had ended.

"Do you remember now, Lucien?" whispered Beatrice; her hunger felt curiously sated. The song was done, and she'd sung most of it—he seemed wavering toward tears. Caressing his shoulders and back, she peeked through the torn fabric of his tunic to see whether in her rage she had envenomed the man. She had not. She'd grown adept at restraining the worst aspects of her monster, like a cobra that could release poison only when it chose to kill. The "sick appetites" she and Moreth indulged in together demanded a certain self-discipline. Belle had loved and cared for this man, or he would now be well on his way to becoming a bloated, toxic, black-seeping corpse. "She...I...We never trusted another man after you," continued Beatrice. "She loved you, man of many names, loved you as truly as I love my husband. You had a chance to redeem yourself when Fate threw you into each other's paths again, in Riverton. Yet you played your game with her again..." Another memory filled her.

Nowadays, Belle takes less work in Menos. She cannot focus on her craft when the sound of every pair of boots crossing the threshold of a tavern causes her to look up and think: is it him? Now she works in Riverton and heads to Menos only when she has been hired to perform at private parties hosted by horrid—though wealthy—Iron nobles. Heathsholme is merely a ferry and a cart ride away, a few hourglasses at most. She can thus spend most of her summers with Galivad, and his high-pitched giggles and great brown eyes are what inspire the happier, jauntier tunes she sings when not in the Iron City. Galivad is so bright and doting a son, so in love with his mother, that he almost makes her forgive the scoundrel who left him to be a bastard.

The sound of boots announces another arrival at the tavern. As has become her habit, she glances at the entrance. A man stands in a doorway glowing with the blood of dusk. Although she can spy nothing beyond his copper shadow, her heart pulls like a leashed animal and identifies the man by his spirit scent, his presence, alone. When he walks over to her, she finds herself unable to play. She ignores the patrons, who are angry that their magikal trances have so abruptly ended. For before her is the wastrel, the scoundrel, the thief of hearts. Although she's readied a million curses and accusations to throw at him, her hands come up empty, and instead they caress his face and pull him in for a kiss.

When their kiss finishes, he grins. "I see that you remember me, Belle."

"I see now that all she was to you was a diversion." Beatrice sighed. "A dalliance to pass the time in your strange and long life. She never had a chance to tell you all that burdened her heart with the weight of a mountain, for you didn't even spend the night that time. You left in the dark, like a rapist. I find that term suitable, as you raped her hope, her wish for any romantic love. How dark her songs became after that, though you never heard another...The second betrayal planted a second seed, which you fertilized with your shite and then ran from. Belle couldn't look at her new son without feeling ripped apart from the inside. So she gave the infant away. To her sister."

Finally, Alastair awoke. "Second seed? S-son?" One of the reasons he fuked with such abandon was that he knew he was sterile. Unable to produce an heir for his *voivach*—his king and biological father—he had felt such shame that he had fled from his Romanisti band. In hundreds upon hundreds of years, he'd never fathered a child. What this woman said was impossible. "I cannot have children. My seed is thin. I'm impotent."

Beatrice's thoughtful air deserted her, and she shook him. "I should not feel the emotions and know the memories of prey I have consumed, and yet magik—damnable as it is—fuks everything!" Her aggression stirred the darkness in her, and she released the man before the monster could get out. She stormed over to the bench and sat. A draft blew up Alastair's tattered tunic, and it roused him to move, walk, and tentatively retake his spot on the end of the same bench. Not sure what to say, the pair remained silent and sighed. Beatrice's tale was far from the strangest thing to have graced Alastair's ears, and he managed to work though his befuddlement.

"You've eaten Belle..." he whispered, then checked to see whether any others were around; they remained alone. "Now she lives within you?"

"Yes."

"Which means that you recall everything she and I shared."

"Indeed."

"And I have a son."

"Two."

A faintness swept over Alastair: the trickster had run out of cards to play to save himself. Even so, he sought some way to free himself of this responsibility. When shite hit the window, he'd found that the most reasonable course of action was always to run and leave someone else to clean it. He'd survived centuries thanks to that code of cowardice. But the pressure of responsibility, the great and powerful memories of Belle, now swept over him so fiercely that he trembled and then shattered in a sob. The last time he'd cried this hard was when Maggie had been tortured—or perhaps when the *yaagha*, the witch woman of the Romanisti, had told him his fruits had no seeds.

"Well, this is a surprise," said Beatrice. "Belle was certain that you'd run, as you always do. I figured I would have to eat the father of my boys and then go explain the mess."

She patted him with her cold hand. He wept and curled further into her icy embrace. They stayed that way for many sands, each perversely pulled to the other. Beatrice quietly tingled from their intimacy, recalling sights, smells, and lustful and heart-warming memories of this man who was not her husband. The thief of hearts, meanwhile, clutched at this cruel simulacrum, this monster, who was nonetheless the only woman he'd ever truly loved.

After his mistress had driven him away from Belle the first time, forcing him to go on an expedition to the grim shores of Terotak, he'd returned to Central Geadhain with a desire to find the woman with whom he'd made music and love. She understood him. She saw things in him that he lied about to all others. However, his quarry moved in different circles now, and whenever a convenient opportunity presented itself to hunt down Belle, his mistress seemed to find yet another errand on which to send him.

Then one day he had walked into the Porcine Belly, a rustic sea-rocking inn built on an old steamboat in Riverton, and found Belle enchanting all those present with her music and beauty. It was as if Charazance had finally decreed that they could unite once more. Their union was not to last, though, not even till dawn. Charazance had torn him from a lover's heavy sleep with yet another demand for yet another service—one that couldn't wait, not even long enough for him to say goodbye. Being a coward, he had convinced himself that leaving surreptitiously would be kinder. It hadn't been. Beatrice's accusation was just: he'd left in the night like a criminal.

Suddenly, a man who had lived on the elegance of lies realized how shallow he had become. Still, he had children—two sons, it seemed—and he'd found Maggie. Was it too late to make a meaningful life? Would anyone want him if they knew who he really was? Furthermore, who was he? He had forgotten himself.

"Stevoch Vastyir," said the man, puffing up, snorting away tears. "Disgraced prince of the Romanisti, and scoundrel of a thousand names. Earlier, you asked for my name—my true name—and that is the one with which I was born. That is the name from which I have run for centuries. But I shall run no longer; I shall lie no more."

Charazance filled him with electric jitters. She'd awakened and appeared amused by his turn in personality, by his suggested gallantry. Evidently, Beatrice was intrigued as well, and she smiled. "I am glad to make your acquaintance. I wish that Belle could have met the slightly less spineless man I now see before me. Bravery is only bluster until it is backed by action, though; you will have to prove you are worthy of being a father."

Stevoch's stomach lurched at the thought—clearly, it was not as ready as his mind.

"I have never birthed children myself," admitted Beatrice, her head bowed. "But I feel the love that Belle had for her children. For both of them, even the one she could not keep. I know that motherhood and fatherhood are bright and sacred gifts that must be protected. You may think me horrible, but I am grateful to have eaten so noble a creature. I am grateful for how she has changed me, and made me mortal."

"Do you know where my children are?"

Beatrice took his hands; hers were bitingly cold, but Stevoch held on regardless. "I do. A miracle of circumstance has already reunited you with one of your sons. You see him every day."

He did? Who?

"A young man," she continued. "A man to whom I have grown attached. A man who feeds me with his songs, his magikal songs—gifts from his mother. You see me with him often. We are rarely apart."

"Galivad?" He gasped.

Beatrice nodded, then slammed him with another revelation. "But he is only the first of your abandoned children. I believe I also know the identity of your second son. While I never watched him grow, never saw intimations of the man he would become, he had one feature that could not be changed by the passage of time…"

"What?" he demanded, grasping at the woman, desperate in a way that exceeded his control and understanding. Beatrice kissed his head. Consumed by one of Belle's fantasies, she nearly kissed his lips, too. The fallen Romanisti prince, too, almost succumbed to love, seeing past the monster of ice to the spirit no facade could conceal. By the Kings, he'd loved her. He had wanted to invite her into his life. Perhaps they could have begun a new caravan, a culture of music and celebration, one not ruled by hierarchies, crime, and expectations of manhood and lineage. However, he'd lost that chance, and she'd lost her life. He and Beatrice began to accept their bitter loss, and instead of relinquishing themselves to passion, they held one another until the memories passed. Afterward, they quickly parted, their faces became serious.

"Our other son…" said Beatrice. "He possessed a birthmark. On his cheek. One he would never outgrow. When she saw the babe, my sister—Belle's sister—declared that it shone like the one true—"

"Star of the North," finished the prince.

Birds now returned and resumed their cheeping, though they did not approach Beatrice.

"Then you think the same as I?" she asked.

A spellsong: a sorcerer of music. The prince knew that a talent such as that could grow only in a garden of true powerful love and art. A vagabond prince and a woman whose voice was magik. Both of his children were royalty, and it was high time they were reunited with their traditions and inheritance—and with their father. Feeling stronger, clearer in his head than he could recall having been in centuries, Stevoch stood, kissed the hand of his departed beloved, and went in search of his family.

"I am a father," he declared steadily.

Beatrice—and Belle—believed his conviction.

VIII

An ominous sky running with crimson—its clouds evoked an air of doom. Elissandra couldn't pull her eyes away. *You must be here, and there. Both places, but in one body. You must be the bird of sun and moon, mother and sword to the Daughter of Fate. Soar from where you are to where you must be.* Whispers of the dream played a game of hide and sneak in her head.

"Mother?" Tessa pulled at Elissandra's dress. "We're supposed to be working on my Arts today, not hunting for omens in the sky."

"Of course, my lambling," replied Elissandra, and bowed to kiss her daughter's head. Eli surprised her by stomping forward and standing near until she hugged him, too. He was now at the age when he was torn between boyhood and manhood; he hadn't yet figured out that a true man could be both soft and hard. *Who will be around to teach him that lesson?* wondered Elissandra. *Not Sangloris. Not me...*

Eli shrugged his mother off in a speck. "C'mon, I'd like to get back to my lessons, as well."

Elissandra righted her grip on the wooden short sword she held, and took a merciless swing at her son. As he hadn't been prepared, she thwacked him soundly on his shoulder—the most important lesson of battle was that one should always be ready. He cried out, and they paused. A few of the Silver watchmen, from whom they'd received the training blades, glanced at the odd, pale trio, before resuming their own vigorous activities. For the most part, Elissandra and her children were left to their own devices. They lingered, like a trio of specters, outside the bustling training ground: where ivory steeds and their riders thundered across the flat escarpment, men whisked from tent to tent, and sorcerers fired crackling bolts into sandbags using bows crafted of glass and coursing wind. She'd come here because war was the discipline of the day, and it was no different with her small three-person army. As soon as Eli shrugged off his soreness, Elissandra launched another assault on her son.

She'd often fenced as a child. Received wisdom taught that a Menosian woman who couldn't defend herself was a corpse waiting to happen. She'd become rather skilled through the years, and with quick, darting blows easily parried the wide, bumbling strokes of her son—she was grateful that the Fates hadn't taken her good hand. Even Sangloris had found her a challenge. Sangloris. She still hadn't told her children about their father.

"Mother, I think I've got it," cried Tessa suddenly and excitedly.

Elissandra and her son exchanged narrowed stares as they walked towards Tessa. The little girl stood not far away, spying on the encampment.

"Mother, I need you to look," said the girl, and tapped her foot, waiting. Gradually, Elissandra and her son relaxed their sparring stances. Tessariel pointed to a group of soldiers surrounding a tent. Their shirts were off and they glistened in the dusk like clockwork soldiers of bronze. The warriors were enjoying a sand's respite around a campfire. There was a lone woman amongst them, and she wore only her cotton camisole. "Watch the woman," whispered Tessa.

The girl squinted her eyes so hard in concentration that they were nearly shut. Sight was not necessary for shadow-puppeting, the magikal art of slipping a suggestion into a person's head. Only a true sorceress of the mind and Fate could bend a person's will. Tessa, who'd never been able to do more than make a mouse walk into a snapping trap, had finally learned to shape the thoughts and actions of larger animals. With a strain that rippled the air around her, she forced her Will upon the woman, and in her quietest voice, she then bade her move. The commands of shadow sorcery must always be spoken: speech made them real, rendered them audible on some level. They had to be sly and quiet, too, like whispers on a breeze, lest they trigger a person's self-preservation instincts. *Get up,* suggested Tessa. *Stretch those tired legs. Walk to the fire, take in a bit of its warmth, then dump your drink in the flames.*

For a spell, the woman continued to laugh and drink bitter warrior's tea with her companions. Tessa had tried some once, and it was awful; she was doing this woman a favor with her interference. Suddenly, the woman sat up stiffly and turned her head as if she'd heard what the young Daughter of the Moon had whispered a sand ago. A moment later, the warrior strode to the fire and tossed her tea into its flames. After that, she sat down as if nothing unusual had occurred. Her company appeared unsurprised by her actions even when she asked for more tea; they were unaware of where her previous drink had gone.

"Well done!" Elissandra rubbed her daughter's head with the stump of her missing hand.

Tessa shied away a little. "When are you going to fix that, Mother? That's not how it's supposed to be."

"Aren't you sharp with your sight today!" said Elissandra, caressing her child's cheek with her stump. "I lost these pieces of myself in Dream. My hand, ear, tooth, and hair now float down the river of time and eternity. What is missing can never be restored, because it is as if it has never been. Only the shrewd Iron mind of the Iron Queen noticed the same dissonance in Fate. Most people think I was born this way. Your perceptions are maturing if you can see the layers of truth and lies that form reality, better than she. I am very proud of you, Tessa. One day, your talents will surpass even mine."

Tessariel grinned, then frowned as another thought struck her. "Why did you lose these pieces, though, Mother?"

"Pick up your blade," demanded Elineth of his mother.

"A speck, my lambling," said Elissandra and turned back to Tessa. "When I had to travel here to reach the Iron Queen in time and stop her from destroying all of this—" She waved her only hand, continuing, "—these pieces of myself were the price I paid for my careless race."

"But you got here. In a day, no less." Tessariel was awed.

"I did."

"Pick up your blade!"

"Not now!" barked Elissandra at her son. Tessa's question had stirred her. Silver-eyed daughter and mother were locked in a trance, focused on each other. Fates hummed, their Seekers buzzed, their hives nearing a secret. A gray shroud fell over the pair, a pall of prescience. They saw and knew only each other.

"How much farther could you go?" asked Tessa.

"To the ends of the land and sea," replied Elissandra.

"What would that cost you?"

"My flesh. My self."

"Would you live?"

"For a time, my spirit would exist outside of death, yes. I would be as unstoppable and radiant as the sun. I could stand against the mad king himself: as a warrior of soul."

"Then that is the answer."

"The answer..."

Thwack! A flat object hit Elissandra's ribs. Their trance fell away in smoky dissolution, and each felt stunned, Elissandra especially, as it had been her body that sustained the blow.

"Ha!" cried the lad. "I gave you ample opportunity to raise your guard. I win. Now you're dead. Dead, Mother. Mother?"

Dead. The gray fog returned, and Elissandra was swallowed once more, sent tumbling from one fugue of prophecy into another. This time, she soared alone through vast, whispering spaces. The river of Dream cast her far and wide, and finally gushed her back into the valley of black rock— back into the Dream where she'd floated over a land immemorial, a scar in Geadhain, and pondered and grieved over the losses of life. With a sigh and tear, Elissandra came back to her children, who huddled around her, afraid.

"No need to fear, my children. I've sorted through something. I know where I must go, and, more importantly, how to get there."

Tessariel's Seekers buzzed a warning to the girl that she could almost construe. Lacking clarity, she knew only that she should embrace her mother more tightly, and she did. When Tessariel opened her eyes, which were teary, her mother looked in that instant as if she were made of mist and light—beautiful, transcendent, and no longer having a foothold in this world. The vision vanished as her mother wiped away her tears.

"We have our training to get back to," said Elissandra, and picked up her sword. She wasted not a moment and swung at her son. Wood clashed against wood; the boy grunted from his mother's brute force. "The strongest minds and bodies will be needed for what lies ahead."

No more questions were asked. The family of seers could sense that war and death were imminent. Eli felt his sweat tingling like droplets of electricity. Tessa could smell a distant rot, like that of a dead rat buried under the floorboards.

Elissandra watched her children wind tight with resolve. She saw their young faces pinch into the countenances of angry generals. They would be ready. She would make certain that they were prepared. She'd brought them here to test them, to make them strong. In days or weeks at most, she would no longer be their teacher and parent, but a ghost.

But Tessa and Eli had given her hope for the future. For now Elissandra understood what must be sacrificed, and how she was to die. She knew how she was going to become the bird of sun and moon.

I am coming, Morigan. I shall save you, so that you may save us all.

Elissandra brought down her sword so hard that Eli crumpled to the ground. Neither he nor Tessa, who had gone back to filling people's heads with suggestions, were bothered by his tumble. The child picked himself up, growled at his mother, and attacked again.

XII

SINNER'S PATH

I

Making it out of Alabion was an ordeal for a spoiled, soft-boned child whose magik did not serve him anymore. The last manual exertions in which Sorren had engaged had been a series of races through the hedge mazes of the old estate—races Vort had always won.

Contrition and guilt filled Sorren when he thought about his brother. Even as icy thorns tore at his newly minted flesh, fanged mammals bit his ankles and numbed him with poison, and furry masses roared beneath the snowy trees that he scraped and tore his hands to climb. For the first time in his life he felt as strong and proud as Vort. He was fairly sure, though, that he was no longer a sorcerer: that spark of him had died with his resurrection. However, the seed Death had planted within him when she had used his body as her avatar remained. Her shadow now infused his being, and its magik didn't require activation by his Will; it was innate. He was now a child of Death: invulnerable, or at least difficult to harm.

Earlier, he'd been bitten by a colorful, lethal snake, and watched his ankle bloat like that of an old woman with gout. But hobbling around for a time appeared to flush out the toxins. Later, while walking across a frozen stream, that same foot had broken the ice, and he had lost his boot and a few toes to a vicious snapping turtle. He had cried a bit, but the bleeding had staunched itself, and the snow had made for a numbing replacement to his footwear. A day later, four little nubs like knots in wood had formed where his toes had been—he had all five now.

I'm coming, my brother. I am coming for you, Mother. These were the thoughts that drove him onward through the pain of injury and rebirth. For despite his body's hardiness, the healing process was agonizing. Indeed, he likened it to experiencing fleshcrafting without ether or sedatives. The cold helped a little, but for whatever reason, even without a boot and despite his shoddy cloak, he never felt cold enough. When his toes grew in, his foot still throbbed, bringing tears with each pulse. When fanged mammals took their turn with his flesh (why was nearly everything poisonous and deadly here?), he was plunged into delusional, sweaty fevers, during which he often harmed himself through carelessness. When he regained consciousness, he'd then find himself trapped in new cycles of pain. A path of torment lay under his feet, and Sorren the wicked—now Sorren the penitent—walked every aching step with humility.

The young witch, Ealasyd, didn't believe he could change. She had called him Viper, after the old legend. Perhaps some of what she said of him was true. He was selfish; he had been the cause of great suffering. Still, even a viper had its brood—fellow serpents. None of his family was without sin: his covetous brother, his voraciously greedy mother. If he were a viper, then they were as well. Also, the golden sister had not experienced the gnawing madness of his imprisonment within himself, within the world of Death's mind. That terror could change a man—and had. Often, as he stumbled through Alabion in a haze of agony, Sorren remembered the lifeless realm he'd wandered while Death reigned in his body.

He flies in a sooty wind over great worlds of ash. Below whistles the blasted nothingness of wastelands where all living creatures are grains of black sand on the desert that reaches in every direction. There are no fossils, no oil, only sand and eternity. There is no sound but that of the wind that bears him. When the current spins and his invisible body flips, he stares at a sky glowing with three red moons: drops of blood on a gray expanse where the stars shine so weakly that it's clear he's seeing only the ghosts of their light from eons ago.

Is this a place? he wonders. Some world of Death's? Perhaps it is the one that first fell to her rule. Its peace is comforting, especially after the intensity of his journey; it suggests a tranquil garden where all sights and sounds are familiar. Sorren soars and spins with the wind. However, a mind—especially a Thule mind—cannot be still forever. And a mind without a body soon thinks of what it is missing. Sorren finds himself thinking of flesh, greenness, and life, of all the elements that cannot be found here—the ones that Death has removed from this perfect vision. Without his body, the vehicle of his ambitions, his desires seem as hollow as the land beneath. How can man desire, yearn for pleasure, without flesh? Questions and doubts assail him. What was it that turned his mother into so cruel a woman? Her love and her pride, he realizes. Why had he even been jealous of Vort? Because he was faster? Stronger? Because his brother had stolen Lenora's heart—and she'd stolen his in turn? None of these reasons hold any weight outside the world of flesh. None of these reasons is cause for him to have murdered and tortured. As Sorren slowly reflects in this void of clarity, a storm brews. What was quiet now becomes loud. Loud with roars from the screaming, bloody mouths of those he killed—loud with the squelching, burbling death rattles of every one of his victims.

As merely ash on the wind, a passenger without control, he cannot escape from the horror of his life. Flesh does not matter! He shouts to ward off the madness. But these faces and hauntings are not flesh, and neither are the agonies he can remember in such extraordinary detail—every bubbling slice with a scalpel, every jitter and warm pissy smell produced by his attempts to fry and magik mutilated women back to life. Names. He remembers the names of every woman he ended: Minenway, Clarise, Eudora, Samantha...He remembers their animal squeals, their final gasps, and the lipstick of blood that each woman wore. When he had flesh, it had been easy to ignore these details, or, somehow, to treasure them as a butcher does the cutting of meat. He felt himself a great and aspiring genius: transcending death through technomagik. He was blinded to his own madness. In the calm of Death, however, Sorren sees himself more clearly than a normal man can ever see himself. I am petty. I am vile. I am a murderer, a rapist. I am filth. Everything I did in my life was wrong. The root of my birth was rotted. I shall never be able to atone for what I have done. There is not enough mercy in all the world.

Wailing with the spirits of his memory, screaming at the horror of himself, and shrieking for the opportunities for light that he had cast into the darkness, Sorren and his wind soar through purgatory. When the wind abruptly stops, the world tumbles like a sandcastle hit by a hurricane, and a green-eyed woman blearily appears—kneeling, whispering to him. Sorren knows that nothing he suffers on Geadhain will be worse than the silent terror of facing himself and his evil in Death's realm.

Thus, as Sorren limped his way through Alabion—a land meant to punish—he was thankful for every gash and tear. His pain was his gauntlet, and there should be no end to it for the crimes he'd committed. Life was a blessing, yes, but for him, it was a prison—and one he was grateful for, after his confinement in the mind of Death. Occasionally, when struck by a transcendent moment of suffering, Sorren smiled.

II

Sorren stirred from his waking nightmare. He was in pain all over: he'd twisted his "better" ankle in a pothole, and then later lost most of his left hand to a hungry thing hiding in a frozen bush. He wanted to groan, but kept his mouth shut—wolves were on the move. They howled and beat drums as they marched, and the icy forest shimmered with wispy torchlight. Sorren hobbled toward a barred window of icicles under a great oak root and then huddled behind it. He concentrated on making himself quite still, although he'd discovered recently that only certain predators noticed him—the carrion ones, the beasts that didn't care whether flesh was dead and green. Another sign that there was something grossly wrong with his body: he hadn't pissed or shat since reawakening to this life. There must be some logic to the metamorphosis he'd undergone, but he couldn't think about that now. Not when there were wolves in the forest.

The thicket thinned ahead, and he could see flames and fluttering shadows. There was a growing din, a cringing chorus of barks, howls, breaking frost, slammed drums, and rattling metal. At least the cacophony muffled the screaming of the victims in Sorren's mind; for that he was grateful. At that moment, a war band rushed through the trees, filling the forest like the rush of water from a shattered dam. There was so much threatening movement in the glittering blackness and torchlight that he reached for his wonderstones, the ones the golden witch said could work miracles. However, his hand paused: to save himself would not be a miracle. The pouch of magik stones was meant to secure the fortunes of others. His die had been cast. He would cower, and if he were found, his unkillable body would know only as much pain and torture as it deserved.

Sorren faced this potential judgment, as around him flowed waves of wolves, half-wolves, whipped beasts in iron collars, snapping mouths, and dog musk. At one point, a woman with a skin of milk shone amid the darkness. Somehow, though, she also resembled a red sun. He'd begun to see fewer shapes and details but more colors lately, as if peering through a lens of fever. The woman and wolf sea moved past him in a chorus of haunting howls. The army of hundreds, or perhaps even thousands, had moved by in sands. Much like other predators in this forest, they hadn't sensed him. Sorren wasn't sure where the wolves were headed, though he figured he would know soon enough. Something about that pale woman who was also a terrible red sun drew him—she seemed cursed in much the same way he was. Like a lost dog, he followed her army down the trail of trampled ruin. At the very least, she'd lead him out of Alabion. Beyond this deadly wood, he'd begin the search for his family.

III

Marks of the army's passage were evident, and Sorren limped his way through the ruts and footprints the beasts had left behind. Smaller trees had been snapped and then crushed into a flattened road. A light dusting of snow concealed its dangers, and he slipped often. Although Sorren was mad—he knew that well enough—his intelligence hadn't dulled, and he made a game of counting the foot, hoof, and paw prints left unfilled by the snow, and tried to estimate the size of the force. Thousands, he conjectured. What was their destination? Menos was obviously out of the question for it had been destroyed.

During his period of captivity within Death's mind, he'd thrice had visions of events transpiring on Geadhain—real scenes that weren't ash and emptiness. Once, he'd seen a roguish man with copper hair and strange eyes of differing colors standing in a graveyard. The man had given him a look of amused pity and said a word or two before Sorren was pulled back into the world of ash. On another occasion, Sorren had stirred from his prison and seen a broken tower dark in a massive smoldering ruin that he knew without doubt was Menos. There would be nothing there for the wolves to raid, for civilization as he'd known it was no more. His third moment of clarity had come at the end of his use as Death's vessel: entirely aware—though through sight riddled and milky as if he'd aged ten thousand years—he'd watched his own decrepit hands unearth the remains of his brother.

Now, no more Death's avatar or prisoner, he reflected on these previous escapes, and began to see that Death's power over her host wasn't absolute. There were times when Death's Will over her vessel's flesh became weak—not weak enough to allow the prisoner to break his chains, but weak enough that he could become aware of the outside world. Perhaps this awareness was all that he needed to reach his brother: to summon Vortigern's soul forth for a new bargain, a better pact. For he knew why Death had made him dig Vort's dismembered remains from the frozen ground: she needed another vessel as his own body had been all used up. And if she needed a new vessel, she needed a new pact, too, an agreement with a living soul. Vort was *alive*—his soul, anyway. Wresting him and his body out of Death's grasp would take a miracle, but he had a pouch of three of those. *I have a stone of wonder just for you, Brother*, he thought. *I hope it will be enough.*

IV

By the time dawn had wriggled its fat fingers through the crystal mesh of Alabion, casting glaring orange and red rays, Sorren had made it quite far. Because he so often drifted in and out of nightmares—visions of ash, screaming faces, the now sickening sensation of viscera on his fingers—he wasn't good at keeping track of sands and distance. So when light set the forest aglow, he realized that morning had come and that he'd managed to cover a great deal of ground.

Well behind him now were the darkest, oldest, and thickest parts of the woods. Less threatening hisses and barks stirred the climes in which he currently found himself. Indeed, none of the usual carrion-hunting cats or scaled hounds had chased him during the night. His continued safety struck him as unusual, as Alabion was never kind to unwanted travelers. He paused to double-check his anatomy to see if anything was missing. Hands, feet, and flesh all seemed intact. The wounds of yesterday, including his limp, all appeared to have mended. When he pulled up his sleeves and trouser bottoms, he spotted nothing save for hairless and smooth alabaster skin. Below his shin, his regrown foot looked flawless, even somewhat gracefully formed—although the nails had been turned blue-black by the cold he couldn't feel. *Curious,* he thought.

You're quite insane, dear chap. Who knows what you're really seeing?

Moving in and out of a daze, Sorren continued. He was making fantastic time. Or perhaps it was simply that the wind now whipping his side gave him a sense of speed. As exhilarating as his sprint was, Sorren didn't lose his breath. Sometime later, as the forest warmed and birds woke up and sang, he noticed a glistening flicker ahead: a river or stream. Sorren raced toward it, thinking he should refresh himself. But this urge was driven by instinct, not by a demand of his body. In fact, as he strode up to the crystal brook that babbled and broke the ice with its chatter, he felt no thirst at all. Many hourglasses of jogging—which had felt like walking—and his throat spoke only of numbness.

When had he last had a drink? He couldn't recall. What about a meal, for that matter? He remembered sipping bitter, liquorice-scented tea back in the sisters' abode, then...Well...Surely, he must have nourished himself afterward. Perhaps because he was paying attention to his stomach, it *disagreed* and then decided to gurgle as if it had something to expel. Within instants, the indigestion had grown violent, but it brought with it no pain. Contemplating these oddities, Sorren squatted in the snow and shat with no concern for dignity. He wondered if it was the cold that made his fingernails look as dark as his toenails. He stared at his very pale hands while a flurry of wet slop fell from his insides—with a fanfare of gas, though without cramping. Sorren's excretion went on for far longer than normal, but his hands distracted him from the nasty business. Then the stench of rotten eggs and spoiled meat wafted up and around him, and Sorren, fascinated, still wiping his arse with a piece of cloth ripped from his tatters, turned to look at what he'd made.

Viscera, a kidney, and strings of fat floating in a gravy of oil stared back at the appalled man. The scrap of arse-wiping cloth that he threw in shock was drenched in black. Sorren fumbled backward, his trousers down and tripping him, his heart racing...No. It wasn't racing—it wasn't even beating, said the Thulian aspect of his mind. The panic drum played only in his head. The trickle of cold sweat on his neck was another phantom memory, a sensation his body was reproducing based on past terrors. That same autonomous reflex was responsible for his gasps, which arose from no genuine hyperventilation. These breaths had a pleasant fragrance: a potpourri of cloves, herbs, and spices used to preserve apples and sweet things.

A man's heart raced. A man sweated from fear. A man felt cold. A man ate, drank, and shat. These rules applied to Sorren no longer. As he finally pulled up his trousers and stumbled to the creek, the shattering realization came to him. There, in a pane of ice like a mirror at the water's edge rippled a ghoulish white face, a grimace of yellow teeth, and a gaze as black as all the evil that had once dwelled in his heart.

The words of the golden sister echoed in his mind: "She stopped the great decay, though she could not remove the piece of Death's great shadow that is within you. Doing so is beyond my sister's power. You let Death in, and now She can never be removed—even if the worst of her power and presence has gone. You are tainted. Or rather, more tainted, I suppose. Is that why you're weeping? Because of what you will become?"

"I have become Death," he whispered, and sobbed, though no tears would come.

V

One boon of his curse was the speed of his new body. By evening, after following the changeling's trampled road, Sorren had covered a great deal of ground—the army was far ahead by now and had shown no indication that it knew of his presence. He felt he was too fast for them to catch, anyhow. Still, he wondered if he could catch them, and how little time and energy of his that would take. An hourglass? A day? On the matter of days, chronexes and time, however, he could not determine the color of the sky or the hourglass, seeing only the land's muffled lightness.

Shortly after his body had evacuated itself of mortal organs, his sight had waned to a cataract-like blindness, a bleary gray through which he now saw the world. Almost everything that had a spark of life possessed an outline in the haze, like a white-coated man walking through a rainy night. Thus he could see the soft, pulsing rods of light that were trees, and the four-legged and fluttering gobs of radiance that were animals and birds. His sense of depth, detail, and shape, though, had been lost. He could no longer see the details and beauty of these creatures. For a man once imprisoned in a realm of ash, a man who longed only to see the world again—all the glories he'd rejected and profaned in life—this was another cruel penalty added to an eternal sentence. A sentence, though, that he knew he deserved. No matter. He was fast now, and strong, which would make his mission to save his family from the depths of monstrosity easier to accomplish.

Sorren came to the balding outskirts of Alabion. Although he still felt drawn by the woman of the red aura and her army of vicious wolf-men, he knew he must go north if he were to find human habitation and information about his family. Whatever war to which the wolves were marching was not his battle—not now or yet, at least. Sorren tore across the wavy field of gray rises and fog, heading for civilization.

VI

Heathsholme was quaint—Central Geadhain's darling, as the locals proclaimed. Looking down upon it, passengers on skycarriages were often struck by the fact that the realm possessed the look of a joyfully made quilt. Red-leafed orchards, yellow fields of flax and corn, patches of blue brocade that were swimming pools and watering holes...all threaded with brown branching roads. Sweet winds blew down from the North year-round, bearing only cool and refreshing properties until winter rose to claim the throne of seasons. When the North wind came, it froze Heathsholme's pools into skating circles and decorated the large trees with grand chandeliers of ice. In the depths of that season, the staunch apple trees finally died. Their fruits fell to the ground and were collected. Their blossoms broke from their branches and filled the air like flocks of migrating winter birds. During this season, families came from the West, South, and East to visit Heathsholme and enjoy great outdoor festivals of food, music, mulled cider, and wine—for which the region was also famed.

Partly on account of the season's coolness, these celebrations happened around great bonfires. At night, when the happily drunk howled at the moon, a primal spirit took hold, and effigies of nameless spirits were burned in the pyres. No one could remember why or how the Vallistheim tradition had been born, only that it was a remnant of the customs once imposed by Taroch. The ancient warlord had been fascinated by the Northmen's rites, and had introduced many of them to Central Geadhain. Vallistheim—the winter festival—was believed to bring bounty and luck in the New Year. Over time, polite society had done away with many of the less pleasant sacrificial details to make the ritual friendlier to outsiders. Now only one cow from each of the barns and byres that rose on rings in the hilled highlands around the heart of the township was cooked in a great feast, without having been ritually slaughtered first.

In the uncultivated grasses past the city proper and its farmlands, a dedicated explorer could find the remains of crumbled churches that had been built to honor the now vanished religion of Taroch's fancies. Runes that the sages had translated into such names as Freyallah, Odric, and Helhayr were found chiseled in the mossy arches of these grounds. These sites of an ancient religion were thought by modern minds to be haunted or perhaps protected by the ancient spirits or warriors mentioned in the stones. It was the sort of refuge where a monster, fearful of being seen, could find sanctuary.

VII

However did you do it for so long, Vort? wondered Sorren.

Amid the ruins, he sat and sulked upon a pile that might once have been an altar and watched the static that he thought must be snow, unable to feel it on his gray skin. He'd spent only two days, maybe three—he was terrible with time now—in the same state of waking death that his brother had lived in for decades, and he didn't know how Vortigern had succeeded in avoiding madness. For to live between life and death was to exist as a ghost in each realm. The living had no color aside from their auras, and the physical world, the soulless elements, were figments the elements of which one could only guess.

Sorren's first encounter with another being had gone terribly awry.

After his race through gray clouds flickering with soul lightning of many colors he'd met his first man, or perhaps woman. He hadn't yet figured out how to discern the intricacies of sex in these fluctuating blobs of colors. The person appeared suddenly during his marathon: a dazzle of color that he nearly missed in the blur. Somehow, he understood that the brightness, and complexity, indicated a person, for the being hovered like a snowflake of white-and-gold starlight. Stopping, he found himself by tall green squiggles of light: trees, as their color was always green unless they were sick. A few gaseous humps that Sorren suspected were hills lay beyond them. Another indistinguishable mound hovered behind the moving rainbow aura.

"Sir? Ma'am?" asked Sorren.

As he hadn't spoken in a while, his words sounded strange and rather loud, even to himself. At once, the figure flared with a flickering muddy-brown light. The aura crinkled and cowered, becoming a doll of crumpled paper. In his new gray existence, Sorren could hear certain sounds quite well. The living produced coursings and thuds: blood flow and heartbeats; this person's had accelerated. What he or she was experiencing was fear. A woman's warbling underwater shriek shook Sorren, and the flickering soul ran off into the gray miasma. He knew he could follow her and catch her in a stride, but he didn't. He'd never chase another woman again; the thought had made his withered prune of a stomach try to force up the vomit it could no longer produce.

Once his phantom sickness had passed, he had rummaged through what he believed to be a cart left behind by the woman. The search was a blind foraging: he couldn't identify even half of the items he touched, but he took what felt like a hat, boots, and a large throw-over smock. In his enthusiasm to make contact with the woman who had so suddenly appeared, he'd neglected to recall that he was now well and truly a horror to behold. Monsters had to hide themselves to survive. Furthermore, he realized his words had actually come out in a screech of gibberish. If everything about his physical body now moved faster, that could well include his tongue. He remembered Vortigern—the dead version of his brother—practicing the careful enunciation of sounds, rolling his gray lips and doing strange vocal exercises in the mornings as he stood in front of a mirror.

"Aaaa...Eeee...Iiiii....Hhhhooooowwww...aaaarrrreh...yyyyoooouuu?"

Too self-involved, Sorren had never taken the time to discover the purpose behind this training. He found himself grateful for the memory, though, and for so many other strengths and virtues of his brother that he could now emulate.

"Please forgive me," said the dead man.

Sorren practiced the phrase, slowing it down on the hitch of every syllable until he sounded like a village idiot. However, he knew that was the speed, the correct tempo, in which he should speak, because the muffled echo sounded not like a shriek but like distantly whispered words. Sorren spent the remainder of the day—he was beginning to be able to tell the passage of time by studying the softer and darker grays—walking the ruins and talking to the little auras that frolicked around him in stone and snow. Their attention, however shy, was a kindness for which he felt a humble gratitude. It was a mercy that they would even tolerate him in their home.

Finally, the monster awkwardly fit himself into the boots and clothing he had stolen from the woman on the road. The hat felt too tight, and the shift hugged him in queer places, but the boots must have belonged to someone with enormous feet, because they fit quite well. He figured his shoddy cloak would conceal at least some of his oddness. He would have preferred to use magik: a phantasm would have solved all of his insecurities. As Sorren had learned, though, when a man died, he apparently lost the passion necessary to spark magik. Sorren was a sorcerer no more: he was merely a dead man. Nonetheless, it was night, the hourglass of his kind, and he needed information on the war and his family. Sorren left the ruins.

After striding a ways through fluffed banks of cloud on the earth that were certainly snow, Sorren paused and looked down into the valley of lights and colors, the beating rainbow heart of spirits, music, and laughter that was Heathsholme. Sorren didn't feel as if he should be allowed happiness, and yet the beauty of the sight clenched his tearless eyes.

VIII

Rhiannon swept her gaze across the rustic tavern a final time. A man lay facedown on a table. A woman and two fellows shared a shady corner; each man had a hand on her leg, which she seemed not to mind. The bard's stool was empty; he'd left for his bed hourglasses ago. Rhiannon wondered if she should do the same. Only the dregs were left, and unless she wanted to make herself a fourth wheel of that trio, she wouldn't be making any coin tonight. They wouldn't pay for it, anyway. *Why buy the spinrex when you can get the milk for free?* went the saying in Eod. In short order, the pair of gents and their giggling spinrex made a windy exit through the door. Rhiannon shivered from the winter they let in and pulled up her stole, then turned back to the cider she would finish before heading upstairs to her chamber.

"That it for tonight, Rhiannon?" asked the apish barkeep.

In rural places, the servers and valets were never as handsome as the ones she'd once seen in Eod: oiled, shirtless brutes of pure muscle who juggled bottles and uncorked them with their teeth. One had been a firecaller and had lit his liquor—and later, her loins—on fire. Rhiannon had been to the western capital only once, and hadn't been able to stay as long as she'd wanted, as she had frivolously spent every bit of coin from her father's inheritance in a span of three days. Even before setting out for Eod, she'd bled money, losing more than half of her fortune's valuation in the currency exchange before she'd even spent a penny. But she cared not. Igor, her father, had been the most worthless kind of man: weak, drunk, abusive. He'd beaten her mother into an early grave and done even worse to Rhiannon. She desired none of his cursed crowns, did not want to preserve his misery-made fortune. When he died, she had thrown him into a wooden box and burned the body. She had been deliriously drunk at the service, and shouted slurs at his ghost, if memory served. Not that any decorum had to be maintained at the funeral—Igor's family had hated him, too, and no one else had come. She'd left his ashes in a heap on the farmland she had sold. Rhiannon was thinking of fists, and flinching from the thought of unwanted touches from meaty hands, when the barkeep nudged her elbow.

"Rhiannon? You finished?"

"Yes, I suppose I am."

The man clasped her forearm kindly. "Are you all right?"

"I will never be all right."

She frowned and stood, then fell back into her seat as a cold wind blasted through the tavern, stirring even the unconscious drunkard for a sleepy-eyed speck. The drunk resumed his nap and so failed to notice the strange fellow who entered. Rhiannon wasn't sure what to make of him. A wide-brimmed hat with a feather in it hid his features in shadow, and the man shyly tipped his face downward, intensifying the effect. Rhiannon could see only a strong, smooth, white chin. She wondered from where he had come. The man's cloak—ripped, threadbare, and gray from wear—spoke of hardship and a long outdoor journey. Slipped over his pauper's jerkin and trousers was what appeared to be a woman's harvest frock with a rectangular embroidered neckline. *Queerer and queerer still*, she thought. What a sight he made. He looked like a child who'd broken into his mother's boudoir, a cross between a dandy, a dame, and also a gentleman, because of his height and carriage. Intrigued, Rhiannon watched the stranger as he walked through the tavern toward her. His steps were long and stork-like, but still graceful enough to suggest good breeding. He approached the bar, folded his large well-groomed, incredibly white hands, and addressed the people beside and before him.

"Greetings. I have come from afar to see the festival. It is rare to find such joy in a world on the brink of madness."

Even his voice had a certain off-kilter elegance. Although he spoke clearly and with sharp inflections, as a nobleman would, his words seemed to carry on for too long. *Greeetings. Afaaar.* Odd. Watchful and silent, Rhiannon arranged the many bizarre aspects of the man in her head. As they were almost shoulder to shoulder, she noticed he smelled of cinnamon and dried sweet fruits. Odder still. She wrapped herself more securely in her shawl—it was as if the man had brought the cold inside with him. The bartender must have been carrying out a similar appraisal, for he rubbed his arms and did not speak at first.

"Can I get you something, sir?" he asked finally.

"Only some information," said the stranger.

The bartender pointed behind him to a wooden plaque with embossed lettering that was nailed above the shelves of bottles. Rhiannon had a peek at an aristocratic nose and cheekbones as the man lifted his head.

"I'm sorry, I've forgotten my spectacles," he said.

"It says, 'You can't stay if you can't pay,'" replied the bartender unpleasantly.

"Oh." The stranger sighed. "I do apologize, but I left all my crowns back at the tavern where I'm staying."

"With your specs?" asked Rhiannon, believing none of it.

"Where are you staying?" pressed the barkeep.

"Down the road…" replied the stranger. "I shall be going, then."

Tired, hunched, and sapped of his royal grace, the stranger rose and shuffled toward the door. Rhiannon, strangely affected by his queerness and his sadness, the broken posture that suggested he was the saddest man in Geadhain, felt torn by his leaving. Rhiannon made a living out of reading and feeding the needs of men, but this one she couldn't decipher. Although he dressed like a tramp, he certainly didn't smell like one. It was possible he was disgraced, or on the run. Anything, no matter how fantastic, could be true these days. She wondered about his story; on an uneventful evening, this stranger was the most intriguing thing around. Perhaps her cider got the better of her, but Rhiannon called to him as he reached the door. "Stay for a drink. My treat. You can pay me with your story. A man wandering alone in a world on the brink of madness, as you call it, must be mad himself."

"A little," replied the stranger, hesitating.

After a heavy, drawn pause, during which the stranger held the door ajar and filled the tavern with bitter gusts, he made his decision and wandered back to the bar. Reluctantly, the barkeep produced a goblet and filled it with the spiced beverage Rhiannon fancied; he did not ask what the stranger wanted. The barkeep slid the drink toward the stranger, then gave Rhiannon a shrug as she produced some crowns. *These will be collectors' items soon*, she reflected as she slid the coins across the counter. The bartender stood there, watching the pair for a while. The stranger didn't speak.

"You can leave us be, Terry," said Rhiannon, and turned to the stranger. Even when not seducing for hire, Rhiannon couldn't subdue her charms. She leaned on an elbow and pushed out her corseted bodice, emphasizing her breasts. She threw back her deep brown tresses, which were curled and luxurious as the hair of a wild mare, and brushed them to one side. She batted her eyelashes and pouted. All of her wiles were for naught, however, for the stranger did not look up from the bottles flickering with lamplight—the ones lower to the ground, as once more he'd hidden his face. The barkeep left the two alone, as requested, and buzzed about the tavern, waking and shooing the drunk, putting chairs atop the tables, and sweeping the floors. It was quite late, Rhiannon realized, well past the witching hourglass.

"Thank you," said the stranger after the long silence. He pushed his goblet toward Rhiannon. "For the drink. I don't think I shall have any, though. My stomach has been disagreeable lately."

"More for me," said Rhiannon, and emptied his cider into her cup. She took a few swigs, which warmed her with bold, tingling fire. "So, where are you from? And where are you headed? You have the look of a wandering man."

"I have wandered far, yes."

"From?"

The stranger pursed his blue-gray lips. At length, he said, "Menos."

"Ah," she sighed. Rhiannon reached out her hand and touched one of his for an instant—but she pulled it away immediately, for he felt as cold and sleek as ice. "You have the look of a Menosian man of means, certain choices in fashion notwithstanding. You're one of the survivors, then. I heard that a few made it out. I thought they would all have been flown back to Eod by now. How did you escape the roundup?"

"Eod?" asked the stranger.

"Yes. Did they not tell you? At those camps or whatnot?"

"I...I don't remember much." His head hung down, and his shoulders slumped. Rhiannon, stricken with pity, touched the cold marble flesh of his forearm, and was hit by another shiver. "I was lost for a while. Very lost. When I awoke, the world had changed."

Benjamin's Ghost, thought Rhiannon. The old bardic song with countless incarnations. In one popular turn, Benjamin was a lad lost in war who returned to an empty tavern in his hometown one eve and struck up a conversation with his childhood love. But this was many years after the war had ended, and his beloved had grown up and was no longer the girl he'd known. She did not recognize him, as it had been so many years since they had last seen each another. At the end of the tale, though, when he turned to leave, he whispered, "You'll be in my heart, forevermore." These, the very words Benjamin had told her before leaving for the war. She had called for him, and he had turned, though truth had broken the illusion, and before her was a rotted, ravaged corpse that reached for her, telling her how much he loved her. It was an awful tale, and Rhiannon quickly banished it from her mind. Still, as she looked around for Terry, who must have gone outside or upstairs, her intense anxiety remained. Rhiannon stopped touching the stranger and tucked her hands in her lap.

"H-how long? Were you away, that is?"

"I think..." The stranger drummed his fingers on the wooden counter. "A few weeks? A month? Perhaps less, or more. I have no idea. I wandered—from what felt like this world to the next, then back again."

This world to the next? Nervously, and with a forced giggle, she blurted: "But you're not a ghost?"

"No. Not a ghost. Just a citizen of the Iron City. Tell me, what have I missed in my waking-sleep?"

Rhiannon relaxed—apparently he was no specter, just a traumatized man. "Not much; the world is rather quiet now. Eod and Menos have settled their ancient feud and are now sworn allies."

"Allies?"

"Against Brutus, who has reportedly left Central Geadhain—though I bet he's not gone far and won't be gone for long. And also against the wicked queen of Eod, who was responsible for the fall of your city. Every mercenary in the known world now tracks that villain and her lover, and they will meet with justice soon." Rhiannon drank most of her cider. Her fingers, belly, and toes tingled with warmth. Her tongue felt as loose as rubber. She nudged the somber stranger. "My name is Rhiannon, by the way."

"Sorren," he replied.

Rhiannon pondered the name and guffawed drunkenly. "The Iron Queen has a son by that name. Though I doubt you're he!" One could not live so close to the Iron rule without knowing of its royals.

"Doubtful."

"Good to meet you, then," she said, regaining her composure.

"And you."

A distant rustling and dragging, like that of wet bags of leaves being hauled by lazy workers, distracted Sorren. He was nearly blind but for his auric impressions and now had difficulties with touch and taste. All surfaces felt fuzzy: if a banquet had been laid before him, he would have made the most embarrassing gaffes, mistaken a napkin for a filet, and he was sure it would taste the same. However, his olfactory and auditory senses now regularly exploded with new and extraordinary information. So, although his vision was impaired, he could perceive the world in an almost three-dimensional manner using his interpretation of colors, sounds, and smells. Thus along with the sloppy dragging he heard, he caught swampish odors and fouler rotten stinks that reminded him of the reek of his recently excreted black organs. It was death he smelled—and it was somewhere close, and moving.

"Pardon?" he asked; the woman had been gently pestering him about something.

"I thought I might have overstepped your bounds of privacy," said Rhiannon. As Sorren stole a glimpse at her misty crimson form—the color of passion and fiery temperament, he thought—he noted a purple twist of melancholy. She continued, "Don't feel that you must answer. I wanted only to understand what befell the Iron City. No one seems to know, and the rumors that I have heard...I mean, they're nightmares. They can't be true. Escaping Menos...I know things must have been difficult for you, whatever your story. I felt a weight on you when you entered. That's why I asked you to stay for a drink. It was probably silly of me to think that ale or cider would cure you of the terrors you have seen."

"Nothing can cure my terrors."

Rhiannon slurped the final drops from her cup and continued her drunken rambling. "I imagine that is true. Doubtful there's enough drink in the world to black out that horror. An impenetrable fog of ash. Noises made by neither man nor beast. The dead risen and hungry for flesh—"

Sorren leaped from his seat and grabbed the woman by her shoulders. "What? What was that about the dead?"

Rhiannon squirmed in his incredibly powerful grip. "Unhand me!"

A hallucination of a bloody squirming woman flashed in the gray field of Sorren's vision: the irrepressible face of one of his victims; Samantha had been her name. Immediately, Sorren released Rhiannon, stammered apologies, and backed away. "I-I'm sorry. I shall go. I should never have touched you."

"Damn right!" Rhiannon threw her chalice at him. As the goblet had no aura, Sorren caught only the shrieking whistle of its toss and so didn't raise his hands to block his face. Rhiannon was practiced at being indignant and hurling objects at men: gents who wouldn't pay, her father when he'd come for her. Her cup struck the stranger square on his head and knocked off his hat, which twirled under a table. Sorren reeled and acted like a man assailed by bats, and Rhiannon at last saw what he'd been hiding: his unwholesome paleness, his sneer of yellow teeth, his eyes of ink-filled glass. Kings above, here was fuking Benjamin himself! He'd lied! He *was* a ghost. Rhiannon was less afraid than she would have expected to be in this situation. Still, she grabbed her stool and pointed its legs toward the monster.

"What are you?" she asked.

Sorren recoiled from the woman. What could he possibly say?

Aaarrggh!

"What was that?" exclaimed Rhiannon.

It hadn't come from the stranger; it was the scream of someone being murdered. The rational side of her terror, the one clutching onto the edge of survival, knew that the scream belonged to Terry. Sorren, meanwhile, could hear the slurping of thousands of wet—or partial—feet walking through mud, snow, and filth. For obvious reasons, Sorren had chosen the most remote tavern he could, a place at the southwest fringe of the city limits where none of Vallistheim's celebratory fires would blaze and reveal his monstrousness. He wondered how many dead, shambling persons it would take to conjure that cacophony. Some of Menos? All of

Menos? While Sorren froze, more screams came, some from far away, others from close by. Straining to listen, he heard a parade of evil: flesh ripping, guts splattering snow, wood shattering, people howling as if on fire, women and the youngest of children wailing—their cries cut short as teeth and bony claws ended them. Evil had arrived in Heathsholme. At last, Death's army had begun its march. What of Vortigern, then? As Death's vessel and prisoner, did that mean his brother was here? Would Vortigern be marshaling the horde?

Rhiannon could not yet hear or smell the rancid cloud as it rolled through Heathsholme, bringing with it a thunder of murderous screams and a rain of blood. Rhiannon had used the moments in which the dead man had stalled—busy pondering or some such thing—to smash her stool up into makeshift weapons. She now brandished a jagged stake at the monster before her. Suddenly, she realized he was not the only threat. Something began thudding against the walls. The door behind the bar that led to the storeroom and cellar rattled; but at least it was barred by a sturdy piece of oak, which Rhiannon didn't think would be easy to break. However, the front door was another matter, and she had no idea what lay past the pensive monster in the winter night outside.

"M-move!" she demanded, thrusting her stake as if it were a sword. "I'll drive this right through you, I swear!"

The man wore a look of bleak sadness. "I would welcome that end. If it were time. If I had performed my penance. But I cannot accept your mercy now. I must find my brother. I believe he may be out there. I shall see."

Sorren strode to the door—on either side of it, the shuttered windows started to flap as things pushed against them. Rhiannon realized what waited for her beyond these walls were likely more horrors, more dead, and probably ones less cultured and sorrowful than this fellow.

"W-wait!" she shouted. "You can't leave me here to die!"

Sorren could, and knew he should. He placed his hand on the door, which felt to him like a thick tangle of cotton. Once he pushed it, the creatures on the other side would flood the building. The putrid musk of their rotting bodies, which filled the room like a cabbage-and-sewage fart, suggested there were at least a dozen of them. Rhiannon's odds were grim.

"Please!" she cried.

There was a certain pining sharpness to a woman's speech before she died. Sorren was all too familiar with the sound, and he noticed it now in Rhiannon's voice. His supernatural hearing amplified the agony into a horn of pleading blown into his head, and he buckled. Sorren was a monster; he couldn't feel mercy. Or at least, that was what his rational self told him. However, Sorren's instinct, his black prune of a heart, made a choice for him and moved his body. A gray wind struck Rhiannon, and she lost her grip on her stake. The wind held her in a basket of ice and smelled sweetly of dried herbs and spices. A spike of fearful realization impaled her: it was no loving wind that had spirited her away; rather, she was trapped in the arms of the dead man. Just as she'd begun to thrash, she was half dropped, half eased down onto a bed of snow. Rhiannon struggled to her feet, swatting at the monster who no longer restrained her. The monster had saved her, taken her far from danger, she soon discovered. Her arms, head, and heart fell in despair as she saw what had become of Heathsholme. Faint, she fell against the scratchy bark of one of the dead trees surrounding the snowy summit upon which they stood.

Down below, Heathsholme glowed with more brightness than the brightest Vallistheim Rhiannon could recall. Yet these were not fires of celebration, but of death and horror. Whole fields laid with straw for the festival had been set alight in what seemed like a blasphemous tribute to Vallistheim. Real people, not effigies, now burned in the wild, consuming bonfire that had spread from building to cart to barn. Small shadows ran hither and thither away from larger spots of moving black. Even through the veil of snow and distance, Rhiannon could tell they were people being chased by the dead. Although nothing made sense when the world broke, there were those able to accept madness in their minds, to find the reason in the unreasonable. Rhiannon was one such person. She looked upon the growing, radiant ruin, shed what tears would come, and numbly said goodbye. *Farewell, Heathsholme. Farewell, city of my troubled youth. I did hate thee, but I shall mourn the bright embers of your flame.*

Throughout her somber vigil, the dead man had remained quiet, pondering. He knelt in the snow, stared, sniffed, and read the colors in the kaleidoscopic chaos happening beneath him in the valley.

"Vortigern is not here. I cannot smell him or sense his spirit. I think that Death divides her army. Perhaps many hands are needed to harvest many fields...or perhaps a number of different enemies are out in search of the same spoils...And what of the wolves I'd seen, and their red queen? I sense now that they are another enemy as terrifying and doom-bringing as Death and her brood. I must find Mother, and warn her," he mumbled.

Rhiannon recognized the name the dead man mentioned: the deceased son of the Iron Queen. Losing her slippery hold on sanity, she hugged her prickly tree more tightly. "What is happening?"

Sorren's black gaze was impossible for her to hold. "To the world? I think everyone is being judged. I think the world and its makers are sick of us ruining their creation. I've been responsible for my share of evil. I'm sick of myself." Sorren stood and strode toward the cowering woman. "I need to know where my mother is. I must find her and let her know of the forces I've seen, and of what has happened to her sons."

"Mother?"

"My apologies. There is a great clarity to your colors; I sense that you understand, but do not accept. My mother, Gloriatrix. The Iron Queen."

"In Eod. She's in Eod, I believe."

She was surprised that her mouth moved, as stunned as she felt. Then, the dead man came nearer and nearer; his shadow fell upon her, colder even than the frost and wind. Rhiannon shivered as fear and shock ran through her in wild currents. Was this it? Was she to die? She closed her eyes, and the strangely pleasant spice of the monster was all around her. Then Rhiannon's arms were pried off the tree and a warmth came over her quivering shoulders and head: a cloak. When she peeked again, the dead man was walking down the white hill away from both her and Heathsholme.

"A kindness for a kindness," he said. As she watched, he ripped off his oddly fitting dress and continued on in his ratty jerkin and trousers. He no longer felt the need to conceal his curse in this age of the cursed. "I see that Death arranges her forces. She will push west. She will move to crush all life and to end this war in the only way she understands: through extinction. I must discover why the changelings move south, too. If you wish to live, you should race straight to Eod, which is the only place on Geadhain with walls capable of withstanding an assault from either army. Perhaps I shall see you there, in Eod. Good luck to you, crimson soul. Good luck."

In a twist of snow and wrinkle of gray, he vanished. *Eod*, thought Rhiannon. She didn't stop to cast another prayer for the souls of Heathsholme. Instead, she ran.

XIII

THE EMPRESS

I

Moreth's prediction of a hard day's march proved true. The Amakri tribe hiked from first light until the sun had vanished behind the range that seemed forever out of reach. From there, it cast a haunting purple glow. Night never brought a darkness deeper than that violet, and a Dreamer in the sky scattered the heavens with stars and a captivating, transparent ribbon of many colors that hung, wavering, above them.

"*Fótac Mágissa* (Witch Light)," said Talwyn to his companions.

The scholar often acted as translator for his company and the Amakri, his working knowledge of the Pandemonian language having quickly surpassed Moreth's. Each of Pandemonia's tribes spoke its own dialect, explained Talwyn when making apologies for Moreth's struggle to understand; it seemed that whatever dialect Moreth had learned was not the one used by these people. Similarities existed between all of Pandemonia's tribal dialects, which was how Moreth had understood the few scraps of Doomchaser chatter he'd figured out on his own. But whatever primeval language lay at the root of all Pandemonia's tongues had been obscured by the unique eccentricities and colloquialisms the region's many different tribes had layered onto it; the language's original form had been lost.

"A wonderful jumble of regional linguistic variations have developed over time," proclaimed Talwyn to his vaguely nodding companions.

While Mouse and Moreth had teased Talwyn during the first part of their journey—he was such an easy mark—they'd come to appreciate his intellect, as well as his ability to withstand their friendly teasing. He was eagerly intelligent without being pedantic. Mouse was of the impression that he was genuinely fascinated with the world. Back and forth Talwyn ran, from Amakri to Amakri, chatting. At times, the scholar engaged in long conversations with Pythius, who walked at the head of the caravan. Mouse was curious as to what they spoke about, as it often occasioned laughter and violent—but well-meaning—slaps from the shaman to Talwyn. Watching him absorb himself in the Amakri's alien culture, seeing him dive without fear into the unknown, made Mouse realize he was a braver person than she'd thought.

For these lands were not safe, and those seeking danger would not be disappointed. Across the tundra ran invisible clefts filmed over with a lace of delicate ice and exposed only by slight furrows in the snow that ran in patterns like dried riverbeds. Mouse found it impossible to spot these perils in the snowy wastes, but the Amakri did not, and were able to prevent the companions from tumbling down into the black, echoing crevasses. It was a good thing that Mouse was not responsible for their scouting. She couldn't navigate an area that wasn't made of concrete and iron. More often than not, she became distracted by Pandemonia's cruel beauty, much as she had been similarly preoccupied in Alabion. As they walked under twists of ice arching over the land like bridges made for frost giants, she gawked. As they passed by a herd of white-coated beasts that looked like winged stallions with horned, reptilian heads, Mouse stared in wonder. The herd of horse-lizards wasn't friendly, and the creatures screeched at the sight of the Doomchaser procession. In a cawing flock, they flapped off the icy summit where they'd been perched and flew toward the tribe, but they were startled away by slingshots and three blasts from Pythius's horn—blasts so loud that snow rumbled down the walls of the valley in which the tribe stood. The instrument had to be magikal.

"*Ourliach fricht*," said Talwyn, after running back with information on the beasts told him by Pythius. "'Howling horrors' is the gist of it. Pythius says that they will pick a man clean to his bones, then eat those, too. Like vultures, only they don't care if you're dead."

Excited by this dreadful discovery, Talwyn dashed back into the line of a thousand strong and was quickly lost. Mouse spotted him again only when he had returned to his place up front with the Amakri leader, but it became more difficult to see him as the day grew darker. Although he was such a small distance away, she missed him nonetheless. In fact, she ached for each of her company: Morigan, her great uncle, the Wolf, and her dear Adam. She prayed to the one inside of her that they were safe. Then, while shuffling along and feeling sorry for herself—which she *hated* doing—it dawned upon her that as a vessel, she should be entitled to certain privileges, certain rights. If Feyhazir was free to use her, then he should submit himself to her wishes every so often. He'd done so when he'd disposed of Augustus and the Broker and sent them to their rightful place at the Red Witches' table. *Time for a second favor*, thought Mouse, and she Willed the entity inside of her to awaken. Feyhazir moved like a brewing, rumbling storm in her body and set her nerves alight with strange titillations.

I have a request. I wish to speak with my friend and your daughter, Morigan, as you have done before. Make it happen.

The inner storm grumbled, roiled, and then settled back into sleep. Mouse couldn't tell whether or not it had signaled agreement, but she felt she wouldn't have to wait very long to find out.

II

Under an ethereal ribbon of emerald, gold, and aubergine Witch Light, the procession stopped for the night. They were to bed down on the cold green stone rather than build an encampment. The Amakri used their baggage to make beds and pillows, though many stayed up late and chose to battle in their warrior circles rather than rest around the campfires. Handfuls of Amakri, burdened by packs, left to forage from what seemed a barren land, and somehow they'd return with sticks, fresh water, root vegetables, burnable moss, and other treasures of the land necessary for survival. One group of Amakri, battle-worn and covered in scars beneath their tattoos, left with Pythius to hunt for food in the frozen jungle. As the party marched out, Mouse was surprised to see Talwyn was not in attendance. In a few sands, a pouting Talwyn kicked his way through the camp toward where Mouse and Moreth huddled in their furs, trying to chat away the cold.

"I'm guessing you weren't welcome on the safari?" Moreth laughed.

"*Adýnamo*," whispered Talwyn, flopping down on the ground before the pair. "It means *weak*. Or lame, or skinny...I don't quite have the translation down, but whatever the nuance, it's not a nice thing to be called."

Mouse patted him on the back. "I'm sorry. I can see how hard you try to make yourself useful."

"I *am* useful, dammit!" cried Talwyn, shrugging off her mittened hand.

"Don't go working yourself up about it!" puffed Mouse. She'd tried to be pleasant, but had already exhausted her shallow well of politeness. A thought flashed into her head. "You don't—I mean, you couldn't be interested in that savage?"

Rising to his feet again, Talwyn spoke down to his two companions. "I find Pythius and his people interesting. I believe they have a connection to the land of a kind we in the West have eradicated or forgotten. Now, hand me your pistol, Moreth. I shall show you how *useful* I can be."

Moreth's composure failed when he thought of Talwyn pointing a technomagikal pistol at anything but his own head—and even if Talwyn did that and pulled the trigger, he'd likely only hit enough skull to disfigure himself. Laughing and near tears, Moreth couldn't find words; however, he managed to shake his head.

A fire stirred within Talwyn, and he was suddenly ablaze with something hitherto unseen in him by either companion: a commanding might. "I am the last surviving heir of the Blackmores. I am a lord and master in my own right. I demand that you give me your weapon, or I shall take it from you myself."

Talwyn's ferocity did not waver, and his glare did not soften. Many Amakri paused in their evening rituals to watch the Westerners' altercation. Moreth felt mesmerized by, if unafraid of, Talwyn's sudden change in behavior. The last surviving Blackmore? How had he not thought of that before? If the scholar survived the trip home, he would indeed inherit tremendous wealth and privilege. Although Menos and its resources had been ravaged, the Blackmores held titles in and collected tithes from many bountiful fiefdoms in Central Geadhain. This bastard child—Moreth was familiar with the official line of descent—could well become a new and influential Lord.

Courteous now, Moreth took his pistol from its holster and placed it in the man's waiting hand. Talwyn gripped the weapon securely and cocked it with a flip of his thumb. He seemed as familiar with its use as Moreth was.

"Thank you," said Talwyn, once again humble and unassuming.

As Talwyn scanned the landscape, Mouse and Moreth exchanged gestures and expressions of perplexity. Talwyn knew what they were doing while his back was turned. He understood the experience of being judged and marginalized; he'd been socially ostracized for most of his life. He was a strong man, though, with an impressive tolerance for punishment. Once he'd settled in Riverton, he'd taken long, exhausting hikes and jogs during his time away from research. Morning's red glow would summon him daily to the beaches of the Feordhan, and there he would swim against its mightiest waves. Although he maintained a safe scientific distance from all things, he believed that to effectively analyze life, one needed to experience it to some degree. Pushing his body to certain limits fit within this ethos. Mouse was incorrect in thinking that his body was a gift of genetics and not the result of devotion to rigorous activity. Rarely did he use his flesh for pleasure, as those that appealed to him were hard to find.

As Talwyn contemplated himself and his abilities, he also searched the sharp valleys, snow-gusting plains, and glowing night sky for a target. Then he spotted a flock of black birds—or birdlike things—flying across the ribbon of Witch Light. What they were wasn't as much of a consideration as the distance, the wind, and the velocity of this weapon's fire. Mathematics being one of his many fortes, calculating such details took only a speck—less than a blink. Hand over forearm, he lined up his sight, savoring his mastery of physics. Talwyn took his time before pulling the trigger. While he dallied, he offhandedly spoke to those watching him. Little did he know that he'd now drawn a crowd far greater than his two companions: many Amakri wanted to see why the man was pointing his small metal stick tipped with blue fire at the sky.

"One of my research projects was for Fulminister Arms," he said. "A Menosian company that specialized in firearms much like your pistol, Moreth. Their products were custom crafted and possessed an enhanced technomagikal T-engine chamber that propelled bullets in a straight line, rather than letting them succumb to the laws of gravity and arc downward. They used newfangled, inexhaustible shells, and surely, your pistol is loaded with something along those lines. Otherwise, you would have run out of iron by now, and I've never seen you oil or care for your weapon and its munitions. Therefore, I'm assuming your chamber compresses and crystalizes the moisture and material in the air—microscopic stuff—into a pellet keratinized in magik, which is then fired with a controlled spark of truefire. An elemental gun, not a crude apparatus of hammer and powder. How do I know of this elegant feat of engineering, you may be wondering? Well, I helped design the modern innovations of this technomagik. I'm forced to admit that the term for your chamber and others much like it—'T-engine'—is a legacy of mine. 'Talwynian Engine' would have served just as well, though I suppose that would have been unnecessarily showy. I handled the prototypes more than the others in the laboratory did; most scientists are terribly afraid of guns and hands-on testing. I became rather a good shot. I bet I could have beaten even my ghoulish brother at the Chasing of the Hart—not that I was ever invited to compete..."

BANG!

A flash of blue sparks and flame lit up the camp.

BANG! BANG! BANG!

A couple of shots followed these three. The flock of black things had been flying many hundreds of paces up in the air, so far away that he could not clearly see them. A smile broke his mask of concentration as five shadows dropped out of the formation in the sky, while a sixth wove and spun in a spiral of death, eventually falling to the tundra as well. The Amakri chattered in awe, then cheered and pointed at the scholar. A few muttered "*mágos* (sorcerer)."

Talwyn turned around to hand the smoking pistol back to Moreth, but the Menosian did not immediately reclaim his weapon. "Oh, and forgive me for my outburst. I hate all trappings of status, to be honest. So much responsibility, so many mouths to feed, hands to grease, and ears to please with compliments. Still, I did use the Blackmore name to get my foot in the door with Fulminister. They wouldn't have looked at me otherwise. Augustus would have killed me had he known. Alas, he shan't be killing anyone ever again." He shook the pistol by its grip, as if it were an unwanted thing. "Are you going to take your weapon? I'm quite finished with it."

Finally, Moreth took back his pistol, stowing it away in its holster. Although Moreth wasn't ready to heap the man with compliments, he did say, "Should you need it again, you have only to ask."

"Thank you."

Having proved his point, Talwyn wandered over to the nearest group of Amakri. The tribespeople slapped him about in that rude, friendly way of theirs and no doubt asked him what further wonders he could work.

"That was a surprise," said Mouse.

"Indeed," replied Moreth. "This land is full of wonders and terrors. I am rarely wrong, and yet I have been wrong about Talwyn. He is more of a man and warrior than we have given him credit for. I was much like him, once: trying hard not to be seen as different, but possessed of skills and feelings no others had. The man's mind is staggering. You'd have to be a seasoned huntsman to make those shots. I shall not test my pride by trying to do so myself. And I was lucky to have a father figure who showed me what was and was not important—Talwyn seems to have figured that out without aid, through his own modesty and brilliance."

"A father figure? You mean the man you traveled with before? In Pandemonia?"

"Yes." Moreth looked away from Mouse, his face wrinkled with sadness. "We shall talk about him another time, if you are interested."

Mouse smiled. "We shall have much time to talk, I feel. Our road is by no means out of track. If you'll excuse me, I have an appointment—someone to meet."

"In your sleep?"

Without answering, Mouse lay down on her side and rolled herself up in her cloak. She closed her eyes and played every trick she knew—counting sheep, counting backward, envisioning a serene, breezy plain—to convince her body to sleep. For if there were any way for her to commune with the Daughter of Fate, it would be in the otherworld between here and there, in the gray spaces of Dream. Mouse knew she and Morigan were indeed about to meet when from the depths of her body arose the tickling storm of music and thunder, the presence of the Dreamer. Powerfully and irresistibly, he told her to *sleep*.

III

Morigan and Mouse meet in an endless field of swaying, golden wheat, its waves stirred by breezes that smell of cotton and flowers. No real place could be this serene: the gray-fringed sky and wavering sphere of sun tell the travelers that they are in an illusion constructed of their hearts' desires. Still a great distance apart, the soul sisters spot each other. Because this is a construction of their fantasies, they meet simply by Willing it to be so. They are carried by a wind that coddles them and then deposits them gently upon the ground so that they stand facing each other.

Morigan looks much the same as she did the last time Mouse was with her in the real world. However, in Dream, Mouse can see deeper into the seer's soul—either that, or in this fleshless realm, the silver light bleeding out of Morigan cannot be disguised. Morigan notices a similar red radiance—the auric color of passion, zest, and honor—leaking out of Mouse's hazy figure, and reflects that her friend's truth is very beautiful.

They hug for a while. Even though they have been apart only a few days, the heartache of their separation resonates as if it has been years. Fake sunshine and the heat of their auras make them warm. When they pull apart, each sees the other has been crying.

"Look what I've done to you," teases Morigan. "You're leaking."

Mouse pushes at her friend. "I bloody well missed you. I didn't think I would. I won't say any more about it. Tears are for widows and whimperers. I am neither."

Morigan regains her queenly composure. She takes her friend's hand, and they walk through the luminous fields, inhaling phantom perfumes of earth and freshness, enjoying the sun on their not-quite faces, staring at each other's hues. When they have walked and basked enough, Morigan asks why Mouse is here. "My friend, my sister…I did not think I could be summoned, and yet you have done just that."

"Your father's gift," replies Mouse. "I consider it his penance for using me as he did, for wearing my flesh."

"Explain," demands Morigan, and the light within her rises like a vengeful silver sun.

As Mouse recounts the tale of her strange abduction, her time with the Amakri, and the relic they now seek, Morigan's sun sizzles into a soft frenzy. Still, she manages to restrain her anger.

"My father told me that the three of you had found safe harbor with the ghost men," says Morigan.

"The Amakri—or Doomchasers, rather. It's a bit complicated."

"Isn't everything? Father called them his eldest children; he's been known to come to Geadhain and sow his seed. So it is not beyond the realm of possibility that they are indeed blood relatives of mine, much like the Daughters of the Moon from Alabion." Morigan sighs. "I am angry that my father has kept information from me, that he decided we must be separated. I'd never have made that choice myself, yet...I think he was right to make these choices. Still, I don't know whether my disappointment is his fault or whether we are the ones who err in expecting empathy, mortal empathy, from a creature who is not mortal, a creature who can only emulate and lust after what mortals feel. I have sensed this in my father: longing. How strongly he wishes to understand us, to be one of us, even. There are some barriers, though, that can never be crossed. Hmm...I do not think he means us any harm. Were it not for our separation, as vexing as it is—especially for Caenith, who feels he has failed us—we would not be able to be in two places at once: hunting relics and saving Eatoth."

"Yes!" cries Mouse, and stops walking. "What of the great city?"

"We're not there yet, though it's just on the horizon." Morigan's light flickers with uncertainty. "During our approach to Eatoth, I have seen terrible visions of doom. I have seen a city in flames, its great waterfalls running red with blood. I cannot leave those people to their fate, not when we might have the power to stop it."

They ponder the gloomy, fractured road that leads onward to the unknown. Their moods cause clouds to form in the sky. Looking up at the darkness, and then at each other, they choose to make the most of this moment away from life, war, and responsibility. They will steal this moment of bliss. As they smile, the sky clears.

"How are the others? Thackery? Adam?"

"Have you ever seen a dog that loses his master, then just sits by the door, staring at it? Well, that's Adam at the moment. He's only just returned to his two-legged form. We had a bit of an incident when he stayed in his other skin too long. I sense that he remained a wolf because he was concerned about how he might behave as a man—or perhaps he simply felt less lonely as an animal…As for your great-uncle…"

On they walk through the field of sunshine and dreams, talking as old girlfriends would, laughing hard at things that couldn't possibly be that funny. The Wolf watches from afar—he never leaves his bloodmate to wander alone when they sleep, not anymore. As the women saunter, he keeps his huge, fuming shadow, a wrathful orange-and-red light, pressed low and invisible in the tall grasses. Mouse's explanation of events does not dispel his unease, his suspicions of the Dreamer. To divide a pack, for whatever reason, is to weaken it. Although he does not have much of an understanding of Dreamers' behaviors, instinct tells him that these creatures do not act with compassion or kindness any more than lions pity the prey whose bones they snap. For now, the Wolf will play the patient hunter: watching, holding his tongue, and biding his time. If the Dreamer betrays them a second time, he will have a new enemy to hunt.

IV

When the procession shuffled to life the next morning, Talwyn remained at the rear with his companions. The glaring sun painted him in a fresh and red-cheeked light. Mouse, too, appeared refreshed, as if she'd somehow had an invigorating sleep on the hard, frosted rock. Moreth found the pair of them insufferable until the kinks finally worked their way out of his back. Age was catching up with him, despite the excellent physical conditioning that wealth had afforded him in the Iron City. He no longer enjoyed such advantages, and he wondered how many years more he could squeeze out of his body before decrepitude, bone decay, and organ failure began to set in. Creaking bones would be the first sign. His father had been stricken by rheumatism just before all the organ transplants and grafts had been rejected by his body.

They continued on through the windy desert of snow until the sun crawled over the sapphire claws of the mountains. The great mountains caught the interest of the three and pulled them out of their spells. After a time, they realized they were all staring at the same landmarks.

"Not everything is impermanent in Pandemonia," croaked Talwyn, his voice rusted and dry. He cleared his throat. "There are the Great Cities, and there are places such as this belt of rock where the seasons change more slowly and according to more modulated cycles. *Idrytikó Aspídar*: the Founding Shield." Talwyn scuffed his feet in the snow until green land appeared beneath his heel. "Pythius tells me that the stone here never changes, not even when the earth's skin melts or when potholes of fire appear. The mountains toward which we're headed are also unchanging, their bones eternal. *Pántus Pétrix*... the Forever Stones. That's why the tribe wanders these regions, because patterns underlie their apparent chaos. Pythius suggests that Feyhazir left the relic here because it would not be destroyed or lost over time."

Talwyn studied the roughly triangular mountains, which bristled with frozen jetties and barnacles of ice like the shells of monstrous crustaceans. He tried to imagine what they would look like in a warmer season. Moreth had no difficulty creating an image of a verdant, mossy range with glass veins of clear water and deep woods in which howling, swooping horrors made a feast of any creature lured into the dark, lush realm. It was understandable that he hadn't at first recognized the place; he'd been there only once, during a time of green fertility. It was there he had met the love of his life and suffered the loss of his dearest friend. Moreth thought of Beatrice—trying to erase her screeching fanged face from his memory—and felt the slave's talisman suddenly dig into his breastbone. A reminder, or a warning. He had never thought he would see this place again.

"Some horrible monsters live there, I'm told," said Talwyn. "We'll have to be on our guard."

"What sort of monsters?" asked Mouse.

"The kind that eat flesh and giblets, raw. The worst kind of carnivore." Talwyn tried to call up the proper phrase. The Amakri had so many names for the beasts: dark mothers, blood sisters, wailing women.

"*Leannan Shide*," said Moreth, beating the scholar at the game. "Blood eaters."

He stared at the mountains and would say no more.

V

A shield of maroon clouds sealed away the stars that night. Soon it would storm, but the procession had covered a great deal of ground by not stopping to rest. They had already reached the foothills of the Forever Stones: slabs of rock that jutted against each other like shattered glass and were covered in treacherous ice. By the light of torches, the Amakri made their encampment in the last of the snowy dunes and green slate that lay before the daunting mountains. They would go no farther now. It was not safe to travel closer to the Forever Stones by night—or so warned Talwyn, on behalf of the Amakri shaman.

Mouse, Moreth, and Talwyn were left to assemble their own shelter for the night, and although theirs was the final tent to be erected and was so flimsy that it shook, they celebrated their victory with congratulations and cold handshakes. Together, these strangers in a strange land were making progress. After their fur carpets and bedrolls had been set up, they took a breath, fought the desire to simply lie down and sleep, and went to find some food. Amakri hospitality appeared to have run its course, and no one had brought them a meal in days. Apparently, they were part of the tribe now and could fend for themselves.

Outside in the brewing storm, they stayed close, battled flurries and winds that slipped beneath their clothing, and sought the nearest campfire. A few Amakri had gathered at the fire pit they stopped by. The men and women nodded respectfully and made room for the travelers on the stones that had been hauled up for seats. Mouse laughed to herself at the notion of lifting frozen hunks of rock after a nearly twenty-hourglass march. She found it incredible how much these people accomplished in the course of a day: hiking, hunting, moving an entire colony of hundreds.

"*Fáok*." (Eat.)

Bowls of sloshing, steaming stew were thrust into their hands by the squatting giantess bundled in white who tended the foodstuffs by the fire. Talwyn hunched precariously on a stone too tiny for his lanky self and tried to balance his food without splashing it. Mouse and Moreth shared a stone, and once the woman had finished passing out food, she waddled over and wedged herself into the space between them. Mouse and Moreth were perfectly willing to accommodate her, especially when they realized that her girth and bow-legged stride were signs she was pregnant. In uncomfortably close quarters, they slurped the Amakri stew, which was always pleasing, if slightly different from day to day depending on what ingredients had been hunted and foraged. Tonight, the meat was beefy, the fat as buttery as caviar, and the spices mostly salt. Mouse, Moreth, and the Amakri woman all finished and sighed at the same time, then laughed at the coincidence. The woman stood, collected the bowls of the others in a stack, and then rubbed her stomach.

"*Eíthex nae eínai mae ischyrí drákos, me megáli kérata, kai oh klímaches tou sidírou—nen eínae mae apó klomó, adýnamo dérmae, ópos aftést agnóstou* (May you be a strong wyrm, with great horns and scales of iron—not one of pale, weak skin like these strangers)," she said.

This caught Talwyn's attention, and he looked up from his meal and tripped his way through an exchange with the woman. What was at first a calm discourse soon turned into an argument, which ended abruptly when the woman threw down the wooden bowls and left in a clatter and a fury.

"You pissed her right off," said Mouse. "What did you say?"

Around the fire, some of the other Amakri were now glaring at Talwyn and shaking their heads, further chastising him, though not as angrily as the woman had. Without replying to Mouse, Talwyn abandoned his meal and walked over to the more moderate tribesmen. With them, he attempted to ingratiate himself in his hapless way—which Mouse was starting to realize might be somewhat affected—and made apologies for his Western assumptions. Within sands, the Amakri were patting him, smiling, nodding, and telling him everything they knew.

Talwyn returned to his companions. He took the angry Amakri's vacant spot and sat down in a huff. "I didn't know whether I had heard her correctly," he said. "I believe she was praying for a child with horns and scales and without our pale, weak skin; she made the latter characteristic sound quite undesirable."

"What's wrong with being like us?" spat Mouse.

"Well, what we consider normal doesn't pass muster here in Pandemonia," replied Talwyn. "Afterward, when I asked her what she meant, she said they placed such children 'into the cruel hands of fate.' I thought she must mean that these unfortunates are cast out into the wild—you know, as is done with the unwanted young women of the Arhad. Those girls are called *khek*, a word also used to describe the shite ejected from a spinrex's arse. They're thrown out of the tribe and left to wander the desert until they die. Aside from the legendary sword of the queen, I've never heard of such a one surviving."

"Awful," whispered Mouse.

"It is," agreed Talwyn. "However, although the Amakri are strong and proud, they are not cruel. The cruelty comes from those who judge from circles of wisdom and privilege; Lakpoli, the city-dwelling Pandemonians, are the 'cruel hands of fate' to which Temupka, our expectant mother, was referring. Having to give up her child, even a weak one born without valuable traits, would be devastating for her. I was a villain for even suggesting such children might be exposed, cast out to die. They are placed under the care of the Lakpoli, as the way of the Amakri would be too rough for a hornless, soft creature to endure. It's seen as a mercy, as the children are saved a life of hardship. I shall have to find Temupka and make an apology."

Kreeech!

The sudden sound was like a sword scraped over slate, and surely came from the mouth of a horror. "Blood eaters," Moreth hissed, leaping up. Panic broke out in the camp. Moreth barked a flurry of warnings at his stunned companions. "Whatever you do, be still and calm. Blood eaters' extreme hunger and lives lived in darkness blind them. They can hear, smell, and taste our fear as it boils through our veins. Our heartbeats and footsteps are hammers upon a metal dinner plate to them—and even a scratch from one of their infernal claws can end you with a fever worse than the ancient plague of Menos. Stay close. They take the weak and isolated. They seek the straggling, lonely prey. We need to be calm, like these brave warriors. We must stand together. We must still our hearts, hold our breathing. We must become the snow and silent winter. They will reveal themselves when the night is still."

KREECH! KREECH! KREECH!

What discordant music the monsters made: singing with the wind, calling to each other. The companions sensed the grating hunger in their pitch, the need to feed. Pythius's magik horn would not deter these beasts, Moreth knew. Their hunger would stop only when they had gorged themselves on fresh red meat.

"I believe it's time for me to borrow one of your pistols," whispered Talwyn.

In a flash, the pistol was in the scholar's hand, cocked and loaded. Moreth gritted his teeth and also readied a pistol. Mouse felt less confident than her fellows. She possessed only a shiny new dagger taken from the *Skylark*'s armory, and it already felt slick in her hand. Although she had the power of a Dreamer within her, he hadn't been much use so far. Nonetheless, she doubted that Feyhazir would let her die. While Amakri scattered for their weapons, the three moved in a tight circle, eyes and weapons aimed toward the twisting sky that echoed with cries. The storm chose this moment to roar, and a white whirlwind descended from above. Within the pale nimbus flickered shadows, darting glints of black that moved as erratically and quickly as schools of ebon minnows. *Those can't possibly be creatures*, thought Mouse. But she was wrong. Moreth immediately fired a couple of shots into the storm; he may even have hit a monster or two, as the sky fell silent. They waited. Nearby, the Amakri, no longer panicking, crouched low upon the ground in the white coats that made them indistinguishable from the snow.

KREECH! KREECH! KREECH!

An inky streak shot from the heavens, touched down for an instant, and then took off again in a puff of snow and black smoke. Whatever the creature was, it moved so fast that it left a trail, a dark smear, in the air. Mouse heard a yelp to her left, and noticed that the white-cloaked man many paces beside her had disappeared—snow still whirled up from the ground marking his absence. Then, his screams rang with the thunder in the storm. By the Kings, he'd been snatched up as if tied to the end of a string. Gone. The blood eaters' cries came again, their throats warbling with gory sustenance. Mouse thought of running for their tent, but she would not leave her companions, Moreth had warned her against running, and the distance between her and the tiny brown dome now felt unbridgeable.

Kreech! Kreech! Kreech!

The world collapsed into terror. All over the encampment, dark comets streaked to and from the earth, causing explosions and noiseless ruffles of sonic force. One, two, ten...Mouse lost count amid the zigzagging confusion. The snowy eruptions and disorienting screams inspired panic in the usually unshakeable Doomchasers. Men and woman who risked being cast out of the tribe for their cowardice ran for the perceived safety of their tents. With a grim calm, Moreth watched as they were pulled into the sky like naughty marionettes.

"Don't run," he whispered with disdain. "Never run. Their thinning of the herd is almost over. Soon they will come for the strong."

They huddled closer. Either Mouse or Talwyn had grabbed the other's hand; they didn't know who had initiated the gesture, though it gave them each strength. The three bated their breath and watched as the storm of black lightning slowed, then stopped. On high, the grisly tearing and screams of the dying ended on a whimpering note. At last from the night came a satisfied cawing and the leathery whoosh and flapping of many great wings. The blood eaters returned for more.

Elegantly, the horrors descended and circled the quiet encampment, where at least a thousand warriors and children stayed motionless as rabbits beneath a great flock of owls. The monsters cawed lazily. Lower and lower they drifted, and the shadows slunk away, revealing forms horrible to behold. Mouse, though, frozen with shock, found herself staring into the face of one that breezed over her: a glowing white countenance with eyes and hair of misty blackness, and the mouth of a lamprey eel. Mouse swore she saw the orifice pucker inward and become an anus ringed with razor teeth. *That's where the meat goes to get squished and chewed into pâté*, her mind shrieked.

Suddenly, the head snapped toward her, and Mouse's heart lurched. Mid-flight, the creature paused, effortlessly hovering while flapping its tattered and fuming wings—nightmare appendages that seemed too thin, slow moving, and ethereal to support real flight. The blood eater made a sensual gurgle and uncurled its shrimplike, emaciated body that was jutting with bones. It clacked its black talons and toenails as if in delight. The creature drifted nearer, spiraling down toward them like a demonic snowflake, spreading its lanky mass and smoking wings as if to embrace her. No. *It cannot see me,* Mouse told herself. It sensed only her heartbeat and fear. Or perhaps it sensed something else...Was that an expression of happiness distorting its hideous, puckered face? Mouse cast off the impression. Indeed, her fancies disintegrated as the acidic wave of the creature's stench drew nearer: the reek of rot, death, and oniony filth. Mouse noticed the butcher's apron of blood spattering the creature and began to gag.

Kreeeech?

It had heard that. The vulture talons reached down—

Pppft!

An Amakri spear pierced the side of the blood eater, and it turned into a black, blurred, shrieking frenzy. Pythius's horn blasted the night, and the Amakri sprang up, hurling spears and throwing nets upon the shadows hovering around the encampment. Moreth and Talwyn heeded the call and opened fire upon the thrashing shape above them, riddling it with a volley of blue fire. The blood eaters' cries of gluttonous ecstasy became shrieks that tore into the ears of the defenders. The blood eater above them dropped with a squealing thud, and Moreth and Talwyn—still holding onto Mouse—ran to the downed beast to finish it. Speared and broken, it continued to drag itself like a dog with two broken legs, leaving a bloody trail through the snow. Its wings flickered like burning paper and added gobs to the ebony drool left by its wounds. As they caught up to the monster, it turned its head toward its attackers and gave infuriated screeches. Then it made a disturbing mewl as its black pearl stare fell upon Mouse. There were slits in its eyes, and they expanded, lovingly.

"In the head," said Moreth. "Shoot it in the head."

The men peppered the creature's skull with bullets, and it slumped and curled up into a smoldering coil. The corpse hissed with foul vapors and within instants had dissolved into a slop of quivering black goo. The three had watched the dissolution with a macabre fascination, but they quickly pulled their eyes away from the spectacle. However, the Amakri had already seen to the security of their people. Warriors could be spotted stomping and spearing entangled blood eaters, or dancing back from the running decay of the monsters' bodies. The three sighed in relief, but soon realized their victory had been a hollow one, for they heard sobbing and moans as the Amakri mourned their dead.

"It was all so fast..." whispered Mouse.

"They may come again," said Moreth. "Usually, the first wave is sent only to test the strength of a herd of prey. More of them will have been held in reserve—one hundred times the number we've seen. A hive of the things."

"How do you know so much about these horrors?" she asked.

As they'd come so far together, and now trusted each other with the most dangerous of secrets, Moreth shared one of his. "I married one."

Before anyone could think of a reply, Pythius arrived. Fast as changelings, he and a band of warriors had sped through the encampment to reach them. The half-naked shaman looked wild-eyed. In one hand, he held his horn and in the other, a weapon that seemed birthed of a cleaver and a sword—possessing the blade of the former and the handle of the latter. The shaman's weapon dripped blackness, and he and his warriors were spattered with the death of the blood eaters.

"*Dýsi Touílio! Skáfos Feyhazir!* (West Sun! Vessel of Feyhazir!)" he called.

Reaching them, Pythius tucked his horn into his waist, threw his weapon straight into the frozen ground—where it hummed and did not move—and then examined Talwyn and Mouse. Pythius made no concessions to modesty, feeling the two from cranny to crevice for injury. Secretly, Talwyn enjoyed the attention, particularly as Pythius had examined him first, before turning to the sacred vessel. One had to relish the finer moments in life, because the rest of it seemed to be monster-hunting and doom. Once they had passed his rough physical examination, he addressed the scholar: "*Isoun apospástike íe danchotheí?*" (Were you clawed or bitten?)

"*Ochi.*" (No.)

"*Kalóc. Afis tous eínaa dilitírio.*" (Good. Their touch is poison.)

As the shaman turned to Moreth, Talwyn confirmed that he, too, was uninjured, figuring he would be a less cooperative patient.

"*Prostimo, Sou écho empistosýni* (Fine, I trust you)," said Pythius, and strode past the three to the pool of ichor behind them. "*Thae to ékan aftó?*" (You did this?)

"*Emes.*" (We.) Talwyn pointed to Moreth and then tapped the pistol that he held, which continued to flicker with sapphire flames until he clicked the hammer off. Pythius watched the flame go out and gasped.

"*Mágos* (Sorcerer)," said the shaman. "*Ákousa t̪is dýnam̪ís sas s̪ímera to pro̪í, kai den pistéyoun. Eínae énas mágos, pára polý?*" (I heard of your power this morning, and did not believe. Is he a sorcerer, too?) Pythius nodded to Moreth.

"*Den eínai arketá.*" (Not quite.)

"*Deíxe mou, enó̪ échoume t̪in tás̪i na to travmatíes.*" (Show me, while we tend to the wounded.)

Talwyn turned to his companions, who had been unable to follow this exchange. "I have been asked to help, though I think the invitation extends to all of us."

They would help, and then they would talk: of blood eaters and of the man who had married a monster. As they were leaving, Moreth glanced back at the liquid corpse and spat upon it.

VI

Moreth's story would have to wait until the encampment had once again been made secure, however. That eve, a host of scowling, spear-gripping Amakri camped outside and watched the skies. The warriors made silent prayers for the wounded whose cries pained their ears. It was in the dark incense-clouded tents that the three strangers from Central Geadhain were most needed, and they spent their evening tending to the gasping, thrashing souls who had been clawed and bitten by the blood eaters.

Mouse and Moreth weren't unaccustomed to grisly battlefield wounds, and they soon learned that Talwyn had spent six months or thereabouts as a surgeon. He had still been deciding on his vocation, he said, though his listeners wondered whether any one cerebral pursuit in all of Geadhain could actually satisfy a man of his intellect. He was a genius, Mouse realized, a miracle worker when it came to medicine. Like many such folk, though, he wanted none of the prestige and attention that came with his gift.

At ease in a crisis, the scholar made tourniquets to stop the spread of blood-eaters' venom. With herbs taken from Pythius's collection, he boiled remedies to sedate his patients, attempting to recreate treatments he'd known in the West. Doctor Talwyn and his Western assistants did the impossible: they saved a handful of Amakri from the screaming death of blood-eater fever. However, survival often came at a cost: even those who'd been lightly grazed could be saved only through the excising of large hunks of tissue from in and around affected areas.

In some cases, a patient could be saved only if one or more of his limbs were amputated. This might affect the tribesperson's pride and harm his standing with his people, but Talwyn didn't care, and he didn't ask. Grim Pythius, who assisted with the bloody surgeries, offered no information on the topic. Once the dissolving, rotten flesh—that resembled the blood puddings Talwyn had once enjoyed but never would again—had been removed, Amakri disposed of the putrid matter by burning it in the fires. Thick smoke and the smell of seared compost soon filled the encampment, but in time the screaming subsided. Those who could not be saved, who far outnumbered those who could, were given a terminal dose of Talwyn's *other* medicine.

This drink was boiled in the largest lidded cauldrons available. It smelled of ether and pine. Inhaling its fumes from a rag would cure all aches; drinking a thimbleful of the liquid was enough to stop one's heart. Within instants of coughing the liquid down, men, women, and children would close their eyes and sink into unconsciousness as their gelatinous bodies were brought toward the great pyre now burning in the center of the camp. Into that belching inferno the dead were cast. Those Amakri not busy caring for the ill or watching the sky sang beautiful, hard-throated songs and made music with rattles and hide drums. Once or twice, when the shaman wasn't around, the companions thought they heard Pythius's horn sounding notes that evoked the long, sad cry of a deep-sea king. They weren't always certain where the shaman was—where anyone was—as a sweaty haze obscured their surroundings.

As the sun rose, as red and angry as the souls of those who wouldn't rest, the great labor at last came to an end. Talwyn, Moreth, and Mouse became aware of their surroundings again, and stood outside of the tents. They'd been watching the whorls in the twisting pyre as if counting the wailing spirits within; they couldn't say for how long they'd stood there.

Their sleeves were rolled up, and they were covered in blood and oils. Although they were without their cloaks, they were warmed by the pyre's rage.

"*Fáoch ka freskada.*" (Food and freshness.)

Temupka had approached them soundlessly and now stood beside them with two peace offerings: in one hand, she held a handled pot of stew with three ladles sticking out, and in the other, a bowl of rags, melted snow, and rock salt for washing themselves. Talwyn and the others accepted the items, and he gave Temupka a nod, which she returned. Their feud now apparently over, the pregnant woman wandered back to the pyre, took up a drum, and shuffled her feet to the music. The companions, tired as they were, still weren't ready to move; their minds were still processing all they'd seen. Moreth stood soberly, while Mouse leaned on Talwyn—each of them watched the dancing, and the whirling twists of ash and smoke that rose to the skies.

"I am sorry for what I said, Talwyn—all of it," apologized Mouse, gripping the pot tightly, gazing at her bloodless knuckles. "You're quite possibly one of the most useful people I've ever known."

"Exactly how smart are you?" Moreth asked, flatly; the question felt overdue.

"I don't know quite how to answer that," replied Talwyn, blushing. "I'm sensitive to too many things in life. I see too much. I hear too much. I imagine if I had Caenith's senses, I would've killed myself long ago; what I know is already a burden. I wish I could turn it off, the machine in my head, but I can't; I simply cannot stop absorbing information, no matter how I try.

"I also am incapable of ceasing to analyze, to parse, to understand completely. Everything I see, I can't help seeing in terms of probabilities, expressions of physical laws, arrangements of atoms—and the intersections of all these and every other force working in or on people and things. Perhaps that's why my personal relationships have mostly been in the dumps; at least, they were until I began traveling with persons equally, if differently, as strange as I am. For one cannot view a comrade, a friend, as an object and hope to develop healthy attachments. Both of you are unique enough to stand out from others of your species—which has made it easier for me to react to you as though you're more than your parts and processes." Talwyn frowned. "Which, of course, you are. That sounds horrible and cold, sorry."

It sounds extraordinary, thought Moreth. "What do you see right now? Tell me."

And so summoned, the machine in Talwyn's mind and soul took the reins. Gazing at Moreth, he saw an unshaven man, clinging to refinement, and, past that, a spiderweb of pink veins around the master's eyes that to some would indicate fatigue, but to Talwyn spoke of fleshcrafting abuse. Quite often, the facial musculature was replaced as men aged and the re-suturing to the skin occurred at set points that caused specific vascular patterns—usually around the eyes and the interior of the mouth. While Talwyn hadn't seen many examples of fleshcrafting in the living, he'd seen such irregularities once while autopsying the corpse of a Menosian diplomat. It'd been poison that killed the diplomat, and such murder had been brought about by one of his Ironguards. In time, Talwyn had identified the cause of death—bloodlily powder—as well as the culprit. For the poisoner, even if wearing gloves and a mask both during and in preparation for the act, would've still suffered from mild exposure to the poison, which was so fine a dust that it spread even when conscientiously handled. Further, bloodlily of any dosage left a telltale darkness around the eyes, as well as made the gums bleed, slightly—a cough, too, would wrack anyone that came in contact with this poison. Talwyn had read the symptoms in a book once, and that fact had embedded itself into his brain—along with every other fact he'd ever learned. During the autopsy, the guilty soldier had been gloomily staring at Talwyn with his charcoal-sunken eyes and repeatedly stifling a cough. In a bit of black Menosian humor, Talwyn had told the young man, "Smile, it's not your autopsy," which had made the soldier nervously grin. Right after noticing the soldier's raw, red gums, he'd asked the young man, politely, "Why did you murder him?" Trapped and stunned, the soldier had confessed in that very room and turned himself over to the Iron marshal in attendance.

"Hold on a speck. What were you doing in the Eastern Front in the company of a Menosian diplomat and an Iron marshal—while working as a field surgeon?" interrupted Mouse.

"A story for another day, my dear."

Part of his curse, Talwyn continued, was that he only needed to see, smell, read, touch, *experience* something once to remember it. Therefore, he knew that Mouse had stubbed her left largest toe three days, sixteen hourglasses, and eight sands past, even though she'd completely forgotten both the pain and the incident.

Likewise, he could use his incredible cognition and ever-growing store of information to accurately deduce historical facts out of present circumstances. For example, as he stared out into the winter waste beyond the Doomchaser camp, from the data and geological patterns he'd observed, he overlaid this time and place with a mesh-framework of warmer seasons: of forests, of grand rocks that had since tumbled into tiny piles, and of great animals striding terrain—creatures reconstructed like wire-form figures in his mind from the bones and beasts he'd known. Talwyn explained all this to his awestruck companions much more slowly than it arose in his mind; to speak as fast as he thought would've made for an unintelligible screech.

"Good Kings!" Mouse gasped.

"Eidetic and a savant of all sciences. Astonishing," exclaimed Moreth. Talwyn blushed from head to toe, and began to wilt in response to their awe at his abilities. "You have my admiration and respect, which are not easily given. I can see you're not one for flattery or vanity, however, so I shall leave the matter be."

"Thank you," said Talwyn, and began to walk. Quietly, he added: "I am glad to have met others for whom my curiousness doesn't offend. I do not think myself above man. Indeed, until all of this extraordinary madness began, I was very lonely."

"Well, you're not now," said Mouse, patting him on the back. "You're the kind of friend I've always wanted. One day, good friend, we need to hit up a betting house and use those skills of yours to rob everyone down to their knickers. Our stew will be quite cold by now. We should head inside."

The company somberly greeted the weary Doomchasers they passed. Travelers and Doomchasers now looked on each other with both understanding and admiration. The strangers had been through battle with the tribe, had lent their knowledge and skills to the community; they were now fellow warriors, bound together with blood. The three walked past Pythius, who was sitting on a stone and explaining to a group of young Amakri where the spirits of their parents had gone. Talwyn and the shaman exchanged glances, a substitute for the conversation that would come when the mourning had ended.

Once back in the soothing darkness of their tent, the men turned their backs to Mouse, undressed, and washed the sour death off their bodies. Temupka, or some other thoughtful Amakri, must have been by, for on the floor lay three bedrolls, upon each of which had been placed a stitched white garment. The three changed into the highlander-styled shifts, which were something like a shirt and a skirt in one and were tied with corded belts. Now dressed, warm, and feeling the pull of exhaustion, the companions rested their heads on their bedrolls and closed their eyes. Sleep wouldn't come to any of them, but they were happy to snatch a moment's peace. After a time, the waft of the stew they'd brought woke their aching bodies, and they sat up and had a cold meal.

"Quite a night," said Moreth, throwing his ladle into the empty pot.

Talwyn sent his utensil clattering into the pot, too. "Although it's been an exhausting day, I think it's time we heard about your wife, and about your travels in Pandemonia."

"Mine is not a love story," warned Moreth. "It is a tale of blood, lust, and hunger."

"I like it already," said Mouse, tossing in her ladle. "Go on, regale us. Leave nothing out. We'll decide what's important and what isn't."

Regale you, thought Moreth. Tales of his time in Pandemonia—of almost any point in his life, for that matter—would disgust any reasonable audience. Mouse and Talwyn, however, had just carved jellied rot off screaming invalids and administered elixirs of death with steady hands. They could handle the truth of his past. "As you know, Mouse, I was a malcontent as a young man. I was a master with too much wealth and ambition, and nothing in the Iron City could sate my desires. Elsa, my mother, ended her life with narcotics. I don't know if she did so intentionally, and I can't blame her if that was the case. Father had finally passed, and the reins of the estate had suddenly been handed to me...I had the world at my fingertips..."

The parties had been exhausting, but nothing like his father's soirees of blood and debauchery. Civilized affairs of string music, dancers, and artists had allowed Moreth to celebrate the death of the foul tyrant who'd spawned him. Father had never allowed proper art—works that were not cast-iron statues of slaves or portraits of himself—in the house, and so Moreth had filled the estate with such creations once he was free of his father's vicious influence. After a time, however, his parties had begun to disappoint the Menosian aristocrats, who were bored by the lack of sex torture and death. Fewer and fewer of them attended his events; his false friends vanished. However, he often saw their slavering faces below the city at the Blood Pits, which he now owned. In his new position of power, Moreth presided over these contests; after a time, he realized the sounds of gristle tearing, men choking, and men screaming had become as pleasing to his ear as the strains of violin music that accompanied his lonely dinners. Brutality could be viewed as an art, if one could achieve the necessary perspective.

Moreth found he liked the new dualities in his nature: he was both cultured and monstrous, manly and effeminate. His father had been only black, but Moreth could embody all the shades of gray, which seemed a far better way to live. And so he'd existed in a blissful state of contrasts for many years. Increasingly reclusive, he spent most of time at home, reading, listening to music, cultivating his senses—and emerging only to visit the Blood Pits. Once a month or so, he summoned a pleasure maiden—or two, or three—or perhaps a man. A kind master, he would allow them to spend the night in luxury, swaddled in silk sheets and glutted with venison, before sending them home with twice their pay. Of course, the extra coin was mostly to quiet any concerns they might have about the bruises and markings that were the outward signs of his curious sense of sexuality—for there could be no true pleasure without pain. In his cellar, he'd built a grand padded room that housed an assortment of instruments that looked made for torture but were softened by rubber tips. In it could also be found great harnesses of chains with fishhooks as small as children's earrings. Often his memories of the glistening, moaning passion, the darkness on the border between desire and agony, were what oiled his rod on the many nights he slept alone. The thought of gloved fingers entering—

"Oh dear," exclaimed Mouse, fanning herself.

"You said I should tell you everything," replied Moreth. "You must understand my tastes if you are to understand me."

"Naturally," said Talwyn.

"Then there's Beatrice," Moreth continued. Taking a deep breath, he lay down upon his roll and looked up toward the place where the bones of the tent met. "You've seen her kind. I'm sure you can imagine her tastes."

Mouse and Talwyn shared a shiver.

"We'll speak of my wife later; there's more for you to hear of my time in Menos," said Moreth.

Boredom had set in for young Moreth, and he now found himself disillusioned by the creative sex and art that had once brought him such pleasure. Before he'd turned to tearing paintings and shooing naked, bloody whores from his manor, he'd tried to engage his interest through other activities. He'd taken up shooting and learned he was a deadly shot. Each week, he'd hired a swordsman to teach him the art of fencing, though he always ended up dismissing these fools once his skills had surpassed theirs. He then sought other tutors who could instruct him in the arts of war. Although he could not predict his future—no men, save the children of the House of Mysteries, could—these experiences were calculated to lead him down one road, to one destined calling: there was something in this world that he must hunt if he were ever to feel complete.

As this hidden awareness grew, he spent more time in the Blood Pits and even swam in the shark pool of Menosian politics. Politicians were easy prey, and melted like buttered toffee when they encountered his clever, educated mind that made a game of tactics and warfare. Moreth played the game to win. He caressed the necessary egos and genitals, killed whatever weaker animals stood between him and his goals, and within months had secured for himself his father's old seat on the Council of the Wise. One day, Gloriatrix herself had summoned him to her austere, gleaming office and congratulated him on his game. She told him that she saw in him something that reminded her of herself. Then he was dismissed, but the seeds of an alliance had been sewn that day.

But alas, despite all these games, his ennui persisted: none of these hunts truly succeeded in rousing him. None of his prey was exactly right. He hadn't found what he needed to achieve satisfaction. Perhaps no such thing existed on Geadhain, and he should settle into the sickening routines of his father. Maybe that was why Father had surrendered to his vices—he knew that life was meaningless and devoid of any real passion. As an Iron Sage and a man of fantastic wealth, there shouldn't have been anything in life that Moreth couldn't obtain. Except happiness: that elusive feeling that neither money nor influence could buy. So it was the hunt for happiness that at last inspired him. He would seek to acquire that which was most unattainable in life, that which his father and most Menosians failed to capture despite their outrageous power.

Would love make him happy? For a while, he tried to answer this question by laying with peasants and duchesses, as many varieties of woman as he could, but he found all Menosian women drab and power-hungry—even the ugly, even the bland. When he had reached the lowest rung on his ladder of shame, he shopped the flesh markets for a bride stolen from one of Geadhain's other realms. Sadly, they were all too terrified and covered in shite and filth for him to give them any serious consideration. Life was not a faery tale: one couldn't make a lady out of a toad. They were all such unformed clay, these women. They were all savage, and not in the way Moreth wished them to be—two-natured, as he was.

One day, feeling hopeless, he bought a dark-haired, full-busted woman and brought her home. Something about her intrigued him: although she was a savage, she didn't quiver or show overt signs of indecency. However, once clean and put in a dress, she behaved like a developmentally challenged adult. She clanged her cutlery awkwardly on his cherished silverware before picking up her quail, tearing it apart, and stuffing pieces of it into her mouth. The sound of her uncultivated chewing nearly drove him to fetch his pistol and end this cruel charade. Instead, he brought her to his crimson-leather room.

Even there, she was an awful disappointment: she refused to cry out, to whimper, to tease him with her suffering. Neither whips nor hooks nor thrashings from a chain drew from her anything more than the occasional grunt. At one point, as he sweated with frustration and paused to catch his breath, the chained slave gazed at him with eyes wide and full of pity. "You poor, sad, broken man," her expression seemed to say. Angry both at himself and at this defiant and saintly woman, Moreth flew into a rage and beat her. After his state of murderous intoxication had passed, he found she lived, but barely. The woman's face, body, and undergarments were all red. She reminded him of mad Ingray from the opera. Somehow, she still managed not to cry out. She would not be broken. Moreth fell and wept, for he realized he'd become his father.

He carried the shattered slave upstairs. He screamed for his servants and ordered them to fetch a fleshcrafter who could make this woman beautiful once more, and then to feed her, clothe her, and hire the finest tutors to educate her. *I am not my father*, he declared to himself. After she had been healed, she would work at his estate. If she were placed elsewhere, perhaps back with the slavemongers in the meat market, her fate would be worse than what he had almost visited upon her. She would live and serve and remind him each day how close his soul had flitted to the darkness.

Mouse leaned in, trembling and enraptured. "What happened to her? The woman?"

"Her name was Elsa," replied Moreth. "I named her after my mother. In order to be a free citizen of Menos, one must first be a citizen of Central Geadhain. Through a series of fortunate circumstances, which I'll discuss in due time, she inherited the Brennoch surname, which belongs to an old lineage of the West. Otherwise, Elsa would have had no family name. None of the people from Pandemonia hold surnames—as I'm sure you've noticed, Talwyn."

"She was a native of this land?" exclaimed Talwyn.

"Indeed," replied Moreth. "Here, each person is known only by one word that reflects the passion of their soul. I'd say her word was mercy. She reminded me not to become a wanton monster like my father. She knew what I had done to her, and yet she treated me with politeness, even respect after a time. I did not understand forgiveness and compassion until she showed them to me. She learned our customs, our language, and lived and worked as a servant on my estate for all her years, until she and her husband—my valet—passed. Her daughter, a dark and comely lass, continued her mother's work, and I arranged for her brother to join the Iron military."

"Wait. However did she cross Geadhain to end up in a Menosian slave market in the first place?" asked Talwyn.

"Meat market," corrected Moreth. "She had been one of a hundred savages caught trying to sail up the Feordhan—Kings only know where they were headed, likely somewhere in the Northlands. Elsa never spoke of the journey, refused to speak of it, in fact. Naturally, our spies in Riverton informed us of the strange vessel long before it escaped the Feordhan and penetrated the Northlands. The Ironguard caught the longboat near Blackmore, then burned it and flew the slaves straight to the Iron City."

"Ghastly how we treat people in this supposed age of enlightenment." Talwyn sighed.

"It wasn't exactly this age," snapped Moreth. "Although not much has changed over the past few decades, I'll admit. I tried to move the rusted wheel of progress in Menos. I signed Gloriatrix's Charter for Freedom. I ensured that a man could win his freedom, and a title of citizenship, from conquering the Blood Pits. After my attack on Elsa—I have never struck a woman since then—I returned to the meat markets, hoping to find more of the exiles with whom she'd traveled. I felt..." He got the word out only after much effort. "Merciful."

Fate wasn't merciful, though. None of Elsa's kin remained after the nightly frenzy of body hawking—none save for one man, that is. He was obviously violent, and his kennel had been shoved to the back of the stage. Moreth was certain that the brown tiger of a man had been present the day before. However, the captive projected a strange calm that made him seem both inconspicuous and threatening. Wandering closer, peering past the feet of the slavemongers and the other slaves, Moreth watched the man gaze from whip holder to master as if he were counting bodies in his mind. If the bars were to suddenly vanish, Moreth knew the man would kill every master and guard present as fast as a spirit of lightning. He'd feel no remorse; he'd do it because he understood he must kill or be killed. This was the kind of man who fought in Moreth's pits. And yet, there was something different about him.

Moreth shouted, "The man in the back—I'll take him. How many crowns?"

"Are you sure?" asked the slavemonger, strutting over and whipping the cage; the man inside didn't flinch. "He killed eight of my men using only chains. Although I suppose you might want him for that kind of thing, your lordship."

Eight men, thought Moreth. He now desired the caged monster more than ever.

Once the two were back at the estate, Moreth had the man hosed down in the gardens before bringing him inside; he had felt it wise to purchase the cage as well. Then the next order of business had been to feed the stringy man, and meat was tossed into the cage. Moreth didn't provide cutlery for the fellow, knowing that any sharp—or blunt—implement might be used as a weapon. Moreth had never seen a man so feral, a man with an animal for a spirit. He watched as the savage ripped apart and devoured his serving of raw steak. Moreth had wanted to see whether he would be willing to eat it. Moreth studied the man's glory. Remove the wind-burned tan, the lines and scars and unidentifiable markings—from claws?—on his short, lean body and he'd likely be a handsome man. Devouring his meat seemed to be a struggle for him, and at one point he coughed up a wad of mucous and meat too big and fatty to be swallowed. It was then that Moreth realized he had no tongue.

Like a voyeur at a freak show, Moreth pulled up a chair and sat in his lavish salon watching the naked man nibble at and gag down raw meat. He couldn't look away: the man was too captivating. Even when the slave walked to the side of his cage after finishing his meal and then pissed on Moreth's exquisite Sorsettan rug, Moreth couldn't summon the urge to reprimand him. Instead, he sat, surrounded by the reek of urine, which grew as the piss was warmed by the rare glow of sunshine coming in through the curtains, and continued his watch. Soon, the man squatted, reached into his anus, and pulled out a treasure—it glittered slightly. A contraband necklace. The man unraveled it, held it for a moment, staring at it, then placed it around his neck.

Afterward, the man glared at Moreth. "Just try and take my treasure," he seemed to say. The man wasn't afraid of him, wasn't even concerned that he was caged. He looked comfortable. A dark thought, a dangerous thought, manifested itself in Moreth's mind: he wondered what the leather man would do if he were to let him out.

Evening hunted through the sky, killing and eating Menos's scarce light; the purple haze would likely block out the sun for the rest of the year. So in darkness, Moreth sat, waiting, watching his pet. Or did he have the relationship backward? Perhaps he was the captive of this quiet, strange creature that prowled the iron floor of his cage. Every motion of the beast had a meaning; his head twitched when he heard a sound from elsewhere in the manor, or perhaps even from the grounds of the estate beyond. Moreth couldn't leave the side of this creature; he was himself in a cage little different from the iron one before him. Moreth realized that the leather man had touched forces beyond those he knew, and his interest continued to grow.

During the night, his valet came and told him that the woman he'd beaten nearly to death had been mended and was now resting.

"Go and stay with her until she wakes," he said to the lanky, gaunt, and striking fellow—a bit like a stork in gentlemen's clothing—whose name was Boris.

"I shall. Will you be needing supper?"

"No."

Boris pointed to the cage. "Will he?"

The leather man sensed his captors were discussing him, and he rattled his empty bowl across the bars of his cage.

"I would say yes," said Moreth. "Meat for him—tenderize or stew it a bit—and a bottle of wine for me."

Boris glanced around, looking for tipped tables or other signs of a burglary. "From where did he get that jewelry? It looks precious."

"Better if you don't know. I wouldn't suggest trying to take it from him."

As if aware of a possible threat to his treasure, the naked man suddenly tested the bars of his cage: he dropped his bowl and shook the metal cube, nearly managing to tip over its hundreds of pounds of iron. Moreth didn't doubt that with a little more effort, he could have done just that, but such shows of rebellion wouldn't amount to much.

"On second thought, two or three of bottles would be a grand idea," shouted Moreth just as his valet was leaving the room.

After the ruckus, the leather man once again began making the rounds of his prison. Wine and meat were brought for their respective recipients, who quickly consumed them. Two bottles soon lay empty on the floor, and Moreth's head was fuzzy with warmth. Perhaps it was his liquored bravado that made him stumble up and offer the neck of the next bottle to the slave. A drink to celebrate his queerness and charm, thought the master. Moreth was not a complete fool, and he brought the bottle only so far. The leather man's eyes glimmered. Too late Moreth realized the danger. In a mere speck, the slave had shot his skinny arms through the narrow bars, grabbed the bottle, shattered it, grabbed Moreth by his collar, and wrenched him up against the hard iron cage. Shards of glass pressed into the softness of Moreth's throat, and he suspected he was about to die.

Predator and prey gazed into each other's eyes. The river of Moreth's life coursed through his memory: sparkling parties, wealth, murders, sex, and the waning, never satisfying thrill of power. For some reason, he remembered the image of his fat father entwined on a bed of writhing whores; his mother and he had walked in on them when he was barely ten years old. It was one of his earliest childhood memories. Moreth had thought he would feel more when facing his own end—more fear, more regret—but he felt nothing.

Do it, he willed the man. *End this empty life of mine. I have squandered my wealth, my advantages, the gifts of Fate. I've found nothing in life that can satisfy me.*

The leather man dropped his glass weapon and released him. Whatever he'd seen in Moreth might not be worth his pity, yet it wasn't worth killing over either. Moreth stumbled away but found he couldn't leave the room, couldn't hide himself from the stare of the man who now watched all his movements. Still hunting him, even from his cage.

Suddenly, they heard a shriek from upstairs—the slave girl screaming bloody terror as she awoke to the agony of her reconstructed body. Moreth remembered the torments that had followed even his most minor fleshcrafting surgeries, and the spectacular wailings of his father during the constant transplants during his final years. When he glanced back at the slave, the man nodded—a gesture of understanding, of respect, though not of fellowship. Was it possible the man had let him live because of what he'd done for this woman? But how could he have known of her, or of Moreth's actions? Could he understand Ghaedic? Did the leather man know of the brutal beating Moreth had given her beforehand? What had this brush with death a moment past been? A primitive, violent leniency for having spared the woman? Certainly Moreth had been spared. Behind the decision of this primal judge was a meaning he needed to find.

Just then, Moreth's story was interrupted when Temupka entered the tent to bring them the evening stew. They noticed with some amazement that his tale had stolen most of the day. They stretched, used the toilet, and ate pensively, saying nothing until the pot was empty. A draught of anxiety and suspense had kept all of them awake, although they had already pushed themselves beyond the limits of exhaustion. After their break, Mouse urged him to continue. "What then? It seems you passed whatever pissing contest that was."

"Not a pissing contest," replied Moreth. "I was given a pardon. And then an opportunity to prove myself worthy of further challenges. He changed me, set me free. He freed me of my guilt, my whingeing, my spoiled aristocratic narcissism, my fear of death. For if you look straight into the Pale Lady's grinning skull and do not shite yourself, you know you are made of the strongest flint. I felt that I, in turn, should set my liberator free. However, there are rules in Menos—rules that must be respected and honored—especially by an Iron Sage. Still, I was determined…"

By placing the Slave in the Blood Pits, Moreth knew he'd made the first payment toward his grand debt. The Slave would not fail, and the odds were a gambler's dream: an unknown, single gladiator against the Blood Pits' finest warriors. Although smaller than all of his opponents, the Slave moved like an evil hummingbird and downed two of Moreth's strongest and longest-serving champions in a day. After that, the crowd became even hungrier, and coins rained into the betting pools whenever the Slave was to fight. Months and months of showering blood followed, the tally of the dead grew to battlefield proportions, and Moreth started to send in duos, trios, and wild animals in order to make the bookers happy.

No matter the odds, the Slave won. He never celebrated his victories. Sometimes, if he had met with even slight resistance from an opponent, he would bow to the corpse of his foe. Otherwise, he would simply set his weapon—he was proficient with every swinging, cutting instrument of death—down upon the sodden earth and walk to his quiet space to await the next battle.

Moreth broke age-old rules and allowed the Slave to live with him rather than keep him in the barracks with his fellows. Such a move was good for Moreth's profit margin, as this apparent advantage riled up those living in the Undercomb, those forced to share bunks, bath, and quarters. The favoritism shown the Slave encouraged men to challenge him, even those who really should have known better: the higher ranking one's opponent, the faster one moved up the ladder toward freedom. Although he appreciated the boost to his coffers, Moreth kept the Slave near mostly so he could watch the beast navigate this unfamiliar habitat. Much to the discomfort of his servants, Moreth allowed the man to wander the estate.

Sometimes, Moreth would realize the Slave had been sitting in a room with him for hourglasses, as still as one of the curtains. Some nights, Moreth would wake in a cold sweat and look for a glint of white in the darkness—he knew the Slave's eyes were upon him. But never did he wake and see the glint of metal, although knives were freely available in the kitchen and many swords were mounted on the walls. The Slave had granted him life, and now, Moreth realized, appeared to be grooming him.

He was always lurking about somewhere nearby, ready to test the senses and reflexes of his host. Moreth began to survey rooms before he entered them, trying to sense the Slave with his ears and eyes; like all gladiators, the man powdered himself with unscented talc, and so couldn't be detected by his odor. Moreth and the Slave were playing an endless game of kitten and cat, student and teacher.

While the two animals played in Moreth's estate, Elsa had regained her health. As he prowled about, checking every corner of the estate for his hunter-teacher, Moreth often came across the fair lady. Now and then, she took lessons with her governess—on language, grace, and poise. The lessons appeared less frustrating for her as summer became autumn. Elsa began making rapid progress in her studies, and come winter, began addressing him as Master El whenever their paths crossed. Moreth, however, felt shy whenever she spoke to him. Wherever Elsa was, Boris was not far away—his responsibility to care for her hadn't ended when she'd risen from her bed.

At first, Moreth noticed only that his valet was teaching Elsa the ways of the waitstaff: polishing, scrubbing, and waxing. Such activities were foreign to her, yet she learned them fast. Then Moreth began noticing that in the darker hourglasses, she and Boris would often sit chatting by lamplight in the kitchen, practicing Ghaedic together. Indeed, many times each week, valet and maid would meet and busy themselves with notes and quills. Moreth, whose hearing had improved since he'd begun tracking his Slave, caught whispers from them well into the night. Their laughter, too, occasionally disturbed Moreth's meditative hunts through the estate. Therefore, it was no real surprise to Moreth when one day, while Boris dressed him, the valet nervously struck up a conversation.

"Master El...If I may?" said Boris. "Uh, speak for a moment. Sorry, I'm not quite sure how to ask this, or even if I *should* ask this. However, I was wondering...I mean, I've been spending time, a lot of time, with our new maid-in-waiting—she doesn't have a lady to serve just yet, but I assume that title will be fine—"

Moreth arranged his cravat himself, as Boris's hands were fumbling. "What are you on about, man?"

The sword of love emboldened Boris, and he straightened his shoulders. "I would like to marry Elsa. We've been courting for some time. I have asked for her hand. I've never asked you for anything except the continued privilege of working on your estate...But I must ask you this: would you, being an Iron Sage and legal authority, officiate the ceremony?"

Moreth smiled. His redemption of Elsa was now nearly complete, and soon she would be both happy and free. Or at the very least free, and she certainly seemed happy. "Is that all? I would be honored."

Thus that winter, Elsa and Boris were wed. It was a beautiful season for a wedding, for the streets of Menos became gray mist-soaked lanes to the afterlife, the gardens were wreathed in fog, and the weeping lilies of the estate cried overly sweet perfumes that caused the eyes to water—though not with stinkeye for once. Only Moreth, a few servants, and the Slave—lurking nearby but unseen—were in attendance. Moreth stamped and sealed the documents related to their union and rights of citizenship. Elsa looked beautiful in her gown of black lace, and she wept beneath her veil—the first emotion Moreth had ever seen her betray. Once her tears had dried, she gave Moreth a slight nod, signaling thanks, perhaps, or forgiveness. Then she and Boris ran off down the treed laneway of the estate to catch a carriage into the Iron City, where they intended to spend many of their hard-earned crowns. They wouldn't actually end up spending a single coin, however, as Moreth had arranged everything for them: a night of extraordinary pleasures they could never have afforded on their own. Guards, too, he'd paid for, as two fools in love and carrying even a bit of coin would be tempting targets for a Menosian thug willing to slit throats.

Seasons, mostly gray and interchangeable, passed. But the Slave's life had changed, for he had at last won his freedom. Down in the Blood Pits, a thousand men had been sent to meet the Pale Lady by the Slave's hand, and so he would now become a man of Menos. There was no celebration for the Slave, no acceptance of his acceptance into society. Rather, he looked at the papers Moreth handed him, crumpled up the parchment into one large ball and then tossed it. Later Moreth unwrinkled the papers, forged a signature and submitted the documents for a *John Doe*.

Moreth and his hunter-father resumed their game, which had now evolved into a test of strength. After he found him, he must fight him. That was the rule, although as was the case with all of the Slave's teachings, no formal instructions were given: the action itself was the lesson. Moreth quickly learned of this new find-and-fight approach after touching his teacher and receiving several blows. After spitting out blood and picking himself up, he saw that his teacher hadn't left: his reward was to try to touch him again.

"Did you need anything else, Master El?" asked Elsa one evening in perfect Ghaedic after bringing him an iced cutlet wrapped in a towel, which she then placed on his swollen eye. Moreth's agonies had forced them to suspend the game that day.

I need you to forgive me, he thought. He knew she had, in her way. She came from people of the same savage code as the Slave: if she had wanted to poison him or end him with a butter knife, she likely would have. So he didn't ask for her forgiveness. Instead, he thought of another service she might be able to provide. Moreth sat up in his chair, groaning. "The man from the Pits, can you communicate with him somehow? I'd like to know more about him, about where you and he came from."

"You're assuming he can be communicated with at all," replied Elsa, with fire to her voice. "We are not the same, he and I. We are as different as master and slave. We may come from another realm, and even if that place is far from our bodies, it is never far from our hearts. In Pandemonia there is an order, too, and he and I do not share the same position. I respect him, and he respects me for the journey we've taken; however, we're not friends and can form no bond beyond the singular attachment of having been enslaved at the same time."

"Elsa," he pleaded, putting down the cutlet, bowing to a knee. "I've never asked or demanded anything of you since...since your employment began, though I beseech you in this request: Will you speak to him for me? Just a few words?"

Elsa looked around warily, as if monsters—or the Slave—hid in the shadows. "Be careful, Master El. Words are the most dangerous weapon of man," she warned. "Indeed you've never asked for much nor anything of my past, and for that I thank you. My past was shameful. I was without pride: here I have found pride. I do not wish to revisit my demons, nor the ones that surely chase your friend. I shall not speak to him." Moreth's heart sank, then rose as her pursed-lips expression warmed with a smile. "However, if you believe he will hear you, I can teach you—as I have been taught—how to speak in a tongue not your own. Then you may ask him himself whatever it is you wish to know."

"Thank you."

Elsa left him.

Moreth's days became busy, and he neglected both his duties in the Blood Pits and his political responsibilities. His enemies on the Council of the Wise plotted, sensing his distraction. He received a shadowbroker-delivered missive from Gloriatrix in which she warned him they would attempt to fill his seat with an ally of their own, and summoned him to a private meeting at the Blackbriar Estate. It hadn't seemed wise to refuse, so he'd attended. Without saying anything definite or incriminating, she offered to assist him in dealing with the vultures who wanted his seat. Moreth agreed, mostly because he wanted to rush back to his manor and sequester himself with Elsa and the Slave. In accepting Gloriatrix's aid, Moreth knew he'd allowed himself to be bought, though she wasn't the worst choice of confederate. By the time the Council met again the following week, two seats were empty, and a handful of potential candidates supported by his enemies had gone missing. Gloriatrix would soon make her move to become not only First Chair but also the first and only queen of the Iron City. However, Moreth was only distantly aware of such developments, picking up occasional tidbits of information from rumormongers, paper-gossip, and shadowbrokers.

He and Elsa finished their lessons in a matter of weeks. At last, he knew the language of the far, far East. Or at least part of it: from one tongue had grown as many broken dialects as shards of clay from a shattered vase, and he possessed only a single shard. She'd taught him what she suggested was the more civilized Lakpoli tongue, as well as a bit of the mishmash that was the broader Amakri dialect of one of the nomadic tribes she'd known. Moreth still couldn't speak either fluently, though he'd learned how to read and write Lakpoli reasonably well. What a curious language: elegant and simple, with small symbols and long rows of black lines.

One day, armed with Elsa's old notepad—stuffed with two languages' worth of scribbles—and an endless ink quill, he went to find the Slave. The man no doubt knew what Moreth and Elsa had been doing. Moreth supposed that was why the Slave had made himself scarce—to avoid this conversation. Search high and low as he might, Moreth couldn't find the Slave anywhere in his estate. He wouldn't have left, that much Moreth knew. Exhausted, he fell asleep in his parlor in the very chair from which he'd first watched the Slave watching him.

It was morning. Eyes were on him when he woke. Before even looking to see where the Slave stood in the gloomy gray room, Moreth fumbled for his pad and quill, but they were not where he had left them. Another test, he realized. He spotted his missing items at the feet of his master, who stood near the window. Moreth understood the game: he'd have to fight to claim them. He assumed this would be the fight of his life, the ultimate lesson—and he was correct. Bookcases were toppled, furniture flung, clothing and skin shredded as the battle raged inside the El manor. The servants stayed clear of the shaking doors to the parlor. Instead, they whistled and went about their business, pretending that a screaming tornado wasn't tearing through the house.

When the dust had wafted away, Moreth and the Slave were as tattered and limp as the bent rod and fallen curtains hanging down like a banner of surrender. The room had been destroyed: Moreth had no hope of finding or even seeing with his bruised eyes the parchment and quill over which this fight had erupted. Then he was lifted and helped to his astonishingly still-intact chair by the Slave, who'd already recovered his strength. Moreth could feel the shadow's breath. He sensed that the Slave was assessing his bruises, his punches, his valor. Moreth despised his original father, and yet he hoped that the man standing above him—the man who had no name and with whom he'd never broken bread, never broken anything but bones—was pleased by the wounded animal he saw.

A note was slipped into Moreth's hand. It appeared to have been written in calligraphic Lakpoli—prettier than anything he or Elsa had ever penned—and he whimpered as he struggled to read it. "You fought well," it read. "You have promise. I shall teach you more. However, you've already learned the most important lesson, which is to fear neither pain nor death."

The shadow abandoned him there: sagging in his chair, bleeding, rasping, and smiling.

Thunder threw him from a dream. Moreth woke in the gloomy salon, having slept in the chair. Ruin surrounded him and he listened to the pelting of rain on glass for a time, then limped to his chamber and cleaned his wounds. He needed to find the Slave. Today, the man allowed himself to be discovered. From his bedroom window, Moreth spotted a black shade haunting the base of the glistening iron-clad tree that stood in the center of the estate's labyrinth of hedges. The Slave looked up at the window, of that Moreth was certain. Moreth threw on a bowler to keep away the stinkeye and hurried through the many corridors of his grand home and then out into the drizzling outdoors. The Slave hadn't moved. He was dressed in leathers and a hooded cloak that had a leafy, stitched quality to it, as if it had been made by and for a hermit.

The Slave gestured him into the shelter of the tree's metal branches, and they sat on a bench together. The day possessed a foggy, maritime odor and brought with it a chill that numbed Moreth's aches. A note appeared in Moreth's hand. He unfolded and read the message, which was written in exquisitely penned Ghaedic rather than Lakpoli this time. "You are a lord of many riches in this Iron land, and yet you do not seem content with your power. I know what you seek, but you must declare it for it to be true. Only once it is true may you hunt it."

"You speak my tongue?" Moreth exclaimed.

The Slave nodded. He scribbled another note while holding Moreth's attention with his wide, piercing stare—so compelling it seemed almost like a form of magik or a natural enchantment, such as a snake's charm. Stirring, Moreth examined the paper; he wasn't sure what had happened to the one he'd held in his hand only a speck ago; he couldn't even tell where the parchment and quill were being kept, as the Slave's hands rested neatly in his lap. "I was once very close with one who listens," read the note. "She taught me how to hear many of the hidden voices of the world and how to speak Geadhain's many tongues—even if mine has been cut. We all have a bit of magik inside of us, and communion with another is a spell any can learn."

"I have spent all this time trying to communicate with you…" mumbled Moreth.

Scribbling. This time, Moreth broke the gaze-trance and saw that small square sheaves and a feather lay under the Slave's palms. The man wrote with the speed of a possessed printing press, moving his hand from left to right, left to right, and filling a line in mere specks. A note was passed. Moreth read it. "If not for the efforts you've made, I would have believed you to be no different from the Iron tyrants of this city. I would not have opened my voice to you. But you helped me find life after I believed myself sentenced to death. Although your quest is dangerous, it is also noble—more noble than the whispers and desires of all others in this cruel place. I will help you find what you seek."

"What *is* it that I seek?" asked Moreth.

A final note: "You will not find it here. These creatures are too weak for a man of your kind."

Silently, they breathed in the burning air of the city and watched as the fog took gray bites out of the land. The Slave's words inspired Moreth. What Moreth wanted and needed was out there, beyond Menos, beyond all realms he knew. At last, the time had come for him to leave this iron cage. He would set forth and hunt his destiny...

"I hadn't realized the hourglass," said Moreth, abruptly breaking off his story and turning onto his side. "Soon it will be dawn. Again."

Moreth had learned how to exist without introspection, to be a creature only of instinct and the present tense. These forays into his history had taken a toll, and a mighty exhaustion clouded him. He wanted to sleep. But Talwyn wasn't about to let such a good yarn end on a cliff-hanger. Having stayed up so late already, drunk with fascination, he felt as enlivened as Moreth was spent.

"Come now, you can't be serious," said the scholar. "What were you seeking? What happened with you and the Slave?"

"I thought I told you that already," replied Moreth grumpily, before burrowing deeper into his bedroll. "I have read you the scroll of my sorrows and sins. I wanted to be nothing like my father. I wanted to find something to challenge me...Thus we came to Pandemonia. I hunted my happiness. I found Beatrice...Not as she is now, but as she was then—like one of those you saw tonight. Or last night, rather—whatever bloody day it is. But everything has a fuking price. I found love, but it came at the cost of a friendship: the Sisters must always balance their scales."

Mouse guessed what it was Moreth was trying to avoid speaking of, and she seized Talwyn's hand and pressed it, trying to stop him from pestering the man. Moreth had returned from Pandemonia with a most exotic animal, a monster in the guise of a lady. He had not returned with the Slave. Mouse had seen the necklace he'd inherited from the Slave, the kind of memento that would be presented only as a dying gift. A few questions remained, but she wasn't sure they needed to be answered. Almost asleep, and now totally free from inhibitions, Moreth spoke once more and resolved a few of her remaining questions. "I shall kill you for what you've done..." he mumbled. "Cage you and torture you and bleed you till you die...Beatrice. My magnificent monster...Bleed you...You beautiful, horrible beast..."

A love of bloodlust and hunger, indeed, thought Mouse.

VII

Talwyn fussed and remained awake. The whirring genius of his mind made sleep impossible. His companions' measured breaths, which sounded like the beats of a metronome, increased his restlessness. He rose in a hurry, threw on an over garment, boots, and gloves, and escaped.

A murderous orange dawn, like a fire rising from the basement of a sleeping house, greeted Talwyn. He had to squint and lower his head, as the glare off the ice-glazed land prevented him from seeing much of anything. Talwyn followed the scent of smoke and the murmurs of voices to a nearby campfire, where men and women hunched on boulders, appearing exhausted but relaxed.

"Proí échei érthech. Eímast asfaleís (Another morning has come. We are safe)," said one of the haggard guards as he sipped a warm, steaming drink.

Morning and light. Creatures of darkness would not hunt in this hourglass.

"Pythíou pae epidiókei (Pythius seeks you)," said the warrior.

Of course he does. Questions aplenty, I'm sure. I have more than a few for him, thought Talwyn. First, however, he wanted to check on his patients, to see how they'd passed the second night after their surgeries. He'd left those attending to the wounded with strict instructions on how to treat and cleanse the excisions and amputations. Still, medicine appeared to be a foreign concept to these people, and, feeling worried now, he rushed through the waking encampment toward the tents circling the ashes of the great pyre of the dead. Outside the ring of black, Talwyn noticed the many unusual piles of stones surrounding the funeral site: they looked like little men with stacks for feet and longer planks of rock for hands. Ash blew in the wind here, and standing still for too long left an unpleasant bitterness in Talwyn's mouth, so he entered the closest tent.

Roughly six wounded and one or two caregivers could fit inside each tent. However, five of the bedrolls he saw were empty. Only bloodied dressings and imprints could be seen where their occupants had lain. Talwyn recalled that it was here that the grisliest amputations had occurred. The smell of singed, cauterized flesh still clung to the leather of the tent. It seemed inconceivable that these folk could be up and walking around—many were missing one or both of their legs. In front of him, an Amakri warrior was busy rewrapping the stomach of a cringing man. He had been one of the luckier fellows of the night, receiving only a concussion and a full suite of broken ribs.

"*Mágos,*" they said, and paused in respect.

Talwyn pieced together a question about the others, making sure to stress the "where have they gone" part.

Frowning, the warrior answered. "*Áfisan. Den tha thélate na tous doúme étsi ki alliós. Den ítan charoúmenos den ítan pléon synoliká kai den axízei.*" (They left. You would not want to see them anyway. They were not happy—they were no longer whole and so of no worth.)

No worth! He had saved their lives. Talwyn stormed off to the other shelters, where more empty pallets, missing amputees, and unconcerned faces told the same tale. Barging out of the last tent, he crashed into Pythius. The strong man stopped him from hurting either of them, and held Talwyn, still huffing, at bay.

"*Épsachna gia esás,*" (I was looking for you), he said.

Surprised by his own strength, Talwyn pushed the man off, then poked his chest with an accusing dagger of a finger. "I-I was looking for you, too! Where are the patients? The-the *asthenoch*? The ones missing their arms and legs, their *pódia kai ta chéria*? You couldn't have sent them away! Even your people aren't that cruel! They're not well—"

Pythius shook the scholar so hard that his brain rattled. Then the fearsome, scowling shaman dragged Talwyn past the stirred onlookers—who tutted at the spectacle—and into a tent. Two Amakri sat inside eating their morning stew, but Pythius roared at them to leave. The men hurried off. Once alone, Pythius approached Talwyn, his shoulders bowed. Instead of making a move to punish the scholar again, he rubbed his smarting wrist.

"*Dýsi Touílio, tóso díkaio. Den íthela na sas mólopes. O laós mou den prépei poté na deis tin adynamía. Den boroúme na afísoume mia prosvolí kai apergía enantíon mou statheí.*" (West Sun, so fair. I did not mean to bruise you. My people must never see weakness. I cannot let an insult against me stand.) Pythius held Talwyn's wrist, and the touch became a caress. Both men shivered, and the shaman pulled away. He continued. "*Rotáte gia tous travmatíes pou koimoúntai mazí mas óchi perissótero, kai tha sou po. Min koitáte epáno mas, tyflómenos apó orgí kai tin krísi. Zoúme ópos échoume zísei edó kai chiliádes chrónia, kai oi trópoi mas eínai giatí fylí mas ypoménei.*" (You ask about the wounded who sleep with us no more, and I shall tell you. Do not be blinded by rage and judgment. We live as we have lived for thousands of years, and it is thanks to our ways that our tribe has endured.)

As Pythius explained, Talwyn realized that once again he had spoken too soon, much as he had during the incident with Temupka. Just as sending the weaker children of the Amakri to live with the Lakpoli was an act of mercy, so too was banishing those too lame to hunt in Pandemonia's most dangerous regions. Of what use would a lame hunter be against one of Brutus's vile Red Riders? How would he be able to keep up with the tribe during their long hikes through lands of fluctuating fire, water, summer, and snow? It was these Doomchasers' own pride more than any pressure from the tribe that made them leave. These invalids were not formally excommunicated and remained true kinsmen of the tribe. An envoy of warriors would march with them to the Lakpoli cities, which would become their new homes. One such envoy had left yesterday morning while Talwyn, Mouse, and Moreth had secluded themselves and listened to the fallen master's tale. Had Talwyn been about, he surely would have seen the procession.

"*Prépei na eímaste ischyrós, vlépete. Prépei na eímaste sklirá. Arithmós mas leptaínei. To aíma mas chánei ti dýnamí tou. Káthe epochí, ypárchoun ólo kai ligótera apó tin ischyrí pou gennioúntai.*" (We must be strong, you see. We must be hard. Our numbers thin. Our blood loses its strength. Each season, fewer and fewer of the strong are born.)

The men sat, and a series of conversations occurred. At last, proud Pythius explained the plight of his people and their own interest in the chalice. There were things the shaman hadn't wanted to share with the travelers. Bashfully, he told the scholar how this quest for the chalice wasn't new. Indeed, for decades now, they'd been on the hunt for the relic. An artifact that was more than a mere cup or symbolic instrument, it was part of the ancient ritual—the Covenant—once made between Feyhazir and the Doomchasers.

In ancient days, when Feyhazir had walked in a mortal vessel and lived with this tribe of Amakri, he'd shared with them his blood and power, which had transformed them into beast-men with thick hides, resilient Wills, and serpentine quickness. But in recent generations, the Dreamer's blood had thinned. Not all children possessed horns and fury; many were soft skinned like Talwyn. Even in Pythius's lifetime, the tribe had produced as many *adýnamos* (weak) as *drakos* (strong)—and the balance continued to shift. It was for this reason that Temupka said the prayer for her unborn child. Talwyn considered the pressure of having to make the decision to excommunicate some members for the good of the tribe, as well as the responsibility of preserving a culture that reached back thousands of years—both rested on Pythius's great, though straining, shoulders.

Talwyn had been a horrible fool.

"For a learned man, I can be quite stupid at times."

Pythius turned and smiled; although he couldn't understand what the foreigner had said, that it was meant as an apology was clear. Staring intently, eyes like two beads of green fire, the shaman approached. He gripped the back of Talwyn's neck and placed his rough, hot forehead against the scholar's. Talwyn froze: because of nerves, their breathing so close to one another, the cinnamon and lavender mixed into the scent of the man's raw sweat—as if the oils he surrounded himself with in his meditations had seeped into his flesh. Prior to this moment, Talwyn had watched Amakri perform rituals such as this, usually before or after a challenge, and therefore he did not feel as awkward as he could have. He even reached up and grabbed the back of Pythius's scaly neck.

"*Den eínai adýnames. Adelfós sti máchi, as páme píso gia na ta pánta pétres kai recalim tin yperifáneia tou laoú mou.*" (You are not weak. Brother in battle, let us go forth to the Forever Stones and reclaim the pride of my people.)

The two men broke apart, sweating, and Talwyn hurried outside to douse himself in winter air. *Time to rouse the troops*, he thought. The mourning had ended; the Doomchasers were going to war.

VIII

Mouse had been about as successful as Talwyn when it came to sleeping, though she hid her restlessness well. After all, she was a talented actress, her skills having been honed during her vassalage as a pleasure maiden and the many years of subterfuge with the Watchers. What had happened to that organization? To Alastair? In Pandemonia, she felt a world away from home. A river of thoughts ran through her head. Carried along on a jostling raft, she did not know which one to pick.

Parts of Moreth's tale bothered her, especially the admission of his predilections. Hooks and whips and bladed things. Mouse had built a hundred Iron Walls within herself to block out the memories of such experiences. The scars on her pelvis crawled like worms when she thought of Moreth's confessions. And what of this Beatrice? Creature of the night? Feaster upon men? What sort of man could tame, and love, such a monster?

We're all monsters, I suppose. Beatrice is not unlike Caenith: each shares a skin with a wild animal.

She still found it strange that Moreth had never suffered and died by black venom during his marriage, especially considering his preferred recreations. Perhaps they had been careful. And yet Mouse had watched the smallest scratch fester into a rancid illness, so she dismissed the notion that any degree of care could have kept him safe—though she could offer no other explanation. When Moreth woke, she would ask him, in the politest way possible, how he'd managed to sleep with a hornet for all those years and never get stung.

She heard movement in the camp. The clanging of weapons. The chatter of Doomchasers. Songs of valor. But it was so early yet. Mouse fought the sneaking sunlight. She clenched shut her eyes, and engaged in a losing battle with the day, and even more so with the beckoning smell of salty, meaty stew that wafted in from somewhere nearby. Any funeral chants had long ago ceased, and Mouse tingled with the intuition that they would soon be moving. She doubted that Pythius would move the whole tribe into the Forever Stones, which meant that only warriors of importance would be going…wherever it was the Dreamer had buried his treasure. She sensed he would have chosen someplace truly horrid. Certainly, she, Talwyn, and Moreth would be going on the quest. Finally, she rose and threw on her garments and boots. *Time to start this mad train up once more. Time to face a horde of blood-hungry wenches on wings.*

Mouse shivered and sat back down. Even the bravest people have instants of doubt, and she couldn't cast the shrieking, flying hag from her mind. Remembering the adoring way it had looked at her brought on a particularly sharp chill…She did not feel ready to march off into a realm of horrors. It came to Mouse that she'd become used to hiding behind the bodies of the strong. Of course, that's exactly what a mouse *should* do when in the company of greater animals: use them as shields. At the moment, though, her biggest, hairiest shield—Caenith—was missing. In his place, she had only two dandyish men—of course, they were rather handy with firearms. However, if their aim failed, she had but a tiny knife with which to defend herself. A small and insignificant claw, she realized, to use against women made of hunger, shadow, and magik.

I need something more. I can't keep relying on other people to save me. What's the point of having the might of a Dreamer, a lord of creation, if I am only a cage in which that power is kept? That's not why I signed this contract. I pledged myself to Feyhazir to gain power and revenge, which comes from violence. Mouse spoke to the sleeping entity, poking him with her irritated Will. *Time to wake up again, darling. The squeaky wheel needs its oil. I won't quail behind some protecting man. I can't sit around waiting for divine intervention if I am to protect myself, and your interests, with only a heartbeat to spare. I wanted power: that's what I asked you for. I don't want magik; leave the sorcery to the others in my pack. What I want is a weapon—one with which I can strike down those winged monsters, one with which I can fell the white wolf who took my father. I have not forgotten the promises I've made.*

The presence shifted and bubbled up within her so euphorically that her head tilted up to the ceiling. She stared at the crossing of bone lines, which suddenly seemed to be spinning like a pinwheel. Somehow, she was rising into that vortex. She twirled and twirled and was lost.

When Mouse awoke, she was on her knees. Strewn around her on the floor of the tent were cards from the deck of Kings and Fates she always carried. She was clutching one card so tightly her hand ached, and her other hand felt just as cramped. Sitting up and beginning to make sense of her surroundings, she realized it was gripping her dagger. Strange: the weapon tingled with a cold current, like a shiver running through ice. Wondering what in blazes had happened, she released the folded card and watched it fall to the floor and uncurl like a flower petal.

Mouse felt she would have remembered this card, which featured a woman in black holding a brand of white sunlight up to the sky. *Imperatrix*, read the scrolled banner under the image. *High Ghaedic?* she wondered. The word looked similar to ones Talwyn used in his academic ramblings. Mouse mumbled her way through it.

"Immm-peer-aah-trix."

The dagger hummed—a low sound, as if a tuning fork had been struck. Moreth grumbled, woken by a sense of danger. Then a star on earth rose within the tent, and Mouse's cry of alarm was consumed by its roaring light.

XIV

CITY OF FALSE GRACE

I

It was dawn when Morigan awoke in the arms of her bloodmate. A bloody sky warned of dark tidings, but she needed no omens to tell her there was darkness ahead. Nonetheless, she wouldn't let the shadow of war dampen her joy. For last night, she'd been with her sister and friend, Mouse. They'd wandered through a field of Dream and eased each other's heartache with conversation and laughter. Soon they would see each other again in Eatoth. She must keep that promise: she must not allow Brutus to defile the City of Waterfalls. Eager and impassioned, she rose from the clinging nest of her bloodmate. Caenith stirred as she left him, and they dressed, kissed, and chased each other a bit while hunting for articles of clothing.

The Wolf had been right, as he so often was—she had needed a rest. They all did, from time to time. Heroes were not clockwork men. They could not be oiled and wound up and sent on quests. They were people—weary, struggling people. Their bodies and spirits were crushed so often that it was a miracle any of them had made it this far without going mad. Heroes often needed to rest even when they didn't feel it unnecessary.

Morigan hoped that her missing companions were enjoying a similar respite, as Mouse had suggested they were.

After they were dressed and finished with their chase, the bloodmates went to find their companions, who had made camp nearer to the shore. Thackery and Adam sat on small stone seats around a pit of wispy smoke. A large piece of well-cooked meat was turning over the fire. Most of it appeared untouched, though the Wolf could hear the gurgle of Adam's belly. Thackery's stomach, though, sounded quite pleased. Caenith helped himself without waiting for an offer, while Morigan told the fellows of her dream. "I saw Mouse last night. She's well, and she sends her regards."

Both Thackery and Adam jumped to their feet and battered her with questions. She answered each and every one. By then, the Wolf had finished all but the bit of meat he'd set aside for Morigan—exactly enough to satisfy her hunger—and washed his hands in the pool. Then they set out. As Adam appeared reluctant to wear his animal skin, and they had the benefit of added time, they hiked hard but didn't race as they could have.

Time was ripening the land's beauty. What had been yellow was now brightening to green. What had been dry now grew damp with life. Soon their toes and ankles were wet from the lush clover—tall as flowers—and the small streams that ran between mounds and through the many gardens of cobalt rocks. The many tiny rivers produced trickling sounds like those of a tub being gradually filled. The Wolf noticed that the little veins all ran in one direction, to a source, a heart. A sweet floral breath blew upon them and carried all of their troubles away for a spell. After a while, they came to a field that resembled an artist's creation. Here, purple growth was mixed in with the emerald sward, white streaks of clouds, black twists of trees like smudges of charcoal, and blue rock-circles of the land. Everything was bold, saturated, almost cartoonish with color. The sun shone a thick and brazen yellow. Cawing flocks scattered from some sudden disruption like splashes of paint. Nearly lost in the kaleidoscopic scenery was a finger of crystal. And yet it shone brightly in the daubed-on environs, even more radiant than Thackery's staff, which he now used to point at the landmark. "Eatoth," he said.

If the place could be so lovely from afar, what would it look like up close? The four ran toward it, eager to find the answer to that question, and to preserve the city's majesty from Brutus's evil.

II

These four travelers had seen Dreamers, changeling hordes, storms of ice and fire, and unspeakable and dazzling events—yet each would have placed Eatoth atop any list of wonders. As they'd raced toward it, the rivulets of water running across the land had become fat, strong rivers that tumbled down a slight rock-torn decline and cut the valley into small islands. The rivers grew ever louder and frothier until they entered a basin, forming a violently tossing lake that would be nigh impossible to swim—a naturally occurring moat. As the travelers slowly crept down slippery rocks and jumped from one safe island of grass and stone to another, they realized there was something strange about the behavior of this water: it defied gravity. From the churning lake, it eddied upward, forming a great aqueous wall. Then, at the height of its spray, it poured back upon itself in a misty cascade as if it were a giant fountain. Fog clouded the terrain, and the waterfall concealed whatever glittering beauties lay beyond it, but the four spotted shimmers through its wavering veil, and those who saw best identified a great wall of crystal or metal hiding behind it.

They ran along with the rustling sea wind; the water was salty and fresh. Their road-tested hardiness made them able to make the daring journey over tiny islands without slipping into one of the spuming white channels at their sides. Before long, they'd entered the deep mists of the basin, and the sun was removed and replaced by a golden suffusion. Then the mist shredded, and they stopped and gawked like tiny ants as a barrier akin to Eod's Great Wall emerged from the haze. Capped with clouds that seemed impossibly high up, it had a facade of crystal and coursing water. It seemed like the cliff a storm-giant might climb; none could fathom how it had been made. His voice barely audible over the grinding ruckus, the Wolf said, "We shan't be swimming across the lake. There are no bridges or paths through the wall, at least not above. However, there are roads and tunnels down below our feet. I believe we may have come at the city the wrong way."

Once they'd hopped a few more islands, the Wolf picked up Morigan—who laughed—and leaped down a steep split in the rocks. When Thackery and Adam reached the spot where they'd vanished and peered down into the rainy crevasse, they saw the pair had safely reached the bottom and was now standing on a damp, pebbly path. Daintily, the Wolf placed his bloodmate on her feet, then beckoned to the two men above. "Come on," he said. "I will catch you."

"Is there no other way?" shouted Thackery. Although he was once again youthful, his stomach flipped at the thought of scraping himself. The echo of his voice was rather terrifying, too—the Wolf was easily two hundred paces beneath him. "What do you think, Adam?"

The changeling grinned at him, then wrapped his arms around himself and leaped. Thackery watched him sail to the bottom and get swept up like a bonnie lass by the Wolf, who gave him a growl of approval. After Adam had regained his footing, they barked at each other happily.

"Show-off," cursed Thackery. "I'm coming…I guess. Catch my staff." He threw it down the crack. "And you bloody well better catch me. Here I come." Stepping out into air went against all his natural instincts, and he could feel his body seizing up and recoiling. "Bugger…I'm just going to have to jump. Kings save meeee—"

Thackery screamed all the way down. A hard meaty impact awaited him. He realized he wasn't dead when he smelled a combination of man, wood, and spice. "Not bad," said the Wolf, and righted his friend.

Thackery reclaimed his softly shining staff and used it to steady his legs and illuminate the darkened grotto in which they'd landed. Raindrops pattered down into the great fanged tunnel surrounding them, creating an endless tin-roof song. The space was wide in some places and narrow in others, but everywhere its height was impressive. Water babbled and bubbled along the path they'd discovered, which was clearly a road—the only evidence of man anywhere to be seen. The cavern smelled of deep earth and wet minerals, and Thackery was even damper down here than he had been above. He looked up, blinking against the constant rain, and spotted the dim wrinkle through which they'd come. "Where are we?" he asked.

"A road," replied the Wolf, beginning to walk. "There are more formal entrances to these caves, but we must have missed them, or perhaps they are not easily found unless one knows where to look. I hear the whistle of winds now that we are down here and away from the roaring monster of the city—those winds are from such entrances, I suspect." He jiggled a fingertip in his ears. "It hurts my head, this land." Morigan touched her bloodmate reassuringly.

After that, the bloodmates remained silent. Thackery puzzled over the idea that a city could have subterranean layers with no conspicuous entrances or exits. This "Undercomb" appeared functionally similar to Menos's sublevel, and surely served similar purposes when it came to transit and city engineering. However, what these people had created was harmonious with nature and must have required a form of technomagik Thackery had never before encountered.

As they moved through the thundering caves, as Thackery watched the currents of water running alongside the road, and listened to the synchronous, musical, measured dripping occurring everywhere, the mechanics of the sublevel became clearer to him. All the water down here ran in the opposite direction from the rivers and falls above—the rivers and falls that somehow did not flood these caverns. It was a system, he realized. One set of pumps took the water away from the city, while another recycled the magik and kinetic force and fed them back into the circuit. He'd heard of technomagikal turbines that produced energy through similar means. Self-sustaining power of this magnitude could easily reverse the physics of a waterfall and make it rush up instead of down. Thackery wondered what other applications these people had found for this font of seemingly infinite magik. Thackery's excitement drove him ahead of the others.

As Thackery passed the Wolf, a spice of library dust and sizzling candles wafted from the sage—the smell of a passion for knowledge and truth. *Am I growing soft?* wondered the Wolf, for he felt a pang when he thought of the autumn-haired fellow who smelled even spicier, and had filled so many of their silences with chatter.

We shall see them soon, promised Morigan.

If your father keeps his word, he replied.

Morigan searched for a retort but could find none. They continued on in silence down the road of water and stone for a great stretch. Fishes and weaving glints of silver swam in the channels beside them. Some of these creatures resembled eels, though they were longer, metallic, and luminescent. They rose and dove in the water as if they were mammals of the sea, and emitted bleating little cries. On the walls crept colonies of crabs that clattered their claws and reminded the Wolf of the crustaceans he and his bloodmate had killed. The Wolf felt certain that his time in Pandemonia and his bond with Morigan had further sharpened his senses. For he could hear the greasy flicking of the crabs' antennas and eyestalks; he could smell their fishy, sardine-like musk. To test himself, he followed the swishing travel of one of the silver eels using only his mind. He tracked the beast for spans and spans until he became bored of the game. In this heightened state of perception, he soon became aware that there were folk in the tunnel ahead, several lazy bends away from where they were. "Three men..." he muttered, peering through the rainy dark and seeing every detail. "Armed with...staves of some kind. Magikal, I suspect."

"Time to introduce ourselves," said Thackery, and then stopped short. "Umm, about that. We're without our Menosian translator and the scholar who has surely picked up half the language by now. How do you propose—"

"I shall be our voice," declared Adam, striding forward.

They arrived at a place where the tunnel expanded into a bulbous hollow. The many rents in the ceiling admitted a bright light, and the streams that wept from above were like banners of glass. As the Wolf had predicted, three men in dark blue robes and cloaks were there, within a circle of falling water. They held glowing staves much like Thackery's, but theirs shone with a blue radiance rather than a white one. To the Wolf, the weapons looked carved of ice, entwined in cottony, cold mist. No fool would rely on only three men—even ones armed with magik staves—to guard a city entrance. But the men themselves reeked of the sulfur of sorcery—great sorcery. "Careful, Adam," he said to the young changeling who dashed to meet Eatoth's defenders.

One of the three defenders responded to Adam's impetuous movement by raising his staff, which suddenly glittered at its tip like a star. With a crackling gust, the cascade before Adam twisted, creaked, and then froze so fast that he nearly smashed into the jagged obstacle. Another few steps, and it would have solidified with him inside. A warning, clearly. Adam raised his hands and calmly spoke. The others couldn't identify the dialect he employed—it was thick, rolling, and ancient, and had harsh k's and a's.

"Please, we come in peace," he said. "We come from very far away. We must have words with your warchief. We must warn him of what is coming for your city—an army of the mad king." The three blue-robed ones said nothing, though the one who'd called the elements lowered his staff. "Do you know of the mad king? He is the enemy of life itself. We have hunted and battled this enemy from sea to sea, and soon he will be at your gates. If you will not hear what we have to say, then you will die."

It seemed his confidence and candor might have convinced them, for the one of the three who'd acted stepped away from the others, strode out of the circular downpour, and tipped his staff. It flashed again, and the frozen cascade in front of Adam melted and resumed its flow. Then the silent sorcerer of Eatoth strode across the chamber. The company quickly pursued him.

At the end of the hollow, the rainfall ended, the thundering dimmed, and the stones dried to dampness. They entered a tunnel so tall that only the Wolf could see its heights; it wasn't difficult to imagine that they were now walking under the lake itself. It became quite dim. The luminescent staves of Thackery and their guide cast the travelers' forms as eerie shadow-puppets on the walls.

Their guide didn't speak; he didn't even look back at them. He walked slowly, strangely lackadaisical for a man who had just been informed of his city's impending doom. Many of the company knew Brutus's horrors firsthand, and the blue sorcerer's calm did nothing but irritate them, and rouse suspicion.

Indeed, Morigan sensed hardly a ripple of discord in the man's ocean of tranquility. She set her swarm upon him and her psychic raiders returned with mostly useless information and imagery of rolling oceans and gently rumbling storms. *A great man. A wise man. One who listens. What she wills, she wills*, they repeated. Either magik or discipline had built in this man a barrier against her prying; she'd need time and dedication to break through the wall in his mind. She possessed no patience for that, and instead asked a favor of the young changeling. "Adam, may

I borrow your trinket? I would like to try my hand—or tongue, rather—at speaking with this man. I have questions for him."

Adam fondled the black stone around his neck. It had become a safety net for him. In recent memory, he'd removed the talisman only when he was a wolf or when he and Mouse stumbled through the occasional lesson on common Ghaedic—he was quite awful, yet made leaps of progress when they were together. Adam hated the thought of words once again becoming gibberish in his ears, of not knowing what his pack said. After a few specks of internal struggling, though, he reluctantly slipped off the necklace and passed it to Morigan.

She thanked him and placed the necklace on. "Excuse me, sir?" The blue sorcerer didn't acknowledge her, so she tried again. "Pardon me? You there. Gentleman with the staff that freezes things." Still no reply.

"The talisman may not work with anyone else," mumbled Adam to himself.

"Adam!" exclaimed Morigan. His voice had sounded smooth, and his speech had been articulate. They came to a halt.

"You understand me?" asked Adam.

"Perfectly," she replied. "I don't know how. When we were on the *Skylark*, you were barely working through your vowels."

"I can understand you, too, which shouldn't be possible," he said. "Not without that." As Adam and Morigan both reached for the talisman around her neck, their hands met just over the stone. Bees buzzed in Morigan's head, and she was lifted in a silver cloud up and out of her body.

Once more she's in the limestone cavern. There's Elemech's pool, and two figures sit beside it. One is the young changeling, kneeling. He is waiting for a gift. Elemech takes her time choosing his present. She leans over while sitting upon her rock and picks through the small pebbles at her feet. It must be the right stone, the right piece of this great rock where she lives, if he is to receive the power he seeks. Elemech choses a stone: flat, shaped a bit like an arrowhead—or perhaps a key, thinks Morigan.

"Are you sure this is what you wish?" asks Elemech.

"Yes," replies the changeling.

"Say it. Declare your desire to the Green Mother, and prepare to suffer all the glory and ruin your decision will bring."

Quite brave—or foolhardy—Adam does not waver. He puffs up his chest. "My wolf-mother wished for me to see the world, to speak with the men in iron and ivory cities. I wish for that too. However, I must understand these animals in order to be among them. I am a foreigner in my pack, and I want to be a friend—"

"Clearly. Speak clearly and true. What is your wish?"

"I want the gift of communion. I want to hear and be heard by the world."

Elemech's stare twinkles with a rarely seen amusement. "Very well." She hands Adam the stone, which is now bound and cased in leather twine—a necklace. Adam slips it over his neck, kisses the stone, and smiles at the sister. Elemech returns his smile, though much of her delight comes from knowing that men always ask for more than what they need.

The Wolf pried Adam and Morigan's praying grasp apart and the Dream ended. After Morigan had returned to herself, she passed the talisman—only a simple necklace, she realized—back to Adam. "You asked for the gift of communion and understanding," she said. "That is what you were given. I don't think this token has any more magik remaining within it. I believe it was more a key than a tool. Its power was spent unlocking your desire."

"My desire?"

"To communicate. With everything, you said. I know not how far-reaching the wish truly is, but it certainly intrigued my mother with its scope," she replied.

Adam thought of the voices he'd heard last night. Perhaps his joy over speaking and interacting with man and nature again had accelerated whatever magik the sister had planted within him. He paled. There could be worse curses, he supposed, than hearing the many voices of land and sea—although at some point he would have to consider what this would mean for his diet. Could he really kill and eat creatures that pleaded for their lives?

"Adam? Where are you, lad?" Thackery lightly shook the fellow. "You look like a hundred troubles in one man. You haven't had a scrap to eat. You have a vacancy in your eyes that I've seen only in Morigan. And you're pale, but you're too tanned to be pale." Thackery looked ahead and made a noise of frustration. "Our guide does not seem to have noticed we have stopped—or perhaps he doesn't care. At any rate, he's now quite some distance ahead."

"Hold a moment," Adam shouted to the shadow far down the tunnel; their guide stopped, clearly understanding him. Unfortunately, Adam's companions could make no sense of the thick syllables that flew from his throat. When Adam resumed speaking to his companions, he did so in Ghaedic—his transition between languages was as fluid as the shifts performed by a master translator. He didn't even seem to realize the shift had occurred. "The sister did indeed grant my wish. But the sisters' gifts always come at a cost or bring unforeseen consequences—and mine was no different." Keys. Voices. Powers. Finally, it was Adam's turn at the wheel of strange, and he'd won one of the oddest prizes at the fair.

"Fair enough," said the Wolf. "Alas, our guide has no courtesy, and Eatoth is in danger; we'll discuss this later." *Soon, Father, you will know your son's claws and teeth*, thought the Wolf. Frowning and determined, he pushed ahead.

In no time at all, they caught up to their guide. Adam asked a few questions at Morigan's behest—where are we going? Whom are we to meet?—but the blue robe made no answer. Their silent journey under the pounding shield below Eatoth continued for many strides, perhaps even a span or two. Gradually, the din quieted, more behind than before them now. They were under the city now, the Wolf sensed. Hundreds of strides up and through the gray bedrock, feet scuffled, cries echoed, and a clatter of mortal sounds played a noisy symphony. Eatoth was immense, he realized—perhaps larger than any of the cities of the West.

Winds bearing woodsy smoke and sultry-sweet oils blew down the tunnel. The Wolf sniffed and tasted what he could, though none of it was familiar. Not long after that, the tunnel's roof dropped, and they began walking up an incline. They passed through a heavily fortified area: two small bastions of stone and a gate that blocked the tunnel from floor to ceiling. The guardhouse had dozens of tiny glass windows, and faces were visible at each one. The Wolf was reminded of the submersibles he'd once seen on the Feordhan. There was a marine-like quality to the gate and gatehouses; perhaps the structures were waterproofed. In this city of water, the guardhouse might even do double duty as a loch. The soldiers visible through the glass were all men, swarthy and strong. Although they glared from afar, the company and their guide were not detained, but they were delayed, as it took many sands to open the grand metal gate.

Light dazzled them, for what lay beyond was a city brighter even than a realm of sunlight and dreams. They wandered past their guide and through the gate, mouths agape, entering a yawning earthen mouth with a carved tongue of stairs that led upward. Dazzling words from the mythic language of Pandemonia had been chiseled into the gold-painted ruts of every step and it was as if the strangers trod upon the glowing prose of a Dreamer; plated, hammered, also dazzling murals hung like metal banners on the walls on either side. The stories stairs and murals told looked fabulous even to these four beings of the fantastic. They depicted a phantasmagoric Pandemonian bestiary: giant fire-belching lizards, women with scorpion tales, men with the heads of bulls, and vistas of sun, sand, forest, and moon that possessed a three-dimensional lure.

In the wide tunnel, the company broke apart and studied the walls with their hands and eyes. Adam was drawn to the stairs. He looked down past his feet to the shimmering stone, and felt awed and frightened when he realized he knew every word engraved on it. *What she wills, she wills*, read the prose near his dirty big toe.

Momentarily, his companions had regrouped, and they now pushed the young man along—his new skill would be needed to communicate with the unimaginable swell of people chattering and moving above. Once the walls met with level ground, the stairs spilled out onto plated cobbles, which had been handset and inscribed. They now stood in a raised stone enclosure with two circular guard towers—a barbican—and men bearing shining weapons surrounded them. Here, though, things were made for beauty as well as for function, and mosaics ran in lengths of hammered metal over brick and down decorative pillars. There was no roof to support, and on the flat tops of these pillars posed elegant carved muses, male and female, that poured water into thin channels below. Even the gateway before the travelers, which was made of curlicues and gothic brass, looked designed to house a nobleman's horses. The four gazed from beauty to beauty, and then their eyes and ears followed the bedazzlement and noise up to the sky.

There, sunlight dashed rainbows through row after row of glass and metal towers so tall that the company had to lean back to take them in. The glass finger that they'd seen from afar was not a single structure, but a combined effect produced by hundreds upon hundreds of towers. A pleasant thunderhead, a gray guardian broken with spots of gold, clouded the city and dampened the already damp company with a sheen of dew. It was humid but warm, without an ocean's cold wetness, although the constant rumbling hiss of the city would not be out of place on an ocean's shore. In the clouds darted handfuls of glass insects—skycarriages of a kind, though smaller and more compact.

As they tried to absorb the extraordinary vista, their guide left them in the circle of armed men. Tall, bronzed, and athletic, they all wore sandals, short pleated skirts, circlets, and baroque chest plates each of which was emblazoned with a lion's roaring face. Every one of them was male and bore a vicious gisarme: they pointed the weapons at the strangers, making no secret of their intent. These weapons—from hilt to hooked blade—were of the same steaming icy substance as the staff of the blue sorcerer. The Wolf assumed they could be made to sizzle skin like a black and lethal frostburn.

Elsewhere in the barbican, many more soldiers watched from their posts with frowning curiosity. Soon the soldiers who had detained the four prodded the herd to one side of the barbican. There, a dozen scowling fellows kept a watchful eye on the travelers. *Some hospitality*, thought the Wolf. *I shall allow you to keep me here, but only for the moment.* He flashed them a smile—full, white, and gleaming with sharp teeth—and they backed away a few steps. Then he snapped his teeth, and they stepped back a few more. Paying them no heed after that, the Wolf splashed in one of the showers falling from the nearest pillar. Then he pulled his Fawn close and dribbled a handful of water into her mouth. Morigan hadn't realized how thirsty the day's travel had made her; her bloodmate had, though.

Thank you, she said. *I feel as if we have walked into the lions' den, and not merely because of the armor they wear.*

The Wolf looked around at his fellows. Certainly, the sight of a tattooed half-naked changeling, a man of power holding a staff twisting with light, and his own large self might be a shock for people not used to their company. Hunting with his sight, he discovered that their guide was now talking to a circle of warriors—he spoke using sign language, which explained why he hadn't replied to any of their earlier questions. Any misconceptions should be cleared up in a moment.

"Oh," muttered Adam, who'd been listening to the chatter of nearby soldiers, who were permitted to speak without their hands, apparently.

Just then, the Wolf caught the sharp onion stink of the changeling's fear and knew that something was wrong. Indeed, the soldiers now reeked of it, too, and their hands were trembling. Everyone's attention appeared centered upon the Wolf. Testing a theory, the Wolf stepped away from the pillar, and their guards shuffled back. "They are afraid," he said. "Of me, I believe. Perhaps my friendly snap earlier was not so clever an idea."

Adam continued to eavesdrop. After a moment, he turned back, looking grave. "It's more than that. They seem to know who you are, great Wolf."

"I?" replied the Wolf.

"And who your father is."

The son of Brutus. It wasn't unreasonable to think that the mad king could have spread his legend of doom and ruin even this far East. Suddenly, soldiers began barking, and the warriors in the background sprang to attention. A hundred gisarmes faced the company in a wall of blades. After arriving in Eatoth as willing visitors, they had now become captives.

III

The men attempted to force hoods and chains upon the company, though their efforts were rewarded with bruises and fractured skulls: Caenith tossed the warriors about like toy soldiers. Morigan managed to rein in her bloodmate, prevent him from committing further acts of violence, but each side appeared hungry for more. It was only Adam's constant attempts at appeasement that succeeded in forging an unsteady peace. After the worst of the commotion had simmered down into grumbles and wounded egos, the blue sorcerer stepped forward, accompanied by a small guard.

The company was then promptly led out of the barbican through a gauntlet of twitchy soldiers.

Once in Eatoth, the company resumed their overawed gawking—they couldn't help it, even though they were conscious of their peril. Over their shoulders, they saw the wall of thunder, crystal, and water. Sprawling along the cultivated streets were weary domes, crumbling amphitheaters, and weathered ruins that had been converted into outdoor gardens and markets; Thackery wondered what the original structures had looked like, and how many centuries upon centuries ago Eatoth had been built. The buildings he could see manifested a wonderful, classic eccentricity. Some had loggias and opulent gold touches that suggested ancient dynasties, while others had modern balconies and clean, regal architecture that looked almost Eodian.

Truly, there was a marvelous symmetry here between old and new, between the towers of crystal and magik—tenements, surely, given the city's size—and the remnants of previous generations. Even some of the street tiles over which they were herded remained unembellished by progress. In and amongst the brass bricks were smooth, timeworn cobbles—stones sanded by millennia of footsteps to a glassy polish. As for the causeways of the city, they spread far and wide, and roads of stone and glass rose like frozen rivers over the city.

Then there were the people—so very many people. Swarms of white, gold, silver, and gaily dressed folk strode, chatted, shopped, and sat on patios. Their movements were like strings of shimmering music, as if they were nymphs attuned to the strains of the impromptu concerts happening on the street or to the songs of the operatic divas who performed in the shells of ancient theaters—their voices higher and with more vibrato than those of the singers of the West. The people of Eatoth were beautiful, carefree, and intimidatingly cultured.

As if trying to hide his barbarity, Thackery found himself shrinking. Strangely, none of the throng beyond the gated-off plaza where they trod seemed to see him, his ethereal red-haired friend, the giant, or the half-naked man—the citizens were too involved in their glorious affairs to notice the unclean things walking out of the garrison. The company weren't led far: they were brought only just outside the portcullis of the barbican and then urged forward a few paces. Their unintentional staring had transformed a journey of a few steps into one of many sands. They couldn't have stopped themselves from hungrily looking around; they were all too overwhelmed by the city's barrage of architectural, technomagikal, and artistic marvels. Even the Wolf was stupefied. While he dragged his feet and sniffed the uncountable, unidentifiable odors—woods, metals, spices, perfumes, and elemental rawness—most of his anger fizzled away.

The plaza in which they now wandered boasted many wonders. Unusual silver eggs lay about, each as large as a carriage and somehow perfectly planted on its curved underside so that it did not rock. Ordered and in rows, the silver ovals lined the courtyard as if a gargantuan sterling hen called this place its coop. They saw no divine bird, though, only more of the unusual eggs zipping about the sky at dangerous speeds. None of the vehicles—Thackery assumed that was what they were—could be spotted beyond the fence in the streets. He supposed they would interrupt the atmosphere of civility.

The company and their guard approached one of the eggs. The blue sorcerer touched the shell of the object, and it cracked almost like an egg, though the shell folded and fell inward in a deliberate pattern. Within specks, a portal had formed. The blue sorcerer went through it, and the guards indicated that the company should follow and suggested they would receive pokes if they did not. They complied and entered a compact space that glowed with the same sapphire brightness as the blue sorcerer's staff. Inside, the rounded parts of the egg were filled with square edges, and plush benches had been installed. The blue sorcerer and two of his guards sat at one end of the egg, the company at the other. Thanks to the Wolf's size, his knees encroached upon everyone. The tilted gisarmes didn't add to the coziness of the arrangement. It was bound to be an unpleasant ride.

A crackling sounded, and the entrance pieced itself together like a puzzle of shattered glass. Of the company, only the Wolf, who was sensitive to every shift and change, realized they'd left the ground. They soon realized the truth, however, for the shell of their vessel was not wholly opaque. As they rose up into clearer, brighter climes, they could see dim and moving shadows upon the walls.

"Holy shite!" exclaimed Thackery. He never swore, but he could find no other words to appropriately describe his shock at discovering they'd shot hundreds of paces into the air without creating turbulence or noise. What sorcery could do that? Was it even sorcery, or some art beyond magik? He whispered, "This metascience...it is beyond anything I have ever known. The theory and mechanics of this craft. I mean, I can't even say for certain that there are parts, moving parts, or any engine in here! I don't feel one."

"There isn't one," replied the Wolf—the close quarters caused his rock-grinding voice to echo, and the guards jumped. "I hear no gears or engines. I do, however, smell the rich, but not unpleasant, scent of magik." He sniffed. "A fresh and clean mist. Like the last billow of winter's breath over a spring lake. A power both elemental and pure."

The Wolf had no more to say, but he'd left Thackery with much to think about. Thackery pondered the nature of a craft fueled purely by magik. The enchantment and sorcery behind such an achievement proved an extraordinary challenge to understand. If he threw away what he knew of magikal theory and technomancy, tossed out the mechanical element entirely, he was left with the phenomenon of a hollow, light craft that flew by elemental propulsion alone. Or perhaps it twisted the wind, manipulated the heat and density of the moisture in the air to create an artificial buoyancy—that would make sense, given Eatoth's mastery of the force and energy of water. Still, he didn't solve the enigma or make any grand breakthroughs in the field of technomagikal engineering during his short mental vacation—mostly because within sands, the ride was over.

As had happened with the liftoff, no one noticed the landing except for the Wolf. Suddenly, the wall crackled, a gust from a high-up place blasted the inside of the vessel, and the blue sorcerer moved out into a bright windy void. The guardsmen stayed behind until the company had left the craft, then followed with their polearms and unspoken threats. They stepped out onto a blustery circular aerie. There were no railings, and the clouds were so near they could see the unusual twists of lightning rolling slowly within them. In an instant, the four were licked from head to toe by rain. A gentle rain, but also a constant one. They stepped gingerly: the slipperiness of the glass beneath their feet could lead to a careless fall and then to a screaming death. At least they didn't appear to have far to go, for the blue robe soon led them through an arch in the side of a cloud-reflecting ziggurat. An astonishingly loud rumble of thunder chased them inside.

Gloom welcomed them. As their eyes adjusted to it, they found themselves in a grand space that once again inspired gasps of awe. Their curiosity was piqued by a change in architecture: unlike the old world down below, these resonant corridors were lined with crystal. Trapped figments of light twisted inside the walls. It was as if the companions wandered the hallways of an alien ship that sailed the stars. Some traces of more classic architecture persisted in the form of heavily frescoed libraries and antechambers that opened off the path that they walked. The Wolf noticed that a few of these secondary tunnels echoed with strange metal music and heat—they weren't forges, but they were certainly places of unfathomable industry. However, none of these places was their destination.

They walked along a dreamy road of glass and stars, consumed by a marveling dread. It was so quiet, their footsteps and even the water dripping from their clothing seemed as loud as the smashing of plates. *Does no one speak here?* wondered the Wolf, though he admitted to himself that he found this respite from noise a blessing. The soldiers in attendance said nothing to one another, and whenever the blue robe passed people, he hailed them using his hand language. Within the ziggurat, the company encountered many blue robes and soldiers. Unlike the soldiers that herded them, these warriors were dressed in flowing white gowns and wore gold circlets of metal leaves and filigree. Instead of polearms, they carried crystalline swords and shields. Their poses were stiff and suggested a potential threat that caused the Wolf to tense whenever he and his company passed. Still, the travelers had never known a place so strange, and their fear came primarily from the knowledge that they were no longer in Geadhain. Adam, who'd known only woodland for most of his life, felt especially bewildered. "Where are they taking us?" he wondered.

Up, thought the Wolf. For he could feel something above—a presence, a force, or perhaps a person. It sat over his head like a storm cloud, fulminous and full of power. Their party soon left the hallway and entered an opulent antechamber much like the ones they'd spied earlier. A rickety, caged metal lift of the kind that could be found in old tenements stood at the far end of the chamber. There were people in the great chamber, but not a single blue-hooded man stirred from his prayers to peer at the company as they passed. Instead, the kneeling contemplatives looked down to where their crystal staves lay on velvet pillows, or kept their stares upon the metal-wrought panels along the wall, studying the menagerie of monsters and heroes. The strangers were of no consequence to the blue robes. They had matters of more importance to ponder than those involving the son of Brutus and his dirty friends.

They created an impression of silent judgment and haughty fervor that lingered within the Wolf. Then he and his pack were inside the lift, and the caged door rattled shut. Once more, the fusion of old and new expressed itself: the squealing, jostling ride took them up past a cupola on the roof and into a shaft of pure darkness. The companions and their surroundings were consumed by the ghostly blue shade cast by their escorts' glowing weapons. Soon, natural light found them, and the lift stopped on a small domed floor.

It was no more than a room, really—one with a gleaming brass floor. Windows filled the walls, and gray seas drifted behind their glass. The chamber was ascetically clean and simple, much like the girl sitting on a long settee—or possibly a bed, as there was a wardrobe nearby. A tilted circlet crowned her head, and a shift hung off her shoulders with a certain lopsided disregard. Her hair was braided and dark. She had the complexion of an Arhadian princess, cinnamon and bronze. She could not be judged either pretty or ugly; her resting expression was a hard scowl that made such a determination difficult. The woman's dark-circled eyes had a pull, as if she were a Dreamer of ravens and secrets.

While the strangers stood there, she gave instructions to the soldiers using hand gestures. The chamber was so quiet, and the storm outside so muted, that even those not of wolfish blood thought they could hear the papery scratch of her fingers on her palms. A moment later, the lift shrieked once more as it descended, carrying the guardsmen. The blue robe remained. He walked to the young girl and stood beside her seat like a golem. In a gesture that seemed familiar to the bloodmates and their friends, the girl tipped her head as if listening to a sound or voice. Then she pointed at Morigan—not at Adam, who could speak her tongue—and beckoned her forward.

The seer understood. Almost at once, she'd sensed in the young woman the prickling of forces that resembled her bees. Morigan came forward and bowed—she felt the gesture was appropriate, as it was clear the woman was of high standing. The girl reached out, touched Morigan's chin to lift it, and spoke. Words and tongues were secondary when two speaking souls communed; they understood each other without the need of a translator. *Daughter of Fate*, said the woman.

Keeper, replied Morigan. More truths entered Morigan's mind in a series of piercing stings. This woman was not young: she was, in fact, far older than she appeared. Ancient. Such vitality was likely the result either of magik or of something from the vault of whispers, secrets, and hidden truths that the woman held in her head behind a tightly warded barrier of Will. Morigan could hear the storm of secrets there, banging like fists on metal. *Are you an oracle? A sorceress? An arbiter of Fates? How do you know who I am?* she asked.

I listen, replied the Keeper. *The world speaks of your tale—and his—with every whisper of wind. How could I not know of you and the son of Brutus? I shall tell my wards and legionnaires to stand down, though, for they do not know how your love has cleansed him. I can see both your light and his animal in each of you. What a divine balance you have struck with and for each other. As for how it is that you and I speak…Anyone can be heard if one learns how to tune out the less important noises: the grunts of desire, the grumbling stomachs of greed. This is no magik, simply a different approach. In the old times, before we became masters of inner silence, we would honor our covenant of silence by communicating only through scribblings on scraps of paper. How crude must that have been! I cannot imagine. This is how two minds should speak. I have heard that there are those in your land who still practice our faded traditions.*

I would not know. Your city amazes me, and these eyes have had their fill of wonderment. It all still sounded like magik to Morigan, but she had other matters to bring to the Keeper's attention, assuming the woman was not already aware of them. *Do you know why I am here, then? Have your winds told you of the omens I've seen?*

It is not just the winds: all of Geadhain speaks. The Keeper smiled in what Morigan felt was a somewhat patronizing manner. *Here in my perfect tower of solitude, I hear nearly all of Geadhain's secrets. Nearly all. Some of her whispers, though, are hidden by dark forces.*

Yes. I have met the ones with whom Brutus conspires.

The Keeper took her hands as if they were sisters. *To which of his allies are you referring?*

The Black Queen: we have come to Pandemonia to unravel her mystery. But there's also Brutus's consort, who walks in Dreams. I have seen them both, and they hunger for your city's ruin.

The Keeper's composure cracked, leaking cold anger. *One who walks in Dreams?*

Yes. She attacked us when we came to your continent. She tried to tempt me into committing horrible acts, but I did not submit to her Will. She is a witch, a temptress who wears a mask of flies and corruption. She is truly horrid, but she is weak without her disguises.

What is her name? The Keeper's hands were hot now, and clenched hers tightly.

I don't know, Morigan replied and the Keeper loosened her grip. *Although I should like to find out. This Dreamstalker influences the mad king; she is part of this war. A general for the dark. I sense that their shared history goes back many chapters...*Morigan paused. What was it that the Keeper held so tightly behind her wall of Will? A flickering image of many trees—perhaps a garden, glowing and bright—the scent of sweet blossoms or a fruit like an apple, and the laugh of a child...Quite violently, the vision was torn from Morigan's head, crumpled, and then thrown away. Nevertheless, the thrust of pain she'd felt in that memory was as real as a sword strike. It was a dark event, the cause of great regret.

The Keeper stiffened, became more guarded. *We can aid you by giving you whatever information you need to continue your quest for the truth,* she said. *Our stores, our hospitality, and the wisdom of a culture that has existed since before the Kings laid their first stone in the West are yours to use. If nothing else, I shall have this ward escort you to a place of rest. You must be tired after braving our lands.*

Now Morigan clutched at her host. *Keeper? Are you not listening? I have come with a warning. The mad king will come to your city. I have seen a possible future, a probable future, in which all of these grand achievements burn and melt to nothingness.*

The Keeper smiled, again regarding her as if she were a child. *Daughter of Fate, Eatoth has stood for thousands of years in the wildest realm of this world; not so much as a rebellion has threatened its peace and prosperity. We are not without defenses, defenses that cannot be breached by the mad king or any of his consorts in darkness. We have a wall of water, and every entrance to our nation is under gate and guard. If necessary, we can bend the elements of our city to our Will: We can call forth storms and thunder. We can flood the tunnels in an instant. Our wards—men of magik and wisdom such as the one who stands next to me—could bring tidal wave after tidal wave down upon our enemies. We could bury them in mountains of hail. Do not underestimate the wrath of water. Like the sea, Eatoth can be tempestuous and horrific. I shall not hesitate to order the execution of any enemy of our city.*

I admire your peoples' accomplishments, and I hear what you say, replied Morigan. *However, you do not know the mad king as we do. You have not watched him and his allies dismantle the ancient civilizations of the West, often by exploiting their leaders' weaknesses and pride. Give men and women the tools of their own destruction, and more often than not, they will do the work themselves.*

We are safe here.

What nonsense! The Keeper was acting decidedly uptight and ignorant in the face of the most terrible threat the world had ever known, and Morigan had reached her limit. As Moreth had told them, one of Pandemonia's great cities had already fallen, probably to Brutus or one of his allies. She countered the Keeper's haughtiness by throwing this information in her face. *What of Aesorath? Once the City of Wind, it is now the City of Screams. I have seen this place. My bloodmate and I traveled there in Dream. At one time, it was a city as great, advanced, and protected as Eatoth. Now it is a city of dead flutes that play dirges for their arrogant masters. It is a graveyard. Do you want Eatoth to suffer the same fate? I am Fate's daughter. I have seen more than one woman should ever see, though I accept the burden of my power. I would not cast prophecies of doom around carelessly. I have never yet been wrong. We must think of how Brutus will strike and of how we can prepare for him.*

Anger wrinkled the Keeper. As reality began to distort, the lines on her face widened, becoming cracks and then fissures. Morigan, suddenly airborne and spinning, fell into these fissures of the past.

She floats in the highest chamber in a stone steeple. Morigan hears winds carrying the distant tolling of bells and other queer percussion music in through the grand windows. There are four windows: the place is almost like a belfry, though there is no bell. Outside shines a golden glory, though the sunlight shrinks from the wicked acts happening here and none reaches beyond the window's ostentatious moldings. Light grazes the little men and gargoyles carved into the stone windowsills and flickers off the polished eyes of the thousand watchers—witnesses to punishment, like Morigan.

A girl screams in the darkest part of the room. Morigan looks to where the shadows fall down in sheets of black from the whirling dusty heights of the chamber. Something wicked is unfolding under that dark curtain, but she cannot see it clearly; this memory resists her Will. Is that a gleam of metal? Is that the sound of meat being wetly cut that she hears between the screams?

The vision recoils from her. Morigan casts her silver servants from their hive. They sting her with whatever scattered memories they can harvest. From afar, she sees two silhouettes sitting on a raised bench in a garden. Although all is foggy, she knows this is a garden by the green hue of the haze and the smell of grass and life. I am glad you came, she thinks, yet cannot say who is glad or why, as the scene is then torn up and thrown to pieces. The keeper of these memories locks them away. Morigan fumbles in the sudden darkness. She hears the scream again. In a spotlight of vision, something pink, rubbery, and small lies in a pool of blood. It has the gleam of an organ pulled from the body, but she cannot say what it is. A wetter, rougher scream—male, this time—joins the first. Then with a whirl and a violent shake, she is returned.

Only an instant had passed while the two women battled in each other's minds. As the Keeper regained her senses, she struggled and wrenched herself away from the seer. Undeterred, and with her bloodmate's reflexes, Morigan wrestled with the Keeper and caught her by the ankle as she crawled down the settee to escape. Immediately sensing the threat of the moment, the Wolf whisked forward just in time to stop the blue robe's staff from striking his beloved. He caught the head of the staff in his hand and grunted as he felt its sizzling cold. Flesh peeled from his palms. Still, he held fast and then rattled the weapon, sending its wielder into a flying tumble. The blue robe landed with a cry some strides distant. The Wolf dropped the staff and stood on it with one of his witchstitch sandals—the material did much to dispel the burn. While the blue robe scrambled up again, the Wolf kept his foot on the weapon. He crossed his arms and shook his head, silently communicating that he although he meant no further harm, he would brook no further interruption. After shaking off their surprise, Thackery and Adam rushed to his side and joined him in making intimidating poses.

Release me! You have no right! accused the Keeper.

Morigan noticed a sweep of blue out of the corner of her eye and felt frost prickle her cheek. Then a whoosh and a man-scented wind saved her from a blow, as she knew it would. Her time with the Keeper would not last much longer, and what diplomacy there had been had clearly reached its end. *What is this tower I have seen in which a man and a woman scream? What is this memory that you keep from me? It burns to be seen. Tell me. I shall find the truth, one way or another.*

Release me, or I shall summon every ward and legionnaire of Eatoth to my defense. You may be the Daughter of Fate, but I am the ruler of Eatoth.

Such hubris—it was a mask for weakness, surely. Nonetheless, Morigan knew that the Keeper wasn't bluffing. Furthermore, she realized she'd overstepped her bounds, and possibly endangered her companions. The beast cooled to a simmer in her veins. She released the Keeper, raised her hands, and backed away. Not quite ready to, or capable of, surrender, the Wolf held his stance and traded glowers with the blue robe and the woman with whom his bloodmate had tangled. It took a whisper from Morigan to calm him. *More secrets and lies, my Wolf. But I have gone too far in hunting them. Let us hope she will not punish us. We still need to meet our companions here.*

Nothing she'd said shocked him; he smelled a sweet fart of deceit wafting up from the Keeper. Puffing, the Wolf kicked the staff over to the blue robe and stepped back, following his bloodmate's example. He did not, however, raise his hands, making them into fists instead. As the blue robe retrieved his staff and righted himself, inaudible instructions were given to him by his mistress. Nothing spoke of the Keeper's mood beyond her stench and the darkness of her eyes, which were blacker now from rage or sorrow. Thackery wondered if they would be thrown in a dungeon for this assault on her Holiness. However, he felt that the Keeper would stand in the way of their mission only if she were truly debased and deluded.

Uneasily, the blue robe came forward. He didn't raise his staff, but walked around the four travelers, waited for the lift to be summoned, then opened the cage's lattice once the platform appeared. A polite escort out was not quite what the company had expected. Whether the chamber to which they would descend would be filled with armed wards and legionaries ready to prod them into whatever passed for prisons in this utopia was a question as yet unanswered. As the lift doors closed, Morigan looked back at the Keeper: her head was bowed, her face stretched in silent sobs. If she could experience regret, then surely she could feel forgiveness and mercy, too. Morigan wished, however, that she knew the secret of the tower, of the blood and the scent of apples. For she felt as if not knowing could damn them all.

IV

After plunging into the deepest silence, the Keeper stirred many hourglasses later. She slipped off her chair, knelt, and slid her hands under the cushions still warm from her body. She reached deep and far, then upward through a tear in the cotton. Her fingertips touched the smoothness of old stone and the furriness of rawhide. A touch was enough. She did not want to retrieve the talisman. She needed to know only that it was still there, beneath her, a reminder of her sins.

The Daughter of Fate had seen too deeply into her soul. She felt naked and ravaged. She wanted to hate the woman, and yet the loathing she conjured was mostly for herself. It was night, and black pearls of water beaded upon the window at which she stared. In the dark mirror, she thought she saw a face for an instant. She leaped up and raced over, but the brown, handsome face with strong lines around the mouth disappeared as her hand touched cold glass.

Spirits were haunting her tonight. She wondered what others would come. Heading over to her armoire, she searched its lower drawers for the potent tincture that brought on dreamless, black sleeps. She squeezed a dozen drops onto her tongue, twice the necessary dosage. She changed into an evening shift—unassuming, white, and chaste. She took a pee and splashed her face in the lavatory hidden behind a cleverly mirrored and enchanted screen that maintained the apparent emptiness of the room. By then, her feet were heavy, and her young flesh ached as if it had not been sustained by elemental magik for a hundred years. She hit the cushions of the settee and continued to descend, falling deeper into a groping dark.

For a while, her dreams were a void. Yet, in the darkness, there came a dissonance. At first it was a chattering and buzzing, almost a whisper. Then words wriggled their way out like maggots. Suddenly, her black dreamscape twisted vividly red and rippled like glistening offal. A force thrashed her awake, and she screamed the words that she'd heard in the buzzing darkness.

"Hear me!" she cried.

The Keeper's echo startled her as much as her nightmare had. She was no longer in her chamber of quietude. During her sleep, she'd somehow traveled through lifts, floors, passageways, and guard points and arrived at the heart of her nation. The Purgatorium. Eatoth had produced no greater achievement than the chamber in which she now stood. She never came here. No one aside from technomancers and watersculptors would or should. The wonder of the immense spinning stone held aloft by a column of watery blue light awed and confused her. Although the arkstone was small in size—about as large as skull—the tube in which it floated magnified its appearance so that those who saw to its care could microscopically examine it without touching it. The mere sight of the arkstone inspired wonder. Glittering with starry sapphire blood, it looked like a grayish-blue moon that had been split with an axe.

The arkstone was clearly an object from the great black beyond. It had not come from Geadhain, but had crashed into her green body when one of the Dreamers fell. It was the source of Eatoth's might, the well from which the city drew its secrets. Through the slow bleeding of the stone, her ancestors had conquered the skies and elements. They'd battled age and illness. All that had been accomplished with a mere trickle of the arkstone's power. She wondered what it would take to exhaust it, for the production of sky vessels, endless waterfalls, and wealth seemed only to skim off its power.

She came as close as she could to the diaphanous pillar that housed this giant force, but she could not really reach the floating object without the ladders and cranes the technomancers used. So, she came nearer and stared up into the trembling column of light within the glass—focusing on the blue sun hovering above. She held out her hands. Divine power, beating like a Dreamer's heart, came over her in invisible waves.

The resonance resounded in the cavernous glass bubble in which she stood, and returned her senses to her. She stepped away from the arkstone's case and no longer wandered aimlessly, but moved toward a black dot in the wall of the grand place. An exit. Why had she come here? There was nothing to see here, no reason to visit Purgatorium unless one was coming for the arkstone.

All the machinery, pipes, and wiring were hidden beneath the hazily translucent floor and walls. She peered through and around the seemingly feeble glass that kept this place from collapsing, and wondered what the rings and shades of earth would feel like if their tonnage fell on her for her sacrilege. With no other soul to echo in this greatness, she felt chillingly alone and her sleeping garment was about as useful as a paper dress in a snowstorm. Again, what had driven her from a comatose slumber down into the bowels of her realm?

She had no answer, but dread was brewing in her stomach. She sat above, and the arkstone sat below. Together Paradisum and Purgatorium ensured balance in Eatoth, much the same way man's baseness and vices were balanced by the morality and wisdom of the Keepers. She must ever remain in her place. She must ever be the watchful and pure mind of their nation. She recalled the former Keeper Superior's harsh mind-whispering doctrines, and the lashes she received for not repeating them properly, smarting from her remembered scorn.

"I, Ankha, the virtuous, the pure, the wise, am Keeper Superior now," she threatened the old ghost. "I hold the lash now. I absolve the sinners of their sins."

But memories of the sins she had committed to don that mantle were neither virtuous nor pure nor wise: the tower, the vilest betrayal, the stink of piss, blood, and fear, and the feel of a wriggling organ in her hand. Memories ruined her moment of triumph.

Frowning, Ankha reached the exit, which was small and clean and had a crystal-hewn door that raised itself as she approached. Two wards stood on the other side, guarding a sparkling antechamber that buzzed with technomagikal tunes. Veins of pulsing sapphire blood rose to the ceiling, and the Keeper Superior questioned for a moment the vainglory of her people, supposedly so beholden to nature. There was nothing natural about any of the great cities' opulence. They'd put the old ways behind them long ago, as she must put behind her any guilt she suffered on behalf of her nation. She threw a thought into one of the ward's heads as quickly and forcefully as the old Keeper Superior would have done; she was the one true and holy queen of Pandemonia now.

Purgatorium is secure. Although Ankha wasn't clear on what she had said to gain access in the first place, she was not concerned they'd question her presence. Still, her strange actions told her she needed to put safeguards in place. Perhaps the seer's warning had been worth worrying over after all. *Triple the wards, and fill the bailey with legionnaires. Post guards around my sanctum. The Kings' War has at last come to Pandemonia.*

XV

THE HUNT

I

"At least we weren't exiled from the city," said Thackery, pouting. It was hard to feel entirely miserable considering the charming quarters to which he and the others had been promptly escorted after their meeting with the Keeper—a meeting in which their attempt to warn the city of its doom had turned into an altercation between the stoic Keeper and her henchman. Here, wide-open doors—polished wood with little squares of glass—led out onto a terrace overlooking a grand piazza of shining brass and stone. When he'd wandered out upon it, seeking to free himself from the despair of his companions, he'd spied a grand crowd milling around on a rambling road. Artisans, street bands, and actors had been performing in the street below. Even now, back inside, he could hear their harmonies.

At the moment, he and his three companions sat in a room with thick trim, luxurious armchairs and couches, and false colonnades that supported nothing but the opulence of this place. Art and false curtains hung on the weary bricks of the old structure. Thackery's three friends wore as much defeat on their faces as he did. He looked around at the frowning, lounging, lost-in-thought folk and decided they were in need of rallying.

Thackery stood up from the bed onto which he'd sunk; the extravagance was numbing, he realized. He clapped for attention.

"Right," he said. "We've come to save the city. I have more faith in Morigan's visions than in the presumptuous proclamations of a leader who seems too isolated in her crystal tower to appreciate the reality of the threat. What are we going to do, other than sit here and sulk?"

"Brutus will come," said Morigan. She stirred in the armchair where she'd been sitting and staring at the fire that crackled beneath the chamber's limestone mantel. In truth, the mantel's unnecessary leaves and engraved golden images of Pandemonia's bizarre bestiary had been distracting her from serious contemplation. None of those monsters approached Brutus in his vileness and evil. Smiling, she looked at her friend and father figure. "You're right, we are wasting time here. The Keeper said that we would have access to the city's resources and knowledge. I'd like to know why Brutus would come here, if this city's defenses truly cannot be breached. There must be a reason. In Zioch, he laid a trap for his brother. In Gorgonath, he set out to replenish his horde. Now he's come to Pandemonia, targeted Eatoth, and we've no idea why. It's an important question, as important as how to stop him. It's dangerous to still be in the dark about his motives. I feel as if we're always following rather than leading. We need to get ahead of him on this. We might even end the Great War, here and now."

"Would destruction and death not be motivation enough for him?" suggested the Wolf. He rose from his chair opposite Morigan and threw a piece of the over-sauced, butter-soft meat their wardens had served them—food made for toothless rats, not wolves—into the fire. "I sense hundreds of thousands of lives and heart-beats here. After having being defeated twice over, my father must be in need of soldiers for his army. I think these bodies would be enough to entice him."

"That doesn't entirely make sense," countered Thackery. "Even if Brutus were to build another army, a horde, how would he return with it to Eod? Transporting his troops would be a logistical impossibility. And yet, I don't believe for a single speck that Brutus's business with his brother has ended. The Black Queen either needs Magnus's body or wants to see him dead if he cannot be claimed. Certainly, Brutus needs an army;

I can't see him and Magnus having a civilized duel to decide the World's fate. What then do the Black Queen and her heinous consorts want here, in this apparently impenetrable bastion of magik and wisdom?" Thackery walked over and touched Morigan's shoulder. "What do you see?"

Morigan shrugged. "The Fates are muddled. As we come nearer to the climax of this war, things become more uncertain. Eatoth will writhe in flames; that much I know. But I do not know whether it will be possible to prevent or mitigate the terrible damage Brutus will cause."

"We have to try," said Adam, and leaped off the couch where he'd been lying and nibbling on fruits. The thought of meat still spoiled his appetite, carnivore though he was.

"Of course," replied Morigan, also rising. The four now stood in a circle. "We shall never surrender to the dark. Let us leave this place and see where my senses, Caenith's senses, and the combined might of our intellect and determination lead us. We shall find no resolutions to our problems if we remain here in this chamber. Night is only a few hourglasses away, so we should hurry."

"We shall hunt and claim this truth," declared the Wolf.

Every soul in the room believed him.

II

Before departing, the company laid out a plan of action. It had been Thackery's idea to seek out archives or museums—they needed to understand the resources and strengths of Eatoth, and quickly. Any museum or place steeped in natural history would be a fertile hunting ground for Morigan: rich in stories, emanations, and spirits. Really, though, what they needed to do was wander, to see where their intuitions, which had guided them through every peril thus far, would lead.

The ward on guard outside their door didn't answer their inquiries, but he did nod and then sign a few words to one of the legionnaires stationed with him. That man—tall and broad, with calves that looked like bronze bricks—then detached himself from his countrymen and offered himself as their liaison for the day: he'd take them to something called the Exhibition, which sounded as if it were a museum, and anywhere else they wanted to go. They couldn't see much of their guide—whose name was Longinus, he told Adam—under his heavy, plumed helm, but the Wolf smelled the fruity tang of suspicion upon him. *More a spy than a liaison*, whispered the Wolf to his bloodmate.

Longinus and his contingent took the company down a winding staircase, a prettier, whiter version of the ones common in Menosian estates. When everyone reached the antechamber at the bottom, the companies split apart, and Longinus walked the four out into a dazzle of white light and sound. It took the travelers a while to adjust to the commotion in the streets. Adam walked up front with Longinus and chatted with the soldier. The changeling appeared enamored by the flourishes of music, art, and culture he saw, and had a question about everything. At first, Longinus replied only reluctantly, but Adam's persistence eventually wore down the stoniness of his manner. Soon Longinus appeared actively interested in showing Adam and the strangers his city. Adam did double duty as both tour guide and interpreter, and relayed Longinus's sightseeing facts to his pack.

They were in the historical district of the city, which contained its oldest bones, reframed and filled with new stone, marble, and metal flesh over time. Powdery walls that might have been standing three thousand years ago served as backdrops to busy outdoor eateries; these were filled with tea tables above which floated odd glass shields that somehow cast cooling gray shade instead of reflecting light. The people of Eatoth didn't seem to drink tea, though: they seemed fondest of mulled and alcoholic beverages that irritated the Wolf's nose with their spice and sweetness. People looked nonchalantly at the scowling giant and his strangely garbed friends before returning to their pursuit of pleasure and conversation. The Wolf had yet to see a person working, other than those who served. And even those service people could often be spied leaning against the bricks, smoking rolled paper things, or chatting with passersby. A civilization of layabouts, minstrels, and fools, the Wolf couldn't help but think.

The only severe notes were struck by the legionnaires who wandered in patrols and the towers—full, as they knew, of wards and keepers—that cast their lucent shadows on the road. Also, in these glimmering dark stretches, the company spotted signs of imperfection in Eatoth's otherwise unblemished facade. Here they saw urchins and vagrants; always dressed in rags, sometimes scarred with a cross-shaped brand on their foreheads, hands, or another visible place; a few were amputees. These cast-off folk lingered in arcade windows or lurked in the narrow cobbled alleys between shops and houses. When they caught sight of Longinus or some other legionnaire, the street dwellers would dissolve into the background like men and women of smoke.

Soon, the Wolf noticed the movements of these vagrants more than he did any of the marks of Eatoth's magnificence. He watched as they surreptitiously slipped their hands into the pockets of the passersby. He felt no need to alert any authorities to their thieving. These folk were clearly impoverished in a nation that had too much for its own good. In one grand square through which they passed, a pack of outcast children washed themselves in a fountain. As soon as Longinus's helmet flashed in the crowd, the children scattered, still naked, leaving much of their clothing behind. The Wolf brought the matter of these younglings to Adam's attention, and awaited an answer from their liaison.

After an exchange with the legionnaire, Adam turned to his friends. "*Amakri*," replied the changeling. Concepts of social status and standing were still rather foreign to him, so he puzzled over what else to say. "He speaks as you and I would speak, great Wolf, of those shamed in our old tribe. They are allowed to live among the others, but denied certain rights and freedoms—much as I was under Aghna's rule. Longinus tells me they are not *Lakpoli*: Blessed. These Amakri we've seen do not belong to the tribes who are allowed to work off their dishonor through labor in the Garden of Life—whatever that may be."

"Vassalage or vagrancy? Those are the choices given to persons not of the city?" The Wolf sneered up at the magnificent towers. "Man always finds a way to piss in his own garden. As for gardens, I am curious, though, as to the one you've mentioned."

Thackery agreed with a *Hm*.

Eatoth possessed even more wonders than did Eod. There was the road, which Adam informed them was called the Ramble. It curved past regal homes and noisy stores boasting great porticos and lattices of vines and flowers. It emptied into vacant plazas that took sands to cross and fluttered with birds. It took them into the cool, shaded, quiet neighborhoods at the bases of the Keeper's towers where they spied more Amakri. While staring at a pair of Amakri—a filthy man and woman who cowered behind a tall urn as they passed—Morigan's sight rippled, and she was sent elsewhere.

She stands in a darkness-drenched place. It is night, and wind and whistling sounds play songs to the moon. Morigan sees two figures much like the ones who triggered this vision tucked very close to each another and hiding behind a pillar. Other details of the room are vague; she senses only that it's staggering to behold in all its echoing grandness. She hasn't been pulled into the past to see this opulence, though: she's here to see the young lovers. Surely they are together, or want to be. Their desire is manifest around them in a red cloud; it's not the brazen crimson of carnality, though, but a gentler hue, softened with pink and white. It is the aura of true love.

A bit startled, Morigan realizes that she knows the young, brown, feline-stared beauty from a previous vision. Amunai was her name. She's a bit older now than when Morigan last saw her in an ancient chamber of knowledge and study. Much like the Keeper Morigan met today, Amunai is both young and ageless—the result of high status in one of the four great cities, Morigan decides. On this day, however, Amunai's usually hard face glows with honey-eyed beauty. The fellow who holds her to his body and whispers delightful words into her ear is the cause of her vitality.

He's a warrior, Morigan knows. A holy warrior something like a legionnaire, although he wears a silver chest plate, the metal twisted and raised in the form of a clawing bird; his cloak is dark, as are his eyes and skin. He's daringly handsome in a weathered, wind-scorched way that makes him appear older than he is.

Soundlessly, Amunai moans as he kisses her ear. She makes an inaudible gasp as his hands caress her breasts. But only for an instant does he act wantonly before lifting and holding her face so that they stare eye to eye. He is able to restrain his passion because he loves her, and wants more than her flesh. They must run away together. They must cast aside their roles as guardian and Keeper. In the chaotic wilds of Pandemonia, they can be whomever they want. Morigan hears him whisper all these things amid the kisses he steals from Amunai. Just then, the holy Keeper breaks her fast from speech. She doesn't implant her words into her lover's head, but speaks with her heart and through her mouth. She cannot contain her passion. "We shall," she promises, and her sultry scratch of a voice, one that must never be heard, arouses and amazes her lover.

They kiss so sweetly and erotically that Morigan is reminded of her first taste of the Wolf. Morigan knows, though, that they are doomed. A shower of warm blood, the shrill of agonized shrieking, and the feel of a rubbery worming object in her hands wake her.

"Amunai," said Morigan as the vision faded.

While in the Dreaming, she'd managed to keep walking a steady path in the physical realm—aided by the Wolf. Although Morigan had only whispered the name, Longinus somehow heard it and tripped. A woman who'd also caught Morigan's utterance looked at the seer with gaping terror, then touched her forehead and each shoulder as if warding off a curse. Morigan felt as if she'd just uttered Brutus's name in streets of Eod. "Adam," she said. "Already our hunt bears fruit. Ask our guide who Amunai is or was. I've seen her twice now. The Fates have declared her importance. I must know."

Adam's mention of the name brought many more ghastly stares and invocations against evil from passersby. Longinus, though, refused to answer any of Adam's questions, and they continued along the Ramble in an unfriendly silence. Finally, Morigan called for the party to stop, not caring whether she made a scene. She stepped in front of Longinus, gazed into the blue eyes burning in his helm, and repeated the name. Each time he heard it, he seemed to become angrier or more fearful. Nonetheless, her bees had found a nectar, a truth, and she would reach into his head and harvest it, if need be. Morigan was about to pick the man's mind apart when he gave a full-body shiver and directed them to leave the street. They gathered in a narrow lane hung with clothes hangers. Longinus looked around at the open windows from which breathed string music and chatter, and then down the mostly quiet path. A young gentleman on a bicycle had paused to talk to his sweetheart, but no others were near. Their isolation satisfied Longinus, and he had a quick, harsh conversation with Adam. Longinus showed great animation for such a restrained man. He crossly tapped his spear upon the cobbles while hissing at Adam. Once he was finished, he went still as a statue. Morigan knew they would get no more from him on the subject of Amunai, at least not through conversation.

"He wasn't helpful," said Adam, turning to the company. "The woman you asked about was a Keeper. She has passed into the Great Mystery now. Our guide says that she is never to be spoken of. Her crimes and sins were shameful. She succumbed to madness and destroyed the City of Wind—"

"Aesorath," exclaimed Morigan. Fates and significances were beginning to align. "We saw the city when last my Wolf and I chased the Dreamstalker together. The Dreamstalker claimed it was her Dream, which means it was a place of importance for her. Perhaps…" Morigan squeezed her eyes and flexed her Will. For a speck, she flashed with silver. In the flickering theater of her mind, she could once again see the dunes and distant spires of a dead, fallen city, taste the iron bitterness of the Dreamstalker's blood upon her tongue, and hear the buzzing symphony of a horrific masked creature as it tried to tempt her to darkness. As Morigan listened to its music, concentrating her wolfish hearing upon it, she discerned a voice beneath the cicadas—a voice that rarely spoke, but had once returned a whisper of love: *We shall.* "She's alive," exclaimed Morigan.

"Who?" asked Thackery.

"Amunai," replied Morigan. "She's the one who attacked me in my dreams. I remember her voice now. As a woman or as a monster, she has the same voice."

The others of the company were surprised only for a moment. The many grim events that had occurred since their arrival in Pandemonia became linked chains in their heads, as they had in Morigan's.

"How is that possible?" asked Thackery.

"Amunai would not be the first we have known to cheat death and destruction," said the Wolf. "Although we do not yet know the nature of the connection between Amunai—the Dreamstalker—Brutus, and the City of Screams, we have now at least found a truth to hunt: a truth that may be the key to Eatoth's salvation."

"Why not ask the Keeper?" suggested Thackery. "We now know what questions to ask."

Morigan turned Thackery and the others away from Longinus; he couldn't understand them as far as she could tell, but she didn't want to include him in their scheming. "I doubt the Keeper will hear us. She knows more than she will admit. I have incomplete visions of her, too, and I sense she is involved in this bramble patch of Fates. When we return to her, we must do so armed with incontrovertible truths. Things she cannot deny."

"What do you propose?" asked Thackery.

Morigan felt enlivened now that they were beginning to uncover clues. While she debated where to begin searching for more, the Wolf made his own agenda. Off he strode down the lane, hunched, slightly feral, and sniffing.

You have awoken something—a trail, a scent, he whispered to his bloodmate. He inhaled a bouquet of roses, rot, and raisins that was wafting down from somewhere very high up, possibly one of the towers. It was the stench of a hidden truth, of love and betrayal. He remembered that scent from the chamber of the Keeper. He wondered what she had been concealing in the floor, or upon her person. *I smell secrets, my Fawn. I hear whispers in the distance like the first leaves of fall kissing the bracken. Go with our companions. Seek the ties between Amunai, the City of Screams, and my father. I shall discover what it is this Keeper hides.*

Where are you going? she asked.

Up...Into the towers. A wind bearing sulfur blew over him, and his ears picked up a drumbeat that sounded like an earthquake. *I hear a strange pulsing song, too. And I smell magik. A magik without compare. I must chase these things as well. I shall find a way to stop my father.*

Go, my Wolf. Let me know what you catch.

They kissed in their souls in a burst of starlight and growling flame. The Wolf scaled the wall of the alley in three great upward strides, startling an old woman in her kitchen, but moving so quickly that she had time neither to scream nor to understand what'd passed her. Longinus shouted as soon as he realized that the Wolf and the wind that had blown past him were one and the same. After the Wolf's departure, Adam did his best to calm the man, who would surely face harsh punishment for losing the son of Brutus. Morigan and Thackery, meanwhile, huddled together and conspired. They soon asked Adam if he could ask their guide to expedite their trip to the Exhibition, this museum as it sounded. It had been Thackery's idea to find a place where people could investigate history and legends without rousing tempers. From what Thackery had heard, Caenith would already be testing Eatoth's hospitality to its limits.

III

In Eatoth, skycarriages were called *theikospor*—"divine seeds" was the closest translation Adam could find—and the vessels weren't permitted anywhere near the ground except in military stations. As the others learned from their busily working translator, the divine seeds ruled the airspace above the city proper, which was more colloquially referred to as the *Metonia*, or Ring of the Repentant. Apparently, theikospor were reserved only for passengers of divine prominence, such as wards. As they were in the company of a legionnaire, an earthly agent of the divine, they weren't permitted to use the seeds for transit. Instead, they had to walk like the common folk of Eatoth. At least that gave the four plenty of opportunity to study the culture that Brutus sought to conquer.

The division drawn between those who traveled by sky and those who walked on foot was not the only sign of how deeply ingrained faith was in Eatothian society. Thackery spied a pantomime occurring behind a line of green-wound pillars in a crumbled amphitheater set back from the street. Several actors wore frightening black costumes and performed primal, sexual gyrations around a half-naked man. The crowd was as quiet as the actors. Some of the watchers closed their eyes and swayed, lost in zealotry or bliss. Of that strange scene, Thackery caught only a glance. Nevertheless, the sense of the silence, the obedient receptiveness to whatever lesson was being taught, stayed with him.

Afterward, he became aware of the significance of other behaviors that he'd previously dismissed. Eatothians often tapped their foreheads, then their shoulders, in a triangular fashion. This everyday blessing seemed used in place of a handshake. He'd seen people make the sign when they bumped into one another, or when they dropped something. He deduced the gesture was intended to invite good fortune and ward off evil.

As the sun was finally pulled away by dusk's red hand, and the shadows of the towers became thick as black lace, bells tolled. The sound was loud and came from some divine belfry, or belfries, concealed in the towers of glass. Like a coat of thunder, the music fell upon the bodies of the company, making them shudder. It reminded Morigan of the voice of a Dreamer, which was all noise, sensation, and a stirring of fear. Indeed, her legs trembled, and she felt tempted to kneel to ease the pounding pressure. But she resisted, knowing the desire was an unnatural one.

She and her pack-mates grasped this truth, even as all those along the Ramble buckled at the knees and prostrated themselves upon the street as if they were a river of domino men and women. They lowered their hands, foreheads, and chests to the ground, allowing the divine weight to oppress them. The three stubborn travelers gaped. On the bells tolled, growing louder and louder. With every beat, the magik from above hammered their heads further into their necks and shoulders. Nonetheless, they didn't submit. They would not submit to magik and rule. They leaned against one another like three hobbled gray dames. In time, the choral judgment faded into echoes, and their bodies were able to unclench. After righting himself, Longinus gave them a disgusted glare.

"We do not bow," said Morigan with enough venom that even though he couldn't understand her, he flinched.

They resumed their walk and continued for a while without speaking. While still muddling through the experience in their heads, they crossed paths with an old woman who had yet to find her feet. She gasped and clawed her way up the low rising wall on the side of the street beyond which citizens sat in a sunny garden drinking and lounging. No one appeared willing to help the woman. Morigan stepped in and quickly hoisted her up, then brought her through an arch into the outdoor arboretum. The old lady smiled at the enchanting stranger, and invoked the three-pointed blessing. Morigan left her sitting on a stone bench from where she could watch the spitting, pissing nymphs of a gaudy fountain. Longinus grumbled a few words, apparently disapproving of the solicitude she'd shown.

"A true believer must stand on her own," said Adam, and thumbed the air in the direction of their guide.

"A truly compassionate kingdom would not slam its people to the ground," replied Thackery. "What do these people even do? Other than contemplate, wander, and shop away their lives? This nation is absurdly lazy for one so technomagikally advanced. I see eating and indulgence but very little work. I'm assuming there are people, somewhere, doing the necessary menial labor. Without contest, I would take Eod and its less-complicated hubris over this nation of fattened sheep."

They returned to the Ramble. However, the systemic zealotry of these people continued to disturb the outsiders. Darkness came on fast and deep, and what stars glittered in the sky behind the veil of perpetual clouds did so like shy maidens. What had been a busy causeway quickly became deserted as folks hurried off to their homes. Musicians packed their instruments into cases. Stages were left draped with cloth like the remains of an abandoned theater.

Soon only the faithless, miscreants, and other unsavory-looking characters roamed the Ramble. These folk never approached the company, likely because they were wary of their strangeness or sought to avoid the gleaming bronze man who led them. Come true nightfall, their path was lighted only by the glow from the windows of the buildings they passed as well as by the radiance from Thackery's emblazoned staff—which he'd rekindled. These lights aside, the streets were bare and black.

Longinus had apparently decided it was time for them to eat, and so led them into a tavern that jutted out of a long arcade. Its solid walls and portcullis suggested it had once been an ancient fortress. The balistrariae, though, had been filled in with tinted glass, and the toothed iron barrier had been capped with pale stone. These touches matched the elegant, white, and plush interior of the tavern. The four drifted between rows of private curtained-off tables, wondering what the mumbling shadows they passed looked like and what the source was of the ethereal harpsichord and flute music they heard. Finally, a silky sheet was swept aside, and they were left alone in an alcove.

There were a number of pieces of cutlery at their places that not even the former Menosian master knew how to use: implements that looked like a set of fine pliers, a small roasting fork, a miniature lance. Morigan might have enjoyed the swooning ambiance more if her Wolf had been present. Together, they could have laughed at the silliness of these tools and the posturing that seemed necessary even for a simple meal. Although he had been silent and hunting all day, his fire-beast growled as she thought of him.

"Fancy," said Morigan, then frowned along with her friends. Poor Adam would be the most hopeless at this culinary guessing game. Morigan turned to the changeling. "I'm not particularly hungry. Can you tell our guide that we don't need all of this; we have not the time for such leisure. For all we know, Brutus could be tunneling under the city right now while we're pondering how to use half the steel beside our plates."

Adam addressed their liaison, who had chosen to stand guard over the three rather than eat. Longinus shook his head at whatever it was that Adam suggested. "The Exhibition is now closed," said Adam, and growled unhappily. "Cruel fox. I feel betrayed, for he says he knew all along we wouldn't reach the place today, given the size of this glass-and-stone forest. Something he calls the holy curfew has begun. We have been told to eat, rest, and only in the morning may we resume our pilgrimage."

A thin and nervous waiter chose the worst possible speck in which to appear. Shaking, he placed an ewer of water, in which floated lemon slices and sweet herbs, and a wicker basket of torn fresh bread upon the table. Morigan scared him away with a silver stabbing stare. *These people have no notion of doom or urgency*, she realized. *Utterly clueless.* She stood up from the table, and indecorously began to stuff pieces of bread into the small haversack hanging off her belt. Then she guzzled away most of the pitcher and wiped her mouth with her hand. "Pilgrimage? We're not here for a fuking sacred walk," she snapped with a bit of Mouse's bile. "What's wrong with these people?"

Morigan stomped over to Longinus, reached up, wrestled with the man—who had only one hand with which to defend himself on account of his spear—and succeeded in unbuckling and ripping off his helm. The fellow beneath possessed a square, solid handsomeness that matched his physique. He appeared older than she thought he would be and dark from sun, nearly as swarthy as an Arhad. His head, though, clustered with faded-gold curls, and his eyes sparkled with sapphire charm.

Trembling with wolfish anger and strength, Morigan shouted at him. "The darkest, maddest monster in Geadhain's history is coming to destroy your city. To enslave the souls of your people. You will all die, or at least most of you will. I shall not be responsible for your deaths by failing to act." She appealed to her companion, "Tell him to have some Kings-damned sense, Adam." Turning again to the legionnaire, she stormed, "I don't care what you have to say, though: we shall not be staying here any longer. He must take us to our destination *now*."

The closer they had come to the Exhibition, this repository of history and fate, the more it had pulled at her like a call of the wild. Perhaps Morigan was simply feeling wild herself, for she threw Longinus's helmet to the floor bringing the music to a sudden halt. While Morigan huffed—in much the same way her bloodmate would have, noted Thackery—Adam explained in hushed tones the urgency of their task.

"I have a duty," protested the legionnaire.

"To your pack, a wife, a child, what?"

"To all of those things."

"I lost my wolf-mother in an instant to a woman that pales next to Brutus's evil. He will eat your mate, and rape your child, then eat it, too. He is the greatest monster of all time. If there was ever a moment to listen with your senses and not your sense, it would be now. Sniff the air, commune with the animal in your soul. Protect your pack."

Longinus didn't sniff the night air, though his skin prickled as Adam spoke. The weary sadness wrought on the faces of the folk surrounding him further caused the hairs on the back of his neck to rise. They'd seen murder, atrocities, and things worse even than what he'd known in the darkest realms of Pandemonia: their expressions betrayed as much. What would the cost of his stubbornness be? Longinus realized he couldn't, he wouldn't, place the lives of his wife and child upon the gambling table.

"I shall take you there. But we do so with stealth, and you must tell no one. If I am asked, and not interrogated by mind-magik, I shall tell them I was coerced."

"Fine." The changeling sealed their understanding by extending an olive branch—Longinus's helm, which he retrieved from under the table.

In a moment, they were again moving through the silk-swaying space of the tavern. On the way out, a waft of something singed to rare, bloody deliciousness seduced Morigan's senses. Today, her bloodmate prowled and succumbed to his primality, and his passion was affecting her as well. Only half-aware of her actions, she slipped behind a curtain, snatched a filet from the plate of one of two shrieking diners, and then rejoined her company. Longinus either ignored the commotion or was no longer concerning himself with Morigan's disruptive behavior. She'd moved too quickly to be stopped, anyway. She was gone and back in a wind with a handful of meat and a bloody smile.

"Are you feeling all right?" asked Thackery as he hurried her outside.

"Fine. Better than fine." She swallowed what remained of her meat in a gulp, then wiped her fingers off on her tunic. "I feel alive." She looked down the bronze-tiled street and up to the fingernail of the moon pushing through the clouds. This was their moon: that of a Daughter of the Moon and a Lord of Fang and Claw—the same one that shone the night they met in Eod. Gazing back to the Ramble, where the witch-moon's shine sparkled off certain stones like shimmers on a lake, Morigan noticed certain steps that were brighter than the others. A path. She knew where they had to go, and would leave the others to catch up. The blood in her belly, the river of fire in her veins, demanded that she hunt. She passed Adam her stolen satchel of bread; she'd heard his stomach rumbling. Thackery knew she was about to leave them, for her form had begun to waver and course with silver light. "Meet me at the Exhibition," she said. "You've been wise, my friend, and something awaits me there. I can wait no longer to hunt and consume it."

She vanished in a shrinking ripple of light, and Longinus uttered what was surely a curse. He'd now lost two of the people it had been most necessary for him to watch. Thackery went to the soldier and patted him on the shoulder. "They don't have much patience, my Morigan and her mate. They'll likely break as much as they fix while they're here. We had better catch up with her to stop the worst of it."

Longinus did not understand what the old man had said, but he set off running down the street towards the Exhibition.

IV

Like a growling wind, the Wolf flew above the heads of Eatoth's witless sheep, who rubbed their arms in the humid day and sometimes looked up as they heard the noise. They never caught sight, though, of the beast himself.

The Wolf prowled the roofs and upper reaches of the city. Below were smells and trails aplenty, but none with the ripped moss and earthy aroma, the bookish spice of ancient secrets, or the rosy fragrance of lies: three scents, three truths, each of which he'd hunt in time. Looking down, he could see the stream of people flowing along the Ramble, which itself ran all around the enormous circular disc of the city. Not a soul amongst the great flock of sheep interested him. They all smelled of sugar and butter. Fat, lazy odors. Their minds were as soft as toddlers, and their spirits were like honey mead—easily drunk, but too sweet and prone to upsetting one's digestion and rotting one's teeth.

For all their culture's dominance over nature, most Eatothians were as dumb as ants. They followed the Keeper and her wards in the glass towers and possessed little spirit or free thought. He was certain that their art was bland and meaningless. The impressions he received of the rituals and social patterns of the flocks of sheep beneath him made him long for the balanced ethics and sorcery of Eod. At least Eod's sorcerers, architects, and philosophers understood the need for nature in their environment and respected an *actual* immortal. They didn't revere themselves as Immortals as did those living in the circle of glass towers that rose around the city's core. He would head to those towers, eventually. But the hunt possessed its own cadence, which must be obeyed. First, he must make for the darkened green circle ringed by the glass towers, which called to him; it was a place of woodland and less-tilled, less-developed land. There, a chatter of life and noise played music happier than the bleating songs of the Ramble.

To make it to the city's green core, he leaped and swung himself up the struts of one of the arcs running across the sky. The labor exhilarated more than exhausted him. He was huffing and wet from excited sweat as he came to the top of a bridge that was really a highway. It was a grand sterling-and-glass road on which streaked speeding silver pods, ones much bigger and more capable of causing injury than the eggs that flew in the sky. Playfully, the Wolf skipped among the silver bullets. He landed upon one of the hovering vehicles heading east toward the green city center—and startled no one inside, since these vessels were technomagikally and not manually piloted. Indeed, in this vast transit system, he sensed neither the heat nor the odor of man. Much of the city appeared to run on a network of intelligence and operations that did not depend on man's oversight.

He thrust his face into the wind. The whistling air seemed as charged as a thundercloud with the static of magik. The Wolf wondered from where the power came and studied the vista before him: the crystal ring containing the towers, the spot of green, the lines like the web of a glass spider crossing over all. The power he sought wasn't up here, he realized, but beneath all this distracting splendor. Indeed, he could once again sense the heartbeat that had begun this hunt: a weight in his stomach, a withering of his balls. It came from below. Still, he wanted to see the green heart of Eatoth, which was the source of the fragrance of moss and soil—a scent so earthy and pure in this sterile city, it was the most compelling of the three smells.

The Wolf stayed atop the bullet until it had crossed the apex of this particular bridge and began its descent. Then, in a fashion that would have looked horrifyingly careless to anyone watching, he sprang and leaped. The Wolf howled as he tore down through the sky in a vacuum of air. Something in the impending night stirred his animalism and recklessness. It also made his beast stronger, and he felt no fear as he fell. As he'd done when he'd dropped into the Iron Mines, he strapped his arms to his sides, flexed the muscles that only he—and possibly his father—possessed, and steered his body through the air as if it were a living glider. When he'd dropped low enough, he abruptly twisted and ripped into a metal strut with a clawed hand. He dangled by an arm, grunting, and then scaled down the underframe and dropped the last hundred paces or so down to a roof beneath him. A cat could not have made a quieter landing. The Wolf looked about. He inhaled the rich pine and soil odors that rose with the steeples of verdant life around him, and let them guide him forward. Then, after creeping to the edge of the flat, tin-shingled square, he looked down.

Dirty working men and women formed a crawling trail in the streets. Some moved with purpose, hauling sacks of clanging items or lumpy bags of food, or tending to the animals that wandered here and there. Hens clucked from wire coops. The pleasing freshness of vegetables, straw, and manure made the Wolf salivate. The buildings here had been built with less care and possessed a more antiquated charm, having none of the brassy ostentation of the Ramble. Apartments had been shoved into old keeps. Markets coughed smoke from ancient forges used for metallurgy and cooking; he knew this from the smell of hot steel, hickory, and spices. In fact, he could sense the presence of many forges ahead, in between tenements, falling towers converted into flats, and fields transformed into marketplaces, which echoed with coarse laughter and raucous, clapping folksongs. Elsewhere, blue, gray, and deep-green trees flourished in every free acre of this region; distant knolls covered with dots of livestock heightened the Wolf's longing for the West even more. He froze for a moment, drinking, tasting, and listening to the sensory feast.

Here at last are the kingdom's serfs—the ones who oil the lanterns, feed the fat little sheep, and probably also build the glass churches for their masters. As he thought this, he watched a large seed like the ones from the highway-of-the-sky touch down in a paved, stripped area of the forest. In a speck, he saw the ant-like forms of many men filing out of a crack in the vessel. They wore tools and craftsman's belts and had the sagging shoulders of people who worked as slaves. However, this place clearly reanimated them, and they laughed as they hurried away from the vessel and off into the hills, the woods, and towards the music. *The salt of the soil. The sweat that lubricates the grotesque machinery of this city. You are its muscles, noble folk. I have seen Eatoth's fat. Now I shall see her heart and her soul.*

Indeed, his hunt felt guided not only by the trio of scents, but by a tingle from groin to brain—a thrum of his bloodmate's prescience guiding him. Still, before moving on, the Wolf stayed for a while in the natural but still uncanny vale, a place surely affected by both magik and science. There was a grit to these people and to the way they lived that the Wolf respected. Leaping from rooftop to rooftop, hiding in the growing concealment of dusk, he hunted for anything else that might be of use to him and his pack. These people haggled loudly. They drank. Lovers romanced each other, although never too indecently, in the streets. Whoever these folk were, they weren't like either the vagrants in the Ramble or the pious residents of the glass towers. Once, the Wolf watched as a naked toddler daringly dashed away from his father, out of an apartment, and onto the street. The child was immediately stopped by a congenial neighbor, who then shared a laugh with the father. He remembered the outcast children running from the legionnaires that afternoon, and wondered at the difference. Who were these folk? They weren't fat and faithful sheep. They weren't vagabonds, either. Another caste entirely, then, which was offered Eatoth's protection but none of its temptations. Perhaps they were second-generation Amakri, and had been born or offered themselves to service. Perhaps the unfortunates in the Ramble were simply too proud to serve; or perhaps they were unable to. Many of them had been missing limbs or the fitness necessary for labor.

Although the Wolf discovered little else in the rural ring of green, at least he'd found people in Eatoth whom he believed deserved protection against his mad father. Content with his discovery, and ready to chase the other secrets of Eatoth, the Wolf looked around while waiting for instinct to seize him. Night had just fallen, and fast. The Wolf spotted a small tower upon the reclaimed keep where he stood—it was now a tavern that reeked of ale and jostled his soles with song. From the roof, he could leap to the lowest strut of the silver-and-glass highway and climb once more onto the bridge.

Suddenly, the bells rang.

They weren't musical instruments. Beneath the metal dinging and donging—far louder and stronger than that of any normal bell—was a crackle of power. The voice of lightning and music commanded him to bow, but he did not. He planted his feet, grunted, and roared up into the sky as the magik's insistence and weight grew and grew. In the end, his scream won out. The beast in him felt that he had chased the song away.

People stirred from their dreamy prostrations: waking upon floorboards, rising from their sore knees, rubbing their foreheads free of dirt from the street. Like a true hunter, the Wolf scurried up an old turret on the roof and studied the creatures as they woke. They were sleepy and disoriented, as if shaking off the thrall of an enchantment. What sort of rulers bespelled their citizens? And to what purpose? The Wolf heard shuffling from the tavern, and leaped up into the sky and was climbing a great metal ladder before the music started.

Once upon the sky bridge, he dashed into the current of traffic. This artery would lead him all the way to the ring of the city where the crystal towers reigned. The moon glowed on high, a pure and virginal half-circle. His blood began to pump faster. It engorged his veins, inflated his head, and filled him near to bursting with strength and perceptions. In the distance, one tower in the ring rose taller than the others and shone like a spear of ivory. The moon had blessed it with light and revealed its importance. If he could have, he would have torn himself free of his man-skin and run down the highway as a wolf. Unfortunately, he would be in need of hands and manual dexterity. His nature, though, could not be wholly restrained, and many times as he bounced from silver egg to tract of gleaming road, he landed with clawed hands and a snarl in his mouth. Wherever Morigan was in the city, he felt she was also lost in the rush and glory of the hunt. He did not call out to her, nor did she speak to him. They were apart and yet one. They would find one another soon.

In what seemed like specks to the Wolf, the ivory tower loomed before him. The shrieking wind should have told him something of his speed, but he was beyond the notions of care, measurements, and caution. Leaping from the highway, he sailed in a weightless acrobatic arc—so light he felt he could fly forever—and then rolled onto a smooth deck. Legionnaires and silver seeds dotted the windy landing pad; none of them had sensed his gently ruffling appearance except in the form of a breeze. All spidery slowness and grace, he crawled on his fingertips and toes.

He distracted two dull legionnaires by tapping on the shell of a silver seed. As one moved to investigate and the other turned to watch, he entered the passage they guarded. The leg hair of the remaining sentry may have prickled, and he may have smelled sweat, wood, and musk, but he thought nothing of it. Inside the tower, all appeared strange to the Wolf: everything was filmed over with gray grain and moving with red and orange hues. The walls were not clearly defined, and he could see through them as if through a fog. The Wolf knew he was perceiving in ways that his bloodmate could, as well as with the heat-tracing and obscurely detailed vision of an animal. How grand a creature she'd made him. How invulnerable and omniscient he felt as he prowled through the tower of mist and glowing souls.

The Wolf's hunt took him through places of study rife with the incense of thought. A being with a less animal mind might have wondered what secrets these purveyors of ancient knowledge hoarded in these vast multi-floored libraries. But the Wolf cared for none of that. Elsewhere in the tower were places of reflection with gleaming gray circles that he thought were pools, fuzzy clouds he interpreted as benches, and a kaleidoscopic scattering of auras—mostly shades of green—that he knew to be plants thanks to their chlorophyll waft. He caught the sounds of eating halls and barracks in the gray echo, though he did not go too near places bustling with people. Instead, he stuck to the shadows and hallways.

As if he were a jungle lizard, he crept invisibly along the walls and ceilings with his hooked claws. The crystal-and-metal skin of the tower was soft as clay to him. At most, he left behind a small trail of powder as he skulked. Even the quietest in this tower would have shrieked upon seeing him in that state—feral, pinching the tiles, his neck twisted round, his eyes gray and compassionless, and on his face a snarl of dagger teeth. He wasn't spotted, however, and what miniscule tracks he left remained undiscovered. Although the Faithful had trained themselves to be silent and contemplative, the Wolf was so attuned to his body that he was able to match his breath and pulse to the single, dominating throb resounding throughout the tower. Under cover of that divine heartbeat, his own would not be felt. He crept toward the beat, wanting to see the beast that possessed such a tremendous organ.

The Wolf's hunt led him downward in a winding fashion. There were lifts that could have aided him in his descent, but the Wolf preferred to take the stairs, as he was wary of making any unnecessary noise or having to dodge elevators. On each floor, rooms ringed the outer edge of the tower's circumference, and an antechamber filled with meditative blue robes and legionnaires sat in the tower's center. In order to reach that antechamber, and the next descending staircase, he had to wind all the way around the main curving passage of the tower. Through these antechambers, he crawled carefully, managing to slip by every guard and supposedly all-knowing sorcerer; they heard nothing of the predator that passed above their heads. He could have slaughtered all of them, and he reveled in the knowledge of his own might. Although he was moving stealthily so as not to be seen or sensed, he was nonetheless able to move quickly. Soon, he came to a point where he could go no lower in the grayness.

There was a lift in the domed swell of a chamber. Several pulsing beings of light, a few so bright that they reshaped reality with their Wills, stood in the space. From his perch, hugging a curved beam in the ceiling, he considered dropping down and killing them all. But he was not his father, and Morigan would not approve of his murdering innocents—and he supposed they might still be considered that, despite their forced indoctrination of others and the caste systems they employed.

Carefully, he scanned the gray fog for another means of reaching the giant heart that thudded through his bones, nerves, and the metal to which he clung. The men guarding this mystery did not know what they had trapped. They could not have understood it or they would not have kept it. What had lured him this deep was a great Will or a magik so incalculable it was nearly a Will. It perhaps lacked soul, for it did not feel wholly living; it was a body of pure light and wonder without a controlling mind. In the wrong hands, such unshaped celestial power could become an apocalyptic weapon.

Thinking analytically had allowed a sliver of the Wolf's logic and consciousness to take the reins from the beast, and it now piloted his body across the cupola toward a shrewdly hidden vent. The Wolf felt around the rectangle, determined to fit inside, and then carefully peeled the metal blinds apart as if they were filigreed wire. He slipped into the hole he'd created, and his slink became a slither. After worming himself through a warm gray passage, the Wolf soon reached a wide drop. He stretched himself across the gap, realized that he fit quite well, and then descended in the manner of a starfish or trapeze artist—moving hands and feet in turn, shuffling lower, never making the slightest noise. In his barking, rabid mind, the descent seemed to take ages to complete.

From down below him came both warmth and light—blue light, somehow bleeding color like an aura. He encountered a second flimsy obstacle placed over a rectangular exit and peeled it away as he had the other. Then he dropped into the blue and beating bosom.

His sight became clearer as his beast succumbed to the wonder his man felt. For in this chamber was one of the oldest mysteries of their world, perhaps of all life in the tree of stars. A fragment of the cosmos. A star trapped in the blue amber of a fractured bit of stone. The Eatothians had bound its divinity through science and magik. The Wolf could sense the restraints placed upon it, could feel its blood being drained through the turquoise arteries that flowed out of the object's cylindrical prison and into reservoirs located elsewhere. He walked over to the arkstone, beguiled by its beauty and hum. With his wolfish ears, he could almost catch the music of stars, the soaring operatic journey this stone had taken past worlds horrific and indescribable.

Abruptly jolted by etheric currents, he realized he'd climbed up the great pedestal upon which the arkstone floated. His hand was curled in a fist, as if he were about to break the glass. He didn't immediately dismiss the idea, and instead debated the possible ramifications of freeing the arkstone, or even of smashing it. A power like this should not be trapped. Whether it was safe to tap the essence of such a star for millennia as the people of Eatoth had done was not the issue. It should never have been used in this way.

It was this arkstone that had made it possible for these people born in a land of chaos and wild magik to build a society more advanced than any nations of the West. Their power had been stolen from the stars. The Wolf wanted to free it. His beast roared to release this catastrophic rapid from behind its glass dam—as his father's would have roared. Of course. He had found the answer he hunted: Brutus wanted this fragment of the heavens for himself. The Wolf knew this, with Morigan's perceptions, with the instincts of his hunter's heart. The Wolf knew that if he had been a darker version of himself, he would have sought this power, too. The sense that it would prove some affinity between himself and Brutus prevented the Wolf from smashing anything. Instead, he touched the glass softly, with the wonder of a boy seeing true magik for the first time. Then he dashed across the chamber and leaped back up into the vent. He did not bother concealing the signs of his break-in—the people of Eatoth would have greater troubles at their doorstep soon enough.

It was time to chase his final quarry, to track the rose-and-wine scent of regret that drifted down every hallway and vent through which the Wolf had passed in his stealthy exploration of the tower; he'd ignored its reek till now. The mistress of this tower had steeped this place in her tears, and in that scented sorrow. She'd Willed more than a hundred years of pain and tortured dreams into the tower's bones. In another century or so, this monsoon of sorrow would cause a *Caedentriae*. Only the darkest, most depraved, and regrettable acts held the power to warp the world in such a way. *What have you done?* he wondered. Prescience and the insights of the witch's moon inspired his reflections, and the Wolf thought of the dreadful, punishing oppression of the bells—like a whip brought to a penitent's hide. For whom was that punishment and flagellation intended? For the people or their sacred Keeper?

The ascent was over in sands. In the antechamber preceding the Keeper's rise, a herd of legionnaires and blue robes had gathered sometime ago; he sensed their steeped-in anxiousness as he approached. Many smelled of sweat and fear; none were down on their knees pondering mysteries. An alert must have been issued—the Keeper was worried for the safety of herself or others. But guards wouldn't stop the Wolf. He slipped in and out of shadows like a snake of darkness, and slithered and crawled along the dome's roof. None of the faces below turned in his direction. When he came to the metal caging surrounding the lift shaft, he pried the bars apart as if they were warm and malleable, then slipped through them. He climbed quite freely through the shaft, using the metal cables as ropes. He did not sway them with his great weight or cause any noticeable commotion among the forces he left behind. As he came closer to the gray hole that led to the Keeper's chamber, he listened.

The Keeper was above; he doubted that she left her gilded glass cage very often. She breathed in short, light gasps: the music of fear. It excited the beast, although he had no intention of drawing blood unnecessarily. Perhaps she knew of his coming, or wisely feared his father's. Either way, he did not slink up into her chamber, but instead leaped to the narrow landing inside the metal cage. He saw a sparse, bare room encircled by silvery clouds. The Keeper's settee radiated warmth from across the room, yet the woman herself couldn't be seen. Her aura, however, glowed and betrayed her hiding place.

The Wolf tore open the grate with one hand and then strode into the seemingly empty chamber while the terrified Keeper watched from behind her invisible screen. First he went to the settee, sniffed around, and then shoved his hand through the fabric and stuffing, and ripped out a piece of stone tied to a leather string. It looked a bit like the necklace Elemech had given Adam. This talisman, though, had a chipped edge, as if it were half of a broken spearhead. Where was the other half? For the Wolf had seen this jewelry before, or another piece quite similar to it. Before he could make the connection, a voice spoke in his head. It was buzzy and echoing—a witch's voice. The Keepers didn't consider themselves sorcerers or wielders of Will, but the Wolf knew a witch when he encountered one.

If you have come to rob me of my valuables, you will find I have little other than my faith and the love of my people. You have already done enough damage, left your claw marks all over my tower. Leave now, before I summon my wards. The Keeper Superior stepped out from behind her glass-and-magik wall. She tried to tremble in rage, but the Wolf saw she was merely trembling.

Assuming she would understand him, the Wolf replied, "Summon your wards, then. I call your bluff. If your magik allowed you to sense me clawing up your tower, then you know where I have been, what I have seen." He stepped forward and shook the necklace at her. "What is this, this talisman of death and sadness? I have never smelled something so infested with grim memories. When you summon your guards, perhaps you can explain to all of us why you keep this thing hidden away—this thing you do not want to touch, yet are still afraid to part with."

That does not belong to you. Ankha gained a spark of courage and stepped into his great shadow. She reached for the talisman that he dangled above her, but was not tall enough to grab it. *Give it back!*

"To whom does it belong?" asked the Wolf.

Give it back!

Suddenly, the moon shone like a sun of the night, and the Wolf saw the Keeper for what she was: a girl. Stripped and exposed, she'd regressed, becoming a screaming, bawling child who'd lost something precious. He suffered tearing flashes the likes of which he'd experienced only through Morigan's transferences. And while his were not as clear as his bloodmate's lucid journeys to and from Dream, he returned to himself bearing Fates. Impressions of silhouetted trees, a man's gurgling cry, shivers of lust and horror, and the tickle of a child's laughter—so distant, though, that it could have been the laughter of a ghost. His strongest impressions, though—he was, after all, a wolf and a creature of physical perceptions—were of the smell of apples, their sweetness, the simple joy of eating them with someone very special, as if indulging in an apple was life's greatest delight. His scowl softened. He knelt by the Keeper, who was now weeping and whimpering. "What is it, child?" asked the gentle Wolf as he folded the necklace back into the Keeper's palm. "Who has broken your heart into such tiny pieces? Why do I smell the golden juice of summer apples, which I have not seen growing anywhere in Pandemonia? I shall ask you once more. To whom does this necklace belong?"

My sister, whispered the Keeper. *Amunai.*

The moon pulsed, his heart raced, and his stomach sank in dread.

V

Morigan's leap into and out of reality took her to the base of the grandest staircase she'd ever seen. At the top of those steps stood a palatial building with pillars and fluttering banners that flashed silver in the moonlight, though they were likely blue. White stone guardians, some nude, others scantily dressed in throws or shoulderless robes gazed down from their pedestals under the shadowed peristyle. The figures brandished giant spears and had touches of metal—crowns, belts, armor. *They are the fabled warriors, founders, scholars, and sages of Eatoth,* thought Morigan, her mind effervescent with knowledge and energy from the witch's moon. She wanted to get closer to them, and vanished in a silver ripple.

In a speck, she stood in the shaded colonnade. She walked and stared upon giant men and women, knowing their names and histories immediately, having no need for the facts inscribed on the copper plates that adorned their square pedestals.

Calginius Rex, she thought as she tapped the base of one great stone man of yore. He was fierce: a man with frown lines heavy even for a stone face, and a brow carved into an entanglement of wrinkles. The statue wore a circlet of gold leaves upon his head and held his spear as if it were a staff of rule. *You were a leader, in a sense. An orchestrator of social change. I cannot say whether what you did makes you a villain or a hero—the line between the two seems so hazy to me these days. You offered the outcast tribes refuge from Pandemonia's ferocity, but only so that they would do the labor that you and your Faithful would not. Vassalage. Protection in exchange for servitude. I suppose the outcasts live happier lives than some of our slaves in the West.* Visions filled her then, of men and women around campfires and a grove that was not far from here. They appeared tired, dirty, and threadbare, but their closeness to the earth brought them comfort. They reminded her of the long-vanished Romanisti people, of whom Mifanwae had sometimes spoken. Morigan realized that some of what she was rhapsodizing over was taking place right now in another's head. *My Wolf,* she thought, but she did not whisper it to him or interrupt him. They were each dedicated to their hunts.

The next statue to which she wandered could have been of the Keeper she'd met today. It depicted a short-statured woman with the most severe gaze Morigan had ever seen upon a statue; its eyes of pitch dark were set into recesses of shadow. Though it was an inanimate watcher, she felt naked beneath its scrutiny. Morigan would not be cowed, however, and she glared back at the austere Keeper. *I know all of your secrets, Teskatekmet, first Keeper Superior. Like your General Rex—the right hand of what would become a righteous army—you molded the unruly masses into a nation of loyal citizens. You turned the worship of nature into your personal theocracy, transformed savage rites into civilized rituals. In the process, you bred obedience into the ones who followed you. What folk would not follow one who could show them such miracles? Aye, you learned that you could use your gift—your extreme sensitivity—not only inwardly, but outwardly, too. You learned that you could use magik and that magik would make you a queen. We are almost kin, you and I, although I disagree with all that you have built. It feels tainted.*

Teskatekmet's eyes seemed filled with black hate. Morigan's wolfish ears suddenly heard voices and footsteps—legionnaires on patrol around the Exhibition. She hadn't seen them yet, nor had they spotted her. Nonetheless, she would prefer to avoid making their acquaintance.

On the long wall that ran beside the colonnade was the shadowy arch of an entrance. She ignored the door, instead stepping into Dream as easily as if she were diving into a gray pool, and then emerging from the ethereal tides on the other side of the wall. The space was opulent, with polished squares of slate, brass bulbs set on poles wound with velvet rope, and a grand fresco on the roof. It was also cavernous and empty aside from a few stone benches, which were designed to strike a primal note amid the elegance. A huge flight of stairs led to a landing where portraits of more of Eatoth's ancient luminaries glared at the intruder from behind glass frames. Morigan took the echoing walk to meet them, sneered back at most of the painted ghosts, and then climbed the stairs to the right of the landing.

As she ascended, she caressed the cool balustrade, and her head flickered with the thoughts and feelings of all those who had touched the same stone. How right she'd been to come here, to this nexus of Eatoth's fate, history, and desires. In one speck, she saw lifetimes upon lifetimes. She watched as the artisans and earthspeakers hewed and manipulated this stone into its pristine shape. She peered into their lives, and wandered down the branches of the families and friendships they valued. Empowered by the witch's moon, and rising every day in her own might, nothing was beyond her ken; she saw *everything*. She felt their stomach-twisting hate for the outcasts, for the tribes who refused to submit to the rule of mind-speaking women and silent men. What they truly felt was fear, a scornful suspicion of people who were not as weak as they, people who did not want to be ruled but instead fairly governed.

When she reached the hallway at the top of the stairs, she continued to caress the railing and see where her thoughts and impressions took her. Chambers boasting monstrous skeletal remains from some of Pandemonia's colossi intrigued her, but not enough that she felt moved to leave the railing and its drip of memories. They were only beasts: they didn't possess the Fates that she sought. She caught wisps of their souls anyway—wafts of their musk and echoes of the terrible roars they had possessed when their bones were wrapped in flesh.

Before long, she wandered down a corridor of windows, most of which had been covered for the night by cinched drapes. The narrow slits of light reminded her of serpentine eyes. For a moment, she was reminded of Eod's queen, heard a rattle, and smelled a puff of cinnamon, sugar, and sulfur. Then the impression passed, and she drifted over to one of the galleries.

In this room, she returned to herself a little and examined the tableaus that rested on small stages about the chamber. Morigan walked to the nearest, a representation of ancient Pandemonia featuring a small line of people wandering through a hostile desert. Black birds with the faces of lizards circled over the wanderers, and the scene stirred her with a sense of impending doom. As she came to a metal podium—a squat pillar upon which was balanced a tilted plate of metal—a glaring light sputtered into life above the desert, the crow monsters suddenly croaked and flapped their wings, and the nomads came to life. It was all simulacrum and illusion. She studied the moving tableau for a while, but it never appeared to progress very far into the future. The crow beasts flew on a loop. The nomads walked on a track hidden in the sand. It was effective nonetheless, and she could almost feel the heat of the sun's phantasm, hear the babble of the wanderers' primitive language, and the whisking of sand off the stage. However, the grit vanished in flickers of gold as it brushed Morigan's boots. What a wanton waste of magik—all this just to tell a simple story. That's what books and imaginations were for. *What people had such magik to squander?* she wondered. The question stirred her hive and made her move, dreamily, to the next tableau; the scene she abandoned fell into darkness and stillness as she left.

"Father," she muttered.

While there was nothing of Feyhazir to be seen in the frozen imagery, she was certain he was there. Before her, a rag-wearing woman with heartless black eyes knelt in a wasted garden. The gnarled witch's hand of a tree reached over the small figure. When Morigan came closer to the plaque and pedestal explaining this history, the tableau sputtered into motion. A moon, not a sun, birthed light upon the sad scene. The woman rocked upon her knees: it was Teskatekmet, but here she was young, scrawny, starving. Whispers from the earth could not feed her. As Morigan's fingers grazed the plaque, further scraps of the tale flitted within her. *You were alone. The seasons of Pandemonia were the harshest they had ever been. The land refused to settle, even for a speck, into a shape that could be farmed or hunted for nourishment. Even the grass was poison, and the rain came down as a sleet of fire. You lost thousands upon thousands of those who wandered. You waited for the Green Mother to guide you toward the faintest tease of life. Yet she did not. She does not believe in fairness, only the balance struck by the rule of the strong over the weak. Your people were not strong. They should have died—such was the Green Mother's decree. Yet you set your Will against hers. Your bright and powerful Will. There came a point of such desperation that your people began to eat one another. You, though, refused to eat the flesh of your tribe, and so...you died.*

Mildly appalled, Morigan watched a vision float in above the tableau like fog over a lake. In it, men and women carved up emaciated corpses and gnawed on the remains with a shuddering revulsion. Some wept, some vomited the remains of their kin. Most of them ate and numbed themselves to their wickedness. Eatoth's historians hadn't recorded this vile truth, not in this or any other tableau in the Exhibition.

Morigan's vision faded. She was back in the Exhibition again, and time had progressed in the tableau: Teskatekmet, drained by her hunger, had fallen before the tree. Teskatekmet called out for mercy, once, as she died. After the woman had slumped to the ground, Morigan saw a twist of silver smoke slithering out of a hollow of the trunk—it was a snake, though not one of this earth. *Feyhazir*, she thought. She would always recognize her father regardless of his form. Still, the Eatothians had added the grandeur necessary for a Dreamer's presence, and the tableau thundered with drums, noise, and madly played string music. Feyhazir wound down one of the tree's branches—the longest one, upon which grew a single green bud. Morigan, squinting, watched as the serpent reached the bud and kissed it with his forked tongue. The touch sparked magik, and the green bud fattened, split, and dropped a shining red fruit into Teskatekmet's arms. *The fruit of knowledge*, thought Morigan. The seed of all the ingenuity and bloated elegance of Eatoth had been planted there, with a covenant. Not a fruit, realized Morigan. The fruit was only a metaphor for the gift, the pact Teskatekmet had made with a Dreamer. *My father from the stars is the one who taught you how to do more than just listen. After he brought you to life again and made you his vessel, you learned in moments the secrets master-sorcerers ponder for centuries. Then, resurrected and empowered— that was what you wanted from him, pride and power—you returned to your tribe, and they saw you as a queen from beyond. Soon, you instructed all the Keepers of Pandemonia in how to use their Wills for a more self-serving purpose than being silent maids to Geadhain's aches and woes. You hoped that your tribe would share in your vision, and become great like you. Most did, yet there were those who betrayed your dream, those you denounced as faithless, who would not come to live with you in your cities of stolen knowledge. They wander in exile still, and only use their Wills in the purest of arts—for healing, listening to the land, and aiding Nature's will. Amakri, which means 'scornful" to you, and 'strong' in their language. The forefathers of the outcasts from your new order wouldn't sell their souls for wisdom as you did. But what else did my father teach you? For Will alone could not have erected these civilizations on foundations that change at least every season.*

While she pondered this question, the bees buzzed and her feet moved. She passed various tableaus, paying them little heed. She was distantly aware of scenes of stones being hauled and raised in red, cracked lands—places that would burst with phantom fire if she came close enough to trigger the tableaus to life. She assumed that would be the City of Fire, in an earlier stage of its development. From another tableau, she caught the sparkle of a single glass tower in a small diorama of a city; the place was so quaint, she almost didn't recognize it as ancient Eatoth. Other stories tempted her. There was the creation of industrial mills. Tiny workmen surrounding a honeycombed tower that Morigan knew would make beautiful music when struck by the wind—that was Aesorath, when it was still young and beautiful. And finally, more miniature men lay down tracks for one of the glass bridges she'd seen in Eatoth's sky.

Morigan was unsure how long or far it was she wandered before she stopped at the fated display. It was simple compared to those that preceded it: a crystal floated over a mechanical-looking pedestal about as tall as she. She was immediately drawn to the shard, even though she knew it wasn't real. The mere promise of what this model mimicked was as grand as the moon's pull. Morigan flickered and passed through the ropes surrounding the display. Suddenly alive with light, the shining blue crystal cast carousel shadows about the chamber. She reached out and touched the glass around the object. *One of four,* she thought, her mind exploding with prophecy. *Four great fragments, pieces of a larger mass that fell to Geadhain along with its greatest Dreamer, Zionae. Four stones, four wonderstones...A stone of pure fire in which metals and weapons are forged that are nigh unbreakable. A stone of eternal wind that pushes away the same sandstorms we suffer in Eod and allows men to travel as fast as a breath of* air. *A stone that brings verdure and immutability wherever it is placed. And a stone that can calm the rain, sweeten the water, and cleanse any wound. Your people protected these relics, Teskatekmet. You once revered them as holy, and knew of their celestial origins. They were treasures of such power that the Green Mother forbade their use, warning you in whispers of what such power could do. And then my father tempted you to push your power further: to use the arkstones to inflate your grandiosity, your vision of ruling Nature rather than serving her. Feyhazir, the serpent. Feyhazir, the tempter. Lord of Desire, not Love...I have been wrong. As were you, Teskatekmet. You were to protect the wonderstones, not tap their power. Nay, "wonderstone" does not fully represent the majesty of these treasures, for they came from the vessel that bore Zionae to our world: an ark—the arkstones.*

A gray hand clawed over her sight, and through the mist, she sensed teases of a time and place. She saw a city that tinkled with music and sang with wind, then watched all its astonishingly tall auric flutes and bridges of glass threads crash in upon themselves in an orchestra of ruin. She knew that the cornerstone pulled from this grand and yet delicate creation had been small, but potent—an arkstone's destruction or removal was surely why Aesorath had fallen. Then, the caterwaul of Aesorath's collapse threw her into a second vision, this one of scorching, bellowing destruction, as an infernal fire rose beneath a city of gold and machinery—Zioch, she believed, and that sound must have come from a king of monsters. Zioch was swallowed by a volcanic sinkhole, down the throat of that astonishing beast. The vision then shattered to nothingness.

She was on the floor, breathing heavily. She'd witnessed the end of Aesorath, and she knew as well what that grumbling, fiery apocalypse was—incomprehensible destruction tied to an arkstone. The latter, the monstrous call, she had heard before while watching Magnus's army and hope being consumed by flame. It was the growl of the Elemental of Fire—Brutus's pet.

Her hunt had gone well. She'd found an ancient trail of lies and omens that suggested the nature of Brutus's intent. Although she failed to understand why it should be so, she knew what Brutus wanted, what he would come to Eatoth to claim: the arkstone, a piece of his master. She may have found the breadcrumb she needed to understand the motivations of the Black Queen. Her stomach twisted as she thought about the kind of chaos and evil Brutus could create with a talisman of Zionae's celestial might. She thought, too, about what she might learn if she were able to lay her hands upon that piece of Zionae's flesh.

Some of tonight's revelations weren't as sobering as they were sad: her father might not be as benevolent as he portrayed himself to be. She knew she had to find her bloodmate. And she now heard footsteps hurrying toward her: the lights and noises she'd triggered in the Exhibition must have drawn the notice of the legionnaires guarding this place. She sniffed for Caenith's wood-and-sweat cologne and reached for him with her heart. Then she stepped into a ripple to nowhere.

When three confused legionnaires burst into the chamber, the lights were still fading, but there was no one to be found.

VI

Morigan could take great leaps through Dream, but she instinctively sensed a danger in pushing this art too far. As soon as she started to feel disoriented—unsure of where she was heading, or unclear as to her motivations—she would leap out of the gray flow of eternity and walk until the disorientation passed. The bees proved capable guardians, too, and gave her warning stings when she was being reckless.

First, she appeared in a green and lively woodland that startled her with its crowds, songs, and old homes. Trees and dwellings were nearly indistinguishable. Tents and campfires surrounded one hollowed building constructed around an oaken giant that grew in the space between the deteriorating outer walls. Morigan saw glass towers gleaming over the treetops behind her. She'd taken a bigger leap than intended. Morigan hunkered in the abundant natural growth of the area, staying away from crowds, and waited until her head cleared of vertigo. When recuperated, she vanished; only a shaggy dog laying at the feet of one of the musicians she had been watching noticed her disappear in a flutter of sliver light. It took her nine more leaps, and a few short rests, to travel across Eatoth and reach the tower of the Keeper Superior.

An alien glass rod jutted from the earth in a bare metal plaza before her. She couldn't see the top: it simply vanished into the clouds. Knowing that the Keepers of Pandemonia had built this edifice using forbidden knowledge, though, stripped away any sense of awe. The Wolf was at the top. She could sense her bloodmate's pounding pulse beyond the strange throb of the ground. *I'm coming, my Wolf.*

In the next instant, Morigan stood in a dim room aglow with moonlight. Her bloodmate knelt nearby, and his behavior awakened tender compassion in her. The great Wolf was holding the Keeper, who seemed stripped of all her years and was crying like a newborn. A truth had obviously just been shared; its importance crackled in the air like static after lightning. Morigan's bees were ravenous for more. The stink of rose petals, spice, blood, and sweat—not her bloodmate's handsome odor, but another man's—soiled the room. In great, nostril-flaring sniffs, Morigan took in the smell as she drifted over to her bloodmate. She placed her hand on his hot flesh, and a bit of her beast calmed and returned to its owner. At the same moment, the strange perceptions and halos vanished from the Wolf's vision. His hand touched hers where it rested on his shoulder.

My Fawn. How was your hunt?

Bountiful. I chased secrets and lies. I know what your father seeks. And I have learned something else about my father, though that is another matter.

Brutus wants the arkstone, they said together.

It's a piece of the Black Queen, a fragment of her flesh, said the Wolf—for their touch had told him all she'd seen. *We have found what you need to decipher the aims of our enemy. An object of Fate for you to read.*

Yes...First, however, we must ask this broken bird for permission to use it...

Morigan walked past her bloodmate. She prowled around the weeping, small creature he'd released and wondered how to handle this woman, this product of sinful traditions and lineages.

Be warned. The Wolf glanced at his bloodmate. *The Dreamstalker, Amunai, is her sister.*

I am not surprised, my Wolf. In some ways, Eatoth resembles Menos, but it's far crueler. At least in Menos, slaves know what they are, and there are not those who claim to be holy while committing the profoundest of evils.

Evils?

This society has broken the Green Mother's trust. She sneered. *They were to be the Keepers of Zionae's ancient and forbidden relics, as they hoard all of life's dangerous secrets. But they used this secret—used it to build everything we see here. And my father was complicit in their corruption.* After fighting for peace, for Geadhain, after living so long in war, Morigan was now a soldier. She was a warrior for the Green Mother and for those children of Geadhain who deserved nature's gifts. It was impossible for her to gaze upon the Keeper, trapped in a hideous grief of her own making, with anything other than disdain.

The Wolf rose and came to his bloodmate. His touch and words softened the hardness in her heart. *The children of the cursed bear the sins of their fathers. I smell grief and sorrow upon this little lamb. I nearly choke on her suffering. I do not know her tale. I do not have the delicacy or talent to hear her misery. But I believe that you do. You are kinder than the softest spring wind, even if my beast and the moon bring out your violence tonight. Go to the lamb, hear how she has suffered, then judge her afterward.*

All of Ankha's defenses had crumbled, and her mental wards lay in ruins. As she knelt before the weeping woman, Morigan could see how broken she was. The Keeper didn't even know how to cry properly, so alienated was she from emotion. Her countenance was a twisted mess, and she made sounds like those of an imbecile in agony. "Shh," said Morigan, wiping the woman's snotty face. As Morigan wiped the tears from the Keeper Superior's face, each bead of grief tingled her with knowledge: she knew a name, faces, and so much more. *Ankha*, she mind-whispered. *I need you to tell me about your sister. I need to know why she wants to destroy you, why she allies herself with Brutus and the Black Queen.*

Ankha sobbed so hard that she heaved, and Morigan lost the last vestiges of her callousness and embraced the woman. *Because of what I have done*, said the Keeper Superior. *I killed them both. Her lover and her unborn son. I killed them both so that I could rule, and then I left her to rot in chains.*

Morigan leaned back, revolted. In response, Ankha stiffened, whipped up her head, and seized Morigan's arms. Black and silver stares met, and the darker gaze of the Keeper Superior pulled Morigan into its abyss.

Morigan falls for a time through shrieking gray eddies, as if she's dropped off a cliff and into mist. Although the surroundings seem insubstantial, she lands hard, and her vision clears in a juddering shake. Wait. Someone is shaking her, though she is being rattled too hard to make sense of it. She fights and cries out a little, and a hand is placed over her mouth. There is no further violence, and the bleariness fades. Her sister's brown face clouds into view in the nearly black tent. Amunai's eyes gleam in the dark like those of a terrified animal. Morigan floats out of Ankha's head to view the scene: two sisters wrangling on bedrolls in a dark tent, one atop the other.

"What's wrong?" whispers Ankha.

"I heard mother and father talking," Amunai hisses, and then slides under the covers with her sister. Their parents are only a cloth screen away, and they know to whisper. They settle into a familiar snuggle, Amunai hugging her from behind. For as long as they can remember, they've held each other like this on nights when Pandemonia roars with rainstorms and tears at their tent with hawks of wind. Tonight, her sister's arms tremble, and she smells of nervous perspiration. It's some time before Amunai continues. At last, the words are breathed into the back of Ankha's head. "A Keeper comes. A great Keeper. She is coming to take me away."

Ankha musters up a "Sister..." but her words run out after that.

What comfort can she offer? Amunai's fate has been sealed. As they share everything as if they were twins and not children born a year apart, she knows that Amunai has been hearing susurrations that do not come from the men and women of their tribe. Instead, these whispers come from stones, sand, water, birds, and bugs. Amunai told only her sister, not their parents, of what she'd been experiencing. But the secret had been pried loose by their shaman.

He had gazed upon the two of them the other day while they practiced their grappling and wrestling with the other children. He had stopped and stared deeply, then nodded to himself. He must have spoken to their parents soon after. Outside the great cities, gender rules are not strongly enforced. Men and women can tend to war or crafts. There is one rule for the Amakri, though, alongside maintaining one's honor: women like Teskatekmet who have been cursed with power are sent where they belong. Thus, Amunai will be taken to one of the cursed cities. Her Fate was preordained when she was born a girl who heard the whispers of the world: she will be a Keeper.

"I don't want to go," says Amunai. "I don't want to leave you. I can't believe that mother and father would simply give me into the hands of the witches in the cities. They don't even speak. They stab thoughts into peoples' heads. They're monsters."

"They might be nice, Sister," says Ankha, although she doesn't sound convinced. "And there will be wonders unimaginable. Fruits, even. I know how you like the sugar roots and sweet water we sometimes find—there will be much sweeter things in a city. Do you remember the fruits that mother once traded for from a wandering man? Those golden things with the juice and the little seeds? You'll be able to have as many as you want, I bet."

Amunai remembers the fruits; they were delicious. She and Ankha had eaten one in specks and then fought over the core. "Apples, they're called. And I don't want apples. I want what I know. It's not right. They can't just take me."

But the Keepers of the Great Cities could and would take whomever they pleased. After a girl had been known and marked, her tribe wouldn't want her, or protect her. The old wounds between Lakpoli and Amakri were too deep.

Ankha pulls out of the embrace, turns, and wipes away her sister's tears. "You have always been stronger than I, and smarter and prettier. There is, though, one thing I'm better at: hiding truths." Suddenly, Ankha starts weeping, too. "It started a while ago, before you confessed you were hearing voices…When you came to me, I could not imagine burdening you with my troubles—"

"Your troubles? Sister, are you—"

"Hearing the whispers? Yes."

Neither can control her weeping then. Hope flickers through their grief. Perhaps they will be taken together, be allowed to stay together. By the time their parents wake them, they've made their decision. They're even happy about it. They haven't slept and are blinking against the light of a cold day like captives held long underground. The family, too nervous to eat or move, huddle on the girls' bedrolls, weep, talk, and remember; they promise never to forget each other.

Soon, they hear the shuffling of many footsteps, and people enter the tent and tear back the mothy curtain hiding the family. A woman comes forth in a sweep of charcoal gray and a blast of cold wind. Perhaps she has brought the chill with her, this eerie woman—for her eyes are a winter blue, her hair all gray frost, and her lines like rents in an icy tundra. They can tell that she never smiles; those wrinkles are from scowling. Armed and glorious soldiers stand behind her like pillars of steel and might, dazzling in the sunlight that shines in from outside. The girls' parents cower. Words are thrust into their father's head, and he nods, already defeated.

"The Keeper Superior herself has come," whispers their father, his voice thick with emotion. "She will take you to Intomitath and teach you how to use your gifts."

"We know," says Amunai. "We shall go together."

As soon as Amunai declares this, the woman in gray turns on the second sister a stare of blades. Something else happens, too—a deep cutting inside Ankha's head that Morigan recognizes as a cruder form of the magik, the Will, that women like Elissandra possess. The psychic surgery is conducted without any form of anesthesia. It's brilliantly painful, a ripping inside the skull, and Ankha shrieks and falls into the darkness. Amunai rallies against this injustice, and a second psychic stab renders her unconscious, too. Proud Amakri themselves, the girls' parents become hysterical, but are held at bay, then beaten quiet by a wall of shining, heartless warriors. The family isn't given a chance to say any more of goodbye. The girls are simply taken.

The mists of Dream whirl and part, revealing fragments of time and memory. Morigan sees torment. Teskatekmet's disciple—Isith, the Keeper Superior of this time—enforces doctrine as strictly as her ancient, dead master: through suffering and penance, through the removal of worldly vices, pleasures, and other voices, until only her Will—her desire—can be heard. Intomitath was Teskatekmet's first city, and it is a forge in which she hardened and tempered her ambition. Here the girls shall be forged into Keepers. The City of Flames leers out of a smoldering, tattered memory like Brutus's volcanic beast: Morigan sees geysers of fire and black funnels of smoke that could be towers. Red furnaces and glowing mouths adorn the humpbacked sprawl of this incontestably grand and horrible city. The whole place feels alive, hungry, and red. The girls scream when they see it, but are quickly silenced. When they've become so weakened by starvation and beatings that they're ready to listen to Isith and accept their fate, they spend their days trapped below the scorching city in places that are slightly cooler but still waver in sweltering heat.

Delirious now, they mumble chants and practice verses, but soon they are no longer allowed to speak. The Keeper Superior cracks them with lash and cane when they do. She's cruel, this woman. That is why Isith is able to *rule the greatest of the four cities. That is why she is able to command legions of men and tame the storms of Pandemonia with Will—and the might of the arkstone that is Intomitath's beating heart. She needs to be ruthless and unencumbered by compassion in order to decide who is worthy of saving and who will live in the wilds with savages, raging elements, and death around every corner. This division must be upheld. Except for the blessed few allowed to tend to and feed the Faithful, those who do not agree with Teskatekmet's decree must never set foot in the sanctuaries the original Keeper Superior founded. Most, however, will never know glory, purity from sin, or life eternal (or at least greatly extended beyond its natural span). The savages will never witness ships that do not sail, but fly. They will never enjoy bountiful harvests, never benefit from any of the Great Cities' incredible accomplishments. Or so the girls are told, repeatedly, through mind-speech and whip, while chained to a wall and washed in scalding water for their sins—which the Keeper Superior claims can never truly be cleansed from filth of the desert such as these two.*

Eventually, their teacher and tormentor's lessons begin to take root in Ankha's mind. We are dirty. We are filth. We must be purified, she thinks. In time—whatever days or years have washed away along with her endless sweat upon the floor—she believes almost anything she hears and experiences in the dripping phantasmagoria. She repeats the doctrines without knowing what her mouth babbles into the nauseating humidity. In exchange for her dutifulness, her faith, the Keeper Superior grants her certain freedoms. She's allowed more water than her sister, and spends less time in chains and boiling showers. Does she have parents? Not that she can recall. Ankha has only Isith's voice in her head, the heat, and the cant and words of the faithful. Teskatekmet's ancient Will echoes inside her, and she soon comes to see that it's all she needs.

No matter how far from herself she falls, though, Amunai is with her. Enduring. She wishes that Amunai would not resist so much, for doing so brings her only agony and reprisals from the Keeper Superior.

A steamy twist of years and pain later, Ankha and Amunai are in a garden. They sit on the edge of a square pot that traps a tree resembling a twist of black wire. Other withered, crisped plants bearing bright-red buds form hedges and copses in the rambling arboretum. Everything smells burned in

Intomitath, and the winds are dry and yet somehow sticky. Above them, the sky is tinged crimson-dark by the forges, black towers, and smog. Tonight, though, clear patches float in the darkness like midnight-blue islands, and some stars provide glittering landmarks.

It took a great effort on her part, but Amunai has completed her training. Ankha hasn't seen her sister for what feels like weeks, if not months. They had lost both mental and physical closeness when obedient Ankha excelled at her lessons and Amunai did not. Ankha isn't sure what to feel about her sister. She doesn't recognize the grown woman who sits beside her. Amunai was once always smiling, but all this woman's mouth does is turn down and frown. She could be a younger sibling of the Keeper Superior now.

"Have they said where you will go?" asks Ankha—through mind, not mouth.

"Aesorath," replies her sister silently.

"That is the greatest of the four cities next to Intomitath. They have mastery over wind, music, and the wonders of space and time. You have been given a great appointment. They will build a statue to honor you, I am sure."

"Where will you go?"

"Eatoth," replies Ankha. "I look forward to the wonders of art and agriculture that I shall find there." There's no enjoyment in her mind-whisper, which is flat and mechanical. "How blessed we have been to take this journey together."

"Blessed...yes."

Ankha stands to leave. How sad, thinks Morigan, that love has been beaten and burned from the minds of these women. And yet Fate surprises the jaded seer. Amunai, who appeared as dead in her soul as her sister, now seizes her sister's wrist. "Wait," she shouts into the other's head. "Do not let us part like this. Like strangers."

Ankha fumes with a rash anger. To touch is a sin. They should not be touching. She pulls herself out of her sister's grip. "What are you thinking?" she asks.

"I was thinking that I wanted to embrace my family one last time." Amunai stands, and all the careful walls she has built—the facades to conceal her indomitable emotions—begin to crumble. "We may never see each another again. I want you to remember me, to remember us. I can't even remember our parents anymore. That's how much they've taken. Don't you care? Don't you see?" The mind-whispers not seeming to have swayed her sister, Amunai mouths the words 'I love you.'

But Ankha's mind and soul have been taken too far down the tunnel of despair. If she confronted the reality of their suffering, she would break—again. She's not the strong one, never was. She couldn't hold on to herself through the religious mortifications. Mindwhispering, she says, "I shall forgive your trespass in touching me. I shall not tell the Keeper Superior. Go to your appointment in peace. Hallowed be our place."

The mists of Dream claim Morigan once more, and she is spared the sight of Amunai's weeping. *Amunai, my enemy*, she thinks, before killing any budding compassion. *I want to know what turned you into a monster. Love spurned is not enough to entice the Black Queen. She feeds on the deepest, sickest ruin of a soul.*

The bees then whirl their mistress through a number of pasts. In most, she floats with Ankha in her new clouded-window sanctum. Here, in the silences, Ankha's armor begins to rust, and pain and loss find their way back to her. Ankha never admits this, though, except through an occasional twist of the heart. These pangs come with a certain regularity, however: each season after a harvest, a gift comes to her from Aesorath. It's always a simple hand-carved box crafted of the white-gold stone of the City of Wind and made as light as paper by magik. Within lies a fruit of the city: an apple with a tartness and sweetness so pure that Ankha's mouth waters whenever the package arrives.

Amunai shouldn't be sending such temptations; Aesorath's fruits are used only to make sacramental wine. They aren't to be eaten. Their sweetness is an indulgence, a sin, and a Keeper must be the avatar of faithful virtue. Amunai, then, must prepare her gift in secret. The boxes are all protected with seals only a Keeper could break; the wards who bring them to Ankha believe them to be political missives of the greatest importance. Either they cannot smell the fragrance, or it exists only in Ankha's mind.

The boxes come and come, and Amunai secretly discards their contents—although once or twice, she sins by taking a bite. The cursed, tantalizing fruits inspire a kind of longing and bliss that women fed on lemon water, grain, and a forkful of meat each day couldn't even imagine.

Then one season, the single irregularity in her routine of rule, worship, and duty is broken. No box comes. Ankha is angry about this change, though she only gradually acknowledges her disappointment. Messages are sent via bird and silver pod to Aesorath. When she receives only cold, nondescript, dismissive replies, Ankha feels a skipped beat in her heart—a pang of abandonment. Her parents are dust now, and she can't seem to remember their faces or names. Her sister's gifts, these forbidden fruits, are the only things in her life that speak of any emotional connection. Suddenly, she is weak and small; she realizes what she and her sister have lived through.

She takes a Divine Seed to the City of Wind and is chewed by the rats of her anxiety the whole time. The dazzle of sunlight over golden towers alarms her as if it were a consuming fire, and the music of the City of Wind sounds like the screams of her and her sister in the dungeons of Intomitath. That dreaded Keeper Superior, Isith. She was a monster, Ankha now remembers.

She exits the seed, ignoring the splendor of this most splendiferous city—a place that would awe her with songs, grandeur, and life were she paying heed, or capable of feeling awe. However, all that she needs, all that she yearns for, is her sister, that embrace that she denied Amunai decades ago. The Keeper of Aesorath is informed of Ankha's coming by her bird-like men, who clatter from the metal feathers adorning their breastplates, and peer through helms shaped as hooked screeching beaks. One of the men gazes at her, brazenly, with a confidence that makes her uncomfortable. She's further disturbed when it is he that receives a mind-whisper from his mistress—and not she.

He leads her through an arch and into a whistling open tower that is encircled by cloisters and lets in sunny air from its opened roof. All seems in a state of disrepair—the tumbled rocks, the green runners, the rambling flowerbeds that grow where they want. To honor the Green Mother. And there sits her humble worshiper—no longer the desperate child and woman Ankha once knew but a smiling, radiant nymph.

Amunai welcomes her sister to the dais where she sits and watches birds. Amunai looks slightly rounder around her hips and breasts. Perhaps she's gotten fat from the fruits of apple trees that surround the dais and the garden; the fruit trees, too, grow wild. She munches on an apple as her sister comes to her.

"I am glad that you came," she mind-whispers. "I did not think that my gifts were welcome."

"Is that why you stopped sending them?" Ankha asks and kicks an apple. There are apples everywhere. "These sinful things."

Amunai smiles with her eyes, enjoying the apple. "They're fruits, Sister. Nothing more."

"What of all this kingly magnificence with which you have surrounded yourself?" Ankha asks, having recovered her guard and retreated behind her battlements a bit. The changes in her sister are rather alarming. The Keeper of Aesorath even wears jewelry. A primitive fetish, jarringly crude—Ankha sees something of leather twine and a lump that hangs between her sister's breasts. She continues, "We are not to live in indulgence. We are not to fatten ourselves on the riches of our nation. We are to contemplate. To honor."

"I honor those duties, Sister," replies Amunai. "But I also understand that one cannot preach love if one does not know love." In that speck, she casts a look somewhere behind Ankha. The guard with the fierce gaze—his aura beats with the red pulse of love. Another smaller star throbs in Amunai's stomach; Morigan sees she is with child. Before Amunai speaks further, she dismisses her and her sister's legionnaires. All save for one leave. She stands, slowly approaches, and then holds her sister, who doesn't spurn the advance. It's that surrender to intimacy—for Ankha does not recoil as she did when last they touched—that makes Amunai feel she can be honest with her sister. Amunai continues, "The Keeper Superior is ailing and will soon be gone, Sister. One of four women will take her place. Of that number, two possess the strongest arts. Two have made their nations more prosperous and glorious than at any other time in our history. I speak of you and I and our achievements. The balance of power is shifting. I am told, on fair authority, that the pole of our world will move East or West. It will not remain in the North, in Intomitath, after the Keeper Superior's death."

The impact of the news causes Ankha to stumble a bit, and her sister helps her to sit. Thoughts rail in Ankha's head. The Keeper Superior is ill? A new leader of all cities will come from East or West, from Aesorath or Eatoth. How does her sister know all of this?

"The Green Mother has spoken to me," says Amunai, as if reading her mind. "Each day, I feel her more and more. Whispers on the winds. Songs when a child laughs with his mother. A beat in my—" Belly, thinks Morigan. This, though, Amunai does not confess when she continues: "Do not think this heresy, my sister, but the voices we hear, the Wills our society follows, are made by man and woman. We listen to ourselves. We listen to our egos. I am not some Amakri shaman preaching rebellion against the cities. I do not see us as forsaken. However, we are in need of saving. We have fattened ourselves on pride. We must change ourselves and listen once more to the one true voice."

"One true voice? This is Amakri heresy!" exclaims Ankha, her face a twist of terror. Yet she doesn't rise or call for her guards, as a Keeper should. She trembles, and her sister tightens an arm about her. The warmth of flesh on flesh is unforgettable. Ankha has missed it more than anything. Into that heat, Ankha surrenders and fades. She and her sister sit; they bask in Nature's golden heat, and in the heat of each other. They watch the sand moths—their transparent husks turned crimson in the day—that flutter about like living cinders. The sisters' heads fill with Geadhain's grand, earthy odor. Their ears tickle from the rustle of countless green swords of grass, each movement a whisper. Amunai has never been more right. Geadhain lives, speaks, and can so easily be heard; the Green Mother's message is one of peace. Not since she was a child and the stones first spoke to her has Ankha heard the Green Mother's voice so true. She begins to weep, slowly and with joy. After the spell over her lightens, and the voice fades to a tremble of tranquility, Ankha asks, "How have you done this?"

"I learned to listen, Sister. I cast out false verses. I searched for who I had been before. I found her, that girl. Then I became a woman, and—"

This time, Ankha senses the secret. "What? You became what?" Whatever has transformed her sister, she desires it, too.

Touched, but still with a mother's protective instinct, Amunai does not confess to her pregnancy. "I cannot tell you," she says. "Not yet. I need you to think about what I have said. Stay in Aesorath for a day, a week, or however long you choose. We have been apart for too long. I have missed my sister. See how much of the Green Mother's voice returns to you. Then I shall tell you my secret."

Amunai stands; her legionnaire takes her hand and escorts her down the stairs of the dais. This impropriety—a protector should not touch a holy *woman*—plants a different seed in Ankha. *A seed of righteous anger or jealousy?* wonders Morigan, at the flash of indignation. For Morigan sees beyond the pinched scowl on the woman's face to her desire to have all that her sister has: freedom, certainty, the power to touch another at will, and a fearlessness of reproach. Alas, Ankha is blind to her motivations. As she continues to stare—at her voluptuous sister, at the man escorting her, at this beautiful garden, at all the things she's too cowardly to claim—the darkness grows like a barnacle around her heart. Ankha's mind fills with postulations, and few are far off the mark. The emotion flourishes so quickly; such a powerful sense of hate and betrayal. If Ankha has not already deciphered the source of her sister's reawakened wisdom and exultation, she will soon.

Dream's waters blur, swirl, and wash Morigan onto another beach of time. Amunai and her sister walk through grand spaces. The light gives towers, fortifications, and bridges the look of solid gold. There's so much light in Aesorath that Morigan wonders whether it was misnamed. Men and women chant and hum with the wind and the music brought by the Green Mother. Here, there are no spirit-crushing sounds like the tolling of the bells of Eatoth. These people make art with nature's melodies because they feel Her presence. Amunai has brought this enlightenment to her city. Already, she works against the old order of stone, rule, and worship. There are no separate buildings for the Faithful, for those who have not ascended—no Amakri encampments for those allowed to serve as serfs. Instead, all roam freely from lower courtyard onto skyships, which are built like Aesorath's waterborne vessels but have no sails: the air's currents are their bobbing sea. These ships and their happy passengers sail over the arched bridges between towers of gold and song.

Much of Amunai and her sister's walk passes in a gleeful stillness. Not since their youth can they remember having smiled or laughed so much with each other, though they do so noiselessly and behind their hands. Some things cannot change, not yet. If it weren't for that man who was following them—the favored guard of Aesorath's Keeper, the one who possesses the hard stare—Ankha would be having an inexpressibly wonderful day with her sister. She has no words for how she feels, for happiness was discarded somewhere in the fire, blood, and sweat of Intomitath. But whatever she feels has her tingling and light-headed. Some shade cools her excitement, and she and her sister find themselves in an alcove: a bench hidden behind a rustling wall *of leaves in one of the lower regions of the city, a place a Keeper should never go. But today, Ankha has eschewed the harshest teachings that chains and penance taught her. Ankha needs to know how this glorious impurity in the fabric of Pandemonia's rule has come to be.*

"How is it that a Keeper walks down in the valley of sin?" she mind-whispers.

Amunai squeezes her sister's hands as she replies: "Are we not mortal? Have we not sinned ourselves? Why should a Keeper not walk amongst her flock? A great leader does not seek to be great: she inspires others to greatness. I have opened the gates between Purgatorium and Paradisum. In this city, you will see no difference between holy man and sinner, between those seeking light and those stumbling through darkness. We have all taken journeys in the dark before, Sister. You and I know this."

Ankha shakes her head and forces the memories of Intomitath back down to the depths; she has become quite talented at burying her pains. "But this is wrong. This is not what we were taught," she protests, without conviction.

"Is it? Who is speaking, Sister? You, or Isith? You, or the specter of Teskatekmet?" Amunai snarls, though her face softens in a speck. "I would speak to my sister. I would ask her what she thinks of what she has seen in my realm. As I have said, the Keeper Superior is dying. The arkstone will no longer sustain her flesh. It is time. You and I can be the future. But you must want it. You must remember who we were."

Ankha bows her head. "You are brave. You were always so brave. I could never do this."

"Bravery does not come from one being," Amunai insists as she kisses her sister's hands, and the gesture is not resisted; she further tests the limits by leaving her lips on their skin as she mind-speaks. "Like a chain, each link makes us stronger. That is why we cannot be whole as a nation unless we break down the barriers between us. I am glad you have come to me, rather than force me to seek you out; it says that you are ready to fight this fight with me. For we are stronger as individuals, and as a nation, when exposed to the passions of others."

"Passions?" Ankha gasps and pulls away; the kissing now makes her uncomfortable. She sits on her hands. "We are never to speak of passions; they are gateways to sin. We must be pure. We must—"

Amunai silences her with a raised hand. She stands and forces another kiss upon the crown of her sister's head. As she bends over, the necklace hidden in her tunic falls out—a swinging pendulum of raw black stone tied in leather. Amunai straightens, the legionnaire standing outside their alcove pulls aside the greenery for his mistress, and she is washed and illumed in sunlight, children's laughter, and songs like a spirit of joy. Ankha is cowed by such beauty. Amunai counters, "Passion is not wicked. Punishing people for wanting love is what is wicked, Sister."

After this final admonishment, the leaves rustle closed, and Ankha is left in shadow, left to ponder in the dark. She sits for hourglasses and tries to see her way through the imbroglio. It is dimming outside and purple shade leaks into the sanctuary when Ankha at last stands. She leaves the alcove and goes to find her sister. She feels bright and light with her answer, her choice. She feels brave...

A quick plunge into and resurfacing from the waters of Dream, and Morigan goes deeper into this timeline. She arrives somewhere else in Aesorath—somewhere dark. A night sky with chalked-on, muted stars grants cover to the woman hiding behind the cloister surrounding a broad, seemingly abandoned courtyard. It is Ankha, hunched and skulking like a murderer in the night. She's found her sister. Out in the courtyard, beneath the silver shadow of a gnarled and moonlit tree, are two almost indistinguishable figures. Ankha watches them, and the darkness in her heart is like a smaller Black Star. She seethes with the Black Queen's envy of life and happiness.

Ankha has forgotten all of the bravery she'd only just discovered. She darkly ponders the touching between man and woman, between her sister and the legionnaire that always guards her. Voices of the Green Mother have come to Ankha, tried to soothe her with words and kisses of wind, but she wants none of them. After her sister told her that everything she knew of the world was wrong, after their first reunion since the dark days at Intomitath, Ankha expected more. More answers, more reasons for what happened in the garden. However, what Ankha discovered has merely enflamed her hate and frustration. For her sister indulges in sacrilege after sacrilege while speaking out of the side of her mouth about holiness and true voices. What rubbish.

All Ankha can hear with her Keeper-tuned senses is the wet lick of their kisses, the pulsing of their ardent lust. She cannot see them very well, for the shadows and night offer them concealment. Nonetheless, her mind fabricates what her eyes fail to perceive. The whispers of the snake-tongued monster that has seduced her sister bridge any gaps in her imagination. Quite wantonly, he speaks of Amunai's breasts, her lips, and the valley between her legs while navigating his hands to these places. A flush that is not hate, a sweat that is not fear, covers Ankha as she listens to this forbidden seduction; his husky, tempter's voice—the sound of a man of snake and rock and fire, a demon of which the Keeper Superior preached. But not everything the tempter says is carnal. Now and again, he whispers words that Ankha simply cannot believe, words that pummel the hate from her gut and leave her stunned and reeling. "Child. Our child," he says. Then the hate returns as the legionnaire, the pride of Pandemonia, pulls out an Amakri talisman that is twin to the crude thing her sister wears and speaks of that, too.

"Halves of a stone from the Cradle of Life," he murmurs. "Like those traded in the days before all the tribes of Pandemonia fell from grace. Although I must leave you tonight, my half will remain close to your heart, where it belongs."

As the man of snake, rock, and fire is leaving, Ankha also creeps away. The farther into the darkness she wanders, the further her spirit sinks. Two halves? Where is she in this equation? What of the sister who held her at night? How can she compete with a man's promises, kisses, and lust? What does she have to offer that could rival the passion Amunai will soon feel for her abomination of a child? Ankha feels she has been betrayed and usurped in every way. What meaning can her love have for a woman who has a queendom of glory and a new family of her own? Amunai has broken every sacred law of their land. She is no longer a virgin mother, but a queen of whores. She must be punished.

In that moment, the broken girl, the lost girl that had come to Aesorath to find her sister, changes. Morigan can feel the flagellation, the suffering, and the grief hardening the woman into a deadly diamond knife. The Dream begins to shake. Its host does not wish to visit the worst parts of itself, these dusty, lightless prisons in which it has kept its great wickedness.

Who among you is truly the sinner? wonders Morigan, as the Dream shatters apart like a house of crystal and the shards of reality scatter over a dark room thick with a miasma of torment. The keeper of this Dream has not been to this memory in years. It is hazy, and parts of what Morigan perceives are muffled, skip frames, or have people without shape—men of smoke like her father. A few of these phantom men stand around the walls of an odd, square belfry. The neglect of this Dream obscures architectural details, but Morigan can sense windy rafters and a sad cry to the night—they are still in Aesorath.

Some parts of the Dream are cruelly vivid. Darkness has possessed Ankha. To Morigan, the Keeper's eyes are now the cold black of a shark's. She stands in the center of the chamber near a kneeling, ravaged man in chains. Close by sways a gagged woman held by two phantom men. Amunai.

Ankha has usurped her sister's claim to the throne of Pandemonia. Isolation and abandonment have bred not longing in her heart, but jealousy and malice. Right or wrong, for her there is only the honor of her station. Thus, she has decided she must do what is necessary to maintain the integrity of their nations. She will make the brave choices her sister cannot.

First among those tasks is meting out punishment to those who broke the laws of their order. Amunai's judgment came in the form of an apple of proposed peace, its skin painted in toxic gland excretions that brought on extreme hemorrhaging. The poison treat has since done its work. A few hourglasses earlier, Amunai's mistake—the tempter's seed—bled from her body.

Now that her sister has been purged, her purification can begin. Earlier, Ankha found her sister in her bedchamber, sobbing loudly, and therefore breaking another commandment. Her soul was in need of so much redemption. Amunai refused to leave her bloody sheets or the clot of jelly she cupped and had decided was her child. They gagged and bound her. They dragged her away. Since then, Amunai has not been in need of sedatives. She is calm, because she has been destroyed. Ankha believes that the worst of the talisman's enchantment ended when she snatched it from her sister's neck. Ankha decided that her sister must have been bespelled, somehow, to have fallen so low. Now Amunai wobbles on her feet and stares catatonically while Ankha punishes the inciter of all this sin: the tempter himself.

Although she considered taking his manhood for his crime of savaging a virgin Keeper, she has decided that his tongue has caused more damage. That is what she cuts out while his jaw is pried open with a steel joist. He weeps and screams the most animal noises she's ever heard. However, darkness reigns in Ankha's mind throughout the wicked surgery, and she feels no mercy. Not until she holds the still-squirming lump of spastic muscle in her hands, not until her sister suddenly wakes and begins screaming behind the rags stuffed in her mouth, does Ankha fully realize what she has done. She can find no explanation for the blood on her hands, or for her lurching nausea.

She'd planned to rip off the tempter's talisman, as well as her sister's, but at the moment she cannot look at his glistening, bloody chest without bile filling her throat and nose. Has she not done only what was necessary? What would Isith's or Teskatekmet's choice have been? Surely, either tyrant would have decided on a crueler fate. But answers force themselves into her mind. *My sister. I've killed my sister's child. I am a child. Who am I? I've cut out her lover's tongue. I am a Keeper. I am a monster. I am bound in duty. I am angry that she chose him over me. I am alone. I am nothing. What have I done?*

The thoughts are a storm that will not be quieted. To banish her horror at herself, she casts away the evidence of her evil: she orders the mangled prisoners removed from her sight. The disgraced warrior of Aesorath is to be thrown out into Pandemonia, to live or die among the Amakri. He will never again poison another with his tongue. *Mercy*, the twisted keeper tells herself: *this is mercy*. Amunai, still wailing, is brought to Aesorath's bleakest depths. There she will contemplate her acts in darkness.

It is there that darkness itself will find the fallen Keeper. For in that sensory-deprived torment, a hollow of absolute black, Amunai will reach out to the only being more despicable than what has happened to her. She will call out to the one that feasts upon depravity: the Black Queen. As the Dream crumbles, Morigan reels and is brought into a filthy, lightless pit—a horrid place crawling with flies and spiders. There, a rocking, haggard woman—Amunai—shrieks and bashes her head against the roach-skittering floor. The drumming of her cracking skull, the potency of her grief, and the spattering patterns of her blood have become an incantation, a summoning.

"Blood has been the sacrament. Blood of your body, blood of your child...The wounds in your heart have called me, desolate one. Your sorrow is a feast on which I could fatten myself. What is it that you want? To forget? Accept me into your heart, and I shall eat away the pain but leave the glory of your hate. Your enemies will rue their

existence. If they did not fear your voice before, they will now. Your softest whisper will taint hearts and poison dreams, as yours were poisoned by injustice. I shall eat away the weakness of your flesh, and you will be reborn as my child, my Herald, my Voice. The Green Mother and your people have forsaken you. I shall be your whispers. I shall be your mother. Invite me into your heart."

Amunai, so wretchedly destroyed, does not take even a speck to contemplate the offer. She smiles for the first time since being cast down into Hell. The rats squeal in a chorus of fear and excitement as she cries, "Yes! Take it. Take it all! Take me!"

"You monster," Morigan hissed, casting off the Keeper with a flash of wolfish strength. The waifish woman was thrown hard to the floor. She chose not to recover herself, instead remaining exactly where she'd landed on the stone. A shadow of fury, Morigan stood over her in a speck. "Why? What did you do? Feed her one of her own fruits? Those that she grew for love? For you? Speak for your crimes!" roared Morigan, and kicked the woman in the ribs.

"My Fawn! Hold!" Caenith restrained her.

Caring no more for the decorum of silence, Morigan spat her words. "She poisoned her own sister. She destroyed Amunai's unborn child. She mauled and exiled Amunai's lover. I can see why Amunai surrendered to the Black Queen. If I were so forlorn, I, too, might find that darkness tempting."

While she spoke, the bees delivered some of the pollen of her journey into the mind of her bloodmate. The atrocities that the Wolf saw repulsed him. If Morigan decided to kick the Keeper again, he would not stop her. He might even offer a kick of his own. Still, as a frequent observer of the failings of mortals, he understood what had driven the Keepers, each of them, to madness. The one before him was nothing but a horribly beaten child, in both mind and body. For the leader of a nation of vast power and wisdom, she had little of either. She was a figurehead, confined to a tower, and left to ponder the emptiness of her being for hundreds upon hundreds of years. Ankha surely thought of her sister, had spent an eternity nursing the painful secret scars she had borne since Intomitath. Ankha's innocence had been flogged from her flesh long before she ever visited

Aesorath. What should have been a homecoming, what could have been a rekindling of a flame of sisterly love and hope, had instead become yet another rejection.

Once Morigan had recovered herself, the Wolf, with a shade more civility—although no more kindness—than his bloodmate, picked the Keeper up and helped her to hobble over to her torn settee.

Thank you, mind-whispered the Keeper. On the edge of the ripped-up furniture, she sat down upon her hands, refusing to look at the great shadow.

"Do not think me merciful or forgiving," warned the Wolf. "An animal that harms its own pack is deplorable. You are deplorable. A person should be hardened by their trials. A champion rises when he is knocked to the ground. You only fell further. You must summon our companions, real champions, to your sanctum, as quickly as possible. We shall need all of our strength to defend you and the arkstone."

Defend me? I am in no danger.

"Foolish creature," he replied, all white, snarling teeth. "Do you think your justice will not come? For what do you think your sister bargained with the darkest force in creation? Your doom. Her vengeance. Brutus comes for the stone. Amunai, however, comes for you."

XVI

THE DESCENT

I

"Should you be playing with that?" asked Talwyn, looking at the knife that Mouse held, which glinted dully in the misted sun. He'd been watching her like a hawk, curious to understand the mechanism by which an unassuming piece of metal could be made to spontaneously swallow several tents in a maelstrom of white fire. What a blessing that no one had been hurt and that the tents had been abandoned at the time. Mouse and Moreth had emerged from the ashen cloud with a bit of charcoal makeup, but had not been singed or burned. The cards she often played with had also been salvaged from the ruin.

For most of the morning, Mouse had hung behind the small line of Amakri as she and the warband wove through stone claws and up icy foothills. Now and then, she'd fondled the dagger in its sheath. Finally, she had brought it out and stroked the blade with a thumb while silently mouthing a word of ancient Ghaedic that the scholar construed as *Imperatrix*. She had explained the destruction back at the encampment: how she'd beseeched Feyhazir for power and this dagger was the result. Pythius readily ignored any of Talwyn's concerns, thinking of Mouse's gift as simply another miracle of the divine. Indeed, Pythius and the small band of

Doomchasers chosen to delve into the realm of the blood eaters marched on ahead and cast few thoughts toward Mouse, her weapon, or any perils beyond those of the looming crags of ice on the horizon.

Talwyn asked again: "Should you be playing with that? Imperatrix, or whatever it's called."

"Shh!" Mouse ripped herself from her stupor and pointed the dagger at him. "I wouldn't say that word if I were you. Well, maybe you can. I certainly shouldn't." She placed the dagger back into its casing. "I don't suppose you happen to know what it means. *Queen*, I think, though I'm rather clueless when it comes to Old Ghaedic. There was an image of a queenly woman on the card I'd drawn from my deck before, well, everything exploded. Regardless, it sounds like an unusual name for a weapon."

Talwyn chuckled and corrected her. "A *magik* weapon. And the word translates to *Empress*, not Queen. My dear, you sound uncertain of what you've inherited and of whether or not you even wanted this divine gift."

"I'm not certain of much these days, to be honest. I feel as if we're marching off a cliff with bags over our heads. This plan of Pythius's: that when the time is right I shall somehow, mystically, guide us deep into the lair of these creatures, like iron to a lodestone...It sounds carelessly grim. I feel as uneasy as when I'd learned that my body had been taken for three days." She shivered. "Do you think he'll do that again? Possess me? How else would I lead us? I can't—I won't lose myself."

Talwyn wasn't at ease with the plan himself, which had been discussed prior to their separating from the Doomchaser encampment. For last night Pythius—and not Feyhazir's vessel or that vessel's guardians—had been visited by a snake of smoke in his dreams. Feyhazir had told the shaman to gather a band of his best warriors and to press on to the Forever Stones, then, when the time was right, his vessel would guide them to the Covenant. Faith. It seemed they were operating on blind faith, which no one from Mouse's side of Geadhain possessed; especially as they'd seen how the Dreamers treated their flocks—very much like sheep or cattle. Realizing something should be said to dispel Mouse's dark disposition as she walked along, kicking snow, Talwyn said: "It'll be different this time. I know it. Call it a hunch. Our aims and the Dreamer's aims are aligned. There's no need for him to assume control over your body. When the time comes—however you sense these things—let him know you'll serve him, we'll serve him."

"I suppose I could try that," she replied.

Moreth, who walked beside Mouse and had spent all morning in gray silence, now broke his glumness with a small laugh. "I'm glad all this business with magik daggers and possession is settled. We are entering into the realm of the blood eaters." He pointed somewhere just below the flinty crags looming over the foothills. The companions would have to climb a little more to see the land as it opened, then dropped and hollowed into a grand frozen basin. They paused as the Doomchasers tried to make sense of the prickled and snow-muffled land, akin to a valley of spears with weathered banners and battlements all crumbling and rendered in white. Farther still, a waterfall of shadow poured from the lipped crags at the base of the titanic Forever Stones—a foothill within a foothill, one that looked as if it could be climbed only by giants. Muted by the mountains' grandeur in that lower valley of darkness lay a field of taller points and half-tumbled cylinders that seemed too smooth, too white to be natural obelisks. Even from an extraordinary distance away, that nest of shattered ivory called to them. It radiated in the dark, seeming to promise both mystery and danger. Snowflakes lingered in amorphous clouds on the scenery and tricked the eye into seeing vestigial shapes that were not there. Ghosts. The queer hints of symmetry and construction suggested it had been a city, and a grand one. *If so, how long ago?* Mouse wondered.

After a quick exchange with Pythius, Talwyn clarified the lay of the land for his fellows, telling a tale Moreth had once heard from the Slave. "Pythius calls this *Fantasmoch*, the City of Ghosts. Once, after surviving a great disaster, the Lakpoli and Amakri—at that time, one tribe and not two—lived here. The bones of their civilization have stood as long as all the other stones in this region. Winter, spring, summer, and fall may come and go, but these ruins remain."

Mouse huddled in her cloak as a rough gust of wind blasted the desolate escarpment like a shrieking voice. "I thought that the Lakpoli and Amakri hated one another."

"They do," replied Talwyn. "However, there was a time, before the great cities were founded, when they had not yet decided to live apart. As

Pandemonia is, well, Pandemonia, there were few places with the necessary terra firma upon which any lasting civilization could be erected. The Forever Stones were one such place, and here Pandemonia's various tribes flourished and developed the rudiments of magik, law, and life. The era of this culture is spoken of by Pythius with reverence. He claims it was an age of miracles, brought on by the wisdom gifted to the people by Feyhazir when last he walked these lands. Many incredible and ancient magiks were conceived in this realm. I wonder if any remain..."

"What happened?" asked Mouse, knowing the answer would be grim.

Moreth interjected. He swept his eyes over the scene as he orated. "A schism occurred. When I heard the tale, I was told of the wisdom brought by the *Wanderer*—the Dreamer who travels with us now, I assume. The Wanderer's wisdom showed the people of Pandemonia how to create fire, how to craft stone, sculpt water, and sing to the earth with their Wills—miracles similar to those generated by the runoff energy of four artifacts of incredible power. Wonderstones, a mother lode of the elements. *Arkstones*. However, the miracles of these arkstones came and went as capriciously as the Green Mother's moods; man's magik is always more reliable. Sometimes the stones would pulse and summon terrible storms, or they might flicker and cause every crop in the realm to mature to succulence. They weren't reliable, and were contained, therefore, in sorcerous casings to inhibit their power. That's where the problems began, with bickering over their containment and use."

"Massive wonderstones..." mumbled Talwyn, mostly to himself. Pythius had said nothing of a schism or a fight over relics. "The power—I can see how such volatile magik would best be trapped. I mean, I've only read of these objects and the magik that even the small ones—ones that fit in your hand—are said to contain. If I remember correctly, you told us that a lesser wonderstone was used to free the king back in Gorgonath. How large do you mean?"

Moreth gazed off, deep in thought, and recalled his leathery friend having written down legends by a campfire. He whispered, *"They shone like small suns and were trapped in vessels as great as towers, which could hardly hold them. They lit this corner of Pandemonia like four stars of different colors: red, blue, white, and yellow. Any man could look north on any night and see them. That was why wanderers were drawn to this area: it teased them with wonder.* Legend tells that the Second City—I don't know if there was a First, though I assume there must have been—stood through many of the great elemental seasons of the world: the Long Winter, the Age of Floods...It was the harmonic power of the arkstones—their influence, even when repressed—that kept the city safe. Come the Dry Season, however, the land became entirely barren. Green refused to grow even as the shamans whispered to it, and the whole of Pandemonia was stricken with famine and drought. The ages became so dry that even the veins of magik thinned, and spells to summon water or to call to animals no longer worked as they should. A great and terrible plague struck, as well—and was incurable by magik. It was as if Geadhain wanted the ancient tribes to vanish, to blow them away as dust.

"With sorcerers being quite useless, the obvious solution would have been to use the magik of a relic—an arkstone—to summon endless water. As I said, however, disagreements arose over how the relics should be handled. There were those who believed the relics were sacred and should be used only as objects of reverence; then there were the iconoclasts, who saw the arkstones' power as a means through which to end the decades of drought. A sorceress led the latter faction. I can't remember her name: Teksa...Teresa...Tormet...No matter. Terrible things happened in that era. A civil war. A religious war. When people couldn't hunt off the land, they began to hunt each other..."

"Cannibalism?" exclaimed Talwyn.

"And worse. Amid the strife that erupted, there were also those who simply wanted to live in peace."

"So three factions: iconoclasts, preservers, and peacekeepers," pondered Talwyn. "Of the two most at odds, which won?"

"The iconoclasts, of course," said Mouse.

"Indeed," replied Moreth. "The heaviest hand always wins. Teskatekmet! That was the sorceress's name. She seized the arkstones and her army left the Second City with the relics—all of them. Charged with magik and wisdom that no others seemed to possess, Teskatekmet drew—safely—upon the extraordinary reserves of the arkstones' power, and from that power she and her followers cured the plague, banished the drought, and built the four great cities of Fire, Water, Earth, and Air. I've seen only Eatoth, City of Water, and it's an unparalleled marvel. A strange theocracy is in place there, with caste systems not dissimilar from Menos's, though they are more insidious. My friend and I didn't tarry for long—less than a day's layover to refresh our supplies. He was afraid of...something. And I'd never seen him fear any beast or battle...Anyway, as for the losers in Pandemonia's civil war..." He nodded toward the Amakri, hunched and surveying the ruins. "We've met them, and they haven't had it easy. From what I gather of your conversations with the shaman, and from what I remember of the Slave's intimations about the Great Cities and their ways, each side believes it's been guided by the Wanderer's Will."

Mouse touched her chest, as if feeling the Dreamer there. "Feyhazir. He certainly sticks his finger in a lot of pies."

"What of the third faction? Ones who cared not for the arkstones or for politics and just wanted to live in peace?" asked Talwyn.

"Ah," replied Moreth. "Whatever peaceful folk stayed in the Second City are said to have vanished, perhaps driven off by the blood eaters. It's possible they ended up in Amakri or Lakpoli sanctuaries. We also have wisemen and wisewomen in Central Geadhain who act with many of the customs we've seen in Pandemonia, so surely some of these ancient people must have migrated West."

A whiff of mystery intrigued the scholar. The sequence of these events struck him as important. Were those who remained in the Second City driven off by the blood eaters, consumed by them? Did they vanish? Did they find solace in the West? Or did something else occur that would account for the missing populace? Perhaps he was thinking too much on matters only an archeological dig would solve.

Moreth partially answered the scholar's silent question. "My friend, he spoke of them as if they died—the ones that stayed, not those who may have struck out as neither Amakri nor Lakpoli. Whatever happened, no one knows whether they rejoined their fellows—as we should do, as our group is moving ahead."

Indeed, Pythius had finished his survey of the land and had now started to lead his small party of warriors forward.

"To bring our dialogue full circle—and to steal your thunder, scholar—that's why this is called the City of Ghosts. Linger out here after night has fallen, and you'll become one yourself."

Limber Moreth left the pair of his companions standing at the bottom of the hill. When Talwyn didn't respond to Mouse's nudge, she pulled him along. As they walked through the City of Ghosts, the scholar watched the white drifts for movement and concentrated on the subtle oscillations of the wind, wondering if the missing souls still lingered here. Waiting.

II

Night came on fast. The Doomchasers—three men, three women, and the shaman were all that had come—did not pursue the retreating light at their usual breakneck pace. Long before the day ended, they slowed their steady climb and sought shelter in a crevasse. Pythius paused and examined the ground. Eventually, he determined it was safe. Then began the nimble lowering of members of the war party into the gap to nowhere. The larger of their number barely squeezed through the dark crack. Mouse supposed its tightness would keep out winged, stalking horrors. Never beyond the reach of her own self-interest, she chose to go last after listening for splats or the sounds of people being eaten. Soon, she weaseled her way into the crack, felt someone wrangle her waist, and was pulled down.

Blinking in the darkness, she patted whoever it was that had assisted her into the low cavern. It was a woman, she realized, as she cupped a breast. She quickly apologized. "Sorry. Quite ample, though. Good for you." A glimmer of light lay ahead, and she and the huntswoman walked toward it. Her companion had to hunch over to avoid scraping her head on some of the lower parts of the oddly tilted ceiling, which was higher in some places and lower in others. It was smoothly wrought by men's hands, Mouse realized. White radiance from the light source ahead played off rivets and inlaid images tiled upon the floor and roof.

Her eyes and imagination played the wildest tricks on her. Under the icy glaze of the ceiling, she thought she saw a phantograph: a bizarre bestiary, depictions of men and women, towers of glass, and small suns trapped in cylinders. She realized it was a fresco, and received better glimpses of the intricate craftsmanship when she scuffed away some of the snow at her feet. So focused was she on the ground, she literally stumbled upon the small warband, kicking Talwyn smartly in the heel. "Oh, sorry. The floor. What I can see of it under the snow. By the Kings."

"Incredible," replied Talwyn, who was doing the same shuffle himself, and had examined and deduced much already. He glanced at Mouse with a fire in his eyes. "From the gradient of the ground and the supporting grid work that has been embedded so artfully into the architecture, I'd say this is only a small part of the city. Buried or collapsed. Perhaps from the wrath of the Green Mother. Some of the stone is cracked and buckled, which suggests some manner of seismic event; I can't say for certain, though. The metal elements of this city have been warded against oxidization by magik, surely—although the grout seems to have been treated merely with a patina. Its hue can be just as revealing as the rings of a tree. It's a shame there isn't much more to explore beyond this small pocket of tiles. Well, it's insulting to deprecate such artisanship as *tiles*; these story-piece wonders were wrought by master craftsmen and fablers. I've nothing else to call them though, other than tiles, given their size. I think this was a street, perhaps—from the tiles, the angle, and a few other details. A collapse occurred up ahead. It's all blocked off with snow there. I expect we'll see more of the city, however, as it is into its depths that we shall descend."

It would have required a great deal of concentration to sift through Talwyn's many words. Mouse correctly assumed that the city was old, had fallen into ruin, and left the matter there. She sat with the others on their humps of snow and warmed herself as they did in the crackle of a pale eldritch fire. Sticks and flint hadn't created this flame. It was a disembodied light that hovered above a pit of snow, giving off no smoke or smell, but blowing a balmy heat. It was so warm, in fact, that Mouse quickly removed her gloves and hood, but the snow around the fire and upon which they sat seemed unaffected by the heat. *Magik*, she thought snidely. *Breaking whatever rules it pleases.* The same ivory sparkle of the flame glowed in the gaze of the Doomchaser shaman. It was kind of him to have used his power. Doomchasers were warriors and hunters of the night. They didn't need flames to see. As she considered the notion, she realized that with the exception of their first encounter, in which Pythius had proved his mastery of herbs, and a blast or two from his enchanted war horn, the shaman had practiced little magik at all. Perhaps his abstinence could be linked to the schism of which she had learned.

Eventually, the shuffling scholar abandoned the study of buried secrets, though he knew there would be more ahead, and sat beside Mouse. She could see how the shaman's stare followed the scholar. The man's eyes flashed with intent. Suddenly, she understood why the Doomchaser had used magik in the face of whatever prohibitions had been put in place against it. "Hmm," she said smugly, while passing a finger of jerky to Talwyn.

"Hmm, what?" he replied.

"You can't tell me that you don't see it."

"I haven't the faintest idea what you mean."

"A man as shrewd as you? Bullshite."

"I don't see anything." Talwyn shifted, and looked away from the man whose stare he'd been dancing with across the fire.

"You certainly do."

Trying to be discreet, even though none of the Doomchasers seemed able to understand Ghaedic, Talwyn turned and mumbled to Mouse, "I am a curiosity to him. A stranger with an aptitude for culture. A parrot that amuses him with the clever phrases it makes." While speaking the words he only faintly believed, he flushed as he remembered the Amakri wrestling with him, or tenderly holding his wrist. "This is a foolish discussion in which to indulge. We are on the verge of war. He and I are from two very different cultures. I do not believe that the Amakri approve of my kind of man—"

"Really? I saw two blokes kissing in the encampment the other day. Right there in the winter morn for all to see. They went inside a tent after and made themselves a little fire. And they weren't shy about the noise." Mouse winked. Talwyn blushed. "Listen, I'm not a girl for love, but that doesn't mean you shouldn't be."

"A girl for love?"

"Well, you can be the girl if you like. I suppose you and he would have to work that out at some point." Talwyn turned red as a boiled crawfish. "Nothing to be ashamed about. Perhaps it's different where you were raised." Mouse scratched her head. "Where *were* you raised?"

"A number of places. I traveled a lot," replied Talwyn guardedly.

"All right, Mr. Traveled-a-lot. I'm assuming you've seen any number of cultures and family arrangements. A man or woman can lie with whomever he or she chooses. I know that you're smart enough to not be a bigot. But self-loathing is another matter. It's possible you have a shade of that."

The canny woman had analyzed him as effectively as he picked apart the behaviors and mysteries of the world. Talwyn struggled with what to say. His thoughts hung around him in a black cloud. She worried she had upset the peaceful fellow with her jibes and sniping humor. "I'll just leave you be," she said, turning away.

Talwyn's cracking voice stalled her. "My mother, bless her soul, held on to life long enough to squeeze me out into this world before dying from consumption. I was taken in by women—my mother's working peers—who, too, had been discarded by society. Women of cheap lace and boozy perfume. Women with hearts cleaner than their bodies. They never abused me or mistreated me. They treated me as if I were their son. Such a lucky boy, to have twenty mothers and many sisters. I've never known such love from strangers. They spent their very hard-earned crowns on books for my mind, which was budding even then. I was walking at three months, speaking at six. Doing their accounting by the age of four. The matron passed me the reins, and I ran the place until I was accepted into the Academy at Gloamshire. Before I left, I saw to it that my mothers and sisters would be tended to. I fattened the investments I'd made until each had enough that she could put that sordid life behind her. Now they are grandmothers. A few of them are happy spinsters, and one or two of them have become artists and scholars, one is a professor. I visit my old family whenever I am in Riverton. That's why I so often return. My heart aches for each of their sweet gray heads and the smiles that once charmed a man's honor from his coin purse."

Talwyn looked down, speaking quietly and uncertainly. "I want you to know that I'm not the way I am because I spent my childhood around women, dresses, and sex. I was born this way. I am no less a man for whom I love. Although, I am a better man, a freer man, thanks to the influence of my mothers. When it comes to love, though, I am conflicted. I've seen what men do, what they did to my family. The cuts and bruises. The tears, the murder—though we got that sorry bastard, we did. It is easier, my friend, to avoid tempting one's heart with desire. It is better that I learn from the lessons of my mothers and sisters and refrain from repeating their mistakes." Finished, Talwyn now looked defeated.

Echoes of his tale touched Mouse with a warmth she rarely experienced. He was a lost child, as she was. He was afraid of love, as she'd once been. Mouse stood, and, overcome with sympathy, kissed the man's coppery head. Despite their road weariness, he smelled of a baby's talc and fresh scalp. What a pure and innocent soul. He deserved to be happy. She hovered, smelling, as people do when sniffing infants. Then she pulled away before she could feel truly absurd. As she leaned back, she whispered, "It's a wonderful story, Talwyn. You should not be afraid to share it—or yourself—with anyone." Hovering near him for too long gave her the impulse to inhale his baby fragrance once more. "Kings, you smell wonderful, too."

Mouse left the scholar to find Moreth. With the aid of the tunnel's white hues, she spotted his lurking shadow not far from camp. Talwyn remained by the flame conjured for his comfort, and when Pythius glanced his way, they resumed their dance of stares.

III

Mouse sidled up next to the shadow that stood in the dark. She'd found Moreth just where the cavern ended—sealed by a heap of snow and rubble. For a while, she watched his white measured breaths. Everything about the man was controlled, which was why she was certain the glimmering black lines and sniffles had to be watery eyes and a runny nose caused by the cold. He couldn't possibly be crying. Could he? "Moreth?" she asked, quietly.

After a few snorts and a cough, he replied. "What is it, little Mouse? I was enjoying a moment to myself. We've been stacked upon one another like tinned fish these past weeks. A man needs to breathe."

"Or cry. I could leave you to do some more of that, if you'd like," she suggested. Moreth held his breath. Mouse's compassion went only so far, and she'd already exhausted most of her stock on Talwyn. She continued, "We're similar, you and I. We don't like to air our problems. We equate sharing with weakness—with a need to have our pain validated. I know you don't want that from me, or from anyone. But how about making use of the willing ear of a fellow bitter soul?"

Moreth snickered. "That doesn't sound so terrible." A great sigh fell from the master, and with it, much of his pent-up worry. He turned to the wall and touched its surface like a widower caressing his wife's tombstone. In a sense it was a gesture for one he loved, for a man whose tainted, blood-eater-spoiled remains wouldn't even be touched by worms wriggling through the soil. There was nothing earthly left of the Slave now save his necklace, for which Moreth reached.

Touching the talisman opened his heart, and he spoke. "We came here to the Forever Stones to hunt the fiercest of what Pandemonia had spawned. After replenishing our stocks at Eatoth, we took the longest journey of my life, next to this one. We chased the legends that these hardened nomads feared. There isn't much that frightens people who chase doom, people such as this tribe. However, all the tribes of Pandemonia feared the blood eaters. Still, something had changed in my friend during our time in Pandemonia—right after Eatoth. I've seen men quail before destiny, watched them deprive themselves of glory, and his was a darkened frustration not dissimilar. He became a beast even darker than the one I'd known. I worried about him, about where our journey would lead. I should've known. I did know. After all, I'd spent much of my life watching men die." A few white puffs of breath and time passed while Moreth clenched away tears. He slid down the stone and dropped his arse to the ground, then let his legs lazily sprawl. Mouse, silent, and stoic as promised, sat next to him. He resumed. "My father was absolute rubbish, as you know. I wouldn't say that the Slave was kinder. He was crueler in many ways. Still, he cared for me. For my welfare. For my strength. I cared for him. I believe that was why he stayed with me for so long, despite his yearning to die. The proud cannot take their own lives, no matter how far they fall. I think this was the best way for him to die, then. In battle. At the side of one for whom he cared…"

At last, a challenge had appeared. Months of hunting in the wilds of Pandemonia had brought broken bones and deep scars, but nothing of heart-pounding peril. Finally, Moreth and the Slave had found such a dark thrill in the green-canopied vales and moss-backed ruins of the Forever

Stones. The legends were true. They'd met beasts as fearsome as those from childhood nightmares: women of smoke, bloodlust, and shadow. They'd seen the charnel caverns, the winding tunnels spackled in bone, shite, and regurgitated filth. The smell was like that of a sewer filled with excrement from rotted bowels: utter putrescence. Nothing Moreth had experienced in his life, including his father's depravities, had ever repulsed him more than the smell and the warm, greasy darkness of those catacombs. Iron strong, he and the Slave had delved into those sickening hunting grounds and returned with a prize of heads. And now they'd escaped the tunnels and dashed through the primeval thicket, evading the swooping, shrieking nightmare women that ruled the caliginous realm.

In the shadows of an emerald bluff, they hid like bandits in a stony ravine roofed in great rent logs. They peered through the mossy overhanging. For hourglasses, they played their game of stillness and calm, and eventually convinced their hearts that the terror was over, that they need not beat so furiously. They didn't smile. They didn't piss. They barely moved until the sun needled the place with light. When daylight came, Moreth at last felt he could relax and celebrate their victory. He nudged the man who'd been hunched and steady as a turtle for hourglasses. The Slave shuddered, tipped over, and hit the peat-padded ground with a wet smack. The man flopped, black oozing and bubbling from the many seams in him. Moreth's elation twisted to screaming panic, and he threw away their grisly sack of trophies. Alas, the poison had somehow made it into the Slave. How long had the Slave hunkered, weeping on the inside, as his organs churned into melted butter and his eyeballs leaked from their sockets? What sort of son was he that he had not even known his father had been dying beside him?

Moreth didn't worry about secondary contact with the blood eaters' venom; he didn't think the poison worked in that manner, having been told only fresh cuts and bites were lethal. In that moment, he really didn't care whether he lived at all. Life would have no meaning without the man who'd taught him passion. He flipped over his sputtering, farting friend and wiped what ebon goop he could off the lined face. The Slave's gritted, teeth-baring grimace might almost have been a smile. Into Moreth's hands, the Slave thrust an object. Moreth didn't look at it; instead, he held the leathered hand in his and stared into his hunter-father's dark eyes until they lost their shine and grew dull, then gray.

When the Slave was long dead—ash white, black veined, and beginning to turn gelatinous—Moreth examined what he'd inherited. Clenched in his hands was his hunter-father's necklace: the talisman that he always wore, and that suggested that he, too, was cared for by someone, somewhere.

As warriors do with their dead, he buried his friend according to old tradition. The sun crept along, dangerously thinning the light, and welcoming the time when the blood eaters would fly once more. However, Moreth cared not for much besides this moment. He donned the dead man's talisman, and the coldness, hardness, and certainty of the stone reminded him of the stern spirit of his hunter-father. He shrouded the rapidly liquefying remains of his hunter-father in branches and leafy wrappings. As he drew together the final layer over his friend's grave mound, he sang. Another tribute to the old ways, to the days of tribes and wild magik. These were the only story-songs of the West that the Slave had ever tolerated.

Night stained the day with black as Moreth sang under Pandemonia's queer stars. Suddenly, he found he was no longer alone. At first, grieving and tormented, he wondered if this were a waking dream, or if he had also passed beyond. For with him was a woman, white and beautiful, with a stare like diamonds and hair like wisps of frost. Perhaps this was a spirit guide sent to claim his friend. When he stopped singing, she halted her slow crawl from the bushes. The enchantment over Moreth broke as he noticed the black trails—bold against her ivory flesh—that trickled from her mouth. He watched her sniff like a hungry dog the rustling pile beneath which his friend lay. He and the Slave had been warned that the blood eaters were relentless hunters. They never abandoned prey within their hunting ground. This one had come to finish her meal. And so he would finish her. Moreth reached for his pistol...

He was fading in and out, not sure how much of his memories he was sharing with Mouse. Nonetheless, she kept to their arrangement, remaining as quiet as a veiled confessor of Carthac behind a wicker screen listening to all a soul's ills would. Moreth continued. "Have you ever heard the Soldier's Dirge?"

Mouse didn't reply.

"An old tune—they would sing it after the passing of a warrior, back in the less civilized days of sorcerer kings and wars. I guess it's just as uncivilized now. Hmph. Regardless, I sang the dirge over his body after I laid him in the closest thing I could find to holly in this kingsforsaken land. I kept my voice strong against the thrust of sorrow, which can be nausea and pain in one. I didn't realize how tireless these hunters were, though. I didn't know that his killer had followed us that far, not until I finished laying him in green. She was there...A naked woman, white as snow. Feral, besmirched with dirt and twigs, and savagely beautiful. She has the most extraordinary stare, my wife, and the most exquisite body...My song of dark love and grief had teased her into her less horrific skin. She had, though, come to finish her meal—my friend—and that I would not abide."

Several moments passed. Mouse heard Talwyn and Pythius laughing quietly by the campfire. Moreth's next calmly spoken words created a jarring contrast to that happiness. "I shot her at least a half dozen times. The blood eaters soak up bullets like a wet couch. Takes thrice the amount to slow them down as it would take to kill a man. Even then, they won't die unless you shoot the head clean off. As she lay there, writhing at my feet, I considered using however many more bullets it would take to do just that. Perhaps I'm a shallow man, for her beauty spared her. Even then, as a wounded monster, she held on to the shape of herself: her mortal shape, a woman fair. I sensed that she wanted the pain to end. I'd lost the bag of blood eater heads in the bushes somewhere, and I decided that she would be a far better prize. I pumped her full of enough iron to knock her into a bloody sleep, and I returned with her to camp."

He had carried her far from the Forever Stones and all the way back to his camp. Whenever she had stirred, he had sedated her with feliron bullets. Once at his encampment, he decided to remain. Where else could he go? What life awaited him back in the West, if he could even reach those shores? Instead, he stayed for the melting of winter to spring, and then the quick rising heat of the summer that followed—about three months, by Pandemonia's chronex. No nomads or blood eaters wandered into his solitude. Moreth and the monster were alone.

Days seemed to disappear entirely, so engrossed was he in the twisted and sadistic games he played with the blood eater. He'd dug a pit and reinforced it with the bones of some of his and the Slave's greatest kills. Afterward, he'd shackled and thrown the blood eater into it. Then he'd conducted experiments to see what would bring her pain: steel, fire, bullets, whips. He found that sunlight, which these creatures were supposed to fear, merely made the creature hiss and squint for a time. He learned that the beast understood pain and deprivation, though they didn't affect her very deeply. Before long, he discovered this was because her suffering at his hands was overshadowed by an agony far stronger than anything he could inflict: a hunger that knotted her from the inside and made her shriek and sweat.

In time, the line between disgust and desire was effaced. Although he despised himself for the sentiment, he began to pity the beast that had murdered the man he'd loved. His feelings must have been the result of his own pain and deprivation, or some kind of mental illness. Still, she was beautiful, even if she was a monster, even if she howled and sometimes became wrinkled and fanged and flapped in her prison with dark wings. She was his to keep: his curse and his burden. Her animalism, her beauty, and her violence, all made her even more alluring.

Moreth denied the feelings flowering in his heart for as long as he could, but his punishments diminished. He started to share his hunts with the monster, throwing scraps of bloody meat into her kennel, meals she snarled at and consumed in a speck. At least she was an easy pet: she didn't seem to shite or piss. It was as if all that she ate was digested down to the last drop.

Soon, he brought her whole, living meals and studied the orgasmic frenzy of her consumption, an act as lustful as sex. Her bobbing bloody breasts, the way she silkily rubbed her red-greased thighs together as she took that first noisy crunch...Usually, she bit and swallowed the head of an animal in one munch. Occasionally, he masturbated while she devoured. She seemed to know what he was doing in these moments, and sniffed the air for his seed.

When puttering about the camp—checking traps and sharpening blades—Moreth found himself humming that old warrior's tune, the first his monster had ever heard. Whenever he did, he would notice her straining her head up through the bars in the dirt, as if she were eager for whatever squealing thing he might drop into her cage, or sniffing for the fresh paint of his semen upon the ground. Moreth noticed that her frenzy quieted, her beast stilled, while he sang. It was as if it were not a monster, but a woman, who listened.

One day, she startled him by croaking out a few notes herself. Her voice was as rough and sultry as his own, and the awkward duet they performed—she did not understand any of his tongue—was charming. He lowered into her pit some water for her throat, which sounded dry, and this became another ritual of their days and nights. In the evenings, he worked, and they sang. Eventually, they found a harmony together.

One night, after she'd eaten, he'd masturbated, and they'd sung, Moreth stood near the cage. He stood and looked at his monster. She seemed—and not for the first time—a wronged and shivering woman. He couldn't see a remnant of the terror he'd trapped. Guilt and horror wormed in his stomach. He had nowhere left to go and no one who loved him. This woman of ice and terror, the object of his torture and affection, was the whole of his world. He wondered if she would kiss him or kill him. He couldn't read the clouded sentiment behind the frost of her stare. It was time to find out. Time to move and join his hunter-father in the warrior's afterlife if that were to be his fate. It would be a noble enough end: being ravaged and raped by a monster. Moreth could think of nothing more beautiful. He shot the lock off the cage, threw back the bone grate, and then tossed his pistol in the sand. He spread his arms.

"Come to me," he said.

He closed his eyes and listened to the irons rattling in the pit. Malnourishment hadn't weakened the blood eater, for only a speck hence, a chain-clattering shadow leaped from the pit and pinned him beneath icy talons and cold iron chains. By the Kings, she was the coldest thing he'd ever felt. Cold as a coffin of ice. Even her breath felt like winter's cough; his skin shrank on his bones. Her gasps and her scent were sweet: a sickly sweetness like dried apples in a mortuary. *Go on, kill me*, he thought. He had not felt the arousal of pain for some time, and his body and prick stiffened as her claws tightened on his arms and blood welled forth. Then the monster made a strange sound, almost like the ones that accompanied her hunger pangs, but more plaintive and whining. The claws loosened, and talons explored his body like chilled scalpels, shredding the clothing they touched, lacing his skin with red. None of this, though, was meant to kill him. He knew this as his monster pressed a frozen kiss on his collar—just below the beating artery through which ran most of his life—and gently sank her fangs into the meat of his chest. The pain and pleasure of her needles and the suction on his chest made his prick sputter and leak across his loins. When his monster lover had finished her appetizer, she moved down his chest and began to consume his white cooling essence—

"And we lived happily ever after," said Moreth, then snickered.

Moreth's story had paralyzed Mouse with its graphic intensity. She took a few sands to compose her thoughts. "How were you not poisoned by her...affections?"

"I have turned that question over and over in my mind for years. I have found no satisfying answer. If magik comes from the heart, and the blood eaters are creatures of magik, then I would postulate that Beatrice did not Will me to die. Simple as that."

"How have you been together for so long? How does she eat? How have you kept this a secret?"

"Masters with deviant appetites are hardly irregularities in Menosian society, Mouse. I learned, quickly—after an unfortunate encounter with a kindly, wandering Amakri family—that Beatrice would need to be fed, and often. I sang for her every day and especially at night, too, when her pains were worse. After we'd returned to Menos, I did everything in my power to curb her hunger. Music worked, though she needed to be regularly fed a melody or song, and it had to come from the heart—which it did, when I was around her. When I wasn't nearby, she attended orchestras or we hired the greatest performers of the realm to sate her hunger. For many years, we did well at keeping her darkness in check. She appeared to all to be naught but a lady of refined musical tastes. It wasn't until we were visited by a songstress from Heathsholme, that we realized her monster was not fully caged."

Mouse dared to ask. "Songstress?"

"Beatrice devoured her; my wife was weeping and soaked in blood when I came upon the scene. She claimed she couldn't help herself; that she was compelled, as if through magik, her hunger had been so ravenous. If you'd seen Beatrice's torn expression, or her chamber—dripping and red, yet with no remains, not even a shoe about—you would have believed her, too. Elsa, her lady-in-waiting learned our secret. I think she'd known all along what Beatrice was, for Elsa was already in the bedchamber, changing sheets and scrubbing floors, when I arrived. She must have known something of these creatures, or of magik. She told me to take Beatrice to the Blood Pits."

"Why there?"

"A theater of battle and blood, where sweat, valor, and death thicken the air to a fog you can breathe right in, when you can taste the essence of life. I'd never wanted to take my monster there, for fear she would be incensed. However, immersion in death, in passion, was precisely what she required. Beatrice could spend an hourglass at the Pits, watching a few men gut and shite themselves, and be full for a week."

Moreth's head and shoulders fell, the confession of his life finally over. "You may think me a monster, now, like her—though I am merely a man in love. I'd do anything for her. I'd feed her my own flesh. At times, I fully realize what she is, and the urge to avenge my hunter-father wells within me, my hands aching for a pistol. However, I could never end her. She's a part of my hunter-father, a part of what mercy I possess."

"Love." Mouse laughed. "What a mess."

"Indeed."

Mouse leaped up and dusted the snow off her arse. Moreth rose as well. They knew that if they wanted a wink of rest, now would be the time to take it. Weary and suddenly feeling the pull of sleep, they shuffled toward the camp. Moreth took Mouse's arm before they came within earshot of the others. "If anything should happen to me, see that Beatrice gets my necklace and hears how bravely I fought."

Mouse shook off his hand and glared at him. "I don't think so. Tell her yourself. Men doom themselves with those kinds of promises. Think of what she would do in a world without you and live for *that*." She puffed and stomped away, then threw herself into an angry cuddle with a half-asleep Talwyn. "Put your arm around me! Not like that, you're sticking me with your ribs. Move a bit. Yes. Good. Goodnight."

Survive, thought Moreth. If only she fully knew what awaited them, what Moreth had caught whispers of from the huntsmen: the Veins of Death. Moreth had survived them once, though he and the Slave hadn't gone very deeply into them. And it was in the depths that the Dreamer would have buried his secret chalice. For there, no fool, no soul, not even a rat, could survive, and any treasure would be safe for eternity. By a miracle, their small, stealthy party might make it to the chalice, but he doubted that all of their number would see daylight again. *I shall, for Beatrice.* Moreth picked a solitary spot in which to curl up. He didn't lay upon his cloak, but allowed the cold to seep into his hip and shoulder. Its chill made him think of his wife, and he went to sleep dreaming of Beatrice's embrace.

IV

For a time, Pythius watched as the day's first trembling light squeezed through the crack in the ceiling and danced upon West Sun's face. Even in this somber hole, the man shone like gold. At last, he roused the others, they prepared themselves, and then climbed out of the cavern and into the day. A slash of charcoal tore the sky in an angry scar and sealed away the sun. Under that rumbling wound they strode through the valley of white monuments, choosing lower paths with higher obstacles when the storm finally came. They huddled close together and walked in pairs. Talwyn and Pythius led the war party.

Watching the pair as they talked, Pythius nodding thoughtfully at whatever Talwyn said, Mouse reflected that the scholar had been shown great respect since his time as surgeon for the Doomchasers and his display of shooting prowess. She didn't know why she was so concerned about everyone else's happiness all of the sudden, but it gave her a begrudging joy to see them shoulder to shoulder, to watch Pythius gallantly prevent the scholar from slipping.

As the land became higher, they moved more cautiously. Mouse shivered as they strode along icy paths carved through ragged valleys so deep, cold, and dark that light appeared only as a vein of distant white. Mouse heaved a small sigh of relief whenever they emerged from these claustrophobic canyons. They saw less of the city as they wandered. Winter ruled this kingdom and entombed its glory in crystal. Golden shadows occasionally peeked through their prison of frost, and now and then the warband walked over plates sparkling with refractions from artisans' creations. However, the overwhelming sense was that the City of Ghosts was ancient and forgotten: Pandemonia's bizarre ecosystems had spent millennia reclaiming whatever civilization and efforts man had once made here. Mouse felt they would never see the true beauty of the ruins under their feet.

At the head of the company, Talwyn chatted off the shaman's ear. He asked every conceivable question about the ruins and the people who had lived here. A kiss of afternoon sun eventually wheezed itself from the clouds with a windy cough that parted the heavens. Cheery Talwyn took it as an omen. He was easily excited these days. His time with the company had produced memories for which he would be eternally grateful. *I regret nothing. I have finally lived. I only hope that I will live to see more of our world's wonders, for she is a woman I could adore. You're certainly charming as well,* he thought, studying the charismatic and reptilian blue man scowling at his side. At some point, Talwyn had exhausted his current round of questions, and they hadn't spoken in some time.

"*Flévech tou Thanáto* (Veins of Death)," said the shaman suddenly, pointing higher up the foothills to a blurry charcoal smudge under the black awning of the towering Forever Stones. Talwyn thought he could see smaller, rounder spots in this stain. Portals or tunnels, he assumed, and recalled Pythius's telling him of a labyrinth. Knowing this was their destination, he felt his happiness wither. Pythius, undaunted, had not broken his stride while Talwyn gaped. The scholar rushed to his side. After several sands, with their goal approaching, Talwyn's head filled with questions. The scholar's Amakri was now nearly as smooth as the shaman's, and they spoke like kin.

"How far into the Veins of Death must we go?" he asked.

"As deep as the Dreamer buried the chalice."

"How deep did he say it was buried?"

"Deep."

"I'm assuming there will be dangers."

"An army of the worst monsters of our realm." Pythius turned his blue-scaled head and glittered with menace from his crown to his suddenly curled—and fang-revealing—mouth. "According to legend, the blood eaters rule every step of the ruins below, dark places that have endured because they are built of the eternal stone of this land. It is said that in the heart of the darkness lives the queen of their kind, sitting on bones and death and ruling her unholy brood."

Talwyn swallowed.

"I shall keep you safe from her fangs. I have my own," added the shaman with a sly grin and a snap of his teeth. "She is only legend, this queen. Blood eaters are verminous abominations, and breed like rats. They have no organization to their tribe."

You could be so very wrong, thought Talwyn; he'd learned too much of monsters, both legendary and real, to share Pythius's certainty. The truth was often the strangest fiction of all. He changed the subject. "If we find this Covenant, this chalice—*when* we find this chalice—what will it do for your people?"

"It will restore us to our might."

Talwyn understood the population issues affecting Pythius's tribe: the decrease in traits—scale, strength, imperviousness to magik and magikal suggestion—that defined the Doomchasers. As a scholar, he wanted to know the procedure behind a reversal of generational, biological decay. "How? What will you do with the chalice?"

"We shall drink from it," whispered Pythius reverently, gazing skyward. "We shall share the blood of Feyhazir as our ancestors once did. We shall drink his blood from his cup and grow strong."

"Blood? What about Mouse? The vessel?" asked Talwyn angrily.

Pythius placed a strong hand on the man's shoulder. "We would never harm the vessel. Blood does not mean death. Blood is life. Blood is sacrament. Sharing blood is sharing truth and love. We would need only a few drops, not enough to end her life, or even to endanger it. Have you never shared blood with another?"

"No," replied Talwyn.

"I have not either," said Pythius. "When you find the one for you, West Sun, you will know no greater pleasure." Pythius removed his hand, and Talwyn noticed a gray flush on the shaman's cheeks and forehead—embarrassment. "Or so I am told by those who are joined."

I am comforted to know you are as confused as I am by the strange serendipity of our meeting, thought Talwyn. It mystified Talwyn, but it also gave him purpose—something to pursue once they'd plumbed the Veins of Death.

On they walked without food or rest. O'er the gloom of thickening dusk, the stain spread on the horizon. From it rolled forth a dark mist that soon welcomed the company into blackness. What remained of the sun nearly vanished. The iced monuments lost all semblance to buildings, and waves of frozen water rose on either side. Through the crested valley they walked, shivering and clawing their way over this wind-battered land that was determined to break them. They could not stop. They had to race against the setting of the sun they could no longer see. They needed to reach the Veins of Doom before the hourglass of the blood eaters.

Among the hunters and champions, many ears hummed with more than frostbite. The winds echoed with high-pitched whistles, sounds not of nature—the yawning cries of horrors. The smell about which Moreth had warned Mouse started to manifest itself. She found herself looking around the shining black wasteland trying to figure out where something recently alive could be rotting so putridly. Alas, there was nothing, and she knew that the rot spread up from below like the reek of a body in the cellar. The smell underground would be unimaginable. She ripped two long shreds from her cloak and tied a mask around her nose and chin, then offered the remaining material to Moreth. He gave her a smile for her courtesy, but it was strained by terror.

Although their minds and stomachs would not settle, their masks at least warded off some of the stink and protected their cheeks from the snow, which attacked their skin like shavings of glass scattered from the monoliths looming over them. These icebergs were the oldest, blackest things Mouse had ever seen. She glanced at them many times, squinted her eyes against the flurries, and wondered if they were the first mountains ever formed on Geadhain. Moreth, less enamored, battled for footholds and supported Mouse with a necessary hand here and there, as a gentleman should. If it hadn't been for the cold clenching his guts, or his hunger, he might well have vomited from the fear he felt. However, a gentleman kept such concerns to himself. Memories of black-and-white hallways, cloisters of bone hung with tapestries of skin, and songs of a shrieking horde of ravenous women flashed behind his narrowed eyes.

Just before night conquered the land, Pythius discovered another crack in the ice: a part in the waves, a triangular aperture leaning sideways through which they squeezed themselves. Somehow, probably by instinct or the voice of the Green Mother, the shaman knew it would open up again farther on. They huddled in the hollow he'd discovered, which was dimly bright with the funhouse glimmer of so many mirrored-ice surfaces. The faces they saw in the walls were distorted and grim. Everyone knew not to speak this close to the lair of the blood eaters. The Doomchasers seemed to be expecting something. After a time, Talwyn's curiosity could no longer be restrained.

"Are we waiting for something?" he whispered to Pythius, who had hunkered down beside him. Pythius pressed a finger to Talwyn's lips, a gesture kinder than the shaman's usual rough behavior that quieted the scholar at once. Then the shaman tapped his ear and pointed to the gray crack leading back into the waste. It appeared they were to wait and to listen.

They settled back on their haunches and watched the clouds of their breaths. Mouse found the patterns calming until she heard—and felt—a rumble. Once, Mouse had disturbed a belfry of nesting bats while waiting for Alastair in one of his clandestine meeting spots. This sound was similar, though amplified and drawn out with torment and hunger. The tremors that shook the cavern came from the stir of hundreds or thousands of ghastly, undying monsters rising out of their nesting holes. Mouse pictured the horde crawling on peaked knees and elbows as webbed-winged things did, then shivering themselves upright at the mouth of their reeking caves and keening to the moon. She didn't need to imagine that shrill thunder, for she and every other member of the war party now plugged their ears to protect them from the cacophony.

The warriors and champions came together, a few stumbling, and buried their heads and formed a circle against fear, cold, and the flock of darkness that was going forth to claim the night. The storm of evil passed without nearing the party's hiding spot. Its cloud moved elsewhere, hunting. Mouse suddenly realized she was gripping two hard objects for dear mercy—Pythius's horns. She quickly released them. "My apologies. I needed something to hold onto. Bit of a fright."

The shaman was not offended and she had apparently not harmed him, but he did raise a hand and shake his head to reprimand Mouse for using her voice. With another gesture, Pythius bade them to stay, then crept to the fracture and listened to the wind hissing by it. Talwyn sensed the shaman was employing more than simply his senses, and his skin prickled with magik. Whatever the divination was, it forecast safety. Pythius returned to the circle, and his warriors stood.

"Tell the Vessel and the pale man that we can now proceed safely," he said, "although our time is limited. We must return to the surface before dawn. We must pray that Feyhazir will guide our steps using both his memory and his vessel. We shall not live if we remain below. The tunnels should be empty now of all but the very young and very old, although they are usually eaten by the pack if they do not grow or die quickly enough. Prepare for the darkest descent of your life." Pythius paused, fought himself for a thought, and then whispered, somehow, right into Talwyn's head, for his lips did not twitch beyond their handsome scowl: *Should we meet again in the eternal garden of the Green Mother, I would share blood with you, Brother.*

Surprised, Talwyn couldn't respond in time; Pythius and his warriors were already squeezing themselves through the crack, and his companions were nagging him for instructions. It was time for war, not moony thoughts. Talwyn turned to his friends. "I've been told we have until dawn—or slightly before that time, I imagine—to recover the relic and flee the caverns. If we have not extricated ourselves by then, we're doomed. A thousand blood-hungry fiends will bury us in that tomb."

"I guess it's time then." Mouse crossed her arms and planted her feet. "Wake up, Feyhazir. It's now or never. You needn't steal my flesh, I submit myself as your champion on this quest. Wake and fill me. Together we shall claim your treasure."

As if she'd spoken an incantation, a crackling gasp of electric wonder expanded Mouse's chest; harmless white sparks leaped from her, striking her companions. A pittance of chaos for the men to endure, while she saw blinding flashes of white, and heard tolling, ancient booms that faded into strains of the kind of string music enjoyed with a glass of wine. The Dreamer was a warm and subtle inebriation in her flesh, and possessed her no more than that. "He has woken," she said.

An announcement that came as no surprise to the two men now gaping at the girl who suddenly had silver stars in her gaze.

V

Mouse drifted. She still felt mostly herself, if a touch drunk, unconcerned, and disconnected from the land around her. This was her destiny, after all: to return to the Forever Stones, to reclaim her treasure. Wait...Whose treasure? Hers or Feyhazir's? She couldn't answer that question with certainty anymore.

Mouse led the warband up something that sloped like a hill, and into a shudderingly warm cave. From where did all the heat come? *From where I am going*, she thought with an uncanny knowing. She followed the heat down the scabrous pipe that had been carved—or clawed—through icy, translucent rock. Soon the paste that Moreth had described became visible. White and brown spackle had been flung upon the walls and ceiling. It hung like melted cheese and emitted a heady stink: a smell of manure and sour vinegar. In the revolting netting, or in the stalagmites of regurgitation they stepped around on the floor, she spotted an occasional bone—a rib, cracked skull, or ossified animal talon that had not been successfully digested.

There was enough space to walk without disturbing the filth: sinewy paths had been made by things worming along the ground, walls, and ceiling. Such horrors were appalling, yet registered with Mouse only as unpleasant. Her master enjoyed all the creatures of the circus, even the hideous ones. More unsettling than the environment was the experience of being two minds in one body.

She could not tell much about how her companions and the shaman fared, as they were behind her. Occasionally, she heard stifled coughs, people spitting as the saliva pooled in their mouths from the rankness. Mouse had no such concerns. No matter where she took them, no matter how dark and fetid the air, she knew no fear. She had come to claim her treasure. Or he had. It didn't matter. She and the Dreamer were one:

lovers, as well as brother and sister. If she looked into a mirror and saw a woman of smoke, she would not blanch. However, the mirrors of ice soon vanished, replaced by plastered refuse.

Every so often, a choice between paths presented itself, but she did not hesitate. She remembered having been here before. A most curious memory, for in it she had meat between her legs and thighs thicker with muscle than her own lean limbs. She'd been a man. These caverns had been less desecrated in that past, too. Still natural, yes, but excavated through glittering sandy-brown stone. Mouse remembered the sparkling aurora cast on the walls by whatever light she'd held. An ethereal fancy, as nothing from the memory was evident now. Now there was but shite and death.

Mouse avoided much of the crapulence through some supernatural agility. To those behind her, she appeared to dance. *Now this is the kind of power I could have trampled Aghna with!* she thought. *Why can't I feel this way all the time?* She knew why, though. Even as a woman splintered from herself, she understood that such a manifestation taxed both her and the Dreamer. Especially her: she was not a Lord of Creation that dreamed planets and music and species into being. She was flesh and bone. Weak. At the moment, though, she felt invincible.

The tunnels always led down. At times, they bisected, trisected, or came to a junction with high and low exits; it was total chaos. The rest of the war party did not enjoy the security of a Dreamer's confidence. Unremittingly proud, the Doomchasers brandished the blades they'd brought and choked on fear and fumes. Pythius bravely conjured a tiny flame in this wicked place, and it hovered in his hand like the ghostly pet of a sorcerer. Moreth fared well enough with a grimace and his gag, and Talwyn quickly made a face-covering for himself, too. Soon, they saw the rancid paste and waste of the blood eaters festered in a guano fungus of ivory grass and toadstool forests, leaning shite-heaps that had accumulated over centuries of defecation. Talwyn decided that Pythius was right: there was no order to the Veins of Death; no brilliant architect had constructed this giant, untended chicken coop. There could be no queen of the blood eaters: no great ruler would ordain such chaos.

Yet as they passed into wider subterranean boils, they saw clear, drier pockets where ten or twenty leathery things might curl and suckle together. Talwyn realized that the place did have some organizing principle—if only a rudimentary one, determined by the needs of the pack. It was stunning to think that Moreth's wife had once been one of these creatures. How had it been possible for her to transform from monster into woman? To even begin to cross that line? For there was nothing of mortal decency in this pit.

And then Talwyn heard the cry of a babe. First one, and then several. The sound pierced the soupy underground and drove into his heart. Mouse didn't hear it, and if she had, she would not have cared or sought to pursue it. In a moment, the cries gurgled and cracked. Thinking children might be being strangled or eaten, he almost charged off to find them. But Moreth halted him, whispering, "We did not go far, my last hunting partner and I—not this deep. Still, I assure you that those are not children you hear, no matter how much like them they sound. They are worms of horror that will one day grow into their mothers. Whatever breathes down here should feel the mercy and justice only of your pistol."

As if on cue, the cries became an undulant warble. Talwyn fingered the gun Moreth had earlier handed him, which hung in a makeshift holster. Quickly, he and Moreth hurried along the weaving roads, and thereafter did not let themselves fall behind for another moment. The wormlings were not the only creatures active in the tunnels. Mouse—with the Dreamer's guidance and an awareness reminiscent of the Wolf—knew precisely when to pause and motion for their company to remain still, when to hunch down in the bone-and-vomit garden. As shapes cawed and lurched through the darkness, Pythius snuffed the disembodied flame he'd been using to reveal the path—he would not light it again until Mouse moved.

Talwyn could not block out the endless horror. The ghoulish gardenias, the fungal flowers, blooming about often skittered with gleaming bugs when he was forced to crouch upon them. Within dripping mucosal chandeliers, he spotted the remnants of Pandemonian species he'd begun to catalog. At least his intellect directed him toward analysis rather than fear. His mind formed meat upon the skeletons and reimagined their shapes in spectral detail. He recalled the names given to each animal—*amnus ignen coulber, terra serpens, dracomusca bestia*. There was no mystery as to how animals so huge and vastly scattered had ended up in a place so deep and low: their dismembered remains told him they had probably been dragged here in pieces.

One enormous serpentine jaw puzzled him, though. And then he recognized it. On his first day of travel with the Amakri—before Mouse's inhabitant had returned to its sleep—he had discovered a scintillating giant rock, curled up like a twist of something tubed and spooled. The spool had shifted and heaved as he touched it, and Pythius had flown in from somewhere and pulled the scholar away as the massive coil unwound itself and slithered away into a riverbank. A creature of its magnitude could not be hunted or lifted. Its glittering shale skin had felt as rough as chipped rock. This was the same kind of creature.

How had that armor been penetrated? How had the great serpent been slain and then lifted and carried in hunks of flesh and bone into this repulsive grave? How far did the blood eaters fly in their hunt? Was any creature safe from them? He worried for a moment about the hundreds of Doomchasers they'd left "safely" encamped beyond the foothills. Perhaps fatter, grander prey would tempt the blood-eater swarm elsewhere this eve.

Despite these concerns, the sleeping hollows they passed vied for his interest. With more than Pythius's weak light, he could have better seen the designs that beckoned him like tarnished and cobwebbed silver. For there were mosaics beneath the grime, elements of the artisanal flourishes he'd seen sealed in ice above. The underground was not merely a network of random caves, but part of the City of Ghosts itself. Whatever infrastructure might be present was buried in death, but Talwyn saw enough through the slathering accretions to deduce the majesty beneath.

He noticed curved braces along the ceiling; their symmetry and placement suggested they were supports. At the junctions to which the party came, the tunnels no longer seemed to divide so haphazardly. The higher, unreachable holes all faced forward—and were not in the ceiling or other awkward places—and could once have been reached by staircase or ladder. Later on, the path through the whiteness led them near one of the empty nests, and Talwyn was given a stark glance at an astoundingly clear portion of the floor where fetid bodies had sweated away the filth. In that glinting circle, he spotted a relief of ornate bronze men who burned in engraved pyres, and of a being with wings and radiant lines of carved light who floated above them. Between the divine and the earthbound souls floated a small mark…He strained his eyes to make it out…A cup. Crudely drawn, compared to the rest of the over-elaborate relief. Dumbly, he peered down and into the nest, until Moreth hauled him forward.

Sin and enlightenment, he thought. *The dichotomy of these people. Technomagik—which denies the supernatural—and faith. The Amakri resolved the issue by choosing to maintain their primitive ways. The Lakpoli have done the opposite. What did the citizens of the City of Ghosts do when their great magik left them, and they could not bring themselves to live like savages? What choice did they make?* Talwyn grew agitated, as he did whenever a deduction began to ripen. In his skull sparked hallucinogenic visions of ruins, ancient people gathering around a bone chalice, and a gray man. Talwyn felt the divine creature was presiding, blessing, giving—

"What's the matter with you?" hissed Moreth; the scholar had been babbling to himself, at times loudly.

"Not me," replied the scholar in a whisper. "There's something wrong with this place, this tale."

"Obviously."

Talwyn risked the war party's fading into a gray oblivion by stopping and quickly confiding his thoughts to Moreth. "Why would the Dreamer leave a chalice here? In this den of monsters?"

"To keep it safe, as the shaman said."

"Would that really keep it safe? Think. A lair of wild animals as guardians? You've seen how these creatures behave. They're barely sentient. They can't be kept as pets. They are chaos and hunger unchained. They're certainly the wildest beasts I've known, your converted wife being a miraculous and solitary exception. These monsters are likely to have covered the chalice in a cement of shite that we wouldn't be able to blast through with a Menosian cannon. So how can the Dreamer be so certain his treasure is safe? After thousands of years? When did he come to this city? After it fell and its citizens vanished, or before?"

"Why does it matter? If the Dreamer claims his treasure is here, then that is what I shall believe. To think otherwise would be hopeless."

Moreth would hear no more of the scholar's words; their wisdom was another trouble he could not bear on his weary shoulders. For Moreth battled the ghost of the Slave. After all that he had seen of the size and power of the blood eaters' horde—back at the encampment and now here, deep in the Veins of Death—he realized that the Slave had betrayed him.

When he and the Slave had come to the uppermost reaches of the labyrinth to hunt, they'd found a few of the creatures nesting. Passed out, really, barely a dash into the dark of a tunnel. The creatures had woken when he and the Slave had begun their hacking and shooting. And while the six creatures had proved worthy adversaries, groggy though they were, the match had been weighted in Moreth's favor from the start. Blood eaters were nocturnal creatures: a man born in Pandemonia would have known the legends told about them. Although the Slave may well have acted out of care for his young hunter, Moreth still felt betrayed. The experience upon which he'd founded his sense of being a man now appeared shaken by dishonesty. *I suppose I should feel blessed to have had a man who cared for me. A man who wanted me to survive. You taught me all that I needed to know in order to live in a world gone wild, as ours now has. If I am given the chance to show your spirit how I can truly fight, I shall.* Moreth hurried to Mouse's side. If there was to be a battle, if Talwyn was correct and Mouse's patron was not to be trusted, he wanted to be front and center in the fray.

But they found nothing to battle. The fact that they remained unscathed in this labyrinth of primeval abominations troubled Talwyn. In fact, it reminded him of their travel before meeting the three cannibalistic hags in the Pitch Dark. Again, he felt as if a repulsing force or Will were being used to steer the company's course and manipulate the heinous local fauna. As the war party continued delving into empty nesting chambers, moving ever closer to the heart of madness, he reflected that the only being with a Will powerful enough to repel such evil was the Dreamer who wore his friend.

Each step farther down was a step into fouler and fouler space. Tunnels swallowed them, shrinking on all sides until the rotten waste was unavoidable and slapped them with wet tendrils. Globs of white paste, fresh and unset, came down in large hunks. These had to be avoided, for some of the excrement had sharp bones that clanged when they hit the roads traveled by the blood eaters. The difference between wall, ceiling, floor blurred. Many a time, Talwyn imagined he was walking inside a giant, diseased squash. The underground possessed a constant song now: the bawling of the wormlings, the splatting and slopping of matter, and other bubbling, licking, and wetly crinkling dissonances. Talwyn and the others were by now immune to the smell, but he doubted that the stink of pigeon shite and compost would ever leave their heads or clothing. Their starved stomachs craved no nourishment and had no urge to empty themselves. Fear was their sustenance.

Surely, they must be getting closer to wherever Feyhazir was taking them. Talwyn, who kept a constantly trickling mental chronex, calculated they'd been at this misadventure for six-and-a-half hourglasses. If they did not retrieve the chalice and leave within the next few sands, they would never escape the underground alive. And that was assuming that dawn would not come earlier than he'd projected. The specter of impending death motivated him, and he dashed to their leader. "How much farther?" he asked.

Mouse looked at him, only partly herself—the other force within her seemed cold and remote, a lone moon over a black ocean splashing in rage. The second force answered him, and he felt utterly insignificant. ***"We are here,"*** said Feyhazir.

The tunnel in which they walked led down and then opened into a large space. All except the Dreamer crept cautiously into its deceptive brightness; its illumination came not from the sun, but rather from glowing spires, stalactites, and barnacles of white waste. They were awed by the chamber, which was as grand as a sea cove and filled with a clammy, foggy air that clung to them. Pools lay about the chamber and bled tributaries to smaller puddles in the belching ivory mere. Many of the pools looked quite deep, and churned softly.

Eventually, a squealing noise emerged from the ghoul's orchestra of drips, splats, and farts. The squeals were faint and came from immature creatures. In the wicked moonlight—for truly, that was what it resembled, thought Talwyn—the bodies of larval blood eaters gleamed as they floated, whined, and swam in their amniotic pools. One blind fishy being in the pool nearest Talwyn rolled as would a more graceful mammal of the sea. What it revealed of itself as it rose, though, had nothing of that grace: black eyes sealed behind a fishy caul, a socket mouth that collapsed inward, stabbing collarbones and a skeletal torso that twisted into a lumpy mermaid's tail. Whatever metastasis it would take for this pupal horror to become a raisin-titted shrieking horror, this was the beginning of her evolution. Vomit rose in Talwyn's throat. He choked it back and whispered what was already clear to all there: "A breeding ground."

In the distance lay a hump, above which a second larger blister dropped from the spiny ceiling. Mouse needed to reach that place. Mouse and her Dreamer dashed between the white rubbish and pools. Stricken by the sight of it all, standing dumb at the point where the tunnel blossomed into the amphitheater of the bizarre, the rest made no move to stop her. Either the path had been blessed by Feyhazir, or they would all soon be dead. Regardless, they followed the Dreamer. Perhaps because of the nearness of death, because there might never be another moment beyond this one, Pythius threw a whisper into Talwyn's head: *If we live, I shall drink to tomorrow with you.*

They had to run, for Mouse and her inhabitant had turned this into a race. It was clear the Dreamer now almost completely possessed his host: she smoldered and burst with silver-and-black fumes. The stumbling war party did its best to focus on the dark beacon. They avoided glancing down at the mewling pools of milk or up at the waxy stalactites amid which hung cawing, shuffling shadows, for if they had, their courage would have shattered.

Now, though, the existence of the softly warbling roost that hung and swayed from the rafters of this profane cathedral wouldn't be denied. Clacking hag-women shrilled like crows as they woke, stirred by the companions or the shivering light of the Dreamer. The company had walked into the heart of the swarm, a breeding ground, and over their heads hung an army of maternal defenders. He didn't dare look up to see, but Moreth remembered that the monsters sometimes rested upside down, like bats, which was how he and the Slave had been able to decapitate so many with ease. Once a blood eater woke, though—even during the day—she was among the fastest creatures Moreth had seen aside from the Wolf.

Moreth felt as if the whole living ceiling were about to collapse upon and consume them in a speck. But for the moment, they were either as yet unimportant—which was unlikely as invaders—or they were protected by the Dreamer's Will.

Indeed, Feyhazir's light had grown into radiance, and the chamber now echoed with chimes and harmonies inconsistent with the songs of propagating monstrosities. The music was a manifestation of the Dreamer's joy and desire. He was excited. Something that was valuable to him was within his grasp.

When the war party reached the pulsing gray-and-black star that was Mouse and her master, they couldn't see for the light spearing the room. They stood, shielding their faces, at the center of the chamber and received an impression of elevated steps, or perhaps a rise, set into a mound. Above the mound was a distended belly of shadow that they could not fully distinguish. A few of them were reminded of an enormous veined and beating heart. It was something organic, massive, and fleshy, but the light and their fear rendered everything indistinct. From somewhere now came an ancient and curious wind bearing myrrh and smoke—the attar of mystery. It swept around the company like a snake of the elements and bound them together in wonder. They all watched the star Mouse had become.

The radiant Dreamer and his vessel ascended the steps to reach his treasure. In the waxen belfries of the hollow, the blood eaters croaked calls not of hunger and bloodthirstiness, but of pleasure and celebration. Atop the mount she'd climbed, Mouse—or the Dreamer—seized the chalice. With that, her world shattered, and she tumbled with the glassy bits down a pit and into the past.

All Mouse knows of prophecy has come from her travels in Morigan's shared visions. Here, she receives only a scattered puzzle of images that aren't nearly as clear—a memory, Feyhazir's memory? A woman in white robes kneels before an altar: her eyes are as dark as her heart, the million cracks on her face reflect great wisdom, and Mouse knows she is a woman of prominence—or was, since she's old and soon to die. A man's hand—as silver as the light Morigan shines, though wearing a black gauntlet of smoke the next instant—caresses the woman's cheek. In the dark space of the brassy chamber behind the woman are fuzzy intimations of row after row of kneeling supplicants, also in white. What is this? A ritual? A sacrifice? Mouse is chilled by the sense of each act occurring before her. The vision twists and Mouse is thrown elsewhere; she hovers, seeing a vista in the distance, a city nestled into a wave of stone. The Second City, she thinks.

As if carried by the wind, a promise is whispered into her ear. It's in a tongue like the Amakri's, but slower and more lyrical. Mouse understands the words, the vow, and that the woman seen a moment ago has spoken it: "I have returned to the city I abandoned. I am broken and old, as are those who cling to these ruins. Once more my body withers. The arkstones cannot sustain me. My people believe I have passed. My flesh is too weak for your Will, Master, and you have found a new vessel just as they have found a new queen. To you and to the world I am dead. As dead as these lost souls, gathered before you—those cast from the tribes of this land. We are all ghosts here.

"But I shall live again. You have given me all that I have ever dreamed, Master. You have raised me from death, and I have built empires that will endure for as long as some of your dreams. So, I shall drink your promise and embrace this new mystery. We shall drink. We praise thee for this new gift, new life, whatever it may be. Remember my name: I am Teskatekmet, the Eternal, and most adoring of your vessels. I wait for your return, Master. I shall wait forever, if I must."

A furious flurry of visions and sounds tears through Mouse: the feel of burning fluid in her throat, the sensation of her limbs stretching in their sockets, painfully changing, as if being made taller on a torturer's rack, and finally there comes a tormented shriek that she knows arises from Teskatekmet. This cry is soon joined by all the newborn shrieking hags birthed in the belly of the Second City, monsters born through a covenant with Feyhazir.

The light settled, though the frenzied cawing continued. The war party, jarred by the noise, saw Mouse doubled over at the top of a tall dais. Pythius and Moreth ran to her. Talwyn followed, though his eyes roamed over the staircase of elaborate silverwork that they climbed, steps miraculously clean of filth, though with railings of slithery mucus. He read everything, deciphered each story the stonewrights and metalsmiths had wrought into their work. In specks, he had pieced together the imagery of chalices, a winged man, a kneeling woman and her flock, withered hags, and curses. *Don't touch it! It's cursed! The people of the City of Ghosts drank from the chalice—just as Pythius would do! They were offered its miracles for a price: to watch and to protect the Dreamer's treasure until he returned.* Damn his mind for always working faster than his mouth.

As he prepared to scream his findings, as he stumbled up to his companions, he looked then at the shadow that dripped warm rain upon him and forgot his every word. He gazed, paled, and fumbled for his gun.

The others had only just noticed the shadow. Pythius bared his teeth and blade at the atrocity above them. Mouse had recovered enough of herself to shriek; a consummate thief, she'd already stuffed the chalice into her haversack. Slowly, the shape on the ceiling, the incalculable accrual of white and black, began to unfurl. Like the petals on a flower of flesh, wings and layers of moldy white skin peeled away from the core they protected. A rainfall of fluid began, and Talwyn, intuiting what was inside, discovered courage and began to shove his companions down the dais. They were off it in a speck.

By then, one of the squealing wormlings that churned like maggots on the surface of the bulbous, terrible sac had fallen and splattered to its death. Mouse stopped screaming. She was unpleasantly aware that she was once again a mortal woman. The war party slipped and skidded away as the placenta broke and a torrent of wriggling, bleating, malformed, prematurely birthed blood eaters came down in a deluge.

Was that the worst of it? The blood eaters hanging in the moldy rafters of the breeding chamber ululated in rage or surprise. "Wake up, you shite! Wake up and get me out of this horror!" shouted Mouse to the Dreamer. However, he would not be roused, producing only a sleepy tingle and an uncontrolled twitch that flung her hand toward her belt. Her knuckles collided with the hilt of her weapon, and she grasped his callous message. *You asked for power. Deal with your own danger.*

"Selfish arsehole!" cursed Mouse. She and her companions formed a tight circle.

"I suggest you ask your master to get us out of this place," said Moreth as they backed away. The collapsed womb, dangling wet folds, continued to squelch and sway. He wondered if it'd finished its birthing.

"He shan't be helping. We are on our own."

"Really?" exclaimed Moreth.

Mouse's reply was drowned out by the dry creaking, then sloppy crash of the juddering sac detaching itself from the roof. It crushed the ancient dais like a mountain fallen on a teacup. Luckily, the war party were at a safe enough distance that they were able to huddle, turn their backs, and shield themselves from the wave of rolling dust and the splashes of the many birthing pools nearby that expelled their squealing contents. The fall and cascading destruction continued for some time, and the war party crawled away from it, eventually blundering upright.

When they looked back, the chamber was clouding and beginning to collapse. White brackets cracked and fell inward, splashing down into the chamber like trees felled in a swamp. The blood eaters—who covered the ceiling in a tarp of bodies—were feeble and uncommonly tame in their defeat, and fell from their roosts like bats struck by slingshots. They hit the rumbling ground dead and were then jostled around.

Somehow, the transgressors in this realm had ruined a delicately balanced ecosystem. Talwyn struggled to determine how. Perhaps now that Feyhazir no longer needed guardians for his relic, the blood eaters' lives were forfeit. Could a Dreamer be so horrifically callous to create and then exterminate an entire species? Yes, look at what Brutus and the Black Queen had done with their disposable grunts made of man, metal, and fire. Talwyn had not the time to explore this quandary or what it meant for the Doomchasers or even Mouse as a servant of this cosmic tyrant, for right then a blood eater, rolled up like a burned moth, bounced down directly in their path. Its black wings spread out—their smoke evaporating—and he saw that it clutched a wormling in its lifeless arms. The grisly larva was attached to the abdomen of its mother through its tail. Talwyn got just one look before a heave of white rot covered the pair, but it was clear that the life of the young one depended on the continued survival of its host, and that the host was dead. No matter the exact cause or sequence, everything down here was dying—the entire foul ecosystem. This at least suggested that the other horrors beyond this chamber were already dead or soon would be.

Braaawk!

A combination of dread and his cursed curiosity caused Talwyn to turn back and gaze at the suppuration of rubble and smoke in the chamber they'd left behind. A shape rose out of the haze; it, too, must have fallen with the unholy mass on the ceiling. What was black and white and trembling all over? It felt like a children's joke, his blundering attempt to describe the abhorrent, fatty mass that barreled toward them. It lurched, slobbering over the rubble like a caterpillar. Some segments of it were armored; others were heaped with a fleshy padding that he couldn't, for a speck, identify. It scrabbled with its multitudinous setae legs, each as black and hard as a fang of rock, and brought more powder and ruin to the collapsing chamber. Its dimensions were impossible to define. It seemed as large and wild as a locomotive that had veered off its track. He picked out a few details in the commotion, trying to make sense of the seemingly inexplicable. Those fleshy plates? Bulbous tumors with small gray dots—breasts, he realized—that clustered like grapes. A smattering of white, withered, and clawed arms flailed about the creature's body. Only a mad man could have discerned their purpose in being. He wondered what that same hypothetical lunatic would have to say about the collage of screaming women's faces—malformed heads with mops of scraggly black hair and wailing mouths—that formed the shrieking head of the beast. He screamed back when the ball of many heads split vertically along a gooey seam, revealing a fissure lined with teeth out of which belched a titanic roar.

These glimpses he caught before being torn away by a strong hand—probably the shaman's. Fear cinched his throat and prevented him from throwing up on himself. Inside his pounding skull, his scientific mind prattled on through the madness. *Lepidoptera sanguinius regina, she'd be called. The blood eater queen. Naturally, a matriarchal society without visible male participants could not exist without a form of asexual reproduction. Having now observed the nesting grounds of these species, I can determine that these creatures go through many cycles of early development. First, the queen incubates her brood, regularly releasing a flow of nascent offspring. She creates enormous quantities of hatchlings, for the blood eaters often suffer losses in their own ranks when their unquenchable hunger drives them to cannibalism. The hatchlings then progress through larval and pupal stages—the latter of which occurs in pools of collected afterbirth and nutrients—before arriving at a young adult phase in which they are old and formed enough to suckle. It is at this stage that both offspring and mother are most vulnerable—*

Oh, would you shut the fuk up! You're going to die!

At last, Talwyn gave in to foaming, screaming terror. He wasn't alone; the others had now seen what was rising out of the chaos and were screaming along with him. They blundered; they were careless. They splashed into the afterbirth ponds, which were like overflowing tidal pools and could hardly be avoided. It was hard to tell who among them had gashed themselves on toppled stalagmites, so smeared were they with blood eater foetuses. One of the Doomchasers disappeared into a ragged rupture that formed somewhere behind them. He thought it was one of the women—he heard her final echoing yelp. He knew she was gone and sensed she would not be the only one to die. A speck later, more Doomchaser curses and hideous screams floated through the destruction, terminal sounds, each one. Pythius's tribesmen had perished.

Mouse and Moreth's dark silhouettes, though, remained beside him, and he could see Pythius running ahead, so at least those nearest to him were alive—for the moment. At least those already dead had been spared the unpleasantness of being eaten by an angry brood queen. And there was still a chance the living might be spared, too, for a black eye winked at Talwyn in the shaking chamber; it was a cave. Where did it lead? Was it still intact? It looked small enough that the Brood Queen would not be able to follow them through it. Within a speck, they had all seen the wavering spot, and as one, they dashed toward it. Suddenly, Pythius, acting as if he were a pugilist, threw out his arms and brought Mouse and Moreth tumbling down. *A clothesline, that's what the move is called*, Talwyn thought as his mind worked faster than his flesh and he slammed into the man, too. All four of them fell into a tangle of limbs. Getting up proved a challenge, as Pythius—as remarkable a wrestler as any of Moreth's gladiators—was attempting to pin them all down.

"*Meínei káto* (Stay down)!" shouted the shaman.

A speck later, a whirlwind of shadow passed over their scuffle. The dark storm landed with a thud that shook them apart, and they rolled helplessly about the chamber. Still, they found their feet in a moment, and spotted one another as outlines in the dusty chamber. Another roar echoed and threw rock down into the just settling hollow. Soon the dust cleared, and the four—no longer afraid, but bitter with warrior's mettle—stared at what prevented their escape. A throw from where they might have been, the brood queen coiled, turning in a circle and half rearing her caterpillar body. The mere sight of the creature was enough to spark hysteria again. A rainfall of destruction concealed her many faces for the moment. Pythius's agility had saved the companions; the four of them would have been crushed if they'd run any faster. None of the champions was shocked to see the flapping, smoldering wings—like those of a dragonfly of evil and darkness—that had sprung up along the back of the horror. They looked too ragged, too flimsy to allow for flight. It was clear, though, that the brood queen was capable of great leaps. One more leap and they might not be so lucky as to escape its tonnage.

"Shite," cursed Mouse.

"Unexpected—or perhaps not, given the winged nature of adult blood eaters. In any case, not good," said Talwyn, stiffening up. He pulled out his gun and aimed, impressed by the steadiness of both his hand and voice. "Moreth, shoot the faces, breasts, and wings. I believe those are the fleshiest parts, the ones most likely to sustain damage."

Mouse already had her blade in hand and was ready to speak the word that would bring fire. "Let's send it to the afterlife. I need cover—a distraction—so I can get close," she spat.

They all knew her Dreamer's blade possessed untold powers. Pythius needed no war marshaling. He felt the urge to spill blood beating like a drum in his heart. He had his tribesmen to avenge, all of whom now wandered the Great Mystery. Although he'd lost his sword, several long splinters of rock lay nearby, and they would do. He roared and threw a granite javelin with a strong, true arm. He summoned his Will, too, and as the fragment left his hand, it glowed like a splinter of volcanic rock. The javelin sailed in a flickering line and speared one of the twisted, shrieking faces in the brood queen's head-of-heads. For an instant, the monster was silenced by pain or perhaps surprise. Pythius roared again, grabbed a second spear, emblazoned it with magik, and hurled it as well—then another and another. Following his lead, Talwyn and Moreth began their salvo of blue fire. In specks, breasts were torn off by bullets, faces were shredded into black pulp, and dragonfly wings were blasted into cinders and smoke.

The brood queen writhed under the assault, perhaps knowing pain for the first time in centuries. She buried her head in her coils, and thrashed her gargantuan tail. Her weight came down as a club of thunder on the land, shaking loose showers of stalactite and petrified shite. A shingle of rock fell and embedded itself in Moreth's forearm, throwing him to the ground; if he didn't remove it and bind the wound, he would almost certainly bleed to death. But instead of doing so, he staggered to one knee, transferred his pistol to his other hand, and began firing. Beside him, the scholar turned marksman loosed a firestorm of bullets. The rapidly emptying chamber of his gun had begun to burn Talwyn's fingers; soon, flesh would sizzle and he'd lose his aim. As for Pythius, he fought, rabid and shrieking, for the honor of his dead clansmen even as the hail of stone fragments cut him and painted him in blood.

Mouse, the most agile of the four, sidestepped the showers of debris and waited for her opportunity to dash ahead into the bedlam. She couldn't wait any longer—any more thunder from the monster, and the collapsing cavern would bury them all.

To near certain death and through clouds of stirred filth ran Mouse, braver than she had ever been—or rather driven by fear. Thank the Kings she possessed such a small body, wore little to no armor, and moved with the nimbleness of a cat. All of the traits that had assisted her as a shadow-broker conspired now to keep her whole. She danced between ground-sundering slams of a fleshy whip, and her calm nature, refined through negotiations with nefarious folk, allowed her to softly speak the correct incantation—*Imperatrix*—while tumbling under the brood mother's rocky talons. She emerged from beneath the shadow of the beast quite wet from its secreting under-slop, but she was dried in an instant by the flame that jetted from her dagger. White at its core and black as its halo, the weapon's flame, the teardrop of its blade, was a manifestation of wrath: cosmic wrath, the wrath of a Dreamer. In the deepest hues of the flame sparkled lights like stars.

The magik's dazzling wonder nearly struck her dumb, but then the shadow of the brood mother came down again, hard and fast. Still, she was the girl that moved through stars and worlds. Wasn't she? Her memory was clouded by another layer of thought, for a flicker of the Dreamer's passion woke within her. The conflict had roused him, or perhaps Mouse had somehow called him forth; either way, he'd decided this was a show in which he must partake. Feyhazir took his vessel's hand and they became partners in this dance. In the strangest twist on the laws of master and vessel, neither Dreamer nor girl knew who led their waltz. Their dance was grand, full of fire and black rain. Together, she and the Dreamer twirled, embraced, and reminisced about distant worlds, people, and places Mouse had never seen. They shared lovers' kisses under showers of noxious gore. They consummated their passion while slicing into heaps of hard fat and shivered, head to toe, from the orgasmic exertion. Mouse wanted the dance to continue forever. She was in love. In love with this power. In love with the Dreamer. How else to describe such joy?

As for the others, the men providing her cover, they watched the nimble girl dodge the smashing bulk of the creature several times while closing in on it, then vanish suddenly. They refused to consider her dead. As soldiers who would accept nothing less than triumph, they fired and threw their hopes and anger at the horror standing in their way. The next instant, Mouse rolled out from beneath the twisted tail of the brood mother; each man swore he heard a song and felt a tingle of melodic music, a harp being played somewhere. Then a light was summoned by Mouse or her master, and the gloom of the chamber was eradicated. With that, something that must be Mouse but looked like an insane firefly with a tail of white heat darted left and right, up and down. The brood queen roared as the firefly scaled the grotesque heights of its body, weaving a pattern of sizzling agony over her flesh so quickly that it took a moment for the pieces of the monster to drop. Finally, there came a monsoon of smoking legs—carved off like rotten fangs—whole gatherings of tits, flaps of skin as long as sails, and dozens of dark dragonfly wings. The firefly shone in the brume it had created. The men ceased their assault and watched.

Mouse, who held the hand of her beloved, realized it was time to end their dance. She returned from her waltz across the universe as easily as if she were waking from a cozy summer nap. Abruptly, she faded into the ugly, confusing scene, saw herself floating above a jiggling, oozing mountain of coils. *I know you*, she thought. *Or he does, rather.* From the center of the mound leered something of a face. It trickled black, its features cauterized; it took her a moment to recognize the head-of-heads. The sound it pushed out from its one working sore—the fissure of teeth, all broken now—was a plea for death. **Thank you for your loyalty, Teskatekmet**, said the Dreamer in Mouse's skull. **Now sleep**. Upon the shattered brood mother, the fallen first Keeper Superior, she descended as a star of vengeance.

The men saw her light blossom and fade into soft explosions. They stared into the flickering smoke and called for her, their amazement turning to worry. Stumbling out of the billows, she appeared. They hurried to her and carried her away from the slag heap. They might yet face their doom, but it seemed possible the worst was over. They stopped to catch their breath once they'd cleared the thickest smoke and then gazed back to the wafts of embers and ruin. Mouse—hesitantly, Talwyn noticed—sheathed her dagger.

"Are you all right?" asked the scholar. He knew not what else to say after witnessing an incident of such incredible, divine power. Mouse looked hale and sound, unscathed by the fires she had conjured. Around her eyes, however—which always betrayed so much about a soul—he saw the tightened anxiety of anger or loss.

"I am fine," she replied, which was the surface of a truth. Beneath, Mouse was conflicted in every manner imaginable. She loved what she had been—a vessel, a star—though she loathed what she had known as soon as she touched the chalice. However, there was no time to consider that truth or its implications, as whatever cohesion had held this underground chamber together appeared to be failing. White slop and tiles of mucous continued to fall, and the near-deafening dribbling, creaking, and groaning made her suspect the ceiling would soon collapse. "We need to get out of here, and I have no idea how."

"Wake up your master," snapped Moreth. "He sent us on this glorious misadventure; he can damn well send us back."

Mouse reached for the hand of her cosmic lover by instinctively touching the dagger. But no answering static ran through her fingertips and bones; no warmth filled her insides; no crystalline music filled her ears. In the battle, she'd somehow managed to summon him, but it appeared he would not be so easily stirred a second time. Perhaps the moment was not right, the fear and passion weren't enough to stir her master. "I think he's gone back to sleep for the time being. I may have exhausted him, so to speak."

"I have no intention of dying down here!" declared Moreth.

While boldly said, the trickling hole in his arm from where a rock spine had been withdrawn, and the manner in which Moreth clenched the maimed limb to his stomach—was that another wound there?—was evident and troubling to his companions. Moreth's behavior seemed especially vexing to Talwyn, who clenched his throat as if aghast while widely eying the man.

"I may be able to find a way," said the scholar.

"How?" asked Moreth.

Talwyn peered around for a while before answering, then set off away from the devastated corpse; there would be no tunneling through that mess. "I believe that I can retrace our steps and lead us back through the underground."

"Impossible," said Moreth reflexively. Then he recalled to whom he spoke: the man that rearranged and viewed matter, physics, and history on a plane invisible to most mortals. "Do pardon me—of course you can."

"There is the entrance we used to enter this chamber." Talwyn pointed to a dimly seen hole past a long field of rubble, blood eater corpses, and slippery wormlings. None of the creatures moved, and as they walked through the dead, the companions were more concerned about being crushed by the crumbling ceiling. Soon the glow and gas of the chamber disappeared, and they traveled along a path illumed by another of Pythius's magikal hand-flames, seeing a familiar pastiche of white mucus that seemed less ready to collapse upon them. All this was comforting after the breeding ground, even the reek of guano. Talwyn walked on for a while in silence. Moreth and Pythius concentrated on listening for predators; they twitched at every gust and groan of the decaying underground. Talwyn was preoccupied with matters graver even than another potential attack.

"You know that the chalice is cursed, do you not?" he whispered to Mouse, who walked beside him. He suspected that Mouse understood the nature of her new treasure. As he'd counted tunnels and cross-referenced them with the three-dimensional phantograph he'd constructed in his mind, he had seen her touch the swinging sack holding the relic many times. She did so lightly, as one would something delicate and dangerous.

Did she know that Feyhazir—her savior, her lover, her patron of vengeance—had lied to them? Yes. Did she know that this entire horrid ecosystem had come from a promise made in blood with an elderly, powerless Teskatekmet, and the outcast ancient people who'd never chosen a side in Pandemonia's war—the people of the City of Ghosts? Indeed, for she'd witnessed the truth herself. Teskatekmet's desire had been fulfilled by the Dreamer: she wanted to live, to endure as a legend; alas, how twisted the reality had been. What of the lost people of the City of Ghosts? With what lies had Feyhazir seduced them into drinking from his wicked cup? Teskatekmet...she pitied her the most, since she didn't know these other victims beyond shadows in a vision. Teskatekmet, the brood queen, could have crushed them. Had her obstruction been a plea? An angry demand for recognition after thousands of years of condemnation and horrific servitude? Mouse felt a stomach-pulling guilt at having killed her for her loyalty, and furthermore, for what that act meant for her own future. *Now sleep*...Was that to be her reward, once Feyhazir was done with her, too?

"I know enough," she muttered, miserably confused. Who was friend and who was foe? That, at least, was a question she could answer. Morigan was her friend. Morigan would have insights. The Dreamer inside of her was a selfish, bitter lover from whom she was unable to wean herself. Grimly, she hurried on through the murk, thinking of nothing but her reunion with Morigan.

XVII

QUEEN'S JUSTICE

I

"I know what I saw, what we survived. The queen of Eod was not the one who destroyed Menos," declared Aadore.

She swore that in the Iron City, she and her family had stared into the face of Death herself, and she was unshakable in her assertion that this being had been the true orchestrator of Menos's doom. She would not be swayed. Not by the compassion and beauty of the King of the North. Not by the cold demands and fury of the Iron Queen. Both leaders stared at her, as if trying to conjure different, more pleasing, truths from her with their gazes and Wills. But she had nothing more to say.

Now free of Menos's fog, her workwoman's mind, always ordering and arranging, had spent the day of air travel and the morning settling into Eod's gracious accommodations and focused on understanding what she, Sean, and the others had endured. Now Aadore was absolutely certain of what had happened. They'd battled a force from beyond: a creature of death, darkness, and doom. There was one pertinent detail, though, that she and the others had decided to leave out of their accounts: she and her brother were immune to whatever power had felled the Iron

City. Sean had already experienced enough torment because of his differences—for what she now realized were her differences, too. Nervous, Aadore hoped that these astute leaders believed her jitters came from her terrible tale and not from any secret she kept.

Perhaps they did know she was withholding something. They retreated to a corner of the chamber and hid behind a billowing veil of white curtains. The room possessed many such ostentatious details, which Aadore found distasteful after decades of Menosian culture. Ornamentations of waves rolled along the moldings, and along with the hangings, gave the chamber a swaying feel. Wind swept in over a windowsill of sanded mosaic tiles, each one like a chip of glass. The light made the chamber far brighter than Aadore felt it needed to be. She wondered if Sean found his room just as bothersome as she did.

They hadn't seen each other since landing on Eod's rather glorious anchorage—a hint of the bedazzlement to come. There, they had been met by a group of Ironguards and Silver watchmen. The soldiers had then politely separated the survivors from each other and escorted them to separate chambers. Aadore assumed that Sean, Skar—who refused to surrender Ian—and Curtis were safe, cared for, and just down the hall. But when she'd once peeked out into the hallway—again unnecessarily flashy with its trellis of light and verdure—she'd discovered soldiers, one from Eod and one from Menos, stationed outside her door. Neither man had been willing to let her leave, though they inquired whether anything could be brought for her comfort.

Later, a physician had come and inspected her for fever and injury. He declared her fit and determined that the wound on her shoulder was healing well. After these events, Aadore had paced and paced. She'd watched the sun stretch its golden arms through the glory of Eod. She'd put her ears to the impregnable walls, which echoed with the earthy hollowness of a canyon but shared no whispers from her family, who might be on the other side. At last, the door had opened. As soon as Aadore had realized who had entered, she'd bowed.

Aadore had no idea what the monarchs were discussing now—possibly her fate. They spoke in hisses she couldn't hear. They appeared quite angry, at odds with each other. She assumed this must be a common occurrence.

"I don't believe it," whispered the Iron Queen.

Magnus glared. "Four stories, four accounts, all containing the same details. Then there are accounts from other survivors—none as clear as these—that tell of a figure in the fog that called to them, or a general commanding legions of walking dead. So either Aadore and her friends are highly practiced agents of yours, mine, or a third unidentified power, or they are telling the truth."

"What truth?" the Iron Queen drove a finger into her palm as she raged on. "That my city was demolished by otherworldly forces? By a man in black? A nekromancer? Who is this being? How could one creature hold such power? Why choose now, when all the world fights to maintain its balance, to strike?"

"You have answered one of your own questions, Iron Queen," said Magnus darkly, and the temperature of the chamber lowered a degree or two. "Our nations have never been so fractured. Never been so weak. Look at the two of us—driven into an alliance merely to sustain the frailest illusion of order. Do you think I relish this arrangement any more than you do? We find it mutually despicable. Still, we must find common ground now, if only to cling on to the slimmest chance of survival. This would be a perfect moment to unseat us." The prickle of cold left the room, and Magnus attempted a broken smile. "It seems we may have chosen the wrong enemies in our lives."

The Iron Queen appreciated the Immortal's frustration. A little venomous candor did much to appeal to her good graces, though she still had every intention of unmaking his kingdom once the war ended. She nodded her agreement; one could better insert the knife into the back of a "friend." "Who could this shadow power be?" she asked. "We know of your brother, and the spirit with which he has aligned himself—"

"A Dreamer, according to Alastair's report on the events in Alabion; events further confirmed by a sage."

"A sage? Pfft. Hearsay from the mouth of a traitor, then—and I don't mean the shadowbroker."

"It is the only information we have received regarding the powers that move beyond our sight. Your brother, Thackery, has been a loyal servant to Eod, and despite your tensions with him, I would ask that you respect and use his name in my presence."

"I shall never respect his name," she spat. "I would not ask you to forgive your brother for his sins any more than you should presume to pardon Thackery for his. He is a traitor to Menos and to his family. If I see him again, I shall order him to be shot. Do not think you can stay my hand; the warrant for his punishment was signed in blood decades ago."

"You cannot decree deaths in my kingdom. I am the law," threatened Magnus.

A ripple of thunder from the clear skies outside startled Aadore. The monarchs were causing a scene—and possibly supernatural phenomena—that whispers no longer contained. As a lady's maid to an Iron lady, Aadore was used to being party to situations above her station. Before either of the two most powerful persons on Geadhain could spill the sort of secrets a low-caste woman would be killed for knowing, Aadore rose from the chair where she'd been sitting during the argument. She interrupted the monarchs politely with a slight cough and a curtsey. "Pardon me, Your Highnesses." Stares of frost and iron found her, and she kept her head low. "If I may, I shall leave you to your discussions and see how my brother and companions fare in their new arrangements."

"Yes, get out," said Gloriatrix.

Magnus was kinder. He came and escorted the girl—with very cold hands—to the door. "If you mean the three men and the child who arrived on the skycarriage with you, then you will find them all in this wing. They are all healthy and without the fevers that some of the other survivors suffer; those countrymen have been given over to the care of Menos at Camp Fury. Tell any watchmen you encounter that you have the king's permission to wander here, there, or anywhere you will. Take a vessel into the city, and see if anything of our culture appeals to you." The king's beauty and soft-spoken compassion astonished her, made her feel as if she were under a kind of spell. Aadore realized he'd opened the door for her and that she was holding his hands as if he were her sweetheart, and that she had been doing so for some time.

"Oh! Yes. Thank you, Your Majesty." She bowed again, then had to apologize as her nerves made her knock heads with him. Aadore left before the king's charisma encouraged further accidents.

"We have the chamber to ourselves," said Gloriatrix, as the king closed the door. "Now's as good a time as any to figure out who plots against us. If your queen—"

"She is no longer mine," snapped Magnus.

"If Lila is not the villain—which I am still disinclined to believe—who does that leave for our rogues' gallery? A nekromancer?" *Only Sorren might have that power—but he wouldn't...*She ceased that line of thinking; the burden of her son ruining her kingdom could crush even her. Sorren was missing, not a genocidal murderer. Besides, Aadore had referred to Menos's defiler as Death, and not a man—so perhaps it was an entity wearing a man's skin. She needed to understand more of these ancient powers that visited Geadhain.

The king claimed Aadore's vacant seat while Gloriatrix paced and tapped her chin; her mind began to weave probabilities. "We know of at least one shadowy celestial force, the one who calls herself a Black Queen..." *My title, you upstart. I shall be crowned Black Queen yet.* "What is her relationship to you and Brutus?"

"Pardon?" The king heard her, naturally. Thus far, he'd maintained a purposeful ignorance surrounding the ties that bound immortal brothers to divine entities of evil and madness. Zionae claimed to be his mother. He could not deny this lineage, as he possessed no explanation for his creation.

The Iron Queen stopped her pacing. She detected a wrinkle of panic in the king's handsome face. "These dark celestial beings...they play with powers of life and death. They chain the oldest elementals like dogs, crystal hocus-pocus notwithstanding. They wear men like puppets. I know of only one man in this world who can work such wonders. One man whose very existence..."—*taints,* she wanted to say, yet settled for—"influences our natural world. You. Already twice today, you've made me shiver from your mood. I don't appreciate the irritation." Gloriatrix knelt so that she could stare into the king's face; he would not glance at her, and the chill in the air had returned. "See, there—you're hiding something. A secret all tied up tight. The world betrays you, Everfair King. I have yet to do so, and if you expect our alliance to continue being cooperative and candid, then you must tell me what you know of this entity and of others like it."

Anger or fear made the king shake, and the room's chill became a breathable mist. "I shall tell you what the Black Queen—or rather, a child she wore like a sock puppet—told me when I met her at the pass of Mor'Keth, the Fangs of Dawn. She told me I was her son."

The Iron Queen gasped. "Your mother?"

"That is what it claimed, yes."

After a moment, Gloriatrix sloughed off her shock and again began striding across the room. Ideas whirled in her head, and she conjectured aloud. "What sort of creature is she? This Black Queen?"

"Wicked."

"No, we are all capable of wickedness. What was she when she was not yet wicked? What drove her to darkness?"

"I know not. Nor do I think we can apply mankind's psychologies to primeval entities that do not figure even in myth. Forces such as those do not think in mortal terms."

"Perhaps. Or perhaps we are the ones who have complicated things, and the natures of these ancient forces are simple. Fundamentally, each element knows its purpose. Rock endures. Fire burns. Wind blows. Water flows. Elements cannot be misunderstood, though they can be lyricized by man."

"The Black Queen's purpose is to corrupt and destroy."

"So we believe. I would like to know *her* purpose, not what we perceive it to be."

"Thackery also believes that truth to be crucial, and he, a brave young witch, and other champions have thrown themselves into Pandemonia's maw in search of it." The king sighed, and the cold wind veered out the window once more, returning the room to muggy warmth. "If you are to understand the Black Queen, you must know more than what I have told you. Know that I have withheld certain facts because we have not always been in the same position of measured honesty with each other as we are at present. I shall tell you of the letter that Thackery sent me from Alabion. In it, he told me of his journey, the losses suffered and successes gained. The Sisters Three provided them with scraps of a creation myth, a tale of the great makers who crafted all that we know, see, and touch in this world—down to man himself. The Black Queen, who has another quite exotic name, was one such creator. Possibly the greatest of them all."

A fallen creator of the cosmos? It was not the most fantastic balderdash the Iron Queen had heard recently, and she found it much easier to digest in this time of chaos and war. Gloriatrix was bothered more by the repetition of her brother's name in this recounting of events, of his importance and perceived heroism. Nonetheless, she felt at ease with only the king and none of their cabinets around. Graciously, the Iron Queen let the mentions of Thackery pass and settled across from the king upon the messy bed that the handmaiden—of the Lady El, she'd learned during the questioning—had clearly been throwing herself around on. She felt an appreciation of that hard woman, though. They shared a similar edge and willpower. Aadore had survived Death itself, if her story could be credited. As asinine as was the thought, perhaps Death was the culprit. She resumed her pondering aloud. "These mythic forces that have come again to our world...What kind of influences do they wield? You, from what I have witnessed, wield powers of wind, thunder, and cold without effort. A lord of storms, one might say. The Black Queen—"

"Zionae is our foe's true name," said the king.

"Foreign, indeed. She would be a lady of corruption and rot, if you've spoken truly. Now, to define our other foe...What the handmaiden spoke of: the destruction, the charnel stink, the doom, the living dead..."

"Death," said the king, solemnly.

"The Pale Lady herself."

They'd reached the same conclusion. Hearts racing, mouths dry, they knew this was the answer. Inconceivable though it was in a world of reason, Death had come to Geadhain. And this wasn't the first warning they'd received of her coming. "Elissandra," whispered the Iron Queen.

"She warned us of Death," replied the king.

"Death is our newest enemy. The one who moves in the shadows. The one who ruined Menos," muttered the Iron Queen. What this meant for Lila's sentence would have to be discussed later. Right now, and until all of her and Magnus's speculations had been proven, she would let the judgment stand. "We shall need to confirm this, somehow, before I rescind my claim on your former queen."

"I would expect nothing less from you," replied the king.

She took that as a compliment. "I shall spread word to the blood houses that your Hammer is not to be killed on sight. His guilt, too, is now in question."

Magnus nodded. For a time they sat, ruler with ruler, and contemplated the motes that dazzled in the folds of sun like milky lines of stars. They were not as lost and dull as they appeared: both were using their silence to create extraordinary stratagems. Their alliance was hardening into something constructive. It was still volatile, though, like a treaty signed in truefire ink and left sitting by the stove.

Once they'd completed their meditations, they arrived at a plan merely by staring at each other, each knowing what the next course of action should be. The rulers leaped up and hurried from the chamber. Elissandra must be found and interrogated for her wisdom. The Mistress of Mysteries' ramblings were not ramblings after all.

II

"Leo!"

The shout hailed the watchmaster as he jogged down one of Eod's long—he'd thought empty—corridors. At first he tried to lose the hailer, yet the call came again, and he recognized the voice as his brother's and knew he wouldn't escape. Leonitis hastened to the next alcove: a forested cloister sporting hedges, delicate chairs, and great false ceilings of light pouring radiance. It was vacant, and he ducked into the shrubs and stashed away his satchel of contraband. He popped out of the alcove just as his puffing brother caught up to him.

"Why are you racing? You know my knees aren't as good as they used to be," huffed Dorvain. But there was a smile on his chipped, pugilist's face: nose broken and mashed, cheekbones lopsided—although his dark beard covered most of that. Leonitis found his brother's smile as alarming as all of the man's recent behavior. The great brute was now conspicuously nice to him whenever they met.

"Why are you chasing me down?" replied Leonitis rudely.

Dorvain punched Leonitis's shoulder. "Come now. I could ask what you're doing wandering down Kissing Lane. The only men who come down here do so looking for afternoon repasts of the sweaty and slippery variety. You don't have anyone in the bushes there waiting for you? Do you?"

Dorvain pushed past his brother and peered into the alcove. All Leonitis could see was the dimple in the branches where he had shoved the sack. Nervous, he made an appeal. "No, nothing like that. You know I like women. I just haven't found the right one. I wish you would stop teasing me about being a man who likes men. If I were one, I expect you would welcome my beau home for brews and arm wrestles as you do with me."

Suddenly, the watchmaster blushed and hung his head. "I would."

Dorvain dragged his feet over to one of the tiny chairs and sat in it. As he looked so pitiable and ridiculous—a large man sitting in a child's piece of play furniture—Leonitis softened. *Rebellions can wait a sand, and this one won't be starting without my contribution of firearms*, he thought. Leonitis also took a chair too small for his large body. In a speck, he and Dorvain were knocking knees.

"Ow," complained Dorvain.

"We picked a terrible place to have a conversation," said Leonitis. They laughed. "Now, Brother, why have you chased me down today?"

"I feel as if I've been chasing you all the time, of late," said Dorvain, and frowned again. "Ever since this war started, you've been...Well...I mean..."

"I've been *what*? Busy? I am master of the King's Legion. I have as many responsibilities as you."

"I know that!" cried Dorvain, and warmed red with anger. "Too busy for drinks. Too busy to head to the tavern and sweet talk every comely wench we see. I'm not good at that game myself, Brother. The ladies flock to you with your golden braids, pretty eyes, and poetic promises before giving me a second glance. I know you're busy! Too busy playing soldier-spy for a mad queen—"

Leonitis matched his brother's rage, though his flame was cold. "Lila's not mad. She may be the sanest monarch we know. What I did in her service saved our city. What I did saved hundreds of thousands of lives. I shall not allow you to disparage her in my presence. She has guided us into our roles as heroes and men."

Dorvain stood and threw his chair across the stones with a clatter. When truly angered, they often fought like this: passionately, violently, with fists instead of words. Many a chamber had been torn apart by their brotherly storms. Although Leonitis was tempted to bash the puffing bull before him, he had no real desire today for their game of wrestling, which would leave them exhausted but finally ready to converse. Why must their fists express their love? Why could they not just speak like men? Leonitis's time in war had changed him. There was enough violence in the world without adding more.

Sternly, Leonitis said, "Pick up your damned chair, and sit your arse down. *Now.*" Unsure, feeling a bit slapped down, Dorvain wandered off and retrieved the chair. Then he sat as he'd been told. Once his brother settled, Leonitis resumed his reprimanding. "Should we get to the meat of your anger? I shall assume that you're upset that you and I have not spent much time together in recent months."

"You could say that, yes," mumbled Dorvain as he played with the straps on his armor.

"We have responsibilities, Brother. Duties to which we are summoned, duties that are greater than our wants and needs. Duties that demand conviction for deeds both dark and good. Lila served our city and saw that it was protected against the Iron threat. Lowelia did the same. I proudly played my part in Eod's defense. And this you must hear and understand: I regret not one of my actions, and I shall defend our queen and our city whenever that duty is demanded of me again. Do not forget what she has done for us—her two precious shells washed up on the shores of Carthac. Lila has shown us more kindness than any woman, ever, and that includes our missing mother. The queen stepped into that role, and acquitted herself admirably. Shame on you for your thoughts."

"I...I..." Dorvain's voice failed him.

Leonitis stood and strode to the bushes. No longer did he care whether his brother suspected he was up to further subterfuge—the whole of Eod would know of the king's crimes and guilt in a matter of hourglasses. After rifling through hedges, he extracted the sack and slung it over his shoulder.

"Should I ask where you're going?" asked Dorvain quietly.

"To do what must be done. To bring justice," replied Leonitis, and left his brother in the garden. There, the watchmaster debated his worth, his purpose, and his conviction, which seemed feeble next to his brother's valor.

III

The discovery of the Mistress of Mysteries' whereabouts required a long hunt through the palace. Elissandra was on the move today. First, she had been seen in the White Hearth; a servant reported that she had dined there. However, the Iron and Everfair monarchs didn't find Elissandra at the long tables of the White Hearth. What they did find was a trail of breadcrumbs—literal breadcrumbs, scattered over a bench. She'd left only moments before.

As the morning waned, the monarchs also somehow just missed Elissandra and her younglings sparring at the watchmen's encampment on the outer precipice. Later, the white witch managed to evade the monarchs' grasps once more at a theater, a concert hall, and even an indoor glade intended for silent contemplation, where Gloriatrix's cursing drew stares that quickly found the floor when their owners realized who was present.

Confusion and ambiguity had been left in the white witch's wake. Either Elissandra didn't want to be found, or this was a most devious ploy to encourage collaboration between the two monarchs. The latter was certainly far-fetched, but it could not be denied that Magnus and Gloriatrix spent more time that day working toward and focusing on a common goal than they had in any of the weeks of bickering that had come before. Not having their aides present—those facsimiles that spoke for their masters—allowed the rulers to see each other as more of what they really were. Ironguards and Silver watchmen, two of each, still attended them. However, when the monarchs decided for the sake of expedience to take the secret tunnels bored through Kor'Keth, they felt it necessary to dismiss them.

"Go find something to do. I no longer need a shadow," said Gloriatrix, as she and Magnus stood outside a vine-woven gate leading to a crack in the mountain. The crevasse looked deep and thin, precarious and dark. The Iron Queen's guards had warned her about entering the rift. At first, her soldiers appeared unwilling to abandon her, even by command. "If I have to ask again, it will be with new Ironguards to replace the ones who lost their lives for the dishonor of disobeying their queen."

The Ironguards bowed and backed away.

"You may leave me as well," Magnus said to his silver guardians. Magnus's soldiers hesitated, much as their Iron counterparts had. "If we meant to kill each other, we would have done so already. We are allies, and an alliance cannot survive without trust. Now go."

You have more than a bit of hard frost in your manner, Magnus, thought the Iron Queen. *Not such a wimp and a waste after all.* Perhaps he would be a tolerable ally in this war. She swallowed such compliments, however, and concentrated on the route they took once through the gate—its twists and turns, its branching passages. In her spider's mind, she wove every detail. Her recall would come in handy later, when she chose to use Kor'Keth's secret passages for nefarious transit.

They were headed toward the King's Garden, the last place Elissandra's ghost had been sighted. It was a beauty the Iron Queen had not yet made the time to see. She was generally so unmoved by nature that being anywhere outdoors seemed a painful waste of her sands. As light and trickling music reached her eyes and ears, though, her dusty, neglected raisin of a heart beat a few times in joy. Magnus creaked open a wiry lattice gate bejeweled with glittering purple flowers that breathed lavender and minty scents. This hedonistic richness prepared the Iron Queen for the forest of variegated trees, of many colors and species, both leafed and pined. There were also rivulets of liquid glass that were creeks, faerytale bridges made of crystal lace, and an effusion of perfumes that battled one another for the greatest sweetness.

"I wonder if we've caught her this time," said the Iron Queen.

She didn't possess an inner compass or instincts for tracking people down, but finding someone constantly on the move surely required constantly moving oneself, so she set off, although without any particular direction in mind. The ancient arch leading into the palace's twilight halls was not far away—she spied it through the shimmering bush—and the monarchs made their way toward it. Once there, they asked the guards if a woman and two children had passed that way at some point earlier. One watchman said yes. One appeared unsure. Gloriatrix deduced that the man's confusion was an aftereffect of Elissandra's amnesic presence—her magik that muddled minds and Fates—so she and Magnus began to search the King's Garden in earnest.

It certainly felt as if Elissandra were there. The birds warbled odd songs, but did not chirp or caw. The brooks sounded more whispery than babbling. There was no one about, although it was a bright and balmy day. The place felt under a spell. Elissandra had that effect on nature; she stilled and unnerved it with her presence.

The monarchs passed over bridges, wound through short hedge mazes, and neared the place where the forest thinned. Their intent was to scout the edges and then come back, tracking in lines, to see where in the interior the white witch and her children were hiding. At last they were rewarded for their efforts. They came to the fringe of the King's Garden, where the many burbles of glass rolled down and over a chasm of stone, and saw a woman—very white and colorfully garbed, with a stumped hand—and two equally spectral children in black watching the lens of pearl power over the sky. The Witchwall had not come down. Magnus hadn't even begun to tackle figuring out the formula according to which it had been made, the complications that would attend its subsequent unmaking. The Witchwall diverted Magnus's attention as he walked ahead. Suddenly, he realized he'd reached the grass-laden circle where Elissandra and her children sat upon a squat plinth of stone. The white witch and her children stared at the pearl light above them, as did the king.

"Elissandra, Magnus and I have been looking for you," said the Iron Queen.

"Isn't it nice?" replied Elissandra. She didn't turn, and gathered her children closer.

"Elissandra," commanded the Iron Queen.

Elissandra lashed her head about like a snake and hissed at the Iron Queen: "No rudeness. Not here; not now. You'll ruin the flower of peace with your incivility before it has a chance to bloom."

From the shine in her eyes, and the slight static in the air, Gloriatrix knew that Elissandra was in the thrall of Fate. She hadn't left her dreamy, half-awake state since coming to Eod. Perhaps the flow of prophecy, growing into a raging rapid as the end times neared, was slowly driving the seer mad. Elissandra turned around again and resumed her sky watching. The Iron Queen tried a softer tactic. She crept forward, knelt, and whispered to the seer. "The king and I know what you have seen. Others have validated your vision. We know of the great shadow that has cast itself over Menos." She waited for a reply, assumed the seer still wasn't listening, and then added, "Death."

"Sh, sh, sh," cooed Elissandra softly, then pressed her children's heads into her breasts, covering their exposed ears; they obeyed, eerily, like dolls. "We cannot speak of this now. I wanted to speak of it earlier, and you should have found me then. Now, I have peace to make."

"Peace?" asked the king.

"Peace with my sins and sorrows. Peace with my children. Peace with my end," replied the white witch.

Gloriatrix felt a tectonic shift in her buried emotions: shock, a fear for someone other than herself. "You speak as if you were going to die."

"I am," replied Elissandra. Elissandra then uncovered her children's ears and covered her children with kisses. The white witch stood, had her children take hand and wrist-stump, and walked around the rock to the monarchs. She released her children, and the macabre little people moved, unbidden, to the Everfair King. The strange children entangled Magnus's thoughts with their gazes, which reflected mysteries, magik, and secrets. They slipped their cold hands into his icy ones and began to lead the king away. "Please watch them for a moment, Magnus. I need to speak to Gloria."

The children didn't take the king far; the Iron Queen could hear the three whispering behind her somewhere. Once she and Elissandra had some privacy, the seer kneeled and joined the Iron Queen on the grass. The seer swished her hand through the green blades and smiled at some augur or another. It was sands before she spoke. "I have served your reign and been loyal to you for all of my years," said Elissandra at length. "I have helped steer the Iron City through its darkest crisis—a voyage not yet over, though started and guided by hope. I would make one request of you, Gloria. Woman to woman. Friend to friend. For I believe that is how we should define a relationship such as ours."

Gloria restrained a welling up of sentiment. "What can I do for you?"

"I need you to look after my children. See that they are provided with the wealth I was to claim from your empire. Ensure they are given the freedom to choose their path in life and society—freedoms we never had. We were denied them by life, by the men we chose, by our culture." Elissa took Gloria's hands and caressed them, and the Iron Queen's tearless front nearly shattered. She'd rarely been touched so warmly, and not in perhaps a hundred years. "You may have a chance, Gloria, to rebuild what you have lost. I can think of no opportunity so precious. You may be able to change who you were through who you are to become."

Misplaced sentiments, thought Gloria. "If I cannot change?"

"Winds will blow, running water will wear away the hardest stone. What refuses to change will suffer a crueler erosion. We all must surrender to the elements. Lift our hands—" Elissa raised their hands, fingers interlaced, into a splash of sudden light. "Spread our arms—" The seer parted their hands and embraced the day; Gloria mirrored her. "And rejoice in our bodies becoming dust, wind, and nothingness."

Embarrassed now, Gloria lowered her hands. Her lip trembled. What would she do without her conspirator in this great game? How would she outwit her enemies without the seer's insights? Who else could slam back adderspit as well as Elissa? (Unpredictable, fair-weather Beatrice aside.) Here, Gloria realized, was the only friend she'd ever made, other than her brother when they were young. She realized she was listening to Elissa's final will and testament. Bitterness claimed her. "I shall not rejoice in your end," said Gloria.

"No." Elissa smiled. "It is not your way. Know that I have chosen my time. I shall be the bird of sun and moon. I shall become one of the champions of this war. They say there is honor in being a hero; there is fear, too. However, the honor in sacrifice is true." Elissandra relaxed her sun-saluting arms and again took her friend's hands.

"When?" asked the Iron Queen.

"Soon. The time for me to be brave is soon."

Gloria sighed. She had more questions, important ones, but even matters of Death and the War of Wars could wait a speck. She held Elissa's hands. The breeze came on hot, but it was pleasant. Silver birds fluttered over the spires of Eod. Whenever the creatures landed nearby and strutted about, they reminded Gloria of gulls. Close inspection revealed them to be mangy, though—beggar kings. They must be confused as to where salt water was, as they were in the middle of a desert. Still, the tenacity of these creatures unexpectedly moved Gloria. They were no different than she. Lost and foraging in a land not made for their tastes. And now she was to lose another of her flock. She wondered, plainly and honestly, how many more losses she could bear. *My realm, my friend, my sons. I am a queen who fights for a throne in a land of ashes.*

"You can still fight for your sons," said Elissa, who'd heard the whispers of Gloria's thoughts. "I have seen them."

"What?"

Elissa clenched the Iron Queen's hands. A jolt of flesh-prickling power ran through each woman. "Alive or not alive. I feel worms over my face. I also taste fresh air as if rising from a grave. I am dead and yet reborn. I am lost and yet hunted. I hear their names: Sorren, Vortigern. My little Blackbirds. Two blackbirds, lost and flying in the storm. You can be the one to guide them home. Just open the cage, Gloria, and they will fly into your nest. I feel them…I hear them. One running, one screaming. They're almost here."

Blackbirds. Gloriatrix's nickname for her children had been shared with no one, ever. Although Elissandra had implied earlier that at least one of Gloria's children was alive, she had offered nothing substantial or incontrovertible regarding Sorren and Vortigern's fates. Gloria gasped. "In Eod?"

"Yes. Both Blackbirds come. They are drawn to you, even though your heart rebukes love." Elissandra slumped and nearly fell over. When she gazed at Gloria again, the seer appeared wan and spent. "That was my gift to you. Whatever I said. The voice of Fate has left me, though I would urge you to remember my each and every word. You must honor what we have discussed for my children—that, I remember more clearly than your gift."

"I shall," vowed the Iron Queen.

The friends sat and chatted. Once or twice, they even smiled. The children could be heard playing some game of hide and sneak with the Everfair King; his cutting laugh suggested he was enjoying the diversion. The sun rose, and gold burned on a sky soon to be set with evening fire. Death? Who cared about that bony wench? It would be a beautiful sunset tonight. The Witchwall magnified the colors in the air as a lens of crystal casts light. Already, beams of crimson and clouds as bright as bronze warmed that most immovable heart: Gloria's. Perhaps she and Elissandra could watch the sunset together, thought the Iron Queen. It might be their last.

"Death," said Elissandra suddenly, and massaged her stump. "Horgot's death came shortly after he'd lost his hand—ironic. We must speak of Death now, and not my passing. Such information is why you've come."

She and the Iron Queen had been gleefully discussing the Second Chair's end when the shift in Elissandra's tone stung the Iron Queen like a slap. It was time to face reality. She stiffened up. In a speck, three shadows arrived behind her: two small, one cold as a winter door open at one's back. The children must have been summoned by a secret command from their mother, which they then relayed to the king.

"I was told it was time to talk," said Magnus.

The children of the white witch joined their mother, standing at her shoulders like matching ravens. *You may stay, my lamblings,* Elissandra mind-whispered. *You, too, must understand what we face. It is also time for me to say what each of you knows must be said.* Tearing up, the children shook their heads. *No tears; no fear. Each of you will live and ensure the survival of our line. You will be children that honor your mother and father, not weak, slow-born creatures with minds of putty and bodies of fat.*

Yes, Mother, the children replied; their tears stopped.

Magnus recognized that an exchange had taken place, a parley between minds. The family of witches now gazed at him and Gloria. "I have seen Death," declared Elissandra.

"The Pale Lady," said the girl.

"The Queen of Bones," said the boy.

"She builds an army from the dead of Menos," continued Elissandra. Nearness to her final hourglass imbued the seer with cosmic clarity. Details and contexts hitherto shrouded were cleared of their fog. She saw the patterns of destiny—the weaving threads of Fate—that surrounded each man, stone, breath of wind, and fleck of dust. Indeed, the whole of the world had become so suffused with music, light, and movement that it appeared to be howling with a harmonious fire. She knew things she would never have known without Death's reaching hand. The truths spilled out of her in a stream. "She should not be here, Death. She has broken the ancient laws."

"What ancient laws?" asked Gloriatrix.

Elissandra's children were touching their mother, and they, too, were consumed in the fire of prophecy. Redness scoured their sight, the world twisted, and filaments of power were strung between every obstacle in sight. Tessa spoke for her mother. "Three laws. What is not of this world cannot exist in it, not without a vessel. By entering into a vessel, a Dreamer debases its own power, for its greatness can be wielded only so well with our crude hands. Finally, a Dreamer can rarely own a vessel completely without the living presence of a man's soul—the two must exist in tandem. These are the three sacred laws of the pact; it is an exchange, really. A trade of power for weakness and tangibility. Still, no Dreamer can manifest in our world without the risk of becoming tainted with mortal sentiments. Death's lengthy stay in her host—the Iron Queen's son, Sorren—has corrupted her: he was afraid and weak, and that weakness of character has passed into her. Death sees only wars and conquest. She's become driven by her fear of Zionae's impending rise. She thinks to cleanse the world with ash."

"She possessed my son?" exclaimed Gloria, many eccentricities and heinous traits of her dear Sorren coming suddenly into focus. "It wasn't his fault then, all the terrible things that he did?"

Compassionately, Elissandra said, "Vessels are not only chosen, they are also sometimes born. A perfect storm of want, need, and power, creates the potential both to wake a Dreamer from sleep and for a mortal to be a vessel to hold them. Your son was made to serve the divine, but he chose to serve a dark one. Many of his actions were his own."

Gloriatrix whimpered, then bit back further weakness.

Magnus pressed on. "So Death—" Only slightly did he struggle with the concept of an entity so dire striding through their world. "—has built this army out of fear, and to destroy Zionae?"

"Zionae, her potential vessels—you and your brother—all who worship the Black Queen," said Elissandra. "Death does what she believes is right, though her justice leads to only one judgment."

Magnus asked the important question: "Death is the one who destroyed Menos?"

"Yes," said the three.

"Through the body of the Everfair Queen, Death threaded her Will," continued Elissandra, her hair billowing in a wind no one could feel. "As your bride was not a vessel, and couldn't be claimed, she wore down the queen's great resolution with a storm of dark whispers. She tormented the queen with visions of your torture at Brutus's hands. Death manipulated the queen into doing what she did not have the power to do herself; Death could not have raised a city of the dead with Sorren's magik, and her dark miracles worked through him, alone. Again, Death was bound by the Laws of the Pact, and Sorren was already weak, ruined, nearing his end as a vessel. Death has since found another vessel—one much stronger, one in which she can flex and cast her might like none before."

Elissandra glared at Magnus. "You seek to know whether the Everfair Queen is guilty of this crime..." Magnus felt every beat of her pause. "I would say she is no guiltier than the soldier numbed by bloodshed who murders when given a command. If one is left to drown in blood and darkness, that becomes all one knows. You left her, Magnus. Whether you knew you were abandoning her or not, the pain was real. When you leave a creature to face strife on its own, it is either destroyed or grows greater through its trials. Your queen conquered her darkness. She has changed into something hard, a shard of amber. Her stone complements the shard of obsidian that now shares her heart. The shining innocence you knew and desired cannot be reclaimed. I think she is more beautiful now. You will have a chance to see and decide for yourself—"

"My king!" a voice cried. A speck later, a mousey, spectacled man in gray interrupted the gathering. It was Rasputhane, wetly disheveled from exertion. A skycarriage gleamed in the woods far behind him. "My liege, you must come at once. Our city has been breached."

"Breached?" exclaimed the king.

"By whom?" demanded Gloriatrix, equally aghast. Standing, she scanned the city for smoke, fire, or signs of chaos but saw nothing.

"Your queen," whispered Rasputhane. "And an army of Arhad."

"Come again?" asked Gloriatrix.

"You heard me," replied Rasputhane, and began to hurry with the monarchs toward a skycarriage that had stealthily landed along the precipice. "She's come back to Eod; she waltzed right in through the Southern Gate. Her army is one, maybe two thousand strong."

Magnus repeatedly tripped over his tongue, trying to discover words. At least his feet proved more capable. Still, he possessed no voice at the moment. The Iron Queen was more communicative. "How could this have happened?" she demanded.

"We don't know. Some minor disruptions and chaos occurred at the Faire of Fates sands back: noise, harmless fires, nothing you'd note from way up here; I still don't have a full report. Now, like the smoke clearing from a magikian's stage, I've been told that an army stands where none had been before. It is said that your queen holds the whole of the Faire of Fates hostage with some kind of enchantment. It is possible that she had agents on the inside. I can't see how any fool manning the gates would have allowed her army through otherwise. We've sent patrols of watchmen into the Faire, and none have reported back."

"Magik? Enchantment? A coup?" asked Magnus, finally.

"Something like that, yes," replied Rasputhane.

They reached the skycarriage, and the pale-faced watchmen stationed by the stairs bowed and then motioned the monarchs up and into the vessel. Gloriatrix cast a look back at her friend—her only friend—who was now merely a lonely white dot on the green, and wondered if she should have dragged Elissandra along.

As the skycarriage lifted off, Elissandra, with her omniscient gaze, noted that Gloriatrix and the king peered out the window portals: lost, white, and afraid. His demons barked at the door and would soon be let out. Flickers of Fate drifted around her in a firefly cloud, and silver threads laced land and sky. Magnus wouldn't have enjoyed her forthrightness over what was to come in the Faire of Fates. Instead, she shared her insights with her children. The three witches watched the world of fire together, and planned how Tessa and Eli would survive the floods and lightning bolts that would strike Eod with a storm of doom—beginning with the arrival of Magnus's vengeful wife. Such anger Lila had returned with; all three shivered from the fury of it. A dreadful thirst filled the queen that could be slaked only with blood justice.

Should we go and see, Mother? asked Tessa.

We can watch from here, my lamblings, replied Elissandra. *We shall see nearly everything aside from the earthly details, which do not matter as much as those of spirit. And when the sun sets, when the fury of queen and king has been spent, we shall see it.* The children swallowed; they were afraid of *it*. Elissandra gathered them close once more. *Do not fear, my lamblings. It will be a grand event. Tonight, the War of Wars will begin. If you look to the sky, you can almost see the herald of the war. A slick gleam of darkness. A smudge of ash floating in the heavens. It's almost here. We are running out of time. Do not be fearful, but look to our doom, and gain from it your strength.*

Stealing a bit of their mother's fearlessness, the children looked. Gazing through the wavering gauze of Fate's weave and the shine on the Witchwall was no easy chore. But their stares were bright silver knives, and they cut through the splendor, through the atmosphere, and out into space. In the vacant dark, they saw it: hovering, pulsing, and curling with tendrils of black light.

The Black Star.

IV

"You seem remarkably at ease for a woman involved in a rebellion," said Lowe.

"That's because it's not my first, I suppose," replied Dorothy.

She and the seamstress hunkered down on one of Eod's ancient battlements. Noon's rich shadows, reaching everywhere the beams of light did not, made the women black as villains. Given the dust-coated bunks, the windowsills covered in cobwebs, the racks emptied of spears, and the military cleanliness and order of a place so clearly disused—bedding folded, not a single personal article or scrap of paper to be seen—the mater assumed this had once been a barracks. From here, men could head up or down into the passageways within the Great Wall, which was a city all to itself. This particular wing, placed along the Southern Gate from which no threat ever came, could easily have been forgotten for one hundred years.

Regardless of the neglect, the women kept their voices to a whisper and moved little from the banded chests they'd claimed as seats. Once, poor Dorothy had started coughing from her allergy to dust. She appeared to have that condition under control now, though, aside from her perpetually pink eyes and the occasional sniffle.

Dorothy's remark had hung in the air for what Lowe felt was a respectable period of time. Lowe handed Dorothy her flagon, which was filled with liquid courage—brandy—and hoped that would make the woman more talkative. Although she could have offered the seamstress one of the delicious, butter-sweet treats from the large wicker baskets near their feet, she did not; they'd be needing those later. Dorothy gave the brandy a sniff, liked what she smelled, and had a few swigs.

"Not your first rebellion?" asked Lowe.

"We have all wanted to change something in our lives once or twice," replied Dorothy.

Carefully, Lowe asked: "What is it that you wished to change?"

"I wanted to change myself. My feelings." The seamstress sighed, and played with the silver-and-white tunic she'd woven, one identical to the one Lowe wore and to the light uniform of Eod's infantry; it looked as if it had been sewn by a royal tailor. She was no such woman of stature, though. What riches and talents she possessed, she'd earned after crawling from the desert and clawing scraps of whatever she could lay her hands on or fairly earn: food, clothing, favors owed. Eventually, she had enough scraps to make a home and then a business. She considered how to explain all of this to the mater. "Rowena," she finally said. "The sword of the queen. Do you know her?"

"Yes."

"I know her story very well. She was blessed to have been found in the desert before all the water ran out of her veins. Twice blessed to have been found by Her Highness and taken in through the great White Gates of Eod—these very stones beneath us—and into the wonder of the city. I can imagine her jubilation. Her sense of triumph." Dorothy clenched her tunic. She looked as if she wanted to tear it. "Well, some of us *khek*—that's the Arhadian word for shite, by the way—were not such favorites of Fate. We either died in the desert, or we found the white mirage of Eod on the horizon and wept when we did. Then we wept again when we realized that the mirage was no more welcoming than the scorching terror we'd left."

"You...You're a cast-out child of the Arhad?"

"One of many." Dorothy sniffled and pinched shut her eyes to hold in tears. "Too many...Three of us were sent into the desert that season: Ashrafa, Cassala, and myself. Ashrafa dried up in a day. We left her bones for the buzzards and took her waterskin as if we were murderous thieves. Survival makes you into a terrible person. I think you understand a bit of that yourself; I sense that in you. Cassala and I made it to the white mirage: the dreaded and desired city of the Everfair King. Every Arhadian child knows the legend of the golden-haired bride stolen from her rightful husband by the Everfair King. We were warned that in Eod every indulgence and sin was for sale and we would become just as corrupt as she.

"We came in through the gates and met the strange Silver guardians of Eod. Every lie about the city shattered. Men were kind to us: they looked us in the eyes and asked what they could do for our comfort. They treated us as if we were men ourselves. It was an unforgettable courtesy, it filled us with a warmth that made us giddy. I don't think that Cassala ever forgot that warmth. She soon forgot me, however."

Lowelia leaned in, glowing with concern. "I'm sorry. Were you close friends?"

The seamstress glared at the mater. Proud and firm, Dorothy rose in her seat. "We were lovers. That's why she and I were exiled. We were caught sinning together. Only a kiss—that time—though it was enough to make us worthless as wives, and useless even as sewn slaves. Our tainted love damned us, but also somehow freed us. You would think that in the City of Wonders, a love such as ours could have flourished. Yet here is where it died. That first soldier that showed us kindness...Hmph. Cassala never forgot his generosity. Nor his hands, his voice, and all the other virtues of the man. She could not stop fawning over him. I realized I was a convenience to her. I was what she had wanted at the time. An escape. So what have I learned? After spending years wishing I could transform my feelings as Cassala did, I stopped. I stopped lying to myself. I accepted that I am who I am, even if that means I might remain alone. I have learned that we are perfect in our evils and faults. What I would change is the unfairness of a world that dictates who we are to be before we ever have the chance to take that journey and decide for ourselves. Perhaps then Cassala wouldn't have been so confused. They're married now, and we used to see one another for tea every few months." Dorothy turned up her nose. "Once her husband discovered our past, our get-togethers ceased. She has several children, last I heard. I would have liked some myself, children, but you can imagine the complications. I'm too old now. A spin-rex past her prime and empty of milk."

Lowelia laughed, dispelling any awkwardness. "I'm the only cow in the pasture myself, so I know the feeling. Still, we old dames have more fight in us than some of the young—those who haven't had to battle for an ounce of decency or morality in all their lives." Lowe stood and offered the other woman her hand. "Tell you what, if we don't end up in shackles after today's escapade, I shall take that tea with you. Once a week, schedules permitting."

There was no offer of romance in the mater's steel expression, and Dorothy was quite done with all of life's starry-eyed pap. But a friend would be nice. Dorothy shook Lowelia's hand. Then the mater helped her friend to her feet, and they made anxious circles of the room while being tempted by the waft of the narcotic-laced pastries. *We shouldn't eat those,* they thought, tempting as they were, or they'd be on the floor sleeping when their co-conspirator arrived. Soon, the sun started to fall, and twirls of golden light ran red. They waited.

The door creaked open. A huge hooded man entered carrying a sack.

"You're running a little late," snapped Lowe.

"I was delayed for a sand," replied Leonitis. "And I needed to check on the other relays and deliver their arms."

"Give it here. Let's see what you've made off with." Dorothy beckoned the legion master over to the nearest bed. There, he carefully removed the contents of his bag and laid them across the mattress. The Menosian firearms gleamed like black horns against the dusty sheets. They were frightful-looking weapons, ornately hooked and embellished with sharp curves that would wound a hand if improperly gripped. Luckily, Dorothy had sewn some workman's gloves for them. The seamstress already wore her pair, and she picked up a firearm, steadied it on her forearm, flicked back the hammer with a thumb, and pointed the flame-tipped weapon slowly about the room.

As the legion master changed himself into the garb of a lesser servant of the crown—a silver-embroidered watchman's uniform—he commented on Dorothy's ease with the firearm. "You seem familiar with the weapon."

"A lady should know how to defend herself," replied Dorothy, then made *pew, pew, pew* noises. "I took an archery course back in the day, though this looks far more enjoyable."

CREEK.

The door was pushed ajar, but there was no wind inside the fortification. Leonitis was caught with his pants half on, and in a moment of unusual clumsiness, he stumbled and hit the bed. What a blessing that Dorothy was such a calm woman; otherwise, her finger would have twitched and she would have shot the arm-waving giant that entered their secret enclave. Giantess, she realized, for the lack of facial hair and the delicate eyes told her this was a woman. She then recognized a face she'd seen in phantographs and printed news: brown, masculine, and with short-cropped hair. Rowena, sword of the queen.

"You came." Leonitis gasped from the floor.

Last night, a letter had arrived at Rowena's quarters, slipped under her door by a shadow. The scrape of paper over stone had been enough to wake the vigilant Sword. Not that she slept with any great serenity these nights with Menosian murders and cannibal priestesses wandering her fair city. After she'd bolted out of bed and thrown open the door to try to catch a glimpse of whoever had been creeping around outside of her chamber, she'd noticed the note by her feet. A single sheaf of paper, upon which was written: *If you wish to ensure that our city is not consumed by darkness, if you wish to become a sword to cut the night, a sword for your queen, then meet us tomorrow, at sundown, at the place where you spilled your first blood.*

This reference to a location would have been vague and indecipherable to anyone save herself: *much* blood had been spilled by her hand, and in many places. However, during Rowena's first day of training with the Silver Watch, she'd gotten separated from the other warriors—she'd not yet developed her metropolitan compass—and wandered up and into the southern barracks of the Great Wall. There, she'd become even more disoriented. She remembered swiping at a cobweb while climbing a flight of stairs and losing her balance. Then had come a tumble, a crack to her face, and a gushing, hot darkness. She had awoken in the barracks below, which featured more lavish arrangements—gold-trimmed armchairs and a crackling fire. A cold compress had been placed upon her face, and she'd clutched at it and applied more pressure to her swelling nose. She'd tasted iron all down her throat, and known that her nose had been broken—for the first, but by no means the last, time. The embarrassment of that moment had taught her never again to disobey or stray from her comrades. The man who had tended to her, the braided and handsome Ninth Legion Master, had dismissed her error. "It's a soldier's life to be cut and bruised," he'd said. He had an unblemished chin and sculpted beard; from what she could see, he shouldn't be able to understand even the concept of imperfection. And yet, they'd sat there, slowly chatting and eventually drinking away her pain. It was a memory she would never forget.

"I knew it was you," said Rowena.

"How's the nose?" asked Leonitis, as he righted himself and his trousers. "Ready for another smash or two?"

"I would do anything for my queen." Rowena smiled. It seemed as hard as the rest of her. "I am glad that you summoned me to this..."

"Rebellion," said Lowe.

"I do apologize, though," said Dorothy. "I don't think I have a disguise for you."

Rowena puffed proud. "I am the sword of the queen, and if what's been insinuated in last night's missive is true, Leonitis, then my mistress is returning. I have no need of chicanery. I shall fight for her with honesty and honor."

"How about a gun, at least?" suggested Dorothy. "We have one to spare. A bit more threatening than honesty or honor, and I don't see a sword anywhere on you."

Striding over and pushing past Leonitis, Rowena sized up the smart-talking brown woman. Dorothy withstood her scrutiny, and they decided, much as animals do, that they were of the same survivalist species. "Arhadian, I see," said Rowena.

"The same as you," replied Dorothy.

By then, Leonitis had finished adjusting his clothing. He tucked in his tunic, holstered a gun in his belt, and took a deep breath, as did everyone in the room. They stared at the thin windows, watching the creep of orange light to red. At last, the moment arrived. Dusk was the signal. A fire in the sky and a storm blowing in from the South. They could feel it then: Lila was drawing nearer. They almost thought they could smell her: a perfume, a spice of myrrh, cinnamon, and mystery. The four, either smelling the enchantment or imagining it, stole down into the garrison. They were quiet for the moment, but in a speck they would be making chaos.

V

The great may sometimes be unseated by the actions of the small: soldiers, farmers, cooks, serfs—people a man bloated with power and a sense of his own superiority would never look at, let alone expect to see betray his magnanimity. Taroch's downfall had been triggered by an angry maid who'd slipped a feliron tonic into his broth one evening. She hadn't been a rebel; she had not been angered by Taroch's growing regime of terror; she had been no Eodian or Ziochian loyalist. She was, simply, a woman upon whom the warlord had once forced himself, and she'd acted in revenge. History had forgotten her name. Nonetheless, her small act of defiance had incapacitated Taroch on the eve of what was supposed to have been his grandest moment. It was the night he, his great army, and the great sorcerers at his command had gathered at the edge of Kor'Khul's sandy border, in the hills of Ebon Vale to restore the desert to its fabled verdancy. They would then ride that green road straight to Eod, which was not yet fully protected by its great wall.

Crossing the desert without transfiguring it was not an option, as Taroch's army was not composed of Arhadians. The catastrophic terraforming spell was also a testament to the Sorcerer King's vainglory: he would do what Magnus couldn't or wouldn't; he would transform the dead land into a paradise. This stubborn pride was what brought the enfeebled, poisoned warlord out of his tent that day, what made him stand in his circle of sorcerers, peers, and generals to wheeze and squeeze no more than a few green sprouts from the soil and some beads of sweat from himself. The sprouts quickly withered. Geadhain was stubborn, too, difficult to alter through terraforming; not at full strength, the warlord was unable to conduct or amplify the powers of his circle. What was to have been a grand panoply to his empire became a mocking defeat. After this, he was no longer seen as a man who might challenge the Immortals; he was only a man.

In the days it took for Taroch to restore his vigor so that he could attempt his great sorcery again, the brother kings mobilized. They came in from the West with silver riders, and they came up from the South on black steeds armored in golden plate—mounts as strong and determined as their masters. Brutus and Magnus themselves led the forces, and fire and ice struck Taroch in a deadly pincer. The warlord's entire force was exposed, and it was already confused and lethargic without his leadership. It's said that the blood from this battle turned the stones of Ebon Vale, once the Vale Ban—the White Vale—black. Taroch was routed. More than half of his force was destroyed, and in the ensuing campaign, he was whittled down from would-be-Immortal to fallen rebel and outlaw. Proud to the end, Taroch didn't allow himself to be caught. Instead, he hanged himself from the rafters of a nameless roadside tavern in Southreach.

Lowelia contemplated that history, which she'd chatted about with Rasputhane one evening, as she and Dorothy strolled upon the bastion aside the towering gates of Eod. In dusk's shade, the lean keep seemed of darker stone than the ivory wall from which it extruded, though it stood nearly as tall. The building was connected to a second identical keep on the great door's opposite side by an interior parapet walk, which edged slightly out of the wall and was lined with long windows. Dead center above the parapet, thrusting out from the wall like an enormous spherical sconce, was an airy dome supported by pillars. It looked as if it were a place for divine contemplation—though Lowelia knew it was a gatehouse, with levers and mechanisms that controlled the doors of Eod. Lowelia knew she had but a few sands to climb to that dome.

She assumed that the lookouts along the crenulations and walkways atop the wall had already been subdued by Brock's crew—posing as stonemasons—as no alarm had been raised. The fire show in the Faire of Fates was scheduled to start any time now. *Hurry*, she thought, giving the soldiers standing along the wide steps and framed arch of the bastion a smile that disclosed none of her anxiety.

The watchmen didn't smile back, but stopped the women, asked why they'd come, and quickly searched them. Were they to encounter any problems here, before hatching their assault, Leonitis and Rowena watched from somewhere in the marketplace behind them; they would send one of the esteemed soldiers forth to demand that the ladies be let inside. Likewise, an officer or two turned to the rebellion's cause waited by the second bastion to intervene in a similar manner. No contingencies were necessary, though, after Lowelia had trotted out her name and explained her royal mission of charity. The watchmen seemed satisfied; they didn't investigate her story or check the baskets beyond lifting the linen and salivating over the fragrant sweets beneath. Lowelia promised the gents that she'd leave one for them in the barracks; she didn't want either man to slump over outside and cause panic too soon. She felt eerily calm, like a contented, prepared murderer, as they ushered her into the cool darkness of the bastion.

Within the great wall, the hubbub of the market was muted. A short hall expanded into a square chamber, which was crammed with stacked beds, tables, and bodies. As soon as she and Dorothy made an appearance with their wicker baskets of cheer, soldiers leaped from their cots and threw down cards, dice, swords—whatever they'd been playing at. Within specks, dozens of hungry men held twists of golden dough coated in powdered sugar, honey, and cinnamon.

"We've come as field feeders," Lowelia said with a smile to one grizzled and suspicious watch captain. "Remember those, from the ancient wars? The lasses who'd flit around the trenches like spirits of nourishment, offering water and sustenance to tired men?"

"I don't," declared the captain.

Lowelia offered him one of the twists. "We're here on official business; note my regal threads. We have no water, sadly, though there's sure to be plenty around here. As for these, I made them myself! Straight from the White Hearth, and made with *love*, by order of the king." *And with a dash of blue arrowhead venom—enough that you should all be asleep in ten sands.* She shook it again. These were old-world sweets, once a national pleasure taken with tea, and their allure couldn't easily be resisted. Finally, he accepted, grumpily retreating to a bunk in the long chamber to chew the treat.

The field feeders continued their charitable work, giving unctuous smiles to the men relieved to be granted this moment of kindness. By the time they'd wandered to the end of the chamber and reached the stairs winding up into the gatehouse, only a few soldiers hadn't partaken of their baked treats. Leonitis and Rowena would be along in a sand to take care of those who'd chosen not to inadvertently sedate themselves. Meanwhile, other rebels, dressed as watchmen, would be causing chaos in the marketplace; nothing fatal, she hoped, though guns would be fired, carts set ablaze, and citizens terrified into a riot. Such was the cost of revolution: the forecast of blood spoiled none of Lowe's courage. The now friendly, stuffed, and happy captain barked his permission for them to pop into the gatehouse. The pair of watchmen standing before the staircase heeded his command and took treats from the field feeders as they passed.

Dorothy and Lowelia hustled up the square stairwell, counting sands, exchanging strained looks, each listening for sounds of a rebellion. Thus far, their timing had been perfect. They came to a long hallway flickering with lines of dusk, then raced down the abandoned path to another stairwell, this one circular, and emerged into a rotunda with curved pillars, artistic frescos of maidens, warriors, and monsters, and a floor of white tiles. Only two watchmen were posted here; usually, there'd be six. But Leonitis had provided them with valuable information, and the rebels had chosen to strike during the changing of the guard. The reinforcements due to come and take these watchmen's places would, instead, soon be sleeping below. The second keep and its soldiers should now be under the care of another group of field-feeding rebels.

Aside from two watchmen, there was nothing in the grand cupola for the ladies to see save for two great cranks set into pedestals on either side. Ahead, two soldiers leaned on the balustrade and peered through the pillars down into the churning marketplace. Neither seemed alert or alarmed. Good. Still, one turned her head at the noise of the huffing invaders.

"Who are you?" she asked, warier than any of her male compatriots had been. She kept a hand on her glass-and-steel sword; as with all the watch's weapons, it was both enchanted and sharp enough to hack off an arm in one sweep.

"Field feeders," said Lowelia, holding up her basket of temptations as she walked toward the soldiers. She didn't have far to go, and she saw a shuffling to her left as Dorothy no doubt fished for the pistol hidden under the napkin that lined the inside of her basket.

"You." The soldier shook a gauntleted finger; her fellow guard turned now. "You're the queen's old handmaiden. The one that pretended to be her. Mater Lowelia of the Hearth. What are you doing here?"

"We're here on official business." Lowelia left her basket hanging in the crook of her elbow and raised her hands. "We're here to bring refreshments to the weary."

Bang! Boom! Hiss!

Just then, a shot rang out in the marketplace, followed by a powdery explosion and a thread of fire and smoke. The soldiers whipped around, but when they turned again—out of a prickle of battlefield premonition—they found that both women had dropped their baskets, spilling cinnamon twists everywhere, and now stood armed with sleek, black, flame-tipped pistols.

"Doesn't seem as if you'll be getting a twist," said Lowe, no longer all smiles and charm. As she kept her gun trained on the edgy soldiers, Dorothy momentarily stowed her weapon, then struggled to lift and secure a heavy black-banded board over the staircase. She finished in a sweat, and pulled the rung a few times, determining it would take a small battering ram to open it again. Screams had begun to whirl in the smoky air outside. A few more explosions came, though they seemed muffled and distant from this height. Four tense combatants watched one another. Dorothy, again brandishing her weapon, rejoined her co-conspirator. She turned her head for a moment to whisper something to Lowe, and in that speck, the second soldier dropped to his knee, reached down to his boot—

Sharp as an eagle, Dorothy saw the movement, then shot him.

Earlier, she had lied when she'd spoken of archery lessons. She'd had training with firearms after a hate-hazed summer during which she'd debated hunting down Cassala's husband. It felt cathartic to shoot someone. The flash, the powder, the ozone scorch—even the sound of hot metal tearing through metal, bone, and flesh—were elating rather than terrifying. She shot only the man's leg, which was enough to knock him to his arse and send the knife he'd been reaching for clanging away. The soldier groaned and slid down the balustrade, leaving a bloody trail. He'd likely live, if he received medical attention soon.

"It's time," Dorothy said, and swept her gun toward the watchwoman. "Open the gate. Lowe, you'll have to get the other one; I don't think that fellow is having his best day."

Lowe hurried to the crank and tucked away her gun, knowing it would take all of her strength to set the gears—even oiled in magik, as they were—in motion. She'd need assistance, too, but the watchwoman had planted her feet and was taking a moral stand.

"I won't be party to an assault upon our city," she said. "I won't shame my husband by becoming a criminal."

Shame my husband? wondered Lowe, and Dorothy's face twitched and revealed an ugly anger. She worried that the watchwoman was about to be shot. Instead, Dorothy reprimanded her with her tongue, not a bullet.

"Husband?"

"Fiancé, actually, and he's a soldier, too. None of you will get away with this, whatever chaos it is you're sowing."

Dorothy stepped forward, aiming at the woman's face; the watchwoman stumbled back a bit, afraid. "We're all noble, lass. But when it comes down to it, when push comes to shove, we value life over decency. A wedding or a funeral? Which do you want your beau to attend? Your choice. I'm giving you three specks to decide. One...Two..."

The watchwoman raced to the second pedestal, nodded to Lowelia, and started cranking. From below came a long, pained machine yawn—louder even than the growing brawl occurring in the garrison or the marketplace—that rumbled through the feet and groins of all nearby. The gates of Eod were rolling open. Up in the gatehouse, they felt the change mostly in their hearts, though. Lowelia, Dorothy, and even the watchwoman toiling on her crank paused for a speck, smelling spice, feeling a rush of angry passion in her veins that drove her further into her exercise: a sweat, a zeal, an enchantment. Dorothy grinned, for it was the smell of vengeance.

In the chambers below them, Leonitis and Rowena had also caught the scent, and were inspired by a sudden fury that filled their veins. They toppled tables and battered men—some quite sleepy and defenceless—twice as vigorously as they had before. They tore through the faltering lines of Silver watchmen like bulls through a glass kingdom. They used only their pommels and fists—their honor held them back from murder—but they would not feel sated without blood on their knuckles. In their hearts, they knew what had happened, what dark muse had inspired them.

The queen had arrived.

VI

A song blew in from the desert. At first no one really heard it. Carried on sandy notes, the cloud of music and myrrh arrived at Eod with a gusty vengeance. Tents in the Faire of Fates shuttered their counters and pinned down their tarps. Merchants pulled signs off the thoroughfare, and if they didn't, the thin advertisement boards were tossed down the flagstones like cards. Eod hadn't known such a storm since the Clash of the Kings.

Then the pandemonium began: a cart that burst into flames, horses slapped by mysterious strangers and sent into frenzies, firecaller incendiaries that blasted harmlessly but produced blinding smoke. Stands were kicked over. People tripped and toppled one another while scattering for cover. The Silver watchmen that were still around fired guns into the air and shouted at citizens, serving only to intensify the terror; sometimes, citizens even saw the Silver Watch fighting amongst themselves. The world had suddenly ceased making sense.

Most of the Faire was soon bare of folk, who now huddled behind safer walls of stone. Men, women, and even babes craned their necks to stare out their windows at the haunted marketplace, which was now dancing with flame, smoke, and sandy plumes. White wisps wandered through the orange obscurity—either watchmen, good or bad, or ghosts. Their city had become like a graveyard. What now threatened their peace?

But they did not stay in hiding for long, no. A music called to their minds, a beat stirred the people from their cowering comfort and made them want to brave the gritty maelstrom to find the source of this enchanted melody. Men and women threw on hats, scarves, and clothing generally worn in what passed for winter in Eod: a carefully controlled season with warm rains and a single snowfall on the winter solstice. Bundled up and shivering with sinister anticipation, people strode through the streets. Occasionally, they would meet another such sand walker near a burned heap, who seemed to be headed in the same direction, who'd say something about a pull, a call, and a scent that could not be defined.

Indeed, something was here, in the storm. Within a short time, the stragglers had formed a larger body, one that continued to grow. Soon, a throng had gathered in the whistling marketplace. They stood around empty shops. They filled the platforms that firecallers or other performers might use. Now a crowd of a thousand silent and shrouded shadows, they waited.

The song grew louder, and voices could be distinguished in the wind's sibilation. In the distance loomed the tall, hazy arch of Eod's Southern Gate, open to the desert, to friend or foe, for the first time since Eod's creation. The Eodians held a patient vigil. Even sellswords and a few of the black-veiled Terotakian murderesses stood tranquilly about the Faire. These strangers, however mercenary, also wanted to know whence that beautiful song had come.

Women's voices carved the sharpest pitch in the song, but there were harmonies of youth and deeper notes from men. It was sung in Arhadian, a language with which most were passingly familiar, though not many of the lyrics could be understood. For this was an ancient tune, conceived in an age when Eod had been young and queenless: a song about the red glory of life and sacrifice that was sung by women and wives, the true backbone of their tribes. Those who could understand the lyrics realized the words had been changed, inflections added, meanings revised. The Arhadian women mentioned in the song were no longer merely mothers and caretakers, but teachers and warriors themselves.

The crowd listened, enraptured, and inhaled the wind.

VII

Through a whirling storm, the queen's army marched, singing. The three thousand newly born warrior women had learned the *Mitra Ich Zenzeth*—the Mother of Warriors—in their desert encampments. It was the ode they had sung while practicing, daily, the martial skills taught to them by the queen's fearless bloodmate: the obsidian knight, who shouted and demanded from them absolute commitment.

The queen's army didn't mind taking orders from a man, for this one understood the concept of equality. He'd sacrificed his title, his life, and what he'd believed to be his honor to be with the queen. Such a cost should be repaid with respect. Aided by the enchanting spice, the inspiring power of the queen, these women of the Arhad had swiftly mastered the strikes, lunges, and drills of their obsidian commander. Within days, they had attained a finesse usually possessed only by battlefield veterans. From morning till night, drunk on the queen's venom, they'd hurled their tireless bodies upon the living shield of her bloodmate. They'd showered him in a rain of spears that would have killed anyone else.

When the warriors weren't fighting, they were singing; they practiced the taunting terror calls of battle and knew how to shriek and trill their enemies into submission. Today, however, they sang the *Mitra Ich Zenzeth* and were as calm as those who awaited them in Eod. Their day had come. The queen was to be restored to power, and all wrongs would be judged.

When the army could be clearly seen by Eod in the mist of sand, it was as a wave of all the colors frowned upon in Arhadian culture: lusty reds, regal blues, and many yellow golds. The army might have been a great band of minstrels. The minds of the army had also been coaxed to greatness by the queen's enchantment, and the thousands sang as harmoniously as a choir. The fallen queen, astride a pale and willowy spinrex as beautiful as a steed, rode next to a large, dark, and mounted knight.

As soon as she'd known she would need mounts for her army, and that such a beast existed—praise the Mind in his omniscience—she'd summoned the albino outcast and the whole of its herd to her side with a wind of spice. There were fewer barriers to the exercising of her power than she had expected. Holding people in complete thrall fatigued her as would have any grand magik, but she no longer needed to bespell or beguile her army into obedience. The people behind her, the ones carrying her woven banners showing an amber snake wrapped around a hunk of black stone, were proud to hold her symbol aloft; they had not been coerced. A few had left once she'd relaxed her enchantment. They'd fled to other tribes or doomed themselves to wither in Kor'Khul. She had decided they were not worthy of marching with her. If a man was not ready to leave behind all that he had been, how could he become something new? Every snake must shed its skin, harden its scales, sharpen its venom and teeth in order to grow into a mature predator. Lila no longer hid her strange inner self, but reveled in her reptilian charms whenever the viper stirred in her. Even now, marching toward her destiny, she effused a light mist of gold into the air and bared her fangs whenever she smiled. This happened often now that she, Erik, and her tribe stood united.

Are you ready, Navigator Lila? asked the Mind.

The white hump of Eod with its strange pearl lens pierced the whitish-brown haze that had fallen over the desert. She believed she'd conjured the sandstorm, too; Magnus was no longer the only Immortal who could influence the weather through his mood. Bold from her power, and from the steadiness of her obsidian bloodmate, she replied, *I am ready, yes. Thank you, my child.*

Now and then, when sentiment struck her, she referred to the Mind as her child. Old habits were hard to break, and she'd been stepmother to hundreds, if not thousands, of orphans in her lifetime. The Mind reminded her of these outcasts, although his innocence and urge to constantly impress her with facts and wisdom made him even more lovable. She wondered how her other orphans fared with the task of preparing for her arrival. They had only to open the Southern Gate and then restrain or incapacitate a few dozen soldiers. Once she drew closer, her poison would subdue any further resistance.

Her saboteurs must have succeeded, for as the army descended into a valley of lazy dunes scattered with red puddles of dusk and the city came into view, she saw the gate was open. The formidable doors that protected Eod from incursion lay wide enough apart to accommodate a flood of her warriors. Magnus would have no choice but to parley once they occupied the whole of the Faire of Fates. The altercation need not escalate into outright war. She'd come with an army, though, and she wouldn't hesitate to stain Eod red if the Iron Queen or her miscreant advisors tried to stand in the way of a discussion between former husband and wife.

VIII

The skycarriage carrying the monarchs touched down outside the tempestuous Faire of Fates. The watchmen had thrown up a slipshod barrier of carts, stalls, and coaches, but it appeared to have been abandoned along with the watchmen's weapons, which shone like half-buried treasures on a beach in the sandy heaps brought by the storm. The monarchs and their meek party of defenders stepped off the glass steps of the skycarriage and were immediately struck by a sense of dread.

"Where are the watchmen?" shouted the king; it was hard to hear him over the wind. A speck later, he sneezed. "And what is that smell?"

"Or that song?" asked the Iron Queen. A chant could now be heard: Arhadic voices, melodious, and in unison. Gloriatrix's single Ironguard, who'd been waiting for her on the skycarriage, felt like inadequate protection. Empty crowes stood parked, distantly, around the perimeter that had been laid, though the Ironguards to whom these ships belonged, and the additional men she had commanded, through farspeaking stone, to meet her here from Camp Fury were nowhere in sight. She took her lone Ironguard's arm once they entered the desolation, and pursued the king, his guard, and the gray mousey fellow, all of whom had already taken off into the whirl. "Wait! Is this safe? You fools! Where are your soldiers, Magnus? Or mine?"

"We should wait for reinforcements!" warned Rasputhane as he tugged at the king's arm. "Sorcery is at work here. Gorijen and his legion are on their way. We must not proceed so recklessly into danger."

The king made no answer. Instead, he opened his mouth and inhaled, producing an uncharacteristic guttural, animalistic snort that was reminiscent of his brother. He tasted the layers of spice, the hints of vanilla, and sweeter herbs. He flushed with the warmth of alcohol and the pleasure of a fair-sung tune, one much less ominous than the echoing Arhadian war chant. Magnus didn't recognize the song: it had been modified and was now unfamiliar even to its own culture. But it spoke of honor and women and warriors.

A wall of bodies soon hindered any attempts to hunt the source of this enchantment. Hundreds of folk blocked the marketplace, staring dumbly, mouths agape. Clearly bespelled, they didn't respond to Magnus's appeals, and he had to push his way through them. Among those enthralled stood a few of his own gawking, unarmed soldiers; he assumed the rest of the watch was likely in a similar dazed state. He didn't bother attempting to break the enchantment. He had lost Rasputhane and possibly also the Iron Queen and her escort. He cared not. He needed to reach the scent and song.

Finally, Magnus finished his charge through the mortal wall and came to a wind-swept court that lay before an arch that yawned to take in all of the desert. Open: the gates of Eod were wide open. So many women in tattered rag-scale armor stood along Eod's great wall that he paused as if he'd been impaled on their primitive polearms. How many were there? A thousand? Two thousand singing women? There were boys and a peppering of men in the ranks, too. He felt thousands glaring at him, as if he'd wronged each and every member of the army. Their judgment and spite seared him like the dying sun.

Spinrexes cawed, though their calls drowned under the weight of the war song. Under dusk's brush, it seemed as if the whole of the Faire of Fates were ringed and painted with ghostly crimson warriors. The majesty of the force humbled the king. In that moment, he felt he'd already lost, although no confrontation had yet taken place. He couldn't swallow his astonishment. Indeed, the spectacle and the shock had the dizzy king gazing at everything but the golden shimmer before him. The shimmer, and a ripple of black, rode forth.

"Magnus!"

It was Erik who hailed him; the timber of his voice, so close to Brutus's, was unmatched and unmistakable. He and another rider trotted across a great stretch of cobbles before anything more was said. The singing army ceased its music, and a dreadful silence fell upon the scene. About halfway between the wall of Arhadians and the gathering of Eod's people, the riders stopped and dismounted. Scowling, Magnus recognized the two warmasters: Lila and his foster son—yet, each was radically changed from the person he knew.

Erik possessed a spine of pure flint, and he strutted with the assured pride of a black panther in his den: exotic, unique, and deadly. Lila appeared as shining as ever, but her shine was too strong. A scintillation of light off some manner of skin disfigurement dazzled the king. The air around her sparkled, too. Dressed in the resplendent gold tatters of her army, she was no longer the woman he'd known: she'd been mutated by eldritch energies. He would not call her ugly, but she was no longer his. A painful dagger of reason stabbed him with the fact that she'd shed those aspects of herself that he'd known and loved. The blade thrust deep as he noticed the bundle that she cradled by her breast. *A child?* he thought, infuriated. Even when he realized that not enough time had passed to bring a child to term, he felt no less betrayed. "What have you done to my people?" he demanded. "What have you done to yourself?"

Suddenly, the queen was closer; Erik as well. She'd traveled in a slithery flash. Erik, though, had simply moved far faster than a normal man should. Regardless, his queen and his son were both now before him: his twin banes. Magnus could see their whole glorious transformation written in their stares and bodies. Bloodmates: they who breathed, twitched, even blinked, as one. Their betrayal sickened him. He found Lila's scent—also tainted, sweeter and spicier—nauseating.

"I have done nothing to these people," replied Lila. "Only those who have something from which they want to break free can fall under my thrall. I am surprised that *you* have nothing you regret."

I am not enthralled, thought Gloriatrix. *I am all that I need to be.* She'd left her Ironguard some ways back in the midst of the comatose horde and crept toward the front. She'd been smart enough to take her guard's gun, and she remained inconspicuous, using the immobilized folk as cover.

"Is that why you have come?" spat Magnus. "To throw your union in my face? To humiliate me? I am humiliated. I am broken. I never believed I would see the day that my most trusted child seduced my wife. Have neither of you any shame?"

"Shame?" Lila laughed, and her fangs and forked tongue flashed at the king. "We came so that I could deliver a message from the dead that may yet win this war. We came because we were declared villains, declared honorless, and we are neither. We came because we were repudiated by this kingdom—one I built as much as you did—and forced into a hunted exile. I came to clear our names and to face the man who wronged me."

Thunder rumbled, and lighting began a white dance in the dusk. "Wronged you? You fuked my son! Surrendered your virtue to him! I have been betrayed by both of you, beyond measure." The arrogance of a man destined to live forever flared up within the king. "I should smite you for treason! Matrimonial treason. The betrayal of honor!"

"You may try, but you will fail," threatened Erik.

Lila checked her bloodmate with a secret word that Magnus sensed but couldn't hear himself. Softly, but not kindly, she whispered, "You betrayed me before we were wed, Magnus. By promising yourself—your soul, your everything—to another."

"Another? You are mad," said the king.

The queen of snakes and spice circled her former bloodmate. "I have seen the past through the eyes of the silver witch. She showed me your life with your brother. You two bled, fed, suckled, and who knows did whatever *else* to each other. It was beautiful, what you and he shared. And untouchable. You loved him long before you ever played the game of loving me, a normal woman. I could never fill your spirit as he did. Yet now that he is a beast unchained, you shun the wretched aspects of his nature. You have wed yourself to a beast, and his bride you must be. I have wed myself to honor, and his name is Erithitek. Calm your thunder and storm, for they are no greater than mine."

Suddenly, the sandstorm that ruffled through the Faire went from fickle to violent. From the deepest desert hollows, sand, rock, and grit—the essence of Lila's rage—was conjured. The storm gathered in an instant, turned the sky brown, then rolled over Eod in a hateful wave. Either the stinging assault or Lila's absorption in her enchantment stirred the catatonic audience from their fugue.

Anger, shattered pride, and a haunting sense that Lila's accusations were not entirely unwarranted summoned an answering fury in the king. A crackle of thunder ran through the clouds, and a wind that glimmered with shards of ice wailed down. Sandy torrents scoured stone and flesh, and hail pelted the marketplace. People shrieked and ran for cover; they felt that another day of reckoning had come. Many were horribly bewildered as to why it was they were outside in the Faire of Fates, apparently under assault from both the elements and an army of rag-tag warriors that was barely visible in the shearing of light, winter, and sand. The queen and Magnus were lost in the chaos.

Gales pummeled Erik, and winds threw him far, but he found purchase in the maelstrom by sprouting claws of obsidian. Slowly, he crawled toward the juddering pocket in the hurricane where he sensed the golden light of his beloved, where the scorned Immortal lovers stood unscathed in the heart of this horrible upheaval.

"You ruined me!" screamed Lila.

A runny tentacle of sand flung itself from the wall of wind that encircled the sorcerers. It was demolished by a spear of lightning and scattered the calm space in dust. There was no confusion over the ruination of which she spoke. It was clear to both which event it was that had utterly destroyed their marriage.

"I was not myself!" insisted the king.

"Were you ever? Were you ever honest with me?" asked Lila, and the howling sandstorm brought by her anger ebbed to a wheeze so that she might hear his excuse.

Magnus answered with his heart. "No."

With that, each of their storms fell apart. An emerald flash crackled through the air, and the hail eased into a drifting snowfall. It was lovely, as if the winter solstice had come early to Eod. The whiteness offered some of the light stolen by the hourglass. In the soft glow, the king saw that Lila had returned to a form closer to the one he'd wed: golden, enchanting, and without scales or serpent's charms. But that reptile, too, he valued and respected now, for it had always been inside her. Magnus took a step toward the memory of who they'd been for one thousand years, and hoped that enough mercy remained in this remade woman that she would be able to appreciate his regret.

"I was never honest with you," he said. "Or with myself. I wanted to be a man, but I cannot be what I am not. I used you to weave an illusion of happiness for myself. And for a time, we *were* happy—or at least as happy as two people deceiving themselves can be." Reaching out to her, he gingerly touched her cheek, a gesture that had once made them smile. Now, they both frowned, and his fingers felt cold to her. "An illusion. You feel it, too. You wanted escape, and so did I. What we built, however—this empire, our legacy—does not have to end with our love. I know what you want to hear, Lila. I am sorry. I am sorry I hurt you. I am sorry I lied to you—as sorry as you have been to live that lie—for so many centuries."

Navigator Lila, though his matrix is extraordinarily complex, I detect the measured heart rate and lowered phosphorus levels of a resting conscience, said the Mind from the tight cradle of her arms in which it had weathered the storm of the king and queen.

"I know," said the queen, to both that entity and her former husband. Here was an admission that their love was finally at an end, that Magnus rued his actions. With that release, she sighed. Magnus, sensing her sentiment, pressed his forehead against hers in a final expression of what had now faded between them. Lila sensed their fragile harmony was about to be broken; she felt a clenching of rage in her heart—it wasn't her own, but Erik's. Stumbling, she stepped away, turned, and before she could mind-whisper or stall him another way, Erik manifested in a black blur.

"Don't touch her! You have lost all right!"

The voice sounded as if it came from someone wailing from the bottom of a dark hole: powerful, elemental, born of rock. Erik? Magnus couldn't place it, and a speck later, any attempts to place the voice were cast into the dirt as he was thrown to the ground like a toy soldier by a ton of solid matter.

The Everfair King, crackling with arcs of emerald power, rose from the ground. He spat blood and glared at his attacker with eyes that mirrored the black and green thunderstorms that had so abruptly gathered above. Through the majesty of his anger—a sheen of green rage that licked at his form—Magnus saw a creature armored in obsidian plates that fumed with a golden light not unlike his aura. A sorcerer?

Lila, standing aside from the clash, carefully backed away. In a few flickers of magik, she'd slithered back to her warriors. While she and Magnus had just forgiven the unforgiveable, she felt pulled in two directions by her heart. She could have made a plea on behalf of Magnus to Erik, though she strained to speak in mind or with mouth to deny her knight his vengeance. Was this not her vengeance, as well? Whatever Magnus's reasons, and pardons, the savagery of his raping her would never be eased. Erik had come to extract a bloody retribution from Magnus akin to what he had wrought upon his queen—if not sexual, than passionately violent. In truth, Erik's heart was her heart, and so she knew they'd both come for blood. Blood would be the font in which the three of them washed away their sins. Violence was not only a man's work, though he would do it better than her. She wanted Erik to beat her former husband as she'd been beaten, and she stopped denying her thirst. Lila's face hardened, her scales subsuming her beauty. Accepting that this was how it would have to be, Lila inspired her army with a wind of spice, and she and the Arhadians gave their voices to sing the warriors' war song, hoping to see Erik claim the triumph he deserved.

As king and obsidian knight circled one another, Magnus at last identified the man under the monster: by the monster's familiar battle stance, and by the cold concentration in his ebony eyes—those had changed, though, lost all flecks of blue, and were blacker than space. "Erik," he hissed. Thunder groaned and split the night.

"I am the knight of the queen of Eod," declared the obsidian knight, stomping a craggy hoof that shook the ground as terribly as had Magnus's thunder. "Do not call me by that name. Ask my pardon for your transgressions, and I may let you leave this place without causing you grievous harm."

"Without harm..." The king's rage built and exploded. Suddenly, the skies flashed and roiled, and a rain of electricity fell from the heavens in a twining nimbus. Power engulfed the king. Magnus vanished into the luminous pillar. However, the light quickly waned into sparks and thin dancing twists of lightning, and from the smoldering hollow where once a handsome king had stood strode forth a warrior of winter. The king's glassy armor shone like the Witch Lights of Pandemonia—all the many shades of his soul from white to teal to crystal green. In gauntlets more talon and icicle than metal, he clenched a blade pulled from an arctic forge, one that seemed too large to be wielded so lightly. It smoldered with his wrath, steamed with a freezing power. A horned helm of emerald ice hid all but the king's pulsating green eyes and twisting black hair. Magnus could have been the lord of the winter hunt himself: a primeval Dreamer conjured from myth.

When the king spoke, his voice, too, came out distorted, echoing and crackling like permafrost. "I see that you have grown," he said. "New weapons, new courage. You would never have raised a hand to me before; you quailed when last given that opportunity. In a sense, I am proud. I see that Lila's blood—my blood—has changed you. In all of my lifetimes, I never thought to bear a child through ritual rather than love. We are now more father and son than ever before. Very well, my son. If you believe yourself to be the child no longer, come! Let us see how strong your fists have grown. Challenge your father!"

Over the city, now rendered heinously bright by the Witchwall's scintillations, the storm continued its dazzling rumble. The warrior women matched nature's beat with their song of valor.

Elsewhere, the Iron Queen, Rasputhane, and what remained of the Ironguard and watchmen who hadn't fled had found one another at last. They crouched in the creaking remains of an outdoor theater. A barricade of broken wood, beams, and curtain tatters gave them no real protection from the storm about to begin. Gloriatrix had refused to be taken back to the skycarriage. Besides, it was too late to flee, and she wouldn't risk taking off with the elements as temperamental as they were. Here they would stay, as witnesses to an historic moment. It was the end of a dynasty, Gloriatrix felt—which was only fair, given that her own kingdom lay in ruins. All should be reduced to ash; all should be rebuilt. She smiled as the first emerald hammer of lightning struck the flagstones with an explosion of black dust.

The king charged. More heavenly hammers struck the land, and the stone man stomped and stomped, causing the spine of the world itself to shake. Gloriatrix was thrown down—losing her gun—and caught by Eod's spymaster. She shook off his assistance, using him primarily as a climbing post on which to stand and look out upon the vibrating land.

What could even be seen through the foggy storm descending from the heavens? There was dust—a coughing, eye-watering quantity of it. There were flashes of green and gold light going off that would have tempted her toward delirium had it not been for the mesmerizing dance of two jewels in the chaos. One was black, the other emerald. They reminded her of the shooting stars she and Thackery had once seen on the clearest night she'd known in Menos. But these were men, or powers that wore man-like forms. She heard their weapons of obsidian and ice smashing against each other. The calamity unleashed torrents of snow and pelted her with a rain of scorched soil. In specks, she was filthy and covered, and yet she could not look away. For it was too exhilarating, being in the presence of real divinity. As hard as Rasputhane—shocked and concerned for her safety—and her Ironguards tried, they couldn't convince her to sit down.

Lightning thrashed in a web from above, and it became impossible to determine which storm was where. Then, in a moment that would be remembered forevermore, a black meteor launched itself on an angle from the billows like an arrow flying in reverse. It hung—glinting, growing a golden flame around itself, and growling, she thought—and then retraced its arc to the earth, landing with an impact as heavy, fiery, and great as expected. The shockwave vaporized the cloud below, blasted apart the storm above, and forced Gloriatrix to the ground with a slap of heat.

Her head rang; her eyes watered. She had the taste of blood in her mouth. Still indomitable, she stood with the rest of her groaning company and looked past the crumpled and scattered wreckage across a sparking, flame-twisted, and pockmarked square. Even in the midst of so much devastation, the warrior maidens sang; she could hear them now that the thunder had stopped. Indeed, they sang on because the battle was not yet over: through the ash and fires, the king and his son still danced. Gloriatrix wondered if the Immortals had stopped their dance for even a moment as the world skipped a beat. She assumed they hadn't, for they parried and spun with a speed so great their movements were difficult to distinguish.

To her, they were garlands of black, gold, and green—incredible spirals. They threw each about like glowing rag dolls; their aerial acrobatics defied the laws of physics. Into the sky they leaped, hovering like a star of two colors. Gloriatrix feared the consequences of another fall, and this time braced herself, but when the star split, one half—the green one—was cast into the wall above Lila's army. There, it bounced back from a dusty impact and tackled the black bolt already hurtling in its direction. The streaks twisted, rolled across the sky like ribbons in love, then veered downward and carved a smoldering rut in the flagstones before breaking apart. On sky, on land, it didn't matter: the Immortals were stuck to each another, bound by their anger, apart only for instants. The dance, the renewed and booming thunder, and the lights were a divine pageantry.

Certainly all the people of Eod had climbed out onto their roofs and turned their eyes toward the spectacle.

The fury of the conflict seemed to be waning, the blows the two exchanged less apocalyptic. Perhaps they had become aware of the damage they were doing: the Faire of Fates was now a wasteland, and no doubt there were many lying injured, if not dead, among the tarred heaps. Magnus's rage had overpowered his compassion.

Occasionally, the Immortals froze in a wavering tangle, and she could see that they now looked much as they had at the start of the battle. In those moments, she heard them barking at one another, though their voices were rumbles and blaring crackles, and she could make no sense of them. Soon, she realized that the battle was indeed slowing, that most of the fight was taking place on land rather than in the sky, and that she could finally see the shapes hidden in the blurs. She didn't dare approach the coruscating pit in which they still battled. Nor would she test her feet on a split land still trembling with tiny earthquakes from their blows. Sadly for her, she wasn't privy to their confessions.

"I loathe you." Erik grunted. In one hand, he clutched the sizzling blade of his father, dark blood pouring over his obsidian-gold knuckles. Sloppily he swung at his father with his free fist. Erik's armor was chipped and much of its shale plating had been cleaved away: what remained gleamed with a polish of blood. Magnus's icy mail had been shattered. Half a helm, a vambrace, and the whole abdomen of the king's breastplate had been carved away. Blood concealed his paleness, but not the glittering fragments of shattered emerald buried in his flesh. Neither warrior could continue this for much longer. The king's blade had been whittled down to a thick wick of light. Erik's hands were numb, and he was sure he was missing a finger. He hoped it would grow back. The pain didn't bother him. Rage pushed his extreme tolerance even further; he'd fight for Lila forever if he must. "You never deserved her," he spat.

"You speak the truth," huffed Magnus.

With a groan, Erik pushed them apart. Spent and shocked, he fell to a hand and a knee. Erik's rocky plating crumbled away from his muscles, leaving him nude and defenceless. Magnus, at last released from Erik's astonishingly strong and determined grip, staggered and also slumped to the ground. Only the flickering brand of the king's weapon prevented him from collapsing: he rested both hands on its hilt. He Willed away his armor, and it faded from him in a shimmering wind. He knelt before his son—a real and true heir to his strength and power—in bloody rags and spoke his heart's greatest secrets. There was no longer thunder in his voice.

"You feel that I have wronged you, by dishonoring Lila," he whispered, "and I have. I defiled her. I allowed my love for my brother to blind me. I took her; I did not earn her. I see that now, although that wisdom will help neither of us heal our wounds. I do not believe we can ever be healed. Know that I have always acted with virtue as my goal, Erik. In my quest to be a man, I built many houses of sand that are now being swept away by the black tide that comes for us. I thought we were stronger. As a nation. As a family. I lived in a prison of my own illusions. I do not blame you for what you have done. In fact—" Magnus coughed and gave his son a bloody smile. "I am proud of you."

Erik's anger rose at this kindness. "You ordered us hunted. You turned the whole of Geadhain against us."

Magnus nodded. "You stole off with my wife and destroyed a nation. Are you upset that I judged you before you could speak? Guilt has too many shoulders to fall upon here, Erik, and I had nothing but vagaries to offer the ruler of the Iron City, who had shown up on Eod's doorstep—after being foiled in her destruction of it. Another ambiguous crime, though not as damning or clear-set as the lives you and Lila claimed in Menos. At least Gloriatrix never had her chance to reap our people. Thus, what was I to tell the Iron Queen of this tragedy when I knew so little of its details myself? I had, at most, two people with faltering phantasms impersonating my missing wife and possibly treasonous aide who themselves couldn't vie for your or Lila's innocence. Do you think Gloriatrix is a reasonable woman? That she would patiently wait for a logical explanation for Menos's holocaust and the menagerie of deceptions left in Lila's wake? Not until recently did we learn that Lila was not entirely, perhaps not at all, responsible for the atrocity. Nonetheless, blame must be placed upon a head lest all heads be removed. I had no choice."

"Wait." Erik shook his head and managed to look at Magnus without hate. "You know of the spirits that tortured Lila?"

"I know something of your tale, yes. This morning, the Iron Queen and I heard a ghastly account of survival from four unbreakable souls. They validate and vouch for your innocence to a degree. I expect there is more for you to confess and to share with the allies of Geadhain—the ones who seek to preserve Her, for reasons either wicked or good. I have buried a thousand-year grudge against the Iron Queen's nation for the sake of a future. If you have the strength, Erik, my child, my son, I must ask that you wait before testing your impressive power against me once more. I know you must hate me, and yet this is what we need: unity. Hate will not win this war. That is the Black Queen's weapon."

"I don't hate you..." mumbled the knight. He was fighting back tears. All the trapped frustration of his exile, of his feelings toward Magnus, toward Lila, and now of this catastrophic release nearly broke him. He was obsidian, and he was the rock for his queen, and yet...she was happy. From within, he felt her spirit: that lightness and peace that had first touched him in a stable in Eod. They were free, their blood-debt paid and extracted, and she wanted him now to surrender to peace. But he wasn't sure he knew how to surrender. Everything in life had been a battle: his survival, his honor, earning his place with the woman he loved. How could he simply stop fighting? Then Magnus rose, and his blade vanished into starry crumbs. The king dragged himself forward a few steps and offered his son a hand. Erik gazed at the pale offering—still unclear as to what he should do.

"We can never be the same," the knight declared.

A melancholy smile afflicted the king. "Although I have lived forever, I am only now realizing one of life's most painful secrets. The decay of life, Erik, is what makes it precious. I would not ask you to change. I would not reverse my damning decisions. Not one. For in that fault, and the damage that you and I have caused, there lies truth and beauty. The leaves must turn; the fruit must rot. What we have been must die. Perhaps one day, something green will grow from what we have left behind." The king paused, and seemed twice as somber. "Though I shall not pray for it."

It was a soldier's promise, to endure and suffer, rather than to ignore the pain, and Erik respected it. He took Magnus's hand and stood. Those watching from afar, who saw the naked man and nearly-naked king rise and walk back toward the now silenced army of the queen, felt no shortage of astonishment.

"I don't understand," exclaimed Rasputhane as he clung to the arm of the Iron Queen. "What of Lila's crimes? What of the murder pool?"

Gloriatrix quickly shook him off like a pest. "You are sniveling. It is disgusting. Speak to your king if you want to be kept abreast of the changing winds of war. The true enemy of Menos was revealed early this morning by survivors of the calamity. If you were a spymaster worth his salt, you would know that by now. Furthermore, I hereby declare the murder pool officially null and void. I shall have to make other plans for the restructuring of the Menosian diplomatic circle. Those plans certainly do not include our most recent enemy's spymaster. If you'll excuse me."

The Iron Queen spotted some of her aimless Ironguards, including the one whose gun she had stolen, and commanded them to escort her to sanctuary.

Displaying a greater sense of authority than people presumed him to have, the spymaster issued sharp commands to the lads and ladies of the Silver Watch. They had been loitering around in the destruction, dumbfounded, but at the sound of his commands, these consummate warriors stiffened, focused, felt new determination. Once his contingent had been assembled and rallied with some of Gorijen's late-arriving legion, he'd issued orders for groups to scour the marketplace for those injured or worse. Then he went to meet the king.

By then, Magnus had covered much ground and was somewhere amid a ring of warrior women and men. As he drew closer, the queen's army appeared even grander and more intimidating, and Rasputhane's force seemed tinier. Before the wall of glaring Arhadians, they tread like worried mice. It was rather eerie, how little conversation he heard among the ranks of the queen's army. Their discipline was impressive, as strong as that of the silver folk at his side, and he could not fathom where, or even how, Lila had assembled such a force.

The spymaster found the red-and-white spot that was his king. Magnus stood near the gate, whistling out into the desert. The former Hammer, nude but for a cloak wrapped around his waist, was at his side. Magnus, too, had been clothed in a ratty crimson cloak. Behind them, assessing, calculating, was a sultry enchantress who Rasputhane knew quite well: Lila. Past the queen leered the stone-faced female horde. Their stoniness deeply unsettled the spymaster. At least there was a more pleasant smell here, which he found strangely soothing, like a room of incense. However odd it sounded, he felt as if the smell came from Lila. She studied him, a snake watching a rat, as he left his contingent and approached the softly talking dignitaries.

"My king. M-my queen?" he said uncertainly, and bowed.

Magnus and the queen traded glances that spoke of agreements already made, then the king turned to his aide. "Your queen, yes—although a redistribution of rights, titles, and responsibilities will be written into a charter when peace provides us an opportunity. For the moment, Lila remains our queen, and I remain your king."

Suspicious wording, thought Rasputhane, that signaled tumultuous changes in the royal cabinet; hopefully, there would still be need for a spymaster. "As you say. I shall inform our criers and presses." He imagined that tomorrow would be their busiest day yet. "I've sent legions to assess the damage to the Faire of Fates and to our citizens." Magnus's shoulders slumped. "I've seen no bodies as of yet—a miracle. If I may, I have a few further questions, mostly about how to communicate our message about the great return of Her Highness...You see, Gloriatrix has dismissed the charges against the queen—"

"Has she?" Erik laughed.

"Yes," continued Rasputhane. "She speaks of another enemy, a greater one. I'm beginning to lose count of how many of those we now have."

"Every ancient force in creation," said the king, cast in gloom.

"All right—we shall need to devise a plan for battling *everything*. However, for the moment, let's address the giant spinrex in the room: the queen has returned, is no longer an enemy of Geadhain, and has brought with her...an army? To aid in the defense of our nation? Is that a credible enough explanation?"

"It should suffice," replied the king, and turned to Erik and the queen. Through this brief discussion, the new bloodmates had drifted slowly and steadily together, drawn by currents of attraction. They now stood as a pair of obsidian and tawny statues, perfect in their complementary beauty.

(Rasputhane noticed this, too, and knew then that all of the rumors of their affair were certainly true.) Magnus continued, sounding pained. "I would ask that you and Erik stay to defend what we have built."

"What we have built..." muttered Lila, and she surveyed the city, studied its silver highlights and valleys of towers and perfect houses. Was that happiness on her face? Rage? Rasputhane couldn't read her inscrutable stare or emotions, though they were intense.

Erik studied the city as well.

"Yes," said Lila and Erik in unison.

"Good," said Magnus. "You will understand if we have no immediate room for your army within Eod. I believe that setting up an encampment beyond the Great Wall would be best. Possibly—"

Lila interrupted him with a sting of venom. "My people will not be told where in the desert we may rule. We shall make our camp in the West, close to the Salt Forests, so neither our ways nor yours will be infringed upon."

Unperturbed, Magnus continued. "Well said. Distance will give our citizens time to adapt to yet another great power becoming entrenched outside Eod."

"What of the movements within?" asked the spymaster. "We have a city full of murderers and thieves who will be extremely annoyed that their bounty has been called off. I don't believe the Iron Queen will move to control any chaos caused by her capriciousness, which means that the responsibility for maintaining order will fall upon us."

"As it always has," said the king, and held his chin in thought. "The mercenaries will need to be routed, peacefully. Although..." As the sentence dangled, Rasputhane intuited that he would not like what Magnus said next. "They are men and women made for murder. I am sure that a few of them have honor buried under their callousness. We have all stepped onto the side of darkness before, and the bravest of us have returned from that journey."

"You're not suggesting..." Rasputhane didn't complete his thought; the notion was madness.

"The gears of war are oiled by choices," said Magnus. "We shall offer these mercenaries a choice. Either they leave our city in fair standing, or they stay and are conscripted into the service of Eod, the service of Geadhain. For we are the final bastion against my brother."

"You cannot turn hired murderers into valiant men," warned Rasputhane.

"We can all become valiant, or ignoble, when faced with our ends," countered the king. "Give them the choice. We need all the able and sword-wielding hands we can find. You do not know my brother. None of you understand him as I do. He is the ultimate hunter. Even his failures are merely steps toward his future triumph. He will have learned from each loss he has suffered, first in Zioch and then in Gorgonath. When Brutus comes for Eod—now all that remains to bind our continent together—he will bring a force he believes to be invincible. Look out into the desert, and picture every wave of sand bearing a crest of hideous soldiers, men twisted by his Will, and forged in metal and fire. Look up to the sky, and imagine a moon of blood."

The circle followed the king's narration. Except for Erik, they couldn't see past the soldiers that clustered in the arch of the Southern Gate; somehow, though, they felt as if the dunes flowed with red and black ants. When they gazed up at the emerging outline of the moon, they imagined redder hues in the iridescence of the Witchwall. Here Rasputhane's witch-tinged stare saw farther and more clearly than the gaze of the obsidian knight. He peered into the stream of Fate and saw ripples of danger—or rather, a spot. "What...is that?" he asked.

It was so incredibly far away. For an instant, he almost believed a piece of dirt had blown into his eye, for the thing stuck in his vision like a spot caused by staring at the sun. The spot was black, and it did not fade. A convulsive shiver racked him and twisted his stomach in a knot. His bowels dropped, then clenched in fear. He couldn't say why he was so terrified. Not until the dignitaries—monarchs, broken comrades, and even the Mind in its sightless way—described the mark in the heavens.

"Black," said the spymaster. "Something black."

All of the minuscule entities peering up at the cosmic event—however great their earthly power—sensed their insignificance in the face of the dark weight that was descending. In prophecies and on scrolls of flesh, by doomsayers, soothsayers, and witches, they'd been warned of this event.

In their souls, they all knew what was occurring. A shift. A changing of the order. The end of this era. For there, pulsing, lowering, and soon to hang clear above Geadhain, was a star. It was a star unlike any known celestial body, for it was made of darkness and antimatter, of hunger. It was a reflection of the Black Queen, who had at last returned to devour her home. The leaders quivered, Magnus most of all. They were not entirely sure what evoked in them the horrific terror of being devoured in a chattering jungle, the most primal of fears, but they knew the threat was real.

Then the presence from the depths of eternity spoke to her son. Finally, her cosmic body had drifted near enough to the veils that separated them to reach down through the millions of spans of space and air and slip a whisper into her son's ear. Magnus heard it as if she stood beside him, dripping madness and evil. **"You see me, my son. At last we are to be together. We shall begin the great work, the grand feast of which I have dreamed for ages beyond ages. Your Will remains strong, but it cannot resist me forever. I see that you are now unchained by love; you want to be filled. Good. We shall eat them first, the ones you loved. Passion makes for the sweetest meat. Surrender, my son. I shall fill you. I shall be your love. Surrender now, and save yourself the agony of being devoured."**

"Never!" declared Magnus.

He shrieked and threw up the strongest barrier he could conjure in his mind. Those around him were pushed back by a dazzling burst of green light and a hammer of freezing wind. When the pocket of whirling smoke separated, they saw Magnus curled in the dirt. He wouldn't rise or answer them.

XVIII

DEEPEST TRUTHS

I

Beauregard was amazed at how much he'd come to detest a man about whom he knew so little: Gustavius. Throughout their entire lengthy flight, they'd discussed next to nothing. Astonishing, considering they'd each recently dived into a waking dream of a nightmare civilization: the Mortalitisi and their wicked city, Veritax. Incredible, as they'd learned that everything they believed about their world was unfounded, and that reality was in truth ruled by crystals, elements, and divine beings.

Alas, the Iron lord wanted to discuss none of these things, and Beauregard spent most of his time in the skycarriage pondering these conundrums himself, while also wondering how to coax more secrets about these mysteries from Amara. He hated visiting her like this, as a spy more than a friend. As he arranged his thoughts, they passed over the scraped majesty of Mor'Khul with its charcoal twists, black valleys, and scorched earth. He remembered then why he had undertaken this duty: Amara must speak for the sake of the world. The Iron Lord sat and glowered on the opposite couch; his silence wasn't so oppressive when Beauregard remembered the real problems they faced.

When the flight landed in the heights of the Silent Peaks, and Beauregard and the Iron Lord walked along the zigzag of rocky road that led to the distant gray keep, he felt as grim and determined as his scowling companion. Monkish, gray-robed men bearing quarterstaffs met them at the gates of the bastion. They weren't greeted—and these men wouldn't have spoken anyway—but they were led immediately into the keep, as though they'd been expected. The Faithful escorted Beauregard and Gustavius through hallowed and quiet stone halls. Occasionally, a wind or rustle disturbed them, but all was as still as Beauregard recalled. Soon, Beauregard and Gustavius sat in Amara's quiet sanctum, awaiting her arrival. The Keeper had been detained: she had been overseeing rebuilding efforts below and hadn't been at the fortress when they arrived. She had had to be summoned, explained one of the Faithful in a note.

Today, fewer candles tempted a devastating fire in Amara's grand study. Still, one wrong gust of the wind, and the flames would spread from the fluttering stacks of papers to the heaps of scrolls that lay in organized chaos around him. Beauregard saw wisdom now in the fact that all of the shelves of this library had been carved out of stone; he wondered how many fires this ancient room had survived. He considered posing the question to Gustavius, but knew he would meet with no response. Boldly, he stared at the ghoul instead. *Who are you?*

Even hunched in the light from the sanctum's great window, the man appeared as if rendered in gray. Even sunlight couldn't relieve his pallor. In the light, he looked older, however, written in lines. A handsome fellow, perhaps, with a longish face and a full, groomed gray beard. Age be damned: the Menosian still possessed a muscular heftiness to his frame. Indeed, Gustavius was quite a large and menacing man. He barely fit upon one of the small stools that had been given to him and Beauregard for their wait. Beauregard couldn't place the man's ethnicity. The man's coloring suggested that he must hail from some place without much sun, or perhaps from a land where one needed to conceal oneself from the elements and therefore had no color at all.

"It is impolite to stare. Men are often killed for choosing the wrong object for their attention, for seeing the wrong thing," said Gustavius.

"I would like to believe that there's no threat of that between us," said Beauregard. The silence thereafter stung. However, the lad would not be daunted; his curiosity was too great. "Where are you from? I cannot place your features or accent."

Beauregard received a considered look from the man. Gustavius stood up, still glowering, then finally responded. "I am from the North. In the land where I was born, a man did not speak to one whose respect he hadn't earned. If he did so, he would learn his lesson—usually only once—through a fist. We do not know one another, spellsong of the king. We are not friends. We are but temporary allies until this war of wars ends, and we can once again engage in less catastrophic conquests. Make no mistake, either: Menos has not truly fallen. The Iron Empire will rise from the ruin into which it has been cast. I do not know you. I do not respect you. You are still my enemy, though I must tolerate you until I am allowed to call you that openly once more. In my homeland, our discussion would have ended days past with your missing teeth and my sore fist. Perhaps also with your corpse lying in the snow. That is all you need to know of me."

"Point taken," said Beauregard.

Engrossed in this exchange, neither noticed Amara's sudden appearance until a shadow drifted to Beauregard's side, and Gustavius turned towards it. Beauregard turned, too, as the youthful, olive-skinned, dark-eyed Keeper fluttered a small note against his ear.

"Hello again, friend," it read. "I am sorry to have kept you waiting."

"Is this the Keeper we are to meet?" asked Gustavius, and looked the young woman over as if she were a naked slave at auction. "She seems young, and unwise."

Beauregard leaped to her defense and to her side. "She is neither of those things. And we must respect the silence that these people cultivate; we must not use our voices." Amara strutted over to the Menosian and thrust a pad and quill at him.

The Iron lord took the items but then tossed them on the floor. "I shall not indulge in ridiculous ceremony. The fate of our world is at stake. You speak to her—or rather *write*. I expect to see each and every correspondence that the two of you share. I shall occupy myself with silence, then. Although I shan't be meditating."

With her hooked hands and huge eyes, Amara looked like a vengeful owl. Beauregard took her elbow and walked with her to her dais. She was trembling and gritting her teeth. This was the angriest he'd ever seen her, aside from the moment she'd learned of the duplicitous diplomatic warning from the former queen of Eod. He wondered if her anger would be further enflamed when she found out about his service to Magnus and to the kingdom that had betrayed her—if the silver-and-white garments hadn't already given him away. While she collected herself, Beauregard went to collect the discarded notepad and quill. A missive had been prepared in his absence. He read it. "I see you have not come in the spirit of friendship, that you are a ship caught in the tides of war. I see that crows now fly with the silver doves of Eod. I had heard of this aberration, but I did not believe that our world had become so imperiled that people would be driven beyond common sense. You cannot trust the crow. It is a trickster."

No sooner did Beauregard finish reading this than Gustavius loomed over him and snatched the note. "Perhaps she is wise after all," he said. Amara shook a fist at him, and he laughed, booming and rowdy as a drunk. Finally, he at last showed some respect and made the gesture of locking his lips with a key.

Amara wrote something else for Beauregard. The other note had been snatched back from the Iron lord and had vanished somewhere—into a candle, thought Beauregard. "It's good to see you, friend, hero of my people. I've forgotten neither you nor your father's sacrifice. We have a garden in his honor that I would like to show you one day."

Tears threatened Beauregard as he read her words. "One day," he wrote, and they shared a smile and squeezed each other's hand.

Amara burned that message and was again writing. She handed Beauregard her message, no longer smiling. "I am sorry that we cannot meet to honor your father. I am sorrier, still, that you need something from me that I cannot give."

What followed was a rapid exchange: notes written and then passed from Keeper to spellsong to Menosian to Keeper to flame, in a vicious circle.

"You know why we are here?" asked Beauregard.

"You wish to ask me something about my order," Amara replied. "I can hear the need, the pounding of your desire. Not for pleasure; I believe valor is your aphrodisiac. You want to know a secret."

"I do. I must know of the *Ioncrach*. Ones larger than the one I used to free the king."

Amara hesitated, and took great care penning her short reply. "I cannot speak of those."

But she'd confessed much about wonderstones, elementals, and Brutus's possible involvement with these forces during their tense preparations before Gorgonath's siege. Beauregard reminded her of this slip: "You already have. I know of the wonderstones, and something of the elementals—more now that I've seen the horror of Veritax."

Amara went snow white after reading his reply. "You should not seek this knowledge. Ever."

"I must."

"No." Amara slipped her arms into the sleeves of her monastic garment and gazed off to the side. Dust glittered in the light like faery folk. The happiness of the Keeper's reunion with the hero of Gorgonath should have eased her anger. However, the Iron shadow lurked in this very room, and Beauregard demanded that she say what must never be said to those who could not truly listen. Her friend was not familiar with the sinister nature of secrets. A single whisper, a forbidden ritual revealed, and whole empires could topple, entire lands verdant with the Green Mother's kiss could be razed. Beauregard didn't realize the dangers involved in the knowledge he sought. Certain evils should be buried in time. Certain wonders, the most powerful ones, must be forgotten, for they stirred dark intentions.

That was why Keepers were the caretakers and archivists of all the world's dangerous magik. They were never to use these miracles themselves. They were holy, above the temptation to abuse the Green Mother's secrets. She'd heard of a mad Keeper in the East, where stood the greatest cities of those who listened, whose people had fallen from their path, abused the Green Mother's trust, and succumbed to temptation. The mad Keeper had destroyed her city, erased thousands of years of wisdom and irreplaceable secrets. She'd done so by calling upon the very power that

Beauregard wanted to understand. His curiosity alone could unleash a catastrophe. However, he wouldn't leave, and she didn't look at him or ask him to.

The Menosian deduced that the tight-lipped priestess would certainly be more forthcoming if he allowed her and her friend a little space; whatever she shared with Beauregard, he could twist—literally—out of him later. Gustavius wandered off to snoop through the aisles of must and mystery. When Amara finally gazed at her friend, he saw there were tears in her eyes. By the time she had finished wiping them away with her sleeve, Beauregard had scribbled a note.

"We have only moments until the crow returns. You must tell me, Amara. I know that your order protects what it fears man will use only to destroy himself. However, whatever the secret, whatever that power, Brutus has it, and we cannot fight a war against a black miracle without having one of our own."

She held onto the message, unwilling to burn it just yet, her hands shaking. Beauregard wrote another. "Please. Or we are doomed. Everything you wish to protect and preserve is doomed."

Amara's training, although kinder than the indoctrinations of the East, had armored her heart against coercion or temptation. She burned his papers while softly crying. Beauregard caught her hand as it hovered in the smoke. He didn't grip her hard, or passionately, but she felt a tremble of love: soft love, meaningful love, the kind that romance and broken hearts would not dilute. "As the king's man, I shall be on the frontlines of the final war," whispered Beauregard, tempting her anger, showing his heart, as well as manipulating her with guilt. "I shall probably be one of the first to die."

Is this how it happens? wondered the Keeper. Did the first step into damnation begin with mercy? If so, then she was about to become the greatest sinner of her age and order. For she sat up, threw off her objections and tears, and quickly wrote down everything she knew of the wonderstones: the arkstones and the legends that told of ones even older than those—the wicked talismans of the Mortalitisi. She hoped that this secret would save her friend. It would be worth it, even if she had damned herself. Furious scribbling began.

My friend, any time a divine—or infernal—entity comes to our world, it must be made manifest through the real: as a blood moon, an asteroid, a tidal wave of fire. It cannot come and go invisibly like the wind. Legend says that when Zionae last came to Geadhain, a fragment of her cosmic mass, the Black Star, descended to our world in an ark of heavenly stone and fire—what the ancients referred to as a meteorite.

While much of her great ark deteriorated in the fall, four pieces survived the crashing inferno. These pieces were taken by the ancient people of the land where they had fallen: Pandemonia. The ancient tribes enshrined and honored the relics; such was the way of the Keepers even then. Our earliest legends speak of Zionae's kindness, her generosity: she gave us these relics to use for our protection, and the relics did protect the ancient people from the worst of the seasons of the world. However, when the Season of Dust began, and Zionae's benevolence and vessel were long departed, the shadow of the arkstones no longer offered enough protection; the ancient people starved, rotted from a black, incurable fever, and died. It's said that they began to eat each other once the worst of the hunger and madness set in.

Eventually, they fought over the power of Zionae's gifts—whether it should be enshrined, or instead tapped and used. We do not know exactly who inspired those who argued for the latter course...A whisperer. A wandering sorcerer without a face. We do know that he taught a wicked woman of my order, Teskatekmet, how to harness the incredible powers trapped in the arkstones. We know this whisperer was real, and that he must have been a demon, for no man or sorcerer of Geadhain could have had such knowledge. Many of my ancestors sailed from our homeland to other lands. They wanted nothing to do with their mad countrymen, with relics of the ark, and the seduction of their power as promised by Teskatekmet. Much of my ancient tribe remained in Pandemonia, though, embroiled in civil war. In the end, the warmongers amongst us took the arkstones for themselves. The bounty was split between them: one arkstone was taken north, one south, one east, and one west. There, they were used to build empires of obscene power. The people did not worship the stones, though; instead, they revered the kingdoms and achievements built through sacrilege.

Later, one of the great cities fell to madness, and one of the arkstones was split. A mad Keeper split it, or so the story goes—though I am not sure how an eternal object could be sundered. Perhaps a combination of grief, magik, and insanity created the perfect tool for her task. We who listen believe that the Black Queen, transformed into a vengeful mother by the abuse of her gifts, came to the mad Keeper and offered her the power needed to break the stone, to end its magik: without it, Aesorath was unmade in specks. Or perhaps there was something in Aesorath that Zionae feared, or wanted no other to claim. Zionae giveth, and she taketh away. We cannot say why. We do not know why she has returned to Geadhain, not as a bearer of life, but as a bringer of death. I have as many questions as you when I consider our fate and past.

Know, too, that when I say that an arkstone is eternal, I mean that it can never be lost, only fragmented. Destroying an arkstone would unmake any enchantments cast while it was whole, but it wouldn't destroy the power of whatever shards remained. I have heard, from voices in the East, that these shards were sought for by the leaders of the Great Cities, but never found. Now Aesorath is merely avoided as a cursed reminder of how pride condemns us to fall. However, the danger remains. A power so great endures. One tiny shard would have the might to chain the Elemental of Fire, at least for a time. Imagine what evils a mad Keeper and a mad king might do with the shards they hold; we've seen some of this dark future already, here in Gorgonath. How many shards were salvaged from Aesorath? At least one. Nothing else could chain the Father of Fire. With a whole arkstone, one unblemished and unbroken, Brutus could command the elemental to cover the world in fire— nothing, save for the sleeping wyrm of frost, would be capable of cooling his rage.

No sooner had Beauregard finished reading Amara's final words than Gustavius returned from his poke about the library. Amara stole and burned the last in her series of messages more quickly than a shady gambler swapping dice. Nonetheless, the words remained branded in the spellsong's mind.

Beauregard knew that for a long time, possibly her whole life, the Keeper would feel guilt for having written these notes. He felt guilty, too, as if he'd forced her to sin with his sugary pleas. As he and the Iron lord were leaving, he ran back, bowed, and kissed his friend's cheek. He couldn't speak his apologies, but he wanted to express his contrition. *You need not suffer. I shall bear your secret with honor and see that you are not defamed*, he thought. Beauregard was unclear how much of the sentiment penetrated Amara's cold facade. When he glanced back, she was touching the faded impression of his kiss and staring down at the floor.

II

The trip through the keep's gray and quiet hallways was as brief and unreal as an afternoon dream. Once inside the skycarriage, Gustavius pestered Beauregard over what secrets he kept, but the lad remained reticent. He watched Gorgonath's vividly painted towers fade with a sense of measured sadness, and spoke not a single word in the many hourglasses of flight it took to arrive in Bainsbury.

From above, and obscured by the looming hand of night, the land looked as glum as Beauregard's mood. Below, things weren't much different; once they had landed, they walked among the tin-patched byres and brushed their knees against the sheep that had escaped the thin fences and taken charge of the mucky, winding roads. Even then, Beauregard only grumbled at the lazy creatures to move. Regardless of the fickle day, which waffled between drizzling and torn bright skies, Bainsbury was a rural treasure. Beneath the waft of recent rain and soil, the air smelled of green: freshly broken grass, daffodils, lavender. A good salt breeze drifted in from the rolling glory of the Feordhan, too, and the two spotted the river hiding behind hillocks and houses. Mud soon covered the men, but the salt air and charm of Bainsbury eventually enlivened Beauregard, and he managed to smile at passersby, who bowed and seemed to know of his appointment with the king. They mostly ignored the grim giant walking with him.

Beauregard's renewed confidence waned after he mounted a frontier-style porch and noticed a few of the wicker baskets and yellow forsythia plants that his mother so adored. Tabitha must possess something of his real mother's—her sister's—verdant and magik thumb, he realized; she always had plants around, and they survived well into the colder season. He took a breath and loudly rapped on the wood of her door. It was time to speak of Belle, Devlin, and Galivad.

No answer or sounds came from inside the house. A tune floated toward the pair, though—a tingle of music. It was a folksong from Willowholme, and perhaps another glint of the faery heritage that existed in Tabitha's bloodline. She'd never sung when Devlin was around, as his father had been opposed to revelry, and Beauregard had annoyed his father with his own antics and strumming. What a lovely voice she possessed: a bit hoarse and smoky, yet certainly female. The men followed the tune around back to a sparse yard where a lean woman in a white apron and blue frock was stringing up laundry. The woman's tousled sandy hair was nearly the same shade as Galivad's; they were all related, it seemed. She was an aunt to him and his brother, though, not a mother. How it stung Beauregard to have all these truths exposed and whirling in his chest like a nest of bees; he had to let the secrets out. As Tabitha's back was to the men, she leaped when she turned to retrieve more clothing from her basket and noticed the shadows standing in her yard.

"Beauregard!" she cried, and ran to him.

Rather embarrassingly, she pecked him in kisses. In a moment, she noticed the gray, sour hulk and the absence of Beauregard's father. Forthright as ever, she asked, "Who's this lug? And where is your father?"

"He is an envoy from the Iron City, which is an ally of the West now, as you surely know," replied Beauregard. Then he held his mother firmly by the meat of her arms, which were no longer as meaty, he found. She looked thinner but beakishly pretty now that the sallowness of starvation from her wasting in Willowholme had been banished by nourishment. However, the lad didn't know of her trials any more than he'd confided in her of his time in the Summerlands. Mother and son realized they each had agonies to share.

Gustavius wandered past the clothesline and leaned against the backyard's single tree. He'd noticed something in the ripple of misty green and blue in the distance that he felt he should watch. But really, he was giving the mother and her son time alone with each other; he knew what bad news looked like. Beauregard and Tabitha walked to the shade of the house and sat upon two spindly chairs. They held hands for a while without speaking and watched a pair of blackbirds—pretty things, though heralds of grief—dancing on the dewy lawn. The fool creatures had no idea winter would soon be here, and yet they could not be blamed for their ignorance, considering the continued good weather. Like those silly birds,

Tabitha sensed she had been ignorant of the truth; she had been trying to find comfort in the long letters she received, despite that they avoided any mention of her husband.

"You first," said Tabitha, finally and bravely. "I already know this isn't a casual visit. Tell me how your father died."

Grief fell from each as Beauregard described his journey in the Summerlands. He shared his experience as honestly as he had with Amara. No horror or wonder was spared; his mother deserved to know. When he told her of Devlin's confession upon the battlements, of how he wasn't their biological son, Tabitha swallowed, clenched her jaw, and closed her eyes as if in pain. In a moment, that passed without a whimper. She kissed the hands of her son when he completed the crescendo of his tale of war, loss, valor, and death. Then they hugged.

"He died more bravely than I ever could have imagined. More bravely than a hero. My dear big old bear..." she whispered.

"My father," said Beauregard, and then sobbed.

After a while, they rose from the embrace. Bainsbury's false spring appeased them with its symphony of cricket flutes and rustling trees. The sky seemed darker than its usual spotty overcast gray could account for, and no more flashes of sunlight appeared. The Menosian had vanished, but there was a black imperfection on one of the distant hills that could be him.

"What of you, Mother?" asked Beauregard.

Their relationship would never change, no matter what truths were revealed; both the life they had shared and Devlin's sacrifice would ensure that. Tabitha smiled with melancholy kindness. "Oh, I was given the mercy of the Everfair King and sent here to live in reasonable peace. But it's hard to accept stability in one place when you know the rest of the world is being thrown into chaos. So I've never felt at ease here. You know of what I speak, don't you? The shiver in the world. Geadhain is afraid, and I am afraid with Her."

"I do." He wished he could say more, but he hadn't been able to make sense of the spiraling, escalating doom himself. Even the answers he had been ordered to seek had stirred only further questions. Arkstones. Mad Keepers and civil wars. A wyrm of fire and a wyrm of frost. And what in the blazes had Amara meant about *infernal* powers? Perhaps it had been a slip of the tongue, but his intuition told him otherwise. Was a demented Dreamer not enough of a threat to Geadhain? What could more seriously damage the shreds of peace a man wove together from life's tatters? *The king sent me to find a means to end Brutus, and I have found neither that nor much else we could use against his brother. Every mystery has a mystery. Every past is splintered. I am already sick of being so ignorant, so small,* he thought.

Beauregard's mother had no difficulty divining his moods. "You take a moment and breathe away your troubles, my son," she said, and patted his knee. Tabitha stood. "I shall make us tea. The first step toward feeling better is feeling warmer, and it's suddenly gotten cold out here. I shall fetch myself a shawl, I think."

Tabitha left, and soon the sounds of clattering dishes and weeping resounded through the thin walls of her house. When she returned to her child, however, she was quite poised, if a tad red around the eyes. A knitted woolen shawl hung upon her shoulders, and she carried two saucers and cups of tea, slightly milky and unsweetened, as Beauregard preferred. She sat, and they heard a grumble from the somber clouds. A stiff wind blew the steam from their drinks into their faces. Tabitha blinked as a wet, cold fleck struck her eye; at last, there was snow. The rainy season had ended: winter was here. They sipped their tea and watched the season change.

"You don't seem troubled," said Beauregard.

"By the weather?"

"Don't be smart, Mother."

Tabitha glanced down, watching the ripples in her cup; she saw a sad and weeping woman behind the steel mask she wore. "I can't be troubled. I don't have the opportunity to grieve right now. I made a bit of a mess inside a moment ago—you might have heard that. However, none of us can take a moment's pause for tears, burials, or love, even, until the War of the Kings has ended. I feel as if the atrocities in the Summerlands and Gorgonath were but playground skirmishes. I cannot imagine what will happen when Brutus and Magnus, with their awesome power and fearsome armies, clash. I could very well be destroyed in that inferno. We all could. You certainly have a spirit of luck on your side, though, my son. If I am to depart and join my husband in what comes after, then I shall leave you as he did: honorably, bravely. I hope to live on as a worthy memory. I won't have you thinking of me any other way."

"I shall always remember you that way, Mother."

"Good."

It was strange to know one's parent as an adult, as a fellow mourner, as a flawed and yet somehow perfect person. Winter gave a hiss from the clouds as it cast a gentle white breath upon Bainsbury. Elsewhere, farm folk could be heard urging their stubborn livestock off the road—they seemed to be bleating and putting up a terrible fuss for the farmhands. Beauregard didn't feel the need to ask his mother anything more about what consumed her mind. She was strong and capable. She blinked only occasionally as the snow flew into her eyes. He remembered her hardiness; he had missed it. After they had drunk the last of their tea, they sat with cold cups and cold hands waiting for nothing in particular, for the hourglasses to pass and the emotions within them to settle. Beauregard did not know how long he'd be able to stay. At least until dinner, he decided. Neither he nor the Iron lord had eaten today, and soldiers couldn't live merely on tea and bloodlust.

Just as Beauregard began to question where his unwanted attaché might be, Tabitha spotted the black dot again; it was easier to see now that the land was whitening. "Your gloomy companion," she said, then squinted. "Running. I'd recognize a large man's jog anywhere—your father, bull that he was, ran like a cart off its horse."

Beauregard stood, and Tabitha quickly collected their cups and placed them on their vacant seats. The pair strode past the flapping clothesline and the tree that was now buckling under the rising, unpleasant wind. Behind them, one or many of the porcelain cups or saucers blew off the chairs and shattered against the wall of Tabitha's house. Mother and son dashed through the field feeling the sickness of danger. Grass and wind whipped at them. Winter had given up any attempt to be subtle, and spurts of snow interspersed with spattering gobs of freezing rain ran over their faces like spittle. Tabitha could now smell a fishy, putrid stench like that of the rotten skin of Lake Tesh—it wound her nerves into spirals. Something wicked was stirring.

As she and Beauregard climbed a small hill, they lost sight of Gustavius, who'd just descended a mound. A moment later, Tabitha clutched her son's arm, and the two of them reeled back as the Iron lord charged toward them. Gustavius's shout blasted through the drizzling howl of the weather. "Back, you fools! Back to the skycarriage!"

Tabitha and her son had survived enough terror to know not to question a call of danger. Smaller and nimbler than he, they were able to match the furious racing of the Iron lord. Behind them, the land roiled with unwholesome sounds: thunder, which shouldn't really occur in a winter storm, and noises that reminded Tabitha of gargling beasts. But from how many throats? The noise was loud enough to suggest legions. The fishy scent crept over them now, as if a wharf's worth of gutted fish was blowing in from the East. She wouldn't look behind them to see what caused the smell. Part of bravery was the ability to mentally retreat from madness, and she now did just that.

All around them, the storm pummeled the world: under a distorted shroud of white, they could see only figments of houses and landmarks. A sparkle lay off to the left, beyond the brown watercolor shacks. Tabitha knew it must be one of the king's glorious skycarriages. As they hurried toward the sparkle, the storm smothering the land grew catastrophic: the wind tore in all directions and was a force against which they had to push. Something awful had come to Bainsbury. Something rotten, vile, and—or so the stink suggested—possibly dead. Most definitely, she caught the sounds of burps, half-gasps, and wheezes from a thousand throats: a horde. Although she wondered what a rotting army looked like, she stayed her course in bravery and refused to test her courage with a glance. Whatever the horde was made up of, it moved fast, nearly as fast as the three of them. The skycarriage seemed agonizingly far away.

How they reached the vessel, which had landed in one of the farmer's meadows that rolled between split-rail fences, was a mystery, nearly a miracle. From inside the carriage, a watchman and an Ironguard shouted and waved to them. They, too, must have seen the wave that was crashing down upon Bainsbury.

Beguiled by her moment of safety, seduced by morbid curiosity, Tabitha turned. The hills were writhing and nearly black. An undulating, dark-gray scab was spreading over the whitened-green as quickly as paint running over glass. It colored and defiled everything it touched. Blurred as they were by the storm, it took Tabitha several specks to realize that the uncountable oscillations were the movements of many forms. Every twist and shudder seemed like the spasm of a flagging, decomposed arm—or some other wiggling part of a stumbling, maggot-filled, jaw-dangling, chewed-up monster draped in seaweed that had pulled itself from the depths of the Feordhan.

"The dead!" barked Gustavius, spitting with horror and confirming Tabitha's dread. "Get inside the craft! Now!"

"The dead?" exclaimed Beauregard, also watching as the blackish wave consumed the hills at a pace impossible to believe. Wildly, he waved his arms. "I don't even understand what's happening. And the people of Bainsbury! We cannot leave them! We cannot—"

Beauregard never saw the punch coming—unlike his mother, who had watched silently as the Menosian clenched his fist. In that moment, she had measured the value of her child's life against that of others—many others—with the kind of pitilessness only a mother could possess. Tabitha prayed that her child would never learn of her decision, or that he would forgive her if he did. There was simply no way to save these people from this tsunami of death. Like a wave, it had crested and was now rolling down the valley to her home. The wave of raging, shambling shapes spat from a sea of the darkest doom would be at the nearest house in specks. Within a few sands, all of Bainsbury would be consumed by whatever unholy enemy had just shown itself. Tabitha took what felt like a long look at the churning, wavering atrocity. The scent drove her into the sterile steel skycarriage before the Menosian could decide to round her up as he had her son. The skycarriage shot away from Bainsbury.

Tabitha never made it to a seat, and was thrown around a bit in the short hallway before the vessel reached a decent altitude and steadiness. At that point, she stopped clinging to the handles built into the walls, entered the passenger chamber, and settled on a couch near the feet of her groaning child. Surprisingly, the Iron lord had put a cushion on his thigh for her son to rest his head on. A further shock came when he applied a black satin cloth, with white-knuckled pressure, to her son's throbbing nose. "It hasn't been broken," said the Menosian, as if that should pardon him. "I shall hold him here for a while until the bleeding stops."

Beauregard mumbled a few words, nothing intelligible. Sands trickled by without meaning like the pellets of rain or wet snow cast upon the windows. Tabitha unlaced her son's boots and massaged his feet as she did when he was ill or in need of comforting. This appeared to wake him, but she would have roused him herself, in case of a concussion. He jolted up, threw the rag off his face, batted at the Menosian, and then stumbled to the window. After gazing out at mist and nothingness, he pounded the glass and finally shuffled over to the other couch. There, he collapsed. He snorted blood and mucus. He looked more fearsome than fair. Indeed, as he stared at the two people opposite him, anger and sorrow cast his face in wrinkles that belied his youth.

"How could you leave those people there? To die? At the hands of...I don't know. Evil."

"I watched them rise out of the Feordhan," said the Iron lord, and trembled. "The smell was what drew me, and a feeling, a sense of wickedness. I watched Evil as it rose from the Feordhan. An army of drowned souls. Barnacled, rotten, some of them burned, I believe—though I did not stay to look and linger, and set off running. They could have walked beneath the water all the way from the cinders of Menos. I believe they did." Gustavius shuddered and was done with words.

Tabitha had still to thank the Iron lord for his intervention, as she knew Beauregard would have charged off thinking to save the day. Perhaps by helping to explain, she could repay some of his charity. "Not everyone can be saved, Beauregard. As much as you wish it, as much as you try. It is not war without death. In this battle, the death, the doom...It's only now beginning. Come sit with me."

Tabitha pondered wars, hordes of the dead, and how small she and her light of a child were in this great darkness. With no great solace to offer, she closed her eyes, listened to the rain, appreciated even this bitter moment of safety with her son, and prayed they would have at least a few more days together. Eventually, Beauregard, sniffling and unsure, came to sit beside his mother. They did not speak, though they were together.

XIX

A TRICK OF FATE

I

"I feel as if we've been here countless times before," whispered Thackery.

No one was certain what he meant, but this surely was a strange place. The sorcerer, Adam, Morigan, and Caenith stood apart from the clusters of warriors gathered in an antechamber of crystal and humming silence. The companions had learned this was the bailey before the Purgatorium. It was the heart and bowels of Eatoth, a place that created an ear-throbbing impression of great depth and made one believe in the myths of damnation and enlightenment as preached by the Lakpoli. Ahead, wards and legionnaires assembled quietly in phalanxes—their weapons and stares gleamed with readiness. Aside from Longinus, who'd been reassigned to the company, the rest of Eatoth's Faithful maintained a respectful distance from the outsiders. Morigan sensed that while she and her fellows were being tolerated, they still weren't welcome. She assumed that even a minor change would be viewed as an upheaval by people so used to a smoothly functioning, serene existence.

Morigan's small company stood guard outside the arch and the sealed, glassy door leading into Purgatorium. Morigan's bloodmate was at her side. She shared his frown, his doubts, and even his position—both rested a hand upon the barrier of translucent crystal beyond which throbbed the arkstone. Like the Wolf, she doubted it was any better than a wall of paper. The Wolf had been testing its resilience with slaps of his hands, though, and it appeared to be durable—enchanted and saturated in magik, like all else in Eatoth. As hard as the material was, his father would be able to shatter it in a strike or two. Sullenly, he and Morigan looked at their companion.

"Been here before?" she asked.

"I thought you hadn't heard me," replied Thackery. "I feel as if we've already been in this situation. Peril. Doom. Standing around waiting for tragedy to strike. Another thin edge of hope along which we must walk. Remember, we always find our balance on that precipice. We always make the journey. We shall survive whatever comes." Thackery rose from his hunch and stretched his legs. Adam stirred from his sulk and came over to his companions. The two fellows and Morigan gathered and smiled for the first time since they'd descended to Purgatorium to await the coming of the mad king. Hourglasses had passed while restlessness frayed their nerves. Thackery's hope was a tonic for each of their private despairs.

"It's all coming together," he continued, almost cheery. "Once we've repelled this madman and subdued him, we can cast his demon out. Assuming, of course, that the Keeper Superior stays true to her word and allows us—well, you—to handle their precious arkstone." Now that the company of heroes realized a piece of the corrupted Dreamer lay just in the other chamber, Morigan would soon know everything about their foe: the Dreamer's deepest, darkest truths. "We are ready, my friends. Today will be our moment of triumph."

Inside his bloodmate, Caenith's beast growled and paced. While the others engaged in wistful chatter about Mouse and whatever antics their missing companions might be experiencing, Morigan reached out to her bloodmate.

My Wolf? You fear this moment, don't you?

I know not if I have the strength to conquer him. I know not if I should be here or out on the field of battle.

She understood his anxiety. They knew very little of Brutus's plan. How would he enter the city? How would he—or his army—circumvent the wall of pounding water, or the flooding of the catacombs? Why couldn't she sense anything in the currents of Fate—anything aside from the bodily beat of her fear? If she dwelled on the possibilities, she'd drive herself mad. Morigan didn't insult her bloodmate by attempting to placate him with suggestions that Brutus wouldn't reach the antechamber. Brutus needed the treasure behind them to complete his conquest of Geadhain— that was why they were stationed here. Besides, the wondrous skycarriages of Eatoth could ferry them nearly anywhere in a speck. Brutus might possess speed and ease of movement, but his horde did not—if there were to be a frontline, the Wolf could be on it in sands.

My Wolf, you are not alone. The Keeper Superior is safe, under more guard than we ourselves could give her, and we are close to the only place we know Brutus will strike. At her feet lay a set of great shackles made of crude black iron. The chains looked simple and old-fashioned, but they produced a jolt of power when held against bare skin. Morigan kicked the feliron snake and her companions jumped before realizing there was no threat and returning to their conversation. *Once he has been subdued, these chains should work to bind him and his power until he can be purged of the Black Queen and judged for his crimes.*

Do you truly believe that he can be chained? How can one chain fire and madness?

Once, Morigan would've doubted that even technomagik forged by the Keepers of Pandemonia could bind the king—but earlier on, before they had assembled for war, Ankha had insisted it could. When the Keeper Superior had shown him the shackles, the Wolf had huffed in disbelief and slipped one manacle around his wrist, then abruptly slumped to the floor as if sapped of all strength. The feeling of nausea and lassitude he'd suffered was extraordinary. *Reverse etherocurrent distributors*, Ankha—slightly gloating—had called the technomagikal witchery. Then she'd ordered one of the wards to aid the lethargic Wolf in removing the relic, which were harmless to handle, other than being quite tingly, so long as you weren't the one in the manacle. She'd explained that the technomagik intensified and redirected power away from itself. Essentially, when clasped on a man's wrists, the bindings turned him into a grounded conduit, a lightning rod that discharged magik—his own magik—into the earth. Whether the shackles would affect a full-blooded Immortal as they had his son, whether they'd even be able to restrain a raging giant long enough to place the shackles on, were questions that would be answered only when they confronted Brutus himself. Ankha insisted that the distributors would function as desired and would, through molecular reorganization (which only Thackery understood, slightly), fit a wrist of any size, too, when the time came.

However, these worries were less pressing to the Wolf than thoughts of encountering his father in the first place. As his mind wended through these tangles, Morigan—creeping about her bloodmate's head, not entirely intentionally—sensed the root of his fear. *Ah. I see, my Wolf. It's not the war itself, but what will come after it that concerns you most.*

Yes. My mother asked me to forgive him. I do not know how to forgive one so wicked.

Morigan petted his warm furry chest, then kissed it. She took a long sniff of his wood-and-spice scent. She felt a calm sense of assurance that they'd emerge victorious from any war. She loved him too much to fail. *First, we must best him: only your strength and speed can do that. You must be the one to chain your father, and in that I see a shade of justice. From there, if we succeed, we shall discover our course.*

And if he cannot be chained?

You know the answer to that, my Wolf. What we were made for, what we are capable of doing.

We shall kill him, they agreed.

It would be their last course of action; contemplating it, the Wolf drew his bloodmate in for an embrace. As the Sisters Three had warned, undoing an Immortal would not come without a cost: one of them might die. He wouldn't kill his father if it meant losing her. He'd find another way. He'd beat and bloody his cursed father into such a bleating state of submission that the chains would seem a mercy. While holding Morigan, his heat and growl grew.

As emotions tended to muddle a man that was also part animal, Morigan gently ended their embrace when she felt his rage blurring into other hotter emotions. There would be time for rolling and biting later. They had an Immortal to defeat and a vile parasite to banish from Geadhain. Now was the time.

For her bees were finally now abuzz in the hive of Morigan's mind: a moment of Fate was approaching. An electric tingle passed into her bloodmate, and they stiffened and leaned forward like dogs catching a scent. They stared toward the end of the antechamber. Wards and legionnaires formed a sea of bowing heads as a figure approached. The waves of men parted and revealed a small figure in gray. In the bluish hues of the chamber, she wavered like a woman under water. Or perhaps that was a supernatural reality only the bloodmates could perceive: perhaps no others could see the shadow that dwarfed Ankha's tiny figure or smell the sickening scent of dead love: burnt roses and sweet decay. This was not the Keeper Superior: it was the shade of the Dreamstalker, wearing her skin.

"Who's that?" asked Thackery, straining.

"The Keeper Superior," replied Adam.

"No," hissed Morigan. "It's Amunai!"

"Foul witch!" roared the Wolf.

Over the murmuring discord, they heard Amunai laugh, then speak—her spiteful voice hollow, haunting, as if cast across a chasm of screams. Her buzzing words, the utterances of a witch, could be understood by all in the chamber. "Your perceptions are keen, Daughter of Fate and her dog. But you've misplaced your forces. The Sun King isn't here."

"*Na stamatích tian*! (Seize her!)" cried Longinus, evidently the sharpest soldier in the room. Stumbling legionaries, obviously confused by this Keeper who was somehow not their Keeper and seeing none of the taint of possession that the bloodmates could, took too long to react. The warriors closest to the Keeper leaped and reached for her, but she twisted away and vanished in a wrinkle of black smoke. Somehow, she'd moved as Morigan could, but even faster. The bloodmates next heard her laughing *behind* them, on the other side of the sealed barrier. A great crash and sparking symphony arose from the frame of the arch they'd been guarding, and Longinus and their four companions moved back. The phosphorescent blue veins that lit the antechamber flickered, and the smoke of broken technomagik billowed forth.

After waving their hands through the clouds of singed electrical fumes, the companions quickly determined they were whole and then rushed the door. No amount of prying and grunting from the Wolf or any of the others budged the door upward—as it was supposed to slide—inward, or in any other direction. From the tunnel beyond came another laugh from the spirit that had taken Ankha's body.

"That door is warded with every magik my people know," said the Dreamstalker. "Rituals older than the first age of the Immortal Kings. It cannot be broken by the son of Brutus, or even by Brutus himself. Only a Keeper can pass through Purgatorium's gate. Perhaps you can follow me, Daughter of Fate. Come then, Morigan, if you are brave enough to take the leap. See if you can stop me."

The Wolf roared and slammed the door with his shoulder; it didn't even tremble. Amunai cackled, the sound echoing away. In the smoke and commotion, they had mere specks in which to execute a plan, a sand or more before the arkstone would be taken. How had they been so duped? Where was Brutus? His army? Subterfuge, not might, was the thorn that had crippled the mighty giant of Eatoth.

"Go after her!" snarled the Wolf. "Catch that witch, and carve her up with your blade of promise. I care not if her vessel must die; the arkstone would be a far greater loss. I know another way, a slower way, to join you. Go now, and I shall be by your side soon." As he barked his orders, the Wolf half-transitioned into his other self: his eyes clouded and glowed silver, his hands warped into partial claws. He gripped the side of the arch and began to scale the wall. "Adam, Thackery, keep these fools safe while we defend their city."

Neither the Wolf nor Morigan remained to watch how their friends—and the lone sensible legionnaire—dealt with the mob of wards and legionnaires that now charged toward Purgatorium's door. In a sterling dazzle, Morigan vanished, and the Wolf speedily clawed his way upward and into the ventilation shaft he'd previously used. The hunt was on.

II

After a dash through Dream, Morigan appeared in a whirlwind of silver light. She stood inside a cavernous chamber that trapped the dark weight of the earth under a film of glass. *Fragile,* she thought, *much like Eatoth's greatness, which could be undone by pulling a single pin.* The rest of the awesome technomagikal splendor of this sanctum she disregarded, concentrating instead on the pillar of blue starlight—again trapped in glass—and the dark figure that fumed shadow before it.

Morigan pulled out her promise dagger. She took one tortured moment to think. In times of war, morality was an indulgence. On the battlefield, there were winners and losers, the living and the dead. No other distinctions could be made. It was unfortunate, but unavoidable: the Keeper Superior must die if this invading spirit were to be cast out. Morigan felt no great compassion for the wicked sister, as she'd driven Amunai to seek the Black Queen's evil grace. Perhaps a death sentence for both sisters would be fair.

Morigan took a breath, then stepped into and out of Dream once more. She swung as she glimmered back into the world, and aimed down with such murderous force that whatever her blade met would encounter a blood-fountaining end. Her murderous howl became a scream as she fell to her knees and her dagger struck the crystal floor. The floor remained unmarked, but her assault caused her hand and wrist to shiver with pain. Morigan pounced up, feral, and glared around the chamber.

Amunai snickered from afar—she was now nearly back where Morigan had been. "Daughter of Fate. How special you believe yourself to be. You're an instrument, a weapon—as you have proven through your attempts to murder me. You're as much a hound of war as your bloodmate."

Morigan shrieked and danced into and out of Dream again. She was certain she'd slice the witch this time. Again, she swung blindly into the air. From another safe vantage point, hundreds of strides away, Amunai laughed at her derisively. "Look at you, crude and clawing like an angry cat in a sack. You cannot touch me in the real world, where elements rule! I was the Keeper of Aesorath! The Lady of the Winds. North, South, East, and West all whispered their secrets to me. Our sages had mastered the mysteries of flight before wise men of the West even dreamed they might, one day, fly. We *invented* what you primitives revere as the impossible art of translocation: we sang to the wind and it carried our atoms from one place to the next in an instant. You have no idea what power I possess! I am the wind of the underworld. I blow where I choose as freely as Death.

In Dream, you might be faster, wilier, better aware of which paths to take. But this is my world. My domain. You cannot touch me in the flesh. I am gone, like a breeze, before you can even think of trying."

"My bloodmate will be here in a moment; you should not test his speed," spat Morigan.

"More meaningless threats." The shadow woman flickered about the chamber, leaving trails of black smoke. Amunai gloated, her lunatic laughter resounding in the space like the wails in a funhouse of horror: it was magnified as her shadows appeared and vanished faster than the echo of sound. "I shall thank him, too, when he arrives. For you have done what I could not: unmake Eatoth. As this city falls, I want you to know—and suffer from the knowledge—that *you* have destroyed it."

"Stop your wicked lies!" screamed Morigan.

Slowly, the many wisps of darkness stilled, and the apparitions faded. Now there was only one distant shadow that mocked her. "Oh, but you have. When I realized how strong you were—your mind, your power—and how that would interfere with my aims, I knew your strength was an opportunity. How does the mouse defeat the scorpion? She leads the scorpion to a pool of water, where it sees and strikes at a reflection. The mouse lets the scorpion defeat itself. That is what I have done with you, Daughter of Fate.

"Keepers are the cornerstones of their cities. Their astonishing Wills hold all magik and order in their civilizations together. We are chosen for our Will, and for our mental fortitude against suggestion. We are chosen because we cannot be tainted. We cannot be influenced. Our minds can never be breached. Ankha was one of the greatest Keepers. Her wall of Will could not be broken. I could not reach her with my whispers. Yet you...Daughter of Fate...You shattered her wall. You drew out her weakness. You filled her with doubt. Through the door you opened in her mind, at last I could enter her. When I say that Eatoth falls because of you, I tell no lie."

"No..." muttered Morigan, spinning, though the rush of her bloodmate's anger kept her from falling into a faint. "I refuse to listen to your deceptions. I know what I have seen: the city of Eatoth in flames, the mad king himself standing in the ruins. This is some illusion or trick of yours.

That is all you possess: lies." In a shimmer of silver light, Morigan sped down the river of Dream, before emerging from the grayness and swinging her blade at a furl of laughing blackness. She missed, again.

Morigan turned toward Amunai's fading laughter. She saw the specter hovering near the glass tube that held the fragment of the divine. "Daughter of Fate," said Amunai. "I am good at tricks, about this you are right. I have challenged even Charazance, the Dreamer of Chance, with my latest gambit. For I have deceived not only you, but Fate itself."

Morigan trembled. Her bees flew wildly in her skull, their stingers piercing the matter behind her eyes. Visions made her stumble and clench her head. A city in flames. Amunai whispering into the ear of a horrible shadow: Brutus. An army marching through a blasted desert. How could none of this be true? She'd seen the future herself.

"Fate is only possibility," shouted Amunai, impassioned by her triumph. "If we speak of something enough, if we generate enough Will and unified purpose, then what *could be* becomes what likely *will be*. That is why, instead of sending Brutus to Eatoth, I sent him to Intomitath. I could have sent him to Ceceltoth, too. I wasn't sure to which place he should march his army. I simply knew that I must deviate from all that he and I had planned. I had to surprise myself—in doing so, I would surprise even you.

"Do you know how I decided which of the great cities to assault? I drew straws. Only a few hourglasses ago, to maintain the suspense. A future based on chance! Even now, Brutus and our army of those reborn in fire and Zionae's dark Will move to subdue Intomitath. Who knows if he will win? It would mean another fragment of Zionae's ark, should he succeed. Nonetheless, it doesn't matter. For Brutus will survive regardless of the casualties of his army, and I shall have the arkstone—perhaps even a pair of them. You have been outplayed, Daughter of Fate. You and your filthy dog of a lover. After so much heroism and sacrifice, you and he have lost. Fate and your own arrogance have been your undoing."

Glass shattered. The sapphire gleam of the sun that had been trapped behind magik and glass since the dawn of Eatoth was now free. In the blinding glare, Amunai faded to a blue shadow. Growling, fighting the cacophony of silver blackouts and fragmented prophecies in her head,

Morigan tripped over herself to reach that shadow. Fate was furious with her—images spun and stabbed at Morigan like a flock of swords. She had to reach Amunai. One step into Dream, and perhaps she could make it. Morigan called upon the sum of her Will, her love, her determination, and her tie to the roaring Wolf of fire in her heart, and she leaped. Perhaps something else roared, too—she felt a wind before she became one herself.

She soared across the chamber in a scintillation of magik, and she and another snarling wind—the Wolf, who had just dropped from the ceiling—struck the possessed Keeper Superior in a twin bolt of fury. The explosion of power hurled Ankha's body high into the air, then down to the ground. The twin winds moved with her, ravaging her: claws and dagger repeatedly plunged into whimpering flesh.

Once the two had struck their mark, sands slowed enough to allow understanding. Entwined in the murderous embrace of the bloodmates, the Keeper Superior wheezed her last breath.

Leaving her promise dagger in the glistening abdomen of the Keeper Superior, Morigan crawled away. She couldn't look at the corpse, which resembled a sputtering, dying fish. Even though Ankha was dead, the nerves of her body hadn't yet stilled. The lights in the chamber performed a dance like lightning—erratic, flashing, and blue—and Morigan heard a rumble that she imagined was a thunderous hammer of judgment. When Morigan brought her hands to her face and accidentally wiped her cheeks with the Keeper Superior's blood, she couldn't summon any more of her rage.

"You have never taken innocent life before. I know that, my Fawn. But she was no innocent, and we had no choice," whispered the Wolf. Savage as his nature decreed, he began rifling the body, searching. "Where is the arkstone?"

"I told you he would not be fast enough to catch the Lady of the Winds," shouted Amunai.

The bloodmates flew to each other and stared into the flashing dark. A far-off glint of sapphire light caught their attention. From any distance, it was impossible to mistake the arkstone's glory. Although it first appeared to be levitating, the Wolf noticed the shadow holding the artifact. It was as if Amunai's smoldering soul had simply stepped from her sister's body and manifested as something no less gaseous.

The Wolf immediately wondered whether the darkness had enough meat to its matter for him to tear. She couldn't win. He wouldn't allow this to be the end. Just before he charged, before his bloodmate shrieked at him to rush the witch, he heard Amunai laugh. Then the blue star of the arkstone vanished, the laugh along with it. Eatoth fell into darkness. The Wolf slashed nothing but air. Morigan wept over the body of the Keeper.

The arkstone had been taken. They had lost.

EPILOGUE

"What news?" Elemech looked up from her pool, which revealed nothing pleasant. She noticed that Eean's expression suggested a bleaker forecast than any of her own visions.

Rather than reply, Eean shuffled across the cavern to the limestone table, laid her staff upon it, and sat her tired self down on a bench. She poured herself a cup of water from the ewer on the table. Although the receptacle could conjure anything she desired—such as the stiffest, vilest whisky—Eean wanted to keep her wits about her. They couldn't afford to indulge in drink, sadness, or time wasting of any kind. The time for fun had ended.

While she refreshed herself, her sisters, drawn like moths, came to her. Elemech sat to her left. Ealasyd climbed onto the table and sat there as if she were a naughty pet. She'd brought her toys with her, too. New figures, a pair of them, neither of which the older sisters had ever before seen. The first figure was a man carved of bone. It was beautiful, especially in light of Ealasyd's usual works. Despite his pose of kneeling prayer, his angularity and refinement revealed he could be only one person: Magnus. However, he was bent and humbled, and no longer looked like a king.

"Magnus," said Ealasyd, playing with the ridges of his sculpted hair. "Or rather, the man he will become. A long road is ahead of him. A dark road. I'd rather not see him walk it. But I think there's something nice for him at the end."

"*Siogtine*? (Penance?)" asked Eean.

"I seem to have forgotten what that word means—so possibly," replied Ealasyd.

"Who's that?" Eean tapped the other figurine, which was also well crafted. It was a woman tall and fair. The darkness of her mineral skin—true ebony—concealed finer details. Somehow, though, Ealasyd's fingers had managed to affix two grains of crystalline sand in the sockets of the figurine's eyes. The doll's stare shone with light as Eean picked up the little person and turned her around in her hands. "She seems quite fearsome. Is she wicked?"

"No!" Ealasyd, quite upset, snatched the doll back, then grabbed little Magnus as well. "He needs a proper queen. A queen of night for a king of winter. The one you chose for him last time was all wrong, though she's quite right for another. No, this one will choose him, and he will choose her. That way, there won't be any mistakes. And don't ask if you can play with them, Elemech! I see your talons clenching like a greedy hawk. It's not time for their tale, so you don't get to see. Not for a winter's winter!"

After that, Ealasyd retreated into a quiet game, whispering to her dolls and making them stiffly dance. Soon she was smiling, no doubt having forgotten all that she'd said. However, her sisters had not. They still had much to discuss.

"This is good, Sister," said Elemech. "If she senses echoes of the future, then perhaps we are not all doomed. What did you see in your travels?"

"Nothing that would foretell of the righteous winning this war," replied Eean, dark and grim. "Our shadows have left the woods."

Elemech gasped.

"They are not bound as we are, and they realize this," continued Eean. "I watched our shadows meet and possibly form an alliance with Aghna and the army of wolves. I see three storms coming for Eod, and I know not how many it can endure. Each will wear down a bit of stone, a bit of the peoples' will...Brutus, Xalloreth, and now an army led by our wicked shadows and a vengeful warmother. Man cannot defeat a three-headed horror. One of these storms will destroy what remains of the civilization that holds the Black Queen at bay. I see no survival for those who would protect life and decency."

Elemech made a sudden, passionate appeal. She reached out and took her sister's hand. In that moment, Elemech, the Lady of Sorrows, shone as the Lady of Light. "Sister. Storms come with every season. This one will be the most thunderous Geadhain has ever seen in all its long years. But we must believe in these heroes. We must believe in my daughter and the son of Brutus. Children can right the wrongs of their parents. Such is the law of inheritance. What is ruined can be repaired by the ones who come after. So do not lose hope. Do not be eaten by despair. Pray with me for our children, our hope. I know you can do this, for you have always been the backbone of our family. You have always been our hope."

"Not always." Eean smiled.

The sisters hugged, kissed, and sang ancient tunes. Eventually, Ealasyd added her sweet voice to the duo. For now, all was calm.

—Fin—